I0681752

ZACHARY GOLDMAN PRIVATE INVESTIGATOR CASES 11-13

ZACHARY GOLDMAN PRIVATE INVESTIGATOR CASES 11-13

P.D. WORKMAN

 PD WORKMAN

Copyright © 2023 by P.D. Workman
All rights reserved.

No part of this book may be reproduced in any form or by any electronic or mechanical means, including information storage and retrieval systems, without written permission from the author, except for the use of brief quotations in a book review.

ISBN: 9781774686317 (KDP Paperback)
ISBN: 9781774686300 (ePub)

HE DROWNED IN MEMORY

For the rescuers
and the lost

1

Zachary watched out the windshield as Kenzie drove back to her house. It seemed like a long time since he had been outside. It was very bright with all the white snow on the ground, the branches of the trees also covered with piles of newly fallen snow. It always looked so nice and clean right after a snowfall. Before all the dirt from the roads was kicked up and tracks and trails were stomped down by pedestrians.

Kenzie's car was warm, since she had driven it from home to the hospital to pick him up. It wasn't very energy efficient to heat the little red convertible during the Vermont winters. It lost a lot of heat through the canvas top. But Kenzie's "baby" was her pride and joy, and she insisted on driving it to the hospital even though she could have taken Zachary's white compact instead. She would drive her car through all but the worst of weather.

"Glad to be out?" Kenzie asked. She turned her head to look at him for an instant, her curly dark hair bouncing.

Zachary nodded. "Nice to get out in the fresh air… the hospital gets so stale, recycling the same air over and over again."

"I'll bet."

Zachary had lost track of how long it had been. Five weeks? Six? The days tended to all run together in the psych ward. It was hard to even keep track of what day of the week it was. But he was feeling good now. There was a lot of work to be done, but he tried not to feel anxious about it. He would be fine once he got back into the swing of things. He knew that from experience. Every year, he struggled to get through December, but he could see the light at the end of the tunnel once he was past Christmas. He could restart his life. He'd stayed in the hospital a little longer than he usually did because they had changed his med cocktail around to try to address his heightened obsessive behavior. It was always best to stay under supervision to ensure the med change didn't cause additional problems.

"Do you want to go out for dinner tonight?" Kenzie suggested. "A celebratory supper?"

Zachary's shoulders tensed. He had been anticipating a nice quiet night at home. Supper in the kitchen with Kenzie. Cuddling on the couch and watching an old movie. Maybe going through his mass of accumulated emails to see if he could put a dent in them so that it wouldn't take so long to tackle them the next day.

Kenzie glanced at him. "No? We don't have to if you're not up to it."

"I *could*. I just… was hoping to be at home tonight."

"That's fine." Kenzie smiled. "It was just a suggestion. I thought you might want to be out and about. Restless after being cooped up for so long."

"No. Maybe tomorrow or on the weekend. Tonight, I just want to be… *home*."

It was funny how quickly Kenzie's house had become home. He should probably think about giving up his apartment, since it no longer represented home for him. He really didn't need a separate place. He didn't have a lot of possessions, having become accustomed to living on very little in foster care as a teen. He would see if Kenzie could make some space for his files and the rest of his photography equipment, but none of the larger items like furniture meant anything to him.

There was no point in paying rent on a place where he didn't live anymore.

But it would be a big step. The last time he had moved in with someone and given up keeping separate residences had been when he'd moved in with Bridget.

Zachary turned his focus as quickly as he could to his business. He couldn't spend any time thinking about Bridget. Bridget was in the past. She had her own family and life, and he wasn't part of that anymore.

He would call Heather, his older sister, when he got home. She had been keeping on top of business calls while he had been away. It was the first time that he'd had a business partner to do that while he had been in the hospital. While Heather didn't do any fieldwork, she enjoyed doing skip tracing and some of the other computer work. She had taken over the accounting system for Zachary, entering expenses, reconciling the credit card and bank account, and chasing down delinquent accounts. Her husband was a bookkeeper and Zachary supposed she had absorbed enough from his work to know what she was doing and had someone to turn to if she had any questions about errors that needed to be straightened out.

"We'll stay in tonight," Kenzie confirmed. "I have a lasagna in the freezer. We can throw together a salad to go with it."

"That sounds great. After more than a month of hospital food…"

Kenzie chuckled. "You could probably use a little something to spice up your diet."

Zachary heartily agreed. It took an effort to gain back the weight he lost during his cyclical depressions, not easy with the bland meals they served in the hospital. He needed some real food. Lasagna sounded heavenly.

Walking into the house felt so right. Zachary took a deep breath and let it out slowly, trying to relax all his muscles. He had been a little bit afraid, in the back of his mind, that he wouldn't feel like he belonged there anymore. That he might have lost something during his absence. But everything in the house was just as it should be. Down to his computer on his mobile desk in the living room and his phone charging on the side table. He walked down the hall to put his duffel bag down in the bedroom, but didn't bother unpacking yet. That could wait. The only things in it were clothes. And he would probably want to put them all directly into the washer to get the smell and feel of the hospital out of them.

"This is wonderful." Back in the living room, he hugged Kenzie impulsively, pulling her close against him and reveling in how good she felt in his arms. He was home, and he was with her, and it would be almost a year before Christmas came around again. By that time, maybe with the new med protocol and individual and couple's therapy, next Christmas wouldn't be as bad. He would stay out of the hospital and just have a quiet Christmas at home with Kenzie.

"How is your mom?" he asked, remembering that she had been planning to visit Lisa Cole Kirsch over the Christmas holiday. She'd never really told him how that had gone.

Kenzie looked surprised. She considered the question for a moment, then gave a slight shake of her head. "She's fine."

Zachary studied Kenzie's face. Something felt *off*. But he wasn't going to ruin his first day home by pursuing something she didn't feel like talking to him about. Her parents had always been a sensitive topic.

As were Zachary's.

2

Zachary looked around the kitchen, frowning. Kenzie had taken the garlic bread out of the oven, and he had been planning to slice it for her, but when he reached for the place where the butcher block of knives used to sit on the counter, it was no longer there.

"Uh, Kenz...?"

Leaning over the lasagna in the oven to see if it was done, Kenzie turned her head to look back at him.

"Oh... drawer to your left."

Zachary opened the nearest drawer, then realized it was the wrong side, closed it, and opened the next one over. The knives were there. He chose the one he needed for the crusty loaf and closed the drawer.

"You moved them." He stated the obvious. Was he upset that she had changed something while he was gone? He wasn't sure. It was such a small thing, but it made him feel suddenly awkward, and he found himself looking around the kitchen for anything else that might have changed.

"Yeah." Kenzie lifted the lasagna pan from the oven and put it onto the stove top. She turned off the oven. "I thought it was best to have them out of sight. So if you're feeling bad..."

Zachary remembered how he had put all the knives in the fridge when he had been having thoughts of suicide. It had been too difficult having them out on the counter where he could see them all the time, even from the couch where he sat with his computer. And then later, when things had gotten worse, he had swept them all out of the fridge onto the floor as he wrestled the mental demons who whispered to him that if he just ended his life, he wouldn't have to keep suffering. His cheeks flamed as he thought about it.

But Kenzie didn't bring any of that up. She didn't see the need to lecture him on how he should control himself better or not overreact to his emotional state. He'd heard plenty of those lectures before, though not from her. He wasn't sure whether it was because of her medical training or just her personality that she seemed to understand better than most people. Zachary was silent as he unwrapped the garlic toast and cut it into thick slices. He licked garlic butter off his finger. He could have made his entire meal out of a crusty, warm loaf of garlic bread. Which, of course, Kenzie had known when she had bought it. Like everyone else, she was determined to fatten him up as quickly as she could.

They moved around each other, getting the meal ready. Zachary wanted everything to be perfect, so he stayed focused on what he was doing, concentrating hard on setting the table and putting out the bread and the jug of water, not doing a slap-dash job of it and forgetting something vital like the forks or plates. In a few minutes, they were sitting down together. They dug into the meal, making appreciative noises and enjoying their first chance in weeks to just sit down to a meal together.

"I should set up a time for us to go visit Mr. Peterson," Zachary suggested.

Kenzie nodded. She took a sip of her water. "He and Pat would love to see you. So much nicer to visit at their house than at the hospital."

There were always distractions at the hospital. Too many things that Zachary had to keep an eye on while he was talking to visitors. While he knew he needed to be there, he worried about whether the other patients would disturb his visitors. Someone might have a violent episode while they were there, a psychotic break, and threaten them. It wasn't the best place for an intimate family visit.

Mr. Peterson and Patrick Parker were the closest things to parents that Zachary had. Mr. Peterson—Lorne—had been one of Zachary's foster fathers for a few weeks when he first went into foster care at age ten. While Zachary had not been able to stay in the Peterson home for long, he and Mr. Peterson had kept in touch over the years. It was a couple of decades since he and his wife had divorced, and Pat, a somewhat younger man, had become his partner. They had been close to Zachary through all the intervening years, becoming his chosen family.

"I should call Tyrrell. Maybe he'd like to join us too."

Kenzie pursed her lips. "If you want to."

It seemed like an odd response. She had never been reluctant to have Tyrrell, Zachary's younger brother, join them before. She had been the one who had encouraged him to reunite with Tyrrell, and it had been amazing to have one of his biological siblings in his life again. And Tyrrell had introduced him to Heather, and then later to Jocelyn, their two older sisters.

"I don't think it would be too much," Zachary said. Meeting with a larger group *could* be overwhelming. Especially if one of the members of the group was Jocelyn. Sharp, bitter Joss. But just Tyrrell joining them wouldn't be too hard. Tyrrell was undemanding and easy to get along with. Zachary didn't feel like he had to always be on guard with Tyrrell.

Kenzie nodded. "If you can get him."

"Why wouldn't I be able to get him?"

Kenzie shrugged. She took a couple more bites of lasagna. "He hasn't been around the last little while. Hasn't answered any calls."

Zachary stopped, his fork in front of his mouth. "What? What do you mean?"

"Just that. He hasn't been answering phone calls. But maybe he'll answer you."

"Do you mean… today? He hasn't been answering calls *today*?"

"No. I mean… since Christmas."

Zachary frowned. "But you've talked to him since then, haven't you?"

"No. We've been concerned, but… I've been busy with work, and you, and… other things. I figure that he'll make contact again when he is ready. Until then… best to just leave him to sort things out."

Zachary felt like something had exploded in his brain. Tyrrell had stopped communicating? What had happened to him? He'd seemed fine the last time Zachary had seen him. Tyrrell was always cheerful, easygoing, reassuring to Zachary when he got upset or anxious about something. He was the strong one, what Zachary might have been like if it hadn't been for the fire and everything he'd dealt with jumping from family to family in foster care.

"What do you mean, '*We've* been concerned?' You and who?"

"Heather." Kenzie poked at the lasagna that remained on her plate, staring down at it instead of looking into Zachary's face. "Tyrrell was supposed to go to the hospital with Heather and Joss on Christmas Day.

But Tyrrell didn't show up. She tried to get him then, but couldn't get him to call her back."

"He's not talking to Heather either?" Zachary shook his head. "Aren't you worried about this? Don't you think it is serious?"

"I told you that we *are* worried about him. But there's nothing we can do if he doesn't want to talk to us. He's a grown man. He's allowed to decide who he talks to or doesn't."

"Has anyone gone to see him? Made sure that he's okay? Somebody has *seen* him, right?"

"He has gone incommunicado before. His ex-wife said that he'd gone off the rails a few times... he would disappear for days on a drinking binge. Not talk to anyone. Then come back and act as if nothing had happened and he couldn't understand why everyone was upset about it."

"Has she talked to him? What about the kids? Has he talked to Mason or Alisha?"

"No. He was supposed to have them on Christmas Day. But he didn't show up."

"Don't you think something is wrong?" he asked urgently.

"Maybe... it is getting to the point where I wonder if we want to have the police do a welfare check. But something like that really isn't up to me to do. It should be someone closer to him. His work, friends, neighbors... family."

"We *are* family." Zachary pulled his phone out of his pocket and tapped the contact record for Tyrrell. He listened to it ring, hoping that Kenzie would be wrong and Tyrrell would pick it up and everything would be fine. Maybe there had been some misunderstanding. He'd had a fight with his ex and hadn't wanted to pick up the kids, then had been too embarrassed to go with Heather and Joss and explain why he didn't have them. And he hadn't wanted to talk to Kenzie because she was an outsider. There could be perfectly logical reasons they hadn't been able to get ahold of Tyrrell, but he would answer Zachary's call.

The call rang through to voicemail.

3

Zachary waited for Tyrrell's outgoing message to finish. He wasn't going to hang up and not let Tyrrell know he was looking for him. Tyrrell would be able to see Zachary's name on his missed call list, but that wasn't good enough. After the beep, Zachary spoke.

"Hey, T. Listen... I'm out of the hospital and back home. I thought I might set up dinner at Mr. Peterson's—Lorne's—and you might want to join us. Kenzie says she hasn't heard anything from you lately, so will you call me back? Let me know either way. I want to make sure you're okay."

He paused, thinking about whether he'd said everything he should or whether he'd messed it up and should start over again. He couldn't think of what else to say, and he knew that before too long, the voicemail would hang up on him.

"Okay. So... give me a call. Bye."

He tapped the red button on his phone and stared down at it for a few minutes. Kenzie's fork touched her plate with a soft clink as she continued to eat. He looked up at her.

"What if something happened to him? What if something bad happened, and nobody bothered to find out?"

"I don't think anything has happened to him. His ex says that he's done this before. So even if they did call the police, the police would know that and probably wouldn't put any time into it."

"But just because he has gone on a bender before, that doesn't mean

13

nothing happened to him this time. He could have been hurt or sick. He might have needed help." Zachary heard his volume rising and tried to lower it, but he was angry that no one had followed up. Tyrrell could disappear and no one even bothered to look for him? How could everyone sit around and just do nothing? "Bad things happen," he snapped at Kenzie. "With your job, I'd think you would know that!"

She gazed at him steadily. "I do, Zach. I realize that. But like I said, I didn't think it was up to me. Heather and Tyrrell's ex both knew what was going on. If they felt concerned enough about it, either one could have called the police or gone to check on him. But they both figured that he'd just fallen off the wagon. And you know…" She shrugged, uncomfortable under his gaze. "You know that when we were at the Lodge, someone had a fair amount to drink from the alcohol cabinet in our cabin."

Zachary felt a chill. He'd forgotten about that. So much had happened since then. Both while they were at the Lodge and upon their return. It seemed like it had all happened years ago. *Had* Tyrrell been drinking while they were there? They all knew that'd he'd had a problem with alcohol in the past. He didn't drink, not even a little bit on holidays. But things had been stressful at the Lodge. Had he slipped? They had asked him, straight out, and he'd said no. Zachary didn't like to think that Tyrrell had lied right to his face and he hadn't detected it. What kind of a brother was Zachary if he couldn't even tell when his own brother was lying or in distress?

"Do you think that's what happened? He started drinking when we were at the Lodge, and then… he just let it take over?"

"Maybe. We don't know what has happened before, or what might have been going on in his life at the time. We don't know what has triggered a setback before. But his ex-wife seemed to think that this is pretty normal. Not unexpected."

"But he's been so good for the time that we've known him."

"That's still not very long. It might seem like a long time since you reunited, but it's only been a year. That's not a long time when you're talking about addiction and sobriety. People fall off the wagon after decades of being sober."

"But he didn't just stop a year ago. I thought it was a long time ago. Years ago."

"He never said *when* to me. But with the way the kids were behaving around him… they remember him being different from now. You remember Alisha being afraid to tell him that she had gone vegetarian?

There wouldn't be any reason for that if he was just calm and easygoing all the time. She's known him when he's been different, when that might have triggered a negative reaction. So he was probably still drinking within the past few years."

Zachary *had* noticed how the kids behaved around Tyrrell, but he had told himself that he was just seeing something that wasn't there because of the way he had grown up. Always afraid his father was going to explode. Or his foster fathers. He had been about Alisha's age when he had entered foster care.

But Kenzie had seen it too, which meant it wasn't just something Zachary had imagined because of his history.

"I need to do something." He fingered his phone, wondering if he should put a call in to the police right away. But of course, the Roxboro police wouldn't be able to help him. He would have to talk to the police in Riverbrook where Tyrrell lived. And it probably wouldn't do to just call them. He would need to go there and make a pest of himself. Look in Tyrrell's windows if he wouldn't answer the door and call the police for a welfare check while he was there to increase the urgency. "Do you think… maybe I should call Heather? Maybe she has heard something but just didn't have a chance to mention it to you yet. You've been busy with work and everything."

Kenzie nodded. "I have cookies and ice cream for dessert if you want some."

Zachary sensed she was trying to distract him. With his ADHD, it wasn't that hard, and maybe she was hoping that he would let it go for the rest of the evening. But he wasn't going to forget that his little brother was missing, that he could be in danger.

"No. I'm full. Dinner was really good," Zachary pushed his plate an inch away from himself. "Really hit the spot. But I'm full. And I should call Heather."

"Okay. Maybe we can have dessert later when dinner has had a chance to settle."

"Yeah. Sure. That sounds good." Zachary pushed himself away from the table and stood up. He could tell that Kenzie didn't want him calling Heather to bug her about Tyrrell, so it was probably best if he didn't do it while sitting at the table. It was probably rude to make phone calls at the dinner table but, with cellphones being so ubiquitous, stuff that used to be seen as extremely impolite was now normal, everyday behavior. He'd already pushed it once by calling Tyrrell. He wouldn't repeat it by calling Heather from the table as well.

"I'll… be back in a bit."

Since he didn't have a separate office or bedroom at Kenzie's house, there wasn't really anywhere private for him to retreat to. He decided to use the bedroom, since Kenzie was in the kitchen. It would only take a few minutes to talk to Heather, and then Kenzie could have her room back if she wanted it.

4

Zachary sat down on the bed and tapped Heather's avatar on his phone. It would be nice to talk to her again, though he wished the circumstances were different. He hadn't seen her since Christmas Day when she and Joss had visited him at the hospital. He appreciated the gesture, but it had been difficult for him. Now, at home, without other distractions, it would be easier to focus on Heather and to hear the emotions behind her words.

"Zachary!" Heather's voice was warm and full of enthusiasm. "You're back!"

"Yeah. I guess I am. How are you?"

"I'm just fine. I'm so happy to hear from you. Things are better?"

"I'm on a new med cocktail, and it seems to be working okay. Now that I'm out… I guess I'll really put it to the test. It's never quite the same, at the hospital and in real life. Different stresses, and some medications take a few weeks to reach full efficacy, so you aren't seeing the real effects of them until later on."

"Sounds complicated."

"It is. Be glad that you're not in charge of it. I can't imagine trying to handle the needs and prescriptions of multiple patients. It's hard enough for me to keep track of my own and figure out what is working and what isn't."

"Better the doctors than me. Have you had a chance to look at your email yet? I've been sending weekly summary reports, so that is probably where you want to start. Get an overview of what has been going on before you dive into all of the individual emails from clients and other contacts."

"I will. I haven't logged in to my computer yet. Just had dinner with Kenzie and found out about Tyrrell."

There was only silence from Heather.

"I can't understand why anyone didn't get the police involved," Zachary told her. "That's their job. Missing persons. If he has been missing since Christmas, then someone should have reported it."

"I don't know if he's actually *missing*, or if he's just not bothering to return calls. I don't really have any way of knowing what is going on in Riverbrook. Other than by calling his ex, and I really don't want to push my luck there. She wasn't too happy to hear from me before."

"What did she say?"

"She said that Tyrrell is irresponsible. That him not showing to pick up the kids like he was supposed to wasn't anything new. And that I should just stay out of it and let him work things out himself. He needs to take responsibility for his own life, not have someone coddling him and putting up with his sh—nonsense."

"But has she seen him at all? Has anyone seen him?"

"I imagine someone has. Not Lindsey, though. He's behind on child support and she says that he's probably avoiding her because of that."

"She hasn't looked for him?"

"No. And I could understand what she was saying about not enabling him or trying to take care of him. So I stayed out of the way."

"He could be hurt or sick. He could be dead in his apartment, and how would anyone know if everybody refuses to take any responsibility for him and find out?"

"You're welcome to try. But I don't have any desire to be around him if he's on a bender. And if he is dead in his apartment, I don't want to be the one to find that out either!"

Zachary opened his mouth to snap back at her that it wasn't funny, then reconsidered. She wasn't joking. Since getting married, she had led a fairly sheltered life and was a bit of a hermit, preferring to stay home where she didn't have to deal with the rest of the world except by computer and telephone. She had dealt with enough abuse and trauma in her teen years. She deserved to live free of all of that nastiness as an adult.

Finding Tyrrell was Zachary's job, not Heather's. If he could take responsibility for finding out what had happened to Tyrrell on himself, he was happy to be able to help Heather continue to live the life she had made for herself, away from the ugliness of Tyrrell's addiction and where it might have led him.

"Okay," he told her in a quiet voice. "I'll take care of it. You don't need to."

There was another small silence.

"Thank you, Zachary," Heather said eventually. "I'm sure everything is okay... but I just don't want to be involved in it."

"That's fine. You don't have to. Tyrrell is not your responsibility anymore."

When they had been young, the little children had been the responsibilities of the older ones. Heather and Joss had been mothers to the little brood of Goldman children way before they were old enough to take on such a responsibility.

"Thanks. I'm sure he's fine... What are you going to do first?"

"I've left a message for him to call me. Maybe he will. I haven't talked to him since a couple of weeks before Christmas... more than a month ago. If he doesn't call me back, I'll drive down to Riverbrook and have a look around. See if he is there. Get the police involved if he isn't or if it looks like there was any foul play involved. Then... I don't know. It will depend on what I find out."

"What about the rest of the business? We've got a good amount of stuff backlogged that you should be starting on when you're feeling up to it."

"It won't matter whether I start now or in a few days. If they've waited this long, they'll wait a bit longer. If they can't... then it's better that someone else takes that on instead of me having to worry about getting something done in a hurry. Tyrrell is family. He comes first."

5

When Zachary got off the phone and went back out to the living room, Kenzie was still tidying up in the kitchen. He realized that he had left her with all of the clearing up, not even thinking about it in his concern over Tyrrell's disappearance. She had made most of the meal; the least he could do was help with the clean-up. He couldn't remember for sure whether he had even finished what was on his plate or whether he had just walked off, leaving half of his dinner behind.

"Sorry—I'm sorry, I didn't mean to leave you with everything." Zachary hurried into the kitchen and looked around to see what else needed to be done. "Is there anything else? Can I help?"

Kenzie sighed. "No, it's done now."

"I wasn't thinking. I'll do better. I'm sorry."

"I appreciate it. How was Heather?"

"How was she? Good, I guess..." Zachary wasn't sure he had even asked her how she was. He had just launched into his questions about Tyrrell and whether she had seen or talked to him. Two strikes against him already, and he had only been out of the hospital for a few hours. He had thought that his symptoms were under control, but if he couldn't even show any courtesy to the people around him due to his distraction, then maybe he wasn't doing as well as he had hoped.

"She hasn't heard from Tyrrell?"

"No. And she doesn't want to get involved. I guess Tyrrell's ex talked her out of doing anything. But I can't just let it go."

Kenzie nodded. "That's understandable." She closed the dishwasher, latched it, and pressed a button to start the cleaning cycle. She motioned toward the living room, and they both walked in and sat down together on the couch. Zachary was feeling awkward, unsure whether they were having a serious conversation or if Kenzie just wanted to cuddle and watch TV or had other things in mind. He watched her for any cues.

"You might want to ease into things a little more slowly," Kenzie suggested. "Let yourself get acclimatized first. It seems like jumping head-long into Tyrrell's problems might be a bit much when you're just out of the hospital. Maybe start with your emails and seeing what work Heather has done and what is waiting for you. Then maybe take a trip down this weekend to see Tyrrell on the way to the Petersons'."

There was logic to laying it out that way so that Tyrrell's bender didn't become central to his life, tying him up in knots when he wasn't ready to take on such an emotional job.

But Zachary was anything but logical. He *did* throw himself headlong into things after Christmas every year. He didn't wait to recover from his depression and regain his strength. He just threw himself back into his work and tried to catch up on what he had missed or gotten behind on. And he couldn't pretend that Tyrrell's disappearance didn't bother him and was something that could just be put off until it was more convenient to investigate it.

"Yeah, we'll see," he told Kenzie, "I'll think about that." It was better if she thought he was going to listen so that she wasn't anxious about him all evening and ended up not being able to sleep well before she went back to her job at the Medical Examiner's Office in the morning. She wouldn't know that he was starting his investigation until later the next day. By that time, he would be well into it. She would be able to see that he was fine and that investigating Tyrrell's disappearance wouldn't throw his recovery off the rails.

"Do you want to watch something?" Kenzie asked, nodding toward the TV screen. "Or did you want some time to get work done?"

"Would you mind if I did my email while we watch something? I know that usually we don't do that, but…"

One of the things they had discussed in couple's therapy was to really be present when they were spending time together. Zachary needed to take a break from his computer and business and just spend time with Kenzie and pay attention to her. And it was something he worked hard on, making it a rule for himself that he put his computer away when it was time for them to spend time together in the evening or on the weekend. Zachary confined his work activities to Kenzie's hours at work as much as possible. Sometimes, surveillance jobs took him away from her during the evening, but he tried to keep them to a minimum.

"I think it's fine this once," Kenzie said slowly, as if she were picking her words carefully. "It's the first opportunity that you've had to log on. But... I don't want it to be something that gets you all wound up so that you can't sleep. If it's something that you're not going to be able to pull away from..."

"I think it will be fine. I've been doing pretty well lately."

"But you've been in a different environment. Staying on task at the hospital when you don't have access to a computer or your email or other distractions is not exactly the same as being home."

"No. But it should be fine. I'm not going to start working tonight. Just getting an idea of what work there is to be done." And he wouldn't even start on it the next day. He already knew he would be in Riverbrook.

Kenzie shrugged. She picked up the remote control for the TV. Zachary waited a few seconds, making it look like he was interested in the process of picking something to watch, and then reached for his laptop.

6

Zachary couldn't have said what movie they watched together. There had been so much email in his inbox after being away from his computer for weeks that he had done exactly what he had said he wouldn't and gotten so focused on it that he forgot everything else and probably hadn't given Kenzie any of the attention she had expected.

But he was true to his word and didn't start on his work. He didn't send out any emails, start any inquiries, or set up any new files.

Heather's advice to read her weekly email reports first had been a good one. He appreciated her doing that for him so that he had a sane, logical place to start. He vaguely remembered her saying once that her kids both had ADHD. She had clearly learned some strategies to help them deal with it.

But after reading through her reports and putting them into a folder to refer back to later, there was still lots of work to do weeding out all of the spam and the emails to do with inquiries that Heather had already taken care of and to pare the contents of his inbox down to what he would need to concentrate on once he had talked to Tyrrell and was ready to get back to work.

Before he knew it, he could hear the music for the movie's closing credits and, looking up, saw the names of the actors scrolling up the screen. He hadn't even been aware of most of them having appeared in the movie. He had only looked up once or twice while it was on, a dramatic fight or chase scene pulling him away from his email. He slowly closed the lid on his laptop and put it back on his table. He squeezed his eyes shut a few times to lubricate them. They were dry and scratchy after staring at the screen without a break.

"Good movie; what did you think?" Kenzie asked.

"Uh, yeah," Zachary agreed, forcing a smile and nodding. "Exciting."

There was a bowl sitting on his table where he had probably put it down. A cookie swimming in a pool of melted ice cream. Zachary picked up the bowl and held it close to his body so that when he picked up the cookie, the ice cream dripped back into the bowl instead of into his lap. He took a bite of the cookie.

"Mmm. These are good."

Kenzie was giving him an amused look. One that told him that she was completely aware of how lost he had become in his email review. She had probably tried to talk to him a few times and gotten no response. And the fact that he had no awareness of the cookie and ice cream until after the closing credits of the movie told him that he had been oblivious to her getting up and preparing the evening snack for the two of them and had ignored it when she gave it to him or put it on the table.

Zachary cleared his throat, his ears getting hot.

"Are you going to need some time to unwind before bed?"

He rubbed his jaw. "Uh, yes. I guess so."

"Anything I can do to help you relax?" She put her hand on his thigh, leaning in closer.

Zachary turned his body toward her and put his arms around her before kissing her gently. He was glad that he had put the computer away. Some other important things needed his full attention.

Before going to bed, Zachary took his new regimen of pills into the main bathroom. He arranged them on the shelf of the medicine cabinet. He disposed of all the old prescriptions so that he wouldn't get confused about what he was supposed to be taking. None of the bottles was full. He refilled his prescriptions often, rather than having enough pills on hand to make overdosing a temptation. It would be possible to do harm by combining several together, but that didn't seem to be as much of a problem for him when he was seriously depressed. It took too much mental energy to figure out what combination to take.

He reviewed the label of each pill bottle before he took each one. He had been on enough other cocktails that he was pretty familiar with everything out there. Still, the combination and dosages were new, so he wanted to ensure he got them right until they became ingrained as a habit. Then it would be more automatic.

Kenzie walked by in the hallway as he was taking his night dosages and stopped to talk to him. "So this new cocktail, you think it's good? Think it will help?"

Zachary nodded as he downed a couple more pills. "Seems to be pretty good so far. Not so nauseated in the morning, so that's good." He looked at the next bottle on the shelf and hesitated.

"Take them all," Kenzie prompted.

Zachary didn't like taking all of them every day. He preferred to judge whether he needed anything for anxiety or not. Whether he needed a sleeping pill. He would take his ADHD meds—a daytime prescription, not night—if he were doing something he knew he would need it for, but didn't like to take them every day. He looked at Kenzie sideways, gauging what her response would be if he told her that he didn't need to take all of them.

Kenzie raised her brows.

"I'm just thinking… it would be nice not to have to take a sleep aid tonight, since I'm at home."

"If you do that, you'll be up again at the crack of dawn. You need to make sure you're getting enough sleep for good mental health and to be able to focus on your work."

"But I'm in a good place already. The hospital enforced all that kind of thing. I just don't like the way they make me feel in the morning…"

"And don't like relying on an aid to get to sleep every night. I know. I just think that for the first few days at home, the transition, it would be a good idea not to vary anything. Once you're sure that you're stable, then you can start using a bit of your own discretion."

That was one of the few issues Zachary had with having a medical doctor for a partner. She was too sure that she knew exactly what he needed to do for his own mental health. That if he just followed medical advice, everything would be fine. While there was some truth to what she said, Zachary had been through the cycle of med changes enough times to know what he was talking about and how his body worked.

But he didn't want to have an argument with her the first day back. He had already come dangerously close to that with his comments about how she and Heather should have dealt with Tyrrell's absence. Even if they didn't *argue*, a discussion about meds right before bedtime was likely to degrade to obsessive thoughts and an inability to get to sleep.

He took the sleep aid without any further comment, short-circuiting any more discussion about which route would be best for him to take. Med discussions were fine in the morning, but not right before bed.

Kenzie nodded and walked the rest of the way down the hall to the bedroom. Zachary took the last couple of prescriptions and followed her.

7

As Zachary had expected, when morning rolled around, he felt groggy from the sleep aid. The prescription sleep aid was much stronger than the Benadryl or over-the-counter sleep aids that the drug store stocked and made him feel thick-headed for the first hour or two after he got up. But it had had the desired effect of keeping him asleep for almost seven hours, like a normal person. If the doctors were right and that helped him be healthier physically and mentally, he would have to put up with the adverse effects.

"Morning!" Kenzie rolled over to give him a kiss. "How are you feeling this morning?"

"Great," he lied. "I'm going to have a quick shower to wash away the cobwebs. You work today?"

"I work every day," Kenzie said with a shrug and a little laugh. She was doing better at getting off at least one day on the weekend. Or if she couldn't do that, at least working shorter hours on the weekend, but it was hard for her to tear herself away from her work sometimes. If Zachary's job had been dealing with dead people every day, he thought he would be happy to go home by the end of the day. "I won't be late, though," Kenzie promised. "Dr. Wiltshire knows that you're back home, and I told him I wanted to make sure we had clear evenings for at least the first week or two."

"So unless there is an emergency…" Zachary gave her an out, knowing that things often came up that were beyond her control.

"If there's a zombie apocalypse, then I might have to stay late. But I don't plan to."

Zachary rubbed his eyes and pressed hard on the bony ridge over his eyes, trying to ease the hangover-like headache, considering her answer.

"Wait, would a zombie apocalypse mean that there were more people in your morgue because the zombies killed them, or less because everyone was *undead?*"

"Uh… hmm… good question. I'll have to think about that one. I'll ask Dr. Wiltshire what he thinks." She grinned at the thought.

If she did that, Dr. Wiltshire might just send Zachary straight back to the psych ward. If that was something the medical examiner could order.

Zachary had never met or spoken with Lindsey, Tyrrell's ex-wife. Zachary and Tyrrell were both divorced, and they didn't talk much to each other about their exes. Tyrrell knew that Zachary's relationship with Bridget was fraught. Zachary fought against himself because of his obsession with Bridget even though he was now with Kenzie and worked hard on his relationship with her. He couldn't help that his brain kept going back to Bridget, replaying the things that had happened between the two of them over and over again, imagining what would have happened if they had stayed together, about if Bridget's newborn twin girls had been his instead of Gordon's, about what he would do if Bridget ever decided she wanted him in her life again. Which he knew wasn't going to happen, but he couldn't stop his brain from going there.

But Heather had Lindsey's name and contact details, so Zachary hadn't had to go searching for her himself. He called ahead, deciding it was probably best not to just show up on her doorstep. In addition to the fact that she probably wouldn't want a stranger calling, much less her ex's brother, he knew that she could be working. Showing up at her house without setting up an appointment first could result in his having to wait a very long time to talk to her.

Lindsey was clearly not excited about talking to him. She spoke slowly, with caution, considering her words carefully before she said anything.

"I suppose you can come over around three," she said finally. "I have to be home for when the kids get out of school. But there isn't really much to tell you. I can already tell you the whole of the conversation. Tyrrell is off drinking. Yes, he's done it before. No, I don't know where he goes to drink. He'll come back eventually. Maybe someday, he will hit bottom and be able to stay off the bottle for more than a few months or a year at a time."

"Okay, thanks." Zachary didn't bother addressing his questions to her over the phone. It would be easier face-to-face, where he could watch her reactions and hopefully discern when she was telling him the truth and when she was just hoping to avoid or end the conversation. If he were there with her, she couldn't hang up. And it would be a lot harder to get him out of the house. Not that he wouldn't go if she asked him to, but people found it difficult to do things they thought were rude, and she would be sure to think that kicking him out when he was just trying to find and help his brother was pretty harsh. She would be polite, even though she didn't want him looking for Tyrrell and didn't want Tyrrell back.

Driving on the highway was one of Zachary's favorite activities. The only time that his brain truly quieted and let him just sit and think. He imagined that was what the brain of a normal person felt like most of the time. His time on the highway was a rolling meditation.

And without Kenzie in the car with him, he could go as fast as he liked. He didn't have to get to Riverbrook in a hurry. It wasn't an emergency. He wasn't going to get more done if he got there faster. But he loved to drive fast down the highway, finding a clear lane where he could just fly for ten minutes without anyone pulling in front of him. Or navigating from one lane to the other to avoid the slower vehicles, like a real-life game of Frogger. Kenzie didn't like his speeding, so he always had to slow down to just above the speed limit if she were in the passenger's seat.

As a result, he rolled into Riverbrook much earlier than he should have. It would still be some time before he could go to Lindsey's house to interview her. He input Tyrrell's address into the GPS and navigated to his building.

The area of town was shabby. Not that any of it was upscale. It was a small Vermont town, similar to many others, where people lived in little bungalows or condo units, not mansions. Not big places like Bridget's new house with Gordon or the home that Kenzie had grown up in. Tyrrell's building was similar to somewhere Zachary would have rented. A small bachelor pad or studio apartment where he could sleep, watch TV, and conduct his business. Smaller than Zachary's current apartment. He reminded himself he needed to make sure there weren't any flyers sticking out from under his door. And he should talk to the manager about getting out of his lease.

He circled once, looking at the building and the neighborhood, before pulling into the parking lot. There were no visitor spaces marked that he could see. He found a curb with Tyrrell's unit number stenciled on it and pulled in. He walked into the building and found himself in the security alcove with a panel of buttons and a speaker. He looked for Tyrrell's name on one of the labels, but didn't find it. He located the button which should have had Tyrrell's name or unit number on it and pressed it firmly.

The speaker played a ringing-phone tone and, after the first three rings, Zachary knew that Tyrrell wasn't going to answer it. He hadn't answered or returned Zachary's phone call. Why would he let someone into his apartment? If he was there, he didn't want company.

It continued to ring, until eventually hanging up, an electronic voice informing him that the party he was trying to call could not be reached. It didn't seem to forward to Tyrrell's cell number. Zachary pressed it again, with the same results. He tried a couple of other buttons, but no one answered. It was the middle of the workday. People were either still at the office or had been on other shifts and were sleeping. Or shopping for groceries. Zachary looked at his phone and saw that he still had time to kill. He returned to his car, got in, and drove around the neighborhood, taking note of the grocery, convenience, and liquor stores.

He didn't see Tyrrell out walking anywhere, but he hadn't expected to.

Maybe Tyrrell was at a nearby bar. Or one in an adjacent town, if he didn't want to be seen by any of his friends or neighbors.

8

Eventually, Zachary managed to run the clock down until it was time to meet Lindsey at the house. He was at her curb a couple of minutes before the hour and waited until the clock ticked over to three o'clock before climbing out of his car and standing at her door.

It was a slightly nicer area. Lots of family homes. Mostly leased cars at the curb, four-doors and soccer mom vans. The sidewalk had been shoveled, but still had icy patches. Like maybe Mason had been the one to do the shoveling and had gotten distracted partway through the job or hadn't been willing to put in the work to do the harder sections. Zachary stomped the snow off his boots on the welcome mat at the front door and rang the doorbell. At least he didn't need to worry about waking a sleeping infant.

The woman who came to the door had a pinched white face. She was slightly taller than Zachary, which would help her to feel more relaxed and safer talking to him. She looked tired and quite possibly at the end of her rope. Not wanting to take the time to deal with her ex-husband's issues on top of her own.

But maybe if Zachary could find Tyrrell and get him operational again, that would be good for Lindsey. She might start getting child support money again. Having someone in her life who could take the kids every second weekend to give her some time to pamper herself or run errands without constant questions and interruptions from Mason.

"Hi. I'm Zachary." He waited for a moment, then offered his hand when she didn't say anything. "I'm sorry to be bothering you about this."

"Come in, I guess. Lindsey. Goldman. As you know."

Zachary nodded and followed her into the house, divesting his winter clothes.

The house smelled good. Clean and fresh. The smell of Lindsey's coffee hung in the area, as well as something else sweet. Maybe some leftover Christmas cookies warmed in the microwave? There was the kind of clutter that accumulated in houses with active children. It wasn't messy or neglected, just lived in. He got a good vibe walking in the door.

Lindsey sat down in the living room and motioned for Zachary to sit in a comfy recliner. Zachary settled in. He took out his notebook, which so far only contained Lindsey's contact information and a few observations Zachary had made about Tyrrell's neighborhood.

"I'll try not to take up too much of your time. Can you tell me when it was that Tyrrell dropped out of sight? When was the last time you saw him or talked to him?"

"Before Christmas. I couldn't tell you what day. A few days before Christmas or maybe a week. It was his year to have the kids for Christmas. Although, after what happened over Thanksgiving..." She looked at Zachary and shook her head as if it had been his fault.

He wasn't even the one who had planned the Thanksgiving vacation. That had been Kenzie. She had invited Tyrrell and rented a cabin with enough room for all of them. And it hadn't been her fault that they had gotten snowed in. None of the rest of the stuff that had happened had been her fault either.

"Yeah. Thanksgiving was interesting," Zachary agreed, hoping she would just let it go. "When was he supposed to pick the kids up?"

"Christmas morning, after they'd had a chance to look at their stockings. He was supposed to have a couple of days with them. I knew he was going to visit you at the hospital with Heather and Joss. Kenzie was going to look after the kids while he was there, so that they didn't have to see you in the hospital."

Zachary nodded. He hadn't felt like the psych ward was a good place for the children to spend any time and he'd asked Tyrrell not to bring them.

"So... why didn't he just plan to pick up the kids later in the day?"

"Because I was going to my parents' house. He was supposed to pick up the kids before that so that I would be free to go."

"And he never showed up? Did he call or give any excuse?"

"None." Lindsey's mouth tightened, angry at the memory. Remembering how upset she had gotten while waiting around for him to show up and do as they had agreed. "I called him and left messages, and there wasn't any answer. I texted him. Nothing. Then Heather called, saying that he hadn't met up with them and wondering where he was. He hadn't called them to change his plans either. No one had seen him or talked to him."

"Did he call at all after that? So that you knew he was okay?"

"No."

Zachary swallowed. He made a couple of notes in his notepad, though he wasn't going to forget any of this basic information.

"Have you seen him anywhere? Seen any sign of him? Have the kids talked to him?"

"No."

"He just disappeared."

She nodded. "Exactly."

"Weren't you worried? Why didn't you file a report with the police?"

9

---

ecause I've done that enough times before," Lindsey said, her voice bitter. "I told you; this isn't the first time he's dropped out of sight. This is what he does. Leaves everyone behind worrying about him, wondering if something awful has happened to him. And then a few weeks or months later, he shows up again, all clean and acting like nothing happened."

"You must have talked to him about that."

"Yeah, we had talked it to death. He always promised that he would never do it again. That he would always call me and let me know what was going on, even if it was bad news. Of course, he swore never to drink again, but if he did, he'd make sure that I knew he was okay. And that the kids wouldn't have to worry about him, wondering if their daddy was even alive."

Lindsey's voice cracked, and she grabbed a tissue from the nearby box. She dabbed at her eyes.

"Sorry. I should be a lot tougher than this by now. I can let Tyrrell go. I can let him find his own way, whatever way that is, and hope and pray that he'll find peace someday. But the kids... I hate how much it hurts them. No kid should have to go back to school wondering if his daddy is ever going to come home again."

Zachary swallowed and nodded. That was a pretty harsh experience for any kid to go through. His parents had been drinkers, often getting into knock-down blow-out fights at night after drinking all evening. His father hadn't taken off and disappeared, but one or the other of them was sometimes hauled off to jail overnight. He tried to imagine what it would have been like to have his father just disappear.

"Do you know where Tyrrell would go to drink? Does he have a favorite watering hole?"

"If he did, I would have told you that when you called, instead of you coming here. I'd rather not have to do this!"

"I'm sorry." Zachary's face heated. He knew that he was making things difficult for Lindsey. Tyrrell's disappearance was not her fault. She had divorced the man. She shouldn't have to still be responsible for him. "I just hoped that there was somewhere to start. Maybe a drinking buddy or hangout. Anything about his drinking habits."

"He was a closet drinker. For the longest time, I didn't even know he drank. He hid it, drank on the sly. Who knows how much of our marriage he was completely pickled. It would explain a lot. So I don't know. I don't know who he drinks with or where when he disappears like this."

Zachary nodded. It didn't look like he would be able to get anything else out of her. And he didn't want to extend the interview, causing her pain, when it wasn't going anywhere. "Okay. Does he have any friends I could talk to? And maybe his work number? Someone else might know more. Even though he hid his drinking from you, others might have known about it."

"He worked at K&L Construction. But I doubt he does anymore. He'll have lost that one by now."

"Has he lost a lot of jobs to his drinking?"

"Yes. He's not a reliable worker. Employers can't be expected to keep him on when he stops showing up. I don't know if he's ever been caught drinking on the job, but his... illness has certainly kept him from being able to stick with a company for more than a few months at a time."

"And friends...?"

"I don't know. You could start knocking on doors and have better luck than you would with any leads from me. I don't know who he talks to."

"How about... his best man at your wedding?" Zachary tried. Tyrrell must have had a best friend; someone he had wanted to be at his side for that event.

Lindsey rolled her eyes. "We didn't have a ceremony. He didn't have any family around. I didn't want to blow all of my savings on some big event. We just had civil union at the courthouse. No attendants, just us and a judge signing papers."

"What about Vince and Mindy?"

Lindsey blinked at him. "Who?"

"Our youngest siblings. They were kept together in foster care, so Tyrrell knew where they were. Why weren't they a part of it?"

"Oh. Right." Lindsey shrugged. "They haven't been that close. I think they kind of drifted apart when Tyrrell aged out of foster care. You know teenagers; they don't see the need to stay close. He emails them a bit. He was a lot more excited about being reunited with the rest of you. I guess you miss what you don't have. He had a relationship with Vincent and Mindy, so he didn't value them as much as tracking down the rest of his family."

"Do you have… their contact information?"

Lindsey raised her brows and shook her head. "No. I was never in touch with them. You'll have to track them down yourself." She gave him a wry smile. "Maybe hire a private investigator."

Zachary chuckled at this. "I guess so." He put his hands on his knees, preparing to rise. He had taken enough of Lindsey's time, making her focus on something that she wanted nothing to do with.

The front door slammed open and Zachary heard a burst of children's voices as Mason and Alisha arrived home from school. He smiled fondly. He'd enjoyed getting to know them at the Lodge during their Thanksgiving vacation. It had been fun to be around kids for a little while.

Mason came around the half-wall of the doorway and spotted Zachary sitting in the living room. "Uncle Zachary!" he crowed, and threw himself at Zachary.

Zachary caught him, laughing, and gave him a tight hug. "Long time, no see! How are you doing, buddy?"

"We just got home from school. We're studying a plant unit in science right now," Mason informed him, talking rapidly, "but I think it's stupid to do a plant unit in the middle of the winter! We should do it in spring when we can plant gardens and watch them grow! Don't you think that would be better? It's stupid to have it in the middle of the winter."

Zachary nodded. "Yeah. It would probably make more sense to have it in the spring," he agreed. He thumped Mason on the back and released him. "Hey, you'd better take off your boots. You're melting in here."

Mason looked down at his feet, then shot a look at his mother. "I didn't see! I was just saying hi to Uncle Zachary."

"Go take them off at the door," Lindsey told him tiredly.

"Sorry."

Alisha's approach was more sedate. She had remembered to take off her boots and other snow gear. She looked at Zachary shyly. He opened his arms slightly to offer a hug, but kept the gesture small enough that she could choose whether she wanted to or not. Alisha stepped forward and put her arms around him. Zachary gave her a little squeeze and let her go.

"It's nice to see you too, Alisha."

"Where is Auntie Kenzie? Did she come with you too?"

"No, she's working today. I just came to talk to your mom for a few minutes…" He trailed off, unsure what he should say about Tyrrell or the fact that he was missing or out of contact. From what Lindsey had said, they knew something of the situation, but he didn't want to make them feel worse. "I just got out of the hospital, and I wanted to make sure… that everyone was okay."

Alisha nodded soberly, her face very serious. "Are you feeling better now? Daddy said that you were feeling… very sad. But that you always do around Christmas."

Zachary nodded. "I'm doing a lot better now. Christmas is over and the doctors gave me some new pills to help me feel better. So you don't need to worry about me."

Mason stomped back into the room, now in his stocking feet. He'd shed his gloves and hat but was still wearing his heavy winter coat. "*We* were sad at Christmas too," he informed Zachary. "I cried."

Zachary ruffled his hair. "I'm sorry, bud. It must have been pretty hard for you."

Mason agreed. "Why does our daddy have to drink? Why does he keep doing it if alcohol makes him feel so bad? And makes him forget to come home or pick us up?"

Zachary looked at Lindsey. She just stared back at him, not offering any direction as to where he should go with the conversation. Zachary hugged Mason and pulled him up onto his knee to cuddle and try to explain it to him.

"Because he has an addiction. He doesn't want to, and he's trying to get better, but that means that he stills goes back to drinking sometimes, even though he knows it hurts him and other people."

"Are you here to find him and tell him to stop?"

Zachary nodded, chuckling a little. "Yes. That's about it."

"Good. I want to tell him that too," Mason said boldly. But then his little face crumpled, and he buried it in Zachary's chest. "But I don't like the way he is when he's drinking. He gets really mad. And mean."

Zachary rubbed Mason's back, tears prickling his eyes. "I'm sorry about that. Our daddy drank too. I don't know if your daddy remembers what that was like, but I do. It was pretty scary."

Mason nodded, his head bumping against Zachary's breastbone.

"I'll try to help him," Zachary promised. "The first thing is… I have to find him."

10

Zachary had already been by Tyrrell's apartment and hadn't seen anything helpful there, so he decided to check out Tyrrell's last known job before going back there. Eventually, he would need to get into Tyrrell's apartment to ensure he wasn't there, hurt, sick, or worse. But it seemed prudent to get to K&L Construction before they closed for the day, if he could.

A quick search on his phone gave the address of K&L. Riverbrook was not a big place, so it wouldn't take him a long time to get there. Tyrrell had been lucky to find a place in town that would hire him, especially if his work experience was as checkered as Lindsey had said it was. Zachary had expected to find that K&L was in another town.

The office was not very big. A prefab metal trailer with rough wooden steps placed in front of the door, on a small lot surrounded by a fence so that the company's heavy equipment could be locked up at night. A yellow bulldozer and a few other pieces of equipment were parked around the corner from the front door, and probably a few more were out on jobs during the workday.

As he approached the building, Zachary felt like he had been kicked in the stomach. The sensation was so sudden and powerful that he froze mid-step and stood where he was, trying to catch his breath. He looked around, worried, trying to figure out what had triggered such a strong sense of danger and unease. His stomach cramped, and he breathed shallowly through his mouth, trying to regain control.

There was nothing to be afraid of at the little construction company. He was sure that nothing had happened to Tyrrell there. Zachary just wanted to question them about the last time they had seen Tyrrell and if they knew anything about his problems or why he had dropped out of sight. There was no reason for him to be anxious, and especially not so anxious that he couldn't proceed.

He bent over, pressing his hands to his thighs to keep himself upright. He had no idea what had triggered the panic. He kept looking around, trying to identify the danger. He knew that his instincts, his animal brain, might have caught some danger that his logical brain had not yet processed. Or his anxiety might have been triggered by something completely innocuous, like when he walked into a room where there was a lit candle. Or sometimes, even an unlit one.

He still couldn't see anything that should have triggered his reaction, so he forced himself to take one step and then another, and keep pressing forward to the office. Turning away wasn't going to help him overcome the anxiety. It wouldn't help him advance his investigation into Tyrrell's disappearance either.

It wasn't until he walked into the trailer that his conscious brain finally started to make the connections his unconscious brain had already made.

Jose.

Going to Jose's place of work when investigating *his* disappearance. Jose had been an illegal immigrant who was a friend of Pat's, working for a small landscaping company. There was a superficial resemblance between the office of the landscaping company Jose had worked for and the construction company Tyrrell had worked for. They were probably nothing alike, but both had a small prefab front office with heavy equipment behind them in a fenced lot.

And, of course, the search for Jose had not gone well. He had been the victim of a serial killer. A killer who Zachary had also run afoul of, though thankfully he had been rescued before Archuro had been able to follow through on all of his plans. But he had still left a lot of scars, both physical and mental. Zachary's body had clearly connected the configuration of the landscaping office with what had happened to him later.

Understanding the trigger for his panic helped. This case would be nothing like the search for missing Jose. Nothing had happened to Tyrrell. He had just gone on a bender, like Lindsey said. There was no serial killer this time. Zachary would find Tyrrell and make sure he didn't need anything, maybe help him get himself into a detox program. And then he would go home, knowing that he had helped his brother all he could.

He stood there in front of the office for another minute, breathing slowly in and out and trying to calm the pounding of his heart. He could get through it. Dr. B assured him that the best way to get over the trigger for a panic attack was to face it and push through. It had worked for fire. It would work for other things.

After his breathing and heart rate had slowed to a more normal speed, he stepped up the rough wooden stairs to the door of the office, knocked a couple of times, and tried the handle. It turned in his hand, and he walked into the reception area. Again, very similar to the one at Jose's construction company. Nothing to be afraid of. There were probably hundreds of little industrial offices that followed exactly the same pattern. How creative could they get with such a small space?

There was a man at the reception desk, not a woman. That was different from his investigation into Jose's disappearance. A concrete difference that he could hold onto.

"Hello," Zachary said with a friendly nod, still finding himself slightly out of breath, like he had run up a flight of steps, but pushing ahead anyway. "I wonder if there is a supervisor or owner here that I can talk to about an employee or former employee."

"Who are you?" the man demanded in a less-than-friendly tone. He was tall and spare, gray hair cut close to his head.

"My name is... Zachary Goldman."

"Goldman," the man repeated. "Then I guess I know which employee you're inquiring about." He shrugged. "You may as well just go back the way you came. You're not going to find him around here."

"I suspected as much," Zachary said with a nod, trying to look and sound as sympathetic as possible. "I wonder if you could tell me... what his last day was. When he worked last."

"Been a while. I'd have to check the computer."

But he made no move to do so, shuffling through the papers on the desk in front of him and initialing forms. Zachary shifted his feet.

"I'd appreciate that."

"Your brother left us high and dry." He glanced up from the papers to Zachary's face. "Brother?" he repeated, checking.

"Yeah. He's my brother. Though we haven't actually... known each other that long. I have been away, and I just got into town and found out

41

that he kind of disappeared a few weeks ago. I'm trying to retrace his steps. See if I can track him down and make sure he's okay."

"Why? You think something happened to him?"

"No, probably not. But I'd like to make sure. And help him if there is anything I can do to get him back on track again."

"Nothing you can do for guys like that. They'll just keep messing you up as long as you let them. Need to leave him alone, let them deal with the consequences of their actions instead of bailing them out."

"I'm not bailing him out. I don't know where he is or if he's gotten himself into any trouble. But I need to find out."

"Suit yourself. You're not going to get anywhere."

"Does that mean you know what happened to him?" Zachary asked tentatively. "Did you hear where he went or what he was doing?"

"Out on a drunk, I assume. He told us when he started here that he was in recovery. Said he was on the wagon and working on emotional sobriety, whatever that means. He was a dry drunk. Sometimes we give guys like that a chance. See if they can keep things together." The man initialed a few more pages. He shrugged. "Obviously, Goldman couldn't."

"You don't know where he might have gone or any of his drinking buddies? Anything at all that gave you a clue where he might go?"

"Not my concern. I have a business to run. If he's going to go off like that... nothing I can do about it. He's going to have to deal with the consequences himself. He won't have a job if he ever shows up here again. But chances are, he won't. They never do."

"Did he leave anything here? Did he have a locker where he might have left any personal items?"

"Cleared it out already. Tossed anything that couldn't be reused. Kept the hardhat. Tool belt."

"He didn't have any papers? Photographs? What kind of things did you have to throw out?"

"Pay stubs, mostly. He hadn't worked here long enough to have accumulated a lot of personal items. And we discourage them from keeping them in their lockers. It's a business. We don't need them sticking up naked pictures of their girlfriends inside. Unprofessional." He shook his head. "I don't remember anything of interest in Tyrrell's locker. Sorry."

"Do you think you could look up what day he worked last?"

The man sighed. He raised his head again and studied Zachary closely.

"I *would* ask for ID. Shouldn't be giving out any personal information about former employees. But you look alike. He's not a scarecrow like you are, but his face is the same. His eyes. Real family resemblance there, isn't there?"

Zachary nodded. He and Tyrrell both had the same dark hair and eyes. Similar facial structures. They took after their father. "I have identification if you want it. Photo ID. And I don't need anything else, just the date he showed up last. And if he has any friends in the company..."

"Not really. I had him floating from crew to crew, hadn't assigned him anywhere permanently. If he'd made close friends, I would have kept him on the crew he worked the best with. But he didn't go out with anyone after work. Made a fuss about how he didn't drink anymore. Couldn't go to the bar for drinks after they knocked off for the day." The manager shrugged. "Don't imagine there's anyone here who could tell you where he went when he fell off the wagon."

"Okay." Zachary stood there, waiting. If the manager wanted him to leave, he would have to look up that date on the computer sooner or later.

The man shook his head and sighed again, then turned toward a narrow corridor that led along the side of the trailer to whatever office spaces he had carved out. "Wait here a minute."

Zachary let his eyes wander around the interior of the office while he waited. It was spartan, undecorated. No feminine touches. No inspirational posters or signs outlining the company rules or safety issues. Utilitarian. It was a few minutes before the man returned, an envelope in his hand.

"December tenth," he advised. "That was the last date he worked. Then he never showed up again. After missing two shifts, we terminated him." He held the slim envelope in Zachary's direction. "There's his final pay, if you find him."

"I probably shouldn't," Zachary said, not taking it. If he didn't find Tyrrell, what would he do with the check? Just keep carrying it around with him? He'd rather leave the responsibility with the company. They could mail it to his apartment.

The man twitched the envelope. "Come on. Chances are better that you'll see him than I will. You might as well take it."

"Well, I guess." Zachary conceded and took the envelope from him. He looked down at it, at "Tyrrell Goldman" showing through the window, and nothing else.

11

Zachary took long, slow, even breaths as he walked back to his car in the parking lot. Darkness was gathering and his car sat in a pool of light cast by a streetlight. He had made it through the interview without spiraling into a panic attack over the similarities between the investigations into Jose's disappearance and Tyrrell's. He had kept the memories of that case from flooding back, but couldn't hold them off any longer. When he slid into the seat of his car, he put his hands over his eyes and let go.

His brain replayed his investigations into Jose's work, the other immigrants he lived with, all crammed into a tiny apartment, and the men that Jose saw romantically. Blind to what had been in front of Zachary's face all along, to the man who was watching and stalking him. All of the questions and the driving curiosity that had led to him being taken to that cabin, where he'd been drugged and held and tortured.

"Hey, what do you think you're doing here?"

Zachary straightened with a shock, dropping his hands from his eyes, lids flying open to identify his attacker and protect himself. This time he would protect himself. He wouldn't be taken unaware.

He held his hands out in front of him. A heavyset, sweaty-faced man bent over, peering in at him.

"You can't just sit here," the man told him aggressively. "You're trespassing on private property. Get out of here."

"I was just… resting for a minute."

"You can't sleep here. Go find somewhere else. We don't need your kind around here."

Zachary blinked his eyes, trying to banish the flashbacks once and for all. He focused on the angry man's face, trying to stay fully present. "My kind?" he repeated, not sure what he was referring to.

"Drunks. Junkies. This is a business, not a place to crash."

"I'm not a drunk," Zachary said evenly. "I was just talking to the manager—" he tipped his head in the direction of the office he had just come from. "I was looking for some information on my brother. And then I was just—I had something in my eye. I was trying to get it out."

"You're already changing your story. First, you were resting, now you were washing something out of your eye. Go somewhere else, or I'll call the cops."

"Do you work here? At K&L?"

The man's eyes went to the office, then back to Zachary. "So you actually looked at the sign. So what, is that supposed to impress me?"

"I'm looking for my brother. If you work here… maybe you could help me."

"I'm not here to answer your questions. I have plenty of my own work to do. You worry about your own family and leave me to mine."

"Tyrrell Goldman. Do you know him?"

The man pursed his lips, looking at Zachary speculatively. "Goldman. Yeah, Goldman used to work here. You're his brother?" He shook his head. "Good riddance to bad rubbish, I say. And you look worse than him."

Zachary knew that with his dead white skin and cadaverous face, he didn't look particularly well. He did look like a strung-out drunk or junkie. The man couldn't be blamed for thinking that.

"I've been sick," he informed the man. "I've been through chemotherapy recently."

It wasn't a lie. But it wasn't exactly the full truth either. But it would, hopefully, be enough to turn the tide in his favor. Not a junkie, but a man who was sick, maybe dying.

"Oh. Well, yeah, you look like it. So what are you doing here? Shouldn't you be… resting in bed?"

"Would you be resting in bed if your bother was missing?"

"If he was a piece of trash like Goldman, yeah, I would. I don't know why they bothered to hire him in the first place. Boss knew that he was a drunk. Should have known that he wouldn't be any good."

45

Zachary ground his teeth at Tyrrell being classified as "a piece of trash." He'd dealt with all kinds of bullying and name-calling growing up. People who thought they could get away with it because he was a foster child, because he was always in trouble and tried to keep his head down, because he was poor and they had power on their side. But ignoring name-calling when someone was denigrating him and letting this man call his brother undeserved names were two very different things.

"Don't call him that. You don't know anything about him or what he has been through."

"Oh, I'm supposed to care why he's a drunk? Everybody has a sob story. I hate the way everybody thinks they have the right to use their 'traumatic' pasts to excuse bad behavior. How we're supposed to feel sorry for all of the poor people and addicts because they haven't had the courage to pull themselves up by their bootstraps like everybody else. You think I was born with a silver spoon in my mouth?" The man gestured to himself. Greasy, five o'clock shadow, stained clothing soaked with sweat around the collar and armpits. "Me? You think that anyone ever gave me a chance just because I whined and made a big deal about how badly I'd been done by? No. I didn't have good parents. I didn't have money growing up. But I didn't become a drunk or an addict. I'm a hard worker. Been here a lot longer than Goldman, and I'll be here long after. Because I'm willing to put in the work, and he isn't. He uses it as an excuse to drink and just stop showing up."

"You don't know anything about it."

And to be honest, Zachary really didn't either. He and Tyrrell hadn't talked a lot about what had happened to each of them in foster care. They covered it in broad strokes—who they had been with and for how long—and left the rest unsaid. Tyrrell hadn't given Zachary any reason to think that he'd been abused in foster care, but that didn't mean that he hadn't been. Zachary hadn't told Tyrrell much about the abuses he had suffered either. He tried to bury it, not even to think about it himself. Tyrrell knew of Zachary's mental health struggles and the institutions he had lived in, but he'd never had much to say about his own alcoholism, implying that it was something he had overcome years before and that he was perfectly fine now. And Zachary hadn't bothered to pursue it, to dig down deep enough to find out his story.

"You need to move on," the sweaty man told Zachary, motioning for him to pull his car out. "I don't care what you were here for. You're just loitering here now, trespassing on private property."

"Did you know Tyrrell very well?" Zachary asked, turning the key in the ignition so that the man could see he was getting ready to go, as he had been asked. "Did you work with him at all?"

"He was on my crew a couple of times. But he wasn't a good worker, if that's what you want to know. He just skated by, barely putting thought into anything he did. Figured he was better than anyone else. He had a degree. He was supposed to be this smart, educated guy who was just stuck in a dead-end job because of his addiction. But he didn't know anything. He wasn't any better than anyone else he worked with. He was a lot worse."

Zachary was careful not to show his surprise at these statements. He'd expected the man to denigrate Tyrrell's work, but Tyrrell had a degree? That was news to him. Tyrrell had never said anything about it. Zachary would not have thought that he would be able to get through college with an addiction. Maybe his alcoholism hadn't come until later, when he was looking for a job, trying to put that education to use. Maybe it hadn't come until he'd failed at several jobs and realized that what he had earned through his hard work and study wasn't going to get him anywhere in life. That it had all just been a waste of time.

Zachary had wondered a few times whether he should go to college to upgrade his education. There were night school classes. He could attend programs while still working as a private investigator, as long as he didn't let any surveillance jobs get in the way of it. Money had been a problem up until he had hit a few big cases in a row. Now that he could afford it, he wasn't sure he wanted to. Wasn't sure it would actually get him anywhere in life.

"So, you had a problem with him. You didn't like him."

The man nodded in agreement. "Yeah. I didn't like him."

"What is your name?"

The man folded his arms across his chest. "I don't see how that's any of your business."

"Well, if it turns out that something has happened to him... it's always good to know who his enemies were."

1 2

Zachary returned to Tyrrell's apartment building. Tyrrell's marked space was still empty, of course, so he pulled into it. He went into the alcove with the call buttons again and pressed the one that should be Tyrrell's. No answer again.

He could see that there were more people home. More cars filled the parking lot than had been there previously. He could probably raise a few of Tyrrell's neighbors if he pushed the other buttons.

But would that help him at all? Would it help Tyrrell? If his neighbors were like his co-worker at K&L, they were probably indifferent and didn't pay much attention to Tyrrell's absence or presence but, if Zachary harassed them, they might target Tyrrell when he returned. Zachary didn't want to make things worse for him.

He pressed Tyrrell's button again, holding it down for a few seconds. Of course, that didn't make any difference. He hadn't expected it to. If Tyrrell hadn't answered it the first few times, he wouldn't answer it the next time because Zachary held the button down.

Zachary sighed.

There was no button for a manager. No indication if there were a resident manager to handle complaints. He hadn't seen a sign anywhere outside indicating where he could go or call for help, either.

Eventually, he gave in and looked up the phone number for the River-brook police department on his phone. There was no point in dialing 9-1-

1. The town was probably too small to have 9-1-1 service and, even if they did, he couldn't claim that it was an emergency when Tyrrell had been absent for weeks. Unless he lied and said he had reason to believe that Tyrrell was in imminent danger. And it wouldn't take the police long to figure out that he had deliberately lied and charge him for wasting police resources.

"Riverbrook Police," a woman announced, picking up after one ring. Was it a good sign that she didn't have half a dozen other calls backed up ahead of him, because someone would get on to the case quickly? Or bad because the Riverbrook police didn't have much experience?

"Hi. My name is Zachary Goldman, and I'm in Riverbrook because my brother hasn't been answering any calls, and I'm checking up on him. He's not answering his door, either. I'm worried something has happened to him. Could you send the police out for a welfare check?"

"How long has he not been answering calls, and why do you think there's anything to be concerned about?"

"I've been in the hospital, but the other members of the family have been trying to reach him since Christmas. I just talked to his employer, and the last time he reported to work was December tenth. That's a long time ago, now."

"No one has seen him since then?"

"No."

Not that Zachary had talked to a lot of other people and gotten dates from them. It seemed like most of the family hadn't been trying to reach him until Christmas Day. Had anyone even tried to contact him between the tenth and twenty-fifth? Or did he think that everyone cared so little that no one had even noticed his absence during those two weeks?

"What is his name? How old is he?"

Zachary gave her his information and all of the follow-up details she wanted.

"We will try to reach him before coming out. You're at his home now?"

"Yes. Outside."

"Can you see in through the windows?"

"It's an apartment building. I can't see anything from outside and can't get into the building unless someone lets me in."

She got Zachary's phone number to call him back to report, and terminated the call.

Zachary left the security alcove and wandered around the front of the building for a few minutes, waiting. But he didn't want people to be concerned about a stranger lurking around the building in the dark, so he got back into the car and sat there, hoping that somehow, Tyrrell would answer the phone when the police called. But of course he wouldn't. He would answer a call from his brother before answering one from a number that had no identification or said Riverbrook Police.

Eventually, his phone rang and Zachary raised it quickly to his ear. "Hello?"

"Zachary. Where are you? I was wondering if you were going to be home for dinner."

It was Kenzie, not the police. Zachary looked at the time. He had been thinking about the time of day in terms of when he needed to meet Lindsey and when people would be arriving home from work. He hadn't thought once about Kenzie getting home and wondering where he was. He hadn't told her what he had planned for the day.

"Oh. Sorry, I wasn't thinking about it getting so late. No… I'm not going to be able to get home in time for supper. I'm sorry. I'm not quite back into the routine."

"No." She was silent for a moment. "I thought you would just be catching up on emails and communications with the people who had reached out to you while you were in the hospital. That you would be mostly at home for the first few days, until you got back into the swing of things."

He could hear the implied criticism. He was jumping into things too fast, doing things too soon instead of letting himself acclimatize to being out of the hospital. But he couldn't just sit still and wait. It had been different when he had been in the hospital after they had met two years before. He had been in a car accident then and had needed a lot of physical rehabilitation. It had forced him to take things more slowly.

"I'm not working, actually." Maybe that would ease her concerns, and maybe not. "I'm in Riverbrook. Came to see if I could talk to Tyrrell."

"You're in Riverbrook?"

"Yes. Sorry, I should have let you know I was going out of town. I didn't think about it. Or about the timing."

"So, are you even coming home tonight?"

"Yes, I'll come home once I'm finished here."

Zachary looked around. He would already be driving back to Roxboro in the dark. He didn't know how long it would take for the police to make it there and check on Tyrrell. Zachary would need to file a missing person report. Even if he were done in an hour, it would be eight o'clock or later before he got home.

And he wasn't going to be done in an hour.

"I'll get home as soon as I can, but it might be late. Sorry. I couldn't see Lindsey until she was home from work, so things got pushed back a lot later than I would have liked…"

"Well, Tyrrell is your brother, and if something has happened to him…"

"Nobody else is doing anything about it. I get why they aren't, but… I need to."

"Yeah. But you'll be back tonight for sure."

"Yes. For sure. As soon as I've finished dealing with the police."

"All right. I'll see you tonight, then. How are you feeling today? Has everything gone okay?"

"Yes." Zachary thought about the stress level at Lindsey's house and his panic attack in approaching the construction company office. All par for the course. He'd been able to keep from melting down. The meds were working. "I've been feeling okay."

"Have you eaten?"

"No. I'll grab something when I'm done here. Eat on the way back."

As long as he remembered. He missed more meals than he liked to admit. Between meds that dampened his appetite and being focused on other things, food seemed unimportant.

"Make sure you do. And I still have cookies, when you get here."

"Dessert. I won't forget that."

Kenzie snorted. "Right. Keep me informed, okay? Let me know if you find anything out and when you're on your way back."

A dark car pulled up behind Zachary's, headlights reflecting in his mirror, and sat right behind him.

Zachary agreed and, after goodbyes, terminated the call.

The car behind him laid on the horn. He looked at it in the mirror. It was not a police car. No flashing lights or markings. He looked at it for a minute, waiting to see what the driver wanted. Maybe it was the building manager or security, and they didn't like him sitting there.

He opened his door and stood up. As he walked over to the car, the driver rolled down his window. A man. Scruffy growth of beard. From what Zachary could see of him, a fairly big man. And he wasn't happy.

"Get out of my parking space," the man snapped.

Zachary looked back at his car. "Oh… I'm sorry." But he was pretty sure he had picked the right stall for Tyrrell's unit number. Maybe the man had an arrangement with Tyrrell. Maybe Tyrrell rented him the space and parked out on the street somewhere. Less convenient for him, but a bit of money to help offset the bills. "I thought… isn't this Tyrrell's parking space?"

"Who is Tyrrell?"

"My brother. In unit 201. I thought this was his slot."

"He's not in unit 201. I am."

"You are. Oh. I guess I got the wrong number. I'll move out of your way." Zachary paused. "Do you know what unit Tyrrell is in? We look similar. Dark hair and eyes, he's a bit taller than I am."

"No. Never met him."

Zachary headed back to his car to move it out of the way. There were still several open spaces, but he was afraid that the owners of those spaces would be getting home soon and he would just go through the same process again. He didn't want to irritate everyone in the building. So he parked off to the side, illegally, close to a group of parking stalls that were filled up, so that he wasn't blocking entry to anyone else. The resident of unit 201 pulled into his parking space and got out of his car. He shot an angry look in Zachary's direction.

Zachary walked quickly toward him. "I was just wondering… how long have you been in unit 201?"

"Just a couple of weeks. Why?"

"Do you know the name of the person who was in there before you?"

13

The man shook his head. "Why, you think it was your brother?"

Zachary took a deep breath in and let it out slowly. "I was told that was his unit. And no one has been able to get ahold of him. So... maybe. I don't know. Is there a manager or someone around? The police are going to be here, and if I have the wrong unit for Tyrrell, that could be a little embarrassing."

"The police are coming? Why?"

"My brother is missing. No one has seen him for weeks."

The man raised an eyebrow. "Well... sorry to hear that. I hope everything is okay."

He hesitated before patting his pockets and eventually coming up with a business card and a pen. He wrote a phone number on the back of the card.

"The manager is Gerald. At that number. He should be able to help you out."

"Thanks."

"Hope you find your brother. Good luck."

Zachary nodded and watched the man enter the building. He didn't try to catch the door and enter after him. His phone vibrated, and he pulled it out and answered the call identified as Riverbrook PD.

"Hello?"

"We tried to reach your brother by phone and were unable to get through to him. A car has been dispatched to the building and should be there in a few minutes."

"Thanks. I just got the phone number of the manager from one of the other residents—"

"You can give that to the officers when they arrive. That will be helpful, I'm sure. Is there anything else I can do for you?"

"I'm just wondering… about checking hospitals, the morgue, that kind of thing? If there are any unidentified patients or…"

"The police will deal with that once they have had a chance to do the welfare check. They know what they're doing. They'll help you out."

"Okay, thanks. I guess that's it, then. Thanks for your help."

She ended the call. Zachary didn't feel like getting back into his car, just to get out again in five minutes when the police arrived, so he paced around, keeping an eye out for anything unusual or suspicious, until a marked patrol car pulled into the parking lot. It wasn't like he expected to find any evidence of foul play in Tyrrell's disappearance. But he'd worked too many cases to take it at face value. Weird things happened. Sometimes the most vanilla of cases could turn out to be something much more complex and sinister than it appeared.

But that wasn't going to happen with Tyrrell. He was sure it was just what everyone else kept telling him. Tyrrell had fallen prey to his own addiction. And it was up to Zachary to find him and try to bring him back.

Two officers got out of the police car. One of them was looking at a notepad. "You're Tyrrell Goldman?"

"No, I'm Zachary Goldman. I'm looking for Tyrrell Goldman. I need to make sure he is okay."

The cop nodded. He was an older man. In a bigger city, a man of his age would not have been on patrol. He would probably be a detective or working a desk at the police station. Leaving patrol positions to the younger, more physically active officers. But in a small town like Riverbrook, he might have any rank and decades of experience.

"When is the last time you saw him?"

"Before Christmas. Early December. I talked to his work, and the last day he showed up there was December tenth." Zachary shifted his stance, feeling awkward. "I'm just looking into it now because I've been in the hospital. I didn't know that he'd dropped out of sight."

"What have you found out so far?"

"I don't know of anyone who saw him after that. December tenth. He was supposed to visit me on Christmas Day, had made arrangements with my sisters to come by, but he didn't show up and didn't answer the phone. He was supposed to have his kids for the holiday too, but he never showed up to pick them up."

The cop nodded, tapping his pen against his notepad. "Was he usually pretty reliable about that?"

"I think… he has been for the past year. But he has a history of alcoholism and goes off on binges sometimes."

"Thought I recognized the name." The cop nodded toward the apartment building. "You've buzzed him?"

"Yeah, there's no answer. And I think… this guy here…" Zachary pointed to the car that had pulled into slot 201. "I think he actually is living in the apartment Tyrrell was renting."

"They know each other? Or your brother lost it?"

"I guess he lost it. I got the number for the manager." Zachary handed the cop the business card with Gerald's number on the back.

He looked at both sides of it and then handed it to his partner. "Call him. Get him over here to talk with us in person."

The junior cop looked doubtful. "For a drunk?" He glanced at Zachary. "He's not going to want to come over here. Can't we just deal with him on the phone?"

"No. He will have to leave his beer and his TV and come here to talk with us. Tell us exactly what he knows and what happened to the subject's possessions if he turned around and rented the unit to another tenant."

The junior officer shrugged and walked away from them to make the call with the manager more private.

The older cop was studying Zachary. He looked away from the man's face and squinted at his name bar. Sergeant Fontaine.

"Do you live around here?" Fontaine asked.

"In Roxboro."

"You look familiar. Like I've seen you around here before."

"No. I don't live here." Zachary hesitated. "There was a case I dealt with a year ago that kind of made it to national news."

"A case?" Fontaine frowned. "Are you on the job?"

"On the job" meaning in law enforcement. Zachary shook his head. "I'm a private investigator. I was involved in a serial killer case about a year ago. You might have seen some of the coverage."

"Yeah. Yeah, I think I might have." Fontaine looked suspicious. "I thought you said this was your brother. Are you stretching the truth?

Looking for someone for a client? I want to know the facts here. Don't try to snow me."

"Tyrrell is my brother," Zachary assured him. He patted his pockets and found his wallet. He showed his driver's license to Fontaine. "You see? Goldman. I don't have a client; I am looking for my brother because I'm concerned about him. Someone else should have gotten the police on it while I was in the hospital, but I guess they didn't feel like it was the right thing to do. So…" Zachary shrugged helplessly. "Now it's been weeks and the trail is going to be cold."

"Very," Fontaine agreed. His eyes went to his partner, who walked back toward them.

"Yeah, he's going to come, but he wasn't happy about it," the younger man said. "Like I said."

Fontaine rolled his eyes. "We don't do police work so that people will like us. We do what needs to be done."

The younger man still projected attitude as he stood there, waiting for further instructions or for the manager to show up. Zachary looked at his name bar as well. Moss.

Fontaine asked Zachary a few more questions while they stood waiting for the manager. Zachary was starting to get cold. He slapped his hands together, stomped his feet, and pulled his hat down snugly over the tops of his ears. When the manager, a sixty-ish, balding man, showed up, Fontaine motioned to the building. "Let's talk inside where it's more comfortable."

Gerald grumbled but agreed and led them all in, unlocking the door on the other side of the alcove. There were a couple of upholstered chairs and artificial trees in a lobby that was probably never used by the residents. Zachary didn't sit, but was happy to be somewhere warmer. The temperature dropped like a rock when the sun went down.

"We're looking for Tyrrell Goldman," Fontaine told Gerald. "He seems to have dropped out of sight. He lives or lived here?"

"Yeah, I'd love to find him too," Gerald said. "Didn't pay his January rent, and I had to come around looking for it. After knocking on his door a few times and talking to his neighbors, I entered his unit. Food rotting in the fridge. Air was stale; that door hadn't been opened in days. Left him a note to call me in case he did come back, but he didn't. Cleaned it out so someone else could rent it."

"Do you know what day it was when you went looking for the rent?"

Gerald scratched the back of his neck. "They're supposed to pay their rent a month in advance, the ones who use checks. So that I don't have to go looking for them at the beginning of the month and can just make one deposit. Most of them have automatic e-transfers set up; heckuva lot easier."

Fontaine nodded. "So, at the beginning of December, you were looking for the January check?"

Gerald considered again, shaking his head slowly. "Wasn't as early as that. I've got a lot to do the first week of the month, making sure that everyone is moved in and things are running smoothly. It would have been the second week, at least." He thought about it some more. "Had to advertise for a new tenant, get the place cleaned out and ready for him for January first." He chewed the inside of his cheek. "Maybe the middle of the month. Thirteenth, fifteenth, something like that. I can look up what day I sent a new ad into the paper if you need to know. But he hadn't been there for a while. The food was going bad."

"After the tenth."

Gerald nodded. "Yeah. Definitely after the tenth. I couldn't have got there much earlier than that."

"What did you do with Tyrrell Goldman's possessions?"

"Threw out most of it. Just crap, garage sale stuff. Nothing the next guy would want or that anyone would bother coming back for. I kept a few personal things, just in case he did, but there's not much."

"We'd like to see it, please."

"I have it in storage." Gerald cleared his throat, rolled his eyes, and eventually took out a ring of keys and led them to a back corridor where the apartment mailboxes and utility and storage rooms were located.

"Was there any sign of violence or a break-in in the apartment?" Fontaine asked. "Blood? Door wasn't forced? Didn't look like it had been ransacked?"

"No, none of that. Just like the guy walked out and didn't bother to come back. Maybe something happened to him, I don't know. But I think he just never came back."

He unlocked the storage room door and took them into it. There were several boxes on a shelving unit with names on them. He selected a cardboard banker's box with Goldman written on the end and pulled it off the shelf. "Like I said... there wasn't very much."

He handed the box to Fontaine. It had no lid, and Zachary tried to peer down inside, which wasn't easy since Fontaine was quite a bit taller than he was.

"Let's have a quick look," Fontaine said. He set it down on a folding table and started to pull items out and place them on the table. There were a couple of changes of clothing. A cheap laptop for web surfing or small office jobs. Charging cables. Some mail that had either been left in the apartment or had arrived after Tyrrell's disappearance and been thrown in on top. A largish brown envelope that contained some papers and photographs.

"Can I look at those?" Zachary asked.

Fontaine gave him a look, then started to lay the contents out on the table.

14

All of Tyrrell's accumulated personal possessions fit in that little box, except for what he might have had in his pockets. Zachary looked at the papers and photographs. Tyrrell's old marriage certificate with his and Lindsey's names on it, corners crumpled and dirty. Some family photographs—the children when they were born, lying in hospital bassinets. A couple of happy family shots. Other bits and pieces.

"Do you mind if I take pictures?" Zachary asked, taking out his phone.

"Go ahead." Fontaine shrugged. "All of this is going to go to you if your brother doesn't turn up anyway."

"Thanks." Zachary carefully framed each paper and took a picture of it.

He didn't see any sign of anything from Tyrrell's early life. No pictures of Vincent and Mindy or their foster parents. No awards or report cards from school. No prom photographs or even pictures of Lindsey and Tyrrell together without the kids.

If Lindsey had been telling the truth when she said that Tyrrell had disappeared like this several times before—and Zachary couldn't see any reason she would be lying about that—then he had probably lost any earlier possessions on other binges. Landlords and shelters wouldn't keep them for long. Tyrrell would lose whatever he'd owned.

"He hasn't called or left a forwarding address?" Fontaine asked.

Gerald shook his head. "No. I wouldn't still have this here if he had. That's the rental business, though; people just take off sometimes."

Zachary had worked other missing person cases and he knew it was true. Sometimes life just became overwhelming and people ran away. Teenagers weren't the only ones who took off, looking for a better life. But like teenagers, adults rarely found any happiness in running away. Most returned home within a week, maybe two. But one thing that Zachary had discovered was that they usually stayed close to home. They didn't take off on a multistate journey looking for the gold at the other end of the rainbow like in some budget TV movie. They tended to stay in the area they knew and still felt safe in.

So, where was Tyrrell? Where would he have settled? Did he already have another apartment where he had started fresh? Had he crashed at a friend's, as Zachary had after fire destroyed his apartment? A homeless shelter was a less-likely possibility, barely better than sleeping rough on the street. Vermont winters were cold. Homeless people moved inside during the winter as much as they could. Was Tyrrell squatting somewhere in an abandoned house or warehouse with other alcoholics and addicts? Zachary stared off into space, trying to put it all together. But he had very little to go on yet.

"Mr. Goldman."

He realized that Fontaine was talking to him again. "Sorry—what?"

"Do you want to come down to the police station and file a missing person report?"

"Yeah. I'd better do that." Zachary pushed the button on his phone to look at the time. He needed to get the report done quickly and get home to Kenzie. He didn't want her waiting up for him, or going to bed before he got home, wondering if something had happened to him.

Despite his hopes, things did not move quickly at the police station. They never did, even when he was working with the law enforcement officers who were his friends. The cops in Riverbrook didn't know him. They tended to be suspicious of the fact that he was a private investigator and had worked some cases that had blown up big in the media. They suspected his motives, thought he wasn't really Tyrrell's brother, thought that there must be more to it than a man who had just dropped out of sight. They insisted on dotting all of the I's and crossing all of the T's and going over everything three times, just to ensure they couldn't be accused of making a mistake or not doing their duty if *this* case should go public.

And there were forms. Zachary had known that there would be, but he hadn't actually made a missing person report before and was surprised at just how much they needed him to fill out. His learning disabilities made form-filling extra tedious. He had to write very slowly to form the letters so that they would be legible to someone who tried to read them later. He *could* print neatly, but it took about five times as long as his usual chicken scratch.

He rubbed his eyes and the muscles around them, strained with fatigue. It was a good thing that he'd listened to Kenzie and gotten in so much sleep the night before because, even with seven hours under his belt, he was fading.

"Sorry to take so long with this," a female cop told him in a brisk, unapologetic tone as she went through his forms a second time and asked additional questions, adding her notes here and there as he clarified certain details.

Zachary nodded. He told himself that it was good they were being so thorough. Maybe there was a chance that they would actually help track Tyrrell down, and he wouldn't have to do all of the work himself.

But he wasn't holding his breath.

"And your contact information is correct?" She read Zachary's phone number, email address, and postal address back to him. It reminded Zachary that he needed to stop by his apartment to make sure that no one had left him anything there. There was bound to at least be junk mail in his mailbox. It could really stack up over a few weeks. There shouldn't be anything urgent in the postal mail; everyone used email or phone if it were time-sensitive. But he should check, just in case.

"Yes, that's all right," Zachary agreed. He stood up. She hadn't dismissed him, but he suspected that if he didn't take matters into his own hands, they would keep him busy all night long. "I have to head home. I'll be available by phone tomorrow, and I'll be back here as soon as I come across anything that suggests where he might have gone. Just give me a call if you think of anything else."

"I'm not sure the sergeant has finished with you..." The woman looked at her wristwatch.

Zachary shook his head. "If there is anything else, have him give me a call. I'll have my phone on Bluetooth and can talk while I'm driving home. I need to get on my way before I'm too tired to drive."

"I suppose," she agreed grudgingly. "As long as we can reach you."

"I'll be doing everything I can to find my brother. If you come up with any leads or have any questions, I'll be right on top of it. I want to make sure he is okay."

15

It felt good to get out to the highway again. The drive was cleansing, as if he were showering off all of the accumulated grime of the day. Washing his brain of all of the anxiety and just immersing himself in the driving. His kind of meditation.

And then he was home. The outside light was on for him, and Kenzie was still up, though yawning.

"Come have something to eat," she told him, giving him a quick peck on the lips. "And tell me how your day went."

Zachary went into the kitchen, realizing that he hadn't remembered to stop for something on the way home. Kenzie had probably already guessed that. She started pulling dishes out of the fridge to put a plate together for him.

"You don't need to do that," Zachary objected. "I can fix something myself. Or maybe I'll just have cookies."

"You'll have dinner *and* cookies." She continued to prepare his late supper despite his objection. "You must be exhausted."

"I'm okay. Really. You're probably just as tired as I am."

Kenzie pushed the plate into the microwave, threw a cover over it, and started the microwave cooking.

"Were you able to find anything out about Tyrrell?"

"Not much. Lindsey says that he's done this before, just disappearing and making everyone around him worry, and then he shows up again later. So that's good news if things go the same way this time."

Kenzie nodded her agreement.

"I stopped by his workplace, but he didn't give them any kind of notice. Just stopped showing up. Same with his apartment. He didn't pay the rent and hadn't returned. It's already been rented to someone else."

"That was quick!"

"Landlord cleaned it out as soon as he knew Tyrrell hadn't paid for January and had left food rotting in the fridge."

"I'm not sure if that's legal. Tenants have rights. He'd already paid for December, right?"

Zachary shrugged. "It doesn't matter whether he cleaned it out in December or January; it all comes out to the same. Tyrrell walked out and didn't go back."

"So... do you have any leads?"

Zachary scratched the back of his neck. Kenzie took the food out of the microwave and put it on the table for Zachary, giving him a fork from the dishwasher. She started putting away the clean dishes while he took a few bites.

"I don't know. I have to think about it all... there's nothing immediately helpful, but maybe I can figure something out. I'll call the hospitals near there, see if they have seen Tyrrell or a John Doe that matches his description."

"They can't tell you anything under the privacy laws."

"No... but I can usually find something out." Zachary smiled like he did when talking to nurses and receptionists at the hospital. "I'm charming."

"They're just afraid that you're going to drop dead if they cause any stress," Kenzie returned. "You don't look like you'd stand up to a strong wind."

Zachary's smile grew, and he tried to mask it as he ate leftover lasagna. Maybe she was right. It was more because they felt sorry for him than that he cut such a dashing figure. "Anyway. If he's been there, I should be able to find something out."

"You should leave it to the police. They can actually talk to the hospital in conjunction with a missing person investigation. You filed an official report, right?"

"Yes. Of course. But I don't think they're going to do much about it.

Tyrrell has already been missing for weeks. They missed their chance to do anything in the first forty-eight hours."

"That doesn't mean they won't investigate it."

"It means it won't be a high priority. There are a lot more cases they have a better chance of solving than a guy who disappeared weeks ago. They probably won't do much more than going to his employer to find out if they know anything about where Tyrrell went and if anyone he worked with was close to him."

"Which you've already checked."

"Yeah. Not much there. I can go back if nothing else pans out, actually talk to each of the employees who has worked with him. But the boss is probably right. He didn't make friends there. Didn't work on the same crew regularly. If he'd made a friend, he would have been sure to get himself put on the same crew."

"Mmm. Maybe," Kenzie agreed. "And Lindsey didn't have any idea where he would go? Who he might be with? Tyrrell must have had a few friends. He's an outgoing, friendly guy."

"She doesn't even have numbers for Vince and Mindy. She doesn't know where he usually goes when he's on a binge. No favorite watering hole."

"That's weird. It's so strange seeing Tyrrell in this light. He's always seemed so strong and down-to-earth. I never would have thought—I never did think—that he was still drinking. Or might go back to it."

Despite Zachary being the older brother, since being reunited he'd felt like Tyrrell was the older, more responsible one. He was bigger than Zachary, in better physical shape, and had a wife and two kids. He didn't act like he was down on his luck or still in the thrall of addiction. Everything he said and did gave the impression that everything was fine. He hugged Zachary, told him to eat more, told him that things would be better after Christmas.

"I thought it was far in the past too," Zachary agreed. "When he was a teenager, maybe. That he'd been fine as an adult."

"I guess people don't like to show their weaknesses. Even to family."

"I wish he'd told me more about it. I wish... that I'd asked. But I thought... it was just a part of his life that was closed now and that it would be painful to discuss."

Kenzie sat down across the table from him with a glass of water. No coffee so close to bed for her.

"I guess we're always finding out new things about people, even the ones we think we're close to. People we think we know everything about." Her tone was pensive.

Zachary stared at the food on his plate, not really hungry, but trying to will himself to eat more. His body needed it, whether he felt hunger pangs or not.

"I guess so," he agreed. He was still learning new things about Kenzie and her background. Her family and the things that had shaped their relationships. And as well as he had thought he knew Bridget, it had become evident in the last year that she was a different person from what he had thought. She wasn't as secure as she always pretended to be. And her mind could be changed. Even things she had been adamant about during the time they had been married, like never having children. It still hurt that she had not wanted children with him, but did with Gordon. Maybe that was just an indicator of how bad their relationship had been. How unsuited to each other they were.

"Mason and Alisha said to say hi to Auntie Kenzie," Zachary said, remembering the children.

"Did you see them? That's wonderful. How are they doing?"

Zachary looked from his food to Kenzie's smiling face. It was a moment before her expression changed and she wasn't thinking about Santa and presents, but about their father disappearing. Her expression sobered.

"Oh. Of course. I'm sorry. How were they holding up?"

"They're hanging in there. It's tough on them. I think on Mason especially. He's younger."

"Or maybe Alisha is just better about hiding it. With Mason, everything is all out there. He wears his heart on his sleeve."

"Yes. I'm sure it's hard on both of them." Mason was the one who had soaked Zachary's shirt with tears. But that didn't mean that stoic Alisha, standing nearby, had been any less crushed by her father's disappearance. And by the previous disappearances. Repeated betrayals. Thinking that Tyrrell valued his family less than a bottle of alcohol. Zachary's mind went to his own father.

"I don't think he was physically abusive," he told Kenzie.

"Tyrrell?" Kenzie's expression was guarded. "I don't know. Did Lindsey say anything about it?"

"Not really. She only talks about problems they had in their marriage in general terms. Said that his being an addict explained a lot. She didn't know he was a closet drinker, to begin with. But Mason and Alisha… Mason said that he's mean when he's drinking."

"Poor guy."

"Yeah. But I don't think it was physical."

"Verbal and emotional abuse still hurt and can have long-lasting effects."

"Yeah. I know." It was the words that stayed with Zachary after so many years. Not an isolated fight or beating. His mother calling him incorrigible. Reminding him it was his fault that the house had burned down. His fault that the family was breaking up. That she never wanted anything to do with him again.

16

It was a tough night. Zachary followed Kenzie's suggestions and still took a sleep aid before bed. But his brain was determined to stay awake, whirling around and around with worries and speculations about Tyrrell. Nothing would quiet them and, as he had experienced before, his OCD and ADHD brain easily beat out a sleep aid on a bad night. He got up and paced, not wanting to keep Kenzie awake with his tossing and turning.

By morning, he had decided to call Joss. He'd talked to Heather, but he hadn't spoken to his oldest sibling. And maybe she knew something that Heather did not know, even if it were just an offhand comment that Tyrrell had made at some point.

Any throwaway remark could be the key to finding him.

He wasn't sure what time she usually worked. He knew she worked at a restaurant and that she might work late shifts, so he tried to leave it until a later enough hour, after Kenzie was gone to work, before calling. Joss could be cutting enough when he didn't wake her out of a much-needed sleep.

"Well, look who it is," Joss said when she picked up the phone. "What's going on, Zachary?"

Straight to the point, no opportunity for small talk. Zachary shifted his phone to his other ear, awkward at being put on the spot.

"Hi. How are you doing?" he asked.

"About the same as ever. How about you?" She conceded to at least asking about each other's health. "I guess you must be home again now?"

"Yes. Got home a couple of days ago. I'm doing a lot better. Now that… it's the new year. And I had some med changes that seem to be working better. Hopefully."

"Good to hear. Don't like it when my baby brother is in the hospital."

"I'm your oldest brother," Zachary pointed out. "Not the baby."

"You're all still babies as far as I'm concerned. I changed your diapers, you know."

Zachary cleared his throat. "Err…"

"What is it?" Joss asked brusquely. "Why did you call?"

"I wanted to talk to you about Tyrrell."

"What about him?"

"Have you seen him at all since Christmas? Since early December, actually. Have you talked or texted or anything?"

"No. He dropped out of sight. Don't know what he's up to."

"I'm trying to track him down. Make sure he's okay."

"You're better off just leaving him alone. If he wanted you to contact him, he would have left you that information."

"Something might have happened to him. He couldn't predict that. It's been long enough. I can't just sit around waiting to see if he shows up again."

"Sure, you can. That's what everyone else is doing."

"I know," Zachary grumbled. "But I can't do that. I've dealt with missing person cases before. I know you can't just leave it and hope they return on their own. If he was going to do that, he would have done it by now."

"You're just making things hard for yourself. Why don't you go back to your own business? Get that up and running again. I'm sure you must have plenty of people to call back. You always seem to have cases on the go."

"Yes, and I'm going to do that. But… I can't just ignore Tyrrell disappearing, either. It's important. He's my brother."

"He's important to me too," Joss conceded, "I just… don't see how chasing after him is going to help anything. He obviously wanted to disappear. It's not the first time he's done it. So why not just leave the man alone?"

"We don't know that he's disappeared on purpose, unless you know something I don't."

Joss was silent.

"Well?" Zachary prodded. "How do you know he wanted to disappear? Do you?"

"Because that's what he's done before. It's an established pattern. I know you don't like it; you would like to think that he's not just running away or diving into a bottle, but it's exactly what he's done before. So why would it be any different this time? He'll come back on his own eventually."

"Just because someone has run away before, that doesn't mean that something bad couldn't happen to them. An abduction or an accident. Sick or hurt. He might not be able to remember who he is or what happened to him, so he's stuck as a John Doe somewhere."

"Amnesia?" Joss demanded. Zachary could practically see her rolling her eyes. "Come on, Zach. That's TV stuff. How many of the missing people that you've found had amnesia?"

Zachary cleared his throat. She was right, of course, but he didn't like to be forced into a corner. "None of them," he admitted. "But that doesn't mean it can't happen. Sometimes it does."

"Well, it's your own time and energy to waste. So... have at it, I guess."

Zachary didn't know what to say to that. Reassert that he was going to go ahead whether anybody approved of his actions or not? He wasn't going to change his position, and he was sure that Joss already knew that. She knew him and his stubborn single-mindedness too well.

"How is Luke?" he said instead, changing the subject.

Joss blew out her breath in a whistle. "Luke? Yeah... he's good."

She didn't sound like she meant it. Zachary closed his eyes. What had happened to the teen since Zachary had taken him to Joss? It had been a little less than a year ago, and Zachary thought Luke and Joss had settled in together pretty well. Both had experienced addiction and trafficking, and Joss was helping Luke to turn his life around and build a better future for himself. They seemed to get along together pretty well, despite the fact that Luke was so friendly and Joss so acid. Even though she could see the danger of the life he had been leading and Luke wasn't quite so sure.

"What's wrong? Did he have a relapse?"

Zachary could relate. He may not have a substance abuse problem, but he certainly knew what it was like to give in to his impulses and fall back into the old thinking and behaviors he had been trying to overcome. It seemed like for every advance, there had to be a relapse.

"Not yet, that I know of. But he's… less committed than he was. He talks a lot about people he used to know and what he liked about the life. It's been long enough to forget some of the worst stuff and to fantasize about what was good about it."

"What was good?" Zachary demanded. "How could anything about that life be good?"

"Drugs whenever you need them. Party life. Good strokes from your bosses when you're doing well. Belonging. Knowing the rules. Having everything… planned and scripted so that you don't even have to think about it. Lots of things."

"You can't let him get back into that."

"I can't stop him from doing anything. If I try to enforce arbitrary rules to get him to conform, he'll just run. You know that. He's got no reason to stay here if he's just getting grief."

"But he was doing so well. I didn't think…"

"Anybody can be pulled back into that any time. As long as they have a use for you. He's still young, has a lot of talent and potential."

"If he goes back, they'll kill him. They were trying to kill us when he and Madison escaped."

"If he goes back to them, they'll welcome him with open arms. Don't kid yourself. He's hugely valuable to them if he brings in new kids."

"But he knows what kind of life he would be leading. What kind of life he would be condemning them to. He said that he couldn't do that anymore after turning Madison out."

"And he hasn't. Yet. That doesn't mean that he won't or that he isn't considering it. Madison is gone. She won't stop him from seducing others."

"Can't you talk to him?" Zachary demanded.

"I do. Plenty. But I can't make his decisions for him. That's not the way it works. He's independent. He knows how to live on the streets. He doesn't need me for anything."

"Except to help him beat his addiction and get ahead in life."

"That's not the way he's thinking about it the nights when he's missing it all. When he needs a fix and the companionship and reassurance that he's doing a good job. Then… it's just a long, hard, lonely night."

And Zachary knew how overwhelming those could be.

"Would it help if I talked to him? Do you think he'd listen to anything I said?"

"A teenager? Listen? Not likely. You can talk to him any time you like, but remember... he's traumatized. Normal kids are hard enough to convince that they don't know better than anyone else. A kid like Luke, he's divorced himself from the rest of the world. Don't expect to get anywhere with him."

"Like you don't expect to get anywhere with me?" Zachary asked softly.

"Nope," she agreed flatly. "You're going to do what you think is right no matter what anyone else's opinion is."

Zachary was afraid that she was right. Once he'd identified a course of action, it didn't really matter who tried to talk him out of it. Even changing his own mind was nearly impossible.

He hadn't called Joss for advice on what he should do; he'd already decided that.

"I told you before that you weren't going to be able to change the direction of Luke's life," Joss reminded him. "You did more than I thought you could... but in the end, there's nothing either of us can do to prevent him going back to the life he was living before."

"I guess. But I don't like to hear that."

"Nope. You never did like being told no."

Zachary didn't speak.

"The one I want you to talk to is your friend Rhys. Tell him he's playing with fire, and he's going to get burned. You don't want him getting into that life too."

"No." Zachary had met Rhys on another case, one that Bridget had gotten him involved in. He was a Black teenager, being raised by his grandmother, with an impairment in his ability to communicate. He could occasionally say a few words, but was mostly non-speaking, getting along with gestures, sounds, and a mixture of typed text and gifs on his phone. Like Luke and Zachary, Rhys had also been damaged by trauma, witnessing his grandfather's murder when he was a child—and that was just the beginning. Rhys was very vulnerable, and he had a crush on Luke. Kenzie had said that she had seen the two of them talking together when Zachary was in the hospital and they had both been by for a visit.

"No, he can't drag Rhys into this," Zachary said flatly. He couldn't let that happen.

"Then talk to Rhys. Explain it to him."

"Okay. I will."

"Good. I'd better get going now. I have other things to do."

"Do you have Vince's and Mindy's phone numbers?"

"Vince and Mindy?" Joss repeated, as if she couldn't believe what she had heard.

"I know that Tyrrell was still in contact with them. I thought he might have given you their information."

"No. Neither of them has ever reached out to me; why would I reach out to them? It's Tyrrell who wanted to meet everyone, get everyone together. He's the one who contacted me and Heather. And you. Then Heather reached out to you because of her... assault."

She stopped. Had Joss wanted to meet him? Tyrrell and Heather had arranged to introduce Zachary to Joss. But had that been their idea or hers? Joss didn't sound like she would reach out to anyone who hadn't reached out to her first.

"I don't have their information," Joss said flatly. "You'll have to find them yourself."

"Did Tyrrell ever say where they were? Are they even in Vermont?"

"Hmm. I think so. But I don't know if he told me that or if I just assumed. None of us had the money to travel. I worked my way around the country for a while, but... there wasn't any reason for me to stay in any of those places. They didn't have anything for me."

17

Zachary had a lot to think about as he drove to his apartment. He tried to immerse himself in his driving and not think about any of it, but that wasn't easy. He worried about Jocelyn. She acted tough as nails, but Zachary knew that under it all, she was just as vulnerable and scared as he had ever been. She had lived a hard life. A desperately hard, dangerous life that could have killed her many times over. She had lived with predators who used every means possible to control her and make her conform to their wills.

And yet, she was still Joss. Still the tough little girl who had helped to raise him. Had protected him as much as she could from their parents, keeping him out of their way. Making sure that he had food and clothes and didn't get bullied too much at school.

He wanted to help her and ensure that the second half of her life was happier and easier than the beginning.

Luke and Rhys.

There was another problem that was going to be a challenge. How would he convince Rhys to stay away from Luke and not let himself be victimized by him or the people he worked with? Rhys wasn't completely naive. He was the one who had put Zachary on to Madison's trouble with the human trafficking ring to begin with. But Zachary had no doubt that he would let the stars in his eyes blind him from seeing what Luke was and what he could do to Rhys.

But Tyrrell first. Zachary was relieved not to have found him dead and moldering in his apartment. He could have died from alcohol poisoning. Or tripping over his own feet while drunk and cracking his head on the corner of the counter. Or passing out and drowning in the bathtub.

It seemed like months since Zachary had been at his own apartment. And he supposed it had been, but not as long as it felt like. The apartment belonged to his before-moving-in-with-Kenzie life. A time that was now separate and distant in his mind. And it was time to let it go. There was no point hanging on to it when he wasn't using it.

He let himself in the apartment door, picking up a sheaf of flyers and other junk that had been shoved under his door. Not as much as he had expected to find there, based on his past experience. He flipped through it to make sure that there wasn't anything important stuck between the sheets of newsprint and tossed it all in the garbage in the kitchen.

On the table was another stack of flyers and a couple of envelopes lying separate from them.

Who had been in his apartment?

Zachary took a quick look around to confirm that he was alone there, locked the apartment door, and sat down at the table. The apartment had been unsecured for a while when the police had kicked in the door, and then it had taken a few days to get it fixed, but since then, it had been sitting there empty. No one else should have been there.

He picked up the letters. One of them was addressed to "Resident," and, slicing it open, Zachary found a "message of hope" from a Jehovah's Witness neighbor. Or someone who said he was a neighbor. Zachary tossed it onto the pile of flyers and picked up the other one.

This one was addressed to him by name. But of course, it had not come through the postal system, or it would be in his mailbox, not inside his apartment. It had been hand-delivered, one way or another.

Zachary tapped it against his hand before opening it. It was light, just a single sheet of folded paper, probably. Maybe another JW message, delivered after his neighbor had figured out his name?

Eventually, he turned the envelope over and slid his finger along the top edge to open it. He drew out the paper and unfolded it.

The handwriting was messy. A lengthy, rambling missive that sprawled across the page this way and that. Difficult to make any sense of. Zachary looked at the bottom of the letter for the signature, frowning.

A single initial.

T

Tyrrell.

Zachary blinked several times in surprise. Tyrrell had written to him? Had he been in his apartment and left a letter on his table? When had he been there? Zachary had never given him a key. Had never given anyone but Kenzie a key. Had Kenzie let him in? And if she had, then why wouldn't she have told him that when they started talking about Tyrrell being missing?

Zachary returned his gaze to the top of the page and tried to decode the tangle of words and letters. He wasn't a good reader at the best of times, with typewritten letters arranged in a neat and predictable way. The mess of words and phrases of the letter would take time to unravel.

After making several different attempts, Zachary settled on a method, typing words from the page into the notes app on his phone as he figured each one out the best he could. He knew that he was probably only getting half of the letters right. Consequently, a lot of the words were either the wrong words or a string of nonsense characters strung together in his best guess that he hoped to work out later.

He was about to tap the next word into his phone when it rang, startling him. Kenzie's picture appeared on the screen. Zachary picked up the phone and held it to his ear.

"Kenzie?"

"Hi. I'm just taking a break, so I thought I would check in and see how you're doing."

She didn't usually check up on him. It was probably a reaction to his having been in the hospital. She wanted to convince herself that he was well and strong, and nothing was going to happen to set him back again. She cared about what happened to him.

"I'm good. How has your morning been?"

"A beast. I needed to get away from it all for a few minutes. We've got quite a backlog right now, and we're still trying to audit all of the cases that people have brought forward after finding out about Nurse Debbie. Everyone wants their case reviewed…"

"That's a lot of cases."

"Yes, it is. I'm going cross-eyed looking for patterns and flagging which ones Dr. Wiltshire should have a look at. What are you working on?"

"I'm at my apartment. Thought I'd better make sure everything was okay here."

"Yeah, good idea. Things could happen while you were gone."

"Were… you here?" he asked tentatively.

"Was I there? In your apartment? No, not lately."

"Did you bring Tyrrell by here once? To leave a letter for me?"

"A letter? No, what are you talking about?" Kenzie's voice got louder and higher. "What letter? Is everything okay?"

"There's a letter here from Tyrrell. On my table. If you didn't let him in, then how did it get here? Did he pick the lock? Get the manager to let him in?" Zachary's anxiety was rising. He looked at the apartment door to make sure that it was bolted and reminded himself that it was secure, not like it had been after the police had broken it in.

"A letter… on your table…" Kenzie's voice got distant. Remembering something. "No—that *was* me. I did go by your apartment, but I didn't have anyone with me. The letter and some flyers had been slid in under your door, so I picked them up and left them on the table for you to look at later. I completely forgot about that. Sorry. I should have let you know there was correspondence for you to review."

"When?"

"When was I there?"

Zachary nodded impatiently. For a smart woman, Kenzie could be extremely slow keeping up with his mental processes sometimes. "Yes. When was this? When did he leave the letter? Before Christmas? After?"

"Uh… let me think for a minute. It was the day you were missing. You checked yourself out of the hospital and I was looking for you, didn't know where you were. So I checked your apartment, just in case."

Zachary breathed out slowly and relaxed his shoulders. That all made sense. Of course she had gone there to look for him. If he wasn't at her house, then where else would he be? Not where she had expected him to be, that was for sure.

"So that was before Christmas."

"Yes. A couple of weeks."

"That would make it… sometime around December tenth?"

"Yes. About that. I can look it up for you later if the exact date is important."

"No, I guess not."

If Kenzie had found it the day that he had checked himself out of the psych ward, then it had been left there *before* Tyrrell disappeared.

"Are you sure? You sound upset. What does it say?"

"I'm still figuring it out."

"Figuring it out?"

"You know how you say that my handwriting in my notebooks is chicken scratch?"

"To say it is chicken scratch would be insulting to chickens," Kenzie quipped. "Especially when I know that you can print neatly when you have to."

"Well… it's sort of like that. So it's going to take some time to figure it out."

Kenzie chuckled. "Yes, if it's anything like your notebooks, you might need some training in hieroglyphics or code-breaking to figure it out."

18

After chatting for a few minutes, Kenzie had to get back to work and they said their goodbyes and continued with their own projects. Zachary went back to the letter and took a couple of minutes to figure out where he had left off. He grabbed a pencil from the kitchen drawer so that he could check off each word or group of letters as he transcribed them.

As he decoded the letter, Zachary's anxiety grew. As he had suspected from the start, it wasn't just a friendly holiday letter. It would have been nice if Tyrrell had left him a Christmas letter, knowing that Zachary wouldn't be able to read it until after he returned from the hospital, but then it would be there waiting for him. Something to warm his heart and know that someone had been thinking of him during the Christmas season even if he couldn't appreciate it then.

But, of course, that had not been the case. Tyrrell's words were dark and hopeless. Lindsey and Joss and the others had all assumed that Tyrrell had disappeared because he had gone on a binge, but as Zachary transcribed the words of the letter, he started to wonder if they had all gotten it wrong and Tyrrell's intentions had been something much worse.

Zachary,

This is a hard letter to write. I know things are bad for you right now so we can't really talk and I don't want to make things worse than they are. It has been a good year for me, meeting you and getting to see Joss and Heather face to face Thought I was on the right track and everything be good even though divorce with Lindsey was final and I don't see kids very often.

But everything is gone to hell When I see myself through Mason's and Alisha's eyes I realize what a monster I have been. Just like HIM. Thought I would be such a good dad but I've hurt those kids so much. (not physically I never beat them but they're afraid of me cause of yelling and stupid drunken behavior) I thought I could still be a good dad and they would forget all of that, but they remember and they always will

And you and Kenzie were right about me drinking again. I made my one year and I thought that was good and meant that I'd be able to stay clean and sober forever they said not to be complacent or I would slip up and I did and now it's all too late and I know I can't be the person I want to be or could be if I was sober

I'm sorry for everything. Wish I could take it all back. Wish I could go back to being the person I was before I started to drink. Before I was broken. Maybe when I was six, and you were still there to tell me everything was okay.

But I can't I can only move forward and there is no future for me. Can't be around the kids like this can't damage them any further. I will be gone so that I can't hurt them or anyone else any more.

Guess I am saying goodbye. I won't see you after Christmas. Will stay until then because I don't want to cause you a setback. But after that I will leave it all behind. I am sorry again. Goodbye.

T

19

Zachary read the transcription on his phone screen and looked back at the scribbled words again, looking for some sign that he had misread it and that Tyrrell hadn't really meant the things Zachary saw on the page. Somehow, he had put his own spin on the letters he saw there and hadn't understood it. It didn't mean what he read there.

But he couldn't kid himself. He might have gotten a word or two wrong along the way, but the gist of the letter, the phrases he had put together, were all correct.

His heart was swollen and hurt with every beat. His stomach had that dropping, queasy feeling of an elevator lurch, only much worse.

With fumbling fingers, he found a pillbox in his pocket and downed a long oblong pill without water. He picked up his phone and the letter and walked out of his apartment and down to the car.

"I need to talk to Dr. Boyle."

Zachary had seen the polite receptionist many times before. He'd been seeing Dr. B at least twice a week, though, of course, he had not been at her office since he had admitted himself to the psych ward at the hospital. He couldn't remember the receptionist's name, though he was sure he should know it. A line creased her forehead as she looked at her computer screen. Her mouth smiled, but her eyes didn't.

"You don't have an appointment today, Mr. Goldman," she said pleasantly. "Did you think you had set something up?"

"No. I need to see her. It's an emergency."

Her eyes went over him, evaluating him carefully. She didn't argue, as he was afraid she would, and say that he would have to set up an appointment and come back then. In a day or two when Dr. B had a free appointment slot.

"Would you wait here for just a moment, Mr. Goldman? I'll need to talk to her."

Zachary nodded, relieved. He wiped at a bead of sweat dripping down his face. He must look a sight, like a wild man or someone with the plague. He felt like he could barely stay on his feet, yet he couldn't sit down and wait quietly, not with his heart hammering like it was. Not after reading Tyrrell's letter.

It was not long before Dr. Boyle came out with the receptionist. She took in Zachary's state with a quick glance and approached him.

"Elizabeth said it was an emergency, Zachary. Are you okay?"

He nodded jerkily, all of his muscles tight and his body coiled for action.

"Come with me. Let's see what I can do to help." She led the way back into her suite of offices, to one that they didn't normally use for their sessions. "Is this okay?"

It seemed a little unreal to be meeting with her somewhere different from usual, but Zachary could handle that, as long as she was there. She probably had another patient in her regular office.

"Do you want to sit?"

He looked at the chair and shook his head, too agitated to sit down.

"Can I take your pulse, Zachary? Is it okay if I touch you?"

He offered her his arm, feeling a little silly about it. Dr. B's fingers rested across his pulse for a second or two, and then she withdrew her hand.

"Wow. That's pretty fast. Are you having a reaction to your meds, or is it something else? I remember you had a bad reaction to one of the meds you were on when you were young."

"No, it's… something else." He fluttered the letter but didn't hand it to her, unsure what to say or do.

"Have you taken anything? Prescription or non-prescription?"

"Anxiety."

"Your anti-anxiety prescription?"

Zachary nodded again, feeling like a bird twitching its head all around to watch its surroundings. "Didn't think I could drive if I didn't."

Her brows went up. "You drove yourself here? I'm not sure that was a good idea in your condition. Get a ride or call an ambulance next time."

Zachary nodded. He probably wouldn't. But he didn't usually try to go anywhere during a panic attack, so it probably wouldn't come up again any time soon.

"What can you tell me about what's going on? Did something happen that upset you?"

"I got a letter." Zachary was holding the letter by the corner with his thumb and forefinger. He squeezed them tightly together, trying to feel the substance of the page between them. He could barely feel it, yet it weighed on his shoulders like a hundred-pound weight. "From my brother."

"From the brother you have met before, or the other one?"

"The one I met. Tyrrell."

"And he wrote you a letter?" Dr. B looked at the trifolded paper in Zachary's grasp. "I thought he lived close by. The two of you get together sometimes."

"Yeah. But he didn't want me to read it until I got out. Home from the hospital."

"He mailed it to your house?"

"Pushed it under the door at my apartment. Not where I live with Kenzie."

She raised her brows but didn't comment on his still keeping two residences. She had to know as well as anyone that he might sometimes need extra space, a retreat to go to if he felt overwhelmed.

"And the letter is not good news."

Zachary shook his head. He held it out toward her, letting her take it from him this time. Dr. B flattened it on the desk and sat down. She looked at the messy writing and frowned, eyebrows knitting as she studied it.

"I think..." Zachary unlocked his phone and slid it across the desk to her with his transcription of the note displayed. "It's hard to read, but I think that's pretty close."

She looked from his phone to the page a few times, then read through the note on her screen. She scrolled it up and down a couple of times, looked at the letter again, and then nodded.

"That must have taken you some work to unravel." She pushed both the letter and the phone back toward him. "You know that you're not responsible for Tyrrell or the choices he makes."

"What do you think when you read that? That he's going to commit suicide?"

"It's a possibility. But it could mean other things too. He might have been drunk when he wrote it and was fine when he sobered up. Maybe didn't even remember that he wrote it. He might find another way to reach out for help from a program or another family member. Call his sponsor, go into detox... there are a lot of options."

"But it doesn't sound like that, does it? It sounds..." Zachary licked his lips. His mouth was so dry he could hardly speak. "Hopeless and final."

"Maybe. That's one interpretation. Only one. Have you tried to call him?"

"He's missing." The lump in Zachary's throat grew hotter, making his voice crack and sound strained. "I've been trying to get him, but no one has seen him since December tenth. He didn't even wait until Christmas like he said he would. These things always happen..." He wanted to say, "before Christmas," but the words wouldn't come out.

Tears streamed down his face and Zachary wiped at them, embarrassed.

"Have you called the police to do a welfare check?" Dr. Boyle asked in a calm, even voice, making no comment about Zachary's messy display of emotion. That helped him to answer in a slightly calmer tone instead of breaking down further.

"I went to his place yesterday, called the police." He pulled a couple of tissues from the box on Dr. B's desk and pressed them to his eyes, trying to stop the stream of tears.

"And I assume they didn't find him."

"He's gone. No one knows where. He disappeared from work. Didn't pay his rent. It's been long enough that his landlord already rented it to someone else." Zachary sniffled and blew his nose.

"You've done what you can. If you've reported it to the police, then it's in their hands now. It's not any fun, but it's a waiting game now, until he shows up or the police find a lead."

Zachary shook his head impatiently. "The police aren't going to do anything about it. He's already been missing for weeks. The trail is cold. They aren't going to put any more manpower into it than they have to.

Make sure he's not a John Doe in the morgue and talk to his boss about when he was in last. That's it. They aren't going to find him!"

"I know it's hard to just take a step back and wait—"

"I'm a private investigator. Finding missing people is something I do. I'm not going to just wait!"

"Seeing your reaction to this letter, I don't think that's a good idea. You need to think about your mental health and how an investigation like that would affect you."

"I'm going to find him," Zachary insisted.

Dr. Boyle studied him. "Why don't we take an intermission? I don't think you're in a good place to discuss this right now. You need some time to calm down, think about it, and see whether you can get some emotional distance. I think that this med regimen needs to be re-evaluated. You shouldn't be this close to a breakdown when you have been taking your meds and had an emergency dose of your anti-anxiety pills already. Have you been sleeping?"

"Yes."

"How much? Did you sleep last night?"

"Last night… maybe a couple of hours. But before that, seven or eight hours every night. When I was in the hospital and when I got home."

She shook her head. "Can you try some relaxation exercises while I finish up with another client? And then we'll talk again."

Zachary swallowed and nodded.

"You're going to stay here," Dr. B said firmly, meeting his eyes as she indicated the office. "I'm not going to come back here in five minutes and find out that you've taken off?"

Zachary hesitated. He didn't want to wait there. Dr. Boyle had confirmed what he went there to find out—that she also read the letter as a suicide note—and now he had to get on with the investigation. If Tyrrell weren't already dead, Zachary needed to find him. And if he were… Zachary needed to find him and bring him home in that case too. He wasn't going to sit around waiting for someone else to take responsibility for his brother.

"Zachary?"

He shook his head. "I need to go. Thanks for your help, but—"

"No, Zachary. No. Stay here. We're not done yet. We need to talk this through."

"I need to find him."

"Five minutes is not going to make any difference."

"Yes, it is," Zachary said sharply. He turned and took a step toward the door.

"You can't drive in this state. Call Kenzie to pick you up."

Zachary took another step. "I'm fine."

"If you leave here in an agitated, unstable state, I am going to call the police. They *will* pick you up."

"For driving?" Zachary challenged.

"For reckless endangerment. I'm telling you as your medical professional, you are not in a fit state to drive. If you get behind the wheel, you're putting the public at risk."

Zachary whirled around to face her again. "What?"

"Call Kenzie to pick you up."

Zachary clenched his teeth. "You can't do this. I'm fine. I'm under control. I'm not impaired."

She just stood there looking at him. Zachary clenched and unclenched his fists. "Let me go!" he insisted.

"Call Kenzie. I need to see her before I let you leave here."

"I'll walk. I'll get an Uber."

Dr. Boyle shook her head. Zachary was not going to be able to talk his way out of it. She'd gotten it into her head that he was too upset to drive, and she wasn't going to accept any other solution.

"Kenzie is working. I can't call her here to pick me up. She'll get fired!"

"I suspect that isn't true. If she is in the middle of something she can't leave, then you can chill here until she can."

"I'm calm." Zachary tried to arrange his face and relax his body so that she would believe him. But did he really think that she would believe he was no longer upset about his brother and the possibility that he had killed himself? Even if Zachary could make himself look calm, she probably wouldn't believe that his distress had cooled that quickly. He would need to go home with Kenzie. Have a quiet night. Convince everyone that he was back to normal again and perfectly capable of investigating Tyrrell's disappearance, just like he had been.

"That's good," Dr. B said. "I'm glad that you're calming down. Maybe with a bit of visualization and relaxation, you'll be able to process these feelings and think more logically. But right now, you're not being logical. You're running into a situation without thinking it through. You're not thinking about the consequences of your actions and, until you do, you are not going to be making good choices."

"You're not being fair." He was a grown man. He wasn't a child or a hotheaded teen anymore. He was a man fully capable of making his own choices. He had proven to her and Kenzie that he could judge when he needed medical intervention and when he didn't. And right now, he didn't need her jumping into his path and preventing him from moving forward.

"Give Kenzie a call and find out when she can be here. Then we'll talk. I'm going to go deal with my other client..." she looked at her watch, "If he's still here. And then I'll be back. And Elizabeth will be watching, if you think you're going to sneak out of here as soon as I'm occupied."

She looked at him, waiting for a response and, when Zachary didn't protest this, walked by him and out the door. She closed it after her and went to speak with her other patient.

20

Zachary paced back and forth across the office. He regretted having come to Dr. B for her opinion of the letter, believing that she could help him to get into Tyrrell's mind and figure out what he would do, what Zachary's next step should be. He knew Tyrrell, and Dr. B didn't. He should have kept it to himself.

But he also knew he was teetering on the edge of a breakdown, as Dr. B had observed. Not entirely in control of his emotions, though he was trying hard to get a handle on things. He still had that sick, plummeting feeling and was afraid that all he would find at the bottom of the elevator shaft was Tyrrell's dead body.

He took several deep breaths. He would have to call Kenzie, however much he didn't want to. Dr. Boyle wasn't going to be satisfied with anything else. Maybe it was unfair but, as more than one foster parent and social worker had told him, life wasn't fair, and he would just have to deal with it.

He walked slowly back and forth, trying to at least calm the tears and the hot lump in his throat so that he wouldn't sound like he was crying when he called Kenzie. He didn't want to panic her or to make her drop everything to deal with his problems, putting her own job in jeopardy. Dr. Wiltshire was a good boss, and Kenzie had told him about Zachary's depression and hospitalization. He had told Kenzie to take time off if she needed it. But saying that wasn't the same as being faced with the sudden absence of an employee he really needed to be there. What people promised and what they really found acceptable were often very different.

One more deep breath, and he touched Kenzie's number on his phone screen, then held the phone up to his ear. He held the phone a little away from his face so that his ragged breathing wouldn't be as loud.

"Hi, Zachary."

"Hey… how is your afternoon going?"

"My afternoon is going fine." Her fingers stopped tapping the keys on her computer. "What's up? Are you still at your apartment?" There was a new note of caution in her tone. Something had already tipped her off. Maybe just the fact that he didn't usually call her when she was working. Maybe over the lunch hour or when it was getting close to dinner and he didn't know whether she would be getting home in time, but not just in the middle of the day for no reason.

"No… I'm at Dr. Boyle's."

"I didn't remember you had an appointment today. Did you tell me that?" More key taps as she probably checked her calendar online to see whether she had forgotten about a scheduled appointment. Maybe to make sure that she hadn't forgotten about a couple's session, which she had done once before when she'd gotten too busy at work. "Zachary?"

"I… No. I didn't have anything scheduled. I came over because I wanted to talk to her about Tyrrell and this letter."

"Oh. Okay… how did that go?"

Zachary cleared his throat. It was closing up again, and he didn't want his tone changing as he spoke to her.

"I was pretty upset. I really needed her help."

"Uh-huh…?"

"And she… says that I can't drive."

"You can't drive?" There was confusion in Kenzie's tone. "Why can't you drive? Are you… impaired?"

"I'm not drunk. I haven't been drinking. Or taken anything else. Except an anxiety pill. She says I'm too upset."

"Oh. Okay. What does she want you to do? Stay there until you've calmed down? Catch an Uber?"

"She said you need to come pick me up." Zachary rolled his eyes and shook his head, hardly able to believe what he was telling her. It was *so* unfair and Dr. B was *so* off base this time. "She won't let me leave here without seeing you."

"Or what?" Kenzie gave a laugh of disbelief.

"Or she'll call the police and have them arrest me for… I forget. Putting people in danger."

"Oh." Kenzie blew out her breath, thinking about it. "Okay… can you give me about twenty minutes?"

"Yes. Of course. But don't rush over if it means losing your job. I can sit here all day if I have to," Zachary warned worriedly.

"I'm not going to lose my job. Don't worry about that. I should be about twenty minutes. Hang in there. You've already taken an anxiety pill?"

"Yes."

"You sound pretty good. I've heard you a lot worse."

"Yeah. That's what I told her. She's just overreacting."

"I take it she's not sitting there with you." Kenzie chuckled.

"No."

"Okay. Hang tight. I'll get there as soon as I can."

***

Zachary returned to the reception area for Dr. B's office. Elizabeth, the receptionist, gave him a warning look.

"It's okay if I sit out here to wait for Kenzie?" Zachary asked.

She nodded her assent and watched him walk over to one of the chairs to sit down. Once he was settled, she went back to her computer work.

But Zachary was still too agitated to sit down. There were a couple of other patients in the waiting room, and he didn't want to look like a crazy person. He should have just stayed in the office where the doctor had left him, but he'd thought he would be more comfortable in the waiting room where he was used to sitting and waiting.

Try as he could to hold the anxiety and restlessness inside, Zachary just couldn't do it. He bounced up out of his seat. Elizabeth's eyes immediately riveted on him, and he was sure she would reach for the phone to call the police if he made a move toward the door. But that wasn't what he intended. He paced the length of the waiting room and back, then repeated the journey another time. He'd hoped that he would be able to calm down again after taking a couple of laps of the room, but the agitation was not going away. His body was primed to run away. To escape the danger that was making his heart pound so hard and fast.

"Sorry," Zachary murmured as he walked past the woman who was waiting for her appointment.

She raised her brows, giving him a wide-eyed innocent look as if she had no idea why he was apologizing and that she hadn't been worried about his restlessness.

"I'm just waiting for a ride," Zachary explained. "She should be here any minute."

The woman nodded and looked down at the magazine she had open, as if what he did was of no concern to her whatsoever.

"Sorry," he repeated to the male patient who was also waiting. Not only was he making them nervous with his anxious pacing and Elizabeth's watchful gaze, but he had probably made Dr. B run later for the rest of the day's scheduled appointments too. Unlike many doctors, she actually seemed to try to stay on schedule, so a patient didn't have to wait two hours for a twenty-minute session.

Zachary glanced in Elizabeth's direction. He didn't meet her gaze, suspecting that if he did make eye contact, she would ask him to please sit down and wait for his ride without disturbing the other patients.

21

Eventually, the door from the hallway opened, and Kenzie stood there, smiling at Zachary.

"Your cab," she offered cheerfully.

But he could read her face better than she knew, and the tension around her eyes told him that she was worried about him.

Zachary took a step toward her.

"Dr. Boyle would like to talk to you before you go," Elizabeth said.

They both looked at her. Zachary wasn't sure which of them Dr. B wanted to see. Him, probably. She would want to gauge how much he had settled down during the time he'd been waiting for Kenzie.

"Dr. Kirsch," Elizabeth said. "She would like to see both of you. Would you wait for a moment? She's just finishing up with someone."

The two waiting patients gave Zachary poisonous looks. Another delay in their sessions. He'd already told them he was sorry. What else was there for him to say?

Kenzie entered the waiting room and looked at the chairs, then at Zachary standing at the far end of the room. She nodded to a chair, inviting Zachary to sit with her. He considered it, but didn't think he could sit. And he was going to have to sit down in the car for the drive home.

Then again, a car drive was usually relaxing to him, so maybe the ride home wouldn't be so torturous.

He walked over to where Kenzie sat down and stood beside her. She didn't tell him that he had to sit down to talk to her.

"You okay?" she asked.

He rolled his eyes. "I'm fine" was not an acceptable answer in their relationship. *Fine* was just a way to gloss over how he was really feeling.

"I want to get out of here," he said instead. "If we just go... they won't call the police if they know you're driving. Why do we have to wait?"

"Well, let's give it a few minutes. Dr. Boyle made time for you when you didn't have an appointment, so you should probably show her some courtesy and wait for a break in her schedule if she wants to see us for a few more minutes."

Zachary grumbled to himself. But she was right. Dr. Boyle had seen him when he'd been afraid he wouldn't be able to get in to see her. She had answered emergency phone calls when he had hit other crisis points. He should show her the courtesy of waiting until she'd had a chance to have her say, even if it was excruciating.

It wasn't an excessively long wait. A patient came out the door and Zachary drummed his fingers on the wall, waiting for Dr. B to come to the door to call him in or for Elizabeth to direct him to go in. Finally, the doctor came to the door and nodded, seeing them both there waiting for her.

"Zachary, Kenzie, this will just take a minute." She said it loudly enough that the other patients would hear and know that they would get in for their sessions before long.

Zachary and Kenzie followed her back to her office. The one they usually saw her in for couple's therapy. She didn't invite them to sit, but perched on the edge of her desk in an informal posture.

"Thanks for coming to pick Zachary up, Kenzie. I hope it wasn't too much of an inconvenience."

"No, of course not. It was fine. I just took my lunch break."

And now they could go home, and Zachary could get on the phone and start calling hospitals and jails and anywhere else that Tyrrell might have ended up, either under his own name or as a John Doe. Maybe he couldn't drive back to Riverbrook now that Dr. B had decided he wasn't fit to drive, but he could still continue his investigation.

"I guess Zachary told you why I was concerned about him. Have you been talking about this case...?" Dr. B looked at Zachary, raising her brows to inquire whether it was safe to discuss it with Kenzie.

Zachary nodded. "Kenzie knows about Tyrrell. She's the one who told me he was missing." He paused. "I wish she'd told me sooner."

"You weren't in any condition to worry about him," Kenzie said. "We were trying to hold on to *you*."

"And what you found today?" Dr. B prompted.

"The letter." Zachary looked at Kenzie. "The letter from Tyrrell at my apartment."

Kenzie nodded understandingly. "What did it say?"

Zachary didn't say anything. Dr. B didn't give any details.

"Zachary was very upset. He made a good choice in taking his meds and coming to see me. Although driving was not a good choice, under the circumstances."

Kenzie looked at Zachary, one eyebrow raised.

"I didn't hit anything," Zachary said. "Or anyone."

Dr. Boyle shook her head. "No. But you could easily have gotten into an accident, considering your state."

"I'm calm now. And Kenzie is here to pick me up, so I don't see that we need to go over it again."

"If I took your pulse now, it would be normal?"

Zachary scratched his cheek. "No," he admitted. "But I can't control that."

"No. And that means that adrenaline is still pumping through your body, and your body and your brain are primed for action. We have seen how badly a panic attack can affect you. No one wants you in the car when that happens."

"If I was going to break down, I would have already."

"Maybe. I think that your medication level has prevented that from happening yet. But we don't know if that will hold. With the doses that we've got you on, I was really hoping to at least reduce the frequency of flashbacks and panic attacks."

"It has. I've been fine. Everything has been stable for a few weeks."

"While you've been in the hospital. A therapeutic setting. Not in the outside world. You only got out yesterday, and we're seeing a huge spike in anxiety and agitation today. I don't think we've got it right. I'd like the hospital to run a few more tests. See where your vitals are right now. Check the levels of the various medications in your blood. Some brain imaging to see if we can tell what's going on. Keep you under observation to make sure that whatever this is will pass and—"

"No." Zachary shook his head. "No way. You want to know why I'm so upset? You don't think my brother committing suicide is enough reason for me to be like this? The meds are fine."

"Suicide?" Kenzie repeated, eyes widening. "Tyrrell?"

"That's speculation," Dr. B advised her. "Zachary is jumping to conclusions. That's my point. This level of agitation and emotion does not—"

"This level of agitation and emotion is exactly right under the circumstances," Zachary snapped, aware that his voice was too loud. He always spoke in a low voice in Dr. B's office. He didn't let himself get angry and explode.

"A drug reaction can make you more anxious. It can make you over-react in ways that you normally wouldn't."

"It's not a drug reaction!"

Kenzie's hand went up, motioning for him to stop and calm down. "Zachary, you're shouting—"

"I do not need to go back to the hospital for a drug review. I just got out!"

"If you're not going to cooperate and do it voluntarily…" Dr. Boyle started.

"You're going to commit me?" he demanded in disbelief.

Zachary wanted to scream at her. He wanted to tear the place apart, throwing her books and furniture around like a toddler having a tantrum.

Both women stood looking at him, eyes wide. Dr. Boyle with a flat, immobile expression, determined to do what she felt needed to be done. Kenzie looking shocked and overwhelmed, but not angry like Zachary felt. He was furious. He had come to Dr. B for help, and she was going to make him go back to the hospital. Back to the psych ward that he'd just left. A failure.

"I haven't been involuntarily committed since I was a teenager," Zachary growled.

"Then think this through. Would I be suggesting it if I didn't think there was reason to be worried? Yes, I agree that you have reason to be upset. But I'm uneasy about how quickly your behavior has degraded. I think we need to step back and review. Just a few days. Just to be sure that everything is okay, and you are stable."

"I wouldn't have signed myself out if I wasn't stable. The doctors at the hospital agreed. They were monitoring me. They talked to you. Everyone said I was fine with the new cocktail."

"And you were. While you were at the hospital. Let's just be absolutely sure."

"And if I don't agree... you *Title 18*."

She gave a little shrug and quirk of her head. If he forced her, she would make it involuntary. And then Zachary couldn't sign himself out. They had him for 72 hours to evaluate and decide whether he were a danger to himself or others. If he signed in voluntarily, he could leave when he wanted to. If they didn't see anything that indicated he was a danger, he could be out the next day instead of waiting for three. And who knew what those extra two days might mean to Tyrrell?

He swallowed and looked at Kenzie. Her eyes were still wide, and she swiped at a tear that escaped the corner of one. He hated what he had done to her; being hospitalized and Kenzie having to worry about whether he might harm himself. Worrying about whether he was ready to be released from the hospital. He had assured her that everything was fine and he was ready, and now Dr. B was saying that he had been wrong.

"Fine." Zachary swallowed again and licked his lips. "Fine, then. I'll go voluntarily."

22

Dr. Boyle said that she would call ahead to the hospital to give them a heads-up that Zachary was coming back in and to get started on the testing required. Going back to the hospital just ramped Zachary's anger and agitation level even more. They didn't normally do any extensive testing on a new drug protocol. They watched him for any obvious reactions, noted any behavioral changes, and had him self-report how he was feeling. If he felt good and wasn't showing any adverse reactions, it was a win. They didn't usually do blood tests unless he were on a drug that specifically required it. Brain imaging was something he'd only heard of being done for experimental drugs when they wanted to see what changes they caused in brain activation.

He couldn't believe that Dr. B would push it so far. She should be able to understand that he was simply worried about his brother and what might have happened to him.

Zachary remained stoic on his way out of the inner office, through the waiting room, and out to Kenzie's pristine red convertible. There was no riding with the top down in the middle of Vermont winter, but Kenzie didn't put her "baby" into storage while it was cold. The car didn't hold any heat with its canvas top and, when Zachary slid into the passenger seat, it was as chilly as if it had been sitting outside for hours, though Kenzie had just been driving it ten minutes before.

He pulled his seat belt across his hips and buckled it with a snap.

Kenzie was slower getting into the car and getting herself buckled in. She looked at Zachary.

"Are you okay?"

"Obviously not."

"No. I know that. I mean... tell me what you found out about Tyrrell."

Zachary took a deep breath. At least *Kenzie* was concerned about the only thing that was important to him right now. "I'm worried... that he was planning to commit suicide."

She nodded gravely, her serious brown eyes meeting his. Zachary choked up and looked away. Without saying anything further, Kenzie started the car, played with the heater settings for a moment, and then pulled out.

Zachary tried to relax, to let the purr of Kenzie's car's engine lull him into a calmer and more centered place. But relaxing meant dropping the mask and, as soon as he released the superhuman hold on his emotions, the tears came again. He kept his face turned away from Kenzie and checked the glove box. He found a pocket pack of tissues conveniently stowed there, pulled a few out, and did his best to stop the flow. Kenzie didn't drill him with questions or tell him that he was being a baby like Bridget would have. She just drove to the hospital without comment. She stopped in one of the paid parking lots, away from the doors, and they sat there in silence for a few minutes. Zachary managed to slow the tears, but not to stop them.

"I shouldn't be crying," Zachary told her hoarsely. "I've got no reason to. Maybe it *is* the meds. Sometimes they make you emotional."

"I think you have plenty of reason to be upset. Don't beat yourself up about it. Is that the letter?" She nodded at Tyrrell's letter, still pinched between Zachary's numb fingers.

He handed it to her. Would she read it the same way as he had? Or would she say, like Dr. B, that there could be other interpretations? That it didn't mean that Tyrrell had been planning to kill himself.

Kenzie held the page close to her face and squinted. "You weren't kidding about the chicken scratch! This is *worse* than the handwriting in your notebooks. How could you read a word of it?"

Zachary pulled out his phone and unlocked it. Closing the phone app, Zachary again brought up his transcription of Tyrrell's words. He handed it to Kenzie.

She read through the transcription and, as Dr. Boyle had done, checked between the words on the screen and the words on the page to see if she could untangle the words as Zachary had. She rested her hands in her lap, holding them.

"Yeah. I can see why you found this so upsetting."

Zachary swallowed, the lump in his throat painful. "I'm not just *agitated by my meds*."

"No. You're actually holding it together pretty well, all things considered."

He appreciated her words of support. He mopped at the tears on his face and in the corners of his eyes and got out more tissues to blow his nose.

"I can't take three days off for a med review. I don't *need* a med review."

"Let's see how much they can do today. It doesn't take long to do blood draws. You can talk to the doctor and explain the situation. The extra stress and emotion. Maybe he'll just want to bump up the dosages a bit and see if that's enough to help you handle the situation."

Zachary nodded.

"If you're admitting yourself, you don't need to stay the whole 72 hours. Just see how it goes. If you can get a nap in, maybe you'll feel better. A good cry and a nap can do wonders," she told him with a smile and encouraging voice.

"I'll sleep in the chairs while I'm waiting." They were bound to keep him waiting for a few hours. Even an emergency psych consult never really seemed to be considered an emergency.

Kenzie took her key out of the ignition and reached for the door. Zachary stopped her. "I'll go in myself. You need to get back to work."

"I can come in for long enough to make sure that you get checked in and settled."

He shook his head. "I can do it on my own. You're on your lunch break. If you get right back to the morgue, it won't be like you missed any time at all."

"I *can* take the time. Dr. Wiltshire will understand."

"I'd rather you didn't."

Kenzie sat there for a moment, looking at him. He waited for her to say that she didn't trust him. That she needed to walk him in to make sure he got where he was supposed to and checked himself in. That he couldn't go off and investigate, breaking his promise to Dr. B.

"Okay," Kenzie said finally. She reached over and they hugged awkwardly across the center console. She pressed her cheek against his, kissed him, and murmured a goodbye in his ear.

They drew apart. Kenzie looked at the phone and the letter in her lap. "I guess I should hold on to these?"

"Yeah. Can't use my phone in there. No point in having it locked away. Maybe… you can keep it with you in case Tyrrell calls back. Or if Lindsey thinks of something…"

"Sure," Kenzie agreed, nodding briskly. "I'll do that. Take care, okay? I'll stop by after work, but I don't know if they'll let me visit. Or you might be busy with tests."

Zachary nodded. He popped the handle to open his door. "I'll see you tomorrow."

23

It felt strange to be back in the psych ward again when he had just left there. He had left believing that he would not be back for at least another year. Maybe longer if he could get through the following Christmas. He didn't spend every Christmas there as an adult, not like when he was in foster care and had returned to Bonnie Brown every year, unable to tolerate being around Christmas decorations, candles, and happy families. Or worse yet, overstressed families fighting about Christmas decorations.

Zachary didn't like the hospital ward, but he didn't hate it either. He knew that if he couldn't handle things in the real world, or if his depression got too deep and he were considering harming himself, that they would watch him and keep him safe and provide the stability and support that he needed to get through the last few days or weeks before Christmas.

Just like taking medicine. He didn't look forward to it, didn't like it, but knew it was necessary to keep himself well and safe.

He normally found a certain amount of peace in the ward, in a place where there were rules and routines for everything.

He saw one of the nurses turn her head quickly as he approached, escorted by an orderly from the emergency room.

"Zachary?"

Zachary raised his eyebrows and sighed, giving her a grimace. "Hi again, Val."

"Did you forget something?" she teased. She nodded to the orderly. "Thanks, John. I'll take it from here."

John nodded and retreated.

"Dr. B wanted me to get checked out," Zachary explained. "She was worried about… a setback or a reaction to my new meds."

"Okay," Nurse Val nodded. "You can go right back to the same room. We haven't had time to rent it out to anyone else yet. What kind of setback?"

Zachary ran his hand over his face. "My brother is… missing. And he left me a note."

Nurse Val frowned. "The brother who visited you here? A suicide note?"

"It's… ambiguous," Zachary admitted. "He doesn't say straight out… but a lot of times, people don't."

"No, of course not. They talk around the problem. Use euphemisms. Pretend that if you don't name it, it won't happen. People act like if you use the word suicide, it might encourage someone to attempt suicide." Nurse Val shook her head. She studied Zachary's face closely as they walked toward his hospital room. She could see, Zachary was sure, that he'd been crying, his nose bright red and eyes puffy. Despite how kind she always was to him, he couldn't find a smile of appreciation and reassurance for her. She touched him lightly on the back for an instant, then pulled her hand back. "Well, I think you're doing pretty well under the circumstances. But the extra stress certainly could be more than you're ready for yet, just settling into this new cocktail. Would you like me to pass anything on to the doctor?"

Zachary shrugged. "Dr. B was going to call about the testing and follow-up she wants. Just…" he shook his head in frustration, "tell him I'm okay, and I'm not going to stay. Tyrrell needs me. I need to find him… wherever he is and whatever he's done."

Val nodded sympathetically. "Okay. Well, you know yourself best. I'll see if Dr. Boyle has sent orders over and we'll try to line everything up as quickly as we can. What have you taken today? Everything in your morning med list?"

"Yes. And emergency anxiety."

"Good. I'll note it down. Anything else? Alcohol? Over the counter? Recreational? Herbs?"

Zachary shook his head. "Nothing else." He rubbed his temples. Crying always gave him a terrible headache, and the panic attack and adrenaline rush that was now fading away made him just want to sleep. "But I could use a Tylenol."

She nodded. "I'll see if we can get you something. Have a rest here for a bit, and then we'll have someone lined up to do the blood work."

"Thanks." Zachary sat down on the edge of his bed. "Could you call Kenzie? Let her know I'm settled?"

She tapped the side of her head. "Already on my list."

Zachary did fall asleep, but not for long. He slept heavily and then woke up feeling groggy and hungover. He stared out the window, trying to estimate the time. It was afternoon, but didn't feel very late. Like he'd only been asleep for half an hour.

He didn't want to get up or move around, and he didn't have anything to do. He could go to the visitors' room to get a book or a pack of cards, but he didn't get any joy out of reading. It was just a chore. Something that helped to pass the time a little less slowly than lying in bed staring at the ceiling. Instead, he thought about his case, trying to divorce his emotions and analyze it logically.

If it wasn't his brother, what would his recommendation be to a client? Keep looking? Or had he exhausted all possible avenues of inquiry?

He hadn't memorized all of Tyrrell's letter, but tried to recall as much of it as he could.

The fact that Tyrrell had disappeared before his self-imposed Christmas deadline actually felt encouraging. If he had made and followed through on a suicide plan, then it should have been on the day he had picked. It didn't feel right to Zachary that he would switch to December tenth instead. Disappearing on or shortly after December tenth felt spontaneous. Like he'd been distracted from his plan or someone had pulled him away from it. But then where was he? In detox? It was a possibility. Zachary could follow up with detox programs when he got out. They might not tell him anything officially, but he thought he could talk them into giving away whether Tyrrell were there or not. He could ask Kenzie to check with other medical examiners in the state to see if they had any John Does matching Tyrrell's description. He thought she might do that for him. Or even as an official part of her job. Tyrrell had been reported as a missing person, after all.

He still had to check with the hospitals to see if Tyrrell had been admitted to one of them. Maybe he'd been in an accident and was unconscious or couldn't remember who he was. It didn't seem likely that he would disappear without at least seeing the kids for Christmas. They were important to him. Zachary had seen that when Tyrrell talked about them and when he'd brought them to the Lodge for Thanksgiving. He might have thought that he was the worst dad in the world but, as far as Zachary was concerned, that position had already been taken.

He hadn't done a deep dive into Tyrrell's social media accounts. He might find something there. A hint as to what he'd been considering after Christmas, a friend or two that might have an influence over him or know where he might have gone, clues as to his state of mind around December tenth.

And what about Tyrrell's email? He knew Tyrrell's email address and provider and might be able to guess at his password. It was likely to be one of the kids' names or his wedding date, or some combination of them.

There were still plenty of avenues left to investigate.

24

The staff wasn't happy when Zachary announced that he was checking out in the morning.

"Your blood work was fine," Julianna, the nurse at the desk told him, "But Dr. Boyle wanted some other tests run as well that we haven't been able to schedule in yet. And you should at least have one therapy session before you go to make sure that the doctor is in agreement that you are safe to be checked out."

Zachary shook his head. "I signed in voluntarily. I don't need a doctor's approval to sign out."

"But it would be good to ensure that everyone is in agreement that it is safe…"

"No one added any flags to my chart, did they? I've been calm. I haven't done anything to endanger others. I'm not having suicidal thoughts." He raised his brows. "You know I check myself in if I need to."

"But the other tests that Dr. Boyle wanted…"

"Call me when they're scheduled and I'll come back in for them."

Julianna rolled her eyes and gave him a frustrated glare. "Zachary…"

"Nurse Julianna," he said evenly.

"You took your morning meds?"

"Yes."

"And you'll come back if there are any changes? If you think that the medications are not doing their job or you have new symptoms?"

"Yes. I will. Or I'll call Dr. Boyle and see what she says."

"We would miss you if you never came back."

"I thought you didn't want me to come back. You want me to be well."

"That's not what I mean. I mean if you... *couldn't* come back."

Zachary nodded wearily. "I know," he agreed.

"You're going to need to sign some forms..."

"You sure you can't just use the ones I signed a couple of days ago?"

"No. The administrators would kill me. Especially since you got sent back after the last time."

"I didn't get *sent* back," Zachary corrected firmly. "It was voluntary. Just a check-in to make sure that my blood levels were okay."

She shook her head, knowing that it was because Dr. Boyle had insisted, that Zachary had nearly had a breakdown within two days of leaving. But Zachary wasn't going to let them derail him. He had a job to do. He wasn't going to sit around doing nothing in the psych ward until they finally admitted that he was fine.

It took time to sign all the releases that the legal department insisted on for liability purposes, but then he was free. Zachary walked out into the brisk, chilly air and took a deep breath of his second taste of freedom that week. It had been hard-fought and was all the sweeter for it.

But it was cold. January was not the best weather to be spending any amount of time outside. But Zachary did not have his phone and, therefore, his Uber app, and he wasn't going to wait around for a taxi. One would think that taxi service would be faster, now that they had competition in the driving business, but they seemed to get slower and slower instead of faster and more efficient.

Instead, he jogged to the nearest bus stop, knowing that in the early-morning rush, it would be arriving every fifteen minutes. He stood there, feeling the cold concrete through the bottoms of his thin shoes, stomping his feet to try to prevent his toes from going numb. It was twenty-five minutes before the next bus arrived, and his fingers were so cold it took forever to tease the change he needed out of the zippered section of his wallet and deposit them into the fare box. The bus driver had pulled out before Zachary finished, and he had to hang on to a pole while he deposited the rest of the coins.

The driver nodded. "Have a nice day."

Zachary sat down and watched out the window for his stop, waiting for his numb fingers and toes to start thawing out.

No one paid any attention to him. He blended in with the commuters, shoppers, and other riders. No one worried about his being an escaped psych patient or commented on his thin, unshaven face. People preferred not to look at those who were down on their luck, and three days' growth of whiskers was one of Zachary's best tools to make himself invisible. When he had been with Bridget—not that he had ever ridden on the bus with her, but when they had gone other places together—people had looked at them all the time, smiling at the pretty woman and probably wondering what the short, skinny, rough-looking man was doing with her. Bridget had never realized that people didn't smile at everyone the way they smiled at her.

He got off the bus close to Dr. B's office and went to find his car. There was, luckily, no ticket on it and it had not been impounded. Maybe Dr. B had told the security staff to leave it alone.

Even though the seat was cold when he slid into it, Zachary immediately melted into the bucket seat of the compact. It was nothing fancy. It was supposed to be just as nondescript as he was, in fact, but it was his and he always felt more at peace with the world when he was in the driver's seat. Maybe that was the only time he really felt like he was in control of his life. A car meant freedom.

He ran the engine for a few minutes, letting the heater do all of the work defrosting the windows instead of getting out to scrape off the frost. Eventually, when he could no longer see his breath and the front and back windows were both relatively clear, he put it into gear and drove to the Medical Examiner's Office.

He hadn't called Kenzie to let her know that he had checked himself out of the hospital already. How could he? She had his phone on her. He could have borrowed a hospital phone or one belonging to a nurse, but he hadn't wanted to chance a lecture from Kenzie about how he was checking out too soon too. She'd been kind to him the day before, not criticizing him for any of his choices, and he hoped to keep it that way.

Instead, his old friend Martin Ash checked him through security on the main floor where the police department was located, then took the elevator downstairs. No one else got on the elevator, so he had it to himself and there wouldn't be anyone else to demand Kenzie's attention when he got there.

Her office was at the outside of the medical examiner's suite, public facing so that she had to deal with inquiries and help people fill in forms to make their requests for records while she completed the rest of her work. But it was usually pretty quiet at the desk. Not a lot of people requested records from the morgue.

His shoes were quiet, only squeaking slightly because of the wetness from the snow on the sidewalks, so Zachary cleared his throat as he walked toward Kenzie's desk to give her warning that someone was approaching. He didn't want to startle her. She paused in her typing and glanced in his direction. Then she smiled and pushed back from the desk.

"Zachary! How are you doing? I wasn't expecting to see you this early."

"I wanted to get to work."

Kenzie leaned across the desk to give him a quick hug and peck on the cheek. "You must have been waiting for them to check you out as soon someone got there."

Zachary shrugged. "Yes."

Kenzie patted her pockets, then bent over to open a drawer and paw through her purse. She pulled his phone out and placed it on the counter in front of him. "I guess this is what you came for?"

Zachary smiled, glad to see that she hadn't left it at home. He had asked her to keep an eye on it in case he got any calls, but he hadn't been sure if she would. He tapped the wake-up button and saw that it was fully charged and the only missed call was from Heather.

"It's been pretty quiet," Kenzie said. "I suspect Heather is still acting as gatekeeper."

Heather had taken it upon herself to redirect all business calls to herself while Zachary was in the hospital, helping who she could and explaining to those who needed fieldwork done that Zachary wouldn't be available until the new year. It was good to know that someone was looking after his clients, so they weren't all wondering why he wasn't picking up their calls.

"I'll give her a call and make sure nothing is urgent. But everyone is going to have to wait while I look for Tyrrell."

Kenzie nodded. He could tell that she was biting the inside of her lip, trying to decide what to say to him. He waited.

"How long are you going to take for that?" she asked. "What if you run out of leads?"

"I haven't run out yet. It will take… however long it takes."

Kenzie's lips pressed together and she nodded. She had probably had enough time to figure out that this was what was most important to him right now, and he wasn't going to be distracted from it by other jobs. "Well… good luck. I hope… that everything is okay."

"I don't know if this is something I can ask you, but… would you check with the other morgues and see if anyone has a John Doe…?" He didn't finish the sentence. Kenzie knew what he was asking. He didn't want to jinx it by saying the words. *A John Doe who matched Tyrrell's description.*

Kenzie pursed her lips, then nodded. "I'll make some time. I'll send out an email blast to everyone this morning, but you know that no one will bother to follow up today unless I call them. If it isn't marked urgent, they'll put it off."

"Thanks. It would be good to know… that he isn't in a cold room somewhere…"

Kenzie nodded soberly. "Yeah. It will ease my mind too."

She leaned forward to give him another kiss. "Good luck."

Zachary embraced her briefly, though it was awkward across the desk. "Thanks for everything."

It was comforting to know that Tyrrell's disappearance weighed on her mind too. He felt like no one else was taking it seriously. Someone should have reported it back on December eleventh. Or maybe the twelfth. It shouldn't have been another month before anyone responded to his absence.

He slid his phone into his pocket and headed for home to start investigating.

25

Zachary took a deep dive into Tyrrell's social media accounts, looking to see what his last posts had been on each platform, looking for any pattern or anything that might have indicated his state of mind or what had been bothering him. What had happened? Had he run away? Been in an accident? Been abducted?

He knew that the cops would say it was very unlikely that Tyrrell had been abducted. Grown men didn't get kidnapped. But it wasn't true. Jose and the immigrants hadn't just dissolved into thin air. They had been deliberately targeted, tortured, and killed. Being an adult and male did not make a person immune to violence.

Most of what Tyrrell had posted on his accounts had been jokes and memes. Fun stuff. Light. Nerdy. He had also posted messages of concern or encouragement to friends who had been struggling with the Christmas season or other challenges. Zachary copied down their names and URLs for future reference. He would follow up on them later. Tyrrell had also said how excited he was to see his kids over the Christmas vacation. The year before had been Lindsey's. She'd had them home all Christmas Day, and Tyrrell had only had a weekend visit, just like the rest of the year. His friends posted congratulations and encouraging thoughts about his being able to have them for Christmas.

What had kept him from them? What had happened to keep him

away from the two kids he claimed were the most important people in his life?

He had been drinking at Thanksgiving. He had confirmed that in his letter to Zachary, had admitted that when they had asked him about the liquor in the cabin at the Lodge, he had denied drinking and said he was still sober when he was not. Zachary had wondered at the time but, when Tyrrell denied it, had pushed the unwelcome thoughts away and ignored the feeling of dread that had blossomed in his stomach. There had been too much else going on to spend his time worrying about whether Tyrrell was telling the truth or not.

Lindsey had said he was a closet drinker. He'd kept it away from everyone, including her, so Zachary couldn't be blamed for not seeing any warning signs. If Tyrrell's own wife hadn't known the difference, how could Zachary be expected to?

Tyrrell hadn't posted much between the Thanksgiving vacation and December tenth. As if nothing at all had happened, even though the murders and their rescue had been posted all over the news and social media.

Maybe because he didn't want Lindsey to be reminded about it or to know the full extent of what had gone on while they had been there. How much did Lindsey actually know about it? Had Tyrrell been trying to hide that too?

Eventually, Zachary decided he wasn't going to get anything else out of Tyrrell's public posts and turned his attention to email.

The first thing to do was to check to make sure he hadn't received any emails from Tyrrell while he'd been in the hospital that had gotten lost in the sea of emails he'd been swamped with. And that nothing had mistakenly gone into his junk mail folder.

But he and Tyrrell hadn't exchanged emails very often. Zachary preferred talking over typing and reading. He didn't find any emails that he had missed during December. The last thing he had from Tyrrell went back to November.

He went to the login page for Tyrrell's email provider. How many wrong passwords would they take before locking his account? He checked a few references before making any attempt. It looked like he was safe as long as he didn't keep trying from the same device, but cycled among trying to log in on from his phone, tablet, and computer. He typed a list of names and dates in varying combinations, then ranked them in order of likelihood. Unlike with most of the missing person searches he did, he knew something about Tyrrell and the way he thought, and that gave him an advantage. He typed in Tyrrell's email address and tried the first password.

Predictably, it failed. Zachary typed an *X* beside it and tried the next one. It too failed. He would try one more, and then switch devices. The list was long and, even though he had ranked them by likelihood, he found his eyes drawn down the list to a string that combined Mason's and Alisha's name with the year of Tyrrell's wedding. He typed it in. A circle spun on the screen, but it didn't immediately reject the password. He crossed his fingers, hoping that Tyrrell didn't have two-factor verification set up. He didn't have Tyrrell's phone or any other devices to confirm it.

Then the screen flashed and quickly resolved into an email inbox.

Cracked in three attempts—not bad! Zachary skimmed the list of email subjects. Lots of spam and advertisements. Not a lot of personal correspondence. Hundreds of emails sitting there unread. Tyrrell hadn't accessed his email in a long time. Wherever he was, he wasn't using his phone to keep up with what was going on in his email inbox. But a lot of people didn't check their emails regularly and, if Tyrrell was feeling bad, he might not have any motivation to look at it.

Zachary had a sense of deja vu as he started to scroll through the emails, looking for anything important. Just a couple of days before, he'd been doing the same thing with his own email inbox. Catching up with the life that he'd abandoned for several weeks. He wanted to be able to leave everything as he had found it, but knew that there was no way he would be able to find what he needed just by scanning subject lines. He set up a temporary folder and started dragging all of the spam and bulk emails into it in order to dig down and find anything that might be important. He watched for the names of family members. Heather, Joss, even Lindsey or the kids. And for names that might be repeated. Some emails had replies marked, and Zachary switched to the sent folder to see the conversations Tyrrell had found important enough to reply to before his disappearance. He set up another folder and dragged all of Tyrrell's most recently sent emails into it. He worked through the recipient names and ran them through searches, pulling out any recent emails that Tyrrell had not responded to and dragging them into the same folder. He switched to Tyrrell's inbox again and continued to work his way through it, dragging most of the emails into the bulk folder he had set up.

Following this protocol, it wasn't long before everything that had been sitting in Tyrrell's inbox was sorted between the two folders. He went to

the important folder and set up subfolders, dividing the emails into correspondence with family, friends, and vendors or services. The family and
friends folders were quite small. Zachary read through each email thread
carefully. He stopped when he had read partway through one thread,
looking back up at the top to see who the contact was.

Vincent.

Zachary stared at it for a moment, trying to process it.

Not Vincent Goldman, but Vincent Miller. But the email exchange
sounded like a couple of brothers talking to each other. Someone in a
pretty close relationship, anyway. Could Vincent Miller be *their* Vincent?
Their little brother?

Zachary searched for Goldman in the sender field, and saw mostly
emails between himself and Tyrrell. There were a few with Joss, but they
were pretty sparse. Maybe she preferred to communicate by phone, as
Zachary did.

He searched for Miller and, as well as pulling up conversations with
Vincent Miller, there were also conversations with Mindy Miller. There
was no way it was a coincidence Vincent and Mindy Miller had to be
Vincent and Mindy Goldman. They had apparently taken on the name of
their foster family. Maybe they'd even been adopted.

Tyrrell had never mentioned this to Zachary, and he himself still went
by Goldman. Did that mean that he was estranged from his foster family?
Did he go by both? It wouldn't do for Zachary to only search for Tyrrell
under the name Tyrrell Goldman if he sometimes went by Tyrrell Miller.
He scribbled a note in his notebook and continued to read through emails
and perform searches, building a picture in his mind of the period of time
before Tyrrell had disappeared.

He made some more notes. Then he clicked on Vincent's name and
found a contact card that included Vincent's phone number. Mindy's had
been set up as well. Zachary wrote them into his notebook, and then put
them into his phone as well.

His little brother and sister. The ones that he hadn't seen or talked to
since the day of the fire on Christmas Eve when he was only ten years old.

26

Vince and Mindy wouldn't remember him. Vince had only been four and Mindy two. Tyrrell could remember Zachary, having been six at the time they were separated. But his recollections were spotty, remembering one or two things about that night vividly, but not a lot about what things had been like growing up in the Goldman family. Vince and Mindy would remember even less, if they remembered anything at all. He was sure Mindy would have no recollection at all of her first family. She wouldn't remember anything about how Zachary used to help take care of her, coaxing her to feed when she wouldn't take a bottle from anyone else, changing her diapers, carrying her around on his hip to keep her quiet when their mother was trying to sleep. She had not been an easy, happy baby.

He had their phone numbers. He needed to call them and see if they'd heard anything from Tyrrell. If Tyrrell needed somewhere to crash because he'd lost the apartment, what better place than on his brother's couch? Or in his sister's spare room? Just because it wasn't mentioned in the email conversations, that didn't mean that Tyrrell had not approached one of them. If they saw each other face to face, there wouldn't be any need to mention it in an email. And if Tyrrell had needed a place to crash, it was more likely that he would call his brother or show up on his doorstep than send an email inquiry about it.

Zachary had never tracked down anyone in his family. He knew that he was the reason the family had been broken up. His mother had made it very clear that it was primarily his fault. She couldn't manage him while they'd been living in the house and, now that there was no home to go back to, she didn't want anything else to do with him. Mrs. Pratt had tried to talk her into keeping the kids, or dividing the kids between her and their father as they went separate directions, but she had been adamant. She didn't want anything more to do with them.

That had hurt Zachary worse than the burns from the fire.

The burns would eventually heal and not cause him further problems. But the pain of her rejection was something that would never go away.

He had not searched any of them up because he hadn't wanted to face that kind of rejection again. He didn't want to hear from his brothers and sisters that they didn't want him in their lives. He had left them alone, believing that he would never see any of them again.

And then Tyrrell had found him. Tyrrell was the first one who had reappeared in Zachary's life, giving him heartfelt hugs and slaps on the back, repeating over and over again that he couldn't believe it. Tyrrell had also searched out Heather, and they had been talking to each other for a while before Tyrrell arranged for the three of them to meet face to face so that Heather could ask Zachary for his help on her old assault case if she felt good about it.

And then Joss. She was the first one to show any bitterness toward Zachary. But he had quickly discovered that was pretty much her default outlook. She had a heart. The tenderness was still there, buried deep behind the hard-as-nails exterior. But she didn't show it often and didn't trust Zachary just because he had once been her brother.

Tyrrell had been in contact with Vince and Mindy all along. But he'd never suggested to Zachary that they would like to meet him, even just by phone or email. Why would they want to meet someone they didn't know, especially knowing his history?

But this wasn't about Zachary, it was about Tyrrell, and they had grown up with him and clearly cared about him and kept in touch. Zachary would just have to swallow his anxiety and self-consciousness and do what had to be done.

He tapped Vince's number into his phone. Maybe he should wait until a better time. If Vince worked regular hours, he would be at work, and Zachary didn't want to interrupt him there. But he could just as easily work evenings or nights. Without knowing anything about him, Zachary couldn't speculate on what his schedule was anyway. He had to start sometime.

It rang a few times, and Zachary was trying to decide whether to leave a voicemail message or not. Would that be weird? It would give Vince a chance to think about it and make a choice instead of just being ambushed. But if he weren't interested in talking to Zachary, maybe being ambushed was the only way that would work.

Maybe he was one of those people who didn't answer the phone if they didn't know the caller ID and it didn't matter how many times Zachary called, he would ignore it every time until he knew who it was.

"Hello?"

Zachary was startled. His brain stuttered, trying to get on script. "Uh... hi. I'm sorry to bother you, and if this is a bad time, you can call me back later. Or I can call you."

There was a moment of silence on the other end, probably Vince waiting for Zachary to tell him exactly who he was and what he wanted. Because Zachary hadn't exactly announced himself properly.

"Tyrrell?"

"No!" Zachary hadn't realized that his voice and Tyrrell's sounded similar. "This is—I'm looking for Tyrrell, actually—this is Zachary." It felt weird and incomplete for him to introduce himself by his first name. "Goldman."

But that was probably weirder.

"Zachary." Vince's voice went up in tone. He sounded so grown up. So much like an adult. Because, of course, he was, but, at the same time, he was still four years old in Zachary's mind. "How did you... well, I guess you're a private investigator, so you have ways of getting people's numbers."

"I got it from Tyrrell's email. I'm trying to find him... did he maybe crash with you?"

"No. I haven't heard from him in weeks."

"Do you know whether Mindy has?"

"I'll three-way her. Hang on for a minute."

There was a series of beeps, and Zachary was just listening to himself breathe. He had talked to Vince. And he was going to talk to Mindy. After so many years, decades of not seeing or hearing from them, he would have spoken to all of his siblings. The rush he got from the thought made his heart start pounding harder and faster, but it wasn't a panic attack. It was something else.

It felt good.

"You there, Zachary?" Vince's voice sounded in his ear.

"I'm here."

"Okay, we're all on. Say hi to Zachary, Mindy."

"Hi," a young woman's voice joined Vince's. She giggled awkwardly. "Hi, Zachary."

"Hi," Zachary echoed, holding on to the moment, breathing shallowly in case they might both disappear like the wisp of a dream if he were too loud. "It's nice to hear your voice."

"You too," Mindy agreed. "So... what's this? You're looking for T? Tyrrell, I mean?"

Zachary sucked in his breath, startled. "I call him T too. Umm... yes. No one I've been able to talk to has had any contact with him since December tenth. Did either of you hear from him after that? December tenth."

"No," Mindy said. "I tried to get him at Christmas and New Year's Day, but he didn't answer and didn't return my calls. I just figured he was... being Tyrrell."

"What does that mean?"

"You know... he drops out of sight for a while sometimes. Or gets distracted by a new project and forgets to call you back... Or he gets it into his head that we don't really want to talk to him. Never mind that I called him, so what makes him think I don't want to talk to him?"

"Oh. Okay. And Vince... you haven't heard anything?"

"No. Sorry."

"Do you go by Vince? Or do you want me to call you Vincent? I assume it isn't Vinnie anymore."

"Vince is good," he confirmed. "What about you? Always Zachary? No nicknames?"

"I prefer Zachary. Sometimes people call me Zach... and that's okay. I'll answer to it."

"Fair enough."

"If this is something that Tyrrell does sometimes—dropping out of sight—do you know where he usually goes when he does that?"

"I don't really know," Mindy said. "He drinks, you know. He's an alcoholic. But he doesn't like people to know that he does, so he... kind of hides out."

"I don't know who he drinks with," Vince agreed. "Not with me. I don't know any of his drinking buddies."

"Do you think... we could get together?" Zachary asked. He wanted desperately to be able to see them face to face. To see their facial expressions and body language, not just to hear the words they were saying. There might be other things he could pick up if he actually met with them. And to see his baby brother and sister after all of these years... "I don't know where you live. I can come to you if you're in Vermont or nearby."

There was silence for a moment. He didn't push the question, letting them think about it instead. He heard an alert bing on one of their phones and realized they were probably texting each other. Keeping him out of the loop while they discussed it. He waited.

"I suppose," Vince agreed. "You're all the way north, though. You don't want to come all the way here. How about meeting in Clintock? That's more central."

"We don't have to meet halfway. I enjoy driving. I don't mind coming to you."

"Clintock," Vince repeated. Maybe he wanted neutral territory. Not to invite a total stranger into his house. Not to tell him exactly where they each lived, though it wouldn't be hard to figure out now that he had their names and phone numbers.

Zachary nodded. "Clintock is fine," he agreed.

It wasn't where he preferred to meet. He had grown up there, mostly, and he'd had to go back when investigating Heather's case. It had been painful seeing the places he had lived, the places he had been bullied and abused. And where Heather had been hurt too. But it didn't hold the same kind of memories for Vince and Mindy. Maybe their memories were of family outings and ice cream cones. Pleasant, warm feelings.

"I don't know what your schedules are like. Is there a time we could meet today?"

"I could swing tomorrow," Vince said. "I'm already booked up today. Mindy? How about you?"

"We could do supper," Mindy suggested. "You still have to eat, don't you?"

"Supper today?" Vince made an indecisive hum. Zachary hoped that he would give in to Mindy's suggestion. He didn't want to have to put it off another day. Vince and Mindy were probably the people who knew Tyrrell best, other than Lindsey.

"It's Tyrrell," Mindy urged. "I've been worried about him too. Zachary is a PI. I'm sure he can find him."

"Well, okay," Vince conceded. "Supper, then."

He and Mindy tossed around a few suggestions and eventually settled on a restaurant they both liked.

"Is that okay with you?" Mindy asked him. "Do you like Chinese? Some people don't."

"It's fine. I'll see you there."

27

Zachary looked at the time on his phone after hanging up. He would have to head out before too long to be in Clintock in time to meet his siblings for dinner. He was going to be meeting his brother and sister for the first time in decades. He was glad Mindy had talked Vince into meeting the same day. He didn't know if he could have slept if it hadn't been scheduled until the next day.

He tapped the phone to call Kenzie. She picked up almost immediately.

"Zachary?" Her tone was sharp. She was obviously worried that something bad had happened. He'd had a breakdown and had to go back to the hospital again. Or he'd found out bad news about Tyrrell.

"It's okay," Zachary assured her. "I just talked to Vince and Mindy."

It took her half a second to connect who Vince and Mindy were. "Your brother and sister?"

"Yes. I found their numbers in Tyrrell's stuff."

"Wow! That's great. How did it go?"

"It was pretty short, but they both seemed... nice." Not angry like Joss. Neither one seemed to think that it was Zachary's fault they ended up in foster care like they did. Neither seemed upset about it. They might not have reached out to Zachary, but they had been responsive enough to calling them. Cautious about letting someone new into their lives, but maybe that's how people who had been raised in good homes thought.

They didn't just jump into new relationships without consideration. They thought about whether it was someone who would fit in their lives or not.

"I'm glad. This is a red-letter day for you."

If only it hadn't been because he was looking for Tyrell. Just a call from Vince and Mindy because they wanted the chance to meet him.

"Yeah. I'm going to meet them for supper. I would wait and take you along, but I don't suppose you can break away from the office yet."

"You're eating now?"

"Driving. Soon. We're meeting in Clintock."

"Oh. Yeah, you don't want to be out there too late, then. No, you go ahead and meet with them yourself. I'll go with you next time. When it's just a social visit."

"Are you sure? I could ask them to change the time."

"No. Go ahead and do what you set up. You know that it's harder for you the more people there are. Unless you think you need me for moral support. But I'd rather stay out of the way."

Zachary was glad for the drive to Clintock. The highway driving soothed his racing brain and helped him to not obsess over what he was going to say to his brother and sister over and over again all the way there. He was calm and focused, even though he was still worried about what they would think of him and what he would say and if he would find out anything that would help with the investigation into Tyrrell's disappearance. It was a momentous occasion, a red-letter day, as Kenzie had put it. But it could go horribly wrong.

He was in Clintock before he was ready for it. And glancing at the time on his phone, he saw that he had misjudged how quickly he could get there. When he didn't have Kenzie in the car to slow him down and remind him not to go too much over the speed limit, he tended to go a little faster.

He drove around for a few minutes, remembering streets he had lived on, schools he had attended, and many of the other things that had happened there. He was glad he didn't live in the same town anymore or any of the others that he had spent time in as a child or teenager. He wasn't sure how he would keep from being overwhelmed with memories.

As it was, he still had to deal with memories of his life with Bridget. Maybe someday, he and Kenzie could buy an acreage or a house in another of the nearby towns to have more physical distance between him and Bridget and their shared memories.

Eventually, he didn't want to see anything else in Clintock, and he found the restaurant that Vince and Mindy had suggested. He wasn't sure if it was new or just new to him. It wasn't like he'd eaten at a lot of restaurants when he had lived there. Few foster families would dare take their kids out to a restaurant, especially not the type that Zachary tended to end up in, where they were experienced in dealing with children with serious behavioral problems.

He walked into the restaurant and looked around, but didn't see any faces that looked familiar. He assumed that Vince and Mindy would bear some resemblance to him, Tyrrell, Joss, or Heather. They all came from the same stock. A hostess approached Zachary, smiling. "Table for one…?"

He shook his head. "I'm meeting friends. I don't know if they're here yet, I think I'm still too early. Do you have a reservation for Goldman? I mean…" Zachary scrambled, trying to recall it. "Miller?"

She looked at the form in front of her. "For three?"

"Yeah."

"Come this way." She escorted him to a table and placed menus on it. "Do you want to order a drink now? Or wait for the others?"

"A water, please. I'll order something else when they get here."

"I'll have someone bring it to you." She smiled pleasantly and left him there to his thoughts.

Trying not to look like he was impatient, Zachary scrolled through his social networks on his phone, glancing toward the door every few minutes. While he didn't want to look like he was anxious, he also didn't want to look more interested in his phone than in meeting his siblings.

He heard the door open again and looked up. This time, it was a man and woman of approximately the right age, the woman with long dark hair and the man sporting a blond buzz cut. Zachary stood up, and they saw him immediately. Mindy pointed, and the two of them approached.

"Zachary?" Mindy asked, tilting her head to the side slightly as she studied him.

"Yes." Zachary put out his hand to shake, not wanting to force unwanted closeness on either of them. "Mindy, it's great to meet you. Vince."

Mindy shook, but then pulled him closer to put one arm around his shoulders, keeping her body slightly separated from his. "Nice to meet you, bro."

Vince kept it to a handshake, but nodded his head in agreement. "Yeah. This is… this is really something."

They all sat down. Zachary studied the two of them. He couldn't see the children they had been when they had been separated. Too much time had passed. With Tyrrell, he had recognized the eyes, still exactly the same as six-year-old Tyrrell's had been. With Heather, it had taken longer to catch a glimpse of the little girl he had known. Almost a teenager when they had been separated. Every now and then, he saw a spark of that little blond-haired gamine. Joss was nothing like she had been and nothing like their mother. Her face was prematurely old from smoking, drinking, and drug abuse. Sharp lines, almost anorexic, after being on drugs for so many years.

He closed his eyes for a minute and pictured Mindy, scrunched up in his arms as he fed her a bottle, coaxing her to take it, tricking her by getting her sucking on his finger and then sliding the nipple into its place. Of course there was nothing of that baby left in the woman seated across from him. He thought about Vince with a teddy bear or truck, following the older kids around, determined not to be left behind. The way he pursed his little mouth in determination.

There was just a shadow of that determination on his face again. Zachary smiled at him.

"You look a lot like Tyrrell," Vince observed. "But skinnier."

"Yeah. There's a resemblance."

"You don't look like me. Neither of you does."

Zachary nodded in agreement. He didn't know what else to say.

A waitress came over and took their drink orders. Mindy lifted her brows at Zachary's soft drink order. "Are you… 'on the wagon' too?"

"Not exactly. I don't drink much because it can cause problems with my meds. Some of them. Safer to just not have any."

Though he was hoping to share a couple of glasses of wine with Kenzie one evening and see how his night went. At the Lodge, when he had been out of his meds, they'd had a very pleasant time self-medicating with a couple of drinks. Nothing excessive, but it had definitely been better for their physical relationship than the drugs that tended to suppress his drive. His and Kenzie's intimate relationship had been turned upside down by the torture he had endured at the hands of a sadistic serial killer and the meds he needed to take to stay on an even keel.

"Zachary?"

He shifted his attention back to Mindy, blinking and shaking his head slightly. "Sorry. Trip down memory lane."

"It's a bit weird, isn't it?" she agreed. "Though... maybe more so for you. For me... I don't remember anything from before foster care, so it's like meeting someone that you always knew existed but have never met before."

"I remember you," Zachary said, nodding. "I remember feeding you and changing your diapers."

She got pink, laughing. "Well, isn't that great!"

Zachary chuckled. "All of the older kids helped with the younger ones." His own ears were burning, probably bright red.

"I don't know if I remember or not," Vince said, tilting his head to one side and then the other, looking at Zachary. "I mean, you didn't look like this, of course..."

"No. Heather says I look 'just the same,' but I think you can take that with a grain of salt."

"Unless you were a very ugly child."

"Vince!" Mindy elbowed him.

Vince grimaced. "I didn't mean you're ugly. I just meant that your face on a child's body..."

Mindy elbowed him again. They all laughed.

The waitress brought their drinks, and they browsed over the menu. But the two of them already knew what was good on the menu, and Zachary agreed on the approach of ordering several different dishes to share. That was always best at a Chinese restaurant.

Orders placed, Mindy looked at her brothers, growing more serious.

28

"So, we know a little bit about you from what Tyrrell has said. I don't know if he's shared anything about us with you?"

Zachary shook his head. "He really hasn't done anything more than mention being in touch with you. I figured you wanted your privacy."

Vince and Mindy exchanged looks. Zachary tried to interpret them, to figure out if they were hiding something or if there were something they wanted to share. But he wasn't sure. Maybe a combination of both.

"It's probably more that Tyrrell knows us better," Mindy said. "Since we grew up together. He was really excited about finding you and told us everything he could, but he wouldn't have been excited about us since we were... the siblings he already knew. We were old news. He'd never been without us for long."

Zachary nodded. "Maybe that was it."

He suspected it probably went deeper than that, but it didn't matter. Now they were together and could find out about each other firsthand.

"You guys were all together growing up, right? And the two of you go by Miller."

They looked at each other and nodded. "Yeah. We always wanted the same name as our parents. They really did raise us, not... *your* mom and dad."

"Right. You probably don't even remember *them*."

"No. We were always with the Millers, so…"

They didn't offer whether the Millers had adopted them or whether they had just assumed their names. "But Tyrrell… he didn't change his name? I mean, I haven't ever seen his ID. I just assumed he went by Goldman. Doesn't he?"

"Yeah," Mindy agreed. "Tyrrell was always different."

More exchanged looks, communicating with each other without speaking, feeling out what they were going to tell Zachary and how they would say it.

"He had trouble from the time we were placed," Vince said. He drummed his fingers on the table. "I guess we all had issues. But Tyrrell was the oldest, had been with our bio parents the longest. He acted out a lot. Mom and Dad—the Millers—said that we had some trouble settling in too. We did a lot of the stuff that kids coming into foster care do… crying, throwing things, wetting the bed. But we still had each other. We hadn't lost everything. Tyrrell… he got in trouble a lot at school, talked back to the Millers and wouldn't follow their rules, no matter how many times they imposed consequences. Mom said he was really smart, but he acted wild at school. Made friends with the wrong kids. Got in fights."

Zachary had experienced a lot of disruption at school too. Being in a new place with new rules, trying to make new friends, being bullied. A lot of the stuff they blamed on him had really been started by the bullies. But the teachers and administrators didn't see what kind of people the bullies really were. Zachary was new and an obvious choice for the role of troublemaker. As much as he tried to behave at school and at his foster homes, he was always getting off on the wrong foot.

His learning disabilities and ADHD didn't help. High anxiety and what doctors later diagnosed as PTSD magnified everything. All of his worries, emotions, and reactions. Being constantly hypervigilant. ADHD meds helped him focus better and stay in his seat at school, but when he started rebounding from them at home around suppertime and before bed, the ADHD symptoms returned ten times as bad, right when he was supposed to be studying or doing his homework. He constantly fought, cried, or argued with his foster siblings, parents, and tutors.

"But they didn't take him away and put him into… Bonnie Brown or another home," Zachary said. "He was still allowed to stay with you?"

"They had him into programs all the time, but not residential. After school, weekends, holidays… they'd put him into another camp or group or therapy… or just respite to give the Millers a break. It was pretty tough on them," Vince explained.

"And him," Zachary pointed out.

"I guess. As kids, we didn't really understand what was going on, and I don't know how much Mom and Dad did. They didn't really know much about things like attachment and complex PTSD back then. It was all just… discipline. Tough love. Trying to… get him to settle down and be a part of the family."

"To break him."

Mindy held up her hands. "It wasn't like that. They love him and always just wanted him to be a real part of the family. But he didn't want to be."

"He *couldn't* be."

She shrugged. "Maybe you understand it better from his perspective than we ever could. When we were little, I couldn't understand why he was always mad and refusing to follow the rules and wasn't close to Mom and Dad like we were. Everybody kind of thought he was just a brat, or later, a rebellious teen. Our parents did everything they could, but he was sort of…"

"A lost cause," Zachary finished.

They both just looked at him. Even now, Zachary wondered how much they understood about how it must have been for Tyrrell. About how his brain chemistry was actually different from theirs because of the things he had gone through. That it wasn't a choice to be damaged. He just was.

"When did the drinking start?"

Mindy looked at Vince. Not about a shared secret this time, but calling on his recollections. He was older. He probably remembered it better.

"I'm not sure," Vince admitted. "I guess there was a lot of stuff going on that no one bothered to tell us because we were just kids. They wanted to shelter us from it. And maybe they didn't know when he started drinking until later on. It's always been something that he's tried to keep hidden."

"When he was a teenager?" Zachary suggested. "Drinking with friends? Or did he start raiding the liquor cabinet before that?"

Vince's lips pressed together and he shook his head. "I don't know.

Really. Mom and Dad did have alcohol around, so he might have started with stealing from them. By the time we were teenagers, there was no alcohol allowed in the house. Not even cough syrup. So they knew then... but Tyrrell had already been in and out of a few different programs by then. Boot camps, that kind of thing."

Zachary nodded. He'd seen it happen. He had been in and out of Bonnie Brown from an early age; it was easiest to just send him back there, where they knew him and he knew and understood the rules and routines. There wasn't any point in trying those boot camp programs, which were mostly for kids who were with their biological families or long-term placements like Tyrrell had been. Kids with a family who really wanted him to be a part of it. Not kids who were throwaways, who it was easier to dispose of than to try to reclaim.

"But it wasn't all bad," Mindy said. "You know, he did really good in some of those programs. They got him back on track with school. He got his grades up and graduated and even went on to college."

"Yeah. I heard he had a degree."

"Did he tell you that?" Mindy asked. "He doesn't usually talk about it. Like he is embarrassed about it. Or doesn't think he deserves it."

"No, I heard it from someone else."

Mindy nodded. "Yeah. I don't know why he would never talk about it. He worked really hard to earn it. It wasn't like someone just handed it to him, you know. He got scholarships and bursaries, and he worked over the summer to earn money for tuition. We didn't have a lot of money, and he wouldn't let Mom and Dad pay for it. Said to keep the money for us." She looked in Vince's direction. "To make sure that we could get a post-secondary education too. He was always really good to us."

Zachary smiled, his heart swelling at Tyrrell's generosity. "It was always up to the older kids to look after the younger ones."

The waitress arrived balancing a huge platter filled with smaller dishes. She smiled and greeted them cheerfully and set everything out on the table, pushing dishes and glasses around to make room for it all. They all dished up.

Mindy looked at the small servings on Zachary's plate. "I thought you said Chinese was okay. If you don't like it, you should have said so."

"I just don't have a very big appetite. Because of the meds. It's hard for me to eat much at a time."

"You could eat more than that," Vince countered.

Zachary shook his head. "This is a lot, actually. I might have taken too much."

They rolled their eyes at each other.

"So, what was it like?" Mindy asked. "Living with... our biological family? Your mom and dad and all of the kids?"

Zachary swallowed, looking down at the food.

Zachary took a deep breath and blew it out. He should have been expecting that. He had come to learn more about Tyrrell and to figure out the directions he should go to find him but, of course Mindy and Vince would be curious about the family they had come from. The home that had produced their rebellious older brother. The parents they had escaped.

"Well, I guess you know from whatever your social worker told you and how Tyrrell behaved that it wasn't the best home. Things were pretty tough. It was nice having brothers and sisters to play with and get help from. I missed that when I went into the system. Never had that connection again. But the rest of it… Mom and Dad got drunk and fought with each other. They were really strict and… disciplinarians. Mom had, I guess, postpartum depression every time she had a baby. Wouldn't want to get out of bed for weeks afterward, so we had to try to look out for you ourselves. I guess that's why we were all so close. We looked after each other. Tried to keep each other out of trouble."

"And then when they split us up, Tyrrell didn't have that anymore."

"No, I guess not. He had you, but he would have known that he needed to look after you. You weren't old enough to do anything." Zachary looked at Vince. "You guys probably played together, though. You and T used to play together."

"Yeah, we did. I don't remember a lot, but I remember playing with cars together, playing cops and robbers running around outside, stuff like that. We got bikes when I was five and T was seven and were a menace to the neighborhood."

Zachary smiled. He remembered having a bike at home. It was probably one of the girls' cast-offs, but he didn't know the difference. Or maybe it had been stolen from someone else. He remembered the freedom of being able to bike around, riding to the park or the store or other places that had previously been out of range on foot.

Vince put down his fork for a moment, frowning. "Our social worker didn't say anything about any of that." He raised his brows at Zachary. "She said... that our mom was sick and couldn't take care of all of us. And our dad had to work, so he couldn't. That's why we were placed with the Millers."

Zachary stared at him, trying to comprehend this. "But... you knew about the fire. You knew why you were really put there."

"We knew there was a fire," Vince said slowly, "and that's why we didn't have a *home*. But that we wouldn't be able to go back, even when they rebuilt the house, because our mom was sick."

"She was... not sick. Not that way. Not like she had cancer or something. She was overwhelmed, I think, having to take care of six kids. And she and Dad drank. There was... lots of violence."

"So social services took us away."

"No. It was Mom." Zachary shook his head. "Tyrrell didn't tell you this? I talked to him about it."

"Tell us what?"

"About... how she broke up the family. She said that she didn't want us anymore. Couldn't handle us. Me especially." Zachary stared down at his plate. "I caused so much trouble. She said I was incorrigible. That it was all my fault."

Mindy leaned forward. "That *what* was your fault?"

"That we had to go into care. With me burning down the house..." There was a lump in his throat that was difficult to speak around. "That was the last straw. She didn't want anything to do with us."

Mindy and Vince were both staring at him, open-mouthed. Zachary felt sick. He had assumed they knew all of this. Their history. Why they had entered foster care in the first place. The social worker and their foster parents would have explained it to them. Tyrrell would have told them about the fire if they couldn't remember anything about it themselves.

Especially after Tyrrell and Zachary had reunited and Zachary had helped fill in the gaps in his memory.

"You burned the house down?" Vince repeated.

Zachary closed his eyes. "Yeah. I was… I decorated the tree after everyone went to bed. Put out all of the other decorations. There were candles. Mom said we would light them on Christmas Eve, but they had a big fight… I thought she would be happy if everything was done, and everybody could have a… a magical…" He swallowed, unable to get the word *Christmas* out. "A magical day. Like on TV."

"So you lit the candles," Vince filled in.

"Yeah. Last time I ever lit a fire or handled matches." He took a drink of water, trying to irrigate the desert in his mouth. "Ever."

"We didn't know that." Mindy shook her head. "I always thought… it must have been electrical wiring or a lightning strike."

"No. It was me."

"That must have been awful for you. But no one was hurt. That was lucky."

Zachary nodded. He didn't push up his sleeves to show them the scars. Maybe one day, he would tell them that part.

"I can't believe that a mother would say something like that, though," Mindy said, shaking her head. "That's just… it's cruel. I can't imagine anyone saying that to their child. And she just… got rid of us? Like a litter of kittens?"

"I suppose we should be happy she didn't drown us," Zachary joked. But the joke fell flat. He knew it wasn't funny.

"Maybe our social worker didn't know what really happened," Vince suggested. "She might have gotten the story wrong. Misunderstood what had happened. Why we were in foster care."

Zachary chewed the inside of his cheek. "I thought… Tyrrell said that you had Mrs. Pratt. To begin with, anyway. Didn't you?"

"Yeah, that's right. Mrs. Pratt."

"She knew what happened. She was my caseworker too. She's the one Mom talked to. Told her that she didn't want us back. Mrs. Pratt brought her to see me at the—brought her to see me, to see if she would change her mind about giving up on the family. And she wouldn't, said that she didn't want to ever see us again. That we shouldn't be a family… that I should be in jail."

30

T hey were all silent, trying to reconcile the truths they had each
grown up with.

Zachary immediately understood the fiction Mrs. Pratt had
told the children. What benefit would there be to telling them that their
parents simply didn't want them anymore? It was kinder to tell them a
story that would make them feel better. A mother who was sick and
unable to give them the care they needed. A father struggling just to make
ends meet. Close enough to the truth.

But he wondered whether she had told the same fiction to the Miller
parents. Had they thought they were getting children from a loving home
devastated by illness? If so, it was no wonder they couldn't understand
Tyrrell's behavior. Zachary knew that many of his issues stemmed from the
abuse they had all suffered. They had grown up in a war zone, anxious
about any raised voice, any hint of trouble. There had been physical abuse
and neglect, money spent on alcohol and cigarettes rather than putting
food on the table. The older children had tried to protect the younger children from the abuse they themselves had suffered, but were not always
successful.

"I don't know what to think of this," Mindy said. "How could they
not tell us any of this?" She bent her head and ate a few bites of her
Chinese food as if it were a chore she had to do. "And…" she looked up at
Zachary. "Tyrrell knew this?"

Zachary thought about it. What Tyrrell had remembered when he and Zachary had been reunited on Christmas Eve a year before. What things he had already known and what Zachary had needed to tell him or remind him of.

"He knew… some of it. Not everything. He didn't know what she said to me about not deserving to be a family. That was after we were split up. But he knew… that they fought. He knew that the fire was… because of me. He would have known that it wasn't because our mom was sick." He rubbed the space between his eyes that was beginning to throb with pain. "He was six. Maybe he believed what they told him. But he knew… to be scared. He knew about hiding when they fought. And about…" Zachary swallowed painfully. He couldn't get another bite of the restaurant food down. He took another gulp of water. "He knew about calling 9-1-1. And what would happen if the police came." Those things, he knew. He remembered Tyrrell asking, that last, horrible night if they should call 9-1-1. And Zachary had told him no.

Everything would have been different if he had said yes. Zachary probably wouldn't have had the opportunity to put out the Christmas decorations and to light the candles. Would his mother still have put them into the system if the house hadn't burned down? In another day? Another week? Or would they have stayed with her?

Sooner or later, he was sure that one of his parents would have killed the other. Maybe it was better that things had happened how and when they did. The little children got put into a loving home while at least two of them were still young enough to heal from the trauma. None of them had had to witness one parent killing the other. Or deciding to take out the whole family, as some parents had been known to do. At least Vince and Mindy had survived relatively unscathed.

Mindy reached across the table and touched Zachary's hand tentatively. "I'm sorry."

Zachary swallowed and licked his lips and tried to find something to say.

"I'm sorry that all that stuff happened to you," Mindy went on, "and that you had to explain it to us. I didn't mean to make you… relive something horrible."

Zachary shrugged as if it didn't matter. He used his knife and fork to cut pieces of meat and vegetables into smaller bits, so that it looked like he was eating, but he knew he wouldn't be able to get anything down.

There wasn't much more to say. Mindy and Vince had told Zachary about how they had grown up and how Tyrrell had coped in foster care. Zachary had told them more about where they had come from. What they had escaped, but Tyrrell had not.

Zachary had his notepad out and was jotting down the bits and pieces he had learned from them.

"So… T went to college and got a degree. In what?"

"Uh…" Mindy frowned, trying to recall the details. "Behavioral Science." She said it with an uptick in tone, as if she were asking a question. Vince nodded his agreement.

"Behavioral Science," Zachary repeated, trying to write it down but miserably failing in remembering how to spell 'behavior.' "So… what's that? It sounds like… FBI or something."

"They have a Behavioral Science Unit," Vince agreed, pointing at Zachary. "I used to tease Tyrrell about that, when he was going to school, and when he eventually earned it. Used to ask him if he was going to join the FBI."

"It's like… social work, addiction, psychology, that kind of thing," Mindy contributed, still frowning. Then she gave a little shrug and rolled her eyes.

Zachary raised his eyebrows at her. "Tyrrell studied addiction?"

"And passed with flying colors," Vince blurted, earning another sharp elbow to the ribs. He laughed and then looked away, maybe embarrassed by his own behavior. "I know, it's bizarre, right? I mean, he's learning this stuff at the college level, but it doesn't help him to overcome alcoholism himself? He needed it… but he couldn't use it in his own life."

"He stayed sober all the way through college," Mindy offered. "That's the longest he's ever gone. A few months, a year, and then he's off on a binge again. If he understands how it all works, why can't he use that?" Her voice was intense, filled with frustration at her brother's self-destructive behavior.

"Addiction is complex," Zachary said lamely. "It's not just about… choosing not to have a drink."

They were all silent, Mindy and Vince still pushing food around their plates and picking at what was left. Zachary had given up on his. He wrote down notes and questions, trying to see through everything Mindy and Vince knew about Tyrrell to the key that would lead Zachary to him. They had already told him more than once that they did not know where he went to drink or who he drank with. What further help was any of the rest of what they had told him?

"I'm glad that I found you," Zachary told his younger siblings. "Do you mind if… we stay in touch? Even though you have another family?"

"Sure," Mindy agreed, and they both nodded. "We've kind of left it all to Tyrrell. He was really the one interested in finding everyone, in making all of these family connections. But yes… I'd like to get to know you better."

"He was the one who found Heather and Joss too, right? Have you met either of them?"

"No." Mindy glanced over at Vince. "Not any of the others."

Zachary cocked his head, struck by the wording of her comment. Not "either" of the others, but "any" of the others. "Any?" he repeated. "Heather or Joss?"

Mindy nodded. "Or the others."

31

There was something in Zachary's ears, like a humming or a buzzing, only he couldn't identify what it was. He couldn't exactly hear it, but it blocked everything else out too, so he suddenly couldn't hear the buzz of conversation in the restaurant or anything other than the sound of his own heartbeat.

He stared at Mindy, trying to reconcile her words with what he knew. He had to make sense of it somehow. Mindy must have meant that the Millers fostered or adopted other children as well, and Tyrrell had been in contact with them, had been concerned about not losing touch with the other children he had grown up with.

Zachary tried to form words, but couldn't get them out. He took a drink of water. He could see Vince's and Mindy's mouths moving, their glances toward him, but he thought they must be communicating silently again. He swished a mouthful of water around his dry mouth, swallowed it, and cleared his throat.

"What others?" he asked.

"The other brothers and sisters."

"Tyrrell's? Other foster kids?"

Mindy shook her head. Her brows were drawn down in concentration, but they made her look angry or grumpy instead of studious. She sighed and sat back in her seat. "I can't believe Tyrrell didn't tell you."

"Didn't tell me what? What other children are you talking about?"

Maybe Tyrrell had fathered other children with a woman other than Lindsey, and Mindy was talking about them. Tyrrell's kids. That would make more sense. Maybe Tyrrell was even shacked up somewhere with another woman. He was free from Lindsey; there was no reason he couldn't be. He might have other children that he hadn't told Zachary about.

But why wouldn't he have told his brother about them? He had been eager to tell him about Alisha and Mason. Keen to have Zachary meet them. If there were more, Zachary would have been happy to meet them too. He couldn't figure out why it would be a problem for Tyrrell. Even if they were older or the same age as Alisha and Mason, who was Zachary to judge? He wasn't the morality police.

Mindy scratched at a piece of dried food stuck to the table. "Tyrrell did one of those DNA tests. You know, where you can find out information about your ancestry, but they all connect to big databases now where everybody else who has had their DNA done—and has made it public—shows up. So you can find out that you have a third cousin in Russia or that your grandpa fathered a kid in Vietnam, or whatever."

Zachary's brain caught on Vietnam. Tyrrell hadn't been to Vietnam. No one he knew had served in Vietnam or even visited it. Certainly not anyone in his family.

"Well, you know, he did it so he could find out more about your family. The Goldman family. Where they were from and if he had any blood relatives around here. He was hoping that you or Jocelyn or Heather would have done yours, and it would be a really easy way to connect with you. Because you can just message each other and say, 'Hey, we both submitted DNA to this database, and you must be my long-lost brother…'"

Vince snorted. He was sitting back, arms folded. He clearly disapproved of Tyrrell having done what he had. Maybe as foster kids, they had been warned never to have anything to do with their biological family. Despite being told that they were in foster care because their mother was sick, maybe they had been told that Zachary didn't want to meet them or that their identities had to remain a secret if they wanted to stay with the Millers, or some lie like that. Or maybe Vince had divorced himself from his biological family, believing that he was better off with the Millers, and it was best not to ask questions or to dig into the past, in case he didn't like the answers he found there.

Mindy looked at Vince, waiting to see if he had something to say, but Vince shook his head and waited for her to continue.

"And none of you had registered in any of these databases, but there were other hits. Other people who had registered who showed up as brothers or sisters."

"How is that possible?" Zachary said stupidly. He knew all of his brothers and sisters. There had been six of them, and now he had been reunited with all of them. There were no more children in their family.

"Because your parents didn't stop having kids," Vince said, his voice hard.

"They stayed together? With each other?"

Mindy shook her head. "Not with each other. With other people. So there are half siblings. But... they are still siblings. Still biologically related."

Zachary tried to wrap his mind around this. It wasn't like it was the first time that the thought had occurred to him that his parents were still young enough when the family broke up that they could have had other children. As a kid, he had fantasized about having more family. If he couldn't be reunited with the brothers and sisters he knew, then there could be others. Or even just kids he got along with in his foster families. Kids who were more than just roommates or passing acquaintances, but who felt like real family, like Tyrrell.

But he hadn't thought seriously about it as an adult. His parents had to know what a mistake it would be to have more children. Hadn't their experiences taught them anything? His mother would understand that having another pregnancy would send her into the throes of depression. His father would know that he didn't want rug rats underfoot and throwing up on his things. Kids just made noise, fought with each other, and got in the way. He knew that he would rather spend his money on drinking than kids, so why would he have more?

"Why would they have more kids?"

Vince shook his head. "I didn't really think about it before. I mean, people do. They get together with someone new and decide to start another family. But... that was before I knew what you were saying... if they were such bad parents the first time, why would they go on and have more?"

"I don't know." Zachary shook his head in wonder. It was amazing to find out that he had more siblings than he had known about. But when he thought about the way they had lived before the fire, he was horrified.

Why would his parents go on having other children? "Do you... know them? Have you met them?"

"No. We were happy with our family." Vince made a gesture that took in himself and Mindy, and maybe the absent Tyrrell as well. "We didn't feel like we needed to meet anyone else. It was Tyrrell. All Tyrrell. He was so determined to... find *everyone*."

When Zachary had first met Tyrrell a year before, Mr. Peterson had commented on the need of foster and adopted children to make biological connections, to feel anchored and to know where they had come from. Tyrrell had brushed this idea off without much comment, saying that his biological connection had been to his children. That he hadn't been as driven to find his siblings or his parents.

But his actions belied that statement. He was the one who had searched out Zachary. Who had searched out each of his siblings. Zachary was the private investigator. It would have been natural for him to track down his family members, to know where they were, even if he decided not to contact them. But he never had. Tyrrell had been the one to track them down and bring them back together.

"So Tyrrell has met them? All of them?"

"I don't know if he's met *all* of them," Vince said. "But he's met some of them. And there could be others... not everyone registers their DNA in these databases or makes it available for family matching."

"Do you know their names? Where they are? How old?"

Vince chuckled darkly. "As far as I know, they're all younger. But I don't know. I'm not sure Tyrrell would have told us if he found older siblings other than you three."

Mindy looked at a sparkling watch on her wrist. "I guess... we're going to be here a bit longer. You want to get coffee or a nightcap?"

32

It was much later than Zachary had expected before he was finally on his way home. He called Kenzie on Bluetooth once he got into the car, reaching her just as he merged onto the highway.

"Hey. I was expecting you home," Kenzie said. "I guess things must have gone pretty well if you were visiting this late. Were you there until the restaurant closed?"

Zachary laughed. "Actually, yes. And hopefully, I haven't had so much coffee that I have to make a pit stop on the way home."

"Well, at least you won't fall asleep at the wheel. How are you doing?"

"Okay. I'll tell you about it when I get home."

She didn't answer for a moment, then agreed. "Sure, of course. It will be easier to tell me everything when we are face to face. But it was okay? You're not upset?"

"It was okay."

She probably didn't fail to notice that he didn't say he was not upset.

Zachary didn't think he was upset, but he wasn't sure what he was feeling. He was feeling somewhat unsettled. But he wasn't sure how to describe it or if there was even a word for the kind of stress and letdown and confusion and disappointment and excitement that he was feeling. It was all mixed together so thoroughly.

"Drive carefully. You're not too tired, right?"

"No, I'm not tired. I'm never tired while I'm driving."

"Well, not usually, but sometimes it does happen."

He knew that he'd fallen asleep when they had been on their way to the Lodge. Not while he was driving, though; Kenzie had already taken the wheel when he conked out. But she had noticed that he was too tired to be safe anymore. It was a good thing she had taken over before he drove off the road.

He cleared his throat. "That's different. I was still recovering."

"I know. And now you're just out of the hospital and on new meds and trying to get used to a new schedule. You could still have problems. Just pay attention. And if you start feeling like you might be too tired, pull over. Give me a call. I can come to get you. Or you can walk around or stop at a convenience store for more coffee. But don't just keep driving."

"Okay."

"Okay?" she persisted, wanting to hear it again, wanting him to be more emphatic in his response so that she knew he had really heard her and would take her advice.

"Okay. I will," he agreed.

"Don't forget, I've seen what happens to people who fall asleep at the wheel. And to the people who happen to be in their way."

Kenzie did have a slightly different perspective on things that could kill a person than the average girlfriend.

When he got home, he sat in his car in front of the house for a minute, reviewing the day in his mind. It had been a long day. Was he any further ahead than he had been when he had first started? Did he have any concrete evidence that would help him to find Tyrrell? There were directions for him to investigate, but he didn't know where any of them would lead him, and if they would lead him toward or away from Tyrrell.

He hoped that the others were right, and that Tyrrell's disappearance was just the same as his other disappearances, the results of a binge. But was it? Or had something different happened this time? If it was a binge, was it just the natural progression of falling off the wagon when he had been at the Lodge? And had it just been the stress of the things that had happened at the Lodge that had made him start drinking again?

Or was he just assuming that Tyrrell had started drinking again at the Lodge because that was where he had noticed it? It was entirely possible that he'd been drinking for days or weeks before that. He was a closet drinker. He had plenty of experience hiding it. At the Lodge, it had been different. Tyrrell only had one source of alcohol, unless he had also brought some with him. He couldn't go out anywhere to get more, so he'd had to consume what was in the liquor cabinet in the cabin. And that was what Zachary had noticed. If Zachary hadn't been looking for something to calm his nerves in the absence of his medications, he probably wouldn't have looked at the bottles and noticed how the levels had gone down and wouldn't have been tipped off to Tyrrell's drinking. Tyrrell certainly hadn't looked or acted drunk.

Zachary had shut off the car and was starting to get cold. He climbed out and walked up the front sidewalk and into the house.

"The conquering hero returns," Kenzie quipped, smiling at him.

She was in her cozy pajamas, a blanket pulled over her lap as she sat on the couch, either watching TV or doing something on her phone.

"Hi." He bent down to kiss her, then sat beside her, pulling her over to cuddle against him. She was warm and soft, and he loved the shower-fresh smell of her. "Sorry to be so late."

"You couldn't very well leave in the middle of the discussion. Then you would just have to go back again tomorrow or some other time to finish. I take it you must have found a lot to talk about?"

He noticed she didn't ask whether he had gotten any leads on Tyrrell's disappearance. Being reunited with his younger siblings was important in and of itself, whether he'd gotten the information he needed or not.

But it was Tyrrell he couldn't stop thinking about. Tyrrell who needed his help. Or not, as the case may be. Was he just voluntarily missing? Part of the street population or living out of his car or a shelter? Was everyone else right, and Tyrrell would eventually show up on his own and act as if nothing had happened? Or was he being held against his will? Or worse, hurt or sick?

He leaned his head against Kenzie's. "Did you… have any time today to talk to the other morgues?"

She took his hand in hers and gave it a squeeze. "I would have called you right away if I had found anything. I talked to almost all of the Medical Examiner's Offices. I left messages with any of the ones I couldn't talk to directly. No one who I have talked to has had any John Does matching Tyrrell's description."

"Okay." Zachary blew his breath out. "That's good."

Of course, Jose and the other men that Archuro had killed had never shown up at the morgue, either. Because he had carefully hidden the bodies after he had finished with them. The medical examiner was still trying to identify the various remains that the police had managed to locate by searching Archuro's properties, the land around them, and Santiago's cemetery. Who knew how long that would take. Maybe most of them would never be identified. He had targeted undocumented immigrants. While Zachary had provided the police with a list of all of the men that John Mwangi had thought were the victims of the same serial killer, they didn't have pictures, DNA, fingerprints, or even good descriptions of all of them. Some of the killings went back years, and the friends or families of those missing men could no longer be identified and tracked down.

"It is good," Kenzie agreed firmly. Maybe she knew where Zachary's mind had gone. "So... did you have anything to tell me about Vince and Mindy? You said you would tell me about it when you got home. Unless you're too tired. Did you want to head to bed and talk about it in the morning when you are fresh?"

"No. I don't think I'll be able to get to sleep for a while yet. I need to unwind first."

"And take your meds. Maybe you should take them now so that they have time to start working before you go to bed."

Zachary shrugged, but didn't get up to get them. It was probably a good idea, but he didn't like changing his routine. He was used to taking them right before getting into bed.

33

He started at the beginning, telling her about meeting Vince and Mindy and the discussion that followed in pretty much the order that had taken place. He told her about Tyrrell as a child and youth, the trouble he'd gotten into, and the lies that the social worker had told.

"If that's what she told their foster parents too…" he trailed off.

"Then they didn't have a hope of giving Tyrrell the support he needed," Kenzie finished. "They didn't have a clue why he was behaving the way he was."

"Maybe it wouldn't have made any difference. Maybe they didn't understand trauma and attachment back then and would have approached it the same way whether they knew the reason for his behavior or not. But…"

"They had at least a vague understanding of the effects of abuse on a child. Maybe not as well as they do now, and maybe they didn't have all of the same therapeutic choices as they do now. Still, they would have at least had some understanding of the fact that he was scared and traumatized instead of just being… bad. A wayward child in need of correction."

"Yeah. But who knows. Maybe the parents knew everything, and she only kept it from Vince and Mindy so that they wouldn't feel bad about their biological mother not wanting them."

"That would be pretty crushing," Kenzie agreed. With her arm around

Zachary's neck, she stroked his head and face. "I'm sorry that was something you had to deal with. On top of the fire and your injuries, in addition to being taken away from them, you had to deal with your own mother's cruelty. Face to face, not just told to you by someone when you were old enough to understand."

Zachary shrugged, not wanting to talk about that pain. He had told her about it before. He might not have talked much about how it had affected him, but she was an intelligent woman with a medical background, and she had seen how damaged and dysfunctional he was.

Kenzie waited. Not forcing him to tell her about his feelings, just waiting to see what else he had to tell her. Dr. B had encouraged them to get comfortable with silence. With leaving open spaces in the conversation so that they each had a chance to contemplate and offer something new without feeling like they were being interrogated. There were things he didn't want to talk about, but there were also things he wanted to share, that he hoped she could help him to process.

"There's something else. Tyrrell was the one who wanted to find the rest of us. He's the one who tracked me down, and Heather and Joss."

"Sure. He seemed like it meant a lot to him. And I know it meant a lot to you too, even though you weren't the one who went looking for him."

Zachary never could have looked for the others. Not when he knew how his actions had ruined their lives. It was good that Tyrrell's disappearance had forced him to reach out to Vince and Mindy. If they weren't interested in searching out their other siblings, it might have been a long time before they were reunited with Zachary. Like the TV shows he had seen where adoptees from the same family were reunited at seventy or eighty years old.

"He did one of those DNA searches to see if he could find us through their DNA matching database."

"But he didn't really need to do that. Not that many Zachary Goldmans in Vermont."

"Vince and Mindy said that... he found other siblings."

Kenzie turned to look at him, surprised. "*Other* siblings? You don't mean Heather and Joss, I gather."

"No. My mom and dad apparently... had more children after they broke up." It was easier to say that they broke up than that they had dissolved the entire family and put them into the care of the state. It made it sound more normal.

"Oh, wow. How many?"

"I don't know. Vince and Mindy weren't interested in meeting them. Only Tyrrell. I don't know how many there were or from which parent. How many were in the database, or how many he contacted."

"Because there are probably kids who hadn't sent in their DNA either."

"Yeah. It could be one of these cases where a dozen or more kids are scattered across the state. Or the country. Who knows."

"You could have some interesting family reunions!"

"You're telling me." Zachary nodded.

"So, how do you find these other siblings? I assume you're going to. Do you have to submit a sample to their database? I guess that would take weeks to get results, and you wouldn't want to have to wait that long. Can the police get access to the results?"

There had been a lot of stuff in the news about whether it was ethical for family DNA search companies to provide information to the police when they asked for it. Whether they needed a warrant and what kind of information they would be required to provide. And there had been legislation passed in some states, including Vermont, about whether the police were even allowed to use familial DNA in an investigation.

"I don't need to go to the police with it," he told her, hoping that it was true. "I have access to Tyrrell's email account, so I should be able to see who he was in contact with. I didn't know before to look for anyone but Vince or Mindy. I've already started to sort through some of his emails, but haven't gone back any farther than December. These siblings he found must have been before that. Maybe even before he found me, because I think he did the DNA search in hopes that it would lead him directly to us. Me and Heather and Joss."

"So he might have been in contact with them for more than a year. He never mentioned it to you?"

"No. Maybe he thought I would be upset. Or jealous. I don't know. But if he has another family... maybe they know something about where he is."

Kenzie nodded slowly. "You sometimes hear about bigamists who have two separate families that don't know about each other. I guess it could be the same with birth families and foster families... and other biological families. Tyrrell could have two completely different lives. He may not have been comfortable with letting them cross over."

"It's just weird. Because they're my family too. Or biological relations, anyway. You would think..."

"You never can tell what is going on in someone else's mind. Maybe he thought that if one family rejected him, he would still have the other. Maybe he has secrets from them. And secrets from you."

Zachary nodded. "I just wish he'd said something. I feel kind of… like the kid who doesn't get picked for a team at school. By his best friend."

Betrayed. Why would Tyrrell not have shared that part of his life with Zachary?

34

Zachary took his meds and did his best to get to sleep. He could feel them kicking in, but his brain didn't slow down enough for them to take effect. He realized that he was just waiting for Kenzie to fall asleep so that he could get up and log in to his computer to do some more research into Tyrrell's disappearance. He'd already made up his mind that he wasn't going to sleep. Finding Tyrrell was more important. Saving him from whatever force was keeping him away from his family.

But what if the thing that was keeping him away from his family was more family? How was Zachary supposed to judge which was more important?

What did it matter which Zachary thought was more important? The decision wouldn't be up to him. It was up to Tyrrell. If he didn't want to be with the siblings he had grown up with, but instead wanted to spend his time with the others he had found, Zachary wouldn't have any say in it. It was out of his hands.

He couldn't know whether that was the case until he found Tyrrell and talked to him face to face. If Tyrrell didn't want to talk to him, at least Zachary would find out at that point.

Kenzie's breathing was long and even. Zachary lay listening to it for a few minutes, both to make sure she was fast asleep and would not wake up when he got up, and to see if her regularly paced breathing would convince his brain that it was time for him to go to sleep too.

But he felt like bugs were crawling under his skin. He couldn't keep lying there any longer. He needed to get up and do something. He slipped out of bed and grabbed his clothes, pulling them on as he made his way to the living room so that he was nearly dressed by the time he got there. He pulled on his socks as he waited for his computer to finish waking up.

He didn't look at his own email inbox, but went straight to Tyrrell's. He first checked on any mail that had arrived since he had looked at it last. There was a good amount of spam, as there had been before, and Zachary just dragged it out to the appropriate folder. He half-expected there to be an email from Vince to Tyrrell, warning him that they had told Zachary his secret. But apparently, it hadn't occurred to Vince to do so, or he knew that Tyrrell wouldn't be checking his email. Or maybe he realized Zachary would see it before Tyrrell. Zachary had told him that was how he had gotten Vince's contact information.

There wasn't anything personal in the inbox after Zachary finished going through all of the spam and bulk mail. No one expected Tyrrell to be there. No one thought that he would return their emails.

That probably meant nothing. Just that email wasn't Tyrrell's preferred mode of communication. It wasn't Zachary's. It was much quicker for him to deal with people by phone than reading and writing emails.

He searched for "DNA" and ended up with a whole raft of emails from multiple companies regarding his DNA profile and matches with relatives. Zachary looked at the status line. *1-50 results of hundreds.* He rubbed his temples, trying to figure out how to process that many emails. Did that mean hundreds of different matches? Hundreds of people they were related to? He couldn't even comprehend that many relatives. He had grown up in a family of eight. And then he had lost them all. The prospect of having hundreds of relatives was overwhelming.

He clicked on the most recent "You have a new match" email, hoping it would give him some idea of how to proceed. Would it say right in it that the person was a brother or a sister? There was little information in the email, just pointing him to an online account for the DNA database company. He clicked. At the login page, he filled in Tyrrell's email address and the password he had used for his email login. It didn't work. Rather than trying more passwords, he just clicked on the "forgot password" link, filled in the email address again, and clicked Send. There was a ding in

Tyrrell's email, and Zachary opened it and clicked on the new email from the DNA company. He clicked a link, set the new password to be the same as Tyrrell's email password, and got in.

There was a button for DNA matches up at the top, and Zachary clicked it. The screen refreshed and then filled with row after row of names. They appeared to be sorted by priority, putting Tyrrell's closest DNA matches at the top, with more distant relatives farther down the page.

Up at the top were several rows with "possible sibling" listed as the relationship.

A couple of them had photos attached, and Zachary stared at the strangers who, according to their DNA, were blood relations. Maybe his brothers and sisters. He clicked, and the profiles were scanty, with no family trees attached. There were a few with Goldman as their last name. Zachary wasn't sure what his mother's maiden name had been. Had he ever known it? Back when he was in school and still living at home, he might have. But if he had, it had been lost during the intervening years, when he had passed through so many different families and each had, in some way, overwritten another piece of his past. The mental space required to remember the details of a new family and to find some way to relate to them had made him lose track of his own family, at least the less important parts of it. He kept his siblings' faces and names carefully protected, but extraneous details about his parents and about extended family members, if he had ever known of any, were gone.

There didn't seem to be any email addresses or phone numbers attached to the DNA match records. Had Tyrrell recorded them somewhere else? In his contacts database? Zachary opened his contact list and searched for the names of the siblings, but they did not appear on the list. If Tyrrell had connected to them, it must have been another way. Zachary returned to the DNA company and found an inbox in the top right corner. He clicked on that and found a long list of contact names down the side, some of them bolded with numbers of unread communications beside them. Zachary clicked on one randomly.

A conversation threaded down the page, only the headings of the first few messages visible. "Are you there?" and "You haven't responded," at the top. Zachary clicked on one of the emails farther down the page, expanding it. A conversation between Tyrrell and Jason Tooley. There were details confirmed between them about Berk Goldman, Tyrrell's and

Zachary's father. And apparently, Jason Tooley's as well. He was younger than either of them, which was as Zachary had expected. A child his father had produced after the family dissolution. He couldn't help being a little bit relieved that Jason hadn't been fathered while Zachary's parents were still together, though he couldn't say what difference it made. He already knew the kind of person his father was. It didn't make any difference whether he was adulterous or not. What mattered was the way he had behaved and treated his children before the family had been broken up.

Zachary backed out and clicked on another conversation. Tyrrell and Mary Smith Burns making arrangements to meet each other.

To meet. So, Tyrrell had gone on to meet at least some of the siblings.

Zachary didn't know why the feeling of betrayal was so strong. The other siblings, Mary Smith Burns and the others, were just as much Zachary's blood relations as they were Tyrrell's. Why wouldn't he want to see them and maybe learn something? To make as many personal connections as he could. The larger his support network, the better.

He stuffed the feelings down. It was exciting, learning that he had a larger family than he had thought. Maybe, like Vince and Mindy, they were less damaged than Zachary had been. Normal people without the same issues as he and the older kids had. And Tyrrell. Why did he have to be afflicted with alcoholism? It wasn't fair, after all he had been through with his biological family and having such a difficult time settling into a foster family, that he'd had to deal with addiction as well. Not just a few scrapes as a teenager, as Zachary had hoped at first, but ongoing problems.

Zachary didn't want to contact the siblings through the DNA website. He didn't want to pretend to be Tyrrell and he didn't want a record of his investigation inside of Tyrrell's accounts. He would put everything back to the way that it had been when he found Tyrrell. Other than the new password on the DNA database login. But it was easy enough to forget a login password. Or for the company to say that you needed to set a new one because of a data breach. If Tyrrell tried to log in, he would hopefully just think that he had forgotten a password or hadn't recorded that he had changed it. Since it was the same password as Tyrrell's email, he might even cycle through several common passwords that he used and hit on it. If not, he would just do a password reset, and everything in his account would be as he had left it.

He wrote down each of the names of the new siblings, and birth years if they were available. Where available, he saved their pictures to his hard drive to upload them into an image search engine and find their social networks.

He was a private investigator. It wouldn't take him long to find contact information for each of them outside the limits of the DNA database.

35

Zachary awoke later on the couch, one of the throw blankets pulled around him. He blinked blearily at Kenzie, who bent down and kissed him on the cheek.

"You got some sleep?" Kenzie asked, though the answer to that was obvious.

Zachary straightened his body out, stretched, and sat up slowly. He rubbed his neck, trying to massage away any cricks from sleeping in such an uncomfortable position.

"I guess it all caught up eventually," he admitted, and covered a yawn. "The sleep meds. I couldn't settle down, but I must have closed my eyes at some point…"

"And zonked. You were snoring to beat the band. Thought I had a saber-toothed tiger in my living room. It's probably too soon to ask you how you're feeling this morning."

Zachary nodded. It took him a while to feel human after he woke up in the morning, then to analyze his body and determine whether he felt better or worse than any other day.

"If you're still tired, why don't you move to the bed? You'll be a lot more comfortable."

"I won't go back to sleep now."

"You sure? You were still pretty deep under, for you. Don't overextend yourself. You were up late."

"I'm sure. Want to make some calls this morning, catch people before they get too busy."

"Just be careful. Sorry, I don't mean to be a nag. Just want to make sure you're taking care of yourself."

"I'm fine." He met her eyes. "The trip back to the hospital was unnecessary."

"Okay. I'll leave you alone. You're the best one to know your own limits." She put up her hands, indicating her surrendering of the issue, and turned toward the kitchen. "I'm putting on some coffee. Do you want it before your shower?"

Zachary noticed belatedly that she had already showered herself, damp curls still clinging around her collar. That meant it was quite a bit later than he usually woke up. The effects of the sleep aid or his body adjusting to his new, out-of-the-hospital activities. He would prefer to just wash his face, comb his hair, and slap on some deodorant to jump back into his work, but Kenzie's mention of a shower was probably a subtle nudge that he was noticeably in need of one, so he'd better not skip it.

"I'll have half a cup before."

Kenzie nodded and measured grounds into the hopper. The machine would make single cups, travel mugs, or a full carafe, and they generally went through a full carafe in the morning. They waited while it brewed, making small talk. Kenzie didn't bring up Zachary's siblings, letting him think about it and be in control of whether he wanted to talk about it some more. They ran through the usual pleasantries about sleep, the weather, and the newest bodies in the morgue. Zachary drank a full cup of coffee instead of a half and headed for the shower.

"I'll probably be gone when you're out," Kenzie advised. "Have a good day. I'll see you tonight."

"Okay, see you then."

"Date night, if you can swing it."

"Is it?" Zachary thought about the week and realized it was Friday. "Right. I'll try not to get stuck doing anything that will make me late."

He should probably put date night in his calendar, if it wasn't already there. Something to remind him that he had a commitment that night. He tried to keep it all on his phone, but sometimes even when he had an appointment reminder, he didn't pay any attention to its noises and vibrations. They needed to make an ADHD phone that would actually reach out and shake *him* when he had to be somewhere.

His shower was brief, though he did stand under the spray for a while thinking about the discoveries he had made the previous day and night and planning out how to follow through on it all. When he got out, Kenzie was gone as predicted, on her way to work or maybe already at the office. She had a better temperament for office work. She was good at showing up at regular hours, following a routine when she got there, and keeping Dr. Wiltshire and the rest of the support staff on track. Zachary didn't really mind the idea of dealing with dead bodies. For him, they were the key to solving some of the really difficult cases. But the rest of Kenzie's work, the administrative stuff, and the years of school it had taken for her to get there, that would have done Zachary in.

He sat down at his computer, pulling on a shirt and then sipping another cup of coffee. The first order of business was to see if he could catch Rhys before school. Zachary looked at the time and decided that it would still be too early for any classes to have started, so he sent Rhys a message.

Hey, can we meet later today? After school?

Three dots appeared on the screen almost immediately as Rhys composed his answer. A brief reply, a thumbs-up that the two of them getting together would be fine. More dots appeared, and then a large, red, capital *Y. Why?*

"Just want to see how you are. Glad to be out of the hospital now."

Rhys sent back a gif of an adorable kitten asleep on its back, limbs splayed out. Affirming how relaxed and happy Zachary was about getting out of the hospital, Zachary assumed.

Just like that, Zachary confirmed back. Though it wasn't exactly the truth. He wasn't sure he'd ever been as relaxed and happy as that kitten. If he had been, he'd clearly been well-drugged at the time. *OK. Will come by after school. Fourish?*

Rhys posted a ticking clock and *c u*

Zachary turned to the next job at hand, which was to get back in touch with the cops in Riverbrook and see if they had made any progress on the investigation. Which he assumed they had not. They would have far more urgent things on their list than following up on some cold, voluntary disappearance. But if he harassed them enough, they might do some basic work on the file just to get him off of their backs.

He looked up the number for the Riverbrook Police Department and tapped it to put the call through. It was answered by the receptionist or officer of the day. "Riverbrook Police Department."

"Hi, I'm looking for Sergeant Fontaine. Is he available?"

"Not sure if he is in right now. I'll put you through to his number."

Zachary waited while it rang. Fontaine probably wouldn't answer, even if he were at his desk. After a few rings, however, there was a click and a brusque, "Fontaine."

"Sergeant Fontaine, it's Zachary Goldman. Tyrrell Goldman's brother? The missing person?" He knew that Tyrrell was probably not first and foremost in the cop's mind, and Zachary's name had probably been long forgotten.

"Ah," Fontaine said. "We haven't really had much time with the case yet. I'm afraid I don't have anything to report back to you."

If it had been a fresh case, the abduction of a child or a senior wandering off, they would have been right on top of it, with plenty of investigation done in the first twenty-four hours. But an adult not identified as high-risk who had been missing for weeks? That was a different story. Just about everything else would take precedent over it.

"I know this is not the only file on your desk," Zachary said. "And I don't want to be a pest, but I wanted to keep up on what you're doing and what I can do from my end."

"Just leave it to the police. There isn't anything for you to do other than to let us know if your brother calls you or shows up again."

"I'm a private investigator," Zachary reminded him. "I'm going to keep investigating it as long as I've got a direction to go."

Fontaine gave a growl. "We are not in the business of cooperating with private investigators."

"No. I'll do my thing, and I'll let you know if I come across anything that might be helpful to the case. But it's best if we're not duplicating efforts. Have you been able to check with the hospitals, or should I call them?"

"Yes, we've been in contact with the hospitals. Goldman hasn't been admitted. No John Does that match his description."

"And he hasn't shown up in the morgue. I already have confirmation of that."

"How would you know that?"

"I have a contact."

"We haven't had confirmation of that yet, but if you have, then go on."

"He doesn't show up in your system? As being arrested?"

"No. Though he does have a record. You know that, don't you?"

"I know he's been a missing person before," Zachary said cautiously.

"I'm not talking about being a missing person. I'm talking about his arrest record."

"Oh. No, I wasn't aware of that. Is it recent?"

Who knew how many times Tyrrell might have been arrested as an older teen. If he'd been rebellious and doing alcohol and drugs, he could have a lengthy record. Though Zachary thought he must be back on track again at that age, for a while at least, because he had gone to college and earned that degree. And since college? How many times since then had he been on the police department's radar?

"Nothing in the past year," Fontaine said carefully, obviously watching how much information he gave Zachary. "But there have been... a number of incidents."

"Are they all for the same thing?"

A pause while Fontaine considered this as well. "More or less."

If Tyrrell had been arrested for anything, it was probably DUI or disorderly conduct. So if Fontaine said they were all more or less for the same thing, Zachary figured he was safe in assuming they all had to do with his substance abuse issues.

"Okay, thanks. That's good to know. But he's not in the system right now..."

"No. No one that we have been in contact with has any idea where he might have disappeared to. But... there's no hint of foul play."

"He might be voluntary," Zachary agreed, "but we won't know that until we find him. Are you able to make inquiries about whether he's been admitted to any of the detox or drug rehab programs in the state?"

"That would be a lot of work, with probably little return. If he were in rehab right now, you would probably know about it."

"Maybe." Or maybe Tyrrell felt too guilty to tell anyone. Or he didn't know if it would "take" and didn't want to get anyone's hopes up.

In truth, Zachary doubted Tyrrell was in any kind of rehab program. The letter didn't make it sound like he was going somewhere to get better. It sounded like he was giving up on sobriety or having anything to do with his family. Fontaine was right; it probably wasn't worth the time it would take to make all of those phone calls.

"Have you checked Tyrrell's license plate?" Zachary asked, remembering a note he'd jotted down the night before. "See whether he has any parking tickets or if it's in impound? If he has a bunch of parking tickets from the same place, that might show where he goes to drink…"

"It hasn't been ticketed or impounded recently. I haven't examined the historical tickets. Might be worth looking into if he has a place he always goes. I'll have someone look into it later."

"Okay… well, thanks for putting up with me. I have a few leads to check out… it turns out that there are some other family members he'd found through a DNA search. Maybe one of them will know something."

Fontaine grunted. "Sure. Let me know if something comes up."

36

Z achary had the list of siblings in front of him, with the contact details that he had managed to pull up for each of them. It wasn't surprising, he supposed, that someone who put their DNA into a public database and used their legal name for their username was easy to find on social media and in phone directories.

Jason Tooley was the sibling trying to contact Tyrrell to find out why he had suddenly gone quiet. He seemed like the best bet for Tyrrell to reach out to. He wasn't apathetic about finding a new DNA relation, unlike Vince and Mindy.

He supposed that Vince and Mindy didn't need to find biological relations as much because they had grown up with each other. They always knew where a biological sibling was and could talk to each other whenever needed. Even though he had grown up in the Millers' home, Tyrrell had not felt like he belonged there. It sounded like he had spent a good amount of time separated from them, put into some program or respite care. He remembered their biological parents well enough to not feel like the Millers were his "real" parents and had missed the other siblings. Even though Zachary wished Tyrrell had been happier, he couldn't help feeling more warmly toward him than to Vince and Mindy because he had not forgotten Zachary and the older girls. He hadn't been satisfied with arrangements like the youngest children.

He took a few deep breaths and tried the first phone number beside

Jason Tooley's name. It almost immediately went to a recorded voice saying that the number was no longer in service.

That wasn't an unusual event when trying to find someone based on information that was several years old. Maybe nothing saved to the internet was ever completely lost, but that didn't mean it was all correct or that nothing had changed. That was why Zachary always searched out all of the phone numbers he could the first time around. It was faster to assume that one or more of them would be wrong, and having to conduct repeated searches was not as efficient as getting the whole list of numbers the first time if he could. He went on to the next one on the list.

"Hello?"

"Hi. Is this Jason Tooley?"

"Yeah. Who is this?"

"My name is Zachary Goldman. I think you've been in touch with my brother, Tyrrell Goldman? Have I got the right Jason Tooley?"

"I'm the only one I know of. Yeah, I know Tyrrell. What's your name?"

"Zachary."

"Zachary. Yeah, he's mentioned you. What's up? Is everything okay with Tyrrell?"

He sounded young. Younger than Zachary had expected. He had unconsciously been envisioning a man around Vince and Mindy's age. But of course, that was wrong. They had not been conceived until after the fire. After his parents' break-up.

"I'm actually looking for him. I was hoping that maybe you had seen him and he had crashed on your couch. I guess not."

"No. Why would he come here? He's got a place of his own in River-whatever. What do you mean you're looking for him? You guys are in touch, aren't you? He sounded like you were pretty close."

Zachary sensed there might be a little jealousy in Jason's tone. Wondering why Tyrrell was so close to Zachary? Thinking that Tyrrell was spending more time or energy on his relationship with Zachary instead of his relationship with Jason?

"I haven't seen him for a while. I've been in the hospital. And it turns out that while I was in the hospital, he kind of dropped out of sight."

"Did you call him?"

"Yes." Zachary rolled his eyes. Why was that the first thing everyone asked him? Of course he had called. Tyrrell wouldn't be missing if he answered his phone. "I've called him, and there is no answer. A number of us have called him. And I went to his work and his home. He hasn't been to work since early in December, and his apartment has already been rented to someone else."

"They took his house?" Jason asked in surprise.

"Well, he had an apartment, not a house, and yeah… he stopped paying rent and didn't show up. Left food rotting in the fridge. The landlord cleaned it out and rented it to someone else."

"Sheesh." Jason blew out his breath. "You think he's okay?"

"I don't know. That's why I'm looking for him. I need to make sure he's all right." Zachary hesitated. "He left a letter for me while I was in the hospital, so I didn't get it until I was out. And he sounded pretty down. I'm really hoping that… it wasn't a suicide note."

"He wouldn't do that, would he? Tyrrell wasn't depressed. He was always up."

"You can't always tell. With some people, it's obvious when they are depressed." Zachary couldn't help thinking of the image of himself that looked back from the mirror as December approached. Drawn, pale, with dark bags under his eyes. But that wasn't what everyone was like. Some people hid it well, clowning around and cheering for everybody else while they were dying inside. "I didn't know that he was having trouble either. I thought that he might have started drinking again, but I didn't realize… how he was feeling about it."

"He was drinking?"

"Yeah. Started again sometime before Thanksgiving."

"I thought he was cured of that. He said he didn't drink anymore."

"He'd been sober for a year, or about that. But that doesn't mean it's permanent. People slip up. Fall off the wagon."

"And some people never get on it in the first place," Jason inserted, a non sequitur. Was he referring to himself? Someone else in his life? It certainly sounded like an observation of something he'd had close experience with.

"That's true," Zachary acknowledged. "So…" he wasn't sure where to go from there. "I guess that means you didn't know that he was off the wagon or where he went."

"No, man. I didn't know anything about it. Just that he'd stopped responding to me online. I didn't know if that was because he was busy and hadn't signed in lately, or if I'd said something. Maybe one of his *other* siblings had talked him out of it, said that he shouldn't be communicating with those of us… born on the wrong side of the sheets."

The antiquated expression made Zachary chuckle. Was Jason a reader of historical fiction? Or watching Downton Abbey or one of those other TV serials?

"I didn't even know about you until now," Zachary said. "I was talking to Vince and Mindy. They're the ones who told me about Tyrrell submitting his DNA. I… had no idea that either of our parents had more kids after the family was split up. I guess I thought that since they'd failed at parenthood the first time, they wouldn't have any more."

"Yeah."

Zachary cleared his throat. "So, do you have contact information for any of the other siblings? I don't know whether you grew up as an only child or whether you have other brothers or sisters growing up with you?"

"Yeah, I had a couple of sisters. There are others… but I haven't met everyone yet."

"Could I get their phone numbers and email addresses? Do you know if Tyrrell kept in contact with either of them?"

"I think it was mainly me, but the others might have been messaging him now and then too. We mostly called or texted. Going through that DNA site was awkward. You had to always be logged in, and you don't get a notification when there are new messages. I went back there a couple of times, though… When he stopped, I thought he might have lost his phone."

"I wish that was all it was."

Zachary tried to think of what else to say to Jason. He'd said all that he had planned to. Jason didn't have anything else for him. But it seemed rude to just end the conversation there when he'd only just met the other man. He wanted to explore more.

"You don't know anything about where Tyrrell would go or who he drank with, do you?" Zachary asked. "I guess if you figured he was sober, you didn't know any of that."

Jason made a noise of hesitation. "He didn't talk about that. I just thought it was in the past."

"Yeah. I always thought that it was longer ago. Like when he was a teenager or something. I didn't realize that it was so recent, or that he hadn't had any longer sober periods…"

"I knew he was drinking a year or two ago. I remember that. But I thought he was done with it." Jason sighed. "I guess not. It isn't that easy."

"No."

"Listen… you want to get together? I'm not sure if the girls will want to meet, but I think it's cool… having these other siblings. I always wanted a different family, and here I had one all along."

"Sure, yeah. I wouldn't mind getting together. I'm kind of busy with this investigation right now, but… maybe getting together to talk would trigger something. One of us might remember something that didn't seem significant before."

"Worth a try, right?" Jason asked, perking up. "You wouldn't like to overlook a clue if one of us holds the key to finding him."

Zachary didn't say anything.

"Sorry," Jason said, "that makes it sound like it's all just a big joke, and I didn't mean it that way. I'm just… excited about the possibility of getting together. I didn't mean it to be disrespectful of Tyrrell."

"It's okay. Where are you? Do you want to set something up for later today?" Something twigged at the back of Zachary's brain. He was going to ignore it, but it nagged away at him, and he eventually tried to figure out what it was. "Oh… I have a commitment later on today. So maybe late today or tomorrow would be better. I'd better stick around here until I've met with… a friend."

He couldn't forget the appointment with Rhys. Not after he'd reached out to him to set it up. Zachary pulled up his calendar on the computer screen and saw that he hadn't added the meeting with Rhys. If he wanted an alarm to remind him to get off of his butt and get moving, he'd better add it in. He quickly added the appointment and then tuned back in to Jason.

"Sorry… I just had to write something down. Do you want to do it late today or tomorrow?"

"Maybe it better be tomorrow. I can see if the girls are free too, if they want to come. Where are you? Where do you live?"

"Roxboro."

"Oh, we're not far away. We could meet there. You got a favorite bar?"

"Not a bar, but there are a few good restaurants. Steak house, buffet, Thai?"

"Steak house sounds good. Haven't had a good steak in ages. Everyone says red meat is so bad, but there's nothing wrong with having it now and then, right? Moderation."

Zachary nodded. "Okay. We'll plan on Old Joe's. I might bring my girlfriend along, if she is free. You don't mind that?"

"Might make the girls more likely to come if they know there will be another woman there. They get so twisted up about *men*, you know. Like every man has designs on them. If you've got your girlfriend there, they wouldn't have anything to complain about."

"I'll see if she's free. You can just call or text me after you've talked to your sisters."

"Our sisters," Jason corrected.

Zachary felt a flush wash over him, followed by goosebumps. He wasn't sure whether he was happy to know that he had all of these other siblings, or if it bothered him. It was weird, that was for sure.

37

I t was hard to concentrate on other things, knowing that he would meet with even more siblings the next day. In the past year, he'd been reunited with all of his sibling group, including Vince and Mindy. And suddenly, he wasn't done at all. There were still more out there. Who knew how many more. It was exhilarating and anxiety-producing, both at the same time.

He spent some time looking over the other siblings in the database. How strange to have their similar DNA highlighted in colorful chunks, the computer telling him that all of those segments together meant that they were Tyrrell's siblings, and therefore Zachary's. Those were things that they had in common, whether there were any similarities in their looks or interests at all. Their DNA still told a story.

Some of them only had usernames that didn't give away their legal names, and they hadn't all responded to Tyrrell's requests for contact. So some of them, even though they had put their DNA into the system and even though the database had matched them up, had still decided they didn't want anything to do with their siblings. Why had they put their information into the system in the first place?

An alert sounded on his phone, and he looked down at it. He stared at the message for a moment before it made sense, and he closed his computer to prevent himself from being distracted by it. It was time to get ready to see Rhys.

His pondering then took a different direction. He had to forget about Tyrrell and his new siblings and the intricacies of DNA relationships and to focus on Rhys. He wasn't looking forward to the talk he needed to have with the boy.

Usually, he liked to visit Rhys. He liked feeling like he was helping and could understand Rhys when others didn't. Because they had both been through traumatic things in their childhoods and were both broken because of it. Communication with Rhys was difficult. He had stopped talking when his grandfather had been murdered. Rhys had been the only witness. He could say a word or two at a time, now and then, but most of the time, he struggled with even that. He used a mix of gestures, pictures and gifs on his phone, and a few typed words or letters here and there. Standardized communications systems, even those designed for those who didn't do most of their communication through speech, did not seem to work for him.

So it was rewarding when they were able to have a conversation. When Zachary was confident that he understood what Rhys was trying to express to him, and they could exchange something meaningful about their feelings and their individual struggles. Rhys knew about some of what Zachary had been through, about his depression and institutionalization from time to time. He knew about Zachary's feelings for Kenzie before Zachary could talk to anyone about them, even Kenzie herself.

And Zachary understood how devastated Rhys had been by the loss of his grandfather, one of the people who had been a parent to him when his mother had not been able to, struggling with her addiction and emotional issues. Now it was just him and his grandma, Vera. His mother was in prison and he only saw her occasionally.

The trouble with visiting Rhys was that Zachary couldn't tell whether he was home or not at a glance. Rhys didn't drive, so there was no car outside to give away if he were home. And Zachary preferred not to sit and visit Vera for an extended time while they waited for Rhys to show up. Vera was a wonderful grandma and was devoted to Rhys. Still, Zachary got the feeling sometimes that she didn't entirely approve of him. It was understandable, with what Rhys had been through and the complications Zachary presented. Vera was always polite to Zachary—offered him food, and called him when she felt like Rhys needed someone to talk to—but there was that little bit of hesitance that told him she had reservations about Zachary and about his playing too big of a role in Rhys's life.

Zachary parked the car and looked at the house. He took out his phone and typed a quick message to Rhys.

You home?

Dots indicated that Rhys was responding. Which probably meant that he was at home waiting for Zachary's visit. Zachary unbuckled his seat belt and prepared to get out.

A gif popped up on his screen. *Honey, I'm home!* the words across a cartoonized version of Lucille Ball.

Zachary got out of the car and made his way up to the door. Rhys opened it and stood there eating a burrito as he waited for Zachary. The tall, skinny Black boy's expression was neutral. Curious, maybe.

"You'd better have a plate!" Vera's voice floated out from the house.

Rhys grinned. He took another bite of the burrito. Before Zachary stepped into the house, Rhys shoved the entire second half of the burrito into his mouth before turning around to face his grandma.

Zachary tried not to laugh. His laughing could set off Rhys, and if Rhys started laughing with the burrito in his mouth, he could choke. That much food in his mouth was a serious hazard. So Zachary rolled his eyes up to the ceiling and refused to look at Rhys's face.

"Zachary, it's good to see you," Vera said pleasantly.

He looked at her, still studiously avoiding looking at Rhys. Was there more salt in her black, curly hair than the last time he had seen her? Zachary himself felt older. "Nice to see you again, Vera. How are you doing?"

"I'm lovely, thank you. Rhys, where is your plate?"

Rhys made a wide movement with his hands, shrugging questioningly. *What? I'm not eating.*

"Don't give me that! You're big enough to get out a plate when you're having a snack. You think I want crumbs or burrito sauce trailing across my carpet?"

Rhys shook his head and indicated the carpet, tidy and unstained.

Vera sighed. "Boys! I'll tell you, it's very different raising a boy than it was girls."

Zachary nodded politely. "Are you still eating, Rhys? Should we go into the kitchen?"

Rhys shook his head and motioned toward the bedroom instead. Zachary followed. "We'll just be in here."

Vera nodded, unconcerned.

In the bedroom, Zachary leaned up against the chest of drawers and tried to figure out how to approach the topic he was there to discuss. He'd been trying to script something out in his mind, but couldn't find anything that was comfortable. It didn't matter what he said, Rhys was not going to be happy with him and he wasn't sure how to express his concerns in a way that Rhys would listen to and respect.

Rhys sat down on his bed, stretching out his long legs and crossing them at the ankle. He made a motion toward Zachary, indicating he should start talking. He raised one eyebrow questioningly.

"How are you doing?" Zachary asked. "I haven't seen you since Christmas. Everything going okay?"

Rhys nodded, not smiling.

"School? Doing okay in your classes?"

He shrugged. Zachary knew Rhys struggled with his classes, especially those that required advanced language skills. He had accommodations so that he didn't have to give long paragraph answers or write essays. Still, Zachary imagined it would be difficult to convince an English teacher that he knew what he was talking about with his limitations. English Language Arts required more than just yes and no answers.

Rhys motioned back to Zachary with one hand. *You?* He motioned up and down the length of Zachary's body. *How are you?*

"Doing better," Zachary said with a shrug and a nod. "I always feel better once Christmas Day hits. They've been working on adjusting my meds to see if something else will help me to... help me with some of the other symptoms. I think they're working pretty good. So far."

He decided not to tell Rhys about Tyrrell being missing and Zachary's investigation. That would take the spotlight away from Rhys and the issues that Zachary hoped to discuss. Rhys wouldn't know anything about where Tyrrell was. They didn't know each other. Maybe they might have run into each other at the hospital one day if both of them had gone to see Zachary. But Zachary couldn't remember both of them visiting the same day.

"So, I was talking to Joss..."

Rhys's face lit up. He smiled, waiting for Zachary to give him an update on Luke. Luke's physical recovery from a gunshot wound was not an issue. He had a scar on his head where the bullet had grazed him, which Zachary was sure Luke was probably proud of. Getting Luke clean and staying clean had been a much bigger deal. And Luke getting over the loss of Madison.

But he had seemed to be calm and in good spirits when Zachary had seen him last.

"I just wanted to talk to you about Luke."

Rhys frowned slightly and nodded for Zachary to go on.

"He's good," Zachary said. "But... you know, he still has struggles. He was with that trafficking ring for a long time, and they messed him up pretty bad."

Another serious nod.

"I wanted to say... that you need to be careful of who you talk to and hang around with."

Rhys pointed to the side, as if Luke, the subject of their conversation was standing there. *Luke?*

"Yes... you need to be careful of Luke."

Rhys folded his arms over his chest and shook his head firmly.

Zachary shifted, leaning a little closer to Rhys, wishing there were another place in the room for him to sit. "I like Luke. He's easy to talk to. He's friendly and charming..."

Rhys nodded his agreement, his eyes shining.

"But with the stuff he's been through, he can also be a dangerous person to know."

Rhys made an *X* with his hands and pushed them forcefully forward and then away from himself. *No way.*

"You know that he brought Madison into the trafficking ring. He was the one who turned her out."

Rhys shook his head and made a motion sweeping everything behind him.

"That was before?" Zachary guessed, making sure he was interpreting Rhys right.

Rhys nodded and made the motion again. He folded his arms across his chest once more.

"Just because we got him away from those guys... that doesn't mean it is over. It's hard to break away from a lifestyle like that. A lot of people just go right back."

Rhys's chin thrust forward. He shook his head and spread out his hands, palms up. *Why would he?*

"Because it's easier to take drugs and do what people tell you to do than to think for yourself and work hard for the things that you want. It's easier to have a relationship with someone because you were told to, and you were told what to say and do to keep them on the hook. And to have drugs and alcohol to take away any pain and regret you feel for what you are doing. Luke wanted to get out… but he also wants to go back."

Rhys shook his head.

"I know it's hard to understand. It doesn't make much sense if you haven't been in that life. But it's easier to be taken care of and not to have to think for yourself. When he does what they tell him to, he gets rewarded." Zachary tried to put everything that Joss had told him about it into words that would make sense to Rhys. "He gets drugs and money and gifts. He gets more seniority in the organization. They tell him what a good job he's doing and give him more of whatever it is that he wants."

Rhys put up his hands, palms up again. *So what?*

"What they want him to do isn't… it's not good for you. You can't just be friends with him if he chooses to go back. He recruits for the traffickers. Gets kids like you to hook for them. Gets them addicted to make them easier to handle. He knows all the ways to entice someone like you. He's been doing it since he was younger than you are now."

Rhys made the *X* again, then motioned from Zachary to the door. *Get out.*

"I'm not trying to hurt you or to accuse Luke of something. I'm trying to explain… why it's dangerous to be too close to him. I don't want him pulling you into this ring. You don't want that. You need to listen."

Rhys reached over and grabbed a basketball from the floor and whipped it at Zachary.

38

Zachary jumped to the side and the basketball smashed a lamp. The huge crash brought Vera running from the living room as fast as the older woman could run.

"What happened? Is everyone okay?" She looked wildly around the room and saw the shattered lamp on the floor, other stuff that had been on the dresser previously scattered on the floor in an arc. She looked at Zachary, brows drawn down as if she thought he was the one who had swept everything off in a fit of temper.

Zachary gave a slight shake of his head.

Vera looked at her grandson, eyes wide. "Rhys? What happened?"

Rhys pointed at Zachary and then at the door. Zachary turned his body toward it. "I'll go," he agreed. "I'm sorry," he murmured as he walked past Vera, embarrassed about the lamp. But it was best if he didn't stop to help clean up. If Rhys wanted him out of there, it was best that he leave before there were any more destruction. Zachary had said what he had come to say.

"Rhys. What is going on here?" Vera demanded, her voice strident. "You did this? You need to control yourself. You can't treat a guest this way. And breaking my things!"

There was a growl from Rhys. No words, just an angry noise of protest. Zachary reached back and touched Vera.

"Walk me out," he suggested.

She looked like she would argue, staying behind to discipline her grandson. Then she changed her mind and followed him. "What is going on? I want to know what's happening!"

Zachary spoke in a low voice as they walked down the hallway and out into the living room. "Rhys's friend Luke is having some trouble," he explained briefly. Rhys was not "out" to his grandmother, so he wouldn't say anything that might hint at Rhys's romantic interest in Luke, but she knew they were friends. "You know that before… he was involved in some criminal activities."

Vera couldn't help but remember the state that Zachary had returned Rhys to her in after the incident where Luke had been shot, which had triggered flashbacks for Rhys of his grandfather's murder. It had been a very difficult time, requiring intensive therapy.

She looked alarmed at Zachary's words. "I thought all of that was over. Luke has been very kind to Rhys. He hasn't been involved with those criminals again, has he?"

"Not yet. But he's having difficulty staying on… a straight path. It isn't easy to make big life changes and stick with them. And if he was to involve Rhys in any of that…"

"I won't let him. I'll ground him from having anything to do with Luke."

Zachary frowned, shaking his head. "I don't think that's a good idea. You see how he reacted to me telling him not to hang around with Luke." Zachary made a motion back toward the bedroom. "If you ground him or punish him for communicating with Luke, Rhys will run straight to him. And if Luke has gotten back in contact with these guys, it would be a very bad thing."

"Then what can I do? I can't just let him be involved with someone who is dangerous to him."

"Rhys already feels strongly about it." Zachary tilted his head back toward the bedroom. "He's too old for you to control him physically, to keep him in this house."

Zachary knew that Rhys was already skipping school and using his bus pass to get around town without Vera's knowledge. Behavior Zachary had discouraged. But he couldn't physically prevent Rhys from making bad decisions either.

"Talk about what a nice boy Luke is. How charming. How much you like him. Invite him to come over if he is in town."

Vera's mouth hung open. "Why would I do that?"

"Because you don't want him to be the forbidden fruit. Make Rhys think about whether what you are saying is true. About whether he wants Luke to be around you. To be here in Rhys's safe place. I've done my best to explain why he shouldn't be spending time with Luke, so it's already in his head. Let him think about that."

"I can't let Luke come here. To know where we live and maybe tell those people where we are."

Zachary bit his lip. There was no point in explaining to Vera that Rhys had already been in contact with Luke over the past several months. Luke undoubtedly knew where Rhys lived and could pass that information on anytime he wanted to. The trafficking ring would not likely want to go in cold. They knew that Rhys and Luke were friends, and they would use Luke to get him to leave home voluntarily.

"Joss shouldn't even be bringing Luke into town. She did at Christmas, but I don't think she'll do it again. She doesn't want him to have contact with those old acquaintances either. So I don't think there is really any danger of Luke coming here if you invite him. But inviting him might be just what Rhys needs to see that he doesn't actually want Luke in his space."

Of course, Jocelyn didn't really need to drive Luke. The young man was perfectly capable of boosting a car and making the trip on his own or calling someone in the cartel to pick him up. They couldn't do anything about that risk. All Zachary could hope to do was to help Rhys see that Luke did not have his best interests at heart and that spending time with him could be a dangerous prospect. Putting Vera and Luke on the same side might help Rhys to realize that he didn't want his grandma near his Romeo, someone who could do Vera harm or use her as leverage.

"I don't know if I can do that." Vera touched Zachary's arm, looking for reassurance. "But… I'll do my best."

"Luke is a lost soul. He's been lost since his own grandma died, leaving him to people like that. Reach out to that part of him. Think about what it would be like for Rhys if you weren't there and he had to survive on his own. Luke is dangerous, but he's also a lost boy."

Vera nodded slowly, her eyes showing compassion. "I didn't know that about him."

"He didn't have the stability that Rhys has had staying with you. He was passed around a lot, subjected to abuse. His grandma was the only one who really cared about him, and when she was gone, he was alone."

"Okay." She swallowed and nodded. "I'll do what you say."

Zachary nodded and left.

He hoped that he had said and done the right things and not made things worse. He hoped that they would be able to keep Rhys safe from the predators.

39

For a few minutes, Zachary just sat in the car outside Rhys's house, resting his forehead on the steering wheel. His anxiety over having to talk to Rhys about Luke and the adrenaline rush from Rhys throwing the ball at him and smashing the lamp left him feeling drained and shaky. While being hit by the thrown basketball would not have seriously injured him, even if it had hit him in the face, Zachary's body and primitive brain had still reacted to Rhys throwing something at him in anger. He had still perceived it as an attack. And having been attacked, abused, and beaten in the past, his reaction was probably overblown.

Knowing that didn't stop it. He still needed to give himself the time to calm down and relax. He wasn't in any danger. He didn't need to escape.

Eventually, he turned on the radio and let the music flow over him for a while. He hoped that Vera and Rhys were not watching him out the window, but there was nothing he could do if they were. He wasn't prepared to drive. After listening to the music for a while, he tapped his phone and called Kenzie.

"Medical Examiner's Office."

"It's Zachary."

"Oh, hi, Zach. How are you doing?"

"Good. Just thought I'd see how your day is going."

"Well, none of the patients have registered any complaints," she joked. "But it's pretty dead down here today."

Zachary smiled, enjoying her banter. "If only they weren't all so cold," he offered. He could have done better, but he'd worn out all of his best dead body humor already. He needed some new material. "You'll be able to make it home for supper tonight?" he asked.

"Date night tonight. I'll be on time. How about you? How is your day shaping up?"

"Good. I... made contact with one of the siblings that Tyrrell was DNA matched with. Jason."

"Jason. And what was he like? You managed to reach him? Or left a message."

Zachary nodded. He started to feel excited about it again, the nervous anticipation of meeting another sibling or siblings that he had never even known existed flooding in to replace the anxiety and panic that he'd felt from the visit with Rhys.

"Yeah. He was interested in meeting me. Tyrrell mentioned me, I guess, even if he didn't tell me about all of *them*. We're going to set something up for tomorrow night at Old Joe's. Maybe him and his two sisters, and you. If that's okay."

"That's not going to be too much at once? Maybe you should just start with Jason, and then meet the others another day, so it isn't as overwhelming."

"No. They should come together. Give each other moral support. It will be okay."

"Are you sure you want me along?"

"Yes. I already asked him if it would be okay, and he thought it would be more comfortable for the sisters if you were with me."

"Okay." Kenzie's voice was warm. "That will be a real treat. You're turning out to have quite a big family, for someone who once told me that he was an only child."

Zachary flushed at the memory. It was easier to tell people he didn't have any brothers or sisters than to explain the whole story to them, telling them about the fire and about being split up and put into foster care. Easier if they thought it was just the usual. An only child. A man who happened to not have any family.

"Seems to me you told me you were an only child too," Zachary reminded her.

It was, after all, easier for her not to have to explain about Amanda, who had died. Less painful.

"I'm sure that's not the case," Kenzie said, chuckling. "But your fib was obviously bigger than mine. Five times bigger. And now with these three more…"

"It's not a lie if I didn't know about them."

She laughed. "Well, I should be getting back to work. I'll see you in a couple of hours."

"You bet. See you then."

Date night. Even though he had put it into his calendar, it had been chased out of his mind by the other events of the day. He should do more than just show up for supper and help decide what they were going to do for the evening. He should do something to actually show her what she meant to him.

Kenzie got home, yawning as she came in through the door from the garage and starting to remove her coat and winter things by the hooks and mat that constituted her mudroom. She stopped and looked into the kitchen.

"What's going on in here?"

She finished hanging up her coat and kicked off her boots and walked the rest of the way into the room. Her eyes went from the flowers in a vase on the table to the flickering tealights along the counter.

"Well, look at this. Is it Valentine's Day already? Did I forget a special anniversary?"

"No," Zachary couldn't dial down the big grin that was stretching his face, pleased with her reaction. "I just thought I should show you… I thought that we should have a nice time together. Really put some effort into it."

He pulled out her kitchen chair and Kenzie seated herself. Zachary poured ginger ale into each of the champagne flutes.

"The last couple of months haven't exactly been a walk in the park for you, but you've been so patient and supportive through it all. I want you to know how much I appreciate you," he told her.

"Well, you're definitely off to a good start. This is lovely." She raised her glass. "To us!"

Zachary raised his glass as well. They each sipped their drinks. Zachary put his down. "This is as far as I got," he said, his face warming. "I didn't make any dinner or order anything. I thought… we could discuss what we wanted and order in. Just relax while we wait for it. Unless you want to go out for something."

"No, this is awesome. What do you want tonight? Any preferences?"

Zachary considered. He always told Kenzie no, to just get whatever she felt like. Which meant that he made her responsible for dinner, and maybe she didn't like always having to be the one to decide. With the new medications Zachary was on, he felt different. He wasn't as nauseated in the morning and the new meds didn't seem to suppress his appetite as much. He wasn't quite hungry, but he was thinking of food and what would be nice.

"I don't know if pizza goes with flowers and candlelight…"

Kenzie looked surprised. "Sure, why not? We don't have to go with fancy French cuisine or anything. I like pizza."

"Pepperoni?"

"How about half vegetarian and half pepperoni?"

Zachary nodded his agreement. "Works for me. I thought you liked pepperoni."

"I do. But I want a choice. Something a bit fresher too."

"Okay." Zachary pulled out his phone and started tapping their order into the delivery app. "Sorry, I know it's no phones at the table on date night…"

"Doesn't count if you're ordering food."

"Good."

Kenzie watched him for a minute. "I'm going to change while we wait. I won't be long. If we're going to relax, I'm going to go all out." She stood up. She moved to the counter, the opposite direction from the bedrooms, and looked down into one of the jars of flickering tealights.

"Artificial," Zachary acknowledged. "I'm not ready for open flames."

"Fine with me. They look very romantic. And they won't burn out if we take a little interlude partway through the evening and adjourn to the bedroom." She waggled her eyebrows.

Zachary grinned. He watched her sashay out of the kitchen and waited for her to reach the bedroom.

"Oh, Zachary!" she exclaimed.

He chuckled and followed her to the bedroom, where he had strung clusters of white twinkle lights and strewn more jars of tealights.

40

They cuddled on the bed, on top of the covers in the warm room. Zachary had pulled on pajama bottoms and a t-shirt which he never actually slept in, so that he would be prepared when the pizza delivery man rang the bell. Kenzie hadn't dressed, but had pulled a robe around herself and cuddled against his side, her head on his arm. She was close to sleep, her breathing long and deep.

Zachary enjoyed the warmth of her body and the room and the comfort of skin against skin contact. He had missed her while he had been in the hospital. He had spent many long, lonely nights wishing he was at home again but knowing he needed to be there for his own protection. Of course, he could have checked himself out, just as he had when he'd gone down to the NICU to check on Bridget's twins.

But the reason he had checked himself in was because of his suicidal thoughts. He wasn't going to try to tough it out at home or to put Kenzie through the stress of knowing he was a danger to himself and she was the only one there to put herself between him and a suicide attempt. He needed to be where the medical staff could help him twenty-four hours a day. Where there was someone to call on when it got to be too much. Kenzie couldn't be there all the time and she wasn't a psychologist. There was nothing she could do but hope he didn't try anything.

He stroked her dark, curly hair, letting his eyes close, waiting for the pizza to arrive.

There was a buzzing from his phone. Zachary turned reluctantly to get it. The pizza guy saying he couldn't find the house or had been delayed? Jason calling to set up a time to meet the next day? He didn't want it to be anyone else. Unless, of course, it was Tyrrell.

At the thought, Zachary's heart started to beat more rapidly. He knew that it wasn't going to be Tyrrell, but with the thought lodged in his brain, he couldn't get it out. He reached for his phone and pulled it to him, turning it to look at the ID on the face of the phone.

Medical Examiner's Office

Zachary's throat felt suddenly strangled. His thoughts jumped to the idea that he had actually picked up Kenzie's phone instead of his own. He knew it wasn't, but his brain immediately started floundering around for an explanation other than the one that immediately came to mind.

He sat up and put the phone to his ear. "Hello?"

Kenzie shifted, groaning. "Who is it?"

"Is this Mr. Zachary Goldman?" asked the voice on the phone.

"Yes."

"I have your name on this file as a point of contact when remains were positively identified."

Zachary gripped the phone more tightly. His eyes burned. A lump swelled in his throat and he couldn't swallow.

"What remains?" he asked, the words coming out in barely a whisper.

Kenzie propped herself up on her elbow, turned toward him, looking alarmed. She put her hand on his arm.

"We have positively identified the remains of Mr. Jose Flores."

It took a long time for Zachary to process the words. *Jose.*

Jose, not Tyrrell.

Jose.

It had been nearly a year since Jose's disappearance and the arrest of his killer. Zachary had assumed that identifying the various remains that were discovered on his land and nearby would be the work of a few days or weeks, not something that was just happening months later.

"It's Jose," he repeated, wanting the caller to confirm this again, and to communicate it to Kenzie. "Not Tyrrell. Jose."

There was a pause before the male voice on the other end came to him again. "Yes, Jose. I don't have a Tyrrell here."

"No," Zachary agreed. He let out his breath. "No, Tyrrell hasn't been found."

"Okay, then," the man said, still sounding confused. "So... these remains have been positively identified. Will you be claiming them?"

"Uh... maybe. I'll get back to you. Can I get your name and number?"

The man gave his information, grumbled for a moment, asking Zachary to get back to him as soon as possible because they couldn't keep holding remains for long, then hung up. Zachary flopped back, his back landing on the pillows but his head thwacking into the wall. He winced, but he didn't even care. All that mattered was that Tyrrell was not dead. They still didn't know what had happened to him. But he wasn't on some medical examiner's table.

"Jose?" Kenzie asked. "Pat's friend?"

"Yeah." Zachary rubbed his eyes, thinking about it. He would have to call Pat and Lorne to give them the information. He had made sure that he was the one on the contact sheet so that he could break it to them gently. Pat especially. He had been the one who had been closest to Jose. He had been the one Zachary had taken the case for. He had hoped to help alleviate Pat's concern. He had been hoping for a different resolution. That Jose had returned to his wife in El Salvador. Even that he had been apprehended by ICE and detained, but safe.

But what he had found was that Jose had been one of the victims of a serial killer who had been killing gay immigrant men for a very long time. They had known for some time that Jose was one of his victims, but with the identification of his remains among those that the police had recovered from on and around Archuro's property, now they had the proof.

"Should I even tell him?" Zachary pondered. "It's just going to make it worse. He's going to have to go through all that grief again, and you know how depressed he got. Can I just... not say anything?"

He knew the answer, but he needed someone else to tell him. He didn't have the fortitude to make himself do it without her help.

"No. We have to tell them. And Pat will be okay. Yes, he will be upset, but he has already grieved Jose. He already knew that he was one of the victims. This will just mean... that Jose can be laid to rest. They'll know what happened to him and where his remains are." Kenzie pushed her hair back from her face with both hands. "Will they bury him here? Or send him back to El Salvador?"

"To his wife, I guess. We need to make sure that he's... home."

"And *is* that with his wife? He left her behind while he came here. Had relationships with other people. Will she still want him back?"

"She doesn't know all of that. Only that he came here to work and then bring her and the kids over when he could save enough money."

Zachary started to think of the logistics of getting the body back to her. How was that done? And what kind of shape would it be in after so many months, even if it had been refrigerated for that long? He had no idea how to deal with such a thing. He looked at Kenzie. "How do we do that? How do we send it back?"

She squeezed his arm. "The easiest way is cremation here and shipping the cremains home. Much easier and cheaper. And his wife won't have to deal with... well, you know."

"Okay. So I'll tell them to do that. Or is that just assumed anyway?"

"You can tell them that. But let's do this one step at a time. You're getting a bit ahead of yourself."

Zachary grimaced. "That's because I don't want to do it."

"I know. But you need to. Don't spend your time fussing and being anxious about it. Just do it without thinking about it any more."

Zachary let out his breath, knowing that she was right. If he put it off, it would bother him all evening. He wouldn't be able to enjoy his time with Kenzie or to sleep when the time came. He would just get more anxious and upset about it until he couldn't handle it anymore.

He looked over at Kenzie. "I'm going to video call. You might want to get some clothes on."

"I think Pat and Lorne can handle seeing me in my robe."

He eyed her, wondering if it were really appropriate. It wasn't like they would be able to see anything, but... "And if the delivery guy comes while I'm on with them—which he will—do you want to be answering the door in your robe?"

Kenzie gave a teasing smile. "Are you saying you *don't* want me flashing the pizza delivery man?"

Zachary snorted. "At least then you wouldn't have to tip him..."

Kenzie laughed. She moved away from him, sliding her feet off of the bed to go get her pajamas on. Zachary knew he didn't need to be worried about her answering the door in some lacy, barely-there thing. Kenzie liked to be comfortable. In the winter, she liked wearing soft, warm flannels. Nothing that would give the pizza guy any thrills.

He took a couple more deep breaths and brought the phone up to face level and tapped the icon to video call Mr. Peterson. Lorne. The foster father who had been there for him ever since he was ten, even when he hadn't actually been Zachary's foster father.

Lorne answered after a few rings, staring intently at the computer for a minute to make sure it connected. He smiled, his round face cheerful as always. The white fringe of hair around his head was neatly trimmed and he wore a comfortable t-shirt. "Zachary! Good to see and hear from you! I was glad to hear that you were out of the hospital. How are you feeling?"

"Good. I'm glad to be out of there, and I think these new medications work really well for me. A few weeks before it reaches full efficacy, but it's working well now."

"Excellent. Good to hear it. They're always coming out with new medicines that work better…"

Maybe someday they would find a drug that could keep Zachary from getting depressed before Christmas. Maybe eventually… he could be almost normal. Except that all the pills would rattle when he walked.

"Is Pat there?" Zachary asked. "I'd like to talk to you both together."

Lorne called over his shoulder for Pat to join him. Kenzie sat on the bed and scooted over to Zachary, putting her head against his so that she could see the screen as well.

"Hi, Lorne."

"Hi, Kenzie." Lorne lifted his brows and gave a teasing smile. "You two are looking very comfortable. Do you have news for us?"

Zachary shook his head soberly, not wanting Lorne to get his hopes up that they were engaged or had some other special announcement to make. Lorne's smile disappeared, understanding that it was not the kind of news he was hoping for. He looked anxiously over his shoulder as Pat arrived.

Pat bent down to see the computer screen and fit into the camera frame. He was younger than Mr. Peterson, still broad and muscled across the chest, someone who took care of his health and his body. Getting more distinguished looking with some gray in his dark hair around his temples. Zachary had taken to calling Pat his stepfather. It was the closest he could get to describing the relationship they'd had since Pat and Mr. Peterson had become a couple.

"Zachary, Kenzie, so nice to see you. How is everything?"

Zachary clenched his teeth and steeled himself for what he had to say. "Can you sit down with us for a minute, Pat?"

Pat looked at Lorne uncertainly, then pulled a chair over from the other side of the office. It was an awkward space to fit both chairs into, but Zachary wanted him sitting for the news. He didn't want to take the chance that Pat would take the news badly and faint or collapse.

"What is it?" Pat asked. "What's going on?"

"I just got a call from the Medical Examiner's Office... He called about Jose's remains."

Zachary's eyes prickled as he saw the color drain from Pat's face. Lorne pulled him closer, a comforting arm around Pat's shoulders, pressing their cheeks together.

"It's... Jose? They found him and... identified him?"

"Yeah. I don't have any details. If his was one of the bodies they collected from Archuro's property or somewhere else. All I know is, he's been identified now. You don't need to wonder anymore."

Pat put his hands over his face. Zachary expected him to start sobbing, but he didn't. He just held them there, breathing, processing what Zachary had told him.

"Thank you for calling, Zachary," Lorne said softly, rubbing Pat's back. "I'm glad that you were the one to deliver the news."

Zachary nodded, unable to think of what else to say. He should say something comforting to Pat. Something about how Jose was at rest now. He was in a better place. Archuro would go away for the rest of his life for the terrible, depraved things he had done and for killing so many men.

But how could any of that be a comfort to Pat? Pat knew that his friend had died under the most terrible circumstances. They had known for months, and now they had confirmation that it was true. That wouldn't make him feel better.

Pat sniffled a few times and pulled his hands from his face. His expression was still one of grief, but he didn't look as devastated as Zachary had been worried he would. He actually did look as if he was a little relieved by the news. A little more at peace.

"Yes, thank you, Zachary. It is a terrible thing... but it's better to hear it from a friend."

The doorbell rang, and Kenzie gave the two a little wave and went to get the pizza.

"I'm so sorry," was all Zachary could think of to say.

"I know." Pat nodded. He swallowed. "So I guess..."

"Kenzie says what they usually do is cremate the remains, and then ship the ashes. It's easier that way. And... his wife won't ever have to see what he did to Jose."

Pat nodded and scratched the back of his neck. "If it's ashes... then maybe it would be okay to spread a few here, too. Just a little. So that... part of him stays in America."

41

It was difficult to get back into the "date" mindset after the calls with the Medical Examiner's Office and with Pat and Lorne. The pizza was hot, and the tealights still twinkled throughout the house. Zachary still felt the warmth and satisfaction of intimate time spent with Kenzie. But the happy mood was gone.

He did his best to focus on the smell of the pizza and how good it would taste, and he gazed at Kenzie in her charming flannel pajamas, but nothing that either of them did could negate the tinge of sadness that remained with them for the rest of the evening. Kenzie seemed to feel it too. Even though she smiled and joked, her eyes were sad, and she was obviously also unable to put Jose's death out of her mind.

The investigation of Jose's death and all that went along with it had been dark days for both of them. It had taken a lot of months to get past the damage Archuro had caused to their relationship with his assault of Zachary. The remnants of that encounter were something Zachary knew he might never be able to shake. It would always cling to him and be a barrier to intimate relationships.

But they did their best to pretend and buoy each other up throughout the evening, and went to bed late, which should have made it easier for Zachary to fall asleep.

Immediately after the assault, Zachary had found himself unable to do much but sleep. He had said that it was just because of his body's need for extra rest in order to heal, but a great deal of it had to do with his brain being unable to process all that had happened, not only with Archuro, but at various times in Zachary's past, incidents that he had previously been able to shove into a hidden room in his brain to forget about them. But Archuro had opened that door and let them all back out again, and it was just too much to deal with.

As he lay in the dark, cuddled up close to Kenzie, the feelings flooded back. Teddy's touch, his threats, and the torture. Other voices from the past; people who had been bigger and stronger than he, in positions of authority, taking advantage of a vulnerable child or teen who had no way to defend himself.

Dr. Boyle had given him relaxation exercises and ways to anchor himself in the present, but she had said that the best thing for Zachary to do was to process those memories. To discuss them in therapy, write them down, or find another way to acknowledge them and get them out. Outside of his head, they would die in the light of day.

But it wasn't day, and Zachary's thoughts were blacker than the night. He tossed and turned, trying to find a more comfortable position. But he knew that whatever position he was in, he still wasn't going to sleep. He was still going to be haunted by those memories all night long.

Kenzie's hand landed on the back of his shoulder. Zachary flinched away, surprised by her touch when so many bad things were writhing in his brain. She felt his tension and rubbed his shoulder and back gently.

"Are you awake?" she whispered.

Zachary took a deep breath in and out. "Yes."

He tried to relax his muscles, but his skin was crawling. The nightmares were too close to the surface.

"Are you okay?" Kenzie shifted her position, sliding her body up against his. She kissed his cheek. "Hey."

"I can't... turn it off."

She stroked his hair and nuzzled him. "You can't turn off your brain?"

"Yeah."

"Did you take your sleep aid tonight? It's probably not a good night to skip it."

"Yes. I took it."

"What about anti-anxiety?"

"I'm not having a panic attack." Zachary was aware that his tone was terse. He didn't need Kenzie telling him what to take and when to take it. He was in charge of his own body and his own medication regimen.

"But you are anxious, aren't you? That's why you're so restless and having trouble controlling your thoughts?"

Zachary didn't say anything. Kenzie rubbed his back again. "Sorry. Just trying to help. I don't mean to interfere."

"It's okay."

Her touch was soothing, now that he was expecting it and was talking to her, rather than being locked into those memories, alone in the darkness.

"Do you want to get up and talk? Is there anything I can do that would help?"

"No." He snuggled in to her, appreciating the warmth of her body, even through the flannel pajamas. "Just... being here."

"I'm not going anywhere," she assured him.

But in a few more minutes, she was asleep again.

When Kenzie got up in the morning and wandered through the living room area to get herself some coffee, she didn't make any comment about Zachary being up already or ask him how much sleep he had gotten. And that was good. She already knew that he'd been having trouble the night before, but they didn't need to talk it through. It didn't need to be the constant focus of their morning conversation.

"We're on for tonight?" Kenzie asked after pouring herself a mug of coffee from the waiting carafe. "Old Joe's, right?"

Zachary nodded. "Yeah. I'm not sure of the exact time yet. Probably seven or so. Jason and the others will need time to get here. And I assume they work. But I have no idea if they work shifts or banker's hours."

"Good. That gives me time to get back here after work and to change and relax for a few minutes."

"Probably. I don't know exactly what time yet."

"Got it. Are you looking forward to meeting them?"

Zachary thought about it. "I guess. Of course. They're family, so of course I want to meet them. It's sort of a strange situation, but I always like watching those reunion shows on TV, where they search out adoptees or whatever and reunite them with their siblings or birth parents. I know it won't necessarily be like that, but..."

She was studying him over the brim of her cup, watching his face.

"But you've always wanted to be reunited with your siblings. So even if they're not the siblings you knew about, you're still eager."

Zachary nodded. "Yeah. Exactly. But… I'm also nervous. I know I don't always present well." He rubbed the whiskers on his chin. He needed to shave before they met. Shower, shave, fresh clothes, all the things that normal people did when trying to make a good impression. "What if we don't like each other? Or they resent me for… something?"

"How did Jason sound on the phone?"

"Good. Friendly. He wanted to get together."

"And did he tell you anything about his sisters? Or about how they would feel about getting together?"

"He didn't say much about them. But he's the one who suggested that they would like to meet me too." Zachary tried to replay everything that had been said. "He thought it would be a good idea for you to come around, so that they didn't feel anxious about meeting a man."

Kenzie nodded. "It can be a bit intense, as a woman, meeting a man face to face without some… backup. They have each other, so that's good, and they have their brother to balance things out. But having a girlfriend with you makes you… safer. Like I'm vouching for you and you won't be trying anything."

"They're my sisters. I wouldn't come on to them." Zachary gave a shudder at the suggestion. That was just creepy.

"You didn't grow up with them. They haven't a clue what you're like or what you might do. And there is sometimes a romantic attraction between genetic siblings who didn't grow up together. Sometimes, you see it in the news, siblings marrying each other before they find out they are related. It's been studied."

"I am not going to be romantically attracted to them."

"No." Kenzie smiled as she brought her coffee mug up to her mouth for another sip. "You're not."

He liked the way that she said it. A little possessive and commanding. There was no way she would let him go to any other woman. He stared at his computer screen, trying to focus on something else to head off a blush. But he was sure she could see his burning cheeks and earlobes getting red.

42

Zachary wasn't sure how he had gotten all the way through the day with all the worry and anticipation. He plugged away at his email and did a few low-level jobs for his actual business. Things he could get done in a few minutes or an hour and get the invoice out to the client. That made it feel like he was accomplishing something, even if they were just little things. A good way to ease back into his job.

He looked over his notes on Tyrrell in between jobs. He scanned his notepad pages and uploaded them to the cloud so that he would have them wherever he was and couldn't lose them if something happened to his physical notepad or computer. He transcribed a few notes or avenues to check. Although Fontaine had said they hadn't found any recent parking tickets for Tyrrell, he didn't know how far Fontaine had looked. Just in town? In the surrounding areas? What if his car had been left or ticketed somewhere outside Fontaine's jurisdiction? They had checked hospitals and morgues all across the state. Might as well look for his car too. Cars could be driven into the lake if the ice cover were not too thick, or left in long-term airport parking but, other than that, there weren't a lot of ways to get rid of one without documentation. Even car wreckers expected proof of ownership, and why would Tyrrell wreck his own car? More than likely, Tyrell's car was where he was, or close to him.

He called a few of the detox programs Tyrrell might have been able to get into without significant up-front costs, and asked for Tyrrell as if he knew Tyrrell was there.

"Tyrrell Goldman, please."

"Excuse me?"

"Tell him it's his brother, Zachary. I need to talk to him urgently."

That was usually enough to earn him a pause while they checked their log-in records to see if there was, in fact, a Tyrrell Goldman registered in the program.

"I'm sorry, there's no one by that name here. Are you sure you called the right facility?"

There were no confidentiality laws preventing a facility from saying someone wasn't a patient. Only if they were. If Zachary ran into one who told him that they couldn't disclose whether Tyrrell was there or not, then Zachary would know that he'd hit gold. Then he could either leave a message and hope that they passed it on and Tyrrell called him back, or go into phase two and show up at the facility. He was even more convincing face to face. If Tyrrell were in a program, Zachary would eventually find him. But he had a feeling that wasn't the case. Tyrrell had already been missing since before Christmas, and most of the programs Tyrrell was aware of were no more than thirty days. A six-week or three-month program was a rarity, especially for a state-funded facility. And Zachary doubted that Tyrrell had saved up the money to get himself into a more expensive program. Not with a casual construction job and paying child support. Zachary had seen where he lived. It wasn't high-end.

When Kenzie made it home, he finally pulled back from work and phone calls looking for Tyrrell. They both got showered and changed, and Zachary shaved. He studied himself in the mirror. Not that much better without the stubble, unfortunately. The partial beard helped to disguise how thin and gaunt his face was. Without it, he looked like he was starving.

Maybe they'd give him a discount at Old Joe's since it would look like it was the first time he'd eaten in a month.

"You're fine," Kenzie commented as she walked by the bathroom door and saw him peering at himself in the mirror. "Nobody cares what you look like. They want to get to know who you are."

"I know." Zachary busied himself with cleaning up the counter and his razor. "I just... wish I looked more like Tyrrell."

Kenzie grimaced and reached through the doorway to put a hand on his arm for a moment. "Maybe it's better if you don't. This way... they get to know you as your own person, instead of thinking that you are so similar to Tyrrell."

"Yeah."

He wouldn't mind being mistaken for Tyrrell's twin, though. He would like to look better, to be less damaged and more outgoing and friendly. He would like to be more comfortable in his own skin.

But that was an illusion. Tyrrell clearly hadn't been comfortable in his own skin. Things had been far different from what they appeared to be.

They got ready and, having a few minutes to kill, had another drink of the ginger ale in the fridge, now going flat. Kenzie glanced in the sink and saw the dishes there.

"Hey, you actually had lunch!"

"Yeah." Zachary chuckled. "I actually remembered to eat."

"Good for you. I'm sure that helps to fuel you through your afternoon. Keep up the energy levels."

"Or makes me want to sleep."

Kenzie shrugged. "I doubt it was anything heavy enough to make you want to sleep. Leftover pizza?"

"Yeah. A full slice of the pepperoni *and* a half slice of your vegetarian."

Kenzie raised her brows. "Does that mean you didn't pick the toppings off of the vegetarian?"

Zachary shifted his feet and took another sip of the ginger ale. "Not *all* of them."

He was good about eating things he didn't like. In foster care, he had quickly learned to chew and swallow whatever families put in front of him, no matter how weird or unpleasant it might be. He might not be able to avoid conflicts with foster parents because of his ADHD and other issues, but he could prevent disputes over food. But at home, when he had the choice, he could pick the toppings off of the vegetarian pizza if Kenzie were not there to see it. That was one of the few positives of eating alone.

Kenzie looked at her phone. "Okay. We shouldn't get there too early if we leave now."

Zachary felt like a dog let off the leash at the dog park. He was raring to go, but was being as cool about it as he could. Now he wanted to run, to speed all the way over to the grill and meet these new family members.

"Did you want to take your car?" he asked Kenzie.

"Well…" She looked him up and down. "I wouldn't mind. If you're offering."

"Sure. You can drive your baby."

192

Kenzie led the way into the heated garage where her car was waiting. No need to wait for it to heat up once they got outside. No frost to scrape. No sliding into freezing-cold seats. Zachary settled into the passenger seat and closed his eyes, trying to keep himself calm.

At Old Joe's, Zachary looked around at the other patrons curiously, looking for faces that were familiar. He hadn't ever seen Jason or his sisters before, but there was still the strong chance that they would look like one of Zachary's other siblings.

There was a group of three standing near the door, conversing. All tow-headed, younger than Zachary, a man and two women. They looked like they were from the same family. Not particularly like Zachary or Tyrrell, but maybe close to Heather, some of her facial features. Maybe something around the eyes.

"Jason?" Zachary asked.

They turned and looked at him.

"Zachary Goldman," Zachary offered, putting out his hand. "Is it Jason? Or have I just made a fool of myself in front of strangers?"

"Well, we are strangers," the man said, putting his hand out to take Zachary's. "But as luck would have it, yes, I'm Jason. And this is Margot and Celia."

Zachary shook hands firmly with Jason, then offered his hand toward Margot and Celia as well. "Hi. And this is my girlfriend, Kenzie Kirsch."

The girls seemed more warmly disposed toward Kenzie, smiling at her and nodding and greeting her. They decided not to leave Zachary hanging, and shook hands briefly.

"This is so weird," Margot observed.

Zachary tried not to stare at them. He wanted to drink in their features, to memorize every bit of them. Still, he knew it was inappropriate to keep looking at them. Like Kenzie had suggested, they might perceive him as a stalker or threat, when he was just interested in their faces.

"We have a reservation," he told the hostess who stepped up to greet them. "Goldman. Party of five."

She looked at her seating chart and nodded. "This way," she agreed, grabbing enough menus for them all and leading them over to a table. Zachary wished for the intimacy of a booth, where he wouldn't feel so exposed. But the booths were not wide enough to fit more than four of them into the bench seats. He shuffled around with the others until he could sit in the chair that gave him the best view of the room, then pulled out the one nearest at hand for Kenzie.

"This is nice," Celia said, looking around. "I haven't been here before."

"They really do have great food," Kenzie offered. "It's been a couple of months since we were here last, but we like to come here now and then for a treat."

How long had it been since Zachary had taken Kenzie there to treat her? He wasn't sure when the last time had been. Before the psych ward, of course. Before their vacation to the Lodge. Before the virus protocol. A long time ago. So much had happened. It was easy to lose track of the relationship, even though they went to couple's therapy and had specific things to work on. Sometimes it was nice to just go out to dinner together. He should get out more often and try to show Kenzie a good time.

"Zachary?"

It was Jason who was trying to get his attention, but Zachary looked at Kenzie instead. "Sorry, what? I was… remembering something."

She raised her eyebrow at him, telegraphing concern, then nodded. "Jason was just wondering whether we live here in town."

"Oh, yeah," Zachary looked back at Jason. "We are. It's good; everything is nice and convenient."

"It's a nice little town," Jason observed.

Zachary wasn't sure whether he was supposed to inquire after where Jason and the girls lived. He decided to leave it alone. If they wanted to tell him more about where they lived, that was fine. But if the women were leery about being stalked or pursued, maybe it was best that he just leave it alone.

Assuming they didn't know that he was a private investigator and already had most of their contact information.

"How long have you two known each other?" Margot asked, pointing to Zachary and Kenzie in turn.

"It's been about two years now," Kenzie said, looking at Zachary for confirmation.

"Yeah, just a little over that."

"How did you meet?"

Zachary looked over at Kenzie, waiting for her to tell the story.

"Well, I work for the Medical Examiner's Office," Kenzie said slowly. "And Zachary came down to fill out a form for some records. We just… something clicked, and we started seeing each other."

"And you've been together since?"

"Off and on," Kenzie said carefully. "It's not like we moved in with each other that day, but we started going out together, exploring, getting to know each other. Not like some TV romance where the couple falls in love the instant they lay eyes on each other. Real life rarely looks like the movies."

"You're telling me," Celia said with a laugh. "I'm still waiting for Prince Charming to come and sweep me off my feet."

Kenzie shook her head. "Don't wait around. See people. Get to know them."

"I know, I know. I'm just joking."

"Relationships take work if you're going to stay together. Both people have to be willing to put the time and energy into it."

43

S peaking of relationships…" Zachary scratched the back of his neck, hoping that the segue wasn't too abrupt. "I was interested in hearing about you meeting Tyrrell. And some more about you guys. Your history together."

Jason looked at his two sisters, then took on the explanation. "Well… you know that we were all registered with the DNA database."

"Yes, right."

"That was Celia's idea." Jason pointed at her.

"Well…" Celia took a sip of her water. "I figured that it was cheaper than getting paternity tests done. We could all just do the test, pop it in the mail, and when the results came back, we would know for sure who our father was. And whether we even all had the same one."

"You weren't sure?"

"Who can be sure of anything? If you believe what you see on daytime TV, half the mothers out there have no idea which man fathered her child. Which is… pretty sad. They all kind of make up their own story about what happened, even if half of it is complete… fiction. They like that guy, so they say he was the father. Or they don't like that guy and want to tell stories about him. Or they want to hit someone up for child support, so they pick the richest guy for that…"

"I guess. Did… your father live with you?"

"No, not most of the time," Jason said, shaking his head. "He'd come

196

back every now and then and crash for a while, but he was usually gone again in a few days, maybe a week."

"To be fair, he was in prison for a fair length of time," Margot pointed out.

They all exchanged looks, but no one laughed like it was a joke.

"What was he in prison for?" Zachary asked. He'd never thought about the possibility. He'd honestly never thought very much about Berk at all. After the family had broken up, Zachary supposed he assumed that his dad would go on pretty much the same way as he had. Maybe going to jail sometimes when he got in an altercation. But he had always gotten out again pretty quickly.

"Manslaughter," Margot said, when no one else answered. She looked at Zachary. "You never knew that?"

"I never saw or heard about him again after we were split up. We were put into foster care, and I knew he could never take us, probably never wanted us. So…"

"He never talked about you guys," Jason said, leaning forward. "We never had any clue that he'd had another family. I guess he figured that since he wasn't in contact with you anymore, he didn't need to mention it."

"Who knows what he thought?" Zachary shook his head. "The family was gone, so I can't see any reason he had to talk about it. It wasn't like he had walked out on our mom."

"Like he did with ours. She made me so crazy. I don't understand how she could be happy every time he came around again. Kids are supposed to love their parents, but I got so tired of her taking him back," Margot said, shaking her head. "I hated it. I just didn't want anything else to do with him."

The others shrugged and nodded, apparently having similar feelings about it.

"When she finally said she was done with him, I was so glad to have him out of our lives. I don't know why she kept it going for so long. If that happened to me now, and some man kept coming back like he could just walk out of and back into my life… I couldn't do it."

"But maybe that's because you already saw what that was like," Celia put in. "You don't know what it was like before we were born or when we were really young. And you don't know much about what happened before that, what her family was like. Maybe she thought that when he came back, things were going to be different."

Margot shook her head. "The first time or two, maybe. But not over and over again. She should have figured it out a lot sooner."

They fell silent.

"Maybe it was the money," Jason suggested. "Maybe she thought she needed that, so she would put up with him disappearing, as long as he helped to keep food on the table."

"Are you kidding?" Celia said scornfully. "He never paid her any child support."

"But he paid for stuff when he came home. Went grocery shopping, paid bills, fixed her car. That's a lot for a single mom."

"Not enough," Margot declared. "I would never put up with a man just for money."

Zachary didn't remember his father coming and going like that, but had he? Or was that a new behavior he started with a new relationship? Zachary could remember specific things that had happened when they were younger, but not a chronology. He had no idea whether his father had been home every night or if he only came by now and then.

He had been there often enough to produce six babies. Assuming they were all his.

Zachary thought his dad had been there every day. At least, the days when he wasn't in jail.

He brought the conversation back around to the DNA testing. "So Celia thought it would be a good idea to see if Berk was really your dad. Of all of you."

They nodded. Celia gave a little shrug. "I never imagined finding other siblings. I just wanted to see that we all had the same paternal DNA. It wasn't because we wanted anything from him. I just wanted to know... where we came from."

Zachary nodded.

"So we all did," Jason said. "Celia paid for it all, just bullied us into submitting our samples."

"I didn't bully anyone," Celia argued.

"Well," Jason gave her a teasing smile. "Maybe bully is a bit strong. She *strongly encouraged* us to submit our DNA. Gave us each a test collection kit and wouldn't leave until it was done."

Zachary smiled at that. Celia was apparently a very single-minded person.

"They all came back, and you confirmed that you were all siblings. But then you looked at the other results?"

Celia shook her head. "No, at first, it was just us. And people that we knew in the extended family. And more distant stuff that we didn't. But over time, other people add stuff to the database. When Tyrrell submitted his, I got a notification in my email inbox. 'You have a match.' I didn't think much of it, figured it was just another third cousin. Until I pulled it up, and it said 'sibling.' That was just bizarre."

"I can imagine," Zachary agreed. He felt like he might have somehow slipped into a parallel universe. It was a strange feeling, finding this alternate family who had lived a totally different life from his, the two never crossing paths.

"Jason and Tyrrell connected, and they talked and met a couple of times before Celia and I felt like it was safe to meet him," Margot said. She swirled the ice cubes in her cup. "We didn't want to meet him if he was like Dad."

Zachary nodded understandingly.

"It was on... it was during a sober period," Jason said, grimacing. "Tyrrell was great. We really clicked, got along together. He was excited to meet the girls. Showed us all pictures of his kids. Margot has kids too. Not as old as Tyrrell's."

Zachary smiled at Margot. More nieces and nephews. He would be excited to meet them, when Margot felt comfortable letting the two parts of her life mix.

"Tyrrell is a good guy," Zachary said. "We were only reunited a year ago, but... he means a lot to me. He always has, but meeting him and being able to talk to him again, that's been amazing. He's helped me to meet our other siblings too, my... full siblings that we lived with before... everything happened."

"You've met them all now?" Celia asked. "I thought you hadn't met the youngest ones yet. Tyrrell said he didn't think you were ready."

Zachary pressed his lips together, thinking about it. What had he done to make Tyrrell believe he didn't want to meet the other siblings or wasn't prepared for it? He had done well with his meetings with Heather and Joss. And Joss—she wasn't easy to get along with. If Zachary had been planning things out, he wouldn't have introduced Joss before Vince and Mindy.

"I met them just a couple of days ago. After Tyrrell's disappearance."

"Oh," Jason nodded. "That's what happened. What did you think? Did you get along with them too?"

"Yes. They're nice people. Didn't grow up the same way as I did, in foster care and institutions. They just grew up in one family, and it seems like they were treated well. So they're… more normal. Having that stability growing up makes a big difference in outcomes."

Jason cleared his throat. "You mean the difference between what you went through and what they did? Or Tyrrell and them?"

"Both, I guess. Tyrrell was lucky to have the Millers take them all in so that he could stay with Vince and Mindy and grow up in a more stable home than I did… but I guess a lot of the damage had already been done. He was six, old enough to remember what had gone on in his bio home. We always tried to protect the younger kids, but… he'd already experienced a lot of the… bad stuff."

Jason and his sisters exchanged looks with each other. Zachary looked away, admiring the furnishings and decorations at Old Joe's, even though he'd been there many times before. He looked at Kenzie and she gave him an encouraging smile.

"So… what was he like to you?" Jason finally asked. "Your father."

44

Zachary took a sip of his water, mouth dry as cotton. He tried to remember whether they had ordered drinks or their dinner yet. He thought that they had done both, but there was still just water on the table. Had everyone picked water, or were they still waiting for their drinks?

Under the table, Kenzie gave his leg a squeeze. She didn't say anything to him out loud, but he knew she was concerned about him and about how difficult the discussion was going to be.

"Things were… pretty bad. Growing up in that house, I knew that we were different than our friends. But since that was what I had grown up with, I didn't really realize how abusive and dysfunctional it was until I'd been in a bunch of other families. Learning from friends and foster siblings and social workers what was really normal and what wasn't."

Jason nodded his understanding. The girls were staring at him. Zachary wondered whether they were expecting him to cry or to blow up. While they tried to look relaxed, he could see that they were tense, coiled for action. Ready to defend themselves or flee from the situation if things went bad. He looked away from them again. He didn't want them to see him as confrontational or threatening.

"He and my mom fought a lot. Not just arguing, but actually beating on each other. Cops would get called and when they showed up, one or both of my parents would be bloody."

Margot's eyes widened. "He would beat up on our mom. But she didn't fight him. She'd run away outside or lock herself into the bathroom. She'd tell us to hide and stay out of his way."

Zachary let out his breath, sighing. Was it better that his mother had fought back? He knew that Berk wasn't always the one who started the fights. Sometimes it was her. And she did not try to keep the children out of the way and protect them. She was just as likely to whip them as he was.

"We had... both of them. I don't like to talk about my mom... I always wanted to go back home, to show her that I could be better than she thought I was. I guess I loved her, but looking back, I don't know why. She was... she was abusive too. Verbally and physically. I guess... she thought it was the only way to handle six kids. Physical discipline." His throat was tight and hot. He took another drink, trying to cool it.

"Traumatic bonding," Kenzie suggested. "You depended on her for your life. You had to love her. To want to please her. It was a matter of survival." Her eyes were compassionate. As he'd said, he didn't like to talk about his mother and, even in therapy, he had avoided talking about her in front of Kenzie as much as possible. She knew about the things his mother had said when she had refused to take Zachary or the other children back after the fire. But he had not told Kenzie that she was physically abusive as well. Not in so many words; but Kenzie had probably figured out that much.

"I guess." Zachary shrugged. "Everybody loves their parents, right? That's what we're taught. That's what the media is always saying. No love like a mother's. Mom and apple pie. All of those... ideals."

"Not everybody loves their parents," Celia said darkly. "I hated him. I hated every minute he was with us. If the DNA testing had shown that he was not our father, I would have been so happy."

"Sorry." Zachary wasn't sure what he was apologizing for. Berk's abusive behavior? Zachary talking about how everyone was supposed to love their parents? But something had to be said, and he couldn't think of anything else to fill the silence.

"Well, he wasn't with us all the time," Jason said with forced cheer. "We were lucky he was such a deadbeat. And for the time he was in prison. Let's hear it for manslaughter charges!"

"What happened, do you know?" Zachary asked. He tried to push down the uneasy worry that Berk might have killed one of his children. Not one of Jason's full siblings, clearly, or he wouldn't be joking about it.

But what if there had been another family? He knew that parents could kill. He'd known that from a very young age, and the fact had been impressed upon him recently with Ben Burton's case and the discovery that his abusive mother had killed her other son. "Who did he kill?"

"I don't really know anything about it," Jason said, looking at the girls to see if they had any thoughts. "I got the feeling it was maybe a bar fight?"

"That or a DUI," Margot said, shaking her head. "I don't know if we were ever told any details. But I definitely got the idea that it was something to do with drinking. So maybe our mom said that he'd had too much to drink and had killed someone, and we were just left to fill in the details ourselves."

Zachary could look up the details if he wanted to. He wasn't sure he wanted to know. "So he was away for a few years because of that?"

"Yeah. Three or four years, I think," Jason agreed. "It was a nice break. We kind of had a normal life during that time."

"And then when he came back, that was when Mom finally decided she'd had enough," Celia said.

They all looked at each other, a current running among the three of them. Something about it raised the hair on the back of Zachary's neck. He looked at each of them, analyzing their expressions and body language for an inkling of what had happened that they didn't want to put into words.

"What?" he asked finally. His eyes were drawn to Margot. She was the one who seemed to want to talk about it the most. He could feel her outrage, a boiling anger beneath the surface. "What happened?"

Margot exploded, calling Berk names, her volume and vehemence attracting stares from most of the restaurant patrons around them. The conversations going on in the restaurant ceased and everyone was silent, waiting to hear what was going on. There was a single laugh, somewhere on the other side of the room.

Jason gave Margot a look, but didn't tell her to mind herself. Celia put an arm around her sister and pulled her close. "We should... maybe we should go to the powder room," she suggested.

Margot looked furious. Not ready to be silenced and to behave like a lady. Celia squeezed her. "Come on. Let's just take a break. Splash some water on our faces."

"Where are our drinks? Didn't we order drinks?"

"I'll ask," Jason said. "You guys go ahead."

Celia managed to get Margot to her feet, and they headed toward the restrooms. Jason looked at Zachary and Kenzie and gave an embarrassed shrug. "Sorry..."

"No," Zachary shook his head. "It's fine. We've all got our triggers and hot buttons. I didn't mean to push."

"Probably best to get it out in the open in the beginning," Jason said philosophically. He looked in the direction the girls had gone, making sure that they were out of the way and weighing his words. "He didn't just hit them. The girls. When he came back after prison... it was worse. I don't know if it was because they were older and looked more mature, or if something happened to him in prison... or just being away from any *company* during that time. When Mom realized what was going on, that was the straw that finally broke the camel's back. She told him to get out and never come back unless he wanted to go straight back to prison. She'd call his parole officer, and he'd be back in prison and facing new charges."

"And even on the inside, they don't look on pedophiles too kindly."

"No."

"She didn't report it to the police?"

"No." Jason sighed. "She's an avoider. Would rather not have to deal with any of the fall-out. Says it was for the girls, so they wouldn't have to testify in court, but I think it was mostly selfish."

"They could still report it if they wanted to." Zachary nodded toward the back hallway where the two sisters had disappeared.

"They don't. They take after Mom. Just want to forget about it. Though you can see... it's not as easy to forget about as they would like."

"No." Zachary was an authority on that subject. "It's not."

"Did he do that to your family too? The older girls?"

"I don't know." Zachary thought back through the mists of time. It was hard to remember a lot of specifics from that long ago, especially since he had closed off as much of it as he could. If Berk had been molesting the older girls, would Zachary have been aware of it? Probably not. It would have been kept quiet, behind closed doors. He thought about Joss's bitterness and experience in being trafficked, and Heather's vulnerability to the foster father in the home she had been placed in. Both were consistent with a history of sexual assault. "Maybe. Neither of them have ever said anything to me about it, but... it's possible."

He felt nauseated at the thought of his father doing that, and his mother letting it go on, if she had been aware of it. And he felt immediately guilty, as if he should have been able to do something to prevent it.

He should have been able to protect his sisters. He should have at least tried. But he didn't think that he had known about it. He had only known about the physical abuse, what he could see in front of him. What he had experienced himself. That had never been hidden.

Jason nodded. "I didn't really know what was going on at the time, or what the fighting was about. But then… he was gone, and I found out little bits over the next few years. Wish that I could have done something about it. That I had known at the time. I just thought that if he wasn't hitting anybody, it was all good."

Jason waved down a waitress walking by. "Hey. We ordered drinks, if you could check on those. And our dinners? We've been here a while."

She looked at him for a moment, then nodded. "Sure. I'll check."

45

Margot and Celia returned from the restroom as the drinks were delivered to the table. Margot appeared to have settled down, but Zachary could see that her eyes were red-rimmed and puffy. He looked away from her, not wanting to draw attention to the fact.

He didn't know if he should say anything about what Jason had told them. He had a feeling it wouldn't go over well if he said that he understood what she had gone through. The circumstances were different, and he couldn't know exactly what she felt like or if she had felt the same way as he had when he was assaulted in foster care or later by Archuro.

"Sorry," he said briefly, "that this is so hard for you. I didn't mean... to cause anyone grief."

"Not your fault," Margot said stoically, looking remarkably like Joss when she pushed him away, refusing to let him get too close. "It happened and it's my thing to deal with, not yours."

"I know, but... I don't want you to feel bad around me. To associate me with that stuff. We'll have a nice meal, talk about good times instead of bad..."

"Build a positive association," Kenzie contributed.

"Yeah." Zachary nodded. "Like that."

Margot rolled her eyes, not impressed with the suggestion. But she didn't argue. Talking about more positive stuff instead of focusing on what had happened to her at the hands of their father was clearly a better idea than immersing herself in the negativity, so she was willing to change the subject.

"You have kids?" Zachary asked her. "Why don't you tell me about them?"

"Yeah, I have two boys," Margot admitted and, though she didn't smile, he could hear in her voice that this was a preferred topic. She picked up her phone from the table next to her, unlocked it, and tapped it a few times, then handed it to Zachary with a picture on the screen. Two boys sitting on swings at the park. Both tow-headed and smiley, mischief sparkling in their eyes.

"Oh, they look like a going concern," Zachary observed, smiling.

Margot nodded, her face softening and the lines around her eyes lightening, even if she didn't give him a full smile yet. "Yes, they're always into something. But they are the light of my life. I don't know where I would be without them."

Zachary showed the picture to Kenzie. She smiled and had a sip of her drink. "What cuties. About four or five?"

"Yeah."

"Can I look at some other pictures?" Zachary asked, finger poised to swipe through the photos.

She held her hand out for her phone and took it back. She tapped and swiped through a few photos, then handed it back. "You can look through that album."

Zachary browsed through the pictures, holding the phone so that Kenzie could see them too. They laughed at pictures of the two smiling children amid big messes, going to the zoo, and sitting on the couch at home, arms wrapped around each other.

"Your mom must be in love with them," Zachary said. "They're her only grandchildren?"

"Yeah, as far as I know."

Zachary raised his brows. "Oh…?"

"After diving into the world of DNA relatives and finding out how many people are discovering deep dark secrets when they start researching their ancestral DNA… I'm not sure I'm willing to believe anyone with anything in regard to procreation." Margot looked at Celia, and they both shook their heads and rolled their eyes over the stories they had discovered. "As far as I know, we're Mom's only kids, but that doesn't mean she couldn't have gotten pregnant in high school and given the baby up. Or donated eggs. Who knows what else. But as far as I know, Bailey and Uriel are the only grandchildren that Mom knows about."

Zachary chuckled. "I guess nothing is as straightforward as we would like to pretend. We've lived in a society that was once so strict about marriage and out-of-wedlock babies, and is now so open about it… Secrets on one end and multiple relationships on the other…"

"It's weird," Celia agreed. "It's like nothing in this world was really what you thought it was."

They all thought about this. Zachary handed Margot's phone back eventually. "They're wonderful," he said. "I love kids."

"You don't have any of your own?"

"No."

"As far as you know," Celia said.

Zachary opened his mouth to argue, then shrugged. "As far as I know," he agreed with a shrug. He rolled his eyes a little at Kenzie, so that she would be the only one who saw it. Trying to communicate with her that he had not been indiscriminate in the past. She knew about Bridget and that she hadn't had any children with him. He hadn't had any other serious relationships. But he had to agree with Celia that sometimes things happened. A night when he'd had too much to drink and didn't remember much about what had happened when morning came around. Situations where he'd been taken advantage of in foster care. There was no way he could account for every possibility.

"Tyrrell has the two; I guess he told you about them. And Heather, she has two, plus one that she gave up for adoption who she was just reunited with recently."

"Tyrrell mentioned that," Celia said. "That's pretty cool too. I guess since he marked his information as private, he won't show up on our charts, but if he hadn't, he would show up as a nephew."

"The family keeps getting bigger." Zachary smiled. He took a drink, trying to hide the smile in case the others didn't feel the same way he did.

Celia smiled, but it was reserved. Not sure yet how she felt about having more relatives. And maybe with what they had gone through with their father, that was understandable. It would make it harder to trust anyone who was related or claimed to be. What if they had inherited that violence or those other proclivities from him? He could see why Jason had said it was a good idea if he brought Kenzie with him. It made him seem safer. Someone else to keep an eye on him and give references for him. Attest to the fact that he was an okay guy.

"And the two of you?" Zachary looked from Celia to Jason and back. "Do you have any plans to start a family? Anyone special in your lives?"

Celia shook her head firmly. Jason gave a shrug. "No one yet."

The waitress arrived with their steaks and deposited them around the table. "Can I get you anything else?"

"Ketchup?" Zachary suggested.

He didn't look at Kenzie, but knew that she rolled her eyes at that. Ketchup with steak and potatoes would have been sacrilege in the household she had grown up in. They'd probably eaten steak blood-rare and paired it with some special wine, and maybe baby asparagus or something else fancy.

Jason let out a loud guffaw. "You see?" he demanded, pointing at Margot. "I'm not the only one!"

"I'll bring you a bottle of ketchup," the waitress promised, smiling at them but not joining in on the laughter.

"You like it with ketchup too?" Zachary asked.

"I know. It's totally wrong. It means I'm a completely uncultured redneck. But it's my steak!"

"What you do with your steak is your own business," Margot told him. "I just wish we didn't have to see it."

The waitress returned quickly with the ketchup, putting it between the two men.

46

Zachary leaned back, putting his hand over his stomach. Way too full. It hadn't been the flavor of the steak or the ketchup, but the company that had made him keep eating when he'd already had enough. He caught Kenzie and Jason both eyeing his plate.

Jason raised an eyebrow. "Not to your liking? Didn't you get enough ketchup?"

Zachary shook his head. "I don't eat very much. This was actually a lot for me. I'm stuffed."

"You're stuffed. You barely had half the steak and hardly touched the potatoes. Even Celia ate more than you did."

"He's telling the truth," Kenzie said. "I was actually surprised that he got that much down. Usually, his servings are about the size of a four-year-old's."

Zachary scratched his neck, grimacing and feeling his earlobes getting red. "Kenzie...!"

"I'm not going to lie to them. Or have them thinking that you're not enjoying the meal, which you obviously are."

"Yeah, but... a four-year-old? I eat at least as much as a five-year-old."

She laughed, and the others joined in.

"I guess... before we go our separate directions, I had a few more questions," Zachary said. It might not be the most graceful conversation shift, but it would have to do. "About Tyrrell, you know. I'd really like to be able to find him."

Jason, Margot, and Celia looked at each other.

"I wish I could help you, man," Jason said. "But we really don't have any idea. Tyrrell... we visited a little, off and on, but he wasn't a best friend or anything. He didn't tell us what he was doing or where he was going."

"He told you about me and the others."

"Yeah. But how does that help you?"

"Maybe he told you other things about his life too. You just don't realize that it could be anything important."

"Like what? His favorite vacation would be to go to Disneyland? You going to fly to Disney to see if you can find him there?"

"It might not be anything like that. It might just be... someone he mentioned a few times. Someone he drinks with. A favorite childhood memory. Maybe where he went to dry out the last time he went into a program. I've only known him a year and... I guess he didn't tell me any of that kind of thing. I knew that he'd had a problem with alcohol, but I didn't realize it was so recent. I never asked him anything about it like I should have."

"We're in the same boat, Zach. I'm sorry. We just didn't talk about that kind of stuff. And when it became obvious that he still had a problem with the bottle, we kind of backed off. None of us wanted to have to deal with that. Not after Dad."

"He never talked about anyone else? Only us kids? And his own kids? Lindsey?"

"Yeah."

"Well, and *him*," Margot contributed.

Zachary shook his head, having missed the reference. "Sorry, who?"

They all looked at each other, no one eager to be the one to answer. Zachary frowned and ran the conversation back in his mind, trying to figure out what he had missed.

"Who do you mean? His brothers and sister, and his kids, and who?" He remembered they had talked about Heather's adopted son. Was that who Tyrrell had mentioned? Another family member that he was eager to meet?

Jason pushed his empty plate away from himself an inch. He lifted up his empty glass and swirled around the ice cubes melting in the bottom.

"Berk."

Zachary blinked. "Berk? He talked about our dad?"

Jason nodded.

Zachary supposed that made sense. He was the common tie between them. That was a subject that Zachary had thought to bring up as well. Comparing their experiences with Berk, what he'd been like as a father.

"Yeah, Berk," Margot said and called him a couple more foul names, but didn't get loud and attract attention like she had the first time. "Tyrrell thought… that he couldn't be as bad as we were making him out to be. That we remembered wrong, or our mom had made things worse, poisoned our minds against him."

Zachary rubbed the place between his eyebrows that was starting to get sore. He knew he was holding himself too tense. The atmosphere of Old Joe's, which had seemed to be warm and inviting before, was starting to feel hot and oppressive. A bead of sweat ran down his back.

"Why would he think that?"

"Because he couldn't remember as much about how things were when he was a kid as you do. He was younger, and in between, that stupid social worker told him lies about Berk. That he was poor and couldn't afford to take six kids or some nonsense like that. She didn't tell them what it was really like."

Zachary groaned and shook his head. "If he wanted to know, I would have told him. He never said he wanted to know anything about him. And I… don't talk about it. I thought he knew."

"Well, he didn't, so he thought that we were lying, and Berk was the one telling the truth. He thought we had been manipulated by our Mom. *Tyrrell* was the one who was manipulated."

Zachary nodded. "I know. Sheesh. If I'd known that he was talking to anyone about it… I didn't even know about you; he didn't mention you. I didn't know that Dad had gone on to have other kids. He must have driven you crazy, repeating what the social worker said."

"It wasn't the social worker so much as him," Margot declared.

Zachary was having trouble making sense of the conversation. Every time he thought he had the thread, he lost it. Something was going on that he wasn't catching. He turned his head to look at Kenzie, wondering whether she were as lost as he was. Was one of his meds clouding his thought processes? Or maybe he was having a stroke. If he were having a stroke, Kenzie would notice, at least. She'd know what to do.

Kenzie gave a slight shake of her head, indicating she wasn't following it either. Zachary was relieved. The problem must be that the siblings had a sort of a shorthand between them. They knew what they were talking about, but it had to be explained to someone who didn't grow up with them and didn't already know what they did.

"He believed what *Berk* told him," Margot told Zachary in a tone that indicated she thought he was an idiot.

Zachary frowned at her, trying to process what she had said and what had already been said. Something was not computing.

47

Tyrrell was talking to Berk?" Zachary finally said, dragging the words out with difficulty. "Tyrrell was…?"

"Yes," Margot agreed, nodding vigorously. "Tyrrell was talking to him. Believing all of the nonsense that Berk was filling his head with. That everything had been fine when you guys were with him. That we were just making things up or exaggerating them because our mom filled our head with lies about him. Poor Berk was the victim, being unfairly maligned."

Zachary cupped his palms over his eyes, blocking everything out. He tried to force it to make sense, but he couldn't. What they were telling him didn't make any sense at all.

"When… where… how was Tyrrell talking to Berk? Where…?"

"I don't know where they met." Margot made a noise, blowing this off. "What does that matter?"

Zachary dropped his hands from his face. "You're saying that now, this year, Tyrrell saw Berk. Face to face? He was talking to him?"

"Last year," Jason corrected. "He was in contact with Berk even before us, so… two years… maybe more, I don't know."

"Why?" Zachary was flabbergasted. He couldn't figure out why anyone would want to see an abusive parent again. Not as an adult, anyway. He had wanted to go back home to his parents when he had been a child, before he had understood that not all parents were like that and really understood how much permanent damage they had done him. But as an adult, Tyrrell had to know that going back to Berk was a mistake. There was no reason for him to do it. No reason at all to go back to the man who had been so abusive.

The siblings looked at him. They had no answer to his question. Zachary covered his eyes again, grinding his fists into them, trying to push everything else out and to think about Tyrrell and why he would have ever wanted to see Berk again.

Tyrrell hadn't been able to remember everything about the home he had come from with the same clarity as Zachary. Just as there were things Heather and Joss remembered much better than Zachary. Tyrrell remembered their parents fighting the night of the fire, but maybe he didn't remember that there had been a physical fight. Maybe he didn't remember that was how it was all the time, with the two of them arguing and hitting, and the children also targets if they happened to get in the way or do something to raise the ire of either parent. Tyrrell had been six, and the older siblings had protected him from the abuse as much as they could. He didn't remember the worse stuff, or had blocked it out. He had been put into the Millers' home and maybe not gotten any therapy until after his behavior got so bad as a teenager. If Mrs. Pratt hadn't told his foster parents all that he had been through, they wouldn't have known what to do, wouldn't have known where the behavior came from.

As the years had passed, Tyrrell had decided to make contact with his family. And he had gone directly to DNA. Zachary and the others weren't in the database of the company that Tyrrell had gone through, but Jason and the girls had been. Tyrrell had contacted them and…

Zachary had to rewind. He was missing a step. Tyrrell had contacted Berk *before* meeting Jason, Margot, and Celia. How? Had they just happened to run into each other? Had Tyrrell's need to search been triggered by running into Berk by accident? Or had Berk sought him out?

Zachary hadn't gone back that far in Tyrrell's email. He had looked at the most recent matches and followed them back to Tyrrell's account with the DNA company. But that wasn't the only DNA matching company. Not by a long shot. They were getting more and more prevalent. And Zachary hadn't even checked the top three or four in the industry. He had stopped at the one nearest the top of Tyrrell's email inbox and assumed that Tyrrell would only have submitted his results to one database. Who would submit their DNA to more than one company?

"Did Berk show up in the database when you guys submitted your DNA tests?"

"No," Celia said, her tone crisp. "Like I said. It just showed that we were all siblings. And there was some extended family. Not Berk. But there were some Goldman relatives, so we knew that he was our father, not some other boyfriend."

"But he wasn't in there himself."

"No."

"Would Tyrrell have submitted tests to a bunch of different websites? That doesn't make any sense, does it? They all have pretty much the same thing; you wouldn't need to do more than one…"

"Zachary." Kenzie touched Zachary's arm, encouraging him to lower his hands from his face so he could see the others. He rested them on the table in front of him, closing his eyes for a moment to try to center himself, then opened them again.

Jason shook his head. "The others are probably a lot more conversant in this than I am, but the databases are all different. They have different pools of results, because there isn't one place where you can add your DNA to all of them simultaneously. And different companies have different tools on their websites. Not just different matches, but constructing DNA of ancestors based on their descendants, browsing genomes, finding out health risks, all kinds of things."

"So you do tests for all of these different companies?"

"No," Celia explained, "You do it once, and you download a copy of your raw genome. Then you can upload that to all of the other websites. You don't have to pay for a whole bunch of different test kits. Just the one."

"If Tyrrell met Berk before he met you… then he must have submitted his to a different testing company to start with."

"Yeah." Jason looked at the others, nodding, and they nodded in turn. "He must have. I hadn't thought about that, but it's the only way it makes sense because Berk didn't show up on our results."

"And Tyrrell contacted him… before he contacted you or any of us."

"Yes. We tried to explain to him what Berk was really like, but he wouldn't listen. Or he would seem like he was, but then the next time he talked to him, he would come back with all of this nonsense again."

Zachary looked at Kenzie, his throat starting to constrict. She recognized the panic in his eyes.

"It's okay," she assured him. "Focus on me. Deep breaths."

"I think it's Zachary's turn for the powder room this time," Margot said dryly, earning an elbow from Celia.

"Do you need to take a break?" Kenzie suggested. "Walk away for a few minutes until you can calm down?"

Zachary shook his head, embarrassed at putting on such a display in front of his new siblings. He took a sip of his water, forcing himself to swallow even though it felt impossible. The cold water helped, and he took a couple more gulps, then looked around for the waitress. Kenzie tried to flag one down.

"Some more water, please?"

The waitress murmured in passing that she would be back with it in a few minutes. Kenzie pushed her water glass toward Zachary. She had been drinking wine, so her water glass was still mostly full, though the ice had melted. Zachary gulped down the top half of it.

"Just breathe," Kenzie encouraged. She put her hand on his back, between his shoulders and, when Zachary didn't object, she rubbed, trying to loosen the tension he was holding there.

"Maybe we should call it a night," Jason suggested, watching Zachary.

Zachary shook his head.

"Give it a few minutes," Kenzie advised. "I think he can manage."

Celia and Margot whispered to each other. Zachary couldn't tell what they were saying. They were probably talking about him. About what a wreck their brothers were, Tyrrell with his alcoholism and Zachary with his obvious emotional problems.

"You don't drink?" Jason asked, his eyes on Zachary's water glass. Everyone else but Celia had ordered something else to drink. Only Zachary and Celia had stuck with water.

Zachary blew out his breath slowly and tried to answer. "Sometimes, a glass. But not..." He coughed and looked at Kenzie to help answer the question, not able to speak naturally yet.

"He can't take alcohol with some of his meds," Kenzie explained. "If he knows or thinks he will need to take one of them later, he won't drink." She patted him on the back. "He's very good about it. A lot of people just go ahead and mix them anyway, which is *not* a good idea."

"How come he's on medication? Is he sick?"

"ADHD, anxiety, depression," Zachary said, "stuff like that." He tried another sip of water. The constriction in his throat was gradually relaxing. "Most of the time... not this bad."

"Don't know why meeting three siblings you never even knew existed before would cause any anxiety," Celia joked. "Or, you know, talking about your abusive father."

Zachary nodded gratefully. "Yeah. It's... just a little stressful." He took a couple more deep breaths, trying to alleviate the feeling that he wasn't getting enough oxygen. Kenzie rubbed his back in soothing circles. "I can't believe... Tyrrell would be in contact with Berk. That he would believe anything he said."

"Yeah. Welcome to the club," Margot agreed. "I mean, I get it that he was pretty young the last time he saw him, but..." She shook her head. Obviously, she felt that Berk's behavior should have left an impression on Tyrrell, no matter how young he had been. He should have remembered enough to know that Berk was not a safe person to be around and that he was lying about his past.

"I'll talk to him when I find him," Zachary promised. "Explain it to him."

"And what makes you think he will believe you?"

Zachary's heart sank. He shook his head. "He has to. I need him to listen."

48

Zachary was glad that he had offered to go to the restaurant in Kenzie's vehicle, so there was no question that she would be the one driving home. He was not as enervated as he was when he had a full-blown panic attack. Still, the evening had definitely been stressful. He was exhausted and just wanted to be by himself and go to bed. But at the same time, his anxious brain was trying to work through the new revelations about Tyrrell and his connection with Berk, and everything else he had learned about Berk that night.

Kenzie drove most of the way home in silence, checking in with him only one time to ask if he was okay. Zachary nodded and stared out the window.

"Just thinking."

When they got home, he didn't know what to do with himself. Hands in his pockets, he paced across to his usual seat on the couch, but he didn't feel like sitting down to use his computer or watch TV, and he turned around and paced back into the kitchen. He wasn't really hungry. In fact, he was pretty full from the steak dinner, but he went to the fridge anyway, looked for anything interesting, then looked through the cupboard. Of course, he didn't actually want anything to eat, so this was pointless.

Kenzie watched him pace down the hallway to the bathroom, decide that he didn't need anything there, and then return to the living room.

"You want to talk, or just go for a jog?" she asked lightly.

Zachary intended to tell her that he didn't feel like talking. He had done enough visiting that night and needed time to process it. But as soon as he opened his mouth to tell her he didn't want to talk, the words started to tumble out.

"I never even thought about him being alive. He was out of my life and I never wanted to see him again. I just… shut him out of my thoughts altogether, like he was dead and buried. I never thought to ask Tyrrell if he'd had any contact with him. Why would he?"

"Considering that in your mind, he was dead and buried."

"Yes. And… he was abusive. You don't go back to people who were abusive."

"But people do," Kenzie pointed out. "That's part of the cycle of abuse. Like Jason and the others were talking about tonight. Their mom kept taking him back, even though she knew he was physically and emotionally abusive."

Kenzie looked like she would say more, but kept her mouth shut. The fact that she held herself back meant that she had been about to say something that might hurt Zachary or make him more upset.

Bridget, of course. Who was Zachary to criticize Tyrrell for going back to his abusive father when Zachary had spent years at Bridget's beck and call, even knowing how verbally abusive she was? He had craved her attention, even if it was negative. Dr. B had suggested that Bridget might be an emotional surrogate for his mother. That Zachary wanted her attention, and he had unconsciously assigned Bridget to fill that role. The mother he could never please. The wife he could never please. The ex-wife. The ex-mother.

He shook his head at this and didn't try to address it directly. Kenzie was right to see the parallel. He was not one to talk about it being illogical to go back to an abuser.

"But… Berk. I can't understand it. What is he getting out of that relationship? He didn't just go back to see him once. Not from what they said. He kept going back."

"I don't know," Kenzie said honestly. "I can't imagine doing it myself. But I would have to guess… he's confused. Vulnerable. Trying to fulfill a dream."

Zachary nodded. He paced back and forth between the kitchen and living room. "I'm going to have to talk to him."

"Tyrrell? You want to talk to him about it? Get him to explain how he's feeling?"

"No. Berk. My dad. If he and Tyrrell have been talking to each other... he might have an idea about where Tyrrell would go. T's been keeping this whole thing a secret from me for a year. He has this whole other life. Two other lives that I never knew anything about."

And more. Tyrrell had his life with Mindy and Vince and his foster parents too. Zachary had at least known about them, but Tyrrell had kept everyone but Zachary and the older girls separate, had never let their lives overlap. He had all of these families, but had any of them given him what he was looking for?

"There are more matches in the DNA database as well," Zachary said. "Other sibling matches. I contacted Jason first because he had been trying to follow up, had been trying to get in touch with Tyrrell. I thought he was the closest, the one who would know best where Tyrrell is."

"It must feel so strange. I mean, first of all, to discover them through this DNA database. But also strange that Tyrrell would be so eager to contact them and then keep them secret from each other."

"It is, right?" Zachary thought that he had a pretty good under-standing of human behavior, even if he hadn't ever received any special training about it. He had lived with and observed so many different people in so many different circumstances. Sometimes his life or well-being had hinged on his being able to understand why they did what they did or what was likely to happen in response to his actions. Sure, he still failed. Usually, when he jumped right in and did something impulsively rather than thinking it over. He couldn't help that; it was part of his makeup. Part of his ADHD or PTSD. But when he was thinking and considering what to do next, he was usually pretty good at predicting other people's responses. "I would think that he would want us all to meet, to get along with each other. To all be one... big happy family."

Kenzie nodded. "I'm sure it is something that makes sense in his mind, even if it doesn't make sense to us."

"I have to find him," Zachary said, the steak dinner feeling heavy and solid in his stomach as he came to the realization.

"I know. We're all trying."

"No. Not Tyrrell."

Kenzie looked at him, frowning.

"Berk. I'm going to have to find my father."

49

Kenzie recognized the seriousness of the situation. She knew some of what Zachary had gone through as a kid. He hadn't told her everything. Nowhere near everything. But he thought that he had told her enough for her to understand that his home had not been a happy place. She had just listened to Jason and the others talking about how abusive Berk was to them and had heard Zachary confirm that it had been the same for him. She had to understand that the very last thing Zachary wanted to do was track down his father. If there were any way around it...

"That will have to wait," she said sensibly. "You can't track him down tonight, so you don't want to get yourself all wound up in trying. Let's have a nice evening together. Let you unwind and clear your head. Get a good sleep tonight. Then you can worry about your next step tomorrow."

Zachary was actually glad for an excuse not to begin the search. It seemed like the worst thing anyone could have asked him to do. He wished there were some other way around it. But Kenzie was offering a reprieve for the evening, anyway. He would do much better with it, mentally and emotionally, if he were fresh and well-rested. Things would go much better.

"Okay," he agreed. He took a few breaths and paced back and forth. "What do you want to do?"

"What do you feel like? Watch a movie? Cuddle? Work out your energy some way other than pacing back and forth?" She lifted an eyebrow.

Zachary laughed. "I don't think I'm up for much more than cuddling tonight. I'm too... My stomach really isn't feeling very good. I shouldn't have eaten so much tonight."

"I was glad to see you getting more than a few bites down. Sorry that it's making you uncomfortable, though."

Zachary held his hand over his stomach for a minute. "I think it's more than just the dinner. I think probably... I'm a little anxious."

"I think probably you're a lot anxious."

He shrugged and nodded. "Yeah."

"That's okay. Cuddling would make me happy, if that's what you want to do. Do you want to take something for the anxiety? You managed to head off an attack at the restaurant, but if you're still feeling anxious, maybe you should do something about it."

"Not yet." While Zachary didn't want to suffer through the physical discomfort and chattering brain that anxiety brought, he didn't want to take something to combat them, either. He wanted to be able to think. Not slowly and methodically like a scientist, but the way he knew his brain worked when he was not medicated—on hyperdrive, going through all of the possibilities. His daytime meds were wearing off and if he didn't need to take his night meds for a couple more hours, he had a window of time during which he could just let his brain run and see what solutions it came up with. If the anxiety didn't eventually start to fade on its own, he could take something before bed and see whether he could calm down and relax enough to sleep.

Kenzie didn't argue. He could sense her disapproval, but she was trying very hard to let him be in charge of his body and medications and not interfere just because she was a doctor and thought she knew what he should do. Or because she cared for him and wanted to eliminate as many of the symptoms as possible. She didn't understand much about how he could sometimes use his neurodivergence to his advantage.

"Let's put something on the TV for a while," Zachary suggested. "That will help distract me."

Partway through the movie, Zachary's phone buzzed. He looked over at it, where he'd left it on his computer table so that it would not be in his hand

and distracting him from watching the movie and paying attention to Kenzie. He was sure that he had put it on Do Not Disturb so that he wouldn't be interrupted by any calls or texts. And he only had a few exceptions to his Do Not Disturb function. He glanced at Kenzie.

"Didn't you switch it over?" she asked.

He nodded. "I'm sure I did."

"You'd better see who it is, then."

Zachary picked up the phone, his mind immediately flying to what might be wrong. Although he knew that no one on his important contacts list had anything to do with his father, other than Tyrrell, Zachary's brain immediately jumped to the possibility that it was one of the DNA siblings, either the ones he had contacted or ones that he hadn't, who wanted something from him or were angry about his searching for Tyrrell and deciding to search for Berk.

But of course, they were not on his exceptions list. If they did call him, they would be funneled to voicemail, and he could catch up with them later. The name on the caller ID was Lorne Peterson.

Zachary swiped the answer call slider. "Mr. Peterson?"

"Lorne, Zachary," his patient voice reminded. "Calm down. I didn't call because something is wrong."

Zachary took a deep breath and let it out. He looked at Kenzie, who was also looking worried, and shrugged. He lowered his voice to something that he hoped didn't sound quite so panicked. "Sorry. Hi. How are you?"

"We are both doing just fine. What's got you so worked up?"

Zachary didn't feel like taking him through the whole case, so he just shrugged it off. "Nothing. I just wasn't expecting your call. It startled me."

"Didn't mean to cause any concern. Pat and I were wondering if you and Kenzie would be able to make it down for dinner and a visit on Sunday. I don't know what Kenzie's schedule is like. Sorry I didn't call sooner, but…"

Zachary covered up the mic on the phone to speak to Kenzie. "Sunday dinner?"

She nodded.

"Sure, that looks okay," Zachary agreed. "Would Pat like us to bring anything? A bottle of wine?"

"No, no. We'll handle everything this time. We're going to have a small gathering in the afternoon. A little memorial ceremony. Just a few people in our circles who knew Jose and wanted to… mark his passing."

"Oh. Sure, of course." Zachary thought about the people he had interviewed while he had been looking for Jose. He had run into some interesting characters, most of whom he really didn't want to meet up with again, even on Pat's turf. "Um... who are you having?"

"Not anyone you met, I don't think," Lorne said. "Some of the men we go to events with. Musicals. Performances."

"Not... Santiago?"

"No, no," Lorne assured him. "And we're not using any of his facilities. Just a little garden ceremony. Oh—Eric Naylor will be there... he is sometimes part of our group. Are you okay with that?"

Naylor ran a high-end second-hand clothing store, which is where Zachary had interviewed him. Not the kind of place where people went thrift shopping, but somewhere they could get a deal on a big-name brand without burning through thousands of dollars. He had not been particularly helpful to Zachary during his investigation, but Zachary didn't think he would be too uncomfortable around him. He, at least, hadn't shown any interest in Zachary. Nor was he a physically intimidating man; slim and fussy with long, tapering fingers.

"Yeah, that should be okay. I'd be fine with him."

"Okay, good. We'll have the ceremony in the afternoon when it is warmer, about three o'clock. Dinner later in the evening, so you'll have time to decompress in between. And dinner will be just the four of us."

Zachary nodded. "Sure. Sounds good. We'll be there."

"You haven't... found out anything about Tyrrell yet, have you?"

"Some new leads... but nothing concrete yet. I have... something to follow up on tomorrow. Maybe it will break the case." Zachary wasn't ready to give him any details yet about his biological family. That was too much. Something that should be saved for a face-to-face meeting. And since they would have one within a couple of days, he wasn't really holding anything back.

"That's good news. I'm glad you're making progress. We consider Tyrrell part of our extended family."

"Oh." This brought a quick tear to Zachary's eye, and he tried to blink it away and stay calm. "That's really nice. Thank you."

"Your family is our family. We'll see you Sunday, then. Take care."

"You too. Take care."

50

Zachary's active brain hadn't come up with anything brilliant while he was watching TV with Kenzie. He didn't feel like he was anywhere closer to understanding Tyrrell and the choices he had made about his family. He didn't have any brilliant insights into contacting Berk, but it should all be pretty straightforward. There must be contact information in Tyrrell's email system somewhere. And even if not, Berk Goldman was not a common name and it wouldn't be hard to run a few searches and find out his last few addresses. Since he had a prison record, he might even have to report to a parole officer or keep his address up to date on the sex offender registry. Just because Margot's and Celia's mother hadn't reported him for assaulting her daughters, that didn't mean that he'd never been caught and held accountable for another sexual assault. Someone else might not have been satisfied with just having him out of her life.

Taking an anti-anxiety pill and sleep aid before going to bed made his waking in the morning groggy and slow. He had breakfast with Kenzie, mostly just staring blearily at his food while she ate hers. After seeing her off to work, he opened up his computer and started to poke around to see what he could find. Kenzie wouldn't likely be gone all day. Usually when she went in on the weekend, it was just for a few hours to catch up on things or help Dr. Wiltshire with something urgent. Even though the Medical Examiner's Office was only supposed to be open on weekdays, they frequently used the weekend to clear any backlog. And Zachary really didn't mind that. They would have Sunday off together, and that would include a highway drive, which always made him feel more relaxed.

He was right, and it only took a few well-placed searches to find fairly comprehensive contact details for Berk Goldman. Zachary transcribed everything carefully, then looked at it again.

It might be easier and more efficient to try calling Berk on the phone rather than driving out to look for him in person. But that also gave him the option to hang up if he didn't want to talk to Zachary. Whether he knew anything about where Tyrrell was or not, he might very well want to avoid any kind of conversation with his oldest son. He would know that Zachary wasn't exactly likely to be bringing him any flowers.

He looked back at Berk's contact information again and decided that a personal visit was in order. The last thing he wanted to do was to see Berk face-to-face. But the thing he wanted most was to find Tyrrell, hopefully safe and sound, and that had to be a higher priority than avoiding his own discomfort with seeing his biological father again.

Overthinking would keep him from acting, so he gathered his notepad, phone, and keys and forced himself to walk out to his car and get on his way.

Snow was blowing across the highway, making the winter driving a little more treacherous than usual. Zachary drove a little more slowly than he usually would have without Kenzie in the car and lost himself in the meditative state that highway driving usually produced for him. He was able to ponder a little on what he would say or do when he met his father, something he hadn't been able to do without significant anxiety the night before. Rather than his anxiety increasing as he approached the event, it started to subside.

Berk Goldman didn't know Zachary. Not anymore. He had known Zachary, the little boy. The little boy he had been before he had entered the foster care system. Before growing up and starting his own business and marrying and having adult relationships. He didn't know anything about the adult Zachary. And if Berk were threatening or unhelpful, it wasn't the end of the world. What was he going to do? He might say that no, he hadn't seen Tyrrell and didn't have any suggestions for Zachary as to where to find him, but so what? He wouldn't be any further behind than he already was. And just maybe, he would be able to get further ahead on the case.

The address that Zachary had found was for a small, rundown four-plex. There were children's toys and engine parts in the yard. One of the units in the fourplex had newspaper taped up all over the windows. Another had a dead, brown Christmas wreath with a red ribbon on the door. And Zachary wasn't sure whether it was actually that year's wreath.

He knocked on the door of Berk's unit several times but was unable to raise any answer. Berk might have been at work, but Zachary hadn't seen anything during his computer searches to indicate that Berk was working. More than likely, he was delinquent on the rent on the fourplex but was squatting there until the landlord was actually able to have him physically removed. It could be remarkably difficult to get a non-paying tenant out of a place. In the meantime, he wasn't likely making improvements to the interior.

Zachary went to the door closest to the children's toys and rang that doorbell. He could hear it ringing inside. In a few minutes, a woman came to the door. She had frizzy brown hair, freckles, and a skinny, mussy-haired child on her hip who was crying about something and squirming to get away.

"What is it?" the woman demanded fiercely. "Don't you know better than to be ringing doorbells in the middle of the afternoon?"

"Uh…"

"You woke her up!" She indicated the child in her arms with a jut of her chin. "Meggie, shut up! Stop that!"

The toddler continued to cry, squirming again to escape.

"I'm sorry. I didn't mean to cause any trouble. Hey, Meggie, it's okay. You can go back to sleep…"

"Go back to sleep?" the woman slapped her forehead. "You think a kid goes back to sleep after they get woken up? Grab a brain, why don't you?"

"I'm sorry…"

"Who are you? What do you want? You'd better not be selling anything, or I'm going to call your boss and read *him* the riot act. Then what do you think is going to happen to your cushy job?"

Zachary wasn't sure how door-to-door sales in the winter would count as a cushy job, but decided there was no point arguing it. "I'm just looking for one of your neighbors," he started, gesturing toward Berks' door.

"Then go ring his doorbell! What are you doing harassing me?"

"I'm just wondering whether you have seen him lately. It wouldn't make much sense for me to hang around here if he's moved out."

"Who?"

"Berk Goldman, the man in unit C." Zachary gestured. "Taller, heavyset guy. Sixties. Lives by himself, as far as I know."

"Oh, that old pervert? Yeah, he's still there. Sit on his doorstep for as long as you like, but don't be ringing my doorbell!" She started to shut the door, but Zachary put his hand out, stopping her.

"Sorry—just wondering if you know, does he have a job or is there somewhere he might be hanging out?"

"How do I know?"

"You might see a work truck? Or he might go out at the same time every day?"

She stared at him blankly.

"No? Is he usually here in the day? You sound like you've noticed him."

"Sometimes he's here during the day. I don't know. Sometimes he's sopping drunk and can't find his own door. What a loser!"

"He lives alone?"

"I told you that, didn't I?"

"No. I was just checking. Does he drink somewhere near here? Or do you know where he picks up his liquor?"

Zachary had looked for empties behind the fourplex, hoping to get some idea of where Berk did his buying or drinking, but without success. If Berk saved his empties rather than throwing them into the trash, then they were inside.

"Get lost," the woman sneered, forcing the door towards the shut position, "or I'm going to call the cops. You're trespassing."

So much for her suggestion that he could sit on his father's steps all day. He suspected that if he did stay there for any length of time, he would be explaining himself to the police. They wouldn't take kindly to his loitering around even if he was a private investigator and the subject's biological son.

Zachary did one more scout around the house, but didn't ring any more doorbells. There didn't appear to be anyone home in unit B. And he suspected that if he bothered the resident of the house with the newspapered windows, he would likely as not be greeted with a sawed-off shotgun.

51

Zachary used his phone to search for the closest bars, pubs, and liquor stores. If Berk was known for being a drinker and was sometimes so intoxicated that he "couldn't find his own door," then he probably didn't go far to drink. He would be known at all of the closest establishments or would have one "usual" place he hung out. He wouldn't be driving far with a habit like that.

The closest bar did not open until the afternoon. If Berk were out drinking rather than working, that wouldn't be his preferred watering hole. Zachary continued to scroll through the list and consider the pros and cons of each location. Somewhere close by, not too high-brow, open long hours. Probably near a convenience store where Berk could pick up cigarettes, a bottle to take home with him, and any other necessities. He had no idea whether Berk was into gambling or pool. Probably not. He probably didn't care about any of the other amenities. Other than girls. Berk would probably be somewhere he could watch women, if not pick them up. Not necessarily a strip club, where the drinks were sold at premium prices and he would get kicked out if he got sloppy drunk, but somewhere that either women would frequent or there were waitresses with skimpy outfits.

The first couple of places Zachary went, the bartenders and other staff shook their heads, not recognizing Berk's name. He was not active on social media, so Zachary didn't have a picture of him and could only give the most general description, not having seen the man for decades and only guessing how he might have changed as he aged.

Zachary went to the pub that was next on his list, though it wasn't the most promising location. More of a British vibe, no cute waitresses, as far as he could tell from the pub's reviews.

Despite it still being morning when he got there, the place smelled dank and sour. Beer and bodies and deep-fried chips. Zachary waited inside the door for a minute for his eyes to adjust to the dimness.

There were a few dedicated drinkers there already. It was quiet, just murmurs of conversation. A few TV monitors hung in the corners of the ceiling, but it was too early in the day for there to be anything interesting on. Poker games and rugby reruns; no one was watching them or even appeared to notice that they were on.

Zachary scanned the room, but there was a heavy lump in his stomach, his subconscious brain having come to a conclusion before he was able to look at any faces. His eyes stopped on a man in a back corner who sat facing the door. He had a glass and a bottle on the table in front of him, working through the whiskey at his own pace so that the wait staff didn't have to keep refilling for him. His face was vaguely familiar. Not the same man as Zachary had known decades earlier, through a child's eyes. More lined, with deep creases running from the edges of his nose to the corners of his mouth, everything turned downward, looking mean and angry.

Berk hadn't lost his hair, but it was peppered with gray, as was the stubble on his face. He was broader than Zachary remembered, with a beer gut straining his shirt. He was sitting down, so Zachary couldn't compare his height to that of the man who had towered over him as a child, but he assumed that he would seem shorter now, since Zachary was taller.

Zachary swallowed and walked across the pub toward Berk. The man's watery eyes lifted from his drink as they caught the new movement. For a moment, he just stared. Then he swore.

Zachary walked up to him, but had no idea what to say. Hello? Introduce himself? Demand to know where and when he had last seen Tyrrell? Nothing seemed appropriate, either too impersonal or making him feel vulnerable. They just stared at each other.

For an instant, Zachary was flooded with memories. All different scenes from his childhood replayed through his mind in a flash. Happy times, anxious times, being hurt and terrified and trapped. Heather had reminded him once of how it felt to be caught in Berk's crosshairs. That horrible, terrifying feeling of anticipating the violence of a punishment. How his father had been God in their household, ruling with an iron fist, meting out whatever consequences he saw fit for their disobedience, for a bad report from the school, or just for crossing his path at the wrong time or knocking over a glass.

But now, he was just a man, and Zachary was having difficulty reconciling the two images. The raging father who had ruled his life and the drunk sitting in front of him, not even bothering to get to his feet.

"Hey, you ready for—" A man coming out from the back hallway where the restrooms were stopped speaking when he realized that someone was standing there who hadn't been there when he had left.

Zachary belatedly noticed the other glass on the table and a mess of coats and outerwear in a jumbled mess on one of the chairs. He turned slowly, his ears attuned to that voice, knowing as he turned around who he was going to see but still not believing it.

52

Zachary!"

Zachary stared at Tyrrell, frozen. Tyrrell's voice was shocked, disbelieving. They both just stared at each other.

Then Tyrrell's face broke into a grin. "Zach, my man! I can't believe you're here!"

He rushed forward and enveloped Zachary in a hug, pulling him close and thumping him on the back. Happy as Zachary was to see him alive and unharmed, he struggled immediately to get out of Tyrrell's grip. The other man stank and he was holding on too tightly. Zachary didn't want to be touched in that pub. Not by anyone. He jerked back and wrenched himself out of Tyrrell's grip.

Tyrrell looked surprised by this reaction. He smiled uncertainly and held one hand toward Zachary.

"Zach. Hey. It's me."

Zachary shook his head. He looked from Tyrrell to Berk and back again.

"Oh, yeah!" Tyrrell exclaimed, once again enthusiastic and eager. He gestured toward Berk. "This is our dad! Can you believe it? Berk Goldman!"

Zachary nodded. "Yeah. I remember."

"Come sit down with us. Have a drink. It's good to see you."

Zachary wanted to do anything but sit down there and talk to the two of them. He fought off the emotions and memories that threatened to engulf him, struggling to anchor himself in the present. The pub was too dark and too warm. It was too quiet, and he felt like everyone's eyes were on him. The floor was sticky. He couldn't seem to move from the spot.

But he had come there looking for Tyrrell. He wasn't going to just turn around and walk out of there again. He had spent a week trying to track down someone he loved who might very well be dead, and the roller-coaster of emotions ranged from fury at Tyrrell, to relief, to mourning the way Tyrrell had fallen. The way that Tyrrell had turned out not to be the man that Zachary had built him up to be. He wasn't strong and whole and healed, with everything going for him and his life put together, aimed at a bright future.

He was broken and imperfect, just like Zachary was.

All because of the man who sat there looking at them, taking another swallow of whiskey.

"Sit down!" Tyrrell urged. "Come on. Sit down with us. This is just amazing, isn't it? Did you ever think you would see him again?"

"No." Zachary swallowed and shook his head. "No, I never thought that I would."

Nor had he ever wanted to. Apparently, unlike Tyrrell.

Tyrrell moved past Zachary to the table. He picked up the coats from the chair beside him and put them on the fourth chair. "There. Come sit here." He pulled on Zachary's arm. Not hard, forcing him to go. Just a tug, encouragement, invitation.

Zachary finally moved, his stiff joints moving rustily, not wanting him to sit down in that waiting chair. He landed in it and, for a moment, just sat there, feeling disoriented and lost in space. He focused on the feeling of the hard chair. The movement of the air from the ventilation system. The background music, so quiet that he hadn't noticed it until then. Maybe the staff didn't even realize it was on. Or maybe the music was coming from somewhere else, inside of Zachary. *Santa Baby.* Why would they still be playing Christmas songs in January?

Tyrrell resumed his seat and again slapped Zachary on the back in a hearty, friendly way.

"Dad, this is Zachary! I told you he was a private investigator. Should have guessed that he would find us here!" Tyrrell laughed, pleased with himself. He picked up the bottle and poured more into his glass. He waved to one of the waiters. "Another glass!"

"No. Just water," Zachary insisted.

The waiter looked at him for a moment as if this were a bizarre cocktail he'd never heard of before, then shrugged and went to fetch a glass of water.

"Water," Berk growled. "No son of mine should be drinking water! Man up and have a real drink."

Zachary shook his head. He tried to answer Berk out loud, but couldn't. Tyrrell took a couple of gulps from his glass.

"This is so cool. All three of us together now. We just need Vinny, and then it will be all of the Goldman men together again!"

"Will it?" Zachary said. "What about Jason? And any others?"

Tyrrell snorted and covered a laugh with his hand as if his secret had been discovered and he was trying to hide his embarrassment. "Oh—you know about Jason?"

"Found him while I was looking for you. And how many others are there?"

Tyrrell shrugged and waved his hand around. "Who knows? Half the state could be populated with them!"

The thought of Berk traveling all over Vermont impregnating unsuspecting women and molesting young girls made Zachary sick. He didn't understand how Tyrrell could think that it was funny. But then, he was drunk. Everything was probably funny to him in this high-flying state.

Berk didn't give any answer about how many of his progeny might be scatted around the state, but he smirked and gave a careless "What are you gonna do?" gesture with his free hand.

The waiter came over and placed a glass of water in front of Zachary. Ice cubes floating on top. A wedge of lime balanced on the rim of the glass. Nice presentation.

Zachary nodded. "Thanks."

He had a sip of the water. Just tap water. Plenty of chlorine. Zachary wanted to drink to moisten his dry mouth but, feeling so heavy and nauseated, he didn't want anything in his stomach. He put the glass back down and squeezed the lime wedge to squirt a few drops of juice into the water to counteract the taste of the chlorine. He stared at the glass, watching trickles of lime juice descend into the water and diffuse into it to become indistinguishable.

"How did you find us?" Tyrrell demanded.

Zachary felt a surge of anger overtake the other emotions. He grasped hold of it and let it lead him into the conversation. "How could you do that? Disappear and leave everyone behind. Let everyone think that you were dead. That you'd killed yourself. You left your house, your job, your *children!*"

Tyrrell's brows dipped down, demonstrating sadness. "You don't know what it's like, Zachary. My life isn't like yours."

"I have things better?" Zachary demanded. "Stuck in a psych ward for weeks? A hair's breadth from suicide?"

Tyrrell waved this off with a careless gesture. "You have Kenzie."

Kenzie. Zachary couldn't argue that she wasn't the best thing in his life.

"And I have an ex too, just like you do. If you cleaned yourself up, you could look for someone else. Make space for someone like Kenzie to come into your life."

"Your ex." Tyrrell rolled his eyes. "She's got money. Try an ex who demands child support all the time. I don't even have enough to live on, and I'm supposed to give her money too?"

"They're your kids! You're lucky to have them! Do you know what I would give to have kids?"

Berk chuckled. "Havin' kids isn't exactly hard. Unless you're... not a *man.*"

Zachary opened his mouth, furious, but nothing came out.

What *was* wrong with him? Bridget had said no to kids. But he could have insisted. He could have at least tried to talk her into it. Gordon had apparently managed to do it. The two of them now had newborn twins. Two precious little lives that Zachary would have done anything to protect from harm.

And what about Kenzie? They had never talked about children. Zachary knew that she wasn't ready for kids now, not as she was trying to get established in her career and to move up the food chain, to someday be a medical examiner with a morgue of her own and people working under her. But would she want kids in the future? Or had he ended up with a second woman who never wanted to have his children?

How could Berk end up with children by half a dozen women all over the state, and Zachary kept picking women who didn't want any?

"You need to assert your dominance," Berk told him, eyes glittering. "You don't ask. You tell her. You take what is yours. None of this wishy-washy politically correct 'talk it out' crap. Are you a man or a mouse?"

Zachary shook his head. He wasn't a predator. He would never be like that. He would never be *that* kind of a man.

Berk eyed him, waiting for him to say something, and had another sip of his drink.

"It's a different world today," Tyrrell whined, not exactly standing up for Zachary, but maybe defending his own weaknesses, "It's a lot different from when you were younger. Acting like that now... would just get us thrown in jail."

Berk shrugged. "Ain't that different than it ever was. But you're going to let that stop you? You don't change the world by being meek and mild. If you want the world to accept men being men, instead of these scraggly little hipsters that are showing up everywhere now and the so-called men in business suits preaching their kind of politics, then you have to act. Get out there and say what you want, instead of sitting at home, complaining that no one is giving you what you want."

Tyrrell nodded, accepting this. Looking as though he agreed with it on some level. Zachary shook his head. This wasn't the Tyrrell he knew. That wasn't the kind of person Tyrrell was at all.

"You have two wonderful children," Zachary told him. "Don't forget that. Don't run out on them. Do you know how much they want you to come home? To know that you're safe? What kind of a Christmas do you think they had, wondering whether you were alive or dead?"

"I can't go home to them," Tyrrell pointed out. "I don't live there. Their mom does. And if she wants to raise two kids by herself, she's welcome to do that. She doesn't want me around. So fine. I'm not around anymore. She can do it by herself. She can do everything by herself."

Zachary just stared at him. Tyrrell drank down a few swallows and reached for the bottle again.

"They'll get over it," he growled. "I got over losing my family, didn't I?"

Zachary blinked and shook his head. "No, you didn't. You never did."

Tyrrell didn't argue the point. Maybe even so deep in his cups, he realized that Zachary was right. He had spent the last few years chasing family. His father, the siblings he had known before the fire, the siblings he never knew he had and were new to his life. He just kept adding more and more people, looking for that feeling of a family. He had confessed to Lorne Peterson that the reason he'd wanted children was to feel like he had a family. A complete little unit.

But that had not worked out. Tyrrell had gone badly off the rails.

He might not be able to mend fences with Lindsey, but that didn't mean that he couldn't still be a part of Mason's and Alisha's lives. The law allowed him that. Lindsey hadn't snatched the kids and run to the other side of the country to live under assumed names until they were grown. They were still there, with Tyrrell taking them on weekends and every other holiday.

53

Zachary saw Berk watching something behind him and turned to look. He didn't like sitting with his back to the door, but the seat Tyrrell had cleared for him was in the wrong position, and he wasn't going to sit next to his father.

Looking out the front window of the pub, he saw something he hadn't noticed before. A school field across the street. A class of girls ran around the field, despite the winter temperatures and the snow on the ground. Most wore long track pants, but a few showed off bare legs under shorts. Everything coordinated in the school colors. A private girls' school? No wonder Berk had chosen that location and sat facing the window.

"You're disgusting," he told Berk, the words popping out of his mouth before he was even aware of them.

Berk chuckled and seemed to be completely unoffended. Zachary looked at Tyrrell.

"You want to be like that? Like him? You think he is some kind of role model for you?"

Tyrrell rolled his eyes. "So he likes to look at the girls. He's not a bad guy."

Jason had warned Zachary that Tyrrell didn't remember what Berk had been like when they lived with him.

"He is," Zachary told Tyrrell in a lowered voice, though unless Berk was mostly deaf, he would still be able to hear what Zachary was saying. "I get that you don't remember what it was like at home, but believe me, this is not a guy you want to pattern your life after."

"You can't believe everything people tell you. I believe what I can see with my own eyes." Tyrrell gestured to indicate Berk. Clearly, he was just an inoffensive older man. A drunk. Not someone who went around harming anyone. He'd had wilder days when he was younger. Tyrrell had too. He'd been put through programs and was now older and wiser than he had been as a teenager. People changed.

"You did see it with your own eyes. You just don't remember. How he used to whale on us? How he and Mom used to have knock-down, drag-out fights until the neighbors called the cops and carted one of them off to jail? How he put drinking and all of his desires over putting food on the table for us? You saw it. Don't let anyone tell you any different."

Tyrrell shook his head, bemused. His eyes were glazed and far away.

"You're not remembering right either," Berk told Zachary. "I don't know who's filled your head with all of that nonsense. It never happened."

"The hell it didn't! I remember!" Zachary jumped to his feet. The table wobbled and his glass fell over, spilling water over the tabletop and down to the floor. Zachary set it upright again, forcing himself to handle it carefully when he would have preferred to throw it across the room. At Berk's head. "I was there and I remember what it was like. Not because anyone told me that was what happened. I *remember!*"

Berk just shook his head, looking amused. "That's the problem with all of these therapists and headshrinkers. They implant false memories. They ask you if your parents ever hurt you or did anything to you, and then they put the images in your head, making you think that it really happened. When it never did."

"No." Zachary looked at Tyrrell. "You told me you could remember the night of the fire. You said that you remembered *Santa Baby* being on the radio before I put you back to sleep again. When you were awake because they were fighting so bad and you wanted to call the cops."

Tyrrell cocked his head slightly as if trying to catch the notes of the song. Replaying it in his head and thinking about the circumstances surrounding it.

"Come on," Zachary insisted. "What do you remember?"

"Whatever was planted there by the cops and the psychologists," Berk said, his eyes still on the window behind Zachary. "Because neither of us did anything to hurt you kids. Zachary is the one who burned the house down. Why don't you ask him why he did that? He's the one that hurt everyone, destroying our home so that we had no place to live. Farming the kids out to foster care because there was no way for us to house them all."

"No," Zachary snapped. "That is just a lie. No psychologist told Tyrrell what to remember. He remembers what really happened, don't you T?"

"I… I don't know," Tyrrell said. "I remember the song. I remember us talking. About the snowman. You said we would build a snowman taller than me."

Zachary nodded. That was what they had done the morning after they were reunited. They had gone outside and built a snowman. Not taller than their heads, but it was something that had re-cemented their relationship as brothers. A shared memory and the completion of that promise from decades before.

"You *were* fighting," Tyrrell said slowly, looking at Berk. "You and Mom… over… something about Christmas. The decorations?"

Zachary opened his mouth to answer, then closed it. Tyrrell needed to remember on his own, not to have someone feeding it to him. Seeding his memories, as Berk had suggested.

"The tree," Tyrrell said, remembering. "Putting up the tree. Getting it decorated. Right?"

Zachary nodded.

Berk ran his fingers through his hair, making it stand up slightly. "Who doesn't argue over decorating the Christmas tree?" He chuckled. "You can't go by those Christmas romance movies where everyone works together to create a perfectly coordinated Christmas tree and then puts the star or angel on top in some lovely ceremony. That's just crap. It doesn't happen that way. The cords are tangled and half the lights don't work, and it's figure it out or go to the store to get more. And we didn't have money to buy more. They were all cast-offs as it was. Then you've got the kids underfoot, grabbing at everything and trying to put all of their favorites on the tree, and fighting over them and getting bloody noses. All of these stupid paper crafts from school that don't belong on a tree in the first place." He swore and rolled his eyes. "Whoever thought of Christmas trees should be shot."

As Zachary remembered it, the bloody noses hadn't been from the kids fighting with each other over tree ornaments.

54

Zachary fell back into his seat. At the mention of the paper crafts from school, he couldn't help remembering the different Christmas shapes cut out of paper with scribbles on them that he had carefully placed on the tree after everyone else had gone to bed. He'd made sure that there were ornaments created by each child on the tree in roughly equal numbers. He had spaced them around the tree, tucked them between branches, and done his very best to create that lovely Christmas-tree vision that he had seen in dopey Christmas movies on the TV.

And the paper crafts, when they had caught fire, made the whole thing go up like a torch. He saw it blazing, saw the curtains catch fire, saw dropping embers fall to the carpet and start it on fire. All around him, everything in the room had been burning. Black smoke filled his eyes and lungs, and he couldn't find his way out of the room. He had yelled his throat raw, trying to wake everyone up and get them out of the house. He had tried to squeeze himself under the couch, wrapped his arms around his face to try to create a breathable pocket of air and keep the flames from reaching his face.

"It's okay," Tyrrell said. "Zachary. Come back. It's okay."

He pulled Zachary's fingers from where they were clamped around the table and pressed a cold glass into Zachary's hand. He gulped, trying to douse the flames that singed his throat. The firemen had come. They had rescued him from the burning room and taken him to the hospital for treatment. And he had never seen his home or family again.

The drink would not put out the flames, went down hot itself but, within a few seconds, the flashback was starting to dissolve, the panic to recede. Zachary drank more, trying to wipe it all out. One day he would be able to talk about it without flashing back. Dr. B assured him of that.

One day.

"You okay?" Tyrrell sat with his hand hovering over Zachary's back, as if unsure whether he should pat or rub it, or if maybe that would make things worse.

Zachary needed to know that he was real. He grasped Tyrrell's other arm on the table, feeling the warmth and solidity of it. Not a fleeting vision. Something that was actually there in front of him. He hadn't imagined finding Tyrrell. He was right there.

"I found you," Zachary murmured. "I did. You're here."

"I'm here," Tyrrell reassured.

Berk watched them with distaste. "What a pansy! What a complete nut job I have for a son."

Zachary shook his head and let the words flow by him. What did he care what the old man said? He had not chosen to meet him again. The only reason he had searched for him was to find Tyrrell. And it had worked. He had found his brother safe and sound.

"He's not a nut job!" Tyrrell snapped back. "Do you have any idea what he's been through? He could have been killed in that fire. And then you and Mom abandoning us? How could you do that to us? How could you put us in foster care and not even care what happened to us?"

Berk shrugged, smirking again. He looked out the window, across the field, at the girls, who were now huddled in a group, getting instructions from their teacher or coach. "That was your mother's doing. Nothing to do with me. She's the one who arranged for it all. She could have taken you if she'd wanted to." His eyes left the window to focus on Zachary again. "But with one like this, why would she do that? Always in trouble. Always the first one to stick his hand in the oven or punch out a window. It's a wonder it didn't happen earlier. And the rest of you were nearly as bad. It was only a matter of time before you all followed his example. As soon as you could walk, you were all getting in trouble. The older girls…" He licked his lips. "They were different. More mature and put together. Didn't have all the issues you boys did." He rolled his eyes and swore at the memories. "Thought you must have had a missing chromosome or some-thing. One of those things that make babies be born morons."

Zachary was reeling under his words. It shouldn't have affected him, after hearing how his mother spoke about him when she had come to the hospital with Mrs. Pratt, telling them both that she wanted nothing to do with Zachary anymore. That he was hopeless, incorrigible, a discard.

Tyrrell jumped to his feet, swinging his fists and shouting at Berk. Incomprehensible, but loud, disrupting everyone's conversations. Zachary struggled to get up and stabilize himself on his feet, but was too slow and wobbly to do anything about Tyrrell's attack.

Berk stood up and just shoved Tyrrell away from him, acting bored and unconcerned with his son's reaction. The bartender and one of the waiters hurried over to put a stop to the altercation. They pulled the wildly windmilling Tyrrell back, shoving him into the wall.

"That's one," the bartender warned. "You want to get kicked out of here?"

"I'm sorry!" Tyrrell started immediately to weep messily, tears flooding down his face, mouth open, ropes of drool descending to his shirt. "What's wrong with me? Can't I do anything right?" He swore and begged for God to strike him dead. Zachary wobbled over to him and touched Tyrrell on the shoulder, trying to calm him.

"T, T, it's okay. Chill. Let's get you out of here, okay? Let's get you back somewhere you can sleep this off. You'll feel better after that."

Actually, it was doubtful that he would feel much better, but he would at least be able to stay in better control of his emotions. Zachary looked at Berk. "Where is he staying? With you?"

Berk shook his head. "In his car. Drunk tank if he gets rousted."

Zachary thought about those searches he had asked Fontaine to do to see if there were any tickets on Tyrrell's car in other cities.

"Okay, okay. I'll check you into a hotel," Zachary told Tyrrell.

On the one hand, he wanted to take Tyrrell home, to try to get him to see the benefit of getting dry and starting over again. To have him under Zachary's roof so that he knew that he was okay. But he wouldn't do that to Kenzie.

The bartender touched Zachary's arm, shaking his head. "You're not driving anywhere. Not in this condition." He'd obviously seen Zachary's flashback or staggering to his feet and thought he was impaired.

"I'm not drunk. All I had was water."

But he knew that what Tyrrell had given him to drink and to pull him out of the flashback had not been water, and they would be able to smell the whiskey on his breath.

"I'll get a ride, then. Tyrrell. Come on. Come sit over here while we wait." He tried to pull Tyrrell toward the front door. They would grab the table closest to the door to get Tyrrell away from Berk and make a quick exit.

Tyrrell protested, trying to turn back to Berk, still weeping.

"Stop it. Come on. Come sit with me while I get us a ride and get you somewhere to stay tonight."

"I want to stay with my dad."

55

Zachary shook his head slightly in disbelief. He wasn't terribly impressed with this new, drunk version of Tyrrell. He wouldn't have talked like that if he'd been sober.

"You need to come with me. I've missed you. I haven't seen you since I got out of the hospital. You didn't even come at Christmas. I thought you were going to."

Tyrrell collapsed into a chair at the table Zachary guided him to. He immediately covered his face, continuing to sob.

"I should have come! I knew I should go see you! You would be all alone at the hospital." Tyrrell gasped and blubbered. Of course, Zachary hadn't been alone for Christmas. He'd had several visitors. Christmas Day was always a new revelation to him, a testament that he could start over again, despite the black despair and certainty of disaster that plagued him as Christmas Eve approached and darkness fell.

"So come visit with me now," Zachary encouraged. "You can tell me all about it."

He could see his car parked in the lot outside the pub. He glanced over at the bartender, wondering whether he would be able to get Tyrrell out to his car and drive off before they had a chance to figure out what he was doing and write down his license plate number. But he figured his chances of accomplishing that were pretty low. The bartender was watching him like a hawk as he dried glasses and, as soon as Zachary made for the door, he was bound to approach if he didn't see someone arriving to pick them up.

He sighed, irritated, and tapped the Uber app to order a ride.

"I couldn't come," Tyrrell explained. "I was feeling so bad, and Dad would have been alone for Christmas. I couldn't leave him alone, could I?"

"Instead, you abandoned your kids? They were looking forward to spending time with you."

"I did them a favor." Tyrrell sniffled loudly. "They don't need a dad like me. A dad who can't stay sober. Who is... abusive. They're better off without someone like me. I should spend the time with him," Tyrrell indicated Berk in the back of the pub. "I'm just like him."

"You're not like him. You're nothing like him," Zachary assured him. He leaned in, trying to look Tyrrell in the face. "I've seen you with Mason and Alisha. I didn't think that you were..."

"I've never hit them. I'd never do that. But... when I've been drinking... I yell. I get really mean. I'm impatient and I say things that..." he shook his head, "I can't forgive myself for."

Verbal abuse, Zachary could believe. He was relieved that the abuse wasn't physical. But at the same time, he knew how much words could hurt. It was still his mother's words, when she had told him that he wasn't wanted, that hurt him more than remembering what his father had done to them. The words had cut him to the quick and stayed with him for his whole life. The beatings had all blurred together and faded into the background.

"They still need you. You still want to spend time with your dad, right? Even after everything he did. Even though you haven't seen him for years. Don't make your kids miss you like that."

"I'm not... I shouldn't even be their father. I can't take care of anyone else. I can't even take care of myself. Look what a great job I'm doing. Living in my car. Spending all day drinking. How is that acting like a grown adult?"

"It will be okay. Things will look better in the morning. When we get you sobered up and can have a real talk, we can work on fixing things. Getting you better."

Tyrrell smeared tears around his face. He really was a mess. "I can't do that to my kids."

"Have you done any therapy? To help you with this?"

Tyrrell shook his head. "They always said that therapy was just an excuse or a bandage. That it didn't really help. The only thing that would help me was…" he let out a long, shuddering breath, "taking responsibility for my own actions and working harder. If I just… put my mind to it, I could do better."

"Who told you that? Your foster parents?"

Tyrrell nodded.

"Well, that's totally wrong. You can't just make up your mind not to have PTSD or addiction. You can't just decide that you're never going to have any issues again. Therapy can help. It can help you work through your problems, and you can even do family therapy with the kids to improve communication. Help them to understand what's going on with you and to give you guys strategies for dealing with each other when things get too hard."

Tyrrell bowed his head, just shaking it back and forth. Zachary rubbed his back.

"Come on, T. It's going to be okay."

"I'm a failure. A complete waste of space. I've never done anything for anyone. I wish I'd died in that fire."

Zachary had wished it himself from time to time over the years, when things got really bad and, looking back over his life, he wasn't happy with how little progress he had made and all of the people he had failed. But it struck him to the heart to hear Tyrrell, his baby brother, say those words.

"Tyrrell, no. That would have killed me. I'm so glad that you all survived, and that you hunted me down and met with me, and that I got to meet all the others. That's amazing. It's amazing how you have been able to find so many people to include in your family. I never would have. I had no idea."

"I know how you talk about him, and I'm exactly the same. I'm exactly the same as him."

"No. You're not. Do you hear yourself? I was there. I remember. He beat the snot out of us. Acted like we were only there to bother him. He killed someone and went to prison for it. And you talked to Jason. You know what he did to the girls."

Tyrrell wiped his eyes and looked up at Zachary. "What? What do you mean?"

"That he…" Zachary stared into Tyrrell's eyes, hoping for some recollection so that he wouldn't have to tell Tyrrell himself. Had Jason and his sisters *not* told Tyrrell? Zachary had had to worm it out of them. Maybe Tyrrell, with Berk whispering in his ear, poisoning his mind, had not been a safe person to reveal it to.

"That he abused the girls. Touched them. I don't know how far it went; I didn't ask. That's when their mom kicked him out."

Tyrrell turned his head to look at Berk, still sitting in the back of the pub, watching them or watching the schoolgirls out the window. As if he could tell by looking at Berk whether these accusations were true.

"No, he didn't! He wouldn't do that. No one ever said anything to me about that."

"Maybe because you wouldn't listen to anything else they told you about him."

"They're making it up. Half of that stuff they're saying they just made up. Their mother, she told them all kinds of things, and they're just repeating it. They poisoned him against Berk."

"Berk is poisoning you against the rest of us."

Tyrrell stared at Zachary. He shook his head, but didn't say anything.

"Then why won't you listen to what I'm telling you? You are not like him, and you don't want to keep hanging around him and letting him influence you. Look at everything you've thrown away! Things that you worked really hard for. Stop listening to him."

"You don't know what it's like."

"To be you? No. I don't know what it's like to be you. But I know what it's like to be me. I know what it's like to have a parent who beats you like that. Two parents who beat you like that. I know what it's like to lose your wife and any chance of having a family with her. I know what it's like to grow up in foster care, being used and abused by everyone who crosses your path. And to live in places you wouldn't sentence your worst enemy to. Places where you are a number and they'll drug you out or knock you around if you step out of line."

Zachary stared back at Tyrrell, willing him to hear and understand.

"I know what it's like to be your brother, T. And I still want to be your brother. I still want to see you, whether I'm in the hospital or you are. Whether you're managing your life okay or are hitting bottom. Just like you were there for me, right?" He touched Tyrrell on the shoulder. "You've been there for me. Let me help you too."

Tyrrell sniffled and sobbed. He grabbed a handful of napkins and tried to wipe his face and clean himself up. Zachary nodded and tried to help him. "We'll do a better job at the hotel. Where is your car? Is it close by?"

"Can't drive like this," Tyrrell pointed out sensibly.

"I know that. I just mean… to get you some clothes to change into… toiletries… whatever you've got in the car."

"Oh." Tyrrell sniffled and wiped his nose. He nodded. "It's just around the corner."

"Okay. We'll have the driver stop there so you can grab your stuff."

Tyrrell nodded, his head moving up and down in an exaggerated way like a bobblehead.

Zachary watched out the window for the arrival of their ride.

56

Zachary managed to find Tyrrell's car, though it wasn't exactly where Tyrrell thought he had left it, and to get what he figured Tyrrell would need for a night or two out of it. The Uber driver watched them with suspicion but didn't drive off and leave them there.

"He'd better not throw up in here," he said as Zachary maneuvered Tyrrell back into the car after getting his things.

He hadn't had a chance to suss out how drunk Tyrrell was when they had first climbed into the car. Now, after watching Tyrrell staggering around and hearing him make repeated weepy apologies, he had an idea what he was dealing with.

"We don't have far to go," Zachary assured him, hoping that Tyrrell wasn't prone to carsickness when he was drunk. Looking at his phone, he read off the address.

The driver nodded. "That the SleepEasy?"

"Yeah."

"We'll be there in five minutes." He sounded relieved, hoping as Zachary did that with only five minutes in the car, the odds of Tyrrell not being sick were pretty good.

Zachary concentrated on keeping Tyrrell upright and calm, reassuring him that everything would be fine. He watched out the window as they moved through town. He wanted to be far enough away from the pub that Tyrrell wouldn't get it into his head to walk back there and continue drinking with Berk, but close enough that Zachary could walk or Uber back once Tyrrell was asleep to pick up his own car. Tyrrell might get a ticket if his car weren't moved in the next twenty-four hours but, from what Zachary had seen inside the car, it wouldn't be his first one.

When they pulled up to the SleepEasy, Zachary got Tyrrell out of the car, thanked the driver and made sure to tip him well and give him a good rating on the app, and went to the front desk to book a room for the day. It was too early for check-in, and the manager at the desk eyed Tyrrell dubiously.

"Rooms aren't ready yet. They still need to be cleaned. And him…" he shook his head. "I don't think so."

"He needs somewhere to sleep it off. And he couldn't care less if the room has been cleaned or not. I'll pay for last night and tonight, if that would help. On *my* credit card," he assured the man.

"We can't really do that," he said, but he started typing information into the computer. "I've got a room in the back that wasn't used last night. But you pay for two nights."

"Yes. Sure."

The man looked at Tyrrell, swaying back and forth. "You're staying with him? You'll clean up after him?"

"Yes. I'll make sure nothing is damaged or left in a mess. You can put a damage deposit on it," Zachary suggested. "Like with a non-smoking room. Pre-authorize it on my card. If anything happens, you're covered."

"If I get complaints that he's disturbing any other guests, I'll call the cops."

"Of course."

He probably wouldn't. He would probably tell them to get on their way first, and only call the cops if they refused. It was best not to have police tromping through the hotel, attracting attention and making guests think there was something wrong.

"No alcohol in the room."

"Good grief. Absolutely not!"

The man at the desk gave a slight smile of amusement.

Tyrrell seemed to focus on this part of the conversation, however. He leaned on Zachary, breathing his foul, whiskey-laden breath in Zachary's face. He could practically feel the sting of the alcohol on his skin. "Zach, Zachy. I need a drink," he said urgently.

"No, you don't, T. You can have a nap. Then when you wake up… we'll start sorting this out."

"But bro… You don't know what it's like. I can't do that. It's too late. Let's stay down here at the lounge." He motioned to the dimly lit restaurant that was clearly not open yet. "We can talk over drinks."

"We need to go up to our room first," Zachary pointed out. "Put your clothes away."

"But…"

"Shh. Let me finish booking the room." Zachary pushed Tyrrell away slightly and moved his hands over to the counter so that he still had something to stabilize him. He shook his head at the clerk. "Let's get this done as quickly as we can. Put whatever deposit you want on my credit card." He pulled it out and handed it over. "Give me a room key. And when he's down," he jerked his head in Tyrrell's direction, "I'll come back and give you whatever other information you need."

The man nodded and worked away at the computer. He looked like he was getting used to the idea now and didn't think it was such a bad one. He prepped a room key while waiting for the printer to spit out its papers, then slid one of them across the counter to Zachary to sign the credit card authorization. He had included a hefty cleaning deposit. Zachary signed it without any objection and pushed it back.

"Room 220." The clerk handed him the room key. "Come back down when you've got him settled." He looked toward the big glass doors where Zachary and Tyrrell had entered. "Do you have a car?"

"I do, but it's not here yet. I need to go pick it up later. I'll give you the details."

"Okay." The clerk raised his brows. "Good luck," he encouraged, giving a small nod.

Zachary was pleasantly surprised by his change in attitude. "Thanks."

Zachary had intentionally picked a hotel that was not expensive enough to have a stocked minibar in the room. That would have been disastrous. There was a soft drink vending machine in the hallway on their floor, so Zachary purchased several drinks and filled an ice bucket for them. It would be important to keep Tyrrell well-hydrated as he sobered up to prevent as many physical symptoms as possible.

Tyrrell complained all the way to the room about needing to go to the lounge or a bar to get another drink or to return to the pub where Berk was to keep him company.

"He gets lonely," Tyrrell told Zachary plaintively. "He's an old man and he doesn't have anyone anymore. He likes to have someone to keep him company."

"It's not a good place for you to be right now. You can send him an email or text later on when you're feeling better."

"He shouldn't be there all alone. He likes it when I'm there with him."

"I'm sure he does," Zachary agreed. To Berk, Tyrrell would be evidence that he hadn't done anything wrong. If he had been such an awful person, then would his son have wanted to sit there keeping him company? If he was a bad person, Tyrrell would want to stay as far away from him as possible. But he clearly wasn't. It wasn't his fault that he'd been abandoned by everyone else and lived a lonely existence.

But once they reached the hotel room and Zachary suggested that Tyrrell sit down, he flopped onto the bed and closed his eyes. Within a few minutes, he was snoring loudly. Zachary watched him for a few minutes, making sure that he was sleeping deeply enough not to be bothered by anything happening in the room, and also making sure that he was on his side so that if he did get sick, he wouldn't choke.

He pulled out his phone and briefly browsed through his new emails, then gave Kenzie a call.

"Hey," Kenzie answered quickly. "I thought you would be home. Everything okay?"

"Are you back from work already?" Zachary looked at the time on his phone. Kenzie had put in half a day and had returned home, thinking that they would be able to spend some time together. And the next day, they had the memorial and dinner at Mr. Peterson's. He blew out his breath, trying to decide how to handle things. "Sorry... a lot has happened. I found him."

"Your father?"

"Yes, and Tyrrell was with him."

"Oh! That's great! I'm so glad that he's okay."

"Me too." Zachary hated to think of how many times he had wondered over the past few days if he would find Tyrrell alive or whether something had happened to him. Dead by his own hand, killed in a bar fight, kidnapped and killed by a serial killer, dead in a ditch somewhere. The possibilities unrolled in a long list. All the things that could happen to a person, especially to someone who was depressed, drinking too much, and didn't care. "So... I've checked him into a hotel. Going to try to sober him up today, stay over, and then see how things go in the morning. But we've got that thing at Mr. Peterson's tomorrow."

"Yeah. You told them you'd be there, and I think it's really important to Pat."

"I'll be there. I'm just not sure whether I'll have time to drive back to get you and then back to their house. I'm not sure how long it will take to get Tyrrell upright in the morning, and I don't want to leave him by himself. If I do, he'll just go back there and start drinking again. I'll have to bring him with me."

"Oh. I see." She sounded disappointed. They didn't like to spend all night apart. Zachary tried not to do too much night surveillance, so that, other than when he was in the hospital, he was at least at Kenzie's house, even if he couldn't sleep. It was comforting for him, and he assumed for her too. "Okay. I'll drive down and meet you at the house, then."

"Good." Zachary breathed a sigh of relief that she wasn't too upset about it. "I'll get there as soon as I can, but like I say, I don't know how long it will take to get Tyrrell moving."

"I don't hear him. He's there with you?"

"Sleeping. Passed out."

"This early. He must have really been tying one on."

"Yeah. I think… that's probably all he's been doing for the past month. Just… drinking all day with Berk."

"That's strange. They… get along?"

"Yeah. I know. I can hardly stand to be near him. Berk. But Tyrrell seems to think that they're buddies. That… Berk never did anything wrong."

"He was pretty young at the time of the fire. Wasn't he just five?"

"Six. Yeah."

"He probably doesn't have very many independent memories of Berk. Just whatever he's been told."

"And between the social worker telling them that he just couldn't raise them as a single dad and Berk telling Tyrrell that everything was just peachy when we were all together… he thinks that Berk was just a victim of circumstances. He doesn't think there's anything wrong with them hanging out together. Though he's gotta know what drinking does to him! He's gone a year sober, so he knows the difference."

"Addiction is a nasty disease. Tyrrell isn't thinking about it clearly and making logical comparisons and decisions."

"He's just trying to drown himself."

"More or less… yes."

Zachary sighed. "I'm sorry I won't be home tonight."

"Me too. But you need to take care of your brother. I get that. Do you think you'll be able to get him into a program?"

"I don't know. Right now… he's fighting me every step of the way. I'm hoping that once he sobers up, it will be easier."

57

Zachary hadn't planned to sleep away from home. Still, being used to surveillance and other jobs that took him away from home occasionally, sometimes unexpectedly, he was prepared. He had a "go bag" in his car with the essentials and, while he missed not having his computer with him to get some work done, he did have his phone, which would do in a pinch.

While retrieving the car, he made a few calls to the people who might care that Tyrrell was now home and safe. Most of them were less concerned than Zachary had been, assuming that he would show up again once he got himself straightened out. Lindsey thanked him coolly and promised to let the children know he was safe. Zachary couldn't bear to think of Mason and Alisha going to school each day, not knowing whether their daddy was dead or alive. They needed to know that he was alive, if nothing else. Hopefully, they would feel better knowing that Uncle Zachary was doing his best to look after him.

Tyrrell slept for several hours but, partway through the afternoon, was beginning to sober up. He moved around restlessly, snorting and asking Zachary random questions, and eventually propped himself up in the bed, his back against the wall, looking around.

"Where are we?"

"Hotel."

"This isn't some detox program?"

Zachary looked around the room. He was pretty sure that the detox programs Tyrrell could get into did not put that much money or thought into interior decorating. Even though it was an inexpensive hotel chain, they still had paintings on the wall, coordinated furniture, and a carpeted floor. Zachary assumed that detox rooms would be more like the institutions he had spent time in. Easily wipeable aluminum and melamine furniture. Tile floors. Plain white or green walls and acoustic tile ceilings. No artwork unless there was some mural painted by previous residents as part of their therapy. Such things made a good impression on donors and administrators.

"It's a hotel room."

"So I can go?"

"Where are you going to go? Back to the pub to start drinking again? At least spend a few hours with me sober and tell me about what's going on with you."

Tyrrell rolled his eyes and made a face. Clearly, being sober and talking about himself were two things he did not want to do.

"I missed you at Christmas," Zachary said. "I was expecting to see you. You were going to come with Heather and Joss."

"Yeah, I meant to… but things didn't work out that way."

"You said in your letter—which you could have given to me instead of sliding it under my apartment door—that you were going to wait until after Christmas to… do whatever it was you were planning on doing. Is this it? You just wanted to go off and drink yourself silly with Berk?"

"You don't know what it's like."

"Then tell me. I'm asking."

"I couldn't. Things happened. Just like with you, you wanted to be able to stay home for Christmas with Kenzie, but that didn't work out either."

Zachary nodded. That was the truth. He had hoped that he would be able to hang on, to tough it out at home as Christmas Eve approached. He had managed to stay out of the hospital the year before, with Kenzie and Tyrrell to lean on, but it had been close. He had hoped to build on that success but, instead, he had ended up crashing sooner than expected. With the virus and the anti-viral treatment protocol, his physical reserves had been wiped out, which had a significant impact on his mental and emotional state. Then going off of his meds while at the Lodge, and all of the stuff that had happened with Bridget and the twins—there had been no way. There had just been too much for him to deal with, and he had spiraled down into depression and suicidal thoughts much faster than expected.

"Yeah. You can't control life circumstances. Or mental health. Sometimes… things just happen and you lose control."

Tyrrell nodded eagerly at this. "Exactly," he agreed. "And it was just too hard. I couldn't deal with it all. I couldn't wait until Christmas. I just had to… escape."

"Your letter sounded suicidal. Were you? Or were you just planning to go see Berk all along?"

Tyrrell looked around the room again as if he expected something to have changed. He sucked his cheeks in, considering Zachary's question.

"I don't know. I was down, and struggling, but it was more… the temptation to drink than to kill myself."

"You really scared me. I thought that you were dead somewhere. No one had seen you. You hadn't been in contact with anyone or told them where you were going. The last communication I had from you… it sounded like you intended to commit suicide. I thought we had lost you."

Tyrrell thumped the mattress beside him with his thumbs. "It would have been better if I had. Then at least, this would all be over. I'd be done trying to fight it. To keep it from everybody. I wouldn't have any more responsibilities. I could just… not exist."

"This isn't the end. I know you're feeling pretty bad right now, but that doesn't mean things won't get better. When I'm in the hospital, in the psych ward and it's Christmas Eve, or a few days before that, I can't see any hope. I can't see any light at the end of the tunnel, just darkness in every direction. What would you tell me?"

Tyrrell sighed. "That things would be better after Christmas. You'd start feeling better again and be able to go on. But there is no Christmas for me, Zachary. There isn't one magical day when I'm going to start feeling better again. I'm just going to keep feeling bad, and keep fighting the cravings, and keep giving in. And then feeling worse for giving in. There is no getting better."

"You were doing better. You were sober for a year. Longer than that. You were seeing the kids, and working, and you had your own place. You had me and the others to talk to."

"It's all temporary. It never lasts. The longest I ever lasted was when I was at college. That's some kind of joke, isn't it? Most kids go away to college and binge drink. I go to college and stay sober. Some kind of backward. But in the end… what did that matter? I can't use my degree. I can't even stay sober when I know all the stuff I learned about addiction for my degree. I should be able to overcome this."

"Knowing what addiction is doesn't change what you went through as a kid. It doesn't change your genes. It doesn't change the cravings to go back to—" Zachary cut himself off, realizing that he was talking about his own addiction rather than Tyrrell's. "You need help. You need to get into a program. Do you go to AA? Do you have a sponsor?" Zachary hadn't seen anything in his email that seemed to indicate a sponsor in the wings.

"No. We studied that in school. There are a lot of different programs that can help; AA isn't the only one. Not everyone believes in abstinence. People have been successful with moderation."

Zachary resisted asking how that approach had worked for Tyrrell. "Maybe you need more than that. A support network. Instead of hiding your drinking from everyone, be honest and talk about how hard it is, and how you're doing, and what is or isn't working. Just dropping out of sight like that... deciding you couldn't handle it and going to drink with Berk instead of fighting it anymore... it wasn't just hard on me. Mason was crushed. Alisha too. They need their dad. Even if you're not perfect. Even if you screw up sometimes."

"Screw up sometimes," Tyrrell snapped. "You have no idea. Screw up all the time. You think you know what it's been like, but you don't. You don't know what it's like to be a dad, and to see that you just can't do it. That you're a failure at it and just end up hurting your kids."

Tyrrell held his head. Zachary had picked up a bottle of Tylenol at the nearby convenience store, and nudged it in Tyrrell's direction. There was a glass of water waiting on the nightstand beside it. Tyrrell shook his head.

58

Tyrrell just stayed there, hunched over, his hands over his face and fingers pressed into his temples for a long time, not moving or saying anything.

"He's a good guy, Zachary," he protested, as if Zachary had been lecturing him on how he needed to stay away from Berk. Which Zachary wished that he could do, but he knew only too well how Tyrrell would receive it. Like Rhys, Tyrrell wouldn't take Zachary's advice as to whom he should stay away from. "He really is. He's a lonely old man, and I like being with him, and the way he talks about how things were when we were young."

"I know you remember them fighting."

"But everyone fights. You and Bridget fought."

Which didn't exactly recommend the practice.

"How much do you remember?" Zachary tried to keep his voice neutral. To invite Tyrrell to tell him about it rather than suggesting he would confront Tyrrell over any detail he got wrong, that he was just looking for an opening to jump all over him because of his choices.

"I remember…" Tyrrell's brow furrowed.

For a long time, he was silent. Zachary looked down at his phone and waited. They had all night and into the next morning if they needed it. Zachary could wait until Tyrrell was ready to share.

"I remember things differently… when I'm with you than when I'm with him."

"Which one do you think is right?"

"When I'm with you, or with Heather or Joss, then I know what happened and how abusive he was, and I remember specific things. And that makes me feel *worse*. I don't want to be like him. But I can't help it. It's built into me. All of his shortcomings. I see myself and the way that I treat my kids, and I know that I'm a monster on the inside, just like him."

"You're not a monster. And you're not like him."

"He's an alcoholic."

"Yes."

"Just like me. And he was… he was abusive."

Zachary nodded.

"And I am too. You think I don't see the hurt and fear in my own kids' eyes? The way that they look at me and expect me to explode and to get after them, maybe even to hurt them. I can see that in their eyes."

"But you haven't. You haven't hit them." If Tyrrell was telling the truth about that part. "Nothing we could ever do would stop him from hitting us. You're not like that. You care about your kids."

"He does too. You haven't heard the way that he talks about us, about how he loved us when we were all at home."

Zachary searched his memory for any recollection of tenderness from his father. There had been the occasional happy interlude when Berk had decided to teach him how to make a paper airplane or lift a candy bar from the store. But tenderness? He couldn't remember Berk ever tucking him into bed. Or telling him he had done something well. Maybe that was just Zachary. Maybe he was the only one who couldn't do anything right.

"T… I don't know. I don't think he's telling you the truth. He might like hanging out with you and drinking, but when we were kids…" Zachary trailed off. "He says he loved us?" He shook his head. "I don't know, I don't think he did. We were in the way, and he said so plenty of times. When I was in foster care, I wondered why they'd had so many kids. Why they didn't just stop at one or two, and maybe that wouldn't have been so hard for them to manage."

Tyrrell frowned at Zachary, unsure where he was going with it.

"I think it was the money. Claiming more dependents. Being able to qualify for food programs, get lower taxes, and get into city programs that were subsidized. I think… the only reason they kept having children was to take advantage of the financial programs."

"That doesn't make sense," Tyrrell said.

Zachary shrugged. "I don't know. I never had any kids that I could make claims against. I don't know how it all works."

Tyrrell shook his head stubbornly. "No. You're wrong. He cared about us."

"Like he did Jason and his sisters? Dropping in on them every now and then, beating on their mom, and then taking off again? Molesting the girls?"

"That's not what happened. You need to listen to him tell about it."

"You can't believe what he says. He's just trying to make himself look better."

"Jason and the girls are the ones making up stories."

"Why would they? What do they get out of telling you about it?"

"Sympathy. They just want... they didn't want me to have anything to do with Dad, so they made up stories about him."

"What they said about the abuse *weren't* stories. Ask Joss and Heather if you don't believe me. They remember more than I do."

Tyrrell rolled his head back, banging it into the wall. Zachary winced in sympathy. Tyrrell rubbed his forehead slowly, the headache obviously bothering him. But he still didn't take the proffered Tylenol and water.

"You said that when you're around us, you remember," Zachary said. "So you know it's true. You know he wasn't the kind of dad who was just happy to be home with his kids at the end of the day. He was the kind of dad who wanted his beer and his easy chair and the remote, and if anyone got between him and one of those things..."

"I know," Tyrrell moaned. "I know you're telling the truth. But... I like the way he talks about it better. It's like... he had a family that meant something to him. That I was his son and he was proud of me."

"You know it's all lies. That what you remember when you're with us is the truth."

"A person can have too much truth," Tyrrell said, his tone angry. "There are times when it's just too much. When we were in that cabin, and I remembered what he was like, and I saw how I was with my kids... I just couldn't take it."

Zachary swallowed, feeling guilty. They had invited Tyrrell to the Lodge. He and Kenzie had no idea that being with Zachary stirred up negative memories and emotions in Tyrrell. He had never mentioned it before.

It was Zachary's fault that Tyrrell had started drinking again.

His fault that Tyrrell had been in a cabin stocked with alcohol.

His fault that Tyrrell could not be around Zachary without thinking about their past and comparing himself to their father. Thinking himself a failure because he was not patient enough. Not perfect.

"T… I'm sorry. Neither of us meant for that to happen. It was just supposed to be a nice family vacation."

"I know. I'm the one who wrecked it. Not you."

But Zachary couldn't help but see his own fault in it. "We need to get you dried out. Get you back in recovery again," he told Tyrrell. "You want to be able to see the kids again, don't you? To be a part of their life? No matter what our dad chose to do, you can still choose for yourself. Don't abandon them like our parents abandoned us."

Tyrrell started to cry again. Not the messy, loud weeping he had done when drunk to the gills. But tears ran silently down his cheeks and he stared at the wall opposite him, looking hopeless. He sniffled and his breaths shuddered.

"I love my kids. I do."

"I know. That's why you need to do what you can to get your life under control again. I'll help you all I can. But you have to let me know if what I'm doing is making things worse, because I don't want that."

"The best thing for them is if I just stay out of their lives."

"No. You know how much that hurts."

"They still have their mom. They can grow up to be normal. Not *damaged* like me."

Zachary shook his head, frustrated. He knew he couldn't talk a drunk into sobering up. He shouldn't even be trying. Tyrrell had to decide for himself if that was what he wanted.

"How about we order in something to eat?" he suggested. "How long has it been since you ate something solid?"

Tyrrell snorted. "Look at yourself before asking that question."

"I'm going to eat too. Come on, let's just relax for a while. No pressure. No lectures. Let's just be together for a while."

"Okay," Tyrrell agreed with a sigh. "We could just go downstairs. There was a restaurant…"

"No." Zachary wanted to keep Tyrrell away from alcohol as much as he could.

But if Tyrrell didn't see the light pretty soon, Zachary was going to lose his chance.

59

They ordered pizza. Tyrrell would eat and seem fine and cheerful for a few minutes. Then he would break down again, holding his head, weeping, rocking back and forth and explaining to Zachary how horrible he felt about everything he had done, both to his kids and to Zachary and the rest of his family and friends when he had disappeared without telling anyone what was going on. Eventually, the tears would wind down again. He would be calm, blow his nose, maybe even laugh at himself in a sad, regretful way, and then have another slice or a few more bites before breaking down again.

Zachary watched and listened patiently, wondering how much was emotional and how much was the result of the alcohol and maybe other drugs he had taken and the effects of withdrawing them from his body.

And then Tyrrell slept.

He was clearly exhausted by all the crying and emotion and, since he was in a safe place with a full stomach, his brain decided it was time to shut off and just let Tyrrell heal for a while. Zachary watched the TV with the volume low. He texted with Kenzie and a few others, rotating from one conversational thread to another.

His phone started to buzz and, looking down at the screen, Zachary saw that it was a call coming through rather than a text.

Lindsey.

He connected the call. "Lindsey?"

"Zachary. Umm… hi. Is it a good time?"

Zachary nodded. As long as he kept his voice low, Tyrrell would not be disturbed by their call. "Sure. He's asleep."

"I know I was short with you when you called, and I'm sorry about that."

"It's okay. He's put you through the wringer just as much as he has me. More so; this isn't the first time that you've had to deal with it, and you have the kids to worry about too, and their feelings and reactions."

"Yeah. It's hell. Christmas this year was…" She sighed. "More tears than I can remember for any other Christmas. They didn't want anything except their dad."

"I'm sorry about that. I wouldn't even have called you, because I know you don't want to have to deal with his stuff, and it isn't your responsibility to make sure that he is safe or that he isn't drinking or anything like that. But I thought… you deserved to know that he was safe. And for the kids to know that he was… still alive."

"I appreciate that. I know I was a grouch with you. When you came here to talk to me too. It's just that this keeps coming up over and over. It isn't something that we can ever leave behind, and it wears me down so much."

"Yeah. I can believe it." Zachary himself was exhausted. Worse than when he was fighting his own demons. At least then, when his body finally gave in, he could sleep. But he didn't want to go to sleep while he was looking after Tyrrell, in case Tyrrell woke up and decided to go down to the lounge or to disappear again. Zachary had to be vigilant and watch over his brother. Even though logically, he knew he couldn't stay awake forever and couldn't actually stop Tyrrell from doing anything if he put his mind to it. Tyrrell was bigger than Zachary and his desperation would make him stronger than ever. There was no way for Zachary to physically overcome him. He just hoped that he could keep talking to Tyrrell and get through to him.

"Okay, well… I just wanted you to know that I appreciate what you've done and letting us know that he is okay. I'm sure that Tyrrell appreciates it too." Then she seemed to reconsider what she had said and laughed. "Or not. He isn't exactly appreciative when someone tries to change his mind or tells him he is drinking too much."

Zachary chuckled. "No. He hasn't exactly thanked me."

She laughed again, rueful.

"Lindsey… I hope you don't mind me asking, and if you don't want to answer, that's fine. I'm just wondering if you can tell me anything about his drinking. When it started, or when you figured it out. If his relapses are triggered by anything in particular."

"He tends to get triggered by the kids," Lindsey sighed. "And trust me, you do not want your kids trying to take responsibility for their dad's alcoholism. They think that if they just do everything right, he won't start drinking again. And, of course, that's not true. He'll always go back to drinking, whatever they do. But it is true that it's usually something to do with the kids, their behavior, home stresses, that triggers him."

"That's not their fault. He has a lot of family stuff he's trying to process. From when he was a kid."

"I know. You know, when we first met, I didn't know about any of that stuff. I thought that the Millers were his real parents and that he'd had a normal childhood, a brother and a sister, and that everything about his past was normal. I didn't know anything about the abuse and the fire and his other siblings until after we got married. Even that he'd been in foster care. He kept it all away from me."

Zachary tried to picture that. "Wow. I don't know how I would ever do that."

"He's a master at covering things up. I didn't know anything about the drinking for the first few years we were married. I knew that he had mood swings, that he went through these dark periods when he was thinking about his past, but I had no idea he was drinking."

Zachary had assumed from what Tyrrell had said and his cheerful disposition that the alcoholism he'd mentioned was years in the past, something that he had suffered with as a teenager and long since overcome. Tyrrell had fooled him too.

"When did you finally find out?"

"When Mason was born."

Zachary knew there was more and waited for the story.

"I had a lot of problems with the pregnancy and Mason was premature. We almost lost him. He was born so early and they didn't know if he would make it. I was sick and sore and trying so hard to hold on to that tiny little baby. And Tyrrell just disappeared."

They both breathed for a few seconds, thinking about that. Zachary tried to picture it. He'd been in the NICU with Bridget's twins in December, so it wasn't hard to visualize Lindsey beside an incubator with a tiny baby struggling to live. How much she had needed Tyrrell's help and support, and instead, he had taken off.

"He said he needed to go to the restroom… and then he never came back. I was frantic. I thought he'd had a stroke or something. Got mugged, maybe, or hit his head. I couldn't wrap my mind around the idea that he would just walk out of the NICU and walk out of the hospital and disappear, leaving me there to deal with Mason's care and the doctors. Everything on me."

"That must have been awful."

"It was. I already had a toddler at home; my mom was looking after Alisha. Here I was with a second baby in the NICU and a missing husband. I reported him missing, and the police believed it. They didn't believe that a young husband with a brand-new baby struggling to survive in the hospital would just take off. We all thought that something horrible must have happened to him."

"It did," Zachary pointed out. "Just not what you thought. Or when you thought."

She blew out her breath in a whistle. "I suppose so. I never thought about it that way. But at the time, we had no idea about his alcoholism or all the stuff from his past. I knew by then that he'd had some challenges as a teenager, but that's all. The rest didn't come out until later… after he reappeared."

"He came back on his own?"

"He always has, sooner or later. There's really no point in trying to short-circuit the process. Sorry." She obviously knew that was exactly what Zachary was trying to do. "I think he just has to go through it. Travel through the darkness to wherever it is he can find some peace for a little while."

"Yeah." That had been Zachary's experience with his cyclical depression as well. No amount of new medication or therapy seemed to be able to cut it off. Certainly no amount of wishing or arguing about it. His brain was just going to keep putting him through the process over and over again, year after year.

"The police couldn't find any sign of him. They were really ticked when he showed up again. More than I was, even. I was so relieved, because I'd thought that something had happened to him. He was dead in a ditch somewhere. I was just so relieved that he was back in one piece. I was happy to take him back and pick up where we had left off. Pretend that it hadn't happened and that we had weathered the storm together. That was probably a mistake. I should have had a big blow-up with him then. Laid it all on the line and told him that wasn't an acceptable response to stress. Instead, I made it okay, and so he kept doing it."

"I doubt it made any difference whether you accepted it or not," Zachary disagreed. "He's not an alcoholic because he chooses to be."

"He chooses his actions, no matter what his genes or his traumatic past are. Where were you this December?"

Zachary was startled by the question, which seemed to come out of left field.

"Uh… in the hospital."

"Voluntary, right?"

Zachary nodded, his mouth dry, and managed to make a noise of acknowledgment that she could hear.

"When you have your problems, you know to go to the hospital and they'll help you. He could do the same thing when he wants to escape and is thinking about drinking again. He could go to AA or a treatment program or to the hospital. He's had a dozen therapists in the time we were married. He could go to any one of them and get help. But he doesn't. It's easier to run away and hide. Have his little fantasy and pretend that he doesn't have any responsibilities."

"Did you have any idea that he'd been drinking with his—our—biological father?"

There was a pause as she processed this. "Are you kidding me?" she asked in disgust. "Talk about dysfunctional. That's just sick. Why would he?"

"I guess because Berk likes to drink and likes to hang out with Tyrrell and tell him about how much he loves his kids and that back when we lived at home, everything was hunky-dory."

"And Tyrrell needs to hear that he wasn't rejected."

"I guess so." Zachary wouldn't mind hearing from one of his parents that he wasn't a total failure, wasn't incorrigible as his mother had told him all those years ago. But at the same time, he wouldn't want to be around either one of them. Just seeing his father had been creepy and uncomfortable.

But however much Tyrrell needed to hear that he was loved and accepted by his father, he also needed to know that he wasn't Berk, that he wasn't doing the things his father had done to traumatize them in the first place.

"Well… I'm glad he has you," Lindsey said. "There probably isn't anyone who can understand him better."

60

When Zachary hung up after talking to Lindsey on the phone, he just sat for a long time staring into space. He didn't look down at his phone when it buzzed as responses from his various conversations arrived. After a while, the alerts ceased, and he was alone with his thoughts and Tyrrell sleeping on the bed.

He knew now what had triggered Tyrrell to start drinking again and what had triggered this disappearance. What had made him go running again, not even able to wait until after Christmas so that he could see the kids and have a nice holiday with them.

And both were Zachary's fault.

Tyrrell had started drinking because they had thought that it was a good idea to stay at the cabin together for Thanksgiving. Tyrrell had been forced to sit in the same cabin and the same room as Zachary, reliving his traumatic childhood memories, while at the same time trying to deal with his own children's increasing demands in the middle of a power blackout.

And as if starting him drinking again after a year of sobriety weren't enough, Zachary had triggered his escape response by placing Tyrrell back in the NICU. Zachary had unintentionally pulled his own disappearing act when he left psych and went down to the NICU to keep watch over Bridget's twins. And when Kenzie had figured out where he was, she had brought Tyrrell with her. They had left him to watch over and protect the babies while Zachary went down to the cafeteria with Kenzie to eat and talk things through. All of the responsibility for not just one tiny, vulnerable infant landed on Tyrrell's shoulders, but for two of them.

Tyrrell had done well. He should have been proud of himself. But being in the NICU with the twins must have triggered flashbacks to Mason's life hanging by a thread in the NICU when he had been born. Tyrrell felt all of the responsibilities and his inadequacies closing in around him and did what he had done then—run away and hidden from them.

And that was all on Zachary.

Just as the break-up of the family had been Zachary's fault when his ill-considered decorating of the tree and lighting the candles had resulted in the devastating house fire. He couldn't blame that on anyone but himself.

Zachary watched Tyrrell breathing, his chest rising and falling rhythmically. Zachary's heart hurt and he wished that he were home with Kenzie and didn't need to think about all the bad things that had happened not just to Tyrrell, but to all of his family because of what Zachary had done. Even Berk being free of his first family, able to hook up with Jason's mother and to have a second family and wreak havoc in their lives.

All harm caused by Zachary's choices.

61

Zachary hadn't been thinking about clothing appropriate for a memorial service when he had gone looking for Berk, nor when he and Tyrrell had picked up clothes from Tyrrell's car before going to the hotel. And of course, a suit wasn't something packed in his go bag in the car. Come to think of it, he probably didn't even own a suit. He couldn't remember the last time he had worn one. If he'd been thinking about the memorial service, he would have at least packed a nice button-up shirt and something other than blue jeans.

But by the time he could get Tyrrell out of the hotel and hit the road, he was already worried about making it to the memorial service on time. Tyrrell had slept heavily and been difficult to waken, even late in the morning. And he'd been in a foul mood when he'd gotten up; grumpy, with a hangover and plans to start drinking again as soon as possible to combat these conditions.

It took a while to talk him down and get some food and water in him. He explained about going to the memorial service being put on by Pat and Lorne. He coaxed Tyrrell into going as a show of support. Lorne had said that Tyrrell was family, and Zachary did his best to use Tyrrell's hunger for another family to get him to agree to go to the memorial with Zachary rather than just heading back to the pub where he knew his father would be drinking.

But they were finally headed south, Zachary keeping one eye on the time and the other on the speedometer.

He had hit the edge of town and was only a few minutes from the house when Kenzie called. Zachary glanced at the phone screen and answered on Bluetooth.

"Zachary." She sounded relieved that he had answered. "I was getting worried. Are you going to make it?"

"I'll be there within five minutes. I'm in town."

"Oh, good. I'll see you in a few minutes, then."

Zachary said goodbye and hung up. Tyrrell was wearing sunglasses, but he rubbed his forehead like he was still getting a headache from the sun.

"How long is this going to be?"

"I don't know. I suspect an hour or something like that. And then we'll have a break before supper. If you want to get in a nap."

He couldn't see why Tyrrell would need a nap after how much he had slept since leaving the pub but, if he was withdrawing from the alcohol, maybe he would just want to sleep.

"Don't want a nap," Tyrrell growled.

He didn't say the other part of the equation that Zachary heard in his head. All Tyrrell wanted was a drink. And if Tyrrell was determined, there wasn't anything Zachary could do to stop him. He had agreed to attend the memorial out of consideration for Lorne and Pat. Zachary wasn't sure whether he could prevail on Tyrrell to stick around the rest of the afternoon and have dinner with them as well. Tyrrell's car was still back in Riverbrook, but that wouldn't stop him from walking or catching an Uber to whatever watering hole was closest.

Zachary glanced sideways at him but didn't say anything.

In a few minutes, they were at the Peterson home. Zachary couldn't park as close to it as he usually could. There were a lot of unfamiliar vehicles parked along the curbs, which meant that they had a good number of people for the memorial. He was glad that they would have a lot of support.

He couldn't help remembering the protests, the media attention, and the window broken by a rock when word of Jose's disappearance and the possibility of a serial killer targeting gay men had hit the news. A horrible note had been wrapped around the rock, ranting about how people didn't want a gay couple living in their neighborhood. Even though Mr. Peterson and Pat had lived there happily for over a decade already. Mr. Peterson had told him that it was just hate mail from a stranger, that he knew it wasn't from anyone who actually lived there. And he seemed to have been right. There didn't seem to be any lasting bad feelings against them from the neighbors. Zachary just hoped that the memorial for Jose would not cause a backlash.

They were met in front of the house by Mr. Peterson, who smiled broadly upon seeing them and gave Zachary a hug. "Glad you made it! Cutting it a little close."

"Sorry, we got away late."

Zachary was glad to see that Mr. Peterson was not dressed in a tux or something fancy or formal. He knew that the group of men had attended musical performances together, some of them very classy, and he'd been a bit worried that all the guests would be dressed formally except for him. But Mr. Peterson was in slacks and a polo, with a warm coat thrown over top. No tie. No tails.

Mr. Peterson offered Tyrrell a hug too, and the two men clasped, murmuring to each other. Mr. Peterson directed them around to the backyard.

Zachary knew Pat was a gardener and kept up the flower borders in the front yard, but he had never spent time in the backyard. It was Pat's space, and Zachary usually spent time indoors with Mr. Peterson. They talked, looked at each others' photography, and ate.

He had expected the backyard to be plain and bleak in the winter. Yard and trees decked with snow. But the yard was very large and looked almost like a fairyland with ornate arches, winding paths, decorative rock piles, and trees cut in topiary shapes. The trees and branches, the bones of the yard, all seemed to work together. There were a couple of circular areas that he thought must be ponds or water features during the warmer months. Although it was only mid-afternoon, the clouds and shorter winter days meant that the daylight was already fading, but the yard was not dark and gloomy. White twinkle lights were wrapped around every tree, fence, and arch, and the pathways were lighted by lines of tiny lanterns.

"Whoa." Zachary stopped and stared at the yard, spellbound. He felt like a child seeing his first electric train set. After a moment of Zachary standing there, frozen on the path, Tyrrell tugged on his arm.

"Let's keep moving. We don't want to block anyone behind us. Looks like everyone is gathering over there."

There was an open area where chairs had been set out. Not cold metal chairs, but cushioned, and the snow on the ground had been partially cleared so that people wouldn't be sitting with their feet in the snow.

"Go ahead," Zachary told Tyrrell. He patted his pockets until he located his camera. He was oblivious to anyone around him while he checked the settings and started snapping photos, capturing each part of the yard before the light changed. As he finished up and headed back toward the seating area, his path was blocked by a large, broad-chested man.

Zachary blinked, looked up, and focused on Pat's face. Pat smiled and gave him a brief hug. "We're getting ready to start."

"This is beautiful. It must have taken you hours."

Pat nodded. "Thank you. I'm so glad you could make it. Thanks for making the time."

Thinking of Jose, the man he had sacrificed so much to find, even if it was in death, Zachary gave Pat another hug, patting him on the back. "Of course. Tyrrell is here too, and Kenzie got here ahead of us…"

Pat nodded, eyes twinkling. He pointed out Kenzie and Tyrrell in the seated audience. "Kenzie's right there, saving you a seat."

Zachary quickly joined her, feeling a little embarrassed that he was one of the last few stragglers to make it to his seat. But he'd had to get some pictures before the light faded.

"Isn't it beautiful?" Kenzie whispered as Zachary sat down next to her. "Who would ever have thought a garden could be so beautiful in the middle of Vermont winter?"

"Pat is amazing."

"He really has a knack."

Pat stood in front of the audience, Mr. Peterson at his side, and welcomed everyone out. Zachary's focus quickly drifted from Pat, taking in the whole of the garden once more and then looking around at the audience. He recognized Eric Naylor from the clothing store and a few other people that he thought were neighbors he had seen around before but, on the whole, he didn't know Pat's and Lorne's friends. Kenzie tilted her head toward a couple of women on the front row, one close to Pat's age and one older. His sister and mother. Zachary was glad that they had come to support Pat, especially considering the number of years he had been an outcast from the family. But things had changed after his father had died, and he had been able to recommence a relationship with Suzanne and Gretta. Gretta good-humoredly referred to Zachary as her grandson, and he didn't object. Pat really had been like another father to him from the time he and Mr. Peterson had started seeing each other when Zachary was a teenager.

"Glad they're here," Zachary whispered.

He tried to catch the thread of what was being said about Jose, but couldn't focus on it.

His eyes were pulled back to Naylor, and he remembered interviewing the man in his store, confronting him with his relationship with Jose. But Naylor hadn't been the killer. He wasn't the one who had kidnapped and tortured Jose. And Zachary.

Zachary's breath caught in his throat as he was pulled down into those memories. He closed his eyes to shut them out, but that never worked. He floated, anchorless, above his body as Archuro worked over him.

There was a hand on the back of his neck, a light touch, bringing him back to himself.

"You okay?" Kenzie whispered.

Zachary nodded. He leaned forward with his elbows on his knees, staring down at the frozen ground. Kenzie rubbed the back of his neck and ran her fingers over the short, stubbly hair at the back of his skull. She knew he liked it, that it was a safe touch. He put one hand on her knee and she put her other hand over it, warm and comforting.

Zachary didn't hear much of what was said. It was too hard to listen to them talk about Jose without picturing what had been done to him. Archuro had described his rituals to Zachary in graphic detail, so Zachary knew. He breathed slowly, trying to keep nausea at bay.

It was definitely getting colder as the memorial drew to a close, despite the padded seats and cleared ground. Zachary was getting stiff from sitting there in the cold and holding himself tense.

He lifted his camera as Pat opened a small container the size of a perfume bottle and sprinkled it in front of him slowly, so that the contents were caught by the wind. The fine powder sparkled in the lights. Zachary wondered whether ashes always did that, or whether Pat had mixed glitter in with them. The effect was magical, and everyone seemed to be holding their breaths until it dissipated. There was music and there might have been a prayer. Eventually, everyone was standing up, talking and preparing to say their goodbyes.

"Do you want to go inside?" Kenzie suggested. "We'll have the chance to visit later when it's just us."

"Yeah. Let's do that," Zachary agreed.

He and Kenzie and Tyrrell retreated to the house to let the rest of the mourners finish paying their respects.

62

Pat and Mr. Peterson seemed worn out after the memorial and decided on naps before supper. Kenzie asked if she could get supper together for everyone.

"No, no," Pat told her. "I made everything ahead. I'll just warm it when I get up. I won't sleep for long. It's just been… a very emotional day. I need some time."

"I'm quite capable of warming up," Kenzie persisted. "If you just point me at what you want me to do, I'm happy to help."

Pat shook his head firmly. "You guys could probably use some time to decompress too. Don't worry about it." Closing the conversation, Pat turned toward the bedroom where Mr. Peterson had already retired. He stopped and turned back to Zachary. "Zach… did you get any footage of me sprinkling the ashes? The videographer said that the light was too low for him to get anything clear."

Zachary nodded. "I'll borrow Mr.—Lorne's computer and see how it looks. I can play with the lighting and contrast and see how much I can bring out."

"No rush. But that would be great if you were able to get anything."

That gave Zachary something to do while the others napped. Even Tyrrell said that his head was killing him and he hoped a nap would help. Zachary directed him to the guest bedroom and was glad not to have to babysit him to keep him from looking through the cupboards for anything to drink. Kenzie curled up on the couch and was snoring softly within a few minutes.

The aroma of creamy chicken soup and what smelled like fresh garlic toast eventually tempted Zachary away from fine-tuning the video on Mr. Peterson's computer and back out where the others were gathered.

The table had been set, probably by Kenzie, and Pat was setting out the serving dishes. He grinned at Zachary. "Was it the garlic bread?"

Zachary looked at Kenzie, feeling himself flush. "Are you telling all my weaknesses now?"

"To Patrick? Yes. Definitely."

They all laughed. In a few minutes, they were seated around the table, hungrily inhaling the savory smells. Zachary looked surreptitiously at Tyrrell, remembering the night before and how Tyrrell kept breaking down as they were eating the pizza. He seemed much more stable today, and Zachary hoped that was a good sign. Tyrrell didn't show any signs of breaking down in front of the others.

He was good at hiding his feelings.

Mr. Peterson raised a water glass—there wasn't any wine on the table as there usually was—and waited for silence. "To family," he said simply. "Even if none of you around this table are related to me by blood, you are still my family. Thank you so much for sharing this day with us."

Zachary nodded. They all raised their glasses, then drank.

Tyrrell set his glass back down on the table and looked at it. His gaze was so intense that everyone around the table was drawn to look at him. He noticed their gazes and tried to laugh it off, leaning back in his chair and looking away.

"How can this be a family?" he asked after a minute, while everyone sipped spoonfuls of the soup. "None of us grew up together. The only ones related are Zachary and I, and we've only known each other for a year. How can this feel more like a family than the people I was raised by or people who share my DNA?"

"Because we care about each other," Pat offered. "No one here expects anyone else to be perfect or to carry the full load. We all… choose to be here and to support each other."

Tyrrell dragged his spoon through his soup, but didn't raise it to his mouth. "I don't think you'd feel the same way if you knew all the stuff that I've done."

"We all have regrets."

Tyrrell shook his head. "I'm not talking about 'regrets.' I'm talking about really bad stuff. Hurting people. Disappointing everyone. Abandoning all my responsibilities. And more. If you knew… I don't think you would feel the same way."

Pat looked at Mr. Peterson. He was the one who had experience as a foster parent. Experience dealing with hurt kids. Mr. Peterson took a few sips of his soup, pondering on it.

"Tyrrell… I'll bet that no one is harder on you than you are yourself."

"No one else knows everything," Tyrrell pointed out. "So how could they be?"

"Even if we knew all of the details, we wouldn't be as hard on you as you are."

"I know what I deserve. And it isn't to sit around a table like this and be counted as family."

"You don't have to earn it. You're family just because you are who you are. And because of the kindness you have shown to Zachary and to us. Look… I dealt with a lot of kids in the years Lilith and I fostered. And they were always hard on themselves and didn't believe they were worth anything. Being discarded by your family or being taken away from them causes a wound. They all came to us broken. Not a single one was untouched by it. What you went through was traumatic." Lorne's gaze shifted to Zachary. "We had hoped to be able to do something for Zachary, but he was one of the most traumatized kids we ever took, and we couldn't keep him. It was too much for my wife and she was concerned about possible danger to the other kids in the home. We just didn't have the resources to help him."

Tyrrell nodded, already aware of this history. "Yeah."

"You came from that same home. I doubt if you were any less traumatized than he was."

"He was ten. I was only six. He'd had to go through a lot more than I did."

"You came from the same place. You were both harmed."

"Vinny and me are only two years apart. And he's just fine. He grew up just like a normal kid in a normal family."

"He probably has a number of issues too. Maybe better hidden. But even kids as young as he was when he was removed are likely to have issues. Did you ever get any treatment?"

"Like therapy? My mom and dad didn't really believe in it. I went through other programs. Like boot camps and addiction treatment programs. I was usually doing pretty good when I graduated from them. But once I was back with the family again, things just fell apart." He pushed the soup bowl away from him, the soup untouched. "That just goes to prove that I was the problem. Not the Millers. Not the home that I came from. Me. Because whenever I was on my own, things went sideways."

"You need support. It's not too late to start therapy now. And AA or another addiction program."

"They've never stuck."

Mr. Peterson sighed and looked down at his meal, brows knit together.

"And maybe they never will," Zachary said. "Am I ever going to stop being depressed? Getting suicidal before the anniversary of the fire? I don't know. I'm not counting on it." He looked at Kenzie, who seemed ready to argue the point. "I'm getting more engaged in the therapy now. Choosing to go instead of being forced to. Going as a couple. I think... I don't know if it will ever change my brain, the way I think. But it's given me some more coping strategies. More ways to talk to Kenzie and have a better relationship."

Tyrrell rolled his eyes and let out a puff of air. "I don't have anyone. It's too late for me and Lindsey."

"Yes, but... some family sessions might still be a good idea. You're still a family, even if you're not together. You still want a relationship with the kids. And you still have to talk to Lindsey and work things out with her, even if you don't live together."

"She wouldn't."

"I think she would. I've talked to her a couple of times, and I think she'd be willing to try."

"I don't know. We've never talked about it. And that wouldn't stop me from drinking. Or messing up with the kids."

"One step at a time. It *might* help with the drinking. And it would help you deal with the kids and co-parenting." Zachary knew he was overstepping his bounds. He didn't actually have experience overcoming alcoholism with therapy or with family therapy and parenting. But he knew Tyrrell needed to try something new. Something other than just running away.

Tyrrell shook his head and picked up a piece of the golden, buttery garlic bread and took a bite. He looked surprised. "This is *really* good. Why haven't I tried this before?"

Kenzie looked from Zachary to Tyrrell and back again. "Oh no, we've got another one. We're going to have to make a loaf each if anyone else wants any."

Pat laughed. "Noted!"

Zachary helped himself to another piece of garlic bread, even though he'd been trying to be polite and eat more of the chicken soup rather than just pigging out on the bread. "Sometimes... trying something new can be good," he told Tyrrell, around a mouthful of bread.

63

enzie had taken a day off work so they could sleep over at the Petersons' and to give Zachary a chance to see Joss before they headed for home.

He met Joss and Luke at the little coffee shop in the bookstore, where he had met with her once before. She seemed to prefer meeting him away from home, maybe so that she didn't have to worry about making sure the house was presentable, or maybe because home was her sanctuary and she didn't want it invaded any more than necessary. Zachary wasn't really sure. But if she felt better meeting him for coffee, that was fine with him. Anything that would smooth Joss's rough edges a little.

Zachary didn't for a minute think that Joss was a bad person or that she was willfully rude or hurtful. She'd just been through so much that she didn't see the point in sanitizing or sugar-coating what she had to say. People could take her at her bluntest and most acid, or not at all. It was probably a defense mechanism. Show people the worst and hope that it would scare them away, and she wouldn't have to deal with hurt feelings or put all of that effort into maintaining a relationship.

Kenzie had suggested before that it was probably easier for Zachary to deal with Joss if he were by himself than if she went along. Zachary knew and understood Joss's background. Kenzie's privileged upbringing was obviously an irritant to Joss, and she didn't hesitate to throw out barbs about it. It was a lot easier for Zachary to talk with Joss if he weren't constantly trying to defend Kenzie—even though she was a big girl and could defend herself. That fact wasn't going to stop Zachary from jumping between them.

Luke had come along for coffee. Zachary wasn't sure why. He had expected that Luke would have his own interests and better things to do than to talk to his guardian's brother. Luke greeted Zachary with a friendly, familiar smile. They sat for a few moments in awkward silence after placing their coffee orders, looking at each other and trying to decide where to start.

"So, you found Tyrrell?" Jocelyn asked.

She was one of the people that Zachary had texted about it. She hadn't responded, even just to acknowledge his text. "Yeah. He's safe and sound. He and Kenzie are at the Petersons'."

"So he *did* just disappear because he wanted to."

"Yeah… I guess so. But it could have been something else. He could have been hurt or sick."

"But that wasn't likely."

Zachary shrugged. He'd had to track Tyrrell down. They had both known that from the moment he contacted her to find out if she knew anything. There hadn't been any question of it.

"Glad he's okay," Joss conceded. Then, after a pause, "Is he?"

"Is he okay? Yeah. I think so. For now. But it's been so difficult for him… do you know where he was…?"

She shook her head.

The waitress returned with their coffee order and handed them their cups, speaking in a bright voice, her movements quick like a bird's. Joss drank a couple of swallows of her coffee, even though Zachary's, when he tested it, was still boiling hot.

"No," Joss said. "Where was he? Some dark tavern somewhere."

"He was living out of his car. Drinking in a pub with Berk."

Jocelyn's brows rose up her forehead.

"Who's Berk?" Luke asked.

"Our father," Joss told him.

"Oh." Luke shrugged, not finding this to be as interesting an answer as he'd hoped for.

But Jocelyn was clearly as shocked about this as Zachary had been. "Drinking with Berk? Why would he be doing that?"

"I don't get it. He runs away because he's afraid he's becoming like

Berk, but then he runs *to* him. Drinks with him. Listens to his lies about how everything was fine when we were kids and he loved us."

Joss's eyes looked intense enough to burn holes right through Zachary. Luke tilted his head, listening.

"Loved us," Joss repeated in disbelief.

"Apparently. Or at least, loved Tyrrell. I don't know if he's said that he loved all of us."

"Blech." Joss spat like she was trying to get something bitter out of her mouth. "You've got to be kidding me."

"You guys didn't get along with your dad?" Luke teased, his eyes dancing.

"I'll tell you how I'd get along with him if *I* met him again," Joss told him. "I'd like to get my hands on a nice PKM, and then I'd use the full one-hundred rounds to cut him in half both directions and reduce him to a pile of hamburger meat."

She sipped her coffee.

"That's what I would do."

Zachary widened his eyes at the graphic violence. He looked at Luke, who appeared to be only mildly surprised at this suggestion.

Luke shrugged. "It's probably a good idea if we don't give her one," he told Zachary.

"Yeah."

"I would *not* sit down with the man and drink with him," Joss clarified, in case they had missed her point. "Unless it was to toast his last remains."

Zachary nodded. "Okay. I wouldn't either. But I don't know about the machine gun."

"You use your weapon of choice; I'll use mine." She tossed her hair. "It's all fantasy anyway. I'm never going to meet him. He'd know better than to contact me."

"You were only thirteen when we... left."

"Too young to get my hands on a machine gun then," she said with regret.

"You felt that way then? Before the fire?"

"It's been a longstanding fantasy."

Zachary thought about Margot and Celia and sighed. He supposed he had his answer about whether Berk had always been predatory.

"How do you... put that aside and just... carry on?" Zachary asked, unsure how to put what he wanted to know into words. Despite the horrors that Joss had been through, she blended well. She worked a regular job and owned or rented a little house, and seemed just like anyone else in the quiet suburbia around her. As far as Zachary knew, she didn't suffer from any crippling mental illness as he did and had overcome her drug addiction. He didn't think it was just because she was a few years older than he that she seemed so mature. He wanted to know the secret.

"I… compartmentalize," Joss said. "I just put all of that 'dad' stuff in a box, and I shut it away. And I don't think about it unless someone like you brings it up. And now that you have, I'll close it up and put it away again."

Zachary was not unfamiliar with stuffing his feelings. He had forgotten a lot of what had happened to him as a child and teenager. He thought about Tyrrell, about how he said he could forget unless he were around Zachary or one of the others, and then it would come back to him. Joss made it sound easy. She was well-practiced, but even she said that things could bring it back to her.

Luke was nodding at Joss's explanation. "Separate yourself from it," he suggested. "Like it happened to someone else. That's the best thing to do."

"Is that what you do?" Zachary asked.

Luke shrugged. "Sure. I don't want to think about it if I don't have to. Avoid making memories in the first place if you can. If it's too late, then forget about it. Rewrite it. You can *change* what you remember."

Joss pointed at Luke. "That's what you've been doing. Rewriting what happened when you were with the organization."

He blinked at her, saying nothing.

"I won't rewrite what happened to me," Joss said strongly. "I'll remember what Berk did to me. And what the traffickers did to me. That's what keeps me from ever going back. If you rewrite it as a fairy tale, you'll end up going back because all you remember is the good stuff."

Luke took a long sip of his coffee, thinking about this.

"Compartmentalize," Joss reiterated. "Don't rewrite it. Just put it away in case you need it again later." She shook her head. "Don't be like Tyrrell, drinking with the enemy." She snorted in derision.

"Yeah," Luke agreed. He rubbed his upper lip, giving it some more thought. Then his gaze shifted to Zachary. He had another swallow of his coffee. "What's up with Rhys, do you know?"

Zachary raised his eyebrows, wondering what Luke had heard from him. That he was angry at Zachary? That he was going to leave his grandma's and run away from home? "Why? What did he say?"

"Nothing." Luke turned his hands palms up, demonstrating that they were empty. "He hasn't been messaging me. And when I message him… he doesn't answer."

"Oh?" Zachary gave it a few beats. He was happy to hear that Rhys had pulled back on communications. Maybe their talk had made Rhys reconsider. "Maybe he's been grounded and his grandma took away the phone."

Of course, Vera would never take away Rhys's phone, an integral part of his communications system. She understood many nuances of Rhys's facial expression and gestures that Zachary couldn't, but they still used the phone for some of the more complex subjects.

Luke shrugged and nodded. "Yeah, that's probably it," he agreed. "It's good he's got a grandma to look after him."

He turned to stare out the window, away from Zachary and Joss. Probably remembering his own grandma, the only person who had really cared for him and tried to keep him safe from harm. It was after she had died that he had been left floundering, anchorless, abusing alcohol and drugs, and getting into other trouble. Until he'd been scooped up by the trafficking ring that had put him to use. Something that, despite his attempts to rewrite history, he wouldn't want to subject his new young friend to. But if he did give in to the temptation to return to that life, he would bring whoever they told him to into the business.

Zachary was glad Rhys had stopped answering him and hoped that Luke would do as Joss suggested, and not pine after the life he'd had in the syndicate.

64

Back at the Petersons', Zachary lounged on the couch with Kenzie and recounted parts of the visit with Joss to Kenzie and to Lorne in his easy chair. Pat was off running errands, maybe buying ingredients for his next culinary creation. Tyrrell sat by the window, a book in his hand. Still, he didn't appear to be putting much effort into reading it, mostly staring out the window into the distance. Zachary had only seen him flip pages once or twice and thought it was just for show rather than that he'd actually finished reading those pages.

Zachary recounted Joss's comments about compartmentalizing old memories, but not the part about how she'd like to make mincemeat of Berk if she ever saw him again.

Mr. Peterson shook his head. "We dealt with a lot of kids over the years, and the ones who were able to deal with what had happened to them and work through it in therapy were the ones who had the best outcomes. The ones who just stuffed all their feelings and memories and pretended that everything was fine... it eventually catches up with them at some point. Sooner or later."

"Joss has been pretty successful with it."

"I don't claim to know all of what happened to her. But from what I saw of her... I assume she has spent most of the intervening years *self-medicating*."

"Well, yes," Zachary agreed.

"That's not exactly a healthy coping mechanism."

Zachary glanced over at Tyrrell. "No."

"She may find, one of these days, that those memories won't stay in their compartments anymore and she has to deal with them."

Zachary's own box of memories had been opened during the assault by Archuro. All those experiences that he had been so careful to push down and hide even from himself had surfaced and couldn't be stuffed away again. Dr. B said that was actually a good sign. A sign that he was healthier mentally and ready to deal with them, as he hadn't been equipped to do as a child. But that hadn't made Zachary feel much better about it. Even after a year, he still fought to keep those resurfaced memories from affecting his focus and daily activities.

<hr>

"Zachary, can you help me pack? I don't want to forget anything."

Zachary looked at Kenzie, frowning. She rarely asked him for help on anything. Certainly, she had always packed her own bags, whether for a weekend trip to the Petersons' or the holiday at the Lodge. She jerked her head toward the bedroom.

"Oh. Sure, of course." Zachary followed. "It's always those charge cords…"

They retreated to the guest room and Kenzie shut the door. Her packed bag was already on the bed. Zachary looked around the room, but it was clear she hadn't forgotten to put anything in it.

"I wanted to talk to you about Tyrrell," she told him.

Zachary was feeling pretty talked-out about Tyrrell. She already knew all of what had happened and what was on his mind. Going over it again seemed more stressful than helpful.

"Okay," he agreed. "What did you want to discuss?" Dr. Boyle would be very proud of him for engaging with Kenzie without whining about it.

"I wanted to offer him the guest room for a few days while he gets back on his feet. And I can help find a program for him. Maybe something a bit different from what he's done before. But I didn't want to do it without talking to you first, in case you feel like it would be a problem, the two of you getting in each other's way."

Zachary felt a rush of warmth and gratitude toward Kenzie. While he had thought about bringing Tyrrell home, he knew he couldn't do it without asking Kenzie first. It was her house, after all. But he didn't want to ask, in case she might feel obligated.

"Are you sure? That would be great, if you're sure it's what you want to do."

"Yes. I want to do something for him, and I don't think that a few days in our guest room would be too difficult for any of us. I'm worried that if he just goes back to Riverbrook, he's going to go straight back to drinking with your father again. If we can get a little distance between them, then at least there's a chance he'll work toward sobriety again."

"What if it doesn't work out? He doesn't want to get into a program and won't get out and look for work?"

"Then I'll be the bad guy. You can tell him that I've had enough and am kicking him out."

Zachary chuckled. "I couldn't ask you to do that."

"You absolutely should. I don't want to be tripping over him for a year while he sits on the couch and drinks. But I don't think he'll stay long. If it isn't working out like expected…"

"He'll run away."

She raised her brows and shrugged. "That's his pattern."

Zachary nodded. "Okay. Let's go tell him."

He grabbed Kenzie's hand, and they walked together out to the living room.

THEIR WALLS WERE EMPTY

For those who would do anything for family

———————————

1

Zachary sat bolt upright in the bed, gasping for breath. The room was dark and he was disoriented. He felt around him for something that he had lost, desperate to lay hold of whatever it had been. A key? A coin? A baby that had slipped out of his grasp. It was important that he find it before it was lost to him forever. He slid his hands under the covers, under the pillow. He encountered Kenzie beside him, but it was a minute before he knew who it was and that she wasn't the thing he had lost.

"Zachary?" Kenzie's voice was sleepy. "What's wrong? Are you okay?"

"It's... no... I lost it..."

"Lost what, hon'?" Kenzie stirred. She turned over to face him, reaching out to touch him in the dark. A hand on his side, then his chest, which was still heaving from his gasps, his heart pounding so hard and fast he was sure she could feel it right under her fingers. "Hey. It's okay. You had a dream."

"I know, but I needed... I needed to hold on to..." He couldn't even remember what it was, that wisp of a dream that had become concrete in his hands that he had been determined to hold on to this time. Not to let it fall from his grasp and dissolve into nothingness again.

"Shh. It's fine," Kenzie murmured. "Try to go back to sleep."

"No. It's here somewhere. I just have to find it..."

He again slid his fingers under his pillow, looking for it. Frustrated, he reached over to the nightstand and turned on the lamp. Kenzie fell back, covering her eyes with her arm and making an irritated sound.

"Sorry. It's here. It's here somewhere." Zachary lifted up his pillow and looked underneath. He slid out of the bed and pulled back his blankets. There was nothing there. No sign of the precious thing he had lost.

What had it been?

He was anxious. How could he have lost it so quickly? It had been in his hands.

Kenzie lowered her arm slowly and was watching him. "It's just part of the dream," she assured him. "It just left you disoriented. That happens sometimes. It might be a side effect of your sleep aid."

Zachary sat back down on the mattress, feeling bereft. What had he lost?

"I hate this feeling. It can't just be the dream."

"Have you had it before? I know sometimes I have part of a dream that sticks with me for a few extra seconds, and it can be a little freaky."

"Yes."

"Just take a few minutes to calm down."

Zachary looked around the room, still sure that he must have missed something. He looked down at the floor to see if something had fallen off of the bed, trying not to let Kenzie see that he was still searching for the lost thing.

"Is everything okay?" he asked her. Though he had woken her up, so she probably didn't know any better than he did. "Did something happen that woke me up? A noise?"

Kenzie appeared to be listening, trying to catch any stray noise that might have startled Zachary awake. A siren in the distance. A tree branch rubbing against the side of the house in the wind. They both listened, but didn't hear anything unusual. Just the usual noises that houses made. Hot air vents. The occasional creaks and pops. Nothing unusual.

Zachary rubbed his eyes.

"Tyrrell," he said suddenly. He turned his head, looking around the room, as if Tyrrell might be there. But he hadn't slept in the same room as his younger brother since he was ten and the house had burned down, and he and Tyrrell had been sent to separate foster families. But Tyrrell was back in his life now, had been back in it for just over a year. And Zachary had brought him home to stay with them while they tried to help him get into a treatment program.

But of course, he wasn't in the bedroom. He was in the guest room, where he had been staying for a few days.

"I have to go see if he's okay."

Kenzie didn't object, just sat there rubbing her eyes. She probably knew better than to argue with him. Knew that when he got into this mood, she couldn't tell him anything. He needed to see Tyrrell, to know that he was okay. To know that he wasn't the thing that Zachary had lost and was still searching for.

Zachary pulled on a pair of pajama pants he had left crumpled on the floor and went to the guest room to make sure that Tyrrell was still there. What if he had left? What if that was what had woken Zachary up, his subconscious brain alert to the fact that if Tyrrell left, he might be in danger. From himself, if not from an outside threat.

He tapped lightly on the guest room door but knew that Tyrrell wouldn't answer it. He would either be gone, or he would be deeply asleep. Not sitting there waiting for Zachary to check in on him and make sure that he was okay. He turned the door handle slowly to try to keep it from squeaking or making any other noise and, when it had turned all the way, pushed it slowly forward.

The room was dark and still. If Tyrrell had gone, he hadn't left a light on behind him to draw attention to the fact that he wasn't there. Zachary tiptoed into the room, trying not to awaken his brother, if he were still there. His eyes had to adjust to the dark again after having turned on the lamp in the master bedroom.

There was a lump on the bed. Tyrrell? Or a couple of pillows and some blankets shaped to look like he was still sleeping in the bed? A juvenile trick, but one that Tyrrell might have used anyway, if he didn't want Zachary to know if he had left.

Zachary reached out and touched the blankets. He expected to feel it all give under his fingers, squashed flat by his touch, but he encountered resistance. Someone was curled up under the blankets. Tyrrell had not snuck out.

Zachary breathed a sigh of relief. For the first time since he had gasped himself awake, his breathing started to slow and settle. More convinced now that no one was in danger, and that the feelings of loss and dread were just that—feelings, artifacts of the dream, as Kenzie had suggested.

"What? Zachary?" Tyrrell turned over in the bed to face him. "What's wrong? What is it?"

"Nothing. Nothing wrong. Sorry. I heard a noise. Wanted to make sure you were okay."

"I'm okay, bro. Just sleeping. Like you should be."

"Yeah. Sorry. I'll go back to bed. You go back to sleep too."

"I plan to," Tyrrell agreed dryly.

Zachary gave his arm a little squeeze, to reassure Tyrrell and himself that everything really was okay, then retraced his steps, closing the guest room door behind him and rejoining Kenzie.

She was dozing even with the bedroom lamp on. Zachary felt bad for waking her up, especially on a work night when she should be able to sleep all the way through and get all of the rest that she needed to be fresh at work.

He sat down on the edge of the bed again, easing down slowly in an effort not to jar her awake again. She made a murmured sound, not really awake, but knowing that he was there.

He probably wouldn't be able to get back to sleep again. And even if he could, he would probably have another nightmare and another waking where he couldn't fully separate himself from the sticky stuff of his dreams. If he stayed in bed, he would probably keep waking Kenzie up again, and she needed her sleep more than he needed his. He was used to operating on just a few hours of sleep.

He turned off the lamp and waited for a moment to see whether that had woken her up again.

"Everything okay?" Kenzie murmured.

"Yeah. It's fine. Sorry. I didn't mean to wake you up again."

"Don't worry about it. Tyrrell is okay?"

"He's sleeping. Shouldn't have woken him up."

"Mmm."

Zachary rubbed Kenzie's shoulder for a minute so that she would think that he was also settling in to go to sleep and would drop off faster. Then, like after putting a baby to sleep, he got back to his feet very slowly so that she wouldn't be aware of the shift in the mattress and wake back up again. Her breaths continued, long and slow and even.

2

Zachary adjourned to the living room, which operated as his office and central hub. He sat down, turned on the TV, found a movie to provide some low background noise, then opened his laptop on his mobile desk. He had checked his email before going to bed, so he knew there wouldn't be much more there. Mostly spam. Not a lot of people emailed him overnight.

After glancing over the subject lines, he closed the email inbox and started to go through his project folders, seeing what he could find to keep him occupied for a few hours. There was a backlog due to the amount of time he had spent in the hospital and then searching for Tyrrell. Zachary had only been back at it again for a few days, so there was plenty for him to catch up on.

It was the first year that he had worked with Heather, his older sister, and she had kept things running while he had been in the hospital. She was a remarkably efficient manager. She had conducted skip tracing and done the easier computer work, had sent out bills, collected on some of the delinquent accounts, and generally kept clients happy while Zachary had been unable to tend to his business. He had thought that his PI business would forever be a one-man business, but it was nice to have someone else helping out. He probably wasn't paying Heather enough. He might have to task her with researching how much he should actually be paying her. Her husband was a bookkeeper and probably had sources for that kind of thing. Heather mostly liked having something to do, since she didn't really need the money as much as she did something to fill the empty hours while her husband was at his own job.

The movie playing on the TV helped to cover up any night noises the house was still making but was not interesting enough for Zachary to pay any attention to it as he did some deep research and looked at the insurance investigation files that Heather had opened for him. He didn't really like trying to catch people defrauding their insurance companies. Still, it was, at least, better than chasing after errant husbands. Or wives. He had made a significant shift away from adultery investigations in the past two years, and he was glad of that. Less surveillance, fewer lives ruined by his pictures, and more time spent on more constructive investigations that might actually make someone happy.

By the time he heard Kenzie up using the shower, the movie had ended. Or maybe two movies; he wasn't sure, since he hadn't actually been watching or listening to any of the action. He got up from the couch, where he had been sitting in the same position for too long, stretched his shoulders and back, and wandered into the kitchen. He put coffee grinds in the hopper, set the carafe under the spout, and started the coffee brewing. He helped himself to a cup once it was finished and went back to his computer, where he checked out his social networks and email again until Kenzie was out of the shower.

She smiled at him, her bright red lipstick looking particularly kissable and dark curls bouncing around her head. "How long have you been up? I didn't hear you get up."

Zachary shrugged. "A few hours."

"You didn't get up after that dream, did you? You got back to sleep for a couple of hours?"

Zachary shrugged and didn't answer to confirm or deny. "There is coffee in the kitchen."

"I can smell it. Thanks."

He followed her into the kitchen, where they worked side by side for a few minutes to prepare their breakfasts. Nothing fancy. A granola bar and yogurt for Zachary and toast with marmalade for Kenzie. And coffee. Then they sat down for their morning visit.

Zachary hadn't realized until they had brought Tyrrell back just how much he valued those quiet breakfast visits. The mornings that Tyrrell woke up early and was prowling around the house and getting his own breakfast or chatting while they were getting theirs, Zachary tended to feel flustered and crowded and just wanted their space back again. But that was selfish. Tyrrell needed them. So Zachary said nothing, but still felt irritated by Tyrrell's presence if he got up for breakfast and much preferred the quiet start with Kenzie when he could get it.

Kenzie watched Zachary open his chocolate chip granola bar in preparation for his breakfast. She smiled, nodding her approval. "So nice to see you eating again. This med cocktail is better for that reason, for sure."

Zachary nodded. It was nice not to be so nauseated in the morning. Much easier to eat if he didn't have to fight his own body to get the food down. And while his appetite still probably wasn't where it should be and he didn't feel hungry most of the time, it was better than it had been with the meds he'd been on the last few years. Which should help him get up to a healthy weight much faster than usual and make his doctors happy.

"It's working okay in other areas too, I think." It was impossible to tell whether it would help him get less depressed before the next Christmas, but that was almost a year away, so he didn't have to worry about it yet. One of the open questions was whether it would help with his obsessive thoughts about Bridget, his ex-wife, and the compulsions to check in on her or follow her. He knew that he had disappointed Kenzie by giving in to those compulsions again when Bridget had been pregnant, convinced that she could not take care of herself and the twins and that she would need him there, close by. He had been the one to call for help when she had collapsed in the garden the day she had gone into labor, so he hadn't been wrong.

Since getting out of the hospital, he had been able to keep those obsessions reined in. But he had been trying to find Tyrrell, so he'd had something else to occupy his anxious brain. Whether he would be able to keep those thoughts at bay as he got back into the normal routine was still uncertain. He was hopeful that the new cocktail would help. And yet worried that it wouldn't.

3

Tyrrell was all right when you looked in on him last night?" Kenzie asked.

They had both kept their voices low so as not to wake him up. Like he was the child and they were his parents, and they wanted to have some time together before he got up and started making demands. But Tyrrell wasn't really that demanding. Not really. The first few days had not been easy as he withdrew from alcohol, but he was doing better now.

"Yeah. He was asleep. Said everything was okay."

"He was asleep but told you that everything was okay?"

"I did wake him for a minute. But he went right back to sleep after. Like when I woke you up."

Kenzie nodded, conceding that she had gotten back to sleep again fairly quickly.

"Do you think… that we'll be able to find the right placement for him?" Zachary asked tentatively.

He had thought that it would just be a matter of finding a good treatment center, calling them, and dropping Tyrrell off. He'd never been involved in the administrative end of getting someone into a program like that. But while it sounded like it should be simple, it wasn't. There were a lot of different programs to look at, weighing the pros and cons of each. Of course, one factor to consider was the cost, but Kenzie had said *that* didn't matter. She would cover it. She had a trust fund and didn't use it very much, so she was happy to cover the expenses of getting Tyrrell clean and sober again.

Maybe with a private program, one that was more expensive, he would get the quality of care that he needed to stay sober long-term. People recovered from addiction. It was possible. But Zachary knew they couldn't force Tyrrell into anything. Even once they found a program that seemed like it was meant to be, they would be faced with the waiting lists. Almost all of the facilities—all of the good, quality programs—had waiting lists. Sometimes waiting lists were months long. Tyrrell needed help now, before he went on another binge.

And when they did find a program that looked promising and was able to take Tyrrell, they would need to talk him into it. If Tyrrell didn't like something about the facility, he didn't have to go. And if he did go, he could just duck out partway through, and Zachary would be left in the position of having to track him down again. Or to let him go.

"I'm waiting for a callback from three different places right now," Kenzie informed Zachary. She told him the name of each of the programs. "If we can get him into any one of those… I think it would be really good. They have good recovery rates in the industry. Good reviews by patients and industry watchdogs."

"And you think that Tyrrell would go into any of them?"

"I hope so. No promises, but he seems like he's willing to try out anything that we think might work."

Zachary turned his head as he heard noises from the guest room. Tyrrell was apparently getting up. Zachary didn't ask anything further about the programs, not wanting Tyrrell to come out of the bedroom and hear them discussing him. He must know that they talked about him, but it still didn't feel right to let him walk in on a discussion about him.

Kenzie took a bite of her toast. "I'm sure we can work something out. It may just take a little longer than we had thought at the start. I naively thought that it would just be a matter of looking up a facility in the yellow pages, giving them a call, and taking him in."

"The yellow pages?" Zachary questioned. "How ancient are you?"

"They still have yellow pages… I think…"

He chuckled. He had no idea whether they still had the big yellow phone books that had been around during his youth. He hadn't seen one in years. Most of his investigative work was in online databases and web searches. Not opening up a book filled of minuscule type.

"Going to be a busy day today?" he asked her.

"Things are always jumping at the office."

"That's sort of creepy, knowing you work in the morgue."

Kenzie laughed, nodding. They both enjoyed a morbid sense of humor about her working in the medical examiner's office.

"How about you? Feel like you're getting things under control?"

"It's a lot easier with Heather helping out. She learned a lot of strategies for ADHD when she was raising her kids, so she has good ideas. I'm not overwhelmed and trying to get everything done at once; I can just work on a certain set of files or tasks... easier to focus on one thing at a time and not be distracted by all the rest."

"That's good. There's no point in trying to get weeks' worth of jobs all done in a day or two. That would land *me* in the hospital."

Zachary nodded. "I could use a couple of bigger files. I don't like to just work on small investigations. I like to have one or two that I can dig my teeth into and then work on the smaller ones around the edges. But of course, anything that was big and couldn't wait, someone else took. So it might be a few weeks before I have the balance I like."

"It will come to you."

"Yeah. It will." He found it essential to say 'no' to the cases he didn't want so he would have the time and energy to take on the cases he did. They tended to come to him when he had room for them. He would keep plugging away at the little ones, his bread and butter, until the right cases came along.

Kenzie finished her toast and was licking off her fingers and swigging down the last of her coffee. "Well, I should be getting to it, I guess."

"You want lunch?"

She hesitated. Zachary had noticed that even though she didn't like to use the sandwich vending machine at work, she also tended not to take the time to make lunch for herself before work. Then she was forced to either get something from the machine or go out and find something else. "No... I'll work something out today. We need to go grocery shopping soon. I need to make up a proper list... figure out what I want to make and what I can take to work."

"If you have a list, I could go pick stuff up."

"No... I don't yet."

And when she did, she probably wouldn't give it to the most distractible person in the relationship. Zachary was pretty good with lists when he had to physically check items off, just not so good at the kind he had to keep in his head. But Kenzie probably thought he was bad at both.

"If you write one, I'll buy everything on it. I won't only get half of them and forget the rest."

Kenzie eyed him. "Hmm. I might have to test that."

"Good. At least give me a chance to show you I can."

Tyrrell came down the hall and into the kitchen as Kenzie was putting her dishes into the dishwasher. He rubbed his eyes, looking remarkably like the six-year-old Zachary remembered him as, other than the stubble. His dark hair and eyes were similar to Zachary's own; genetic traits inherited from their father. Zachary's hair was kept in a short buzz cut so that he didn't have to worry about taking care of it, and Tyrrell's was a bit longer.

"Morning," he greeted, yawning. He headed for the coffee pot and poured himself a mug.

"How are you doing this morning?" Kenzie asked as she pulled winter clothes from the mudroom just outside the kitchen and prepared to leave.

"Fine, I guess." Tyrrell gave a half-smile and shrugged.

"We'll catch up later." Kenzie gave them both a little wave. Zachary stepped forward to give her a farewell kiss, and then she went through the door to the garage and was gone.

Zachary freshened his cup of coffee with what remained in the pot.

"Did you wake me up last night?" Tyrrell asked, frowning at Zachary.

"Yeah, sorry. I had a dream."

Tyrrell nodded and didn't ask anything else about it. He probably assumed that Zachary's dream had been about the fire. And maybe it had been; Zachary couldn't remember enough about it to be sure. He still dreamed of the fire frequently, especially when stressed.

And despite what he would have liked to say, having Tyrrell there did make things more stressful. Tyrrell wasn't a child, but Zachary felt like he needed to take care of him anyway. Make sure that he was kept busy, wasn't thinking too much about the past, didn't start thinking too much about his mistakes so that he wouldn't begin binge-drinking again before they managed to get him into detox. Someone needed to be there all the time; he wasn't as free to come and go as he would have liked.

Tyrrell drank his coffee, eyes far away. Zachary wondered if he were thinking of the fire too. Or was he somewhere else? Maybe beating himself up for the ways he had failed his children. Or remembering the things that had happened when they were both children. He had confessed to Zachary that whenever they were together for any length of time, Tyrrell started to remember what things were like at home. The abuses and neglect that they had suffered. Zachary wished that it wasn't true. And that Tyrrell hadn't told him that. He wanted to be with his younger brother and didn't want his nearness to cause Tyrrell distressing memories.

"We should go out today," Tyrrell suggested, maybe picking up on Zachary's itch to leave the house and not just to stay home playing the part of the responsible brother.

"Out where?"

' "I don't know. We can go out and do something. See the sights. Grab a burger. Go to a hockey game."

Zachary didn't know how many tourist places were open during January. And of course, hockey wouldn't be happening until the evening, and he didn't think leaving Kenzie alone while he took Tyrrell to the nearest NHL game was quite what she had in mind when she had suggested Tyrrell could stay at the house until he could get into a detox program.

"Maybe we can go to the grocery store to pick some things up for Kenzie if she puts a list together. But I have other work to do for now. I have to get back to my business."

Tyrrell sighed loudly and retreated to the guest room with his cup of coffee.

4

Zachary tried to ignore Tyrrell's presence in the house and focus on his work as if he were the only one there. He wasn't there to babysit Tyrrell, other than keeping him away from any booze if he could. Tyrrell was a grown man and was responsible for himself. If he wanted to shut himself away in the guest room all day because Zachary wouldn't take him out anywhere, he was welcome to do that. Zachary had already taken a week away from his business to find Tyrrell and pull him away from his drunken binge, which meant Zachary was more behind than usual after his Christmas break. He needed to get some work done.

He worked through various items on his list, trying to stick to the stuff Heather had identified as the most important and profitable. Still, he did do some smaller tasks in between because he enjoyed them or they were for a client that he particularly liked.

He wasn't sure what time it was when the doorbell rang. Zachary blinked and looked around, waiting at first to see if anyone else would answer the door. But it was apparently still early enough in the day that Kenzie was not back. Zachary wondered at first whether Tyrrell had ordered pizza or called a friend to come over, but apparently not, because there was no sign that Tyrrell was coming out of the guest room to answer the door.

Which left it to Zachary.

He pushed himself up off of the couch and stretched his back, shoulders, and neck. He knew that hunching over his laptop sitting on the couch was not making his body happy. He should get a proper ergonomic chair, a standing desk, or whatever was the newest ergonomic solution.

On a typical day, he would go out to check a few of the errands on his list off. But he didn't want to leave Tyrrell there by himself and couldn't think of a script that would convince Tyrrell to come with him and be happy about it. He couldn't just tell the other man that he didn't trust him to be home by himself and he couldn't drag him around like a puppy on a leash. Tyrrell had been interested in going out, but to something entertaining and interesting for him, not a supply run or to investigate the victim of an accident to see if they really did have a debilitating back injury.

Zachary squinted through the peephole, which did not give him a very clear image of the person outside the front door. He should probably install one of those doorbell cameras or a proper security camera so that they could see anyone who came to the door properly and not have to worry about opening the door to a stranger or to someone dangerous who had followed Zachary or Kenzie home. Zachary knew only too well how easy it was to follow someone.

The man on the doorstep was dressed in a suit. Zachary couldn't see his face well, but it didn't ring any alarm bells. He didn't look like a hood or cartel member, just like a businessman.

He opened the door and looked at the man's face for a moment before realizing why it was familiar to him. He had, Zachary thought, lost a little weight since the last time he had seen him.

"Walter. Uh… Mr. Kirsch. Kenzie is at work. She isn't home."

"I didn't expect her to be. I was hoping to talk to you about something."

"Oh… okay. Come on in." Zachary stepped back to allow him in.

Kenzie's father was still a stranger to him. They had only met a couple of times, and although Zachary knew that Walter loved his daughter, she had been quite resistant to Zachary meeting him. The last time Walter had come to the house, he had hidden a bug in Kenzie's purse to listen in on her conversations. Not something that inspired confidence. Zachary would have to watch him like a hawk and sweep for bugs again after he was gone.

"How are you feeling?" Walter asked, looking Zachary over.

Zachary wondered whether he was asking because of the viral infection that had landed both Kenzie and Zachary in the hospital following the

Halloween ball or whether he knew about Zachary's depression and being in the hospital again over Christmas.

"I'm good," he said, keeping it vague. "They got everything straightened out. Modern medicine is a wonder."

"Good, good. Glad to hear that!"

"Did Kenzie know that you were coming today?" Zachary asked as he sat down on the couch and Walter settled in one of the easy chairs.

Walter waved away the question without answering it. "Kenzie said that you're a private investigator. That you're quite good. I looked into it, and from what I could see from the publicity you've had, she's right."

Zachary shrugged. "I've had some cases that have gone public, so that's good for my reputation." He didn't like to brag about himself, to say how good he was at what he did. He probably couldn't be classified as a *great* detective. He was dogged. When others had stopped, he continued to look and didn't always take things at face value. Those were good traits for a PI. They helped him turn up clues that the police or other investigators hadn't been able to.

"Modest too," Walter said, shaking his head in amusement. "Well, good for you. I don't really need to ask you if you're good because, as I said, I've already looked you up and checked with some references." He smiled. It made Zachary think of a shark's toothy smile and flat, dead eyes. Walter was a politician, Zachary knew. A lobbyist. Very wealthy, very powerful. Not the kind of man who really needed to go to his daughter's partner for anything.

"How can I help you?" he asked politely. He wasn't sure he would help Walter with anything. The last time he had come calling, it had been to pump Kenzie for information on a case that she was working on and to pressure her to use her influence in the medical examiner's office.

Kenzie had not obliged.

And she had been right about that particular case. The governor hadn't wanted the bad publicity that a rogue virus would have if word got out about it. An outbreak before an election would have been bad for him. He was lucky that Dr. Wiltshire and Kenzie had been able to take action when they had, or the consequences would have been much worse.

"I don't want you to think that this is anything big or political," Walter cautioned. "If it was, I would hire a bigger firm, one with good optics and a lot more power behind it. And Kenzie didn't want me to involve you in anything relating to my lobbying; I know that. She didn't want me to bring my politics to the table, so to speak."

Zachary nodded. It sounded like he and Kenzie had already discussed the matter, which helped him relax. He didn't want to do anything behind her back. To be seen as colluding with the enemy. While he was sure Kenzie loved her father, he knew that she didn't get along well with either of her parents and definitely did not trust her father's politics or anything relating to his lobbying.

"In fact, it's so small maybe you won't even want to get involved," Walter said with a shrug. "Maybe it wouldn't be worth your time. It would be a favor to me."

Zachary wrinkled his brow at this. Walter was certainly wealthy enough to pay if Zachary believed Kenzie or the magazines that had profiled Walter.

Walter may have looked into Zachary's reputation, but Zachary had also looked into Walter's. He needed to know what he could about Walter Kirsch and his ex-wife Lisa Cole Kirsch. It wasn't like Kenzie would tell him any more than the bare essentials.

Walter chuckled. "I don't mean that I wouldn't pay you. Of course I will pay your standard—or even premium—rates. I just mean this wouldn't be a highly profitable case for you, and it wouldn't be high-profile."

"I see." So far, everything Walter had to say was as clear as mud. Zachary leaned forward, his elbows on his knees. "Why don't you just tell me about the case, then?"

Walter hesitated. Zachary glanced around the room, waiting to see if he would begin.

"If it's so confidential that you can't even give me the broad strokes…" Zachary started.

"No, no. Of course not. I told you that it wasn't a big deal. I just like to… put all my cards on the table first. And all of yours."

"I don't have anything to put on the table yet. I don't even know what you're here about."

"I suppose not. But what I mean is… I need to tell you that this would be more than just a favor. You know, I guess, that MacKenzie and I have not been close the last few years. I did some things that… she can never forgive me for. Nothing to hurt her, I assure you. Nothing intended to hurt anyone. Just some… choices she didn't believe were ethical." Walter paused as if waiting for Zachary to fill in whether he knew the details. Zachary knew little about the rift between Kenzie and her father, other than that it had something to do with Kenzie's deceased sister and some treatment choices that Walter and Lisa had made.

"Go on," Zachary encouraged.

If he were going to put his cards on the table, then it was time to stop guarding them so carefully.

"I would like to mend fences. I would like to be a bigger part of my daughter's life. I don't think that she would let me do anything for her. She has put her trust fund to use, but that isn't really a gift from me; it is a trust her grandparents set up. I don't think she would take any favors from me."

"Uh-huh." Walter was probably right about that.

"So I can't really do anything for her. She would not accept it. But I can hire you to do what you do professionally and pay you your regular rates. That shows her that... I support her choices..."

Zachary nodded again. He could understand Walter reaching out to Kenzie in this way. The lobbyist was used to exchanging favors in politics, giving to a charity that someone supported rather than to them directly, supporting them on a bill they wanted to get through so that they would later support you on yours, and all sorts of other convoluted bartering scenarios that Zachary was sure he would never be able to follow.

"Okay." Walter spread his hands. "So there it is. I know someone who needs a private investigator. I know that my daughter's partner is a private investigator. I want to give him the business in a way that doesn't compromise any of us but shows my daughter that I value her and her partner."

"So, what is this case?"

5

———

You're a man who likes to get down to brass tacks," Walter said.

He sat back, smiling, looking more relaxed now that he'd opened up to Zachary. Though he had probably still held a few cards in reserve, if Zachary was right about the kind of person he was. A politician never put all of his cards on the table. He had made his opening play. It was the beginning of the game, not the end.

"There is a little sports bar near the statehouse. Nothing big and fancy, just a little place that I like to go to occasionally to relax and forget all about the world of politics I live in the rest of the time. The one place that I go to just hang out and be me."

Zachary looked at him speculatively. Walter did not strike him as the sports type. Or the "let it all hang out" kind.

"What sports?"

"Hmm?"

"The bar, you go there to watch football?"

Rugby? Polo? What did high-class lobbyists go to sports bars to watch? He couldn't see Walter getting rowdy and cheering on any sport.

"Like any good Vermonter—baseball in the summer and hockey in the winter."

Zachary would explore that later. "Okay. What does this bar need my services for?"

"You're getting ahead of me. I haven't even told you that they do."

Zachary waited.

"Okay." Walter sighed. "Bypass the sentimental stuff. Yes. The bar was recently the victim of a burglary. A smash-and-grab type job."

"They called the police?"

"Sure. But they ran out of leads and aren't pursuing it. If the stolen items show up at nearby pawn shops, they'll follow up. But they don't really care. It's just a little job for them, and they have better things to do. More important cases. Which is true, of course. I wouldn't expect them to turn away from murders, kidnappings, or big heists to chase after this little thing. But that doesn't help my friends at the bar."

"What was stolen?"

"Memorabilia. You know that type of place—signed jerseys up on the walls, photographs of the winning team. Pennants. Reminders of the glory days."

"How valuable?"

"Intrinsically, not a lot. That's why it's not a big deal to the police. It isn't like someone stole Babe Ruth's rookie card. The stuff may run in the thousands, but we're not talking millions. And a lot of it is worth a lot less than that. People walk off with stuff. If you have anything really valuable, you have to invest in smash-proof cases, security, stuff like that. For a little business, that's a big investment. They want to surround themselves with happy memories, to provide them to the fans. Make it a comfortable, fun place to hang out. It isn't Fort Knox."

"Do you have a list of the stolen items?"

"Does that mean you're taking the case?"

"I'm still exploring what that would involve."

Walter hesitated. "I should retain you before I show you anything."

"Is the list of stolen items confidential? I thought it was just some mid-range sports memorabilia."

Walter considered this. Eventually, he popped open the slim briefcase he had brought in with him and pulled out a few pieces of paper. He handed them over to Zachary.

He looked down the list. There was a column of dollar values, so he could pick out what the higher-priced bits were and then read the descriptions. But he could not read quickly and he would prefer a few minutes without Walter staring at him to peruse the list.

"There is coffee in the kitchen," he said. "Why don't you go help yourself to a cup?"

Walter shifted forward in his seat, his eyes still on the list he had given to Zachary.

"You aren't going to make any copies of that."

"No." Zachary thought this a little paranoid. Walter was clearly used to dealing with paperwork that was a lot more privileged than a list of stolen property. "I just want a minute to review this."

Walter conceded, getting to his feet and walking into the kitchen. He could still keep an eye on Zachary from there and make sure that he didn't make some kind of copy of the information.

"Uh… the pot is empty. Do you want me to make another?" Walter called back to Zachary when he'd had a chance to look at it.

"Oh, yeah. Can you figure out the machine?"

"I practically live out of hotels. I can probably run any coffee machine on the planet."

"Great. Yeah, go ahead and make another pot."

Zachary probably shouldn't have too much coffee, but he could use at least one more cup to fortify himself while discussing the case with Walter. It would help him to keep his focus.

He shut out everything else to focus on the list of items stolen from the sports bar. He was not a big sports fan, so he didn't know what the various items would go for on the street or in nearby pawn shops, so the column of values was helpful. But he worked a lot with insurance companies investigating possible fraud charges and was immediately suspicious of any list of stolen items that had been prepared for an insurance claim, which he assumed was what he held in his hand. Items could be added and values inflated to reduce the company's losses and how much their premiums would go up once they made a claim. They might have only lost half of the things on the list and planned to sell the other half themselves, getting paid by both the buyer and the insurer.

Nothing jumped out at him as being ridiculously overvalued. It didn't make sense to put things on display that would crater your business if someone walked off with them. As Walter had said, they were more middle-of-the-road memorabilia, not the outrageously expensive collector's pieces.

Walter entered the room to refresh the coffee cup on Zachary's side table, then returned the carafe to the kitchen and resumed his seat in the easy chair. Eventually, Zachary put the list to the side and looked at Walter.

"I don't think it is worth your while to hire me."

Walter frowned, his eyebrows coming together and forming a deep crease on his forehead. "Why do you say that?"

"I will need several days to look into it, mileage to get around, maybe a hotel for a night while doing interviews, and meals. I didn't add it all up, but my bills would eat into the value of anything recovered. Better off just letting insurance pay out."

He knew how much he would have to charge for several full days of work. It wouldn't be quick to track down those stolen items. It wouldn't just be a couple of phone calls.

Walter nodded slowly. Then he shrugged. "That really doesn't matter, though. As I said, they have mostly sentimental value, and you can't put a value on that."

"They might not be willing to pay for recovery for something that only has sentimental value."

"They aren't paying. I am. Out of my own pocket. I want to do this for them. Something you do for friends."

"And you're willing to get nothing back for the money."

"That's why I laid my cards on the table," Walter pointed out. "To show you that I'm doing this for Kenzie. That's what I get out of it. And I get the gratitude of my friends. Maybe a few comped beers the next few times I drink there. It's goodwill, not money."

Zachary was not the type of private investigator who was usually hired to make someone look good. He was hired because someone was grieving. Because there had been an injustice done. Because someone had been betrayed or might be perpetrating a fraud. Trying to wrap his head around the fact that Walter didn't actually want anything concrete from the investigation was difficult.

"So, you're willing to take a loss on this."

"It's like giving to a charity," Walter said. "It gives me a good feeling. It makes me look good. It hopefully makes people like me better. Those are things that have value to me. Maybe you'll be able to recover a few of the items on that list and maybe you won't. Maybe you'll be able to give the police a lead on who was involved in the robbery. Or maybe not. But we will at least have put all of our resources into it, so people feel like everything possible was done."

Zachary considered the list again. He looked back at Walter. "So, do you want a budget and a project outline of what I will be doing?"

"No. Just say that you'll take the case and tell me how much of a deposit you'll need to start. I'll give you all of the details I can and the contact information for the bar owners. They can tell you anything I can't answer. And then… you dive right in."

"I do have other cases that I am working on right now, and my brother is staying with us while he tries to get into—get back on his feet. I can't just leave him with Kenzie to deal with. So it may be a slow start. I'll get the information from you, make some phone calls to the owners, and get as much information as I can from here. Lay the groundwork for the investigation before I go there and start making inquiries."

"That all sounds fine." Walter shrugged. "You know the business the best. I don't. I wouldn't even know where to start."

"I'm not going to have results for you in a couple of days."

"Right. I understand."

Zachary took a deep breath. "Well then… okay. I'll look into it."

6

Zachary heard the guest room door open and looked up. He hoped that Tyrrell wasn't going to come out in his boxers for what he assumed would be a private discussion, but he didn't know what to say to warn Tyrrell that they were not alone.

Tyrrell was dressed. Zachary blew out his breath. Tyrrell looked at Walter and became flustered.

"Oh, sorry, I didn't know you had someone here. You didn't say you were expecting anyone."

"No, it was unexpected. It's okay. Tyrrell, this is Walter Kirsch, Kenzie's father. Walter, my brother Tyrrell."

The two men nodded at each other but did not get close enough to shake hands.

"Uh, just going to get some more coffee," Tyrrell offered. He looked toward the kitchen but didn't move in that direction. "Maybe I should head over to Starbucks so that I'm out of your way."

"No," Zachary's answer was sharper than he had intended. "We just made a fresh pot. Help yourself."

Tyrrell still looked like he would have preferred to go out. But Zachary didn't want him taking off. There was nothing to stop him from changing his mind and going to the liquor store or bar instead of Starbucks. There were fewer temptations to drink if Tyrrell stayed in the house.

Tyrrell probably read all of this in Zachary's manner, if he hadn't figured out already that the reason they wanted him at the house was to keep an eye on him and, if possible, to keep him from going out on his own. He grunted in disgust and turned away into the kitchen. Zachary listened to him pour a coffee cup and go through the cupboards again for something to eat or drink. Eventually, there was the sound of a crinkly wrapper being removed. Maybe a granola bar. It was good that Tyrrell was eating solid food again. But Zachary didn't know how long that would last.

Tyrrell headed back to the guest room, eyeing Zachary as he went through the living room. He was not pleased with his prison, even if there were no bars.

Zachary looked back at Walter, sitting there waiting, watching the little drama with interest. When Zachary looked back at him, he smiled. "How much, then?"

"Hmm?"

"Your retainer. Your deposit. How much to get you started on the case?"

"Oh." Zachary considered and gave Walter what he figured was ten percent of an investigation that took three full man-days.

"Do you want it by check? E-transfer?" Walter asked, obviously not concerned by the amount.

"Sure, e-transfer is good."

He gave Walter his email address and Walter went ahead and made the transfer.

"I'll tell you what I know, but it isn't a lot. Not that there is a lot to tell, it wasn't complicated. The bar is named Barnburners, and I'll send you the contact information for the owners so that you can get any additional details from them. It was a late-night burglary. Window smashed in to get access to the inside lock on the door. Alarms go off. The thieves grab everything they can in two or three minutes and run. By the time the security company and police get there, they're gone."

"Did the police have any leads? Fingerprints? Identity of the thieves? A similar theft in the area?"

"You can ask them, but I don't expect they'll tell you anything. The thieves were wearing gloves, so no fingerprints. They had balaclavas on, obscuring their faces. So pretty hard to make any kind of identification."

"The police probably won't talk to me, but they might tell the owners one or two details, if we're lucky."

"Yeah, you can ask Glen and Janice about it. They'll share whatever they have."

"Were there any security cameras?"

"Yes. But as I say, there was no way to identify the culprits."

Zachary nodded. "If there is video footage, I'd like to see it."

"The police got a copy. The owners have it on a hard drive still. They can show it to you when you get there."

"Or maybe before. They could email it or send me a link to their server."

Walter shrugged. "I don't know all of the technical stuff. You'll have to deal with them on it."

"So how were they informed about the theft? Their security company called them?"

"I think so. Must have been either the security company or the police."

"Right. Late night or early morning?"

"2 a.m. or something like that. A time when they could be pretty sure that no one would be around."

"Have there been any similar robberies in the area?"

"Not that anyone has mentioned. I assume that if there were a bunch of similar robberies, they would have made a bigger deal of it. If it's a gang or a series."

"You would think so. If they noticed that there was a pattern. Sometimes, you have to look pretty closely to find patterns and start to pull them together."

"You're welcome to do that. At least internet searches make it easy to search the newspapers going back a few months."

Zachary nodded. "Not like in the old days when you had to look them up on microfiche."

Walter laughed. "Was that a shot?"

"Of course not." Zachary grinned. He was old enough to remember going to the library and playing with the microfiche machines. He'd never used them in his private investigations business, but he could remember them being around.

He was pleased to get the case from Walter, with money already in his pocket and a chance to help to reconcile Kenzie with her father. He didn't expect an immediate turnaround in her attitude. Still, it would certainly help that he had come to Zachary and offered him a legitimate job at a good rate. If he needed an investigation done, then why not retain his daughter's partner to do it when that was his business? Most of the people Zachary knew personally would never have a reason to hire a private investigator. Or, if they had a reason to do it, they wouldn't have the money. Walter had both, and it felt pretty good to get such a nice case when he was just getting back on his feet. It would help to cover his losses from the time he had been in the hospital and investigating Tyrrell's disappearance. It wasn't like he had a lot of expenses when he wasn't working, considering he was now living with Kenzie. But he still had the lease on his old apartment, which he intended to get rid of soon, but hadn't gotten around to yet.

"You have my number if you need anything else from me," Walter said. When Zachary was about to object that he didn't, Walter motioned to Zachary's computer. "It's with the e-transfer. My email and phone number. And I'll send you Glen and Janice's information when I get back to my computer. Set up a time with them and they'll show you around Barnburners. You can see where the thieves broke in, where the items they stole were, watch the security video, all of that. You'll have everything the police do. Only, hopefully, you'll be able to make something of it."

"I'll do my best."

7

Zachary did what preliminary work he could, creating a project folder to save information to and then checking for any online accounts of the burglary. There were no parallel cases mentioned in the news articles. Of course, that didn't mean that there weren't any, but reporters often picked up on patterns of cases before the police did. He found a few PR articles about Barnburners, probably paid articles that talked about the ambiance and what a great place it was for sports fans to hang out. There were a few pictures of the interior in those articles and in the online reviews that he turned to next. He took note of the pictures and other memorabilia he could see on the walls and tables, looking at the list of stolen items to see if he could tell where the thieves had been concentrating their attention.

Kenzie arrived home from work and, after greeting him briefly, she excused herself to shower and change out of her work clothes. Zachary stretched and massaged the back of his neck and decided that he needed a break from the computer as well. He went down the hall to the guest room and knocked on the door.

"Come in."

Zachary opened the door. Tyrrell was lying on the bed with a book, pretty much all that he'd been doing since they had brought him home. Zachary wasn't sure he was even reading them, but might just be using them as a prop to look like he was busy when he wasn't. Zachary wanted to ask Tyrrell why he wasn't busy trying to get into a program, to at least put some effort into helping himself, but he bit back the questions. He already knew that Tyrrell was an addict. Asking an addict why they were addicted and weren't motivated to do anything else was pointless. Tyrrell might want to stop drinking, but he hadn't had much success with rehab programs, so Zachary could see how that would be demotivating. Kenzie was looking for something. She would find it.

"What's up, Zachary?"

"Oh. I thought I would order in so that Kenzie can have a break tonight. Do you want pizza? Thai? Something else?"

"I'm not really hungry, and I don't suppose you'll be ordering drinks with any of those."

"No. What will you eat?"

"Anything. I'm not going to reject anything put in front of me. But I'm not very hungry, so it probably won't be a lot."

Usually, Tyrrell was the one telling Zachary that he needed to eat more. Now he was stuck, not wanting to eat anything as he recovered from his latest binge. His body wanted only one thing, and that was the one thing he couldn't have.

"Okay. I think maybe it will be pizza. You're okay with that?"

"Yeah. Nothing too spicy and no anchovies." Tyrrell thumped his chest. "Been dealing with a lot of heartburn."

"Sure. No problem."

Zachary left Tyrrell to his reading and opened the door to Kenzie's en suite bathroom, full of steam from her shower.

"Kenz, I was going to order pizza. Is that okay with you?"

She let out a little sigh. "Yeah, that would be great. I'm beat and was not looking forward to trying to pull something together for supper. How about Tyrrell? I assume he's good with pizza?"

"He says he's okay with anything and said yes to pizza. Not too spicy and no anchovies."

"Works for me. Half cheese, half veg?"

"Okay."

He started to close the door, then paused when he realized she was speaking again. "Thanks, Zach. I should be out by the time it gets here. But if I'm not…"

Zachary chuckled. It was a good thing she had a big water heater. "I'll come get you. And squeeze the excess water out."

Kenzie was out of the shower by the time the pizza got there. She was dressed in her warm plaid jammies, and they opened up the pizza in the living room instead of sitting at the table. It was nice to just have a more casual evening. Zachary felt like there was some tension among the two of them due to the added presence of Tyrrell.

Tyrrell helped himself to the first slice of pizza, since Kenzie insisted that he have the first pick as their guest. "Thanks. This looks great." Tyrrell plopped the large slice onto his plate. "Met your dad today."

Kenzie held the pizza out to Zachary for him to take a piece, her brows drawing together in a frown that mimicked her father's.

"What?"

"Your dad," Tyrrell repeated.

Kenzie was sure to be wondering whether Tyrrell was delusional, or she was.

"Walter came by during the day while you were at work," Zachary told Kenzie as casually as possible. It was clear that she hadn't been expecting Walter to stop in, even though he had said that he had first approached her and talked to her about the case. A great detective Zachary was to not even question it.

"Walter. Why did he come here? He knows I work during the day."

Zachary nodded. He picked the smallest piece of pizza and put it on his paper plate. "He wasn't looking for you. He was talking to me about a case."

Kenzie put the pizza box down and looked at Zachary, pulling her feet up onto the couch as she settled in to eat and relax. But her expression told him that she wasn't relaxed.

"Why would he be talking to you about a case? What case?"

Zachary cleared his throat. "A burglary at a sports bar in Montpelier."

"What would he have to do with that? That doesn't make any sense."

Zachary took a bite of his pizza and glanced over at Tyrrell, nervous about having a conversation with Kenzie about her father in front of Tyrrell. He didn't want Tyrrell to think that he and Kenzie didn't get along, didn't want Kenzie to feel like she had to air her dirty laundry in front of him, and really didn't want to get into a discussion about fathers at all while Tyrrell was around. Not after Zachary's recent reunion with their father.

"He asked me if I would look into the case. The police aren't getting far on it but, of course, it is not a high priority. Not really valuable merchandise, not part of a series of robberies, so it is way down on their list."

"But what does *he* have to do with it?"

"I guess it's the bar he likes to hang out at to relax. He knows the owners, and he wanted to do something for them."

And for Kenzie. But he didn't want her to feel like she was being manipulated. Or that Zachary had anything to do with manipulating her.

"He hangs out at a sports bar," Kenzie repeated in a tone of disbelief.

"That's what he said. It's called Barnburners," Zachary added lamely, as if that might make a difference. But he did hope that it would ring a bell with her. Maybe she would remember that he used to go there when he was a kid or that family friends had started it up.

"That's news to me."

"Well… you guys haven't exactly been close the last few years. It could be somewhere that he has just started to frequent recently."

"Of course," Kenzie snapped. "But he hasn't become a completely different person, has he? He doesn't have any interest in sports. He would never hang around somewhere like that."

Zachary shrugged uncomfortably. "People can change. Pick up new hobbies and interests. Maybe he has a… friend who is interested in sports and introduced him to the place."

"A friend?" Kenzie repeated. "Are you saying a girlfriend? You think that he's seeing some woman who has gotten him interested in sports or in this bar? Who owns it?"

"He's going to send me the contact information for the owners. Their first names were Glen and Janice…?" Zachary hoped that she would recognize the names as old family friends and relax. He especially didn't want to discuss whether her father could have a girlfriend and, if he did, how she was influencing him. Men of Walter's age often picked younger women. Not bimbos, necessarily, but younger, more attractive women a couple of decades their juniors. Had Walter recently taken up with a woman Kenzie's age or younger who was interested in sports?

Zachary looked away from Kenzie, trying to find something else in the room to look at other than her accusing gaze.

"I don't know of any Glen and Janice. And if he's got a girlfriend… well, of course he does. It's been years since he and Mother divorced. I wouldn't expect him to go that long without some kind of companionship."

Zachary nodded mutely. In his experience, divorced men usually started looking for companionship very quickly after a divorce. Or before. Walter had probably been through a series of girlfriends, but Kenzie had not been subjected to them because of the rift between her and her father.

Or maybe she knew about some of them and had just not thought to share anything with Zachary. It had been a long time before Kenzie had said *anything* to Zachary about either of her parents. Kenzie preferred to keep her relationships with her parents separate from her relationship with Zachary. And he respected that. He would never introduce her to *his* biological parents. He would never see them voluntarily and certainly wouldn't want Kenzie to meet them.

8

Kenzie took a couple of bites of her pizza, chewing it slowly, but she didn't look like she was enjoying it or even tasting it. Her thoughts were far away.

"What you're telling me," she said eventually, "is that my father has been hanging around some sports bar, which was the target of a burglary, and he wants you to look into it for him."

Zachary nodded.

"As a favor," Kenzie said.

Zachary swallowed. "He is paying me," he countered. "Regular rates."

"But it's still a favor. Right? Because he's my father? He used that to leverage you."

"Well…" Zachary cleared his throat again and looked around for a drink. He didn't know whether it was his meds or the conversation that was making his mouth so dry. He hadn't opened a soft drink to have with the pizza, so he swigged cold coffee from the mug on the side table. "Your name did come up."

Tyrrell laughed. Kenzie looked at him and smiled grudgingly.

"Okay, so that does sound a little ridiculous," she admitted. "I wouldn't expect him to come here and hire Zachary without my name ever being mentioned."

"You and your dad don't get along?" Tyrrell guessed.

"Well…" Kenzie grimaced. She took another bite of her pizza, thinking about what to say. "We don't get along, but we don't fight. I just… stay as far away from him as possible, and he generally does his own thing." She looked at Zachary. "Unless he wants something."

"So it's good that he's hiring Zachary for this job, right? It's a way to reach out to you without disrupting your life."

Kenzie considered. "Well, it's a way to get involved in my life without talking to me. Or getting my permission first." She sent a glare in Zachary's direction.

Zachary held his hands up. "He sounded like he had talked to you."

"Did he say that he had?"

Zachary had been thinking about it as they spoke. "I guess not… he said that he had talked to you about me being a private investigator."

Kenzie snorted. "Maybe in passing. He never discussed this case with me. Certainly, never said anything about this bar he supposedly hangs around at." She shook her head. "He's the kind of guy who never buys a drink unless it will get him something. Unless it is for someone else so that he can keep them captive long enough to convince them of whatever it is he wants."

Tyrrell looked at Zachary and gave a little shrug. He'd done what he could to help Kenzie realize that Zachary had been a victim of Walter's wiles, rather than choosing to do something to aggravate her.

"You've already taken the case," Kenzie said, looking back at Zachary.

"Yes."

"Well, you can un-take it. Tell him that you've reconsidered and you've got too much else on your plate."

"I accepted a retainer."

"So? Give it back. Tell him that you don't want to do it."

"Once I take a retainer, I'm committed. That's my promise that I'll do my best to solve the case."

"But you can tell him that you changed your mind. That you looked into it further and decided that it isn't the kind of thing you want to do."

Zachary ran his thumb over the smooth rim of the paper plate in his hands, considering. "I'd like to see what I can find out. He hasn't done anything wrong by hiring me. I said that I would look into it, so I want to follow through."

It could be hard for Zachary to change direction once he had committed to a course of action. He might jump from one thing to another or follow impulses that weren't always the best decisions, but if he decided to do something, he didn't like to have to change course. And as a professional, he had promised Walter he would find out what he could. His reputation was at stake.

He scratched the back of his neck. "How important is it to you?" he asked finally.

It was a strategy that Dr. Boyle had suggested in couples' therapy. If they had widely varying opinions on something that required a decision to be made, then it was important to know how strongly each of them felt about it. Was it a hill they were willing to die on? Would the wrong decision endanger someone's health or their relationship? Or was it just a preference? Or somewhere in between?

Kenzie frowned, thinking about it. "Well... it's not something I'd risk our relationship over. I want to keep you and my father away from each other to protect *you*, not because I can't stand him. I don't like you taking a case for him. But if you insist on following through... just be warned that you're dealing with someone without ethics."

"Or without your ethics," Zachary suggested.

"Okay, without my ethics. I'm sure he has his own boundaries that he won't cross, but I don't know what they are. I know that he's been more than willing to cross a lot of the boundaries that I would observe. He's out to get what he wants, and he is very diligent in getting it. He'll run over a lot of people and a lot of... moral codes to get it."

Zachary nodded. He knew from the way she had talked about him in the past that the two of them did not have values that aligned. And he'd seen Walter plant a listening device to eavesdrop on his own daughter when she wouldn't do what he wanted her to. That *was* someone willing to go to great lengths to get what he wanted.

"But he cares about people, too. He cares about you. And it seems like he cares about your mother."

"But not enough to stay with her. Not enough to make the relationship work. So is that really love? Or is it just self-serving? He cares about people only to the extent that it serves him."

And that was true of a lot of people.

Zachary nodded. He took a bite of his pizza. "Does it help if I say I'll treat him just like any other client? I'm not going to give him any special consideration because he's your dad. And I'm not going to hold you responsible if he does something like... deciding not to pay my bill and calling the cops when I start harassing him for payment."

Kenzie chuckled. "Well, I don't see him doing that. He's usually pretty good about paying his bills, assuming that hasn't changed. It's more likely that he would… tell somebody that you were investigating them, or tell you that I had asked you to get him involved in the case, something like that. Misleading people. Twisting things around or gaslighting you. That's what I'm worried about."

"I've been warned. If he does anything like that, I'm not holding you responsible. In fact, if he does… I'll buy you ice cream and flowers to say, 'you were right.' "

Tyrrell laughed. "You guys are too much. You're so careful of each other! You're like a couple of kids on their first date, trying to decide what movie to go to."

Zachary looked at Tyrrell, irritated. He and Kenzie had broken up once before because he hadn't been willing to talk about his feelings and the boundaries in their relationship. They were working hard with a therapist to build a strong relationship despite Zachary's issues and their vastly different upbringings and personalities.

"It's called being considerate. Thinking about the other person and working things out," he told Tyrrell firmly. Though he would like to have said a lot more. Tyrrell was divorced and his method of dealing with conflict was to run away and disappear for days or weeks at a time. How exactly did he expect to build a happy relationship dealing with problems that way?

Kenzie put her empty pizza plate to the side and put her hand on Zachary's leg. Not to stop him from defending himself against Tyrrell's words, but an unspoken "thank you" for taking her feelings on the matter into account and talking it out.

"Go ahead and take it. Just remember I didn't want you to get hustled by him."

9

K enzie was moving around the living room and kitchen, tidying things up. Zachary was aware of her on one level, but blocking her out on another. She wasn't trying to carry on a conversation with him. They'd had breakfast separately because Kenzie had slept in and then had a shower, so it was quite late in the morning by the time she was up and around.

But part of Zachary's brain was aware of what she was doing and starting to wonder why she was cleaning. Had she asked him to help with something? Was someone coming over that he had forgotten about? Was she irritated over the mess that two men made in the house now that Tyrrell was there during the day and not just Zachary? He'd been trying to tidy up after himself and Tyrrell if he saw things that were out of place, but he knew that his awareness of the cleanliness landscape of the house was not good. He would walk around a pile of laundry in the middle of the floor half a dozen times before he really saw it and started to wonder if he were supposed to be doing something about it. He often started a chore and didn't finish it because he got distracted by something else. Maybe an insight into a case that he had to write down or do a quick search on before he forgot about it. Or maybe just a bird flying past the window or a motorcycle buzzing down the street. He could remember more than one foster mom or group-home worker slapping him across the back of the head to try to bring his attention back to the chore or conversation at hand.

Zachary stood up abruptly and looked at Kenzie, as if she'd been the one who had slapped him across the head to get his attention. "What's going on? Do you need help?"

Kenzie raised her eyebrows, looking amused. "Good morning."

"Uh… didn't I say good morning to you yet? Sorry. Hi. Did you have a good sleep?"

"It was nice to be able to laze around. What's going on with you? We did say hello earlier, but why the jack-in-the-box act?" She gestured to where he had been sitting on the couch, attending to his work.

"Just noticed that you were cleaning up and… thought I should help. Is something going on today? Or is it just… because we're messy?" Zachary gave a little head-tilt in the direction of Tyrrell's room.

"Is he up yet, do you know? I haven't heard him. But I think we should probably get him up before too long…"

Zachary looked at the time on his phone. "He's usually up by now, but maybe he stayed up late watching a movie. Do you need him out of there? Do you want to vacuum?"

"It's like you're a half-trained dog," Kenzie said with a laugh. "You know you should be doing something; you just don't have a clue *what*."

Zachary nodded, his ears and cheeks burning.

"Alisha and Mason are coming over," Kenzie said in a low, confidential tone. "So… yes, we are having company, but they won't actually care whether things are tidy or not, and I'll probably have to tidy up again after they leave. I'm just full of nervous energy right now, trying to distract myself by doing something physical."

"Alisha and Mason? Does Tyrrell know?" Zachary couldn't fathom how Tyrrell could still be sleeping if he knew that his children were coming over for a visit.

"No, I didn't tell him. That's why I'm wondering if we should get him up. I don't want him to still be in bed when they get here, but I don't want him getting all anxious and stressed out, either."

"When are they coming? In the next hour or two?"

She double-checked the time. "Within the hour."

"Then we'd better get him up."

"Okay… how would you like to do that? He's your brother…"

Zachary laughed at her reluctance, but he didn't really want to be the one to wake Tyrrell up either. He hated waking people up. And Tyrrell wouldn't have any idea why Zachary was interrupting his sleep. "You're the one who invited him to stay over," he reminded her.

"You get in there and wake him up!" Kenzie ordered, miming a slow-motion punch to his shoulder. She knew better than to actually slug him in the shoulder like she'd seen other couples do. He'd been hit too many times by too many different people in his younger years not to react.

"Yes, ma'am."

Zachary marched himself down to the guest room. He knocked on the door and then opened it. Tyrrell was still in bed, in a tangle of sheets, the room still dark with the blind being pulled down.

"Tyrrell! Hey, wake up; we have a surprise for you."

He went over to the window and pushed the blind up to let the bright sunlight stream into the room. He wouldn't shake Tyrrell awake, knowing that he might also have some demons in his past that triggered unexpected violence when someone woke him up abruptly.

"T! Hey, wake up. Guess who's coming over?"

Tyrrell groaned. "What's going on? What are you doing? I was sleeping."

"I know. But it's late, and Kenzie has some guests coming over that you're going to want to see."

Tyrrell moaned. "I barely got any sleep. Leave me alone."

"Alisha and Mason are on their way over. You should probably at least wash your face and comb your hair."

Tyrrell moved around sluggishly, pushing blankets away from his face. "What? What do you mean, Alisha and Mason are on their way over?"

"Kenzie made arrangements, apparently. She didn't tell me either until just now."

At least, Zachary hoped that Kenzie hadn't mentioned it before then, and he'd simply ignored her or forgotten about it.

"Kenzie called Lindsey? And set up a meeting?"

"I guess so. She said they should be here within the hour, so I didn't think you'd want to still be sleeping."

"No." Tyrrell pushed himself up and looked around, blinking groggily. "I'd better... shower and shave."

Zachary nodded his agreement. Alisha and Mason could visit with Tyrrell in the living room and not have to be in the overly warm, sweaty-smelling guest room. But Tyrrell needed to get himself cleaned up and prepared for the visit.

"Okay. I'm up. I'm up."

Zachary didn't leave, waiting for Tyrrell to get on his feet. Even as a little boy, Tyrrell had been difficult to get up in the morning, sometimes crawling back into bed even once he was dressed for school and had his backpack on.

Eventually, Tyrrell got to his feet and lurched toward the door. "Yeah, yeah. I'm up."

Zachary moved to the side and let Tyrrell past him to the main bathroom. "Don't be too long in there."

10

Tyrrell was out of the bathroom, freshly showered, shaven, and dressed in clean clothes in enough time that Zachary could also take a few minutes to freshen up. Kenzie had the living room tidied as neatly as Zachary had ever seen it. He even stashed his laptop and the rest of his mobile office into the bedroom so that it wouldn't be out when the children arrived.

Tyrrell had been pacing up and down the hallway, waiting for their arrival, but still didn't get to the door fast enough to beat Mason's dash to the doorstep. The doorbell rang, buzzing loudly while he held the button down and completing its two-tone ring when he released it. Kenzie was the first to reach the door, Tyrrell behind her, and Zachary hung back to give them space to get in.

"Hi, Auntie Kenzie!" Mason shouted, then saw Tyrrell and, giving an ear-splitting squeal, tackled him like a linebacker. Tyrrell had difficulty staying on his feet. He reached down and grabbed Mason, swinging him up into his chest and giving him a tight hug.

"Mason, my man. Look how you've grown! I haven't been away for that long!"

Mason bawled loudly into Tyrrell's shoulder, answering him in a long wail of words that no one could understand with his face muffled. Tyrrell held him, rocking back and forth and patting him on the back.

"It's okay, bud. It's alright. You're okay. Hey, come on, little man," he ruffled Mason's hair. "It's all okay. Chin up."

Alisha's entrance was quieter. She greeted Kenzie, took off her winter boots, and walked up to Tyrrell. She hugged him, putting her arms around both Mason and her father.

"Hi, Alisha. How are you doing, honey?" Tyrrell shifted Mason around to reach Alisha and gave her a kiss on the head. "There, beautiful. It's so nice to see you guys! How have you been?"

Alisha pulled back, tears in her eyes and escaping in a couple of tracks down her cheeks and chin. She sniffled, trying to keep her emotions under control.

"We've been okay," she told him stoically. "You're the one who ran away. If you'd stayed home, you could see us whenever you wanted to."

"Well… there are rules about when I'm allowed to have you for visits," Tyrrell explained.

"Mom would let you come and see us whenever you wanted," Alisha informed him firmly.

Tyrrell swallowed and nodded. "Yeah, she probably would," he admitted. "I'm so sorry, baby. Your daddy… has some problems."

"You need to stop drinking."

"I know."

She nodded. "Then do it."

There was an answering nod and sobs from Mason. "Please, Daddy, please stop drinking so we can see you at Christmas and not be sad."

Tyrrell kissed his cheek and then held Mason's face against his own, looking anguished. "I'm sorry you were sad at Christmas. I really am. I was… it was a really hard time for me, but I know I made a mistake when I started drinking again and didn't come to visit you."

Mason pulled back from Tyrrell, so he was sitting on Tyrrell's encircling arms, face-to-face with him. He put his hands on each side of Tyrrell's face, holding him still and looking straight into his eyes.

"You just behave," he ordered. "You're a big boy now and you can make better choices."

Clearly, these were words he had heard from his mother or some other authority figure in his life. Zachary felt bad for Mason, recognizing in him the severe ADHD that had also plagued Zachary as a child, making it impossible for him to make the right choices much of the time or to sit and behave and be a big boy when the adults pleaded with him to. And threatened and meted out punishments when he was unable to control himself.

Tyrrell was looking pretty overwhelmed himself. He pulled his face back from Mason's grasp and bit his lip, not able to come up with a satisfactory reply.

"Let's get your winter clothes off now," Kenzie invited. "It's cold outside, so you need them, but it's nice and warm in here. I don't want snow puddles all over the house, so let's get these boots off and find a place to hang your coat."

Tyrrell put Mason down and they helped him get his clothes put away. Alisha followed suit, then they all went into the living room.

"Hi, Uncle Zachary," Alisha greeted, looking a little shy.

"Hi, Alisha. You're doing a great job," he told her, and put his arm around her shoulders to give her a little squeeze. He didn't need to specify what she was doing good at. Taking care of Mason; being the responsible, mature one; being a listening ear for her mother and a voice of reason to her errant father. She was struggling with a hundred responsibilities that would have been onerous for any grown-up. He wanted to make sure that someone let her know that her efforts were seen.

Alisha smiled and put her arm around his waist to give him a squeeze back. "Thanks."

"We have some games," Kenzie offered. "You remember at the Lodge you guys were playing Clue and some other board games? That was fun, wasn't it?"

Mason looked at the TV, which had been turned off, and glanced around the room for a game controller or other electronic recreation. Then he sighed and nodded. "I guess so."

The children sat down to look through the board games that Kenzie had pulled out for them. Kenzie, Zachary, and Tyrrell sat down. Tyrrell let out a long, slow breath, still looking overwhelmed, but a little more in control of himself.

"If you need a break, then take one," Zachary told him. "Just say you need a few minutes and go back to your room to decompress for a bit. It's better than…" He trailed off, not finishing the sentence. Better than having a meltdown? As far as he knew, Tyrrell didn't do that. Better than running away? He didn't want to suggest that Tyrrell was going to run away or felt like it. It wasn't his place to judge or evaluate Tyrrell. He just wanted to support him. "Anyway. I'm not going to stay out here the whole time. I'm going to go get some work done in the bedroom."

"You don't have to do that," Tyrrell protested. "The kids want to see you too."

"You're the one they need to see. And you don't need me hanging around watching you or making you... think about when we were kids."

"I'll stick around if you need a fourth player," Kenzie said. "But if you don't, I have some errands to run and I'm going to take the opportunity to go while I still have enough energy to manage the crowds. I might pick up some supper, depending on how long it takes."

"Thanks," Tyrrell said appreciatively. "This is really great. I don't know if I could have set something up with how I've been feeling lately. I really didn't want to talk to... you know who."

Alisha looked up from the boxes of games. "We know you mean Mommy," she told him with an impatient shake of her head.

Tyrrell cleared his throat and turned pink.

"Anyway... you guys don't need to run away. I don't want to take over the house on you."

"I've got work to do," Zachary said. He stood up to go to the bedroom. Tyrrell might say that he wanted them to stick around, but Zachary knew that when Tyrrell spent too much time around him, especially with the kids, it brought back Tyrrell's memories of when they were kids, and how Berk had treated them. Which made him both more irritable and impatient with the children and more sensitive to the way he was treating them and all of the ways he was like Berk.

Zachary bent down to rub Mason's head. "I'll be back out later. Don't leave without saying goodbye."

Mason nodded. "Okay."

"And I'm going out unless you need me," Kenzie told Tyrrell again.

Zachary didn't wait around to see if she were staying or going out, and went to the bedroom to work on his computer.

Zachary didn't spend a lot of time in Montpelier. Still, it was the least populous state capital in the United States, so it wasn't hard to find his way around, especially with the GPS on his phone to supplement his knowledge from previous visits.

The owners of Barnburners, Glen and Janice McNichol, had agreed to meet him at the bar, even though it was long before their usual opening time. Zachary found the door unlocked upon his arrival and let himself in.

The couple was sitting at one of the tables with their heads together in discussion, seated where they would be able to see Zachary as soon as he got there. Janice stood up to greet him.

"You must be Zachary Goldman."

"Zachary. Nice to meet you, Mrs. McNichol."

She offered her hand. "Janice is fine. If I'm going to be calling you by your first name, you may as well call me by mine."

Zachary nodded and shook with her. Her skin was cool and dry. No sweaty palms on meeting the investigator. Her handshake was firm, but brief. She motioned to her husband, who hadn't gotten up from the table. "And this is Glen. We were just going over the police reports. I'm not sure what you will want to see."

"Everything you've got. And anything else I can pry out of you." Zachary smiled to reassure her that he was just joking, but of course, he would get everything out of them that he could in their discussion. And probably be back with several more questions as the investigation proceeded.

They were a middle-aged couple, maybe in their mid-forties to early fifties. Still young-looking, but with some fine wrinkles that hadn't been there a decade before and gray creeping into the hair on Glen's temples. No noticeable gray in Janice's hair, but she probably dyed it if there were. They looked like experienced business owners, but maybe put a little off-balance by the burglary.

"Why don't you come sit down? I guess we'll start here with what we've got."

Zachary looked at the papers spread over the table as he sat down with them. "If I could get copies or scans of these documents, that would be great. Then I can review them at my leisure and I don't need to spend all of today's meeting reading."

Janice nodded, though she didn't look pleased that he wasn't going to jump straight into the paperwork.

"I can get a better sense of what happened by talking with you. There will be things that you remember that didn't make it into the official reports. Nuances, feelings, suspicions, all of those things that the police don't really want to hear."

"But you do want to."

"If the cops could solve it based just on the facts you have given them, then they would. How long have they been on the case now? The robbery was a week ago?"

"Last weekend," Glen agreed with a nod. His voice was deeper than Zachary had expected. A warm, resonant baritone.

"That doesn't mean that they won't eventually be able to nail your thieves and recover some of the stolen property, but if their identity was obvious, the police would have made some progress by now. Sometimes, investigations like this can take months before you hear anything back. They work on it as they can, but it isn't a high priority, and it takes time to process evidence and make inquiries."

"What evidence?" Janice demanded. "They didn't even send anyone out to take pictures or fingerprints. They told us to send them a copy of the surveillance video and come in and make our statements. I thought that at the police station, they would at least take the time to discuss it with us. You know how they always sit down with the victim on TV and have coffee and go over everything together. But they were too busy. They just nod and open a file and give you the forms. I tried to talk to one of the police about it when we submitted the forms, the Officer of the Day or whoever was there at the desk. But you could tell he didn't want to hear it. The phones were ringing and other people were waiting and they just pushed us through the process. I doubt the officer we talked to would even remember us the day after we were there. And I'm sure he didn't write anything down. Just filed our reports and said that it would be passed on to the investigators."

"You took some pictures yourselves?" Zachary suggested.

"Sure." Glen got out his phone and tapped it a few times to bring up his photo stream. He handed it to Zachary. Zachary thumbed through the pictures, seeing photos of the broken window glass, of stuff that had been knocked to the floor, and empty shelves and walls where the memorabilia had once been displayed. There were quite a few pictures, and he went through each one slowly, thinking about how they would have felt, walking into the business that they had built from the ground up and lovingly cared for, and seeing the devastation the thieves had left in only a few minutes.

"I'm sorry. It must have been awful to walk in here and see all of that." Zachary glanced around the bar. The lighting was soft. The McNichols had cleaned everything up so that there was no sign of the destruction. Some of the blank spaces on the walls had been filled with posters, and a few toys, pucks, and baseballs were sprinkled around on the display shelves. Still, there was far less memorabilia than there had been before the theft. "They didn't take everything. How much of this did they leave behind and how much did you purchase after the burglary?"

Janice looked around and shrugged. "Maybe half and half... we tried to spread stuff out and then purchased some cheaper stuff just to fill the biggest holes. It is going to take a long time to build it back up again if we can't recover anything that was stolen."

"Maybe some of your patrons would donate some of their memorabilia. Collectors tend to acquire too much stuff to display everything. They might be proud to have some of their stuff on your walls, even if it was just on loan for a while."

Janice looked at Glen, who cocked his head to the side and nodded. "Yeah... maybe we could do some kind of donation drive or ask people if they would loan us a few things. We could put up tags to indicate who they were from, so they'd get a bit of publicity."

"Unless they're afraid that it would be stolen too," Janice said. "What if they are worried that we'll get robbed again?"

Glen sighed and looked at Zachary. "We're working on getting our security upgraded. But it's expensive. I don't suppose you have any recommendations…?"

Zachary took a glance around. "There are some things you can do that are low-tech. Bars and bolts. A guard dog. You have footage of the break-in, so you must already have cameras."

"It's from neighbors," Glen said, shaking his head. "We haven't invested much in security before now. I guess the burglars knew that."

"Probably," Zachary agreed. "You should at least get front and back door cameras. And maybe something over the bar." He gestured to the ceiling over the bar in the center of the main room. "You want to have some kind of surveillance of the cash registers in case someone holds up your staff or they are skimming from the till."

The couple exchanged looks. Glen moved a couple of papers off of a notebook where he had apparently been making a list of what follow-up actions to take. Zachary nodded.

"If you beef up security and let people know, I don't think they would be as worried about lending you their own memorabilia. You can get anti-theft anchors to make it harder to walk off with artwork. They aren't infallible, but they help in a smash and grab like this. If thieves can't easily pull them off of the hooks and walk away with them, they won't generally take the time to figure out how to detach them."

"We'll look into that."

"I can refer you to a security consultant if you like. Just let them know your budget off the top, so they don't suggest high-priced solutions."

Glen nodded grimly. "That's the problem. We don't have the money to beef up security and replace the stolen items. I'm worried about a drop-off in business if people decide it isn't a safe place to eat and drink and hang out. So far, business has been fine. Everyone wants to come and gawk and to talk about what happened. But once the novelty wears off… are they still going to come here to drink?" He shook his head slowly. "I'm worried that too many of them will go somewhere else instead."

Zachary nodded, but he didn't want to get into a discussion of marketing the bar. That wasn't his area of expertise at all. And if he didn't have anything to offer, he might as well not waste paid investigative time doing it.

12

Zachary pulled his notepad out of his pocket and opened it up to make some notes. "Why don't you go through what happened the day before the break-in. Was there anything unusual going on that day? Any new customers that you noticed? Any fights or other things that might have distracted your attention?"

"The day before?" Janice shook her head, eyebrows drawing down. "No. How is that going to help you? Like you said, it was a smash and grab. Someone saw an opportunity and just... took it."

"Whoever cased it out was probably in the bar, not just walking by outside and noticing that you didn't have a security camera and that they could smash a window to get access. They probably came in, had a drink, chatted with the staff, walked back to the restrooms and maybe even into the kitchen. Checked out any back exits. Scoped out which memorabilia was worth the most so that they knew what to target."

The couple considered the possibility, looking dismayed. "They were in here?" Glen demanded. "They just walked in here and took a look around so they could come back later and steal everything?"

Zachary nodded. "More than likely."

Janice scratched her head, frowning and thinking back to the day before the robbery. They had been focusing on that night, on remembering how everything had looked in the early-morning hours when they had been called about the burglary. At that point, it was too late and, if the thieves had been wearing balaclavas and gloves, they had probably not left any physical evidence behind to identify them.

"If they were here to scope the place out, then they wouldn't cause a disturbance, would they?" she questioned. "They would want to stay quiet, under the radar so that we wouldn't notice them."

"Maybe. Or if there was more than one person involved, then one might have had a little look around while the other made a scene to distract you."

"There were more than one," Glen admitted. "That's on the video." He squinted at his wife. "I don't remember anything unusual during the day before the robbery, do you?"

"No… nothing specific," she said. "I mean, sometimes we get people being rowdy. That's pretty normal with a sports bar. Their team is losing or they are being obnoxious about a win. Had too much to drink and they just lose all inhibitions. It's normal to have a disturbance here and there. But I can't think of anything unusual that day."

"Have you had any strange phone calls? Hang-ups? People calling for another business or someone who doesn't work here?"

Both shook their heads, looking mystified.

"Anyone hanging around? Loitering inside or outside? A homeless person, someone who asked for a glass of water and didn't spend anything? Someone asking you questions that are out of the ordinary? Maybe about how long you've been in this location or who does your cleaning?"

"No. Nothing like that. It's pretty cold for the homeless to be hanging around right now," Glen offered. "Most of them have found places in more hospitable parts of town. Near the homeless shelter. We don't really… have anything to do with people like that. They don't come in here, and if they do, we make it clear that this is a paying business, not a place to loiter. Paying customers only."

"Who does your cleaning? Do you hire out?"

"No, we do it ourselves. The staff. We have checklists of procedures to be followed every day. Mopping up at the end of the day, checking the bathrooms, wiping down fixtures, that kind of thing. Anything bigger, we usually do ourselves, or have someone in."

Anticipating Zachary's next question, Janice spoke up. "We don't have a company that we usually go to, just whoever specializes. And we haven't had any contractors in the past few weeks."

Zachary nodded. "I'd like to talk to your staff, see what their recollections are about that day, and if any of them are aware of anything unusual happening in the days before the robbery. What time will they be coming in?"

Janice looked at her watch. "Not for a couple more hours."

"Okay. I should probably look at the video." Zachary started to put his notebook away. "How long have you guys known Walter?"

They both looked at him with blank expressions. Zachary raised his brows, waiting for them to understand.

"The man who is paying me to investigate?" he prompted.

"Oh, Mr. Kirsch. Yeah… I don't know, how long do you think he's been coming here, honey?" Glen asked his wife.

"Hard to say. I'm not sure when he started. It's been a few months, I guess."

Zachary kept his expression neutral. Only a few months? What had precipitated the change? When Kenzie had said that her father didn't have any interest in sports, he had assumed that she was wrong. That it was just because she hadn't been in close contact with him for a number of years that she wasn't aware of his passion for hockey or baseball or whatever other sport interested him. Hockey and baseball were the ones that he had mentioned, if he remembered right. But if he had only been going to the bar for a few months, even if the McNichols remembered wrong and it was as long as a year, then what had changed?

Had he started dating a puck bunny? Moved to an office building across the street, and just gravitated toward the nearest bar, not caring what their specialty was or how rowdy the customers might get? Was it a childhood interest that had rekindled as he got older and remembered his younger years and tried to recapture that magic?

Nothing felt right. He had believed that Walter knew the owners. He had talked like he did. But considering the fact that they didn't even know his first name, it seemed unlikely that he was good friends with them.

"He must really like the place," Zachary offered. "For him to be willing to lay out this kind of money for the investigation. I mean, you could probably buy a lot of memorabilia with it, if it wasn't earmarked for the investigation."

Glen's eyes widened, as if it were the first time he had thought about such a thing. Maybe they didn't know how expensive it was to hire a private investigator for a few days. But it wasn't pocket change. Zachary was no longer a wet-behind-the-ears investigator. He'd been at it for a lot of years and had worked his way up to the higher rates.

"He must like it," Janice echoed in a faraway voice.

"He's here most nights?" Zachary guessed.

They both shook their heads immediately. They looked at each other, trying to gauge their answer. "Not every night," Janice said. "Maybe… once every couple of weeks?"

"Oh. I had just assumed…"

She shook her head again, more definitely now. "No. He came in here a few times since the summer. But he wasn't what you would call regular."

"Did he only come in when a specific team was playing?" Zachary suggested. "Or for a certain… tournament or cup?" He hoped that his terminology wasn't too far off.

"No. I never saw him pull for any particular team. He didn't wear a jersey or any other team colors. To be honest…" Janice looked at her husband for his corroboration. "I'm not sure he ever watched the TVs. He would just come in for a little while for a drink or an appetizer. And then… he would leave."

Zachary rubbed the bridge of his nose, thinking about that. He tried to picture Walter there, to see him come into the bar, sit down, and have his drink or snack. And then get up and walk back out. It didn't feel right. He couldn't picture Walter in a team jersey, so that part made sense to him, but what didn't make sense was that Walter was spending his time there at all. Not for a specific sport or team.

"Did he come in with someone else? Did he have a friend or a date? Someone he met here? A friend on the staff?"

"No." They both shook their heads together. "I never saw him with someone else. He would chat a bit with the wait staff, just pleasantries, you know. Sometimes Glen or I are on, so he got to know who we were. That we owned the place. But he didn't… ingratiate himself or anything like that. He wasn't expecting special favors for recognizing the owners. I think…" Janice pursed her lips while she thought about it. "I think he was just a lonely old man, that's all. Maybe some night he didn't want to go back home alone. So he came somewhere to be around people for a little while. Even if he didn't know anyone in particular, it's a friendly place. You can come here and feel like you belong to a team or a club. People crack jokes and involve you in a conversation, even if they don't know you. They assume you're pulling for the Habs and talk about their prospects this year. Just… it's a place where you can come and not feel so alone."

"At least, I hope it is," Glen said, turning his palms up. "That's the type of community and atmosphere that we've tried to foster. When you're here, you're family, or however that saying goes."

345

"Sounds nice," Zachary gave them a warm smile. He could imagine having a place like that to go to. He and Kenzie knew some of the staff at Old Joe's and some of the other local eateries. People recognized you if you were there regularly. And it was nice to be recognized, even if you weren't close friends with them.

"Yeah, it is," Janice agreed. She shrugged. "And obviously Mr. Kirsch thought so too, or he wouldn't have done this." She motioned toward Zachary by way of explanation.

"Yes, he obviously felt comfortable here, and thought highly of you," he agreed.

They looked pleased at his words.

But they were just words. Inside, Zachary was trying to figure out what was going on. Why did Walter care about the robbery if the bar and the people who owned it didn't mean anything to him? He could go and have a drink and a meal anywhere in Montpelier. It didn't have to be the little sports bar.

So why did he care what happened to them?

And even more than that, why did he care about making it right?

13

Zachary made a few notes in his notepad before putting it away again. He followed Janice to the small office in the back, with a computer and a stack of papers in an overflowing basket that looked like it probably only got cleaned out once a year.

"Sorry for the mess," she said, waving her fingers to indicate everything in the room.

It wasn't the messiest office Zachary had ever seen, but it wasn't the cleanest, either. He remembered fleetingly the feeling he had walking into Isabella Hildebrandt's office. Widely known as the Happy Artist. Of course, she had not been happy when he had been investigating the death of her son. Isabella's studio had been a nightmare. Every inch of space was covered with canvases, brushes, paint, or other supplies. Stacked high on shelves in piles that looked like they were going to topple over any minute. The exact opposite of the rest of the house, neatly arranged and maintained by her husband.

"I've seen worse," Zachary told her with a smile.

Janice smiled vaguely in response. He doubted she had even heard what he'd said. Her focus was already on the computer and starting up the video recording they had obtained from one of the neighborhood cameras.

In a few minutes, she turned the monitor partway around so that Zachary could see the black and white video playing on the screen.

It wasn't the horrible, fuzzy images that a lot of the cheaper security cameras captured, but nice, high-resolution pictures with good lighting and contrast. Two figures breaking the window, as Walter had said, and reaching through to unlock the door and let themselves in. There was no sound on the video, but Zachary could tell by the body language of the two thieves that they were aware they had tripped an alarm, whether it was audible or not. Their movements were quick, jerky, with lots of looking around to make sure that the police weren't coming yet. They pushed away anything that was in their way as they grabbed what Zachary assumed were the highest-priced memorabilia, shoving the stuff into duffel bags and what looked like garbage bags. Grab, grab, grab, look around to make sure they weren't yet caught, and then grab, grab, grab again. In a couple of minutes—2:15 according to the timer on the video—one of them grabbed the other by the arm, and they hustled out.

"The security company arrived a few minutes later," Janice said. "Never caught sight of them. And then the police after that. And as you can see, they were wearing masks and gloves, so… there isn't much to go on."

"No," Zachary agreed, looking at the screen where the video had now ended and was sitting waiting to be replayed. "Can you play it through one more time?"

"I'll send you a copy and you can watch it as many times as you want, but I don't think you're going to be able to get anything from it. Unless you can perform some magic on it that the police can't. But I know all that stuff they do on TV with magnifying images ten times and bringing stuff up in reflections is mostly made up. And even if it wasn't, the cops aren't going to be spending much time looking at the video. It isn't a high-priority case. They just need to confirm to the insurers that it was a burglary, watch for any of our stuff to show up in the pawnshops, and maybe keep their ears to the ground in case there is a series of similar burglaries or someone starts talking about it."

"Just play it one more time," Zachary urged. "I'll watch it on my own computer too, but I just want to see it one more time while I'm here. In case there is anything that I have to look at while I'm on the scene."

Janice shrugged. "Fine." She clicked the video again and they watched the same sequence play through. Zachary watched the whole screen, not just focusing on the thieves, but trying to impress it all on his memory. When the video had finished playing a second time, Janice swiveled in her chair and looked at him. "Okay? Anything else?"

"And you've checked with anyone else who might have had a camera in the vicinity? To see if anyone caught the getaway vehicle or its license plates? What direction they went after the burglary?"

"I don't know. I can ask the police if they did that. We didn't go door to door; we just asked the businesses nearby to check their videos to see if they caught the break-in. This one came from the restaurant across the street. I thought it was pretty good. It's just disappointing that it doesn't give us anything we can use."

"Yeah. Well, I'll look at it a few more times. It might turn out that there is something I can use on it." Zachary looked at the time on his phone. "We've still got some time before your employees come in. Could you walk me through the bar and show me where each of the stolen items on the list was to start with?"

Janice rolled her eyes. She didn't think that it would do anyone any good. The police had already told her that the whole investigation was a waste of time. They might be grateful to Walter for hiring someone privately to look into the burglary, but she didn't really think that it was going to come to anything. Zachary would tell them the same thing as the police. That he had no clue who had committed the break-in and theft and they would just have to replace what they could.

"Let me just print off the list again," Janice said with a deep sigh. So much work for something that was hopeless.

Zachary looked around the little office as she tracked down the document on her computer and sent it to the ancient HP printer across the desk. It was a nice little office. Crowded, admittedly, and Janice was definitely behind in her paperwork. Still, Zachary could picture himself retreating to this room after a busy night in the main room of the bar, shutting the door against the music and noise and stink of the crowd and taking a breather. There wasn't any memorabilia in the office, which seemed a little strange. If they were collectors and the items that had been stolen had a lot of sentimental value, then why hadn't they decorated the office as well? Maybe kept an item or two with special significance to them there in the back where they could enjoy them and they wouldn't be a temptation to patrons or burglars casing out the place?

"Here we go, then," Janice rattled the printout of the stolen items. She led the way back out to the main room and started to work her way down the list.

They were mostly arranged on the list by placement. Everything on one wall in a grouping, then moving to the next segment of shelves or the pieces that had been displayed on the tables or the display at the back of the bar. A couple of times, Janice had to consult with Glen, and they discussed which position an item had been displayed in, but mostly they agreed and didn't have any problem telling Zachary where each thing belonged. He didn't write them all down, but concentrated hard as she worked through the list, trying to memorize as many of the displays as possible. He could refer back to the social media and review site photos as well, actually see what was missing with his own eyes rather than having to imagine it.

The door banged open as the employees started to arrive, each bringing with them a rush of cold air from outside.

14

They must have to keep the heater cranked pretty high during the winter, as people came and went all night. Although body heat would help keep the room warm as well.

As the employees shed their outerwear and looked curiously at Zachary, Janice and Glen introduced him and told him who the employees were and the positions they held.

"You hired a detective?" demanded Stacy, a woman with short, bleach blonde hair and numerous piercings.

"We didn't hire him. One of the customers did."

Stacy frowned and shook her head. "Who?"

"He's this guy who comes every now and then. Sits over there," Janice gestured to a table in the corner that was not in a good position to view the TVs and was a little more private than some of the other seats, away from the kitchen and bathroom doors. "His name is Kirsch. Uh…" She looked at Zachary for help. "Mr. Kirsch…?"

"Walter Kirsch," Zachary supplied. He smiled at Stacy. "He has very generously covered my fees so that I can see if I can recover any of the stolen property or figure out who the thieves were."

She frowned, shaking her head. "Walter Kirsch? Who is that? Is he some sports bigwig?"

"No. Just someone who enjoys coming in here now and then and wanted to help out."

"The suit?"

She looked at the other employees, and they all looked back at Janice. She nodded.

"Yes, the suit who sits over there sometimes."

"Weirdo," Stacy muttered.

"Did he ever hit on you? Say something offensive?" Zachary asked, studying her for any clue in her expression or body language.

"No. He was just a weirdo. Why would you come in here if you weren't even interested in sports? Why not go to a bar or a private club for people like that? He comes in here, eats, chats up the staff, touches the memorabilia, but doesn't know a thing about sports. *Any* sports. Why would anyone do that?"

"Touches the memorabilia?" Zachary repeated.

"Yeah. Fiddles, I guess. Or stares at it. I don't know. Maybe he's thinking of becoming a collector. But it wasn't like there was anything that expensive here. Nothing that he would want to buy and display in his fancy-schmancy house." Stacy made a gesture to the limited memorabilia now displayed on the walls and shelves. "It isn't like this is the high-end stuff, the stuff that goes for hundreds of thousands of dollars, or even millions. It's just mid-range, sentimental stuff."

"Maybe he's remembering something from his childhood. Maybe his dad was a sports guy and they used to go to games together, or he went to his dad's sports bar with him, or they had a bunch of memorabilia like that around their home." From what Kenzie had said, Zachary knew that Walter's father had been a wealthy, politically inclined man, much like Walter. But that didn't mean that he couldn't have a hobby. Something that he liked to go out and do to unwind. He wasn't likely to have thrown around a baseball with his son, but maybe they had watched games when they went into the city. "Was there any particular team that he seemed to lean toward?"

Stacy stood with her hands on her hips, looking at him. "So you really are a PI? A private eye? And you care about the stuff that was stolen? I've never met a PI in real life before."

"Yes, I am." Zachary stepped toward her, drawing a business card out of his pocket and reaching out to hand it to her.

She looked him over. "Where is your gun?"

"I don't have a gun. That's a TV thing. In real life, private investigators do a lot of computer work and phone calls. And coming to a scene like this to see if we can find any other evidence when a crime has been committed, or there is something else you want investigated. We're not Magnum or the Equalizer having shoot-outs in parking lots or from speeding cars."

She smiled, chuckling at this. Picturing Zachary in one of those situations, he assumed. And he certainly did not measure up to Tom Selleck on any level.

"So," Zachary ventured, "did you notice that there was any one particular team that he followed or seemed fond of?"

"He didn't watch the games."

"No, that's what Janice said. I just wondered, when you said that he touched the memorabilia, *which* memorabilia it was. Was there a particular team?"

"No, I don't think so…" Stacy thought about it, her voice fading out. "I just remember him playing with the die-cast car that was on that table."

Zachary raised his brows. There had been several die-cast collector's items on the list of stolen items. Those limited-edition reproductions that he used to see on TV or in magazines, that were probably now all over the shopping channel and other paid advertising.

"It was a little station wagon. You know, the wood-grain panels on the sides and team logos on it. The Habs."

Zachary pulled his notepad out to make a note of it. "The Habs?" he repeated, trying to recall a local team this might refer to.

Janice giggled. "You're worse than he is. The Habs? The Montreal hockey team."

"I thought they were…" Zachary frowned, reaching for the name. "The Montreal Canadiens."

"Yeah. The Habs."

He tried to figure out how a team called the Canadiens ended up with a nickname of the Habs, but shrugged it off. It didn't matter why they were known by that name; he needed to stay focused on his line of inquiry.

"Why do you even care?" Stacy asked. "I mean, if he's the one who hired you, then it isn't exactly as if he is a suspect. Mr. Fancy-Pants would never get involved in a smash-and-grab like that anyway. If he was going to steal something, it would be all super-secret and involve a corporate takeover or insider trading or something like that."

"No. You're right. I don't think he had anything to do with it; I just want to know everything about him that I can, especially as it relates to this bar. It could be relevant. He could have an emotional attachment that explains why he was so concerned about the theft and catching the thieves and getting the mementos back. And if he has an emotional attachment, then someone else might too… Or there could be something that was *very* valuable to a Habs fan that wouldn't have been to a…" He trailed off.

"A Bruins fan," Janice supplied.

Zachary shrugged with one shoulder. "To a Bruins fan."

"There wasn't anything that valuable, even to a big fan," Janice said. "I mean, we had game pucks and signed jerseys and things like that. But so does everyone who is a fan or collector. I don't think he had any particular connection with the Habs." Janice looked at the staff members who had assembled so far. "I don't think… did anyone notice anything?"

There were head shakes and murmurs. They looked at each other, but no one jumped in with any insight into why Walter might have cared about the stolen memorabilia, for the Habs or any other team.

15

_____

Well, apparently, that's not important," Zachary said, closing the topic. "Sorry. A lot of being a private investigator is just following rabbit trails. They don't always lead anywhere. I'd like to talk to each employee separately, if I could. It won't be long. No torture or sweating you out under a bare light bulb," he joked. "Just fifteen minutes to talk about anything that happened the day of the robbery and what you remember about the weeks before. I'm just looking for any patterns or the possibility that the bar was cased out ahead of time. We could start with you…?" He addressed this to Stacy.

"Actually, if I could go first," offered Nate, the tall Black barman. "I need to get set up for the evening and can't be interrupted later."

Zachary nodded. "Sure, of course." He looked at Janice. "Should we use your office? Or is there another room? Or just one of the tables here?"

Janice rubbed the creases across her forehead. "I need to get some office work done. We don't really have anywhere else, other than the kitchen or supply room, so if you could just take a table that's out of the way…" She motioned to the booth in the corner. "Why don't you take Mr. Kirsch's table? Maybe that will be good luck."

Zachary nodded. It would be far enough away from the other employees that they could talk quietly and not be overheard. He preferred not to have one employee's comments taint another's recollections. Always best to interview witnesses independently. "Sure, let's go over there," he told Nate.

The man strolled over, his long legs eating up the gap before Zachary was halfway across the room, even though he only appeared to be walking at half the speed Zachary was. Zachary nodded when the other man did not offer to shake hands, assuming that he preferred not to make physical contact. They sat down.

"Thanks for volunteering to go first," he said. "You always need someone to break the ice, and it can be hard in something like this. People are nervous about talking to an investigator, even if it's just a private citizen like me. They're afraid that they're going to get in trouble somehow."

Nate nodded politely. "Sure. No problem. What do you need to know?"

"Were you on the evening before the robbery?"

"Sure, yeah. I'm usually here every night. We have other people who can cover the bar when I'm not able to, but I'm the one who is usually there."

"Do you remember anything unusual happening that night?"

"No. Just a regular night. Nothing stands out."

"I know that sometimes sports fans can get pretty rowdy."

"That wouldn't be out of the ordinary."

"Do you remember any fights or disruptions that night?"

"No. I don't think there were. Maybe some arguments or raised voices, but that doesn't qualify as anything unusual. Just boys being boys." He smiled. "Though we have more and more female fans, and they aren't any quieter than the men. In fact, some of them can be *quite* vocal."

"I imagine so. Any women making noise that night?" Zachary prompted. Nate's mention of women might have been triggered by a memory about the night of the burglary. Something he wasn't even consciously aware of.

"Women…" Nate thought about it, closing his eyes briefly. "Probably, but I don't remember anything. It was just a regular night. Nothing unusual."

"Did anyone get kicked out? Was there any reason to call the police or get a bouncer involved?"

"No."

"Anyone who… ditched without paying?"

He shook his head again. "What about the kitchen? Anyone snooping around the back? Someone who said that they were just looking for a bathroom or going out for a smoke in the alley?"

"That kind of thing happens all the time."

"No one that night?"

"Nothing I recall."

"What about in the weeks before the robbery. Was there anything unusual or concerning? Any phone hang-ups or threats? Someone who expressed anger toward Janice or Glen?"

"No. It's a quiet place. I mean, it's noisy when a game is on, but it isn't the kind of place that the mob or drug dealers hang out. It's *quiet* that way. There's no one making book at the bar or running illegal games or selling drugs out of the back. It's all aboveboard. Maybe it's not family entertainment because of the alcohol, but if it wasn't for that… it's just people getting together to watch a game and cheer for their favorite team. To get together with other fans and have a good time together."

"Anyone loitering around the sidewalk out front, or coming inside just for a look around and not for something to eat or drink or to watch a game? Someone homeless or a stranger? Someone like Walter who really didn't belong?"

"I can't think of anyone recently. The homeless population kind of disappears when it gets too cold. They go somewhere else for help. And the suit… he's the only one I can think of who was really out of place. Maybe the occasional businessperson, but they usually show at least some interest in who is playing."

"Did you ever see Walter—Mr. Kirsch—meet here with anyone? Chat with anyone aside from the wait staff?"

"No, I don't think so. But I'm usually quite busy at the bar; I don't spend any time watching the tables."

"Is there anyone on the staff who is having financial trouble?"

Nate raised an eyebrow, looking at him. "Why?"

Zachary knew that Nate had a pretty good idea already. "In case there is an inside connection. Is there anyone who might be struggling who would see the memorabilia as a possible way to dig themselves out?"

"Nah," Nate shook his head. He frowned, brows drawing down. "Nah, no one would do that. We're like family here. And what is all of that stuff going to get? There isn't anything worth more than a couple of thousand dollars, if that. And you're not going to get that at a pawnshop."

"No," Zachary agreed. "But sometimes a person is desperate, even for just a few hundred dollars. Everything that was taken from here, they'd get at least that."

Nate scratched his head. "Really, no. I don't think so. I don't know anyone's financial affairs. But I mean… there isn't anyone sleeping on the street or talking about getting evicted or going bankrupt. People whine about their problems sometimes, but nothing like that."

"Okay. Well, that's all you can say. You can't know anyone else's business if they haven't been talking about it. Unless maybe their clothes are wrinkled from sleeping in the car, or they're talking about not being able to pay all of the bills."

"I'm telling you, there's no one living like that here."

"If you think of anything that might help me—anything 'off' that happened the night of the robbery or in the weeks before—would you give me a call?" Zachary slid one of his business cards across the table.

Nate looked around before picking it up, as if he were worried about someone seeing him taking it. He tucked it into his shirt pocket. "I don't know anything. I'm not going to think of anything."

"Understood. But if you do think of anything, or see or hear anything, just let me know…?"

16

Two of the waitresses came over to the table after Zachary had finished talking to Nate.

"If you could come one at a time..." Zachary suggested.

"I can't," the younger girl suggested, clutching at the arm of the older one. "I'm too nervous!" She looked at the other woman, making sure that she wasn't going to abandon her to Zachary.

Zachary raised his brows and waited, seeing if the young woman would screw up her courage and sit down with him when she saw that he wasn't a big, foul-mouthed, rough-and-ready private eye like she might have seen on TV. Just a guy, short and slight, non-threatening, asking her a few questions while in a familiar, safe place. But the woman shook her head again.

"I don't want to do this," she reasserted. "I'm sure not doing it by myself."

Zachary wondered how she had the courage to serve people she'd never met before drinks in a noisy bar. Maybe she'd needed the other woman at her side for the first few days there, too, until she'd gotten to know the regular patrons and knew that she wasn't going to screw everything up when she worked by herself.

The older woman finally sat down. "Come on, Martha. It's no big deal."

Neither was very old. Young, cute waitresses were apparently what was expected in a sports bar. Martha was perhaps nineteen and the other woman in her early to mid-twenties.

"I'm Jennifer," the older one introduced herself.

Martha sat down beside Jennifer, both of them across the table from Zachary.

"Nice to meet you, Jennifer, Martha," Zachary greeted, giving them both a warm smile, hoping that Martha would be able to relax a little once she saw that Zachary was no one to be afraid of. "How long have you worked here?"

Hopefully, with some bland, easy questions to start, Martha would let down her guard.

"I've been here a couple of years," Jennifer offered.

Martha had her mouth behind her hand as if she were hiding from Zachary. "Not long," she said, "just a few months."

"How do you like it here?"

"It's good," Jennifer contributed. "Good, steady paycheck. As many hours as you need. Tips are good. It's not like the places where they're allowed to grope you."

"The owners seem nice. Glen and Janice."

Jennifer's eyes flickered toward Glen, who was talking at the bar with Nate. "Yeah. They're good. Never had any trouble with either of them."

Zachary looked at Martha. "What do you think? Is this your first job?"

"I've worked at… like… Subway. But not at a bar before."

"How has it been? Big culture shock?"

"It was a bit to get used to. But Jenn's right… it hasn't been too bad."

"I've worked a lot worse places," Jennifer asserted. "You're lucky to be starting out somewhere they support your rights and don't just expect you to put up with being manhandled or catcalled."

Martha nodded, looking anxious at the idea.

"Were either of you on the day before the burglary?" Zachary asked.

"I was," Jennifer offered, nodding. "Helped to close."

"I was on earlier in the afternoon," Martha said, squaring her shoulders. "But I wasn't on until close."

"How was it?"

"How was it?" Jennifer repeated, shaking her head slightly. "What do you mean?"

"Well, some shifts are good, and some days… it's a full moon or something and everyone is acting crazy or out of sorts… or you didn't get enough sleep and you're dropping everything or forgetting orders..." He shrugged. "Just... how was it?"

"Normal, I guess. Nothing out of the ordinary. What about you?" Jennifer looked at Martha.

"Yeah, I guess. It wasn't a bad day. Not a holiday or a cup day or anything. No full moon, I guess."

Zachary nodded. "You have any customers who gave you a hard time or acted strangely?"

"No." Both women shook their heads together.

"Anyone hanging out where they shouldn't? In the kitchen or back hallway?"

"No."

"Can you remember who was here? Who are your regulars?"

Jennifer and Martha looked at each other. Jennifer offered a couple of patrons that she was familiar with, but shook her head at Zachary. "I don't know how that's going to help you. And I really don't know... who else was around."

"I didn't see anyone casing it out," Martha said, finally offering something on her own. "I would think I would have noticed if someone was acting suspiciously."

"Have you ever been worried about security? Walking back to your car at the end of a shift?"

Jennifer shook her head. Martha shrugged. "I take the bus?" Her voice curled up, like it was a question she was asking him. "So I'm always a little nervous? Kind of paranoid about anyone following me, you know?"

Zachary nodded understandingly.

"When you see in the paper about women getting killed," Martha offered, "Knifed by a stranger or pulled behind the bushes and assaulted, they always say it was one o'clock in the morning and she was going home from work, you know? So... I'm always watching... being aware of my surroundings. Don't wear earphones or anything like that." She looked proud of herself. Like she had prevented an assault just by doing that.

Little did she know how hard it was to fight off an ambush or gang attack in the middle of the night when the streets were dark and lonely. Zachary gripped the edge of the table and tried not to let his brain drift back to when he had been attacked by a group of skinheads leaving a bar after asking questions on a case. He forced a weak smile.

"That's good," he told Martha. "I'm glad that you're being careful and trying to protect yourself. You never know what to expect out there."

"I've told her taking transit that late at night is not a good idea," Jennifer said, "she should get someone to pick her up or get herself a car for a couple hundred bucks. It's not worth getting jumped on your way home."

Funny that scared little Martha hadn't heeded these words. But maybe she just didn't have the means. No one who would pick her up, no savings to put into a car. She might be able to buy a car for a couple hundred bucks, but who knew where a junker like that might leave her stranded. It might be somewhere much worse than a well-trafficked sidewalk between the bar and the bus stop.

"Have you ever had a patron that you've had to report to management? Because he was giving you the wrong kind of attention? Someone you had a bad feeling about, even if you didn't report him?"

"Sure," Jennifer admitted. "But nothing recently."

Martha shook her head wordlessly, her eyes wide. Zachary could see that he would not be able to pursue that line of questioning. Not unless he wanted to cost the bar a waitress.

17

The next couple of interviews had similar results. No one had noticed anything unusual in the day before or weeks ahead of the robbery. If someone had cased the bar out ahead of time, they had done so quietly and without drawing attention to themselves. Zachary didn't think it would have taken more than a few minutes inside to sort out the security concerns. Watching from outside would give anyone the information they needed about when shifts started and ended. It wasn't a bank heist. Any nonprofessional could have pulled it off at least as well as the two who had broken in and made off with the loot.

Stacy seemed to be avoiding an interview but, eventually, Zachary managed to get her pinned down, getting Glen to lean on her, telling her that she could take a break from her prep duties to talk to Zachary. She couldn't give any more excuses, and finally gave in. To begin with, she just stood beside the table, looking as though she might run at any minute.

She was older than he had thought at first. Looking at her close up, he could see the wrinkles around her mouth. Lines running down from her nose that had been camouflaged with makeup. Her hands were dry and wrinkled, yellowed around the tips. No age spots, but she was definitely not in her twenties as he had initially thought.

"This is going to take a bit," Zachary told her. "You might as well get off of your feet while you can."

She just looked at him, her hip cocked, making it clear that she didn't want to talk to him.

"You must get sore feet by the end of the day," Zachary commented, pulling out his notepad to browse through the notes he had made, giving her some time to think about that without any scrutiny. Eventually, she sighed and sat down across from him.

"This is a waste of time. I'm telling you that at the start. You're just wasting your time talking to me and the rest of the employees. None of us know anything about what happened. We've already talked it over, you know? And none of us have been able to come up with anything. No suspects. Nothing suspicious. It was just chance. Bad luck. Someone was walking by outside and saw the memorabilia through the window, and decided it was something they wanted."

"You don't think it was a customer or someone who had ever been in here. Just completely random."

"Exactly. Random. A stranger. Someone who had never even been here before. Well, obviously, because if they'd been here before, they would have done it *then*. Nobody is going to set up some big plan to rob a little place like this. It isn't like the McNichols have any enemies. They're not into drugs or something like that. It's a little mom-and-pop shop. Who rips off someone like that?"

Anyone who wanted to, apparently.

"Little mom-and-pop places get ripped off regularly," Zachary pointed out. "They're easy targets. But they are *not* very profitable targets. Somewhere like this, with all of the memorabilia around, maybe they make a little more, but it isn't likely to have been set up by some kingpin. Someone who needed a fix or couldn't pay the rent this month. Someone desperate for a little cash."

"Yeah, I guess." Stacy twisted her fingers together. She shook her head at him. "I really can't think of how anyone would do something like this. I mean, why target Barnburners? Or the McNichols?"

"It was someone who didn't care about Glen and Janice. Maybe didn't even know who they were. It's easier to rip off a nameless business than it is someone you know, who has been kind to you."

She nodded slowly. "I suppose so. Easier if they aren't anyone you know." She paused. "They really are nice people. Don't think they're involved in anything shady, because they aren't. I know a lot of business-people operate another, less legitimate business to stay afloat, but Janice and Glen aren't like that. They have the bar. They love what they do. They put all of their energy into it."

"They seem like nice folks," Zachary agreed. And they did seem to be very into what they did. He liked to see people engaged in what they were really passionate about. With a business like Barnburners, it could be the difference between a business that failed and a business that succeeded. "I'm sure you and the other employees wouldn't want to see them go under because of something like this."

"Why would they go under because of this?" Stacy furrowed her brow at him. It made the piercings above her eye wiggle in a distracting way. "It's not that big of a loss, and they can claim it on insurance."

"It might increase their rates too much to be worth it. When you take into account whatever the deductible is, what percentage of the actual value they will get to replace the stolen items, and how much their insurance rates will go up after a claim, then it's sometimes cheaper to just take the loss."

"Really?" Her piercings wiggled some more. "I would have thought that a small claim… it wouldn't affect their rates that much."

"Small claims are rarely worth it. Better to save it for the time something big happens. A real disaster."

"Like getting burned to the ground?" Stacy challenged.

Zachary tried to keep his expression flat. But he couldn't help a grimace at the mention of a fire. Having survived the burning inferno of a house fire when he was ten, the mention of a house or building on fire could still send him back there in a flashback. He was doing better, but it was still a struggle to remain grounded and stay focused on the conversation instead of letting himself be sucked into the flashback that threatened at the edge of his vision.

"What?" Stacy asked, apparently seeing something in his expression. "Oh, you mean because it's called Barnburners?" She shrugged. "It's not literal, you know. It just refers to a high-scoring game. Lots of goals. It's called a barnburner."

Zachary nodded politely. He had wondered at the name and what it had to do with sports, and now he knew. "That makes sense. I didn't know where it came from."

"I like it. I think it's more unique than *Top Shelf* or *The Puck Stops Here* or some of the other sports bar names that you see over and over again in different cities. Everyone thinks they had the idea first and don't realize that it's been used a dozen times before."

18

T he other thing that I wondered about," Zachary continued with the investigation, not wanting to get sidetracked, "is whether anyone who works here is having financial trouble. Have you heard anything…"

"Financial trouble? Who isn't? What does that have to do with the theft?"

"Sometimes, someone on the inside is involved. Maybe just bribed to provide a key piece of information or make a phone call. Just a little thing, in exchange for part of the take. I'm not saying that anyone did. I'm just saying that it happens. It's something that I need to consider in my investigation."

"No. No one here would ever do anything to hurt the McNichols."

"They might have thought, like you, that Glen and Janice wouldn't really lose anything because of insurance. Or maybe didn't realize the sentimental value of the things that were stolen, and that they can't just be replaced."

"No. No one here would have helped the thieves."

"You can't think of anyone who might be in financial trouble and be tempted to take a few things to pay the bills? Get them out of a sticky situation?"

She shook her head firmly. "No, of course not."

Zachary nodded. "Okay, well, if you think of anything…" He again slid a business card across the table as he had to each of the other employees. "If you could give me a call. That would be great."

"No." She pushed the card back toward him. "No, really. I'm not going to call you. I've got nothing."

"You might think of something. Or overhear something from one of the others. Or even from a customer or someone hanging out having a smoke at the same time as you."

She looked down at her fingers, tips stained yellow with nicotine. She curled them into fists to hide them from him.

"I don't know anything, and I'm not going to magically overhear anything," she asserted. "Sorry, I just can't help you."

"You don't want to help Janice and Glen? I thought you said they were good people."

"They are. And I appreciate the job here. But I don't work with cops. I just want to be left alone."

"I'm not a cop. I'm just a private consultant, making some inquiries. I'm not turning anybody over to the police. The police have already given up on this case. So whatever you're worried about, it's not going to happen."

"I'm not worried about anything. I just don't want to be involved. Now I've answered your questions. I've told you everything I can remember. It just isn't anything helpful, so I'm sorry. These guys, whoever they were, were just random thieves picking a random target. Okay?" Her voice had risen, causing the other employees to look in her direction while they pretended to be doing other things.

"Okay."

Stacy looked at him. She was prepared to argue. To have a fit, throwing a chair over and stomping off in a tantrum. She wasn't ready for his simple acquiescence. She stared at him.

"Okay?" she repeated.

Zachary nodded and waited.

"So I can go?" She made a motion away from the table, still waiting for him to object or grab her by the arm, to try to force her to do something.

Zachary nodded. "Have a nice day."

She stood up, still watching for him to make his move. Then she marched away from him resolutely and went into the back rooms without a backward look.

Glen was nearby. He watched Stacy go and turned to look back at

Zachary. He didn't get closer to the table, but was already close enough to have heard what was said in raised voices, if not when they had been speaking quietly.

"Sorry about that," he said. "Maybe I should have warned you; Stacy is a bit temperamental."

"That's okay."

"You handled her pretty well. She tends to… provoke people. Get into arguments with her even when they didn't have a beef to start with. Like she's always looking for a fight. Even though she's…" Glen frowned, reaching for the words. "She's small and sort of fragile."

Zachary nodded. He'd seen that sort of behavior before. He knew what it was like to feel that way. Himself against the whole world. Ready to fight everyone who got close to him, whether there was any chance of his winning it or not. Because no one was safe and everybody was out to get him. He might as well start the fight on his own terms and have a chance of controlling some part of it, even if only the beginning. It wasn't easy, fighting the whole world.

"I get it," he said. "I've been there myself."

Glen looked at him for a minute. Zachary knew what he saw. A skinny, short man who clearly wasn't up to facing off against any high school or college jocks. Unless he had unseen ninja skills like in a B movie.

"Yeah? Well, like I say, you managed her okay. I was expecting broken dishes."

There weren't even any dishes out on the table. Zachary didn't know if that meant she would have retreated to the kitchen and thrown them around in a rage there, or if he only meant it figuratively. He smiled slightly and shrugged again.

"You have employees who aren't here tonight?"

"A couple. Not a lot. We run a pretty tight ship here."

"If I could get their contact information, I'll get ahold of them by phone or email and run through the process with them too."

Glen pulled out a leather case from his pocket with index cards held by corner tabs. He started to jot the information down. "You don't really expect to find anything, though, do you?"

"Well… I might. I'm going to work my hardest to. And I'm pretty dogged. I've broken other cases that the police had given up on. Because I don't really like to let things go. I like to put a file to bed knowing that I did everything I was hired to do."

"That's admirable. But not possible in all cases, I would guess."

"No."

Glen looked at the information he had written down, reviewing it to see if he should add anything. He had, Zachary noticed, not needed to look up the phone numbers or email addresses. He pulled out the index card he had written on and handed it to Zachary. "I'll give them a heads-up that you are going to be contacting them."

"That would be great, thanks." It always made it easier if employees knew that their employer was onside with the investigation and they weren't expected to hide anything or protect him. Though there were always those who didn't want to do their bosses any favors and would be more resistant if warned ahead of time. But those guys were in the minority. Odds were that neither of the final two employees would cause him any trouble.

19

Zachary had hoped to get some more investigating done the first day, but there had been more to do than he had anticipated. He couldn't fit everything into one day, but he had known he had several days' work ahead of him. He needed to rest and recharge, or he would crash before he had the case solved.

"Things went well?" Kenzie asked, curious about her father's case despite her objection to Zachary taking it in the first place. She sat down at the other end of the couch, sitting along it, perpendicular to him.

"A good first day," Zachary confirmed. "Had a look around, talked to the owners, most of the employees. Saw the video of the burglary and them snatching what they could and then taking off before the cops arrived."

"Professionals?" she asked.

"Hmm." Zachary had been wondering about that himself. "They looked pretty competent, and they got out of there before the security company was there to investigate the alarm being set off. They got away with a good amount of loot, considering the time they spent there. But I still got the feeling that... there was something wrong." He shook his head, unable to put his finger on precisely what had bothered him about the video. "I watched it a couple of times, and they said they would email it to me so I can watch it again until I figure out what the problem is."

"So you think that they're not professionals? Just somebody who thought there was a hole in their security that they could take advantage of?"

"Maybe. I can't say at this point. It was pulled off nice and cleanly, good planning and execution. But something still didn't feel right." He replayed the video in his head, thinking about it. Jerky, birdlike movements, keeping a close eye on the door to make sure they could get back to their vehicle before someone arrived to put a stop to the looting. The quick, efficient way they had cleared everything out in the allotted time. He tried to slow everything down in his head, but he lost focus. He needed to watch the video again. Probably a few more times. Eventually, he would identify what it was that was bothering him.

Kenzie shrugged. She put her bare feet on his leg, curling her toes against him, then pulled one of the throw blankets over her. She tended to get cold feet during the winter evenings, but didn't like to wear socks or slippers to keep them warm. She smiled at him and wiggled her toes again against his leg, taking advantage of his body heat.

"So... anyone have anything to say about my dad? Why he's so interested in this case? Does he own a partnership share in the bar? Owe them a favor for saving his life one day? Been bewitched or hypnotized to serve them?"

"I don't think so." Zachary pulled one of her feet onto his lap and massaged it.

Kenzie sighed.

"Nobody there really seemed to know him very well," Zachary told her. "They recognized who he was when I described him or the owners pointed out where he would sit when he went in. But no one was friends with him, not even the owners. He knew their names from when they waited on him. That's all."

"So... he's just this mysterious benefactor that decided to hire someone to investigate the burglary of their establishment."

"Yup."

"That makes no sense."

"I know. But that's all I've got so far. They called him 'the suit' or Mr. Kirsch. Didn't even know his first name. Said he didn't wear team colors or talk to anyone about the games that were playing. A friendly guy who came in every couple of weeks or so, had a drink or a snack, and then left again."

"He must have been meeting with someone there."

Zachary shook his head. "They say not. Said that he was only ever there by himself."

"Walter. At a sports bar." Kenzie closed her eyes. "That still makes no sense to me."

"Do you think he used to go to sports with his father? Anything that might make him nostalgic? Any particular team that he might have been interested in once? Even if it was just a passing mention."

"No. He's never been interested in anything like that, thinks it's a waste of time. And as far as I know, his parents were the same way. His dad was high finance, not the type to ever take a day off or relax with a beer and a game at the end of the day."

"Did you ever play sports in school?"

"No." Kenzie pulled her foot out of Zachary's hand and replaced it with the other one. He massaged the arch and the ball of her foot. "To be honest, we were too wrapped up in Amanda's illness by the time I was old enough to join any school sports teams. Amanda was all our family was focused on. Taking care of her, keeping her healthy, finding a way to help her." She shook her head, her eyes shiny with tears. "I was just counting the days until I was old enough to donate a kidney. My parents wouldn't give permission while I was a minor."

"Why not?"

"They said it was major surgery, that they didn't want to endanger my health. What if my remaining kidney failed down the line? They said they would find a non-related donor. That she was okay on dialysis until then. They wouldn't let the doctors bring it up around me. But I didn't need the doctors to tell me anything. I could figure it out on my own."

"They protected you. Didn't want to save one child at the risk of the other."

"Yeah. I think it was pretty presumptuous of them, actually. I wanted so much to help Amanda. I would have given her my kidney a couple of years earlier if they'd let me."

Zachary nodded slowly. Bit by bit, he was finding out more about Kenzie and the rift between her and her parents. It was nothing like his split from his biological parents. She was still in contact with them. But it was hard for her to talk about it. And about what had happened to Amanda.

20

"Do you want to see the video?"

Kenzie blinked at him. "Sure. You're okay with sharing it?"

He usually limited the information he shared with her to generalities or medical stuff that he needed her advice on. He tried to keep anything that might be confidential to himself. But the burglary wasn't exactly confidential. He'd already told her about it. And the video hadn't even been taped by them, but had come from a neighborhood camera. The video might not exactly be public, but it wasn't something that the McNichols could quash, even if they wanted to. And they hadn't had any problem sharing it.

Zachary reached for his computer table and pulled it over to himself. It only took a minute to open the clamshell, find a link to the video in his email, and bring it up on the screen. Kenzie changed position to lean on his shoulder, and they watched it together.

"Wow." Kenzie pushed the button to watch it again. "I wasn't expecting it to be so... violent. I mean, there's no violence against any people, but the way that they rip through there, throwing things down and grabbing whatever they can. It's very visceral, isn't it?"

Zachary nodded, though visceral wasn't a word that he would have come up with. He understood what Kenzie meant by it being violent. Even if no one was hurt, they had shown a certain level of anger and disregard for personal property that was disturbing.

He watched the scene play out again in front of him. The broken glass, the door being opened, the two people moving through the restaurant, grabbing what memorabilia they wanted and letting other items crash to the floor, along with chairs and tables they swept out of their way, not even bothering to walk around the furniture.

Kenzie watched closely. She touched the tip of her fingernail to the screen. "That one is a woman."

Zachary paid closer attention, examining the masked figure. It was swathed in bulky winter outerwear, making it difficult to see its shape underneath. "Are you sure?"

"I couldn't swear to it in court, no. But the way she moves—her gait, the way she positions her body—I'm pretty sure."

"She is shorter than the other."

"And he moves like a man. Maybe they are a couple."

"That would make sense. If they need money for household bills or drugs, they could easily team up to do something like this. Get each other worked up over it. Keep talking about it until it becomes normalized instead of seeming like something they wouldn't consider doing."

They continued to watch the video, replaying it several times. Kenzie shrugged. "I don't have anything else to contribute. You can't really see much, can you?"

"No. But there's still something more that keeps niggling at the back of my brain."

"Sleep on it. Maybe it will occur to you in the morning."

Zachary nodded. He watched it one more time for good measure, but was still left with the feeling that he was missing something, like an itch that was just out of his reach.

Kenzie's advice to sleep on it was good. Still, Zachary couldn't help thinking about the video as he was trying to go to sleep, replaying it in his head over and over again, which was not conducive to settling down to sleep. He knew from experience that doing certain activities before bed would keep him from being able to fall asleep, and he tried to shut off his computer and phone at least an hour before retiring so that he had time to unwind and let his brain slow down before sleep. He should have known better than to think about the video before bed. But once he did, he couldn't stop.

It took a long time to get to sleep, and he wasn't sure when he had actually crossed the barrier between his waking review of the video and then dreaming about it after he had dropped off. He kept dreaming it, analyzing it in his sleep. But as dreams do, it changed. Different people took on the role of the thieves in the dream. Kenzie, Tyrrell, Mr. Peterson, Walter Kirsch. Other masked figures who were bigger and carried weapons. He found himself running into the bar in his dream, trying to save some nameless person who was in the path of the destruction. But how could he defend anyone against the monsters with guns? How could he reach the person he needed to save and get them out of the bar before the inevitable happened? And then the inevitable did happen and Barnburners went up in flames. Zachary's anxiety morphed into panic as he screamed for everyone to get out. The person he had been protecting. The thieves. Walter, Kenzie, Tyrrell.

"T!" Zachary shouted, his voice constricted by the smoke and his own panic. "T, get out! Get out; there's a fire!"

"It's okay. It's okay, Zachary. Shh. Wake up." There were gentle hands on him, nudging him, urging him to escape the nightmare.

"T. We've got to get them out," Zachary croaked.

"Everyone is safe. Everyone got out of the fire," Kenzie assured him. "The firemen got everyone out safe."

He turned toward her and held her against him, his heart thumping wildly. Kenzie snuggled into him, repeating the reassurances. Letting him know that the nightmare was over and he was no longer a ten-year-old trapped in the burning house, screaming at his siblings to get out.

"It was the bar," he told her, trying to get the words out into the open. "This time, it was the bar that was on fire, not the house."

"Well, that didn't happen. The bar was fine. Just a burglary. They'll recover from that."

"And Tyrrell wasn't there."

"No."

"Not you. Not anyone."

"No. No one was there. Everyone you know is safe."

He breathed slowly for a few minutes, paying attention to each breath in and out. When he had been in the fire, his airways had been swollen and painful. It had been hard to breathe, even when they put an oxygen mask over his face. But lying there in bed with Kenzie, his breathing was normal. Cool air flowed through his throat and into his lungs and didn't hurt. He was okay. There hadn't been a fire at the bar; it had just been a dream.

He sat up slowly, trying not to disturb Kenzie, but she reached out and touched him. "Stay here. Go back to sleep."

"Can't right now. I'll get up for a while and see if I can get tired again."

She groaned. "You won't go back to sleep if you get up now."

"It's okay. You can go back to sleep. You need to work tomorrow."

He got out of bed. Kenzie didn't try to stop him. He pulled on pajama pants and a t-shirt and went out to the living room, where he started to go through his notes and review his emails, studiously ignoring the video file.

21

Even though Zachary's brain desperately wanted to watch the video again, stuck in the rut of replaying it in his memory, Zachary resisted. He pushed it as far from his thoughts as he could and let his subconscious mind work on it. That was the part of his brain that knew something was wrong. If he refused to acknowledge it, sooner or later, his brain would be forced to process it and push it back to his conscious mind.

He looked through the "before" pictures that he had downloaded from social media and reviews, along with the "after" pictures that he had taken at the bar. Pulling out the list of stolen property, he tried to match each item on the list to its image in the pictures. Of course, not all of them would have been captured on social media, and they probably changed and were added to from time to time as the McNichols acquired new pieces. But they had walked him through where each one had been displayed, and he worked from his memory and the photos to identify each one he could.

When he had finished, he looked at the after pictures. Not everything had been stolen, of course. Just what the thieves had been able to grab in the two minutes they had been inside the bar. Items not itemized in the list should all still be on the walls, display shelves, and tables.

When Kenzie got up in the morning, Zachary's eyes were gritty, and he knew he had been staring at the computer screen for too long. It was time to blink, put some eye drops in, and have coffee and breakfast with Kenzie.

"Morning," Kenzie greeted, rubbing her eyes. "How are you doing?"

She didn't point out that she had been right about him not getting tired and returning to the bedroom. But of course, both of them had known that she was right at the time. That didn't matter. Zachary had known that he wouldn't go back to sleep if he stayed in bed, either. If he tossed and turned and got frustrated lying there, he would just keep her awake, and she needed to get her sleep in order to function at work. Zachary could always take a break during the day for a nap. Though, of course, that never happened. He didn't sleep during the day unless he was sick or traumatized.

"Good, good," he assured her. "How was your sleep?"

"Great. I went back to sleep. Which it doesn't look like you did."

There were times when he could stretch out on the couch to snooze or had fallen asleep working on his computer, but those occasions were pretty rare.

"No. But I got some work done. Billable hours." He smiled. "For your dad."

"Well, that's good. If the case is going to keep you awake, you may as well bill him for it."

Zachary pressed his lids closed for a few seconds, trying to work up some tears to irrigate them. "How did you know the case was keeping me awake?"

"You said you dreamed about a fire at the bar."

"Oh, yeah. That's right."

"Did you find anything interesting?"

"In fact... I did."

Zachary's next step was a review of social media. Most of the employees at the bar were young, and young people were on social media all the time. He could look at each employee's social networks and construct a timeline. See who had been where at what time. Who was friends with whom. Who might have had reasons to make a very bad choice.

It wasn't hard. In a society that chose to be on camera 24/7, Zachary had no need for warrants for video footage or the police to put the suspects under surveillance. He could find everything he needed right there on their feeds.

There was no need for Big Brother. They had Little Brother, held right there in the palms of their hands and on selfie sticks. Monitoring themselves without any need for an overlord to interfere in their private lives.

Zachary went through each popular social network methodically. It was still going to be a guess, but he wanted it to be an educated guess. He wanted to be pretty dang sure before he started making accusations.

Once he was sure, he would go back to Montpelier.

Zachary scouted out the first address on his list. He was about eighty percent confident that he knew who the culprit was. He walked down the street in front of the building and then down the alley behind it. The garbage bins had been set out for collection, which was a lucky break that he hadn't expected. After glancing up and down the alley to make sure there were no backyard mechanics watching him, he lifted the lid on the bin behind the house and started pulling out the garbage bags.

It was a fourplex, so there was only a one in four chance that any one bag belonged to his target, but he might get lucky. He ripped each open on the ground, spreading the contents out for inspection, then balling them back up in the ripped bag to return to the bin afterward.

He was down to the last bag, not having found anything worth mentioning, when he hit pay dirt. Two black balaclavas and medical gloves like the thieves had been wearing in the security footage. Zachary's heart raced as he looked down at them. He glanced up and down the lane again, making sure that he was not being watched.

After putting everything else back in the bin, he dialed his phone.

"Emergency services. Can I get your name and location, please?"

Zachary dutifully went through his information as he answered each question in turn, waiting for the opportunity to tell what he had called for. It was a good thing that someone wasn't in immediate danger. But then, if the operator could hear a fracas in the background, maybe she would have gotten to the crux faster than she did.

"What is the problem?" the dispatcher finally asked.

"I have evidence that the residents here were involved in a burglary and theft at a bar a week ago. I need someone from the police department to secure the evidence and hopefully to make an arrest."

"What makes you think that they were involved in this theft?" She sounded bored. How many times a day did she have to listen to muddled stories and sort out the real complaints from the nonsense people called in?

"I've watched the security video of the burglary and theft several times and identified them as the most likely suspects. I've just looked through their trash and found the masks and gloves they were wearing during the burglary."

"I see. Where was this burglary and was it reported to the police?"

"Yes, it was. The bar is called Barnburners." He gave the address and Glen and Janice McNichols's names.

"Do you know who the detective assigned to the case was?"

"I don't have his name, no. I haven't been in contact with him."

"Can you hold, please?" she said with a sigh.

She was gone before Zachary had a chance to answer. He held the phone to his ear, looking around again. Before long, someone was going to notice his presence there and want to know what was going on. People could get nasty quickly if they thought someone was up to no good, casing them out or rummaging through the garbage…

22

He was also getting cold and had left his car on the street back around the front of the house. He didn't want to let the gloves and masks out of his sight, but he wanted to leave them there where he had found them. Even if the detective on the case decided it was worth his while to come out to the house and take a look at the "evidence" that a civilian had turned up, it would be at least twenty minutes to half an hour before he made it there.

Zachary should have worn heavier gloves. He'd already spent a good length of time out in the wintry air going through the garbage bags.

He started to pace up and down the back lane, still within sight of the evidence but trying to keep his toes from freezing while he stood there. He tucked one hand under his armpit while using the other to hold the phone to his ear, then switched hands to try to warm up the other.

Winter was not a good time to be doing outdoor investigating in Vermont. It was at least fifteen minutes before the dispatcher finally returned to the call, maybe closer to half an hour. Zachary's ears were hurting, even though he had his hat pulled down to cover them.

"Mr. Goldman, thank you for holding."

"Hi." Zachary was finding himself a little breathless from the cold. "So, are you sending someone out here?"

"The detective on the case isn't available right now, and we don't have any available units. I'm afraid we can't get anyone over to you right now."

"You can't spare anyone to collect evidence that breaks a case? There isn't anyone free?"

"I'm sorry. Everyone is tied up at the moment. We don't have a large police force. We'll send someone over as soon as we can, but it probably won't be for a few hours."

"I can't stay here that long. I'm already frozen."

"We're not asking you to, sir. I'll note your issue and make sure that the detective gets it. And as soon as I have a spare unit, I'll send it over. That's the best I can do."

"So I'm supposed to just… leave the evidence out here and hope that it's still there when someone comes over? It would make more sense for me to collect it… I can swear an affidavit about where I found it…"

"Just leave everything as it is, sir."

"Seriously?"

"Yes, sir. We appreciate your cooperation."

"You really don't want to solve this case, do you?"

Her voice grew testy. "I told you that I just don't have anyone available at the moment, sir. That doesn't mean that we don't want to solve the case. It means we're operating under the restrictions that we have. You wouldn't expect an officer to drop an emergency he's on now, putting lives in danger, to collect your evidence."

"No. I would expect that you would have enough staff to take care of calls as they come in."

"I would too," she sighed. "But that's just not reality. We have to prioritize cases. Someone will follow up as soon as possible. But in the meantime, you don't need to stay there. I have taken down all of your details."

"And I should just leave the evidence here."

"Yes."

Zachary couldn't think of anything else to say. It wasn't like he would be able to talk her into having more police units available. They had to play the hand they were dealt. Shaking his head, Zachary lowered his hand and took off his glove to operate the freezing cold phone. He was lucky that it hadn't turned off in the time that he'd been waiting on the 9-1-1 dispatcher. He'd had that issue before when phones shut off due to the temperature. Working as quickly as he could, he tapped the screen with numb fingers to take a few pictures of the hats and gloves, the garbage bin, and the number on the fence. He looked around for anything else that they might need to put the pictures into context and, as he walked away down the lane, he snapped a few more shots of the alley.

Back in his car with the engine running, he waited for his fingers and toes to start warming up. It hadn't seemed that bitterly cold to begin with, but he had been outside long enough that the cold had really gotten down into his joints. He remembered being on the street a couple of times as a child or teen. Never for very long. He found he didn't like roughing it. Especially not during the winter. Too easy to get hypothermia.

He started to shiver as he warmed up and realized that he had pushed it a bit too far. He'd obviously been colder than he had thought. He'd thought he'd kept his core temperature up to where it needed to be. But with his weight being so low, he didn't have the insulation needed to keep him warm.

Once his fingers thawed out and he stopped shivering, he paged through the photos on the phone, looking them over and deciding whether he needed to take any more. The front of the house? The side? If he were lucky and they were away from home—and so far, he had been lucky on the case—then he might be able to see something incriminating through the windows. Who knew how long it would be before the police got there and whether they would bother to get a warrant based on what he had said on the phone. More than likely, they would wait until they had seen the evidence with their own eyes, and then take time to process what it meant for the case and if they had enough to arrest the couple for their part in the theft.

Once he was feeling pretty toasty again, Zachary got out of the car and took a couple of pictures of the front of the fourplex. There still didn't appear to be anyone around. He walked to the side and took pictures of the door and mailbox. A few envelopes were sticking out of the mailbox, and he pulled them partway out to check the full names of the recipients and the senders. One of the mail pieces was from an auction house. Zachary swore under his breath. He held the envelope overhead against the sunlight and tried to make out any words on the letter inside. But it was folded in thirds and he couldn't see any words.

If they were dealing with an auction house, then the memorabilia they had stolen could already be on the block. It would be risky to sell them again so quickly, but criminals were not known for making good decisions. Criminal masterminds tended to be something from TV, not reality.

He walked around the building, aware that he was leaving footprints in the snow. It would be obvious to the residents that someone had walked the house's perimeter looking in all of the windows.

When he returned to the couple's door, his luck ran out. A woman in a tattered coat stood there, smoking a cigarette, watching him like a hawk. She was tall and round, and she looked tough, like she might have wrestled or done some kind of hand-to-hand combat in the past.

"Who are you?" she demanded. "What are you doing skulking around here?"

23

Zachary's brain raced on ahead, trying to come up with the most plausible approach. Of course, the best thing to do would just be to retreat. Walk back to his car. If she called the police, she wouldn't be able to get them there before Zachary got away from the scene. What if she did get his license plate? The local police were clearly too overworked to stay on top of cases that were not considered priority.

But that would mean abandoning what he had already found out and any chance he had of advancing the case further. The masks and gloves would be gone by the time the police got there. There would be nothing but Zachary's guesses to connect the couple with the robbery. They were good guesses, obviously. But they wouldn't be enough for the police to investigate. Not once the masks and gloves were removed from the scene.

"Oh, thank goodness you're here!" Zachary told the large woman fervently. "Do you have the key? She said someone would be here with the key, and I've rung all of the bells, but there is no one around and I thought... I thought something had happened."

"What key?" the woman asked, frowning.

"To unit C," Zachary gestured to the door. "I'm supposed to feed the cat!"

"What cat? There are no pets allowed in the building."

"Oh... no, I didn't mean that. I meant... they wanted me to check in and make sure that everything was okay while they were gone."

"They've got a cat?" The woman chuckled. "I've got a chihuahua myself. Not easy to keep it from the landlord if he comes around without notice. One water leak could blow us all."

"She didn't want anything to happen to it while she's gone," Zachary confessed. Despite the cold, his face was sweating. A bead of sweat ran down his back as well. "The cat has diabetes, and it's supposed to have insulin shots and be fed at the same time every day. If it doesn't get its shots, it could die." Zachary nodded to emphasize this. "It could; she said so."

The woman puffed on her cigarette and rubbed her forehead, thinking about it. "I didn't know they had a cat. But then, why would they tell me? Everybody has their secrets."

"So… does that mean you don't have a key?" Zachary looked around. "Someone was supposed to be here to give me a key."

The neighbor looked around, but there was no one nearby paying them any attention. Whoever was supposed to have given Zachary the keys to feed the poor diabetic cat had obviously fallen down on the job.

"Maybe they were in an accident," Zachary said. "Man, I hope that nothing happened! If they broke a leg or something and can't get here, then how am I going to get in?" He looked at the house and shuddered. "I couldn't break a window. Someone would kill me. Besides, then the cat would be able to get out."

The woman considered, still looking around for someone to materialize. She scratched her neck.

"The landlord keyed all of the doors the same," she said finally. "He's a lazy so-and-so and doesn't want to have to carry around more than one set of keys and figure out which one it is. We're not supposed to know, but of course, we figured it out a long time ago."

"Does that mean your key would work on this door?" Zachary pointed to unit C hopefully. It would be great if someone would let him into the suite. He didn't plan on getting caught, but if he did, things would be far more likely to go in his direction if he'd been let in by someone with a key.

"Yes," the woman admitted. "But you have to promise me that you're legit. You're really here to feed the cat?"

"Yes. Of course. I don't randomly go around breaking into people's houses."

She nodded, chuckling. Eventually, she leaned toward the door and produced her own keys to unlock the door. She turned the handle and pushed it open. Zachary stepped forward, catching the door quickly so that it only opened a crack. "You don't want it to get out!" he warned. Making himself as small as possible, he slid through the door, pulling it shut behind him.

He had a feeling that the woman wasn't going to stay there. She would come in after him to make sure that there really was a cat and he was there to feed it rather than getting into mischief.

He hurried through the entryway, cut through the living room, and entered the kitchen. It still smelled of whatever they had fried up for breakfast. The suite was warm and comfortable. Zachary went through the cupboards, quickly gathering what he would need.

He was right about the neighbor not being able to stay outside. She had to enter and make sure that he was not telling her a story.

"Well?" she demanded, looking around, "Where is the cat?"

"Fido?" Zachary called loudly and made kissing noises. "Snowball?"

They both stood there and listened for answering footsteps or bells.

"Hiding somewhere," Zachary said, shaking his head. "She said they're pretty shy. I might have to stick around for a while to find them and get their trust."

"It's two cats now?" She demanded. "Or a cat and a dog?"

"Well..." Zachary did his best to appear sheepish and wiped sweat from his forehead. "I'm really not supposed to say. If it is a no-pet building..."

He ran water into a bowl and set it down on the floor while the woman watched. She looked at the brown, pasty glop in the other bowl. "Don't you think that's too much?"

"For two cats?" Zachary looked down at it. "I didn't measure it, but she said to give them enough. You can always throw out what they don't eat, but if the cat doesn't get enough to eat during the day, it could go into shock or something. They have to have enough to eat, and I have to give it the insulin..." Zachary went to the fridge and started pushing things around as if looking for the vials of insulin. He looked over the door at the woman. "Was there anything else? I don't think I'm supposed to let anyone else in here."

The woman raised her hands. "Okay, fine. I'll go. Looks like you've got everything under control here."

She turned and went back out. Zachary listened until he heard the outside door open and close again, then waited a few more seconds to make sure that she was really gone and it wasn't just a trick.

"Fido?" he called again. "Snowball?"

Not waiting for the imaginary pets to show their faces, he pulled the can of refried beans back out of the sink and looked at it. "Thank goodness they like Mexican." He put the remainder of the can into the garbage, burying it under what was already there. As the trash was nearly full, he hoped that they would be taking it out to the bin soon and would not notice the smell of the refried beans. He would clean up the "cat" bowls before he left, but left them where they were in the meantime, just in case the neighbor came back.

It was time to check out the rest of the unit before the suspects returned. He did not want to get caught there. Coming up with an explanation for his presence would be a lot more difficult than fooling the neighbor had been.

24

Zachary left the kitchen, looked briefly around the living room, and then walked through to the bedrooms and bathroom in the back of the unit. The first bedroom looked pretty normal. A queen bed, low to the floor, and a couple of side tables with lamps, clothes closet, items of clothing messily strewn here and there. Lived in. Not tidied up for company. They didn't expect anyone else to be in there. He didn't spend any time searching it. There wasn't space under the bed for storage and a glance at the open closet assured him that there would be nothing to find there. Not unless they had another storage space hidden behind a false wall.

He went to the other bedroom. The couple didn't have any children; he knew that from their social media. The second bedroom should be a guest room, storage, or home office. But as far as he could tell, they didn't have a home business, both of them working outside the home.

At first glance, a storage room. Several stacks of moving boxes that had probably been there since they had moved in together. A few items of smaller furniture or decor that they did not have the space for in the suite. But there were stacks of boxes to his right, lined up along the wall beside the doorway. Bending down to look at them, he saw that shipping labels were affixed to them. Zachary moved the boxes in order to examine each label. Not all addressed to individuals. There were two that were addressed to auction companies. He took out his keys and opened the pen knife on his keychain. He slit the packing tape down the middle of the two flaps and snapped them open.

And there it was. Sports memorabilia taken from Barnburners. He reached automatically for his phone, then paused. There was no point in calling the police; he'd already been told that the detective on the case was unavailable and so was anyone else in the department. There was not even a car available to come and secure the evidence from the garbage bins. There was no point in calling them and having the same discussion again.

He took pictures of the boxes and the contents of the one that he had opened. He stepped back and took several shots of the room, then walked around the suite, snapping photos of the other rooms as proof that he had been there and hadn't just staged the boxes somewhere else. Was there anything else to do? He could send the pictures to the police, and they could arrange for a warrant when it reached the top of their priorities list and come by and pick up the boxes. Then the thieves could be arrested and the case closed.

But that didn't sit well with Zachary.

He could wait and let the police do it right. That was, ninety-nine percent of the time, the right choice. But there was always that last percent or fraction of a percent.

The thieves had already disposed of the evidence that they had been involved in the burglary. That evidence would probably be gone by the time the police got there. The mask and gloves would be taken or cleaned up by someone walking down the alley. Or the couple themselves would see that someone had been into the garbage and would see the evidence of their wrongdoing there on display for all the world to see.

And the rest of the evidence was packaged up and ready to go. The couple had been quick to find buyers for some of the products and an auction house to deal with the rest. It was probably not the first time they had done something like this. They were not likely to leave the packed and labeled boxes in the storage room. They would get home from work and one of them would take them to the nearest shipper and send them on their way. And then all evidence of what they had done would be gone. Zachary would be unable to prove anything to the police. He had the pictures, but that would probably not be enough to convict them. And they might not be able to get back the items that had been sold to third parties.

He went back and looked at the packaged and labeled boxes, running scenarios through his brain. With things as they currently stood, he saw more opportunities for things to go sideways and the memorabilia to be permanently out of their reach than he did for them to line up properly, with the police getting all of the evidence they needed and the stolen memorabilia going back to Glen and Janice.

Zachary pressed his lips together grimly, deciding what to do next.

In a couple of minutes, he had carried the first couple of boxes out to his car, popped them into the trunk, and was heading back inside for another load.

The nosy but ultimately helpful neighbor again stood by the door, her eyes sharp, ready with another barrage of questions. Zachary looked at her, raising one eyebrow.

"Thanks for your help," he told her crisply. "I just have a few more things to take care of here."

"What are you doing?"

"Taking some deliveries to the post office." He stared at her. "I don't see how that's any of your business."

She didn't stop him from going back into the suite, but she was still there when he came out with the next set of boxes. She leaned in to look at them as he walked by. Taller than he was, it wasn't hard for her to see the address label on the top box. She could see that everything was properly packaged and labeled for delivery.

"You didn't say you were picking up any parcels," she pointed out.

"I didn't think I was required to tell you everything I was doing here."

"All you said was that you needed to feed the cat."

Zachary shifted his grip on the heavy boxes and kept walking. "The cat was what I was most worried about. The boxes could wait if I couldn't get into the house. But a cat with diabetes? It couldn't wait, not even a few hours. It could be dead by the time I got in if it didn't get its food and insulin at the right times."

He kept walking to his car and settled the next set of boxes into the trunk. He closed the trunk lid to prevent the neighbor from taking pictures or pulling a box or two out for further examination. One more trip should do it.

He grabbed the last couple of boxes and set them down outside the door. Turning, he took the time to lock the door before closing it again. He was done there. It would be obvious to the thieves that someone had been there, but they couldn't exactly go to the police about it.

The neighbor watched as he trudged back to his car with the last couple of boxes and slid them into the back seat.

"Thanks again for your help," he told her, forcing a smile. "Have a great day!"

She probably wouldn't. Not once the thieves realized what had happened and looked into how someone had gotten into their suite.

25

Zachary made sure he was out of sight of the house and that there was no one around to observe him before tapping the Bluetooth button on his steering wheel and placing an outgoing call to Janice. The call went almost immediately to voicemail. Zachary hung up and tried Glen. His phone also went to voicemail right away. He hung up, then frowned and thought about that for a few minutes.

They were somewhere that they could not answer their phones. Maybe a theater or a business meeting that could not be disturbed. Or maybe they turned off their phones for some quiet time together during the day. That wasn't the usual behavior for a dedicated smartphone user, and Zachary had seen both of them using their phones regularly while performing various tasks. But of course, they could be an exception. One of those few couples who actually implemented the Do Not Disturb or Focus features of their phones.

More likely, they were somewhere phones were not allowed. That worried him, but he couldn't do anything about it. He called Janice once more, hoping that it was just a phone network issue and that it would be answered this time, but again it rang directly through to voicemail. Zachary waited for her outgoing message to finish, then left a brief voicemail.

"Hi Janice, it's Zachary Goldman. I've made some progress on the case and would be grateful if you would give me a call. Thanks." He left his number again, even though she would be able to see it on her screen.

Hopefully, it wouldn't be too long before she called back. Zachary decided to stop and have lunch while he waited. Kenzie would be impressed.

He selected a drive-through so that he wouldn't have to leave the loot alone in the car, and sat in the warm cabin eating slowly while he scrolled through the email and social networks on his phone, waiting for it to ring with a call back from Janice.

But the call did not come. Zachary had waited for an hour and a half and couldn't stand sitting in the car any longer without something constructive to do. There was only so much work he could do on his phone. There was no call from the police to say that they were on their way to pick up the evidence. No call from Janice or Glen, apologizing for being out of reach. He couldn't just sit around waiting for them to get back to him all afternoon.

Eventually, he turned around and headed for home. The memorabilia would keep. It would be safe at Kenzie's house until he could get it to Janice and Glen.

He apologized immediately to Kenzie when she came home and saw the boxes in her living room. "Just let me know where you want me to put this stuff. It should only be a day. I didn't know if you wanted them in the garage or in the office… I just didn't want to leave it in the car because of security…"

Kenzie looked at the stack of boxes and shook her head. "This is everything that was stolen from the sports bar?"

"Well, I haven't itemized it yet. But it looks like it. I wanted to leave as much of it as possible intact for the police. There might be fingerprints on the packing tape, hairs, other forensic evidence…"

"They're really not going to be doing a bunch of forensic testing on a few boxes of recovered memorabilia," she pointed out with a chuckle.

"I know…" Zachary was always disappointed when the real-life police did not imitate those he saw on TV who were always intent on finding and analyzing every last bit of forensic evidence in even the smallest, least significant cases. Because you never knew what might be a clue to a bigger crime, an organized syndicate or serial killer. But of course, Kenzie was right. They would ask Glen and Janice if that was all their stolen property, then close the file. He would be lucky if they went on to arrest the culprits, considering the fact that Zachary had removed evidence from the scene. "But they could."

"They could," Kenzie conceded. "Why don't you put them in the office for now? Just stack them against the wall."

He had thought she would prefer having them stored in the garage, so it was a good thing he had asked. She probably didn't want to risk his bumping a hand cart full of boxes into her "baby," Kenzie's red convertible.

"I'll get them out of here," Zachary agreed.

Kenzie probably wouldn't react violently to things being out of place or somewhere other than where she wanted them to be as Bridget would have. Still, he didn't want the presence of the boxes to irritate her, especially if they reminded her of her father and how Zachary had gone ahead and taken Walter's case when she didn't want him to.

He grabbed a couple of boxes, carried them down the hall to the office, put them down to open the door, and then set them against the wall. The room was small and didn't boast a lot of extra space, so it would feel cramped once he had all of the boxes in place. But at least they would be out of sight. Kenzie didn't use her office very often. Zachary was sure that he would be able to talk to Glen and Janice before then and take the boxes to them.

He made a couple more trips out to the living room and back and had the boxes all neatly stacked out of sight in the office in a few minutes. Kenzie was rummaging around in the kitchen, starting to get dinner ready. They hadn't discussed what they were having, but Kenzie obviously had something in mind, so he didn't make any suggestions and started setting the table. Whatever they were eating, they were going to need plates, cups, and cutlery.

Kenzie filled a pot with water, put it on the burner, then turned to face Zachary, leaning against the calendar.

"I've got a program for Tyrrell."

"You do? That's great. Where is it?"

Kenzie started to fill him in on the details. "They're going to want him right away, which is good, because I think he's waited long enough. If we have to keep waiting…"

Zachary nodded. "He's going to have a setback sooner or later. Once he's in the program, it will be easier."

"He's done really well, but I don't want to tempt fate."

Zachary was relieved that it was a longer program. It had been hard to find one that was longer than 30 days or six weeks. If they could keep Tyrrell in a longer-term program, with some good transition services, he would have a better chance of really integrating the change. Zachary didn't believe in God, but felt like he should send a prayer out to the universe somehow that this time, sobriety would "take" and Tyrrell wouldn't keep relapsing.

"One day at a time," Kenzie advised, meeting his eyes.

Zachary nodded. He took a deep breath and let it out. "Yeah. Take things as they come." Dr. B had given him several strategies to avoid getting overly anxious about things that hadn't happened yet. There was no point in assuming that things would go wrong, or that they would go right, for that matter. It was best to just take each day as it came and be flexible with it.

Flexibility was not something that came easily to him. But Dr. B said it was something he could work on and get better at. He took a couple more deep breaths, looking ahead just one or two days, as Tyrrell was admitted into the facility.

"He should see Mason and Alisha before he goes in. Do they allow visitors during the program?"

Kenzie nodded. "Not for the first few weeks. It's closed until then, just the patients working with the professionals and group. No distractions. No one who might try to pull them away from the program. It would be good if they could see him one more time before he goes in. Maybe talk to him about that?"

"Have you told him about the program?"

She nodded. "I called Tyrrell to make sure it was okay and gave him the main points. I think he's eager to get to it."

"I'll go talk to him, then."

26

He left Kenzie to work on the dinner and went down the hall to the guest room. He hadn't seen Tyrrell since he had arrived home with the boxes, but assumed that he was cocooned in the guest room as usual. He tapped lightly on the door and, after waiting a few seconds, opened it a crack.

"Hey, T?"

Tyrrell was stretched out on the bed, listening to something on his phone, earbuds in his ears. He heard Zachary or saw the movement of the door and turned his head, then sat up and took the earbuds out, tapping the phone to pause whatever was playing.

"Hey, Zach. How's it going?"

"Good. How about you?"

"Fine. Dinnertime?"

"No, Kenzie's just working on it now." Zachary walked into the room and stood a few feet away from Tyrrell, folding his arms and trying to affect a casual stance, not hovering over Tyrrell or giving off any anxiety. "She just told me about the program that she's got you into."

Tyrrell nodded, smiling at that. "Yeah, she's really a gem, Zachary. You really got a winner in her."

"I know. She's amazing." He didn't give Kenzie enough credit. It was too easy to get used to someone, to get used to being around her and her doing things for him, not realizing how much it really was. Kenzie put up with a lot with Zachary's quirks and issues and never yelled and berated him the way Bridget had. Kenzie got impatient sometimes, was curt or said something she later regretted but, as far as Zachary was concerned, she was pretty close to perfect.

"Yeah. You're lucky." Tyrrell's voice was a little wistful. Undoubtedly thinking about his own lack of a partner. How things had not turned out for him and Lindsey the way they had for Zachary and Kenzie. And probably blaming himself for the fact that things had fallen apart, the marriage too stressed by Tyrrell's drinking, two children, one of them with behavioral issues, and Tyrrell's absences whenever things got to be too difficult.

"I was just thinking," Zachary said, trying to move quickly away from morose thoughts about the failure of Tyrrell's marriage. "The kids aren't going to be able to see you for a few weeks, the first little while you're in this program. So you should see if you can visit with them one more time before you go in."

Tyrrell scratched his chin. He hadn't shaven that day. Maybe for a few days. "I don't know. I don't like to ask Lindsey for something like that. It's not on the visitation schedule."

"It isn't yet. But she'll understand that you can't visit with them while you're in a closed program. You don't think she would try to make it work?"

"I don't think I should ask. I've asked too much of her already."

"All she can do is say no."

"She can say a lot more than *that!*" Tyrrell said with a laugh, then looked embarrassed that he had said it. "It's just... I know the kids have school and after-school activities, and Lindsey has work. It's not a good time to be asking for an extra visit. Maybe if it was the weekend, but..."

Zachary stood there, trying to figure out what to do. Was it a hard "no," or was Tyrrell just reluctant to call? If he pushed back, would Tyrrell give in and agree, or resist and be angry with Zachary for interfering with his family relationships?

"What if I called her?" he asked eventually. "If the request is coming from someone other than you, would that be better?"

Tyrrell nodded, looking relieved. It probably wasn't good for Zachary to be enabling Tyrrell backing out of his responsibilities. It was clearly Tyrrell's job to make the call and see if he could visit his kids for a few more hours before going into the program. But they could worry about building responsibility *after* Tyrrell was out of the program. Before, it was probably best to help out where he could and not put more stress on Tyrrell before then.

The last thing they needed was Tyrrell disappearing again before entering the program. Zachary had already spent a week tracking him down. He knew where to look now, but if Tyrrell really wanted to avoid being found, he could find another bar to hide out in. He could go anywhere in the state. Anywhere that he could get to with the gas already in his tank. Farther if he happened to have a working credit card.

"Okay. I'll give Lindsey a call."

"Thanks, bro. I really appreciate it."

Zachary hesitated for a moment, trying to decide between calling Lindsey on speakerphone with Tyrrell in the room, so he could hear her and respond to any questions she might have, or leaving the room so that Tyrrell didn't have to participate at all.

He decided that keeping Tyrrell calm and relaxed was probably best and walked out of the guest room while he tapped the contact on his phone to get a hold of Lindsey.

Contrary to what Tyrrell had thought, Lindsey had been very accommodating about getting one more visit in with the kids before entering the program. She promised to see what she could do about changing her schedule and would pull the kids from whatever their usual after-school activities were to get them some time together.

"It's really tough dealing with them after they get back from a visit," Lindsey confessed to Zachary. "They get depressed, act up, don't want to do anything I tell them to… I know Alisha worries about whether that's the last time she'll ever see him. Mason probably feels the same way but doesn't realize it. It makes me question sometimes whether it is worth setting up visitations."

Zachary tried to think of what to say to counter this. He knew Lindsey wasn't really asking his position, but he didn't want to support the idea of keeping the kids apart from Tyrrell.

"But I know it's the right thing," Lindsey went on before Zachary could say anything. "Even if they are stressed and crabby afterward… at least they get to see him. To know that he's okay and have a bit of a chance to build their relationship."

"Yeah," Zachary agreed, glad that he didn't have to say anything to convince her about it being worth it. He could have argued that the court would force visitation if she didn't allow it, but that would be confrontational and might not even be true. With the right expert witnesses on her side, she probably could convince a judge that Tyrrell's disappearances and temper when he was drinking were detrimental to the children and they shouldn't be forced to see him when it was just doing them more emotional harm.

"I'll get them over there tomorrow, one way or another," Lindsey said. "That will work, right? He'll at least take a day before he checks into this program?"

"I'm sure we can take a day to pack and get ready for it. He said he wanted to see them but wasn't sure he would be able to before the weekend."

"I'll make it work."

"Okay. If you want to just give me a call or shoot me a text when you've worked it out, I'll let him know what time."

"Thanks, Zachary. And... thanks for acting as a buffer between us. It makes it easier for me."

"Oh... you're welcome." He had thought that she would prefer to deal with Tyrrell directly, so he was a little surprised at her comment. Maybe both of them needed an intermediary for a little while. Until they both felt up to talking to each other directly again. He might bring it up to Dr. Boyle during their couple's therapy session and see if she had any advice on the matter. Couple's therapy wasn't really the time to be discussing someone else's relationship issues. Still, he thought he could find a way to make it more relevant to his and Kenzie's relationship. A hypothetical situation, maybe. Or just a question on when it was okay to involve an intermediary when a discussion was difficult.

27

As Zachary was helping to clean up after dinner, his phone started to vibrate, and he looked at it, hoping that it would be Janice or Glen. Dreading that it would be the police and he would have to explain what he had done and why. But instead, it was Walter. Zachary looked at it for a moment as it rang, trying to decide on a course of action.

"I'd better take this," he said eventually, and walked out of the room before answering. "Zachary here."

"Zachary." Walter's voice was ebullient; rich and cheery. "I was just hoping for an update on how the case is going. I know you'll let me know when there is something to report, but…"

"Oh. Actually, yeah, I do have news. I was hoping to reach Glen and Janice first, but they've been out of touch all day." He worried that thought over in his mind for a few seconds, a knot of dread in his stomach. Had something happened to them? Why had they just disappeared from view so suddenly?

It was sure to be something minor. Just a problem with their phone carrier, or a lunch date at the restaurant, after which they had forgotten to take their phones out of Do Not Disturb mode. Nothing had happened to them.

"Well, that's great," Walter exclaimed, apparently unconcerned by the couple's unavailability. "Tell me about it."

"I should start at the beginning. Are you at your computer? Can I do a screen share with you to show you what I discovered?"

"Sure. Send me an invitation and I'll meet you."

In a few minutes, they had switched from the phone call to a web conference, with Zachary sharing his screen with his client.

"You've seen the video, right?" Zachary asked. "Footage of the break-in?"

"No, I haven't seen it."

"Oh, okay. Let me just play that first, then."

Zachary brought up the video and played it full screen. As Kenzie had noted, it was startling in its violence. Zachary was getting used to it, but he tried to see it as Walter would be seeing it for the first time. With no preconceived notions. Not something that he had watched a hundred times before and broken down and analyzed in detail. He let his vision blur and just watched the shapes moving on the screen. Angry or anxious, jerky, watching for the cops, knocking stuff over and grabbing whatever they could of the sports memorabilia.

Walter swore. "That's brutal," he said. "I had no idea of the... ferocity. I just pictured... like you see on TV, on a heist movie. A quiet break-in, moving carefully from room to room to avoid setting off any security alarms... targeting the one thing in the room that they came for. This is far more... feral."

"Kenzie noticed that too," Zachary acknowledged. Maybe mentioning his daughter would help Walter feel like he was getting his money's worth out of this case. An unconscious confirmation that he was getting what he wanted.

"You showed it to Kenzie?"

"Uh... yes. I didn't think it was confidential."

"No. No, of course not. So... there was something on that video that you could use?"

"At first, I was just looking at it for the general stuff—how did they get in, what were they looking for, was there anything to identify who the burglars were..."

"Right. And you found something?"

"Kenzie thought that this burglar," Zachary moved a spotlight cursor over one of the figures in the frozen video, "is a woman."

"Oh. Well... I suppose it's possible. She is smaller than the other one."

"And she moves differently. Kenzie thought she moved more like a woman."

"I'll take her word for it," Walter chuckled.

Zachary knew that he could often tell whether a person he saw on a surveillance job was a man or a woman based on how they moved, without seeing their body shape and without gendered clothing styles. He wasn't sure he would have Kenzie's confidence with it and had not noticed that the person in the video was a woman. Still, he often subconsciously absorbed much more about a person than he realized.

"So, this looks pretty much like you expected it to," Zachary said, moving his spotlight over the walls in the video. "The way that the bar looks, not the robbery itself."

"Sure. I'd recognize that as Barnburners. It's obvious."

"I have some other photos." Zachary opened his file folder and opened up several pictures to look at. "These are mostly from social media and reviews. People who have taken pictures while they were there."

"Right," Walter agreed, but his voice held a note of hesitation. Wondering where Zachary was going with his narrative.

"Compare this photo," Zachary brought it to the right of the video, now reduced on the screen.

They weren't the same angle but showed the same wall and a corner of the bar.

"Are you saying that isn't Barnburners?" Walter asked, confused.

"No, I'm sure it is. But just look at the two pictures. Do you see the differences?"

There was a brief silence as Walter looked at the two photos. It apparently didn't take him long to see what Zachary had. "The amount of memorabilia on the wall. At this point in the video, they've already taken most of the pictures and display items."

"Right," Zachary agreed. He pulled the dot on the video timeline all the way to the left, rewinding the video back to the beginning. "Now watch again and look for that wall."

The opening sequence of the video played again. The two burglars breaking into the bar. Starting to remove the valuable items and putting them into their bags. He froze the video when it reached the same point again.

"Notice anything?"

"They haven't touched anything on that wall yet. They've been across the room."

"Yeah."

"But…" Walter tried to reconcile these facts. "The items on that wall were gone *before* the burglary."

Zachary nodded. "Exactly."

"How could that be?"

"There was too much loot to be grabbed in two minutes by only two people, even with the speed they were blasting through there. This video was staged to distract everyone from when the real thefts actually took place."

"Before that."

"Yeah."

"How much before?" Walter took a sharp intake of breath. "It was an inside job."

"It was an inside job," Zachary confirmed.

"Nicely done, Zachary! Wow. So, the next job is to figure out who did it. Not Janice and Glen, I hope…"

"If you look at the height discrepancy between the two thieves in the video, you can see that it is not Janice and Glen."

"Thank goodness for that. So how are you going to figure it out? It's helpful to eliminate the McNichols, but how do you nail down who it is? There are another half dozen employees, and they aren't all couples, so you can't use the height thing to sort them all out."

"You asked when the actual theft took place. It would have to be between the close of business and the smash and grab."

"Because the McNichols and the staff would have noticed if there was a bunch of stuff missing from the walls during the day."

"Right. So that gives us a pretty narrow window to find alibis for."

"How are you going to do that? Get them to give you proof of where they were? And what about the ones who don't have any alibi?"

Zachary opened another folder and brought up the images it contained on the screen. Each image was labeled with the name of an employee and a time. "These are social media pictures and posts that establish where the different employees were and at what time."

"All of the employees?" Walter asked.

"No, not quite all. But the employees tend to be young people who post regularly on social media which establishes where they were."

"But not everyone posted."

"There were only a couple of employees who didn't post anything on social media during the evening and up until the time of the burglary. But those people still have social media accounts. They just aren't posting as actively as the others or were not posting that night. So there are still social media posts that show them with their best friend or partner."

Zachary brought up a couple more pictures for Walter to see. He didn't say anything at first.

"But only one couple matches the body types on the video," Walter eventually saw.

"Right. This is Jennifer Brown and her boyfriend, Michael Martin. It's not definitive proof, but it's pretty good evidence. It could be someone else with a similar body size who posted fake posts on their social media to cover their tracks, but I really don't think that our thieves would have thought to do something like that. The smash and grab was to cover the actual theft. They wouldn't have thought they needed another alibi on top of that or that she was the only employee not posting to social media during that period."

"Have you contacted the police with this? You've done a fantastic job, Zachary. With all of this, the police might be able to recover the stolen property, or at least some of it."

Zachary considered how much to tell Walter about what had gone down at the fourplex. He probably shouldn't admit to getting into Brown's residence and removing the stolen property. Even though he felt like it had been the right thing and the only way to recover the stolen property with the police being unavailable, it was probably best to keep the details of the recovery vague.

"As it turns out," he said slowly, "I did manage to recover the stolen property. I haven't yet been able to talk to the detective on the case, so he is probably not going to be too happy that I went ahead without him, but I do have the memorabilia here, safe and sound."

"All of it?" Walter demanded.

"I haven't itemized it, but yes, I suspect everything is here. It looks like a professional operation. They already had auction accounts and buyers. They may not have pulled off an operation just like this before, but they're clearly used to selling valuables quickly."

"That's amazing. I assume you've already called Glen and Janice? Have they made arrangements to pick up the stolen property?"

"No. I haven't been able to get ahold of them today. I'm not sure where they are or if something is wrong with their phone service provider. And I should probably talk to the detective before I turn anything over to anyone. He probably won't actually want it. From the way they have been handling this case, I'm not sure he'll even want to look at it. But I should talk to him before handing anything over to the McNichols."

"You just have a box of stolen goods sitting there at Kenzie's house—your house—for pickup?"

"Several boxes. They had already packaged everything up to send to the buyers and auction house. It's out of the way and is fine to stay here until I get everything sorted out with the police."

"That's great news, Zachary. You've certainly been worth your fee. Be sure to get me an invoice for the rest of your time and I'll transfer you the money right away."

Zachary smiled, pleased. At the back end, when all of the work was done, clients sometimes balked at paying the rest of his fees, thinking that since they got what they wanted, it was time to renegotiate the cost so that they didn't have to spend as much.

"I'll be sure to get it to you," he agreed.

28

Zachary slept pretty well that night. His shortened sleep the night before, the action of the day, and the satisfaction of having cracked the case all combined, and he fell asleep soon after his head hit the pillow. There was no need to be replaying the video in his head this time. He had a little bit of anxiety from thinking about exactly how he would explain it all to the police detective when he finally got around to calling Zachary back. Still, he could suppress this worry enough that it didn't keep him awake.

He still awoke before Kenzie, but without nightmares or other sleep disturbances. He rose quietly and moved out to the living room so that he wouldn't wake her, and started in on his inbox and the other work awaiting him. He had more than just the Barnburners file to work on, and now that the burglary case was solved, he knew he needed to get back to the rest.

There were still no calls or messages from the McNichols. Maybe they didn't think he would find anything, so they didn't see the need to call him back immediately. Or maybe their phones were still down and they had no idea that he'd been trying to reach them. Either way, the property was safe for the moment. It would wait until they got back to him.

The arrival of Mason and Alisha in the late afternoon was not nearly as dramatic as the previous visit had been. Zachary was glad to see that things were more normal. The children and Tyrrell were happy to see each other, and the children were reassured that their father was going to get some help for his drinking problem. They probably knew by now that Tyrrell going into a new program wasn't any guarantee of success, but it was at least positive. He was trying.

The weather wasn't too bad, and Mason had seen kids sledding down a nearby hill as they had arrived, so he harassed and cajoled Tyrrell into taking the two of them to the sledding hill. They didn't have sleds with them, but Kenzie equipped them with a couple of flat pieces of cardboard from filing boxes and some large garbage bags, and they would probably also be able to make friends with the kids already out on the hill and get turns on their sleds and toboggans. That was the way things worked on community sledding hills.

"We'll make some hot chocolate for when they get back," Kenzie said, watching Tyrrell and the children traipsing off for the hill.

"I'm sure they'll be ready for it," Zachary agreed. The thought of sledding and coming home to hot chocolate was enough to make him want to chase after Tyrrell and join in on the fun. The last time he had gone sledding with Tyrrell would have been the winter of the fire, with Zachary ten and Tyrrell six. They'd never had sleds of their own and had made do with whatever cardboard, plastic sheeting, or garbage can lids they could put their hands on. He remembered the neighborhood park as idyllic, somewhere the Goldman kids spent a lot of time hanging out and playing tag and made-up games without having to worry about their parents and the unfair rules of the grown-up world. It was probably nothing like he remembered it. Just a broken-down, worn-out little park in a low-rent neighborhood. But for them, it had been paradise.

"Zachary?"

Zachary tore his eyes from the window and looked at Kenzie.

"Do you want to go?" Kenzie nodded toward the distant figures.

"No. I've got work to do, and Tyrrell should have some time with them to himself."

"All right. I'll call you when the hot chocolate is ready, then."

Zachary returned to the bedroom where he had stowed his computer and went back to work. He found it hard to concentrate, his mind repeatedly returning to the children at the park and his own childhood memories. It was strange that they should come back so clearly just from being around Alisha and Mason.

And that made him remember how Tyrrell had said that being around Zachary made him remember home. Not just the good times that they had enjoyed together in the park, but their abusive parents and the violence and neglect that the children had endured before the dissolution of the family. Being with Zachary and then being with his children was a bad combination for Tyrrell, making him think he was a bad parent when he got frustrated or impatient with them. Zachary chewed on the inside of his cheek while he typed, hoping that everything would be okay and that Tyrrell and the children would be able to have a good visit together.

They were gone for about an hour. Zachary heard them return to the house, the door banging, thumps as they removed their winter boots, loud voices rising. Zachary cocked his head, listening, trying to decide whether the children were just excited or whether they were arguing about something.

Kenzie tapped on the bedroom door and opened it. "Come on out for hot chocolate. There are marshmallows!"

"Okay. Everything all right out there?" Zachary was still anxious about a fight, despite the lightness in Kenzie's tone.

"The kids are a bit hyper. That's all."

Zachary nodded. He saved the document he was working on, but left his work out on the bed, intending to return to it after the hot chocolate break. He followed Kenzie out to the kitchen. Mason and Alisha were getting their hot chocolate prepared, adding milk to cool it down and dropping marshmallows on top. Mason was making bombing noises as he dropped the marshmallows in.

"Stop it," Alisha complained. "You're bothering me."

Mason continued to bomb his hot chocolate with marshmallows, splashing hot chocolate on the table.

"Now, look!" Alisha got after him. "I told you to stop!"

"I can do it if I want to!" Mason told her. "You can't stop me!"

"Mason," Tyrrell told him sharply. "Stop bugging your sister."

"I don't have to!" Mason shot back. "I'm not doing anything wrong! If it's bothering her, then she can go somewhere else!"

"Mason, you're a visitor in someone else's home. You should be on your best behavior. We're all going to have hot chocolate, so you need to be considerate of others. Alisha shouldn't have to miss out on hot chocolate because you're intentionally annoying her."

"I'm not intentionally annoying her! She's just being annoyed!"

"Mason!" Tyrrell snapped.

"It's not fair!" Mason shouted, pushing a handful of marshmallows into his cup so violently that the hot chocolate splashed up over the rim of the cup, soaked the front of his shirt, and spread in a puddle across the table. Mason howled. "Now, look what you made me do!"

"Come here," Tyrrell grabbed Mason by the arm and pulled him back from the table. "I can't believe that you're behaving like this. You need to—"

"You made me wreck my shirt. I want my hot chocolate!" Mason protested as Tyrrell pulled him away and he realized he wasn't going to get his treat. "Daddy! I want my drink!"

"Look at me!" Tyrrell shook Mason by the shoulders, glaring at him. "You need a time out. Go down the hall and sit on my bed. And stay there until I come get you. This is…" Tyrrell shook his head angrily. "This is not acceptable behavior."

Mason wrenched himself away from Tyrrell and stormed off down the hall. He slammed the door and set up wailing about not having any fun or having his drink when he was so thirsty and how Daddy was so mean and unfair.

29

Everyone in the kitchen just stood there for a minute, taking a collective breath and trying to figure out what to do. Zachary felt like running into the master bedroom and shutting the door. He hated confrontations and he hated seeing Tyrrell angry at his children and Mason so distressed. Zachary had been a kid like Mason. While he understood how annoying it was to deal with Mason's hyperactivity and impulsiveness, he also understood how unfair it felt to Mason to be attacked just for having a little harmless fun with the marshmallows.

Kenzie grabbed a dishcloth from the sink and started to mop up the hot chocolate that was spreading across the table, trying to move everything else out of the way before they came in contact with the chocolatey pool of milk.

"I'm sorry, Daddy." Alisha started to weep. "I'm sorry, I didn't mean to cause a fight. Mason can put marshmallows in his hot chocolate. I don't care."

"You didn't do anything wrong," Tyrrell told her. "You just asked him to stop making the noise and being too wild." He took a deep breath, obviously trying to calm himself down. He hated it when he lost his temper with Mason.

"But he was just having fun, and I know he has a hard time stopping when he's playing a game…"

"You didn't do anything wrong," Tyrrell repeated. "It's okay. Grab your hot chocolate and sit down. We'll all have our hot chocolate now."

Sniffling, Alisha picked up her mug and sat down on one of the chairs, holding it close to her chest. Tears still streamed down her cheeks. Kenzie squeezed out the dishcloth, rinsed it, squeezed it out again, and mopped down the table once more. The spilled hot chocolate was taken care of. "Don't cry over spilled milk," they always said. But Alisha was still crying, Mason was weeping sporadically in the guest room, and Zachary just wanted to withdraw and be by himself before their emotions became too much for him too.

Kenzie firmly put a mug in front of Tyrrell and gestured for him to doctor it to his liking. She looked at Zachary, still standing in the doorway between the living room and the kitchen. Instead of telling him to come in and get his ready as well, she put the final two mugs in front of herself and filled them both. She added marshmallows to one and pushed it across the table in Zachary's direction. Zachary stepped into the kitchen and picked it up, but he didn't immediately drink it. Kenzie picked hers up and sat beside Alisha, starting a "girlfriend" type conversation about school and what Alisha and her friends had been up to recently.

Tyrrell picked up his mug and took several hard swallows without first cooling it down with milk. Zachary stared down at his hot chocolate. The marshmallows were dissolving around the edges and making a foam over the surface of the liquid.

"Have fun sledding?" he asked Tyrrell, unsure what else to say.

"The kids had fun. I went down a few times, but there weren't a lot of other parents participating, so…"

Maybe Zachary should have gone with them so that Tyrrell would have had someone to enjoy the sledding with. If they were both going down together, Tyrrell wouldn't have had to feel awkward at being the only dad who was acting like a little kid.

He should have gone.

Zachary continued to stare down at his hot chocolate. He couldn't drink it. Not with the big knot in his stomach caused by the fight.

Which was silly. A little childish behavior did not put him in danger and should not be anything to worry about. Zachary wasn't unsafe and neither was Mason. Tyrrell hadn't been physically or verbally abusive to Mason, had just told him to stop, and then had told him to go to his room when things got out of hand. A perfectly valid parental response. Mason's sobs had already chugged to a stop. He was, Zachary assumed, waiting on Tyrrell's bed for his father to come talk to him and then invite him back out to finish his hot chocolate. Zachary didn't think Tyrrell would take the treat away altogether.

But Zachary still felt like things might explode around him, and there was no way he could force his hot chocolate down.

Kenzie was watching him but didn't say anything. She probably understood perfectly well why Zachary wasn't drinking. She was trying to just calm things down and make them nice for Alisha and Tyrrell. The sooner everyone could get back to normal, the sooner Mason could return and they could get on with the visit. No one wanted it to be ruined by a little spat. Tyrrell wasn't going to see his children for several weeks and wouldn't want the visit to end on a sour note.

As everyone started to relax and Alisha chattered with Kenzie, Zachary went over to the sink. He discreetly lowered the mug into the sink out of sight before dumping the hot chocolate down the drain. The marshmallows were not completely dissolved and they stuck in the strainer. He swallowed and turned back to the others.

"I guess I'd better get back to work. That was really nice, Kenzie, thank you." He looked at Tyrrell. "Did you want me to tell Mason he can come out now?"

Tyrrell took a deep breath in and blew it out. "Yes. If he's calmed down, he can come out and drink his hot chocolate." Tyrrell looked at the half-mug of hot chocolate that had survived the marshmallow bombing. "Though it is probably cold chocolate now."

"We can heat it up in the microwave," Kenzie said. "But... maybe it's best if I don't."

"Just leave it like it is," Tyrrell said firmly. "He can deal with it."

Zachary slipped out of the kitchen and went down the hall to the guest bedroom. He tapped on the door and opened it, then looked around, confused. There was no sign of Mason. Zachary looked in the closet and under the bed, then left the bedroom, puzzled. He had heard Mason stomp down the hall and slam the door. Mason hadn't come out, or he would have walked past the kitchen.

Kenzie's office.

Zachary took a few steps down the hall to the next door and opened it. Mason startled and looked up at Zachary, his eyes wide and guilty. Sports memorabilia was scattered in a circle around him, and he had the Montreal Canadiens die-cast car in his hand, running it along the carpet as he made motor noises.

"Mason." Zachary looked at the boxes and saw that they had all been opened, even the ones he had left sealed closed with packing tape. Mason had rummaged through them all, pulling out the bits that interested him the most. "These are not yours. They were closed. You shouldn't have gotten into them."

"I thought… they were toys. So, I could play with them."

"They aren't yours. They belong to a client of mine, and they shouldn't have been touched. That's why most of the boxes were still sealed shut."

"Oh… I'm sorry." Mason started to pick them up and shove them haphazardly into boxes, not taking any care to sort them or pack them properly. He held the Canadiens car up for Zachary to see. "This is really cool. Did you know that the doors really open—"

"Put it away with the others," Zachary interrupted. "It's not to play with."

"Can I show you, though—"

"No."

Mason frowned. He scrubbed at his eyes with his fists, maybe remembering the hot chocolate now and that he was supposed to be upset about something. That was one of the positive aspects of ADHD for Zachary—the ability to be distracted by something interesting and forget all about what he had been upset about.

Except for those times when the obsessive part of Zachary's brain refused to let something go or be distracted by anything else. Anxiety and hyperfocus could overwhelm the distractibility and keep him preoccupied. Like not being able to forget about the video until he had identified what was wrong with it. Or fantasizing about returning to Bridget when he loved Kenzie and wanted to be with her.

"Go on out to the kitchen and have your hot chocolate," he told Mason. "Your daddy is waiting for you."

30

As Zachary worked through the tasks in his email and task list, his phone vibrated. It was off to the side and he was busy with other things, so he didn't look at it at first, planning to just let it go to voicemail. But it occurred to him that he was waiting for more than one person to call him back, so he pried himself away from the page he was looking at to see if it was a call he had to answer.

Janice McNichol.

Zachary grabbed the phone and swiped to answer the call. "Janice. Hey, I've been trying to reach you. But I guess... you've been having phone trouble?"

"I wish that's all it was." Janice's sigh carried down the line. "It's been a pretty rough couple of days."

"What happened?"

"That police detective who is in charge of the burglary case? He contacted us. Yesterday, I guess. It's all running together. I can't keep the days straight."

"Oh, that's good. I was waiting for a call from him too. What did he have to say?"

"What didn't he say? The guy was like a bulldog. He's determined that it was an inside job, so it must have been me and Glen. Or we at least knew something about it or colluded with whoever actually pulled it off, because we weren't anywhere near the bar at the time. He just... wouldn't give it up. He had… phone records from the bar to known fences. He actually called them that. Fences. I thought that was just TV jargon. He said that he didn't believe the video footage was real. He thought it was staged, so we must have done it. We can't alibi each other and we can't prove that we were somewhere other than at home, because that's where we were. We weren't out burgling our own bar. Believe me, at the end of a long day at Barnburners, I don't want to do anything other than go home and go to bed. And that's what we did. We didn't know about the burglary until the alarm company called us."

"It was an inside job," Zachary agreed. "But I know it wasn't you."

"What do you mean? It wasn't an inside job. No one we work with would do something like that to us."

"Your waitress, Jennifer Brown. She and her boyfriend."

"Jenn? That doesn't make any sense. Jenn has worked there for two years. I've never had a lick of trouble with her."

"Well, maybe she was influenced by the boyfriend. Or maybe they got into debt and they needed to make some quick cash. But from what I could tell, they've done this before. Or he has, anyway. He had accounts with auction companies. Had buyers lined up for some of the stolen merchandise."

"No! Jenn would never do that."

"Maybe she was coerced. I don't know."

"You can't tell that detective that she did it."

"I'm going to need to tell him something. He'll want to know how I got the stolen articles back."

There was a gasp from Janice. "You got them back? Really? How *did* you get them back?"

"I went over to Jennifer's house. They were all boxed up, ready to be shipped."

Janice swore, wonder in her voice. "How could she do that to me? I don't understand why or how she would do that."

"I'll show you the video if you're at your computer, and some other photos, and you can clearly see what happened…"

"No. I'm not at my computer and probably won't be for a few more days."

Zachary was surprised. "Where are you?"

"I'm at the hospital."

"Oh, I'm sorry. I didn't know. Did you have an accident? What happened?"

It was no wonder she hadn't answered his phone calls. She'd had her phone switched off at the hospital.

"It isn't me; it's Glen. All of this stuff…" Janice groaned. "You don't know how stressful it's been. I wake up in the morning and I just want to hear that it was all a bad dream. I don't want to deal with it, and it seems like the pressure keeps getting to be more and more, not less."

It sounded as if Glen had had a breakdown of some kind. Janice sounded at the end of her rope herself.

"Has he been admitted? Is there anything I can do?"

"There's nothing. The hospital is doing everything they can and I'm just keeping him company. They're going to do surgery tomorrow. The one where they thread the balloon in through your veins…?"

Zachary blinked, trying to understand what she was saying. He shook his head. "Sorry, what happened? What procedure is he having? I thought you meant he'd had a… that he was under too much stress. What actually happened?"

"He had a heart attack," Janice said, in an annoyed tone that suggested Zachary should have known that.

"Oh, dear."

"Right when we were in the middle of talking to the detective. He's badgering us and insisting that it had to be an inside job and that we must know all about it, that we're just trying to defraud the insurance company or something. Glen is getting paler and paler, and then he just… collapses. Facedown on the table, all gray, it scared me to death."

"I'll bet." Zachary could see it in his mind's eye. All of the pressure from the police, insisting that they must be in on it or know something about it, making threats about what would happen to them, encouraging them to cooperate if they wanted to stay out of prison. And then Glen grabbing his chest and toppling over onto the table, skin gray, eyes lifeless. The detective jumping up and calling for an ambulance. Maybe performing CPR to keep him alive until the paramedics could get there. Police were trained in CPR, weren't they? The police station probably even had one of those mobile defibrillators so that they could shock him and bring him back to life.

"I'm so sorry that happened to him," Zachary said.

No wonder they hadn't bothered to call him back. Being interrogated by the police, then a heart attack and racing to the hospital to try to keep Glen alive and figure out what to do with him. Janice had probably sat by his bed the last twenty-four hours, waiting for some word.

Now the rest of what Janice had said was starting to make sense. Glen was having a procedure the next day to clear out the arteries to his heart. So neither of them was likely to be available for a few days. They had enough to worry about without recovering the stolen goods. Those could stay in Kenzie's home office until the McNichols were able to get their lives back on track. Poor Glen.

"Is there anything I can do? Do you guys need anything?"

"No, we're okay here. But we're not going to be able to deal with this… I guess we'll have to call Detective Shelly back. Explain that we know what happened now. That should make him happier."

"Do you want me to call him? It sounds like you've got a lot on your plate right now."

"Yeah, I would? That would be really good?" Janice's voice went up at the ends of her sentences as if she were asking a question. And maybe she was. Would he call the detective? Would he handle it all so that she didn't have to face him again? Zachary could only imagine how she must feel toward the detective now, after watching him bully her husband into having a heart attack. That probably wasn't fair. Glen probably would have had a heart attack sooner or later anyway if his arteries were in bad shape. But it still must have been very traumatic to watch, and Zachary was sure she would blame what had happened on the police detective.

"If you would give me his contact information, I'll give him a call today," Zachary agreed. "Then you won't have to think about it."

"Thank you! You don't know how much of a load off of my mind this is. Getting the stolen memorabilia back, knowing what happened, getting the detective off of our case, that will be such a relief for both of us."

She sounded so strained, it was a wonder she hadn't had a heart attack too.

"I'll take care of it."

31

Of course, telling Janice that he would take care of it and actually taking care of it were two different things. Zachary didn't relish the thought of facing off against the "bulldog" of a detective. It was going to be hard enough to explain how he had discovered that Jennifer Brown and her boyfriend were the thieves and how he had come to possess the stolen items. It would be that much harder if the detective was a bully. Zachary did not enjoy talking to bullies.

He sat there on the bed for a while, trying to sort out in his mind what he was going to say to the cop that wouldn't sound too suspicious or defensive. It was not going to be easy. He didn't feel like he was getting any closer to a script that would work, so he decided to scrap that idea and just wing it.

When nothing was going to work, it was better to just jump in and get it over with than to spend the day being anxious about it.

He dialed the number that Janice had given him, which wasn't the one that he had been using to contact the police department. Hopefully, the detective's direct line or cell phone. Something that the cop would answer, while ignoring all of the pink message slips that the phone operator had left on his desk. Or maybe they were sent to him as email messages that were languishing in his inbox.

"Shelly!" The voice that answered the phone on the second ring had a snap that made Zachary jump. He was glad that they were on the phone and not face to face.

"Uh, Detective Shelly. I'm glad I got through to you. My name is Zachary Goldman, and I'm a private investigator—"

"I don't deal with private investigators. Talk to our public affairs liaison."

"I was hired to work on one of the cases that you have been dealing with—"

"Don't deal with PI's. I have nothing to say to you. Get your information somewhere else."

"I'm not calling to get information from you. I have information to give you. About your case."

There was a pause while Shelly considered this. Then he sighed, a deep grumble that told Zachary it had been a long day and he really didn't want to deal with a pesky PI, even one who claimed to have information.

"It's about the Barnburners burglary," Zachary explained, hoping to get some momentum going. "I managed to sort out what happened. I can give you the names of the perpetrators and I have the recovered stolen property here."

Shelly coughed explosively. Zachary winced and pulled the phone away from his ear, waiting for the detective to stop coughing. He put it back to his ear.

"Oh, you have the loot, do you?" Shelly demanded. He made a noise that might have been a laugh or another cough. "Well, that's very convenient, isn't it? How much are the McNichols paying you to smooth this all out for them? They have some gall, setting you on me the day after he has his so-called heart attack. They could at least make it look like it took a while to recover the merchandise."

"This is not a set-up by Janice and Glen. They are still at the hospital. Glen has a procedure tomorrow, one of those angio-whatevers. Janice has been by his side the whole time. They didn't know that I had broken the case until today."

"I'm sure. Funny how they didn't even mention hiring you when we were talking yesterday."

"They weren't the ones who hired me. But they knew about it and I had talked to them and interviewed their employees. They didn't know that I had made any progress on the case, so they wouldn't have had anything to tell you. I doubt you asked them if they had a private investigator on the case."

"Of course not," Shelly agreed. "I don't deal with private investigators." But there was a wry note of amusement in his voice this time, maybe acknowledging to himself that he was, in fact, dealing with a private investigator.

"Do you want me to go through the progress on the case with you or just give you the names of the thieves?"

"Are you the one who called and left me messages about evidence in the garbage at Michael Martin's home?"

"Yeah, that was me." At least he'd gotten the messages. Zachary wasn't sure until then that he knew anything about it.

"Well, that was a wild goose chase. I went by there today and there was nothing. Not only that, but it looks like they have cleared out. I don't have enough evidence to get a warrant to get inside, but by all appearances, their suite is empty."

"Sorry, I tried to get you as soon as I found anything. The dispatcher I talked to wasn't able to get any police officers over there to gather the evidence, and I couldn't stay there and sit on it all night."

"If you hadn't interfered, then it would still be there and maybe we could prosecute him, but since you've royally screwed everything up, chances are, we will never find him, let alone be able to charge him with anything."

Zachary set his teeth and did his best not to react to the accusations. "Sorry to hear that he's run. I did my best."

"And how is he related to the bar? I don't believe that this was just a random theft. Everything points toward it being an inside job."

"Yeah. Martin's girlfriend is Jennifer Brown, one of the waitresses at the bar."

"The McNichols spent all day yesterday swearing up and down that it couldn't have been an inside job."

"I'm not surprised. They're quite close to their employees. They didn't have anything to do with it, and I'm sure they would never have suspected Jennifer or any of the other employees of being mixed up in it. They're trusting people."

"You think they didn't have anything to do with it?" Shelly snorted. "I think you should look again. They're the ones who would benefit the most by making an insurance claim for the 'stolen' items. Sell them off and claim insurance on them. Get twice the money. They told me yesterday how they're going to hold a fundraiser to replace some of the stolen stuff. So they get triple-compensated. Not a bad deal."

"Did they say they were making an insurance claim? I didn't think it would be worth it."

"Maybe not if you were only looking at what they would get out of it and the bump up in insurance premiums. But multiply the value of the stolen goods by three, and it's a different story."

He did have a point there. But Zachary hadn't seen any sign that Janice and Glen were involved in the theft.

"Do you want the stolen goods, or should I just return them to the McNichols? I wasn't sure how you would want to handle it."

"I can't drop everything I'm doing to come out there and collect stuff. Are you able to bring it here?"

"I'm not in town, so it can't be today. I'll try to get it to you in the next day or two."

"Where are you located?"

"Roxboro." Zachary gave Shelly the address. Despite what Shelly said, it sounded like he planned to pick it up. "Should I wait, then?" he asked uncertainly.

"Maybe. Hold off for now. I may be able to get a cop from Roxboro out there to pick it up."

And, Zachary supposed, to have a little look around to see what kind of a character Zachary was and whether there was any sign that he or the McNichols had been involved in the theft.

"Okay. I won't touch anything unless I hear from you," he promised. But there was a knot in his stomach as he remembered that Mason had already opened all of the boxes, touched and played with the toys, and repacked them differently.

He'd have to explain that later. He didn't need to do it over the phone with Shelly. Maybe the cop who came to pick up the stolen property would be easier to talk to. He wouldn't be coming into the case assuming that the McNichols were guilty. Unless Shelly told him they were.

Zachary suppressed a sigh.

"I'll have more questions for you," Shelly said. "Give me your contact details and I'll follow up with you when I'm not in the middle of my supper."

"Oh, sure. Sorry about that. I just got a call from Janice, so I called you back right away."

Shelly grunted, which Zachary suspected was the closest he was going to get to an acknowledgment that this had been the right thing to do, even if it was at an inconvenient time for Shelly.

He gave Shelly his contact details. Shelly thanked him and terminated the call.

32

Driving Tyrrell to the treatment facility and getting him checked in had been a little rough. Kenzie and Tyrrell had both told Zachary that he could stay home if he felt like he wasn't up to it. Kenzie wanted to be involved since she was a medical professional. She wanted a chance to see the facilities in person and to talk to the doctors and therapists.

So Tyrrell had a ride and someone who knew what they were doing to check him in. But Zachary felt like Tyrrell needed family there too. Someone who really cared about Tyrrell, deep down in his bones. Kenzie was friendly to Tyrrell and had willingly accepted him as part of her extended family. But she couldn't feel the same way about him as Zachary. They had the same DNA, the same background, the same fierce and protective love for each other.

Kenzie separated from them to take her tour of the facilities, giving Zachary and Tyrrell a small measure of privacy as they said their goodbyes.

They both remained as stoic as possible in the reception area of the treatment facility, where Tyrrell would go on and Zachary would not. Tight hugs and manly slaps on the back. Both of them with determined smiles that were grimaces of pain and sorrow rather than pleasure.

"It won't be long," Zachary assured Tyrrell. "You can't have visitors the first few weeks, but once they say that you can, you're not going to be able to keep me away."

"I figured that," Tyrrell agreed, pretending to be annoyed. He punched Zachary lightly in the shoulder. "I have work to do here, you know. Can't have too many distractions."

Zachary gave him one final hug, holding just a little too tightly and a little too long, until Tyrrell squirmed away.

"It will be fine, bro," Tyrrell assured Zachary, his Adam's apple bobbing up and down as he tried to swallow his own emotion. "Tell Kenzie thanks again for helping me to get into this place."

"I will."

Zachary separated from Tyrrell and walked back out to the car, taking slow, deliberate steps, refusing to allow himself to look back over his shoulder. Tyrrell was right. He had hard work to do. He would need to be strong, and Zachary needed to show that he was too, so Tyrrell wouldn't worry about him.

In the car, he sat down and immersed himself in his social networks, email, and, eventually, cat videos to distract himself from his anxiety over the separation from Tyrrell and whether the rehabilitation program would be more successful than the programs Tyrrell had completed in the past.

Eventually, Kenzie finished her tour and returned to the car. She put her hand on Zachary's knee for a minute before starting the engine.

"How are you doing?"

"Fine."

She waited. Zachary looked up at her. One of the cardinal rules they had established in couples therapy was that they were not allowed to say they were "fine." No covering up real emotion with something fake and more socially acceptable. They could talk about how they really felt or decline to answer, but "fine" was not an option.

Zachary sighed. "It sucks," he acknowledged. "I know that this is where he needs to be and that they'll be able to help him more than anything I could ever do. I'm really glad that you found this program, and so is he. But I'm afraid and... upset that I won't be able to see him for a while... and just... really emotional. I don't think I can label everything I'm feeling."

Kenzie squeezed his knee again and started the car. She pulled out of the parking lot and headed for home in silence. Zachary turned on the radio and found a station that they would hopefully both enjoy. Not that he cared what he listened to. He just wanted to drown out the thoughts that grew in the silence.

"Are you sure you want to be home alone?" Kenzie asked. "I could ask

Dr. Wiltshire for the rest of the day off if you need someone around. Or you could go out somewhere that you won't be alone. Run errands or go see Heather... go for a walk in the park."

"Too cold for a walk."

"You would be fine if you bundled up."

"It's okay. I don't mind being by myself. If I get antsy, I'll go out somewhere. But you don't need to miss a whole day of work."

"Well... give me a call if you need to talk. Or just to take a break from your work. I'm still reachable. I don't have an autopsy scheduled; I'll be at my desk."

"Sure," Zachary agreed. "I'll call if I need to."

She didn't push him any further, just drove him the rest of the way home and dropped him in front of the house.

"Don't forget to disarm the burglar alarm."

Zachary nodded. "Thanks."

While it irritated him to be reminded, her comment was timely. If there were a day that he would walk into the house, forget to punch his code, and be utterly oblivious to the warning beep of the alarm, this would be that day. He couldn't criticize her for reminding him to do something he had forgotten once before—ending up in handcuffs because his name hadn't been on her security company's file. It was now, but he would prefer not to be surprised by the siren of the burglar alarm, having to remember his passphrase while off-balance to give to the security company before the police were alerted.

Once in the door, he carefully punched his code into the alarm system, and stopped and waited for the red light to turn green. He even stood there a moment longer to make sure that the warning beep didn't come on. He closed the door, still watching the alarm panel. The little screen flashed FRONT DOOR CLOSED and then returned to STANDBY. Zachary headed to his computer and got to work on some routine skip tracing. Normally, he had Heather do that now, but he wanted to do something that didn't take a lot of attention, and he could just lose himself in the process.

33

Zachary was working at his computer when he started to get an uneasy feeling. The first few seconds, he tried to push it aside, assuming that it was just anxiety over Tyrrell going into detox. He wanted Tyrrell to detox, so he could just push that feeling away. But it didn't work. His sense of disquiet grew, getting more and more ominous. He looked away from his computer, glancing around the room first but, of course, he was home alone and there was nothing else in the room that should cause him to be anxious.

He turned and looked out the big living room window and, for just an instant, saw movement, off to the side, close to the house, too close for him to get a good view line. He leaned forward into the window, trying to look all the way along the front of the house. Kenzie had the sense not to grow bushes around the windows and entryways where they could obscure a burglar, but the way that the front steps jutted out, he was blocked from seeing anything past it.

But he had seen a movement.

Not a cat or a squirrel. A person. And that person had gotten closer to the house but had not rung the doorbell. If it were a delivery person, then he should have rung the doorbell or at least tossed the package up onto the doorstep by that time and be heading back to his truck. But there was no Amazon Prime truck at the curb, no unfamiliar cars that could be private couriers.

Maybe it was the cop that Detective Shelly had sent by to get the memorabilia, and he thought he'd have a quick look around the house before going in. That was the kind of thing that a cop might do. See what he could find out about the subject before ringing the doorbell. As a PI, that was what Zachary often did.

He stood up from the couch and headed toward the front door, planning to peek out and see if he could catch the cop at it.

But as he rounded the corner to the front door, he discovered his mistake. The cop hadn't gone around the house to scope out the backyard.

And it wasn't a cop.

And the reason that he hadn't rung the doorbell was that he was already inside and didn't want Zachary to be forewarned.

There were two of them.

Zachary turned to make a break for it out the door to the garage. His movements seemed incredibly slow to him, like the slo-mo shot of sprinters bursting through the tape at the finish line of a race. He was only too aware of how long it was taking him to pivot, how many strides it would take to get to the door, his brain already ahead of him, anticipating the need to unlock and turn the doorknob when he reached the door, to jump down the three steps to the garage floor level, and to hit the button that would raise the big garage door, even knowing how grindingly slow it was. How else would he get out?

Could he slide or roll under the garage door as it opened a crack, like in a Star Trek action sequence? Get out of there before the intruders could?

But it all seemed hopeless. Unlike he, the intruders had anticipated his being there and had been ready for his appearance, even if they were trying to take him unaware. They were coiled for action and Zachary was not.

He reached the door between the kitchen and the garage, but he didn't manage to turn the lock and get it open. Even if he had succeeded in doing that, there was no way the big garage door would have opened quickly enough for him to escape.

Strong, hard hands grabbed him from behind, not being careful, not caring whether they injured him. Zachary fought to free himself, flailing, using his elbows, trying to kick out.

But he was no kung fu fighter. Watching Jackie Chan movies a hundred times would not turn him into an expert in hand-to-hand combat or any of the martial arts. He was still Zachary Goldman: small, too thin, awkward and unarmed. One of the intruders had his arms locked behind his back in a few seconds, with only one grunt of protest as Zachary had tried to fight back. Zachary attempted to use the grip the man behind him had on him to kick out his legs and hurt the one now in front of him. But it didn't work like it did in the movies. The man behind him just ratcheted the hammerlock on his arms tighter and let his own weight pull down into his shoulders, so that he gasped in pain and couldn't even think of lifting his feet up to kick again.

"Stop fighting," the man holding him growled. "We don't want *you.*"

Zachary tried to figure out what this meant while the man pulled out a pair of flex-cuffs and zipped them over Zachary's wrists. Then he shoved Zachary away, dumping him on the tiled kitchen floor. Zachary's tailbone hit the hard surface with an explosion of pain.

"Stay there, or I'll hogtie you too."

He ran thick fingers over Zachary's hips and backside and, for an instant, Zachary flashed back, sure he was going to be assaulted, but the man found his phone and slid it out, taking it with him so that Zachary had no way to call for help.

Sitting up straight was out of the question, given how much his tailbone was hurting, so Zachary let himself slump into lying on his side, partially curled up. He listened to them walking through the house.

Each of the bedroom doors was opened in turn. The master bedroom, the guest room, and then Kenzie's home office.

"In here!"

Zachary closed his eyes, concentrating. What did they want in the office? There was Kenzie's laptop, but they had walked past Zachary's laptop in the living room without comment, and it was newer than Kenzie's. She didn't store any valuables in the office, as far as he knew. There was no safe. Just office supplies, a bit of furniture, a few out-of-season clothes stored in the closet. They had walked by expensive furnishings and artwork on their way there.

Then he heard the sound of them going through the boxes.

The boxes of memorabilia stolen from Barnburners.

Was it Jennifer Brown and her boyfriend?

It couldn't be. It had definitely been two large men. Not a woman. Not Jennifer's slender boyfriend. But they could be hired thugs. They looked and acted like hired thugs. Quick and efficient, good at what they did. Not worried about hurting someone, but not there to do him physical harm, either. Zachary had just been an obstacle and could be disposed of however they saw best.

They weren't there for *him*.

They were there for the stolen memorabilia.

How had they tracked him? How did they know Zachary was the one who had come to their house and stolen the objects they had stolen?

Now they were stealing them back again. It was dizzying, wondering how many times the loot could be stolen.

It wouldn't have been hard to track Zachary. Jennifer knew that Zachary was investigating the burglary. He had introduced himself to her, given her his card, encouraged her to call him. There were not a lot of Zachary Goldmans in Vermont. His name wasn't registered to Kenzie's address anywhere, but they probably hadn't needed that. People knew him, knew that Walter Kirsch had hired him, could probably look up news articles online that linked him, Walter Kirsch, and Kenzie Kirsch. It wouldn't take long to figure out that he and Kenzie were a couple and that he would either be living with her or she would lead them to him.

Zachary let his head bump on the tile floor, frustrated with himself. He couldn't have left a much clearer trail for anyone who wanted to find him. They had told everyone that Walter Kirsch had hired him, trying to gain their trust.

The memorabilia Mason had been playing with had been thrown back in the boxes haphazardly, but it didn't take the thugs long to repack the boxes properly so that they could be closed and stacked. It didn't take them three trips to transport them like it had Zachary by himself. Between the two of them, they quickly carried all of the boxes out of the house and were gone.

34

"Hello? Anyone home?"

Zachary didn't know how long he had been lying there on the floor when he heard the voice. He should have figured out by then how to escape the flex-cuffs or have managed to get to his feet so that he could walk out of the house under his own power. But the ape had manhandled him more than he had realized. Between the pain in his shoulders and arms from being cuffed so tightly behind his back, the pain in his tailbone from landing on the floor, and the various other bruises and tender places, he couldn't do much more than kick himself around in circles on the kitchen floor.

"Help me!" he called out, projecting his voice toward the front door.

He heard a low voice, muttering, a radio squawk.

"Help?" he repeated. "I'm in here. In the kitchen. They're gone. It's just me."

It was still a few minutes before the heavy tread of footsteps entered the house, and Zachary strained to look up at his rescuer.

A uniformed cop. Zachary let his breath out in relief.

"Hey..." he greeted weakly.

"Zachary Goldman?"

"Yeah. That's me."

The cop got closer and crouched down. "It's me. Donaldson."

Zachary cricked his neck, trying to examine him from a better angle.

"Oh, Donaldson." It seemed like the cop had come from another world. It had been a long time since he had worked on a case that Donaldson had been involved with, but he was a good cop. Not one of those who had a thing about private investigation as a matter of principle. Only if said private investigator got in the way and went places he shouldn't.

"What happened here? Your front door was hanging open."

"I... uh... a couple of intruders. Home invasion."

"You don't say." Donaldson looked around the kitchen. "You do live an interesting life, don't you?"

"Can you help me?" Zachary asked, irritated.

Donaldson hooked a hand under Zachary's armpit and lifted him to his feet. It was a hundred times better to be standing up instead of curled up on the floor in pain, but the movement hurt his shoulder. Donaldson examined the flex-cuffs and, in a minute, he had out a Leatherman tool and cut the plastic loops that held Zachary's wrists together. Zachary brought his arms back in front of him, his shoulders popping and grinding painfully. He rolled his shoulders and rubbed his hands together, trying to restore the circulation.

"Thank you." Zachary blew out a long breath. "How did you know to come? Did one of the neighbors report it?"

"Nah. I'm not here because of this. I'm here to pick up some stolen property that you apparently recovered."

"Oh." Zachary looked in the direction of the bedrooms. "Well... that's apparently what these guys were after too. I don't know if they left anything behind."

"You're kidding me." Donaldson shook his head in disbelief.

"No... I don't know if it's the guys who initially stole it, and they figured out that I was the one who... uh... recovered it from them."

"You don't know?"

"It wasn't the same people, but these guys acted like hired thugs. Professionals."

Donaldson glanced around the house, then nodded. "Nothing busted. Handcuffed you. No messy stuff. Just in and out."

"Yeah." Zachary nodded. "Five minutes. Let's see if they left anything behind. But I doubt it..."

Donaldson nodded and walked down the hall after Zachary. Zachary minced along, hoping it wasn't too obvious to Donaldson how much pain he was in. The doors to the bedrooms were open. Nothing appeared to have been touched. Zachary stopped at the office and looked in the door.

All of the boxes and their contents were gone, as Zachary had known they would be. He gestured to the empty spot along the wall, where the boxes had left rectangular impressions in the carpet.

"This is where they were. These guys just walked in and took everything."

Donaldson nodded and pulled out a notepad to make some notes. "Detective Shelly isn't going to be happy about this."

"No. But I promise you… this wasn't the way I had planned for things to happen…"

Donaldson walked into the room and looked around. There wasn't much to see. He bent down and picked up a USB drive that had been knocked to the floor and put it back on Kenzie's desk.

"Well, nothing for me to do here."

"Uh… what about the home invasion?"

Donaldson looked at him and sighed. "I suppose since I was first at the scene, I'll have to make a report. We'll need to call the robbery boys in to open a file and take your statement. That's not my department. I was just here doing a favor for a fellow officer." He rolled his eyes. "That's what I get for being a nice guy."

35

There wasn't really much for Zachary to tell the detectives that showed up about the home invasion. He could give only a general description of the two masked men who had come into the house, accosted him, and reclaimed the stolen property. A look at the footprint evidence outside the house showed that there had been a third man outside, who would undoubtedly have snagged Zachary if he had managed to get out of the house through the garage. That made him feel a little bit better about not making it that far. Even if he had been faster, he wouldn't have gotten away.

The detective took pictures of the footprints, but just shook his head at the idea of making casts of them or even measuring them for shoe size.

"You said yourself, they were likely hired muscle. It isn't really going to help us to get their shoe sizes. Even if we were able to identify them, we still wouldn't know who had hired them, and that's the important question."

After looking once at the lack of memorabilia in the home office, the detective shrugged and made motions to leave. "You can drop your written statement off at the station any time. We'll be in contact if we have any questions or hear anything. But these guys were efficient. I think it's safe to say that we're not likely to find them."

"And you'll copy everything to Shelly in Montpelier? Since the stolen property relates to his case?"

"Yes, sir," the detective said tiredly, making Zachary realize that he'd already made this request several times. "I will make sure that Detective Shelly gets all of the details, sparse as they are."

"Maybe there will be something that is meaningful to him."

"Maybe, sir."

Zachary let the detective go, leaving him alone in the house once more. This time he made sure to lock the door and enable the exterior door and window alerts so that he would know if someone entered the house. He knew it was shutting the barn door after the horses were gone, but he felt more secure knowing that no one could sneak in again without his realizing it.

Unless, of course, he was so focused on his work that he didn't hear the alerts when a door or window was breached.

Zachary tried to sit down and resume the work he had been doing when the thugs had arrived, but it didn't make any sense to him and sitting was painful. He paced for a while, just trying to convince himself that he was safe and could get back to work. His brain and body were still on high alert, sure that he would be attacked again. He knew he should be grateful for his brain's hypervigilance; it was one of the things that had gotten him through the years of foster care and kept him safe from more than one abusive parent, sibling, or group home resident. His impulsivity, on the other hand, had dumped him into more than one situation that he could have avoided if he'd been able to stop and think things through. His brain was both his protector and his enemy.

The ring of Zachary's phone made him jump, and he immediately whirled around to face the front door, sure that someone had again entered the house. He blew out his breath when he realized it was just the phone and picked it up. He wasn't in any mood to talk to a client.

But it was Kenzie's name on the screen so, after taking a few more breaths to calm himself down so that he wouldn't sound frantic when he answered the call, he swiped to answer it.

"Kenzie."

"Zachary," her voice was higher than usual. "I just heard about the break-in! Are you okay?"

"How did you hear about it?"

"I work in the basement of the police station. You and I both know plenty of the cops around here. Did you really think that I wouldn't hear?"

"I... no. I thought it would all be kept confidential. I didn't think of anyone telling you. Sorry… I would have called to give you a heads-up if I had known."

"Yeah. It's not exactly reassuring to hear from the cops that your house has been broken into."

"No." There was a pain in Zachary's chest, and he thought about Glen, in the hospital, going through his heart surgery. Zachary's pain, on the other hand, was not a cardiac event, but his guilt over Kenzie's house being violated and over her finding out from someone other than him. "I am sorry. They didn't act like it was a big deal, and I thought they would keep it private."

"I am the homeowner."

"Yeah. Didn't think of that."

"When were you going to tell me? Or were you?"

"When you got home. I didn't think there was any benefit to interrupting you at work. It would just distract you from your job."

Like Zachary was distracted from his. He couldn't seem to get refocused.

"Okay." Kenzie's tone had lowered slightly. Calming down a little bit. Realizing that everything was fine and that he had not been trying to keep the news of the break-in from her. "Okay, then. And nothing was broken? The door or a window?"

"No," Zachary admitted, disgusted with himself. "I left the front door unlocked and the alarm off when I got home. A lot of good they do when you don't use them."

"The detective said that it looked like a professional job. If they hadn't found the front door unlocked, they probably would have used a pry bar. They would have gotten in either way. At least leaving the door unlocked means that they didn't have to break in."

Zachary grunted an acknowledgment. He sighed. "Anyway… nothing broken, nothing to clean up. And you don't have to worry about tripping over the boxes in your office, since they have now been removed."

"Yeah. Not exactly the way you'd planned, though."

"No."

"And you're okay? You must be freaking out. Should I come home?"

"I'm… irritated and distracted. Mad at myself. Don't know that I'll get any more work done today. But I'll manage. You don't need to get off early unless you want to. I guess Dr. Wiltshire will understand if you tell him your house was broken into."

"Yes, I think he'd understand that."

"If you do come home early—and you don't need to for me—just let me know, okay? Shoot me a text."

"Okay…" Her tone was doubtful, inquiring.

"So I don't have a heart attack when I hear the door."

"Oh, yeah. Sure. Have you taken anything for the anxiety?"

"No."

"Think about it."

Zachary waited for more, but apparently, she wasn't going to push it any further than that. "I will," he agreed.

"All right. See you later."

Zachary hung up and considered whether taking one of his anti-anxiety pills would help. He didn't like to take them except when there was a clear need for one. And if he did, he would want to sleep. It wouldn't help him get any more work done, and he didn't want to go to sleep when he should be vigilant about the door and whether the thugs would be back.

Of course they wouldn't. They had gotten what they were looking for. There was no need for them to return. But his brain wasn't ready to accept that. He needed to stay aware and alert, at least until Kenzie got home.

36

Kenzie didn't get off work early, but she did leave work on time, which was early for Kenzie. She sent him a text, so he watched for her car, saw it enter the garage, and was in the kitchen when she entered through the connecting garage door. Zachary had already unlocked the door and disabled the door alert so that she wouldn't have to do anything other than walk in as usual. But once she was in, Kenzie deliberately locked all of the locks on the door and enabled the door and window alerts again before greeting him.

"Hey. You survived. How are you doing?"

Zachary hugged her briefly. His shoulders were still hurting from the way his arms had been wrenched around and handcuffed, but he didn't tell her that. "I'm good."

At her doubtful look, he reiterated. "I know I'm not supposed to say 'fine,' but I am. A bit freaked out over the whole thing, but it was minor. It was over fast. No permanent damage done." He made a motion indicating the rest of the house. "Have a look around. Nothing is broken or damaged."

Kenzie walked around the house, then returned to his side in the living room and gave him a sideways hug. "You're right. Everything looks fine. It even looks like you vacuumed."

Zachary nodded. He had vacuumed the carpet once the wet footprints had dried to remove any traces of mud and dirt, erasing any sign of the intrusion.

"Thanks. That makes me feel better," Kenzie said, looking around again.

Her mouth was tight, though, and her hug had felt rigid. He met her eyes.

"I'm mad," Kenzie admitted. "Not at you. At them. I've always heard about how a robbery makes someone feel personally violated, but I never really understood how much... I'm just furious at them. The thugs and whoever sent them. I just want to kick the crap out of them. Coming into my house like that."

"I'm sorry—"

"Don't keep telling me you're sorry about it. I know it isn't your fault. It's theirs. And my father's."

Zachary looked at her, surprised. He hadn't even thought of being angry at Walter.

"Why are you mad at him?"

"Because he's the one that hired you for this case. This happened because of him. The last time he came here, he put a bug in my purse. This time, he set you on a case that ended up with my house being violated. I just feel like... I'm just furious at him. If he called me right now... he would regret it. Let's just say that."

Zachary nodded his agreement. He wouldn't want to be on the receiving end of Kenzie's temper at the moment. Walter had better watch his step with her.

"I told you that you would regret taking this case from him," Kenzie went on. "I warned you what he's like and that it wouldn't go like you expected."

"Yes, you did," Zachary admitted. "But I don't know if you can really put the blame for the robbery on him. He's not the one who ordered it. It has to be Jennifer and Michael, the original thieves."

"It's still his fault," Kenzie said bullishly. "One way or another. Why did he even want the robbery investigated in the first place? How does it benefit him?"

Zachary frowned and shook his head. "I don't think it does. I think he was just being generous, helping his friends who own the bar."

"That's not like him. He has his own interests at heart one way or another. He always does. If it seems like he's being generous, you can be sure you're not seeing the whole picture."

"I thought he was known for being a philanthropist."

"That's how he would like you to see him, sure. And Mom is. She'll throw money at an organization just because she thinks it sounds like a good cause. But with Dad, it's different. He gives money when he knows he'll get something back, whether it's to do with his reputation, or calling in a favor, or what. I used to just think he was generous. When I was young. But that is not the case."

"Oh. Well, that's too bad. He seems like a nice guy."

Kenzie's expression softened a little. "I do think he's a nice guy," she said. "To the people he loves. But he's also a shark, and you can't ever forget that."

It probably wasn't good for Kenzie to be dwelling on the negatives of finding out that her father was human, so Zachary looked for a way to change the subject.

"Did you want me to make something for supper? Order in?"

She leveled a look at him. "What would *you* make for supper? When have you ever made supper for the two of us in the time we've been together?"

"Well… I'm pretty sure I got out a tub of ice cream that one day…"

"A meal."

"That was a meal," he reminded her.

Kenzie cracked a grin. "Well, that's not going to cut it tonight. So have you got another idea, or are you just angling to order something in?"

"If you want to make something, that's fine with me. But I didn't want to suggest that you should. I know which side my bread is buttered on."

"So far, you don't even have bread, let alone butter." Kenzie finally let him off the hook. "Sure, why don't you order in? Whatever you're in the mood for, I don't have a preference."

Zachary walked over to the couch to sit down and pull the restaurant menus out of the drawer on the side table. An explosion of pain ran from his tailbone up his back, reminding him that he was going to have to be a lot more careful for the next little while. He tried to pull himself back into a standing position to relieve the pressure, but his knees were wobbly with the pain.

37

Zachary!" Kenzie cried out in alarm and rushed forward. "What happened? Are you okay?"

He rocked a little, trying to get back up, but she pressed her hands against his chest and the pain prevented him from rising.

"It's just... it's nothing."

"It's not nothing. You're as white as a ghost. If you stand up, you're going to pass out, so just stay put."

Zachary shook his head. "I just bruised my tailbone."

"Bruised it, my foot! I've seen how you act when you're bruised. It's broken."

"Maybe. But there's not much they can do about that. I'll be fine. It will heal on its own. I just have to be more careful. I sat down too hard."

"How did you hurt it?"

"When..." Zachary tried to come up with the right words to explain that it had been the thugs who had broken into the house. Everything he thought of sounded too frightening. He didn't want to distress Kenzie any further. She would never forgive her father if she thought he was somehow responsible for injuring Zachary. "This afternoon..."

He was able to focus on her face, which was progress, because all he'd been able to see when the pain had overtaken him was a field of red.

"This afternoon." Kenzie sat down beside him and searched his face. "Tell me exactly what happened this afternoon."

"You already know."

"Well, I already know that there was a break-in. And that the thieves stole the memorabilia that you recovered. But somewhere in the middle there... you got hurt, and I don't know how."

Zachary cleared his throat. He tried to change his position again, and Kenzie didn't stop him, letting him squirm around until he found a position leaning over with his weight on his hip, which relieved the pressure on his tailbone.

"When they came in... I tried to run. They grabbed me. I tried to fight." He swallowed hard. "I landed on the floor."

"On your butt."

Zachary nodded, embarrassed. "Very graceful, I know. I'm not exactly the catlike ninja you might have thought."

She laughed. "I never thought that," she confessed. "Besides, you remember that shortly after we met, you had a spinal injury that severely curtailed any ninja-like moves."

"Well, before that, I'm sure I was much more catlike."

"You need to get it checked out."

"I've broken it before. It's one of those things they can't really do anything about. Just be careful how you sit. Get one of those donuts."

"Unless it needs surgery. The fact that you have had a spinal injury before makes this kind of thing dangerous. And if you've broken your coccyx before... you never told me that. How did it happen?"

"Similar," Zachary said curtly. "Fell on it."

She studied him. He didn't want to share any more of the experience with her and had lost interest in joking about it.

"I know you would prefer to just... sit it out..." Kenzie said, one corner of her mouth quirking up. "But I'm serious. You've had a spinal injury before. You've broken this bone before. There could be shock damage on up your spinal cord, compression of the spine from the way you fell, there could be bone chips that need to be cleaned up. You don't want sharp edges close to the spinal cord. So... you need to get it checked out. To keep me quiet, if nothing else."

Zachary sighed. He had hoped to just lie low for a few days and let it heal on its own. He knew it would take more than a few days, and he would have to be careful of how he sat down. But he had thought he could just do as he had done before and let it heal on its own.

"You don't really think it's dangerous, do you?" he asked. "I mean... it's my tailbone. Not my heart."

"Let's just go and get it checked out, and make sure."

"Can't you just look at it?"

"I don't have an x-ray machine."

"I don't really need an x-ray."

"You don't know that for sure. You hope that everything is fine, but you don't know."

"We could leave it tonight. Give it a few days to see how it does. It will probably heal on its own just fine."

Kenzie folded her arms across her chest. "I'm not budging."

Zachary rubbed his forehead. "Okay. Fine. Can we at least eat before we go to the hospital?"

"We can eat at the hospital cafeteria once we get you checked in. While we're waiting. At least we'll have something to do while we wait."

Zachary remembered the hard plastic chairs of the cafeteria. He was going to end up having to stand up all night. "I'd better get a cookie out of this."

"We'll get you a cookie."

Kenzie didn't have a donut pillow at home, but she had some other pillows that they tried to arrange in the car to make the bucket seats more tolerable. Kenzie drove slowly, wincing herself whenever they went over a bump or down into a pothole. Zachary realized partway to the hospital that he should have taken a painkiller before leaving the house. Maybe several painkillers. And maybe he should have put an ice pack on the tender spot.

"I'm so sorry," Kenzie said. "There are so many bumps. They should fix these roads!"

"It's okay. At least most of the potholes are filled with snow."

Kenzie snorted. When they finally got to the hospital, Kenzie did her best to use her influence as a medical doctor to get Zachary seen to more quickly. But apparently, broken tailbones were not a high priority on the triage list, and being a doctor who dealt with corpses did not give Kenzie a lot of pull at the hospital. After confirming with the nurses that they were going down to the cafeteria to eat and would be paged if Zachary's turn came up, they took the elevator down to the first basement level and walked slowly to the cafeteria. It was quiet, only a few people sitting at the tables eating, some of the food already being cleared away for the evening.

38

Zachary was sitting awkwardly in the hard plastic chair, picking at his food and trying to stay balanced on one buttock and hip to keep the pressure off of his tailbone when his pocket started to vibrate. He pulled out his phone, hoping that it would be a message from the nurses upstairs that someone could see him. But it wasn't.

It was a number that he didn't know. Zachary looked at it for a moment, considering whether to answer it or just ignore it. He was at the hospital. He had a good excuse for not answering the phone if he needed one. But it was a Vermont number, not a toll-free or long-distance number, and therefore less likely to be a telemarketer or robocall. He let it go a couple more rings before finally deciding to answer. He put the phone to his ear.

"Goldman Investigations."

"Is this Zachary?"

Zachary froze. The voice was familiar. Slightly older and more gravelly than when he had first learned it, but still recognizable. Berk Goldman.

His father.

Kenzie had been telling him how much she disliked her father and her problems with him. She claimed to love her parents, though Zachary had difficulty reconciling her attitude toward her father with her claim of love.

But for Zachary, it was different. As a child, he had loved and longed to return to his mother for a long time after being put into foster care. But over the years, he had come to realize how toxic and abusive that relationship had been. And he remembered his father more as an angry drunk than anything else. He didn't remember ever wanting to go home because of him. Berk had been out of his life for decades. They'd had no contact since Zachary was ten. Until Zachary went looking for his missing brother and found Tyrrell drinking with Berk.

"This is Zachary," he acknowledged, voice tight.

Kenzie looked at him, her eyebrows going way up at his tone.

"Zachary. I'm looking for Tyrrell. Can't seem to reach him on his phone. I thought... you might know where he is. What's going on with him."

"I don't want you trying to contact him."

Berk chuckled. "Well, he's a grown man and you don't have any say over who he does or doesn't. And I'm still your father, so don't try telling me what to do."

"Stay away from him. He needs to stay sober. He can't do that if you're calling him and drinking with him."

"Oh, so you've decided what is best for him. How about you let the boy make his own decisions?"

"I thought you just said he was a grown man."

"And he is," Berk agreed. "You're the one who isn't treating him that way. You don't have any control over who he sees or spends time with. I've known him longer than you have, and if you think he's going to stop drinking or stop seeing me, you better think again."

"Leave him alone. Don't call again." Zachary lowered the phone and touched the red button to terminate the call. Back in the days before cell phones, he could have slammed the phone down with a satisfying crash to end the call, but cell phones required him to be more civilized. He felt like throwing it across the room to appease his temper.

Kenzie watched him with bright eyes, waiting to see what he would do. He didn't imagine she'd be very pleased if he gave in to his temper and threw the phone. She might think it was funny, but she wouldn't be happy about it. Zachary set it down on the table in front of him and straightened it. He grimaced at Kenzie.

"Bet you can't guess who."

Kenzie laughed. "I bet I can." She shook her head. "He has some gall calling you to get in touch with Tyrrell. He has to know that you have... er... negative feelings toward him."

"I think I made that pretty clear."

Kenzie nodded in agreement. She looked at the food left in front of Zachary. "You want another cookie?"

"Can't. Too full."

She nodded and accepted this. Zachary thought he'd done a pretty good job of eating compared with the period before Christmas and his med change. Especially considering the pain he was in, which was making him a little unsteady and lightheaded.

"Well, if you're done, we can head back up to the waiting room and see how long it is before they call your name."

Zachary pushed himself to his feet and held himself braced on the table for a few seconds, waiting until he was sure that he was steady. Kenzie eyed him.

"Are you sure you're okay? Need a wheelchair?"

"I don't need a wheelchair. It's just a broken tailbone."

"Are you experiencing weakness or numbness in your legs or back?"

"Just a little wobbly."

"That sounds suspiciously like weakness or numbness."

"It's just the pain. It's nothing."

Every time she mentioned the spinal injury he had sustained in the car crash two years before or the possibility that he had reinjured it, he got more anxious and more adamant that he hadn't. It had taken a long time to fully recover from the injury, and he still felt awkward running, walking backward, or any other ambulation than regular walking. Kenzie thought he had stopped his physio too soon and should have worked on those other movements more. But Zachary had just wanted to get on with life.

Kenzie looked at him for a minute, then turned away from him, pointing her body toward the elevators. "Let's go up, then."

Zachary hesitated. The more he thought about his gait and the possibility of facing more physio, the more stuck he felt. He didn't want her watching him and, at the same time, was not sure he could move normally. It wouldn't go over well with Kenzie if he took a step and fell flat on his face.

She was halfway to the elevator before she turned her head to see if he was following. Zachary swallowed and took a careful step toward her. Just a half step to be sure that his legs were strong enough to hold him and he wouldn't collapse without the support of the table.

That was okay, so he took another step and then was shuffling toward Kenzie, more sure of his stability.

"Are you doing the zombie shuffle to be funny?" Kenzie asked. "Because you're worrying me."

"My foot is asleep, that's all."

"One of your feet? Which one?"

"It's just asleep from the way I was sitting. I shouldn't have been sitting that way."

He could tell she didn't believe it. In the elevator, Zachary held on to the rail and flexed and pointed his feet. They were fine. There wasn't anything wrong with them. In a few minutes, they were back in the waiting area of the emergency room. Kenzie told Zachary that she was going to find some coffee, and disappeared. He closed his eyes and waited, sinking into the throbbing pain.

It didn't seem like much time had passed when Zachary heard Kenzie's voice again and she was shaking him gently.

Zachary blinked and didn't catch the name of the doctor who was introducing himself with an East Indian accent. "Dr. Kirsch says that you may be experiencing some spinal injury symptoms," he stated. "Out of an abundance of caution, we want to check this out, and don't want you walking around. A nurse is bringing over a wheelchair and we are going to help you to move to it without putting extra stress on your spine. We don't want a lot of twisting and turning," the doctor advised, putting his gloved hand on Zachary's shoulder and gently keeping him from turning to look for the nurse.

"I've been okay. I fell down hours ago; wouldn't it be obvious by now if there was a spinal cord injury? After the car accident, it was obvious. I couldn't move."

"It can be tricky. It may swell or develop slowly over the next few days. A fall like that can cause some symptoms, but is not likely to be serious. Since you've had a previous injury, we want to look at your previous imaging and compare it to what we will do today. Then we will have a much better idea of what we are dealing with."

The wheelchair that a nurse eventually pushed over had a u-shaped cushion on the seat, which Zachary soon found was to take the pressure off of his tailbone and gave him much-needed relief.

"Fell on your bum, did you?" the nurse questioned loudly, drawing smiles and chuckles from the other waiting patients seated nearby. "Well, most of us have plenty of padding down there," she slapped her own ample padding, "but you certainly do not. We're going to have to get your girlfriend to fatten you up!"

"Actually, you might be interested to know that heavy patients are far more likely to break their tailbones," the East Indian doctor informed the nurse and Zachary. "An obese patient is far more likely to receive a tailbone injury than an underweight one." He smiled in Kenzie's direction. "But your girlfriend should still fatten you up."

Kenzie laughed, and Zachary grimaced, trying to laugh along with them. At least with the special pillow, he could sit and breathe without it hurting so much. The doctor would order a few x-rays, and everything would be fine.

39

Kenzie had apparently made a good impression on the doctor, who saw that Zachary was given a small examination room to wait in rather than being in the curtained area where everyone else was being seen. When Zachary was changed, settled, and waiting for the x-rays, Kenzie joined him again. She looked over him, eyes critical.

"Hey. How are you doing?" she asked sympathetically.

"I should have just stayed home. There's nothing they can do for a broken tailbone. It probably isn't even broken. It's probably just bruised."

"Yeah, I know you're feeling anxious about it."

Zachary shifted, trying to find a comfortable position on his side. "I really want to just get out of here. Can't we go home and then come back if there are other symptoms? If it gets worse?"

"It's bad enough now. I don't want to risk it. If everything looks fine on the films, then we'll go home, and I won't be worried because I'll know it's been looked at properly."

The thought of being paralyzed again, even temporarily, terrified Zachary. He didn't want to have to go through all of that again. He hated to be helpless. He hated having to learn to walk properly again and to do physio for hours to build up the muscle memory and make things like walking, bending over, and reaching feel more natural again. He hated the way people looked down at him when he was in the hospital bed or wheelchair.

"This can't be happening. I just fell on the floor. That's all. It wasn't anything significant. It wasn't like the car crash."

"And hopefully, they'll tell me that I'm just worrying over nothing and send you straight home."

But he could tell that she didn't think so. Zachary breathed harder, trying to suck in more oxygen. What if even his breathing became paralyzed? It hadn't been after the car crash, but who was to say if there was new damage? He couldn't seem to draw in enough breath.

"Slow down," Kenzie advised. "Just take it easy."

"I can't breathe."

"You're panicking."

He tried to listen to her. Tried to slow his breathing, but it wasn't working.

"I think you need one of your pills."

"No. I'm okay. I can…" Zachary tried to do everything Dr. B had told him to help ward off a panic attack. All at the same time, which was confusing and chaotic. He worked on slowing down and breathing with his diaphragm, but that just made him more focused on the feeling of suffocation. He tried to anchor on things in the room. What he could see, what he could hear. He could hear Kenzie trying to walk him through the anchoring exercise, but he was already trying visualization instead. Picturing himself in a calm place. Somewhere he felt safe and secure. Home with Kenzie. In bed. He only had to revise a few things to picture them at home. But when someone started screaming down the hall, his muscles all tensed, and he gasped for breath.

"It's okay," Kenzie assured him. "If it's getting to be too much, take your meds. That's what they're for."

"I want to talk to her."

Kenzie frowned, her brow wrinkling.

"Dr. B. Do you think I could talk to her?"

The frown lifted, and Kenzie nodded. "Sure. She always says to call if you need to talk."

"She won't be in bed?"

"It's not that late."

Zachary motioned to the small locker that contained his clothes and personal belongings. Kenzie looked inside and retrieved his phone for him.

"It's okay to use the phone in here? I'm not going to get in trouble?" he asked.

"If there is trouble, I'll smooth it over."

Zachary fumbled with the phone, trying to find Dr. Boyle's number. Kenzie looked as if she wanted to jump in and help, but she didn't, letting him sort it out himself.

"Do you want me to stay with you, or do you want privacy?" she whispered as the call started to ring through.

Zachary extended the fingers of his other hand to her. She held his hand and stayed by his side as he waited for Dr. B to pick up. Eventually, his therapist did answer, right at the moment when he thought the call was going through to voicemail.

"Zachary. How are you?"

Zachary breathed out in relief. It still took him a few more gasping breaths to answer her, but just having her on the line seemed to help. "Doctor…" A shuddering breath out and another in. "I just… I don't know what to do."

"Okay. Let's talk it through. What's going on?"

"I… fell down. It wasn't any big thing. Just falling on the floor. But Kenzie was worried, so…"

"How did you fall? Did you trip? Or were you dizzy or faint?"

"No… I was pushed. But… that's not it."

"Okay. Why is Kenzie worried?"

"I just bruised my tailbone, and she's worried about… about spinal cord damage because of the accident. The car crash where I got hurt."

"I remember talking about that, yes. So if Kenzie is worried about it, and she's a medical doctor, then you should probably listen to her concerns. Get it checked out."

"Yeah." Zachary licked his lips, but his mouth was dry. "I'm at the hospital."

"Good. Sounds like the right choice. What is it you're not sure about, then? You said you didn't know what to do, but it sounds like you're doing the right thing already."

Zachary cleared his throat, trying not to let his voice crack. There was a hot, hard lump in his throat and he didn't know if he could talk around it. It was silly to be calling his therapist. Stupid to be so worried when he was in the hospital where they could keep an eye on him and make sure that everything was okay.

"Just worried. What if there's damage? What if… I can't breathe?"

"You're breathing now. I think you'll be fine."

"It's hurting. I can't get enough air."

"What do you think you should do?"

"Kenzie said to take a pill."

"You can if you choose to. What do *you* think?"

"I just want… to breathe."

"You know taking your emergency meds will help with that."

"What if it's not anxiety? What if it's my spinal cord?"

"Then you'll be relaxed enough for the doctors to rule out anxiety and get to the real problem."

Zachary swallowed. He could see the logic of her response. Maybe she was right. Maybe they were both right. He just needed to take an anti-anxiety pill, and then all would be well.

"What if it makes me tired?"

"Yes, they often do, don't they? Why are you worried about that?"

"There's so much to do…"

"Your health comes first. Physical and mental. You can't do everything else if you're not well. You will be more productive overall if you're able to be calm and relaxed."

Zachary looked at Kenzie. She interpreted his look and reached again into the small locker to find the box of pills he kept in his pocket.

"Are you still there, Zachary?"

"I'll take one," he told Dr. B.

"Okay. Do you want me to stay on the phone? Or do you want to call me back if you need to talk more?"

"I'll call back."

"Sounds good. I'll be here if you need me. But I think you'll feel a lot better once you take your meds."

"Yeah."

"Good luck with your check-up. You let me know if you need anything."

"Thanks." Zachary did the best he could to muffle the sobs that were creeping up his throat. Sympathy could break him. He could stay strong in the face of anger or an attack, but give him compassion, and he melted into a puddle.

He hung up the phone and took the pill and the water that Kenzie offered him.

"Thank you."

He swallowed enough water to get the pill down, then closed his eyes, waiting for it to take effect.

"It's going to be okay," Kenzie assured him. "You're in the right place. If there is anything wrong, we'll get it dealt with. But like you say, it's probably limited to your tailbone, and you'll be able to go home in a couple of hours, once they've finished looking at the imaging."

Zachary nodded, his eyes still closed. He tried to focus on his breathing, keeping an even rhythm in and out to stay in control. Kenzie stopped talking and let him be. She was probably wondering why he fought it so much. Why he fought having to take a rescue dose or taking all of the other meds every day. She didn't know what it was like to be in his head. To need so much help just to get by and look normal. There were days when he felt like he could be normal, like anyone else, and it was so tempting to just go off all of the meds. But he knew how that had ended up in the past. And he knew, from experiences going on a med holiday to get a baseline or start building a new cocktail, or ending up without any meds like he did at the Lodge, how quickly things would spiral out of control if he did that.

But that didn't mean he had to like it.

40

"Feeling better?" Kenzie asked.

Zachary realized that he was drifting, eyes still closed, and that the crushing anxiety had lifted. He could still think about the possibility of a spinal cord injury, could still worry about it, but the heart-racing panic over the thought of having done lasting neurological damage and not being able to breathe were gone. His breathing and his heart rate were settling down. The tight muscles in his stomach had relaxed.

"Yeah. Better."

"Good." She gave his shoulder a squeeze. "I hate to see you so anxious."

Zachary shifted, still not able to find any position that was really comfortable. But at least he wasn't sitting or lying directly on his tailbone. It was still sore and throbbing, but he relieved as much pressure as possible by lying on his side. They would probably give him a prescription painkiller before sending him home. Zachary wasn't sure he would take it. He always worried about conflicts between painkillers and his meds, having had problems after combining them in the past. And there was always the danger of addiction to the more powerful painkillers. Tyrrell and Berk were testaments to the fact that Zachary shouldn't be messing around with anything that he could get addicted to. Addiction was in their DNA.

"Where's my phone?"

"You just dropped it." Kenzie reached over and picked his phone up from the mattress. She handed it back to him. "Keep yourself entertained. Maybe message Rhys."

"I still have work to do," he reminded her.

Kenzie pursed her lips, looking at him. "I don't know if now is the best time for you to be working."

"I'm fine."

"Those are pretty powerful drugs."

Zachary nodded his agreement. That was why he didn't like to take them every day. But that didn't mean he had to put his life on pause whenever he took one. He scrolled through his contacts and found Detective Shelly.

He was fully expecting it to go to voicemail. Detectives were never there when he wanted them. But Shelly picked up after a couple of rings.

"Shelly."

"This is Zachary Goldman."

"I've been trying to reach you, Mr. Goldman. Where have you been?"

"Oh…" Zachary had noticed that there were missed call notifications on his screen, but hadn't taken the time to see who had been trying to reach him. "Sorry. I'm at the hospital."

Shelly was silent for a moment. "Visiting the McNichols?" he asked eventually. "I didn't think he'd be having any visitors today."

"No. I… I suppose you heard about the break-in at my house. Donaldson said that he was going to talk to you. And I filed a report here in Roxboro. I told them to copy you."

"Yes," the detective's voice was somewhat snide. "I heard about your so-called break-in. Didn't sound like there was any evidence to be collected."

"It was pretty clean," Zachary agreed. "We thought they were probably professionals. Hired help. Jennifer and her boyfriend must have tracked me down and hired someone to—"

"Yeah, I don't believe that load. You think petty criminals would hire heavyweights to go back and steal their stuff back? No way. Not gonna happen. Those kids have cut and run. They're not sticking around here to get caught."

"I know they moved out of the house they were in, but with some work, we might be able to track them. Credit card receipts—"

"You think I'm that inept? Of course we're on top of credit card receipts. They're gone. Hit the road. They didn't stick around here long enough to steal their stuff back. Nice try."

Zachary was stumped. If they weren't the ones who had hired the thugs to retrieve the stolen property from his house, then who was?

"I don't think there *was* any break-in," Shelly said. "The loot just happened to get stolen before Donaldson got there to pick it up? A little too convenient for my tastes. This was a set-up. You returned the stolen goods to the McNichols."

"No! You can check with them. I didn't have anything to do with this."

"Yeah."

Zachary sputtered at the phone. He looked at Kenzie. "He thinks there was no break-in. That I did this myself."

Kenzie took the phone from his hand. "This is the detective in Montpelier?"

Zachary nodded. He reached to take it back from her, but Kenzie kept it out of his reach, and he didn't feel quick enough to grab it back. Everything had the loose, slippery quality that he associated with sleep or anxiety medication.

"This is Dr. Kenzie Kirsch," she snapped into the phone. "What exactly is your problem, detective? How exactly do you think Zachary wound up in the hospital if there was no break-in?"

Zachary couldn't hear Shelly's response.

"Those thugs roughed him up, that's how," Kenzie snapped into the phone. "So don't act like Zachary is making it all up."

Another pause, while she listened to his protests.

"Well, maybe you should ask Donaldson why he didn't tell you all of the details. This is not made up. You call him and you get the scoop. Don't be a jerk and blame the guy who ended up in the hospital."

He said something back to her. Kenzie handed Zachary the phone back, her eyes bright with anger. Zachary took it uncertainly. Donaldson had, he thought, probably thought he was doing Zachary a favor, not exposing him to the humiliation of Shelly knowing that he had been handcuffed and thrown on the floor, helpless as a baby during the robbery. He hadn't anticipated Detective Shelly turning the blame on Zachary and the McNichols.

Zachary cleared his throat, grimaced at Kenzie, and put the phone back up to his ear. "Uh—hi. It's me again."

Shelly swore. His tone was definitely less confrontational. "You were injured in the robbery?"

"Yeah... maybe a broken bone or two, and they're checking for spinal cord injury... just waiting for x-ray now."

"And you're calling me for an update? Put your phone away and take care of yourself. And your girlfriend. She's a little firebrand, isn't she?"

Zachary glanced at Kenzie. "Yeah. I just wanted to make sure you knew about the robbery and the details that I know... which isn't really much. Just that I'm pretty sure they were hired muscle."

This time, Shelly didn't accuse him of making the whole thing up. "Do you have descriptions? I didn't get anything helpful from Donaldson."

"I asked the robbery detective to share with you, but I don't know if they've sent anything over yet. They were masked, so I can't tell you much except size... big goons like wrestlers or football players. No detectable accents. They took pictures of the boot prints, but... that won't tell you much other than that they were big dudes."

"Well, your original thieves didn't hire them. They wouldn't run before getting the merchandise back and, from the paper trail they have left, they ran last night. So not them. Which leaves... Janice and Glen Nichols."

Zachary shook his head. He closed his eyes, feeling drowsy. It took too much effort to open them again. "Not the Nichols," he disagreed. "Why would they do that? I would have gotten the stolen goods back to them or to you, and you would have released it to them. So why come after it here?"

"They couldn't wait. They had already arranged for the stuff to be sold at auction. They had already claimed it as stolen on their insurance. What you were doing threw a wrench in the works, so they had to get around you."

Zachary supposed that what Shelly said could be true, but it still didn't feel right to him. "They weren't the ones that set up the auction. That was Jennifer and her boyfriend."

"It could have been at McNichols's instruction. They might have all been working together."

A little extra money for Jennifer and her boyfriend. Her boyfriend was already in the business, so they were easy to rope into it. Or maybe it had been Jennifer who had suggested the fake robbery to the McNichols, showing them that they could make back more than what had been stolen if they handled it the right way. Maybe she knew that the bar was in financial trouble and went to Janice and Glen with the proposal.

"As an idea, that sounds fine," he admitted. "But... they don't strike me as the kind. And they were surprised to learn it was an inside job. Really upset about Jennifer being involved."

"Or they are good actors. Or what they were upset about was you finding it out. Maybe you weren't supposed to."

Zachary was about to say, "Then why did they hire me?" but stopped himself. Because they hadn't hired him. It hadn't been their idea to bring in a private investigator at all. It had been Walter's idea. He had retained Zachary and given him a deposit before the McNichols knew what was happening. They couldn't very well say at that point that they didn't want a private investigator looking into it, free of charge to them.

"I can't prove they weren't involved," Zachary admitted. "Maybe with a little more investigation, I could find something out. But I don't know if Walter Kirsch will want me to go any farther. I've recovered the stolen property once; I'm not likely to be able to do it again. And he might not want to know if the McNichols were involved."

There were a few beats of silence from Shelly. "Walter Kirsch?" he asked eventually. "That's who hired you?"

Zachary suddenly wondered if he shouldn't have revealed the fact. But it was too late to take it back now. "Well... yes. Barnburners is a favorite hangout..." He felt a little strange about saying it, knowing that Walter hadn't exactly been honest about that claim. "And he wanted to do something to help them out after the robbery."

"Walter Kirsch."

"You know him?"

"Know him? No. I'm too far down the social ladder for me to know him. But know of him? Of course. Everyone in the state knows about him. And everyone involved in politics in this corner of the country. He's a heavyweight. A different kind of heavyweight than the ones who broke into your house."

"Yeah. I guess he is. Kenzie said—"

"Wait a minute, did she say Dr. Kenzie Kirsch? She's Walter Kirsch's daughter?"

"Yeah. That's why he picked me for the investigation. How he knew I am a PI."

Shelly swore. Zachary had a feeling Shelly was reviewing everything he had done in the case, including his accusation that Zachary had reported a fake robbery to hide the fact that he had returned the stolen property to the McNichols. All of the things Shelly could be in trouble for.

"I'm going to go over this case with a fine-toothed comb," he said finally. "If there's anything else to be found, I'll find it."

"Walter is personal friends with the McNichols," Zachary pointed out, knowing that he was stretching the truth slightly. "So you should be careful of any accusations you make against them. And Glen's heart attack... I don't imagine Walter would be too happy about that."

In reality, Zachary doubted Walter would care about Glen's heart attack. He might care if it meant that he didn't get good service at Barn-burners or that the bar had to shut down and he had to find a new hangout.

41

While it seemed like it would take forever for the doctors to get the images they needed of Zachary's back and to review them and decide what was to be done with him, the doctor did eventually return to his bedside to report that there didn't appear to be any swelling around the spinal cord, no fractures to the vertebrae in his back other than his coccyx, and that he could go home and didn't need to spend the night at the hospital.

"There are still some concerns," the doctor told Kenzie, choosing to talk to her about it rather than to Zachary. Maybe because she was a doctor and he thought she would understand better or take him more seriously. Or maybe because Zachary couldn't keep his eyes open. "There could be some inflammation that is not showing up on the imaging. With Zachary experiencing some mild neurological symptoms, it is still advisable to take it very easy. Bed rest for a few days. Nothing strenuous for a couple of weeks. And a trip back to the hospital if either of you has any concerns about continuing or new symptoms."

Kenzie made noises of agreement. "Yes, I'll keep a close eye on him. He won't be doing any gymnastics for a while."

"Call or come back if you have any concerns at all."

"Thank you for your time, doctor."

Zachary was eventually released, taken to the curb in a wheelchair, then climbed into the car without assistance. Kenzie nodded her satisfaction and made sure he buckled in before pulling out.

Zachary watched out the window, his eyelids cracked open just enough to see the lights and shadows of the city at night.

"It's pretty," he breathed. "A long exposure to capture the movement of the lights…"

"Yeah?" Kenzie asked. "I bet that would be nice."

"It would." Zachary rubbed his forehead. "We're going home, right?"

"Yes."

"Back to your house, not the apartment."

"That's right. Why, did you need something at the apartment?"

"No. Maybe Tyrrell can stay there when he gets out."

Kenzie looked over at him. He could feel her eyes on him. "You haven't mentioned that before. Is that what you want to do?"

"Not using it anymore. He's going to need somewhere when he gets out."

"Yes. That might be a good solution. Lets him get back on his feet, but without us hovering over him, trying to direct everything."

"No hovering," Zachary agreed. "You don't hover."

"Well, sometimes I do." Zachary could hear the smile in her voice. "But I try not to."

"You're perfect," he told her. "I don't know how I could be with someone so perfect." He looked in her direction and attempted to put his hand on her leg, but missed. "Especially when I'm such a mess."

"You're not such a mess. You have some challenges." Kenzie shrugged. "But so does everyone. I prefer you."

"Doesn't make any sense." Zachary tried not to slur his words. He didn't want her thinking that he was drunk. "Choosing to be with someone like me? They say women pick men like their fathers. I'm not like Walter."

"No, you're not. I'm thankful for that. I knew I didn't want someone like him."

"But he's a good husband. A good provider. Makes good money, doesn't get mixed up in dangerous situations. Home every night."

"Zachary, you know nothing about my father. He's not a good husband. He and my mom have been divorced for years. And he was never home every night. He's always traveled away from home and stayed in Montpelier near the Capitol. Mom was home in Burlington, and he would be away a few days or a couple weeks at a time. Come home weekends and recesses. Make sure he was around for holidays. But he was never a father and husband who was there for the family. He lived a separate life."

"He's your father and he loves you," Zachary assured her.

Kenzie chuckled. "Sure, he does. Or so he tells me."

"He's like Gordon," Zachary suggested. He rubbed his eyes, thinking about Gordon and Bridget. "Gordon can give her everything she needs. Everything she ever wanted. He's all of the things that I could never be. She figured out what she didn't want while we were married. So she got together with Gordon because he's the opposite of me."

"I'm sure Gordon is no more perfect than Walter is." Kenzie drove for a few minutes in silence, thinking about it. "I don't know Gordon well, but there are definitely similarities. They both get what they want. If my dad puts his mind to something, he's going to get it, no matter what anyone else says. That's how he's always been. But you know what's wrong with someone like that?"

"What?"

"He doesn't really care about anyone else. I'm sure Gordon is devoted to Bridget, but probably only insofar as it suits him to have a wife like Bridget. He wants the beautiful socialite. The perfect children. Now he's a family man. That's the image he wants to project."

"He could have dumped her," Zachary pointed out. "When he found out she is sick."

"But it doesn't hurt him for her to be sick. It just means that people will feel sorry for him. They'll look at him and think he's an angel for sticking with her and taking care of her. But he'll just hire more staff to do the actual caregiving as she needs it."

Zachary remembered Gordon talking about everybody he had to take care of when Zachary was wrapping up the Lauren Barclay case. How he had to look after everyone at his investment banking firm, Drake Chase Gould, and Bridget, and the expected twins.

"How could you do that?" he mused aloud. "How could you be responsible for so many people? It would be paralyzing."

"Who? Are we still talking about Gordon? Do you mean Bridget and the twins?"

"And everyone else. All the people at Chase Gold. He has to take care of them, make sure that they aren't being forced to work too hard. Make sure the firm is not taking advantage of them."

"Well, yes, that would be a lot of people. But I doubt Gordon sees it the same way as you. To someone like Walter or Gordon, people are just… assets. You take care of your assets, but it isn't the same as you taking care of a person you care about. They don't spend any time worrying about whether people are happy or healthy. Not if it doesn't impact them."

Daniel, an employee at Chase Gold, had said that Gordon was a psychopath. Maybe he was right. Maybe everyone who ran a big company like that had to focus on himself and the company's bottom line, rather than the people employed there. Zachary had no idea how he would make a decision that would affect hundreds or thousands of people, knowing that every choice he made would be bad for a certain portion of them. People would be hurt, fired, or have their feelings ignored. But Gordon could make choices without getting bogged down by the minutia. He didn't need to know how it would affect everyone.

"I'm not perfect," Zachary told Kenzie as they drove into the garage. "I'm never going to be like him."

"Good. I don't expect you to be. I wouldn't want to be married to Gordon. Or to Walter. They are egomaniacs. You have more compassion in your little finger than both of them put together."

"And that's good?" Zachary looked at his little finger and thought of all of the times he'd been paralyzed by a choice, worried that whatever he chose, it was going to hurt someone.

"Yes," Kenzie agreed. "That's good. Are you going to remember any of this in the morning?"

"Don't know," Zachary murmured. "We'll just have to wait and see."

42

Zachary slept in late in the morning due to having taken the additional anti-anxiety meds the evening before. He was also very sore after the manhandling by the thieves. Not only his tailbone, but all over. Like he'd been beaten up or hit by a truck. He didn't think that he'd been roughed up so badly when they had caught him, but maybe he hadn't realized at the time how hard he had fought or how many times he had been hit.

He waited until the early morning hours before taking a painkiller, wanting to be absolutely sure that he wasn't mixing it with the anti-anxiety meds. He was extra careful not to mix painkillers with other meds after an incident when he'd been staying overnight with Mr. Peterson, his old foster father. He groaned and struggled to get out of bed to go take something, waking Kenzie.

"Hey, are you okay? What's up?"

"Just need a painkiller."

"For your tailbone?"

"For my everything."

"Oh, poor Zachary. You stay put; let me get it for you."

Zachary settled back into place on the bed. He wasn't going to argue this time. It wasn't about being a gentleman and letting her sleep. She had offered, and he would take her up on it for once.

Kenzie got up and went to the en suite bathroom. Zachary listened to her going through the medicine cabinet and eventually picking what she deemed to be the right painkiller. She returned with a glass of water and a couple of white pills. "This should help."

He didn't bother asking what they were and just swallowed them with the water. "Thanks."

"Do you want anything else? Ice pack? Heating pad?"

"No. I'll just sleep it off."

"Okay." Kenzie leaned in to give him a peck on the cheek and settled back into bed herself. She ran her warm hand over his back, rubbing it in soothing circles for a couple of minutes. Then she stopped and he could tell from her long, even breathing that she had fallen back asleep.

And then sleep had overcome him, and he had slept fitfully until late morning, unable to do anything else. He eventually managed to drag himself out of bed and to the bathroom down the hall. When he opened the door, Kenzie was there waiting for him. She smiled.

"How are you feeling this morning? Like crap, if needing a painkiller during the night is any indication."

"Yeah. Sore. And hungover from the pills." Zachary rubbed his face, trying to wake up properly and focus on Kenzie and his surroundings. But he felt like he was in a dark room and could only just make out the things right in front of his eyes. Concentrating on anything more than a foot or two away seemed impossible.

"Well, back to bed with you. You know the doctor said he wanted you on bed rest."

"I can sit on the couch."

"Nope. Bed. If you want, I'll bring your computer in when you've had enough sleep. But bed rest means bed. Not doing anything to aggravate your back."

Zachary wobbled slightly. She took him by the arm and escorted him back to the bedroom and helped get him settled again. He was sore from sleeping on his side for the past few hours, but he couldn't lie flat on his back or sit up.

"I'll get you some cushions to make it easier to sit later on," Kenzie promised. "For now, try the other side." She helped arrange pillows and blankets to stabilize his position and make him more comfortable. "You need anything else? Hungry?"

"Does this mean I get breakfast in bed?" Zachary teased, his voice still rough and gravelly with sleep. Kenzie did not approve of any practice that would result in crumbs between the sheets.

"Only while you're on prescribed bed rest. This is not going to carry through to weekends," Kenzie responded in a mock-severe voice. It wasn't like Zachary ever slept in or demanded to be served breakfast in bed. She was the one who usually had to coax him to eat.

"Aww," Zachary pretended to be disappointed. He closed his eyes. "Not ready to eat anything yet."

"Okay. I'll check again later. Do you mind if I vacuum? Will that bother you?"

Zachary shook his head. "No. Won't bother me. I don't think I'm going to go back to sleep."

But he was asleep again before he heard the noise of the vacuum cleaner.

When he next awoke, Zachary thought by the angle of the sun through the window that it was around noon. He rubbed his eyes. He never slept that late, even sick. But knowing that he wouldn't be allowed to get up to sit in the living room, there wasn't exactly any point in trying to get up.

"Hey, Zach. Ready for something to eat?" Kenzie asked, coming in to check on him after a while and finding him awake.

"I guess. Don't really feel like anything, though."

"Maybe not, but you're already late taking your morning meds, and some of them need to be taken with food."

Zachary grunted his acknowledgment. He was used to having to plan mealtimes around his med schedule.

"Granola bar?" Kenzie suggested, since it was Zachary's usual go-to choice for breakfast.

"No." Zachary was strangely turned off by the thought of anything sweet. He considered, trying to think of something that would be appetizing but didn't require Kenzie to do any preparation. He wasn't likely to eat more than a few bites. It wasn't worthwhile for her to spend an hour preparing something.

"Maybe… those cheese strings?"

"Sure. You probably want something other than just cheese, though. Yogurt? Cereal?"

"No…" He tried to decide what else he could get down. "Toast?"

Kenzie nodded. "I assume you don't want marmalade on it. Some strawberry jam?"

Zachary had learned in foster care to eat whatever was on offer. But he had to admit that marmalade was not something he had ever developed a taste for. The bitterness of the peels made him wince.

"Just plain. Margarine."

"You're sure?"

He could understand her confusion over his not going with his usual breakfast choices. "Just… nothing sweet right now. Can't stomach it."

"Okay. No problem. Cheese string and buttered toast it is. Be back in a few minutes. Oh—and I found this in my office."

Kenzie handed him a USB drive.

Zachary held it in his palm and looked at it for a minute, trying to remember where he had seen it before.

"Where was this?"

"In my office. It was on my desk, but it's not mine, so I assume it's yours."

Zachary frowned. "No. I… I remember seeing it there. But I thought it was yours. Who else's would it be?"

Kenzie raised her brows and shook her head. "You're the detective. You figure it out."

She obviously thought it was his, even if he didn't remember. And he couldn't blame her. He was easily distracted, lost things without realizing it, or had to spend an hour looking for something he had misplaced because he had left his phone in the fridge or some other weird place. It wouldn't be out of the realm of possibility for him to forget that he'd bought or been given a USB drive for something. He had a vague recollection of Donaldson picking it up off the floor in Kenzie's office. It could have been there for months without either of them seeing it. Partially hidden by the furniture, or left on the desk or another surface and forgotten about.

Kenzie left to prepare his breakfast/lunch, and Zachary moved around restlessly, trying to find a position that didn't aggravate his tailbone or another bruise or pulled muscle.

"Will you bring me my laptop?" he asked when Kenzie returned with a lunch plate bearing one unwrapped cheese string and one slice of buttered toast. She set it on the side table along with a small plastic box filled with his daytime meds. There was still a glass of water on the table, lukewarm from the night before.

"Don't eat over your keyboard."

"I won't. Want to see what's on this drive." He tapped the USB stick against his palm. He could not remember what he might have used it for or who he might have been given it by, but still hadn't managed to dredge up anything from his unwilling brain. If he knew where it had come from, that knowledge was currently lost in fog.

Kenzie ducked out to the living room and returned with his laptop and charge cord. "Food first," she advised. "So you can take your pills. Then you can play on the computer." She smiled teasingly to let him know that she was only pretending to act like she was his mother instead of his partner. But she still wanted him to be sure to eat and take his meds.

Zachary left his computer on the bed beside him, unopened, and reached for his plate. He took a couple of bites of the toast and then washed his pills down with warm water. He peeled a long string off of the cheese and stuffed it into his mouth. He knew that the enjoyment he got from playing with his cheese was juvenile, but what was the harm in a little ritual that encouraged him to eat when he had little appetite?

"Need anything else?" Kenzie asked. "I didn't get you another painkiller. How is your pain level?"

Zachary shrugged with one shoulder. "Tolerable."

"Let me know if you need anything. I'll probably go out this afternoon to get a couple of cushions for you."

"Thanks." As it was, Zachary was going to have to lounge on his side to use the computer placed on the mattress beside him. It would be a lot more dignified and bother his shoulders and back less if he could sit upright.

Kenzie walked back out to continue with her housekeeping chores, Zachary assumed. Or to have her own lunch or take a break before going out to do the shopping.

Zachary turned the laptop around and opened the lid. He logged in to get past the lock screen and then put the USB stick into one of the ports.

Gerry, his computer guy, would undoubtedly not approve of him putting an unknown USB drive into his computer. But they had set his computer up not to autoplay anything that was plugged into it. He could at least examine the file system before deciding what he wanted to do with it. And the USB drive wasn't really unknown. It was his or Kenzie's; he just didn't know which. One of them had been given it and then forgotten about it. People did that all the time, sharing music, pictures, or other files.

It could be a drive with some of Mr. Peterson's photography on it, and Zachary had just forgotten about it.

Or not.

43

Zachary's laptop brought up a file listing for the contents of the USB drive.

Zachary and Mr. Peterson had traded digital pictures plenty of times, and he knew that the list of files was nothing to do with photography. There were several image files, but the names were not formatted incrementally or like anything Zachary had ever gotten from his friend before. And there were too many other types of files mixed in with the images. Word processing and spreadsheet files. Various log or system files. A number of large PDFs. Nothing meant to launch when the USB was put into a drive. He didn't see anything executable.

There were several layers of folders, and he clicked through them, just looking at the file and folder names to start with. Projects, dates, maybe some company names. Nothing that sounded familiar, either from cases that he had worked on or anything that Kenzie had mentioned. He wasn't sure how her files would be named. Still, nothing in the filenames sounded even vaguely medical, and he didn't see any x-rays or colored scans on the thumbnails of the graphic files.

Zachary drilled down another level in what seemed to be a project folder and stopped, staring at the name on a subfolder.

Bieberstein

He gazed at it for a few minutes, frozen, while his brain tried to process its significance.

He had met a Blair Bieberstein on the Lauren Barclay case. A case that he had taken for Gordon Drake. The same Gordon Drake as he had just been talking to Kenzie about the night before. Bridget's new partner, the father of her children. CEO or managing partner of Drake Chase Gould, a new and very successful investment banking company.

Of course, if there was one Bieberstein in Vermont, there must be others. Blair's parents, siblings, cousins. Just because Zachary had never run into the name anywhere before or since, that didn't mean that Blair Bieberstein was the only person in Vermont who bore that name. It was just a coincidence. He had seen other names as he went through the USB drive, and if he hadn't actually known a Bieberstein, it wouldn't have ever attracted his attention. There were other surnames or corporate names on other files and folders, and none of them had meant anything to Zachary. Common names like Brown and Jones. Old Vermont family names. And names that meant nothing to him because he didn't have any experiences to attach to them.

Eventually, Zachary started to click through other folders in the file structure. He still didn't actually open any of the files. Those with graphic thumbnails he studied for a second or two longer, but he didn't have any experience in investment banking or whatever finance documents were in the folders, and the images didn't mean anything to him.

He looked for the names of other employees that he had met at Chase Gold, as the firm was affectionately called, and eventually changed his approach and put several names into the search field in turn. Drake, Chase, and Gould all brought up hundreds of hits. It could be research on the firm. Someone might be looking at a financing or buyout and had compiled stacks of research on them. They could be internal files from Chase Gold that someone had taken home to work on. But even if the files had been copied for a legitimate purpose, how had they ended up in Kenzie's office?

Perhaps one of the thugs had dropped it. It would have been easy for a USB drive to drop out of one of the men's pockets as he bent over to pick up the boxes. If he hadn't noticed, he might have inadvertently left it behind.

But what would a hired thug be doing with hundreds of files of research on Chase Gold?

It seemed very unlikely that a criminal for hire would be carrying financial documents on a USB drive. Unless he'd picked them up at the last office he'd hit. Maybe someone had hired him to retrieve the USB drive, the same way as he had been hired to retrieve the boxes of memorabilia from Zachary.

Zachary tried searching the names of other people he had met at Chase Gold. There were hits, but far fewer. He tried Bieberstein, and the list of files containing his name was lengthy. Zachary tried "Blair Bieberstein," putting the name in quotes, figuring that would foil the search. If the Bieberstein named on the folder he had seen was for another Bieberstein, then "Blair Bieberstein" would not have any hits. But there *were* hits. A lot of them.

Zachary turned it over in his mind. He could open the files and start reading through them. But he didn't like the idea that they might be password protected or that they might somehow leave footprints on his system or send out a beacon when he opened one that would alert someone at Chase Gold about a breach of their security protocols and lead them straight back to Zachary. He'd already dealt with one homicidal maniac at Chase Gold and didn't relish another. Especially not when he was already sore from the previous day's encounter. Whether he had any spinal cord inflammation or not, he didn't need to risk a physical altercation with anyone.

"Bieberstein," Blair answered his phone briskly. "Who's this?"

"Oh, hi. It's Zachary Goldman. I don't know if you remember me from—"

"Sure, I remember who you are. What do you want?"

Zachary smiled at the brusque question. He knew that Bieberstein didn't intend to be offensive by skipping over the usual small talk and progression up to what he had called about. He was just being efficient. Cutting away all of what he saw as unnecessary deadwood and going straight to the heart of the matter. Zachary wasn't exactly a social acquaintance, so why had he called? He must want something.

"I have come into possession of a USB drive," Zachary explained. "It seems to be filled with documents about Chase Gold."

"Came into it how?" Bieberstein asked. "What kind of files?"

"I haven't opened them in case they are sensitive or set off some kind of alarm. There are lots of documents. Hundreds. Whole tree structures, from what I can see. There is a subfolder named Bieberstein. When I search Blair Bieberstein in quotes, I get a lot of hits."

"You're saying that it is a USB drive filled with files about me?"

"No, it obviously isn't just about you. I thought maybe it was research documents that someone had compiled about the company. Maybe they are planning to buy it. If it's not that... then I think it might be documents pulled from your server."

Bieberstein swore. One short, staccato syllable.

"Take a picture of it with your phone," he instructed. "Text it to me right now."

Zachary obeyed, taking a shot of the screen that was currently up on his laptop. He texted it to Bieberstein and then put the phone back to his ear.

"I sent it."

"Hold on."

Zachary waited while Bieberstein checked out the file. Zachary could hear rapid key clicks before Bieberstein said anything. Then another oath.

"Where are you?" Bieberstein demanded when he resumed the call. "I'll come to you."

Zachary hesitated for just an instant before giving Bieberstein Kenzie's house address. He couldn't exactly go to Bieberstein. Not when he was supposed to be on bed rest. Kenzie would kill him if she came home to discover that he had gone out. And that was ignoring the fact that he could aggravate the injury to his spinal cord, which was a risk he was not willing to take.

"Got it," Bieberstein snapped. "I'll be right over."

"Hey, uh, Blair..." Zachary was awkward calling him by his first name. But he didn't want to just address him by his surname and, though he knew that the employees at Chase Gold frequently referred to him as "Biebs," he didn't know whether they did so to his face or how he would feel about Zachary taking this liberty.

"Yes?"

"Listen, I'm on bed rest from an injury. I'll get up and unlock the door for you and disarm the security alarm, but then I'll be back in bed. Just come in and find me. And... be sure to lock it once you're in."

"Roger," Bieberstein agreed, without bothering to ask Zachary how he had been injured. He hung up.

Zachary looked at the time and tried to estimate how long it would take Bieberstein to drive there. He didn't want to leave the house unlocked and unsecured for too long. He didn't want to leave it unsecured at all. The very thought ramped up his anxiety, and he didn't want to have to take another rescue dose of anti-anxiety meds. Not two days in a row. If the house were only unlocked for ten minutes, that wouldn't be a risk. No one was going to know that it was unlocked and no one would try to break in during those ten minutes.

Still, he tried to plan it as closely as he could, doing a quick Google Maps search to see what the predicted driving time was from Chase Gold to the house, then trimming it by a couple of minutes, anticipating that Bieberstein would have a lead foot, wanting to get there as quickly as possible.

He watched the clock closely, then eased himself out of bed and walked slowly and carefully to the front door, trying to keep his back straight and to use the best possible posture, like a model walking with a book on top of her head. He disarmed the alarm, unlocked the locks on the front door, then walked back to the bedroom without looking out the window to see if Bieberstein was driving up yet. If he gave in to the compulsion to check once, he would be checking every thirty seconds until Bieberstein actually arrived. He slipped back into bed, turning the opposite direction from what he had been facing before and moved his computer to the edge of the bed. It took a little shuffling around to get the blankets and pillows into the configuration that eased the pain the best. He continued to click through the file tree structure, looking for any other indications as to what kind of information was on the drive.

There was a rapid knock on the door, followed by the sound of the door opening, closing, and the locks being turned. Zachary breathed out, relieved.

"Blair? I'm in here."

Bieberstein was at the bedroom door a moment later. His eyes swept the room briefly. He grabbed the chair from Kenzie's dressing table and dragged it over to the side of the bed. Zachary had previously compared him to a hyperactive squirrel. Not aloud; just in his mind. Bieberstein was a small man, always moving, some kind of math and finance genius that no one could compare to.

"Is that it?" He nodded to the drive sticking out from the side of Zachary's computer.

Zachary nodded. Bieberstein reached over and pulled it out.

44

Zachary's computer beeped and issued an error warning for not ejecting the USB drive before pulling it out. He clicked the error and then closed the computer lid. Bieberstein sat down on the chair and pulled his own laptop out of his bag. He opened it up, inserted the USB drive, and touched the laptop's biometric sensor to unlock it. His eyes drilled into the screen as he clicked and typed, moving quickly through the contents of the USB drive, exploring what Zachary had already seen. As Bieberstein faced Zachary, his screen was not visible, so Zachary didn't know if he was opening files or just viewing the names and thumbnails.

Bieberstein ran his fingers through his hair. He continued to look at the contents of the drive. He stood up, set the computer down on the chair, and started to pace back and forth. Bieberstein had said that he thought better on his feet. Zachary waited to see what he came up with.

"This is not good," Bieberstein said. "I thought that maybe if they had files on me, they were just headhunters. Trying to see if they could hire me to work for another firm. I get offers sometimes."

Zachary nodded, not surprised. Bieberstein had locked up one of the positions at Chase Gold before anyone else had even been considered, leaving the rest of the interns to fight over the last remaining position. Bieberstein had shot ahead of them with his employment assured. No one wanted him to go anywhere else.

"But this is not a headhunter file." Bieberstein stared up at the ceiling as he strode back and forth, thinking about it. "This is industrial espionage."

Zachary had been afraid of that. "How bad is it?"

"Really bad. This is privileged information that no one outside the firm should have. Or even see. Did you look at these files?"

"I only looked at the names and the thumbnails. I didn't want to open anything and risk infecting my system or setting off an alarm."

Bieberstein nodded his understanding. He muttered to himself, too low for Zachary to understand. It sounded like he was running through scenarios in rapid-fire, looking for the best possible outcome.

"Where did you get this?" he asked. "Can you tell me that?"

"I would if I could... but I really don't know. The house was broken into yesterday. The thieves took several boxes of stuff. That was in the room that the boxes were stolen from. I don't know... maybe one of them dropped it."

"Who were they?"

"They were masked. I think they were hired thugs. Professionals that someone paid to come in here and take those things."

"What did they steal?"

"Sports memorabilia. Some... mementos and valuables that had been stolen from a sports bar a couple of weeks ago. They didn't have a high intrinsic value. I was hired to see what I could do. I recovered them from the people who had stolen them, brought them back here, and then I guess... someone stole them from me."

Bieberstein rubbed his hands together rapidly like he was trying to warm them up. He gazed up at the ceiling, stopping close to Zachary.

"What made them so valuable? Why did they hire you?"

"The memorabilia? Nothing. Some of them had been sold to private buyers already, and some were going to be sold at auction. I didn't look at everything in the boxes, but I didn't see... certificates of authenticity or anything like that. Some stuff was signed. Baseballs, hockey pucks, posters, pictures..."

"Sounds like junk," Bieberstein said with a jerk of his head that might have been a shake or a tic.

"Well... for anyone who wasn't into the teams, I guess that's exactly what it is. I have an inventory list..." Zachary thought about it before opening his computer. Was that classified? Was he sharing private client information if he showed Bieberstein what had been stolen? He didn't think it was secret. And they were each helping the other, trying to sort out a crime that involved both of the companies they were working for. He lifted the lid on his laptop. "You'll keep this confidential?"

Bieberstein widened his eyes. He made a motion toward the USB drive. "*This* is the sensitive information. Not your inventory of stolen property. I'm the one who should be asking you for confidentiality."

"Well then, I guess we both agree to keep each other's information confidential."

Bieberstein nodded his agreement. Zachary took a couple of minutes to find the inventory list. He then displayed it on the screen and turned it toward Bieberstein. Blair looked it over, reading parts of the list out loud very quickly, muttering in between some of the items. He started pacing again, still repeating inventory items aloud. He started reciting the memorabilia by team, with all items for one team in a list. The list on Zachary's screen was haphazard. Bieberstein had, Zachary realized, memorized the list and was now breaking it down and resorting it, looking for patterns. It was no wonder that he was so valuable to the firm.

After repeating the items by team, Bieberstein repeated them again, grouping them together by like item. All posters together, all balls or pucks, all signed photographs, all scale replicas.

"Wait..." Zachary held his hand up.

Bieberstein stopped pacing and looked at him.

"The car. The Montreal Canadiens car. My nephew was here playing. He ended up playing in that room and taking a bunch of the memorabilia out of the boxes. He wasn't supposed to, so that got him in trouble. He was trying to show me the little station wagon. He'd been playing with it on the floor. I just wanted him to pack everything back away so that nothing would get lost or broken."

Bieberstein's head was bobbing up and down, eyes bright as he followed Zachary's narrative.

"He was trying to show me that the doors open and shut. It had little doors on the side and in the back. It was a replica station wagon, so there was space inside for cargo. A rectangular space, about this big." Zachary held his fingers up.

Bieberstein rocked back and forth on his heels, thinking about it. "Just the right size to put a USB drive inside."

Zachary laughed. Was that where the USB drive had come from? Mason had taken it out or dropped it when he had opened the doors to the little car? Then he had left it on the floor when he had packed everything back up. Maybe in plain sight, maybe behind one of the boxes hidden from view until the boxes were removed. But the thugs picking up the boxes would have no idea that it was part of the loot they were supposed to be collecting.

"That's where it came from," Bieberstein said, "but how did it get into the car in the first place?"

45

Then it all started to click into place. Zachary looked at Bieberstein.

"Oh, no."

"What?" Bieberstein asked. He paced across the room. "You know who did this? You know who is trying to bring down Chase Gold?"

"Do you think that's the goal? To ruin the company? Couldn't it be... for a takeover or something like that? Maybe they want to buy Chase Gold."

"Maybe they do. If so, you can get the best price by devaluing the company first. Put it into bankruptcy, buy it as a going concern, then bring it back to life under new management. You get all of the assets at bargain-basement prices, can strip out what you don't want, then build it up again."

Zachary tried to imagine how that scenario might fit. He wasn't a finance guy, but he didn't see how that would work. There had been some other plan.

"Whoever is leaking this information, they have to be stopped," Bieberstein said. "I can try to trace the breach from our end, get a look at security logs and who would have had access to copy this off the system. But I don't know where you were in the chain. Why would someone put a USB drive in a toy car? Were they hiding it?"

"I have an idea," Zachary told him. "But I'm going to need some time to sort it out."

Bieberstein nodded. "More important to stop the leak on my end. If nothing can get out, then whoever your man is, wherever he is in the process, he can't get the information."

"So… you'll take that to Gordon Drake? And talk to the IT guys?"

Bieberstein nodded. "Yeah. He's probably the guy to talk to. Mr. Drake has kind of… kept in touch since the whole thing with Lauren. Much more involved than he used to be. With me, anyway."

"I don't want you to tell him that this came from me."

Bieberstein twirled on his heel and looked at Zachary. "Why not? You're friends with him. He's hired you before. He would be happy that you found this and turned it over to me. He'd be grateful to you."

"I know. It isn't because we don't get along." Though there had been a distinct chill from Gordon since the day Zachary had protected the twins from coming to harm. Zachary wasn't quite sure why. Was it because Gordon thought he should be their protector? Did he feel inadequate or embarrassed that it had been Zachary who had seen the danger before anyone else? Zachary didn't quite understand the change in attitude from someone who had always been warm and pleasant to him in the past. Too warm and pleasant, in fact. Something seemed to have reset Gordon's attitude. But that wasn't why Zachary didn't want Gordon to know of his involvement with the USB drive. "I have my own reasons for keeping this quiet. Do you think you could just tell him that some geek friend of yours came across this and realized that it was sensitive information about Chase Gold? But he's paranoid and doesn't want to be identified?"

Bieberstein smiled. "Are you paranoid?"

"Let's say I am. I don't really qualify as a geek, but… if you could sell that…?"

"Yeah, no problem. And for the record…"

"Yes?"

"You're a lot more of a geek than you think."

Zachary laughed. He might like his electronic toys, but he had never been smart like the kids at school. And never been obsessed or a collector of any of the popular TV or computer worlds. As a foster kid, his concerns had been elsewhere and he'd never had money or the ability to hang on to anything but his most priceless possession. He didn't think that he qualified as a geek. But he took it as a compliment from Bieberstein.

"Thanks. And I appreciate you coming right over here. I don't suppose your bosses at Chase Gold like you taking off and disappearing in the middle of the workday."

Bieberstein waved this concern aside. "I'm not an intern anymore. And they know I practically live there. HR is always telling me that I need to take care of my health and not put in too many hours."

"Better health, better wealth." Zachary remembered the tagline from when he had been investigating Drake Chase Gould.

Bieberstein nodded sagely.

"Still running on the treadmill?" Zachary asked him.

"Yeah. But I use the safety strap now."

"Good idea."

Bieberstein sat down with his computer on his lap once more. He clicked a few times before taking the USB drive out of the port and slipping it into his pocket. He put his laptop back in his shoulder bag.

"Thanks for the information."

"Yeah, you bet."

"You want me to lock up or reset the alarm for you?"

Zachary shook his head. He wasn't going to give the security codes to anyone, especially anyone involved in corporate espionage in any capacity. He knew corporate spy craft was a nasty business, and he didn't want to get caught in the middle of it.

Except he already was.

Zachary didn't want to make the next call. He knew he had to for several reasons. But he was stuck. He couldn't see any other way out of it.

It took quite a few rings before the other party picked up.

"Zachary. I was hoping to hear from you."

"I wonder if you would come to meet with me."

"Well… that would be nice, I'm sure, but I'm sort of tied up today. We can just make it a phone call this time."

"I really need to see you face to face. This is too sensitive to deal with over the phone."

"I'm sure someone in your profession has already checked for bugs," he said dryly. "This line is secure."

"It needs to be face to face."

"I can't just drop everything." A definite note of irritation had crept into his voice. "I have had a very busy day and still have several meetings ahead of me."

"Reschedule them."

"Really, Zachary—"

"This is more important. Trust me."

There was silence on the line while the other party considered this assertion. He sighed in exasperation. "This had better be good."

"Get here as soon as you can."

"Where?"

"Same place we saw each other last."

Zachary hung up.

46

Zachary didn't know how long it would take. He couldn't look up the amount of time it would take him to drive there, as he had with Bieberstein, since he wasn't sure of the starting point. But it would probably be an hour, more or less.

He was still feeling somewhat hungover from the anti-anxiety meds and painkillers. Zachary wasn't normally one for taking naps, but he felt like he needed one. He was tired enough that he could have closed his eyes and drifted off for half an hour or an hour and would probably feel much better when he woke up. But he couldn't sleep knowing that the front door was unlocked and unsecured.

Instead, he lay there, listening to every creak and groan of the house. Listening for a car to pull up in front of the house and for footsteps to walk up to the door. The turning of the doorknob, and then footsteps down the hall…

He was on edge, his whole body coiled for action even though there was nothing to do. It wasn't the same as the anxiety he had felt the night before, wondering whether he was going to end up paralyzed by a spinal cord injury. It wasn't the same as when he worried about Bridget or the twins. It was more raw. Vigilance. The anticipation of danger. Masked men had broken into the house once when he had left the door unlocked. It could happen again.

It was an hour before he heard a car pull up. He couldn't see it, but he heard the door slam shut and footsteps up to the house.

There was a knock at the door. Zachary had forgotten to tell him to let himself in. He shifted his position and contemplated getting up. Standing was not as painful as sitting; he could get up, answer the door, and just stay on his feet for the meeting.

Getting out of bed without sitting on the side was more like falling out of bed onto his hands and knees and then finding his way to his feet afterward. He made his way stiffly down the hall and to the front door.

The door opened just as he was getting there.

"Zachary? Are you there?" Walter looked around the door. Zachary stopped where he was, one hand on the wall to support himself.

"Come in. Sorry, I forgot to tell you to just let yourself in."

"The door was open…"

"I know."

Walter was frowning, studying him. "Is something wrong? Are you sick?"

Zachary didn't bother to answer. "Come on into the living room."

Walter obeyed, settling himself on the couch. Zachary remained on his feet. Not only was it better for his tailbone, but it gave him the advantage of being higher than Walter. A position of power. He could really use the edge since Walter had just about every other advantage over Zachary. Zachary leaned against a bookcase.

"You weren't honest with me about the break-in."

Walter looked surprised. "I wasn't honest with you? What are you talking about? I understand now that it was an inside job, but I didn't know that at the time."

"You weren't in on it?"

"Why would I be in on it? You found the stolen goods, so you know that I didn't get anything out of it. It was nothing to do with me."

"Then it was just bad luck?"

Walter blinked at him. The long, slow blink of a snake, focusing on an enemy. "What are you talking about?"

"I'm talking about the car."

"What car? I'm afraid you've gotten yourself all mixed up over this. I don't know what you mean."

"The replica Habs station wagon."

Walter's eyebrows went up. "I'm not sure I know what you're talking about," he said politely.

"One of the waitresses said that she's seen you fiddling with it, so there's no point in pretending. A little car just the right size to hide a USB drive in."

Walter shrugged. "Just because I may have touched it, that doesn't mean that it is something I would remember. I'm sure you've seen things at restaurants or other people's homes that you don't remember again later."

"If you weren't involved in the theft, then I guess you must have been pretty shocked by it. Not only that there would be a smash and grab at your 'favorite' sports bar, but that it would happen when it did and that the car would be taken."

Walter said nothing, still sitting there looking at Zachary as if he had no idea what he was talking about.

"You never thought that your dead drop would get stolen."

"Dead drop." Walter's face remained blankly impassive. But Zachary could see his jaw clench and a tendon stand out on his neck.

"Everybody wondered why you were so interested in the bar and in the robbery. Why you were interested in finding out who had committed the robbery and recovering the merchandise. Everybody wondered why you even went to the bar in the first place. You were out of place. You weren't interested in any of the sports. You weren't attached to any of the teams. You just went there, had a drink or a snack, and left again."

"Everybody relaxes their own way. I enjoyed the ambiance of the place."

"You needed a place where you could exchange information. I don't know if you were the one leaving the information or the one picking it up. Or did it go both ways?"

"What information?"

"The information on Drake Chase Gould."

Walter stared at him. He gave up on pretending not to know what Zachary was talking about. "Where is it?"

"It's not here."

"It wasn't in the boxes." Walter's eyes scanned the room. Did he think that Zachary would hide it there?

"I think it's time to give up on recovering it. It was a long shot from the start. You must be looking at other ways of recompiling it or getting another copy."

485

"It can take months to put together a package like that. Replicating it…" Walter shook his head. "That's not as easy as it sounds. People lose trust. In a game like this, you have to have trust. Or the flow of information dries up."

"Is that how you see it? A game?"

"Call it what you like. The stakes are high. Higher than you could ever realize."

47

"You want to take Drake Chase Gould down."

Walter's shoulders lifted and fell. He rubbed the back of his neck. "Unless you work in the circles that I do, you don't know the impact that a company like that has nationally and internationally. How many pieces of the political puzzle and the outcomes of bills and sessions depend on what is happening in the financial world. We live in a capitalist society. Everything hinges on money."

"What would bringing Drake Chase Gould down accomplish for you? Are you saying it's still political? Nothing to do with lining your own pocket?"

Walter made a face. "I have all of the money I need. Some things are far more important to me. I am someone who *makes things happen*. I don't know if someone like you can understand that."

Zachary nodded slowly. He understood that he and Walter operated in two completely different worlds. Their paths had crossed with each other, but they didn't really inhabit the same realms. From the beginning of his life, Zachary had struggled simply for survival. He had enough money now that putting a roof over his head and food on the table was no longer a problem, but he still saw the world through that lens. And it was a world that Walter had never inhabited. He had been born with money, as much of it as he needed.

Zachary had glimpsed that world for a short time while married to

Bridget. She hadn't been that wealthy herself, but she intended to be. She had wealthy and powerful friends, and she used them to improve her circumstances. She was well-spoken and beautiful; people liked her right from the start. Zachary wasn't sure why she had married him in the first place. She must have thought that she could mold him into what she wanted her husband to be. She had placed opportunities before him and encouraged him to talk to influential people and get involved in the political games, but that had never been for him. In his mind, he would always be fighting for survival.

That had been Zachary's first glimpse of Walter's world. He had seen more of it when Gordon had come into the picture. Not just to give Bridget everything she had ever dreamed of, but also showing Zachary the mercenary way he ran his business, how he used people as pawns, all while smiling and acting like a benevolent father. Daniel had said that Gordon was a psychopath and Zachary couldn't decide whether this was true or not. Gordon seemed like a nice guy, as did Walter, but were they just wolves in sheep's clothing? Men who had learned how to present themselves to others but who didn't really care about those around them?

Zachary was concerned with self-preservation, but he couldn't imagine not being concerned about the people around him. Bridget and Kenzie had both said it before, but in very different tones of voice. Zachary *had* to help people. He had to rescue them. He just didn't know how else to be.

"Do you even care?" Zachary mused, then realized that he'd said it out loud.

"Do I care about what?" Walter asked, shaking his head slightly.

"Do you care about anyone else? Do you care anything about what happens to the people around you? Or just about yourself?"

"I care very much for certain people in my life. And I want to make the world a better place for them. If I have influence, why shouldn't I use it?"

"And people who aren't in your little circle of friends and family, what about them? You don't care what happens to them?"

"I try to do the right thing," Walter said deliberately. "And I believe that if I do the right thing, aimed at helping those in my life, that the rest will fall into place. I can't be responsible for everybody. They will... take care of each other."

"When you sent two thugs here to get the stolen merchandise so that you could retrieve your USB drive, did you care what happened to me?

How Kenzie would feel about having someone break into her house? How she would feel if I got hurt or killed in the process?"

Walter chuckled. "You hire professionals to do the job they were trained to do. And then you trust them to do it."

"So, no. You didn't care."

Walter motioned to Zachary. "You seem to have survived the incident. To be honest, I didn't think you would be here. I assumed the house would be empty during the day." He shook his head. "I guess I had in my mind that you had an office somewhere that you operated from. Not just... this."

Walter rolled his eyes. Arrogant. Lowering his opinion of Zachary on learning that he just lounged around all day in Walter's daughter's house. Not a true professional, just a hanger-on.

"I heard that you were here when it happened, but they said that they hadn't had any trouble taking care of you. I would never authorize the use of violence or killing someone to get them out of the way. There are always other choices. I have made my living in finding ways to leverage people. Finding ways to change the world one step at a time, to make it a better place for my wife and daughter."

There was no hint of an "s" at the end of daughter. No hint that he had also been thinking of Amanda as he had been working at changing the world.

Walter studied Zachary. "What happened? You don't look good. But then... you don't usually."

"The way they threw me down and restrained me may have caused some spinal cord damage. I'm supposed to be in bed."

"Well, at least sit down," Walter looked slightly alarmed. "I don't want you collapsing on me."

"Sitting is worse than standing."

"I never intended anything to happen to you. I gave you the case, didn't I? Why would I turn on you and try to hurt you? It was supposed to be a simple operation. In and out. Grab the boxes and get out. Faster than the original burglary. Things always go better when you use professionals." He raised an eyebrow, looking at Zachary. "Almost always."

Zachary wasn't sure whether he was referring to the thugs who had injured him or the fact that Zachary hadn't produced the hoped-for results.

"And Kenzie? You didn't think of how she would feel having her house broken into? Scared? Violated? You didn't care about any of that?"

"It was more important to get that information back. More important than some fleeting emotions." Walter held up his hand to stop Zachary from interjecting. "I know my daughter. She may react emotionally to begin with, but she gets over it quickly. She will find a way to move on."

"What about when she knows it was you?"

Walter gazed at Zachary. He pressed his fingertips together in a steeple shape. "I was not planning on her finding out that it had anything to do with me."

He didn't ask Zachary not to tell her. He was used to making things happen, so maybe he already had a plan in mind to keep Kenzie from finding out. And now that Zachary knew... maybe Walter had a new plan for him too.

"I don't want Kenzie to find out," Zachary told him. "I want her to be happy. To have a relationship with you that isn't so... negative. She deserves to have good family relationships."

"Yes. She does."

"Do you know anything about Gordon Drake, the man who owns Drake Chase Gould?"

"Of course. I made it my business to know about him."

"I mean personally. Do you know what kind of a person he is? Or about his family commitments?"

Walter shook his head. "Why would I? It isn't his family life that concerns me."

"He's a family man. Has a wife with Huntington's disease and newborn twin girls. Premature, so they have health issues. And also the Huntington's gene."

Something flickered in Walter's eyes. "That's too bad. That's a tough situation."

"Tough. I don't think you know how tough it is to have a wife who is dying."

"No?" Walter looked at him. "That's so different from having a daughter who is dying?"

Zachary considered. "I don't know. Maybe it isn't. How would you have felt about someone who came gunning for your business while Amanda was sick?"

48

This isn't personal. I told you that. Drake Chase Gould is not good for business in Vermont. Having a big investment banking firm here—it's not what we do. He thinks that he can just pay off anyone in the state. Anything he wants, he can just throw money at it, and it will go away. Take it to the big city. Why isn't he operating on Wall Street like everyone else? Vermont is community minded. Small towns, small businesses, families."

"Maybe because he has a wife and children to take care of. Maybe he doesn't want them in New York and doesn't want to be away from them while he operates from there."

"He needs to take care of his own. That's not my responsibility."

"His wife is my ex," Zachary told Walter. "She *is* family."

Walter rubbed his brow line, scowling. "Why would she be with someone like him after being with you? You and Gordon Drake are nothing alike."

"I know," Zachary agreed. He braced himself against the wall, his legs getting tired and his tailbone throbbing. Were his legs weak just because of the pain in his tailbone? Or was it the neurological damage that Kenzie and the doctor at the hospital had feared?

"You're supposed to be lying down," Walter told him.

"Yeah."

"Where do you want to lie down? The couch? The bed?"

"Bed." Zachary already knew how uncomfortable sleeping on the couch was. And it would be that much worse with his injured tailbone.

Walter got up and took Zachary by the arm. He held him firmly and guided him down the hallway back to the bedroom. He helped Zachary to get over to the bed, and Zachary tried to climb in without aggravating his tailbone, back, or any other part of his body that was bruised or sore, which was basically impossible.

"This is from the robbery?" Walter demanded. "The guys who stole the mementos from you?"

"Yeah. They didn't give you any details?" Zachary thought it was best not to indicate that his most painful injury was his tailbone. That would make it sound like a joke.

Anything could have happened in the robbery that Walter had set up, knowing that he was sending professional criminals to his daughter's house, where they could run into either Zachary or Kenzie. He didn't know their schedules or anything about them. Those goons could have pulled knives or guns when they encountered Zachary in the house. If they hadn't been wearing masks, they would have been faced with the dilemma of whether to kill Zachary in case he could identify them. They could be murderers, rapists, terrorists. Walter had known they were bad news, and he'd sent them into his daughter's house.

"I didn't ask for details," Walter admitted. "I got the report that you had been here at the house but that they had dealt with you. I didn't think I needed to know any more than that."

"They invaded my house. They tackled me, handcuffed me, left me that way. I could have been knocked over the head and ended up with a fractured skull. Had my throat slit. I could have had a heart attack. You didn't care?"

"I didn't say I didn't care. I said I didn't want details."

Zachary heard the garage door motor. Walter stood there looking at him. It was early for Kenzie to be getting home. Walter had probably thought that she was at work and had been counting on the fact that she would be gone until the early evening. He didn't know that she had just been out running errands.

They listened to the kitchen door opening and Kenzie hanging up her winter gear and then coming down the hall. She didn't call out, but looked around the doorway first to see if Zachary was asleep. She saw her father standing there and her jaw dropped open. No words came out.

"Hi, sweetie," Walter greeted, stepping toward her and giving her a hug and a kiss on the cheek. "I'm so glad you're home. I didn't know how long you would be out."

"Just a couple of hours," Kenzie said, her voice heavy with suspicion. "Just running some errands. Picking up a few things for Zachary."

Walter motioned to the bed. "I was just helping Zachary to get settled again. Came over to discuss the case and any progress he had made."

Kenzie looked at him, eyes narrowed. "I thought the case was finished. Zachary identified who stole the memorabilia and recovered the stolen property. That's the end of it, isn't it? It isn't his fault that they were stolen again from here, and I don't want him wasting his time chasing after them again. Especially not while he's still recovering. I'd say the case is done and you owe him the rest of the agreed-upon price, wouldn't you say?"

Walter nodded. "Yes. I just wanted to get a few more details from Zachary. I will send him the money to wrap this up right away." He smiled at her. "I'm not trying to rip him off."

"No renegotiating. You just give him what you said you would, and no more investigating. The case is done."

"Yes, MacKenzie," Walter agreed in a smooth, soothing voice. "I'm not here to ask Zachary to do anything else. In fact," he turned and met Zachary's eyes. "I want to make sure he *doesn't* try to pursue any more action in this case. Not after being injured. Leave the police to clean up any loose ends. I don't think there is any point in trying to trace the stolen articles any farther. It isn't like they were that valuable. I was just hoping to do something for a friend."

Kenzie nodded. "Good." She looked past him to Zachary. "And *you're* not going to pursue it any further on your own, are you? This case has already been enough of a pain. Whoever has those things now, let them keep them."

"It's too bad we weren't able to return them to the McNichols," Zachary said slowly, staring at Walter. "They've really had some bad luck with all of this. The memorabilia wasn't valuable enough to claim it on their insurance. The police detective thinks that they were involved. Glen had a heart attack and is convalescing. I hope they get a lot of donations to replace what they lost and success with their fundraising for anything else. They *deserve* that."

Walter nodded. "Yes, of course. They are good friends. I wouldn't want any lasting harm to come to them because of this."

"I hope things turn out for them too," Kenzie agreed. "It's been quite a run of bad luck."

Zachary rested his head and closed his eyes. Maybe now he would be able to sleep. It had been quite the afternoon. But he thought that, even with being on painkillers, he had done a good job of sorting things out to correct as much of the damage as he could. Drake Chase Gould had back the data that had been stolen, so it couldn't be used against them. He and Walter agreed that nothing more would be done to harm any of the people involved. And hopefully, Walter would make the McNichols whole, donating memorabilia or cash back to them. It would be like none of it had ever happened.

"You should invite your dad for supper," he suggested to Kenzie. "You didn't have any plans, did you? We can just order something in."

"I don't know if I want to have a dinner party when you're not able to participate," Kenzie pointed out. Being forced to make small talk over dinner with her father without Zachary being there to act as a buffer was probably not what she would have planned if they had talked about it ahead of time.

"You haven't visited with your dad for a long time. You don't have anything else you have to do, do you, Walter?"

Of course Walter had said that he had the rest of the day booked up, all kinds of things to get done. But he had made the time to come see Zachary. And he said that he wanted the opportunity to connect with his daughter. They were both going to have to make some adjustments if they wanted to have a good relationship. Kenzie had been doing couples therapy with Zachary, so she should have some good tools in her communications toolkit for finding common ground and being cordial to her father. So that maybe it could develop into something more in the future.

"No, of course I can make time," Walter said. "It doesn't have to be anything fancy. I can drive to the sandwich shop and pick something up, if you like. Do you still like tuna salad?"

Kenzie snorted. "You know I don't like tuna!"

Walter gave a smile, enjoying her reaction. He had obviously intended to provoke her.

"How about you, Zachary? Sandwich shop? Or do you want something hot?"

"You and Kenzie could go out to a restaurant if you wanted to. I'm not really hungry."

"No. I'm not leaving you alone the rest of the night," Kenzie interjected. "Here. Let me help you get more comfortable, and then we can decide what we're ordering."

49

Kenzie had spent longer having dinner and visiting with Walter than Zachary had expected. Zachary had spent most of the time sleeping, his body exhausted by the combination of pain, medications, and the visits with Walter and Bieberstein. He didn't talk much to Kenzie after Walter left. She came in and cuddled with him as best she could with his injury, rubbed his sore muscles for a while, and both of them drifted off to sleep. So it wasn't until the following day that they really talked about how her evening with Walter had gone.

"It actually wasn't a bad visit," Kenzie said, smiling and lifting her eyebrows to express her surprise over the fact. "Usually, when I see him, he wants something. Or even if it is just for a visit, it's on his own terms. He has his own agenda and plan, like it's a business lunch. But last night, there was no agenda. He was just here. And he didn't have a bunch of other meetings to run off to like usual. It was like... being at home again."

Zachary nodded. He was sitting at the table, which made him feel more human and less of an invalid. He could get reasonably comfortable with one of the coccyx-cradling pillows that Kenzie had purchased for him. His tailbone was still sore, but he could sit up for a while. He also found that his back was a lot sorer than he had expected it to be. Kenzie had talked about the possibility of a compression injury to his spine, and he felt like everything had been bruised or pulled. The muscles in his back felt like he had overdone it lifting weights at the gym.

Or what he assumed it would feel like if he had overdone it at the gym, since he wasn't actually one for lifting weights.

He unwrapped his granola bar slowly, trying to minimize the amount of crinkling noise the wrapper made, which he found extra irritating all of a sudden. "I'm glad you had a good visit with him. It's been a long time, hasn't it?"

Kenzie looked thoughtful. "Yeah. I don't know if we've really had a good sit down and just talked about life, what we're doing, and our interests since Amanda died. We've talked, sure, on the phone and the occasional face-to-face, usually at some fundraising event that Mother has roped us both into. You can't actually talk at something like that. Not like last night."

"What did you talk about?"

She shrugged and spread marmalade on her toast. "Just... stuff. Movies, weather, holidays, work. Anything and everything. I've never really listened to him talk about his lobbying. I kind of shut that off, decided that he was dishonest and that I didn't want to hear anything about it. Especially back then, when he was lobbying so much for changes in the transplant system. I was really angry with him for what happened to Amanda."

"But that was a long time ago now."

She nodded. "Sometimes it seems like it was just yesterday. But that was before I even decided to go into medicine. I'd done some college, but then I just drifted. Mom told me that I would figure out what I wanted to do sooner or later, but I wasn't passionate about anything. She had all of her causes and taking care of Amanda, and I just messed around, wasting my time. I wish I had decided to go into medicine earlier, but..." She shrugged. "I guess she was right. I just needed time to figure out what I wanted out of life."

"And you've changed your mind about Walter's lobbying?" Zachary asked, circling back to what she had said.

"I don't know. Like I said, I didn't really give him a chance before. You know, when we were little, I always knew that he was a white hat. One of the good guys. Lobbying for reforms that would benefit society. Not one of the lobbyists who hire themselves out to the big gun corporations and try to pave the way for them to make more money or a bigger piece of the pie. Then I kind of changed my mind. Not a black hat, maybe, but it was a lot darker gray than they had told me as a kid."

"Is anyone really all white hat or black hat?"

"No, I guess not. But I enjoyed hearing him talk last night about what he is doing to help people. Some of the initiatives he is working on sound really worthwhile."

"And did you tell him all about your work with the medical examiner?"

Kenzie grinned. She took a big bite of her toast and chewed it while she considered her answer. "He's not as squeamish as I thought he would be. I guess he's gotten used to the fact that I work with dead bodies. Braced himself for it. I wouldn't discuss the state of the bodies I see or the results of the tests run on tissue and fluid sample over dinner with him like I can with you, but he held up pretty well."

Zachary chuckled. If Walter talked too much about his lobbying or about a cause where Kenzie wasn't on the same side as he was, Kenzie could easily change the subject to the details of her own work. Then they could choose a less controversial topic, like movies or the weather, that they could both agree on.

"I guess maybe he isn't quite the villain I thought he was," Kenzie admitted. "I may have judged him too harshly. Or... maybe he is just mellowing more with age. People do tend to get a little less... intense over time. He hasn't let go of his ideals, but... maybe it was just last night. He just seemed more open. Less opinionated or zealous. Something like that."

Zachary thought back to Walter's comments about Drake Chase Gould. He hadn't seemed very mellow when he talked about the danger that a corporate giant like Chase Gold could be to a small state like Vermont. Maybe he was just learning to hold back his opinions when talking to his daughter. Set aside the agenda for the night and just enjoy being with her for once.

"I'm glad you had a nice time with him."

"Me too."

It was Sunday, so probably not the best day to call Blair Bieberstein back to see whether he'd been able to get anywhere on his analysis of the server logs and tracking back who had leaked the information on the USB drive. But Zachary knew from past experience that the employees at Chase Gold worked long hours, both weekdays and weekends. He decided to give it a try anyway. Kenzie was in her office catching up on some personal emails. Maybe emailing Lisa, her mother, about the visit with Walter.

Zachary tapped the number on his phone. He was expecting to have to wait a number of rings before Bieberstein got around to answering his phone. He would be distracted by whatever job he was working on. He might even completely ignore his phone and Zachary would have to leave a message or call back later. But he'd only heard one ring before Bieberstein picked it up.

"Goldman!" he greeted.

Zachary wasn't used to being addressed that way, but shrugged it off. "Hey. I was just wondering whether you had been able to get anywhere on the data on the USB drive. I know these things probably take a lot more time and analysis, but..."

"Right, right. The USB drive." Bieberstein sounded even more hyper than usual, if that was possible. Maybe he'd just polished off a couple of energy drinks. Caffeine was definitely one of his vices. Zachary still wasn't sure if he went for the harder stuff. They'd discussed meth at one point, but Bieberstein hadn't admitted to being a user himself. "Did some analysis on the servers..." He went off into a long, technical spiel about what he had done to backtrack where the data had come from and who'd had access to it over the previous few weeks. Zachary was quickly lost in the jargon.

"So, where did that get you?" he interrupted when he heard Bieberstein stop for breath and maybe another gulp of his high-octane drink. "Did that get you any closer to figuring out who it was that stole or leaked the information?"

"I'm telling you, man," Bieberstein assured him.

"Okay..."

Bieberstein went through some more of the procedures he had gone through. "But then I got a call from Mr. Drake. He wanted to know what was going on, why I was into the security files. So I explained to him about the leak. I didn't tell him where I got the USB drive," he assured Zachary. "Don't worry. I remembered not to mention your name, just my geeky friend who didn't want to be brought into anything."

"What did Gordon say about it?"

"He's a good guy, Mr. Drake. You remember that he helped me out when I got out of the hospital. Made sure that I was somewhere safe until all of that stuff blew over."

"Yes. I remember. He seems like a good guy." Zachary didn't want to say more than that. Whether Gordon was really a good guy, deep down, or just a psychopath who put on a good show of caring for people. Zachary didn't know and didn't want to speculate.

"Anyway. He pulled me off of it. Told me to get back to my regular work, that he would put the cybersecurity guys on it. We've got a contract with this high-priced IT team. Very good at what they do. I probably should have talked to them in the beginning anyway, rather than diving into it myself. But I thought I would be able to identify who it was that had copied the files initially…"

"You didn't find out who it was?"

"No."

Zachary rolled his eyes. Bieberstein could just have said that to begin with, instead of going through the long narrative of what he had done to try to track the culprits down.

"Will you find out what these cybersecurity guys discover? Will Gordon let you know who it was?"

"No. Not my area, so I highly doubt it. Mr. Drake likes people to stay in their own lane. Security isn't my forte, so he probably won't get back to me on any of it. I'm good at it, mind you. Whoever stole those files did a really good job hiding their footprints. But I get why he wants me to stick to my job. I already bounce between departments and different projects, depending on where my expertise is needed. He has to put some kind of limits on where I am and what I'm doing."

It sounded more like that was what Bieberstein had been told than that he agreed with it.

Zachary sighed. So his one avenue of exploration into Drake Chase Gould had been closed off. He could call Gordon and ask him about what they found out, but since it was really none of Zachary's business and Gordon's attitude toward him had cooled lately, he figured the chances Gordon would tell him anything about it were pretty slim.

50

Zachary was taking a walk around the block when Janice called. He was getting a bit of cabin fever, mainly staying indoors, as it was still too painful to go for a drive in the car, even with one of the special pillows. The bumps and potholes were just too much for him. Kenzie said that he should be starting to feel better before too long and, in the meantime, if he couldn't drive, he could at least go for a walk. Get out, get some fresh air and sunshine, and he would feel a lot better than if he just stayed home staring at the computer screen all day. Just don't slip on the ice and fall on his coccyx.

It was good advice, except that Zachary was now paranoid about slipping on a stray patch of ice and landing again on his broken tailbone. Who knew if it would ever heal properly if he did that. Most of the neighbors kept their sidewalks well-shoveled, so there really wasn't anything to worry about. Still, one or two places had not been properly shoveled throughout the winter and were covered in ice and packed-down snow. They were shiny and slick in the sunlight. Zachary strayed off the sidewalk and into front yards to avoid the super-slick surfaces.

His phone ringing made him jump, which made him panic about slipping and falling. But in a second or two, he had regained his equilibrium and worked his phone out of his pocket, taking off his glove to answer it.

"Goldman Investigations."

"It's Janice McNichol, Zachary."

"Oh!" Zachary smiled. It felt like a long time since he'd talked to her. Ages ago.

"You know, I never did thank you for the work that you did on our burglary—on the theft of the memorabilia from our bar. I know that I wasn't the one who hired you and I was kind of resistant at first, but I'm glad that Mr. Kirsch was able to get you on the case. I feel a lot better knowing that it wasn't just a random burglary. That probably doesn't make sense because you would think I would be more worried about it being random than planned... but I'm not. I feel a lot better knowing that it was someone who had the inside track and that she isn't here anymore. I don't have to worry about it happening again."

"You can have background checks run on people before you hire them. Or in the probationary period after you hire them. If you want to be more sure of this not happening again."

"But Jenn wasn't a new hire. She'd been there for a few years. It was that new boyfriend of hers. And I don't think we can get background checks run on every new boyfriend or girlfriend that our employees hook up with. Jenn passed all of the pre-screening that we did. I don't think you can stop people from meeting someone else who influences them three years later."

"No," Zachary admitted. "You're right about that. You couldn't have known what would happen."

"Yeah. And I don't think the odds are very high of it ever happening again. And Glen is getting some cameras installed inside and outside the bar so that people know they're being watched. If they're being watched, I don't think they'd do anything like that."

"It's a good deterrent. Just make sure it's not the only thing you are relying on. You know how they were able to get in to go through the charade of a smash and grab, so you need to fortify the windows and doors a little better. And be aware of what's going on, anything that seems out of place. I don't know if there was ever any sign that Jennifer was having financial issues or any problems with her boyfriend, or if everything just seemed perfectly normal up until the end..."

"Well..." Janice drew the word out. "Hard to put your finger on anything. But she had changed. She wasn't as happy. Got in late for her shift some days, which she had never done before. But nothing that would have predicted what she was going to do."

"No. But maybe if you knew something was wrong, you might have talked to her, and she might have done or said something to clue you in that everything wasn't right with her. Or *not*, there's no point in what-ifs. You did the best you could, and now you know a few more things you can do to improve security some more. Maybe you prevent a bigger theft in the future."

"That's right!" Janice agreed, sounding happy and relaxed about it. Zachary was glad. He hadn't wanted to make her feel guilty for not knowing what Jennifer had been about to do before she did it. No one could predict the future. "And we might have more that we need to protect in the future."

"Oh? Your fundraising has gone well?"

"It's been amazing. You wouldn't believe it. We got a couple of large donations from anonymous donors. Corporate donations, I would guess, because they're too big for patrons. And we've had a lot of memorabilia donated as well. We published a list of what we had lost on our social media networks. Some of the things that have been donated to replace them are almost identical to the originals. It's amazing."

"That's great." Zachary chuckled to himself, glad to hear that Walter had gone ahead with helping Barnburners get back to where they had been before the robbery. Some of that "almost identical" memorabilia were probably the exact same items as had been stolen from them in the first place. "How about that little die-cast Habs car? Did you get one of those?"

"No. Not yet, at least. They were a limited run. Those things always are because it increases their value. I'd love to get another one, but I don't know if we'll be able to find one. Maybe some time."

Zachary frowned and wondered what Walter had done with the Habs car. Kept it as a trophy? As a reminder of what he had done to get back into his daughter's good graces? Maybe he kept trophies of all of his wins. Or perhaps it had attracted the eye of one of the goons and he had pocketed it before giving the rest of the merchandise to Walter.

Whatever had happened to it, the bar wouldn't miss that one little item. They had been more than compensated for their loss. Though Walter couldn't do much to make up for the cloud of suspicion they had been under or for Glen's heart attack.

"How is Glen doing? Is he still in the hospital?"

"No, they don't keep them for very long. Snake out the pipes and send them home. He's doing pretty good, to tell the truth. Better than I thought he would be. The doctors say it's lucky he found out now about his arteries before they were totally blocked. He's young enough that if he takes care of himself—stops eating fried food and staying up late at the bar, maybe gets out for a walk now and then—that he can probably live a long and happy life. With some young guys, the first time anyone knows they have heart disease is when they have a massive coronary and drop dead."

"Well, good thing that didn't happen to him."

"I guess if you're going to have a heart attack, a police station is a good place to do it. Full of trained first responders. One of those AEDs right there. If he'd been at the bar late at night or out on the highway... he could be dead now."

51

Lindsey dropped Mason and Alisha at the house, stopping for a moment on the doorstep to thank Zachary and Kenzie.

"I appreciate you taking them to see him. I didn't want to visit Tyrrell myself, but what else was I going to do, sit in the lobby while they visited with him in a family visit room? That would be pretty awkward. And driving all the way out there just to sit and wait for the kids... this is so much nicer."

"We were going to see him anyway," Zachary said with a shrug. "I knew he'd like to see the kids, so I figured they might as well come along if it worked for you."

She nodded. "It's really nice of you. I know that it's not always easy to deal with kids who aren't your own, especially when they are..." She looked significantly at Mason and made a face, not putting it into words in case Mason overheard her.

"I get to be the uncle who spoils them," Zachary said. "You're the one who gets to deal with them afterward."

"Well, don't give them too much sugar!" She smiled again in appreciation. "Goodbye, guys. You be good for your Uncle Zachary, you hear me?"

"We will, Mom," Alisha assured her.

Mason, of course, was distracted and didn't answer. He was looking closely at the burglar alarm panel.

"I bet I could figure out your password," he told Zachary.

"Mason," Lindsey said in a firm mom voice.

He glanced over at her but decided she wasn't serious enough for him to pay attention to her yet. "Do you think I could?" he persisted. "I can see which buttons you push most often. It would be like solving a code."

"Mason, your mom is talking to you," Zachary pointed out.

Mason heaved a sigh and looked at her. "What?" he demanded, as if she were the child and was getting on his nerves with her constant questions.

"You be good for Uncle Zachary and Auntie Kenzie."

"I will!" Mason gave another exasperated sigh. "I was just talking to him. You were interrupting."

Lindsey shook her head at Zachary and stepped back. "Have a nice visit. I'll see you guys in a few hours."

Both of the children said goodbye.

"We're going in Zachary's car," Kenzie told them after Lindsey left. "He'll go get it warmed up, and you come with me and tell me what you want to bring for a snack."

She led them into the kitchen to look into the cupboard that Kenzie kept stocked with snacks that Zachary liked, to encourage him to consume more calories and get his weight back up to normal. Zachary went out to his car, started the heater, and scraped frost off the windows. By the time they got out to the car with their snacks in hand, the inside was comfortable.

They were good for the trip out to the detox center, playing on their phones or electronic games and munching on snacks. Zachary enjoyed the highway drive and the fact that he could sit comfortably in the car again, even without the special cushions. Though he was using one since they would be in the car for longer than he was used to, and he didn't want to take the chance that the weight on his tailbone would cause the injury to flare up again, even if it were only temporarily.

He liked highway driving, though with Kenzie and the kids in the car, he had to watch the speedometer and not go too much over the speed limit. Any time he caught the turning of Kenzie's head to look at the gauge, he lifted his foot off the gas to slow it down.

Zachary felt like it had been a year since he had seen Tyrrell. It wasn't as bad as when he had been missing, of course. Finding him while he was out on a drunken binge had been such a huge relief when Tyrrell had been missing for weeks and Zachary hadn't even known for sure whether he was alive.

This time, he knew he wouldn't be facing a sloppy hug and Tyrrell's sorrowful ramblings about what an awful father he was to his kids and that he could never go back to them again. Zachary wouldn't have to face his father. This time, Tyrrell would be clean and sober, and he would have a better outlook on his future. Plans for how to get back on his feet again and be a part of the children's lives.

After checking in at the reception desk, a young man in scrubs met their little group and escorted them around to a family visit room. There was comfortable, worn furniture, some toys and books on shelves, a checkers/chess game set, and a few other things to help keep families occupied during visits.

They waited there, Mason bouncing on the couch and chairs to test them out and rifling through the shelves to see if he could find anything interesting. Knowing how attached he was to his electronic games, Zachary didn't expect him to find anything there that would keep his interest for long. Would things have been better or worse for Zachary if there had been handheld games around when he was a kid battling with ADHD? Being forced to play outside was a common strategy foster parents used. It was probably better to get hyperactive kids out in the fresh air doing physical activities than letting them hyperfocus on electronic games.

Then Tyrrell arrived. Mason squealed and launched himself at Tyrrell, giving him a tight hug and immediately launching into a long-winded explanation of everything he had done since he last saw Tyrrell. Tyrrell reached for Alisha to pull her into a hug as well, kissing her on top of the head and whispering something in her ear that made her smile.

Zachary and Kenzie waited until the kids had taken a little time to get reacquainted with Tyrrell and had settled down into their chosen seats before also greeting Tyrrell and giving him hugs and congratulations for being able to stick with the program for six weeks.

He looked good. Happy and clean and strong. The Tyrrell that Zachary had been used to seeing before he had fallen off the wagon. But this time, Zachary knew that it was partly an illusion. Yes, Tyrrell was getting better, but he wasn't "cured." He hadn't left alcoholism behind years ago, as Zachary had first assumed when Tyrrell had told him he'd had problems with alcohol. It was still very present in his life and something the rest of them would always have to be mindful of.

"How's it going, bro?" Tyrrell asked happily, thumping Zachary on the back as they hugged. "You're looking a lot better than the last time I saw you."

A testament to Kenzie's efforts to get him into better physical shape, eating better, getting a little exercise, and trying to get into a routine that would allow him to get more sleep at night, though that one seemed to be an elusive goal.

"You are, too," Zachary told him.

"Hell, I hope so!" Tyrrell laughed. "Considering the shape I was in before I got here!"

"Daddy!" Alisha exclaimed, horrified. "You swore!"

Tyrrell chuckled. "I'll put a quarter in your mother's swear jar the next time I'm there," he promised. Which wasn't much of a promise, considering that he would probably never be in Lindsey's house again. Maybe to step in the door while he waited for the kids to get ready, but more likely, he'd wait in the car while she got them dressed and packed and then sent them out.

Tyrrell gave Kenzie a quick hug and kiss on the cheek after releasing Zachary. "And thank you for getting me into this program," he told her. He looked like he would say something more but then thought better of it. Maybe he'd realized that Kenzie hadn't just used her medical connections to get him into the program, but had paid for his stay as well. If he acknowledged that he knew she had spent money for him to get into the program, it would mean that he was accountable to her if he ever fell off the wagon again. And, of course, he would probably fall off of the wagon again. Sobriety was not a journey in a straight line.

They sat down and asked Tyrrell all about the program and his progress and plans for the future. He'd had plenty of therapy and career counseling. The facility was associated with several outpatient placement programs, so maybe they would be able to find him a job when he was ready to venture into the world again. Somewhere like K&L Construction, where he'd been given a chance despite their knowing that he was a recovering alcoholic? Or would they help him find a career placement that was more suited to him? Zachary hadn't thought that casual labor and construction were a good fit for Tyrrell. But of course, he took what he could get. Someone with his history didn't get a lot of opportunities.

Mason was playing with a car, getting louder and louder with the engine noises he was making with his mouth. Tyrrell tried to quiet him a couple of times, and they all rolled their eyes at each other, knowing that he wouldn't quiet down for long, but would soon be back to the same volume as he had been.

Zachary looked over at Mason, watching him for a minute. He had been wrong about Mason choosing his electronic games over something more physical. He must have found a toy car that he liked on the shelves of toys in the room.

He was looking at the car in Mason's hand for a minute before he realized that it was not one he had found on the shelves of the visitor's room. It was a little die-cast station wagon with the red horseshoe shape of the Montreal Canadiens logo on the side.

Kenzie had been saying something to Tyrrell about the different therapies offered in the program but stopped speaking, looking at Zachary questioningly.

"You okay?" she asked tentatively.

Zachary stared at the car in Mason's hand, trying to think of the right response to the question.

"Zachary?"

"Where did you get that car, Mason?" Zachary asked.

Mason looked at him, mouth open to answer, and then closed it abruptly. He tried to shove the car back into his coat pocket. "From a friend," he mumbled.

"Mason, come over here."

Mason reluctantly approached his uncle. Zachary put his hands on Mason's shoulders, looking him in the eye. "That looks like the car that you were playing with at my house."

"It's Auntie Kenzie's house," Mason pointed out.

"Yes, it's Auntie Kenzie's house. Isn't this the car that I told you was not yours? That you were supposed to put back in the boxes with the rest of those things?"

Mason's eyes were wide. He looked around the room guiltily, searching for an acceptable answer. Tyrrell's face was red, but he didn't interrupt to reprimand Mason.

"You took it with you instead of putting it back in the boxes, didn't you?" Zachary prompted.

"No. It's like that one, but this one is from a friend." Mason displayed the car. "The one that was at Auntie Kenzie's house didn't have this on it," he told Zachary, pointing to a long scratch along the side.

"Can I look at it for a minute?" Zachary asked.

Mason handed it over reluctantly. "It isn't yours," he insisted.

Zachary looked the car over, then tried opening the side doors and the back door where he knew the USB drive must have been hidden.

The side doors opened out, as Mason had been trying to show him at the time.

But the back door did not. There was no way anyone could have wedged a USB drive into the car.

52

Zachary was watching the TV casually while typing a message to Rhys. Not paying a lot of attention to the TV, but watching it in the breaks where he waited for Rhys to message him back. Rhys hadn't had a lot to say to Zachary since their argument. Zachary hoped that enough time had passed for Rhys to let go of whatever anger and resentment he had and be on the way back to being friends again.

Relationships were a tricky thing. Especially when they involved teenagers, with all of their volatility.

He looked up at the TV screen when the next news story came up. In surprise, Zachary looked at the man on the screen and called out to Kenzie.

"Hey, your dad is on TV."

"What?" Kenzie was down the hall. Zachary hadn't been paying any attention to whether she had been doing work in her office, cleaning the bathroom, or doing something else. He'd been focused on his own thing. "Walter's on TV?"

She walked into the living room and stood slightly to the side, so she wasn't obstructing Zachary's view line, and looked at the screen. To begin with, it was just a still photograph of Walter with a few words about his work on the bottom of the screen and the newsreader announcing the new story about a bill being passed. Then there was a video of Walter talking about the reasons for the bill being passed and the benefits that it would have to the people of Vermont.

"Turn it up."

Zachary thumbed the remote, turning the volume up for Kenzie. Then there was a video of Walter shaking hands with another man. The two of them smiled and posed for the camera, arms around each other's shoulders.

The other man was Gordon Drake.

Zachary stared at the screen, jaw dropping. He looked at Kenzie and then back at the screen in disbelief. "That's Gordon."

"Oh, yeah," Kenzie nodded. She had only seen Gordon in person once or twice. "I didn't know that they knew each other, did you?"

Zachary remembered his confrontation with Walter after the theft of the memorabilia from the house. Walter railing about how bad Drake Chase Gould was for Vermont. The dangers of having such a huge corporate entity making decisions that affected everyone because of their impact on the local economy. Walter had made it clear that Drake Chase Gould was an evil Vermont had to be rid of.

And now he and Gordon Drake were standing arm in arm as it was announced that the bill Chase Gold had sponsored had gone through the senate.

Zachary tried to reconcile the two opposing pictures.

His first thought was that Walter had used the private data from Chase Gold to blackmail or pressure Gordon into sponsoring the bill. That was why he had been gathering information. Not to take Chase Gold down or to take them over, but to be able to pressure and manipulate them into sponsoring the initiative he was lobbying for.

Walter had always seen himself as a white hat, Kenzie had told Zachary. But that didn't mean that he couldn't use a corporate sponsor to push through a law that he saw as beneficial.

But Walter had never seen that data that had been left for him at the bar. Zachary had found the USB drive and returned it to Chase Gold before it had reached its intended destination. Walter had done everything he could to get it back, including hiring Zachary and then arranging to steal the recovered goods back from him. But he hadn't been successful. He hadn't ever laid eyes on those files.

That didn't mean that he couldn't get it from somewhere else. Maybe the person who had leaked it had made an extra copy of the data for safekeeping. Or Walter had gotten more data from another source. Walter could still have the information Zachary thought he had protected.

Looking at Gordon's and Walter's smiling faces and their arms around each other, Zachary had a sick feeling in his stomach.

What if the whole thing had been a setup, from start to finish? What if there had never been any actual corporate espionage? What if it had all been a sham? Walter got one of the thugs to drop the USB drive in Kenzie's office when they stole the boxes of recovered memorabilia. Zachary found it, reviewed the contents, and discovered what appeared to be private information about Chase Gold.

Why hadn't the drive been password protected?

What were the chances that the stolen data would just happen to be about a company that Zachary had been involved with before and had contacts at?

Had Zachary unmasked Walter? Or had Walter set up an elaborate scheme that had placed Zachary in a place of apparent power over him, establishing this secret between them that bonded them together. Something that they both kept from Kenzie.

It was that secret and the injury that had sidelined Zachary that had paved the way for Kenzie and Walter to spend a pleasant dinner and evening together, beginning to heal the rift that had been between them ever since Amanda's death.

Zachary had always been amazed at chess players and how the masters could see so many moves ahead and determined the outcome of the game before it had been played out. Was that what Walter had done? Arranged the chessboard so that there was only one possible outcome of the game?

"We should have Walter over for dinner again sometime," Kenzie said, still watching her father's image on the screen. "This time, with you back on your feet again, you can join in."

Zachary nodded slowly. "Yeah," he agreed. "You should see your dad again."

THEY CAME FOR HIM

To those imprisoned by lies
and the truth

———————

1

———

Zachary's phone rang as he breakfasted with Kenzie. He knew better than to answer it at dinnertime unless it was an emergency, but he didn't usually have to worry about it ringing during breakfast, so he wasn't sure how to handle it. He glanced at Kenzie, who raised her brows questioningly. Zachary decided he'd better at least check to see who it was. It could be Heather, his older sister, calling to let him know that there was a client he needed to deal with urgently. Or it could be Lorne Peterson, his old foster father and long-time friend, who wanted to reach him while Kenzie was still home to invite them over for dinner or let them know something that was going on. It would be rare for a client or anyone else to call him first thing in the morning.

The caller ID was Jocelyn Goldman, his oldest sister.

Zachary's stomach plummeted. He couldn't think of any reason Joss would call him so early. The fact was that she never called him at all. He occasionally called her to see how she was doing, ask after Luke, or let her know that he would be in the area and was hoping to stop in for a visit. But Joss kept herself separated from everyone else, not getting close emotionally.

He swiped to answer and held the phone to his ear.

"Joss?"

"There's been some trouble," Joss said, bypassing any greeting or small talk.

Zachary swallowed. Had Joss gotten herself into trouble? Or had Luke? Was it something to do with Madison, Luke's former girlfriend, who Zachary had rescued from human traffickers? Or with Rhys, Zachary's young Black friend who was romantically interested in Luke? Zachary had been doing his best to keep them apart, but Rhys was a teenager and wasn't about to be told what to do.

As far as he knew, Joss hadn't had any contact with her old life and had been staying away from drugs. Still, he had thought the same of Tyrrell, his younger brother, before he had given in to his addiction a few months earlier. Was *she* the one who was in trouble?

Or was it something completely different? Since Joss kept to herself so much, there could be a hundred things going on that Zachary had no idea of.

He licked dry lips. "What's wrong?"

Across the table from him, Kenzie had put down her toast and was leaning forward, dark eyes worried, echoing his concern.

"Luke has been arrested."

Zachary swore under his breath. What had the boy done now? He knew that Joss had been worried about him lately, concerned that he could be tempted back into his old life. It was difficult to leave behind a life of addiction and almost impossible to leave a crime syndicate like the one that Luke had been involved in. Despite the abuses he had suffered at the hands of his bosses in the human trafficking ring, it was easier to be told what to do than to have to make his own decisions. It was easier to be supplied with all of the drugs and money he needed as long as he lured in new teens and brought in more business. The approval of his superiors was almost as strong a drug as the substances he had been addicted to. With long experience in the life herself, Joss had tried to explain to Zachary what a battle it would be to keep Luke not only clean and sober, but away from sex trafficking and the cycle of abuse that he had become accustomed to.

That was beside the fact that Luke had been making the organization a lot of money and they would do whatever they could to get him back if they knew where he was living now.

"What for? Drugs? Or...?"

"I wish that was all it was," Joss said with a sharp laugh. "If it was only that simple."

How could it be worse than that?

"It's murder," Joss told him baldly. "He's been charged with murder."

2

"M urder?" Zachary repeated, his stomach tying itself into even tighter knots.

Kenzie's eyes widened. For an assistant in the medical examiner's office, murder was part of her everyday life. It was what had brought them together initially, as Zachary had been investigating the death of Declan Bond. But the deaths that she was involved with were not usually anything to do with anyone they knew.

There was a deep sigh from Joss. "Yeah, murder. You know that's what I said." Her tone was irritated. She had probably been up all night. And undoubtedly, she didn't really want to have to deal with it all. Zachary was encouraged by the fact that she had called him, but wasn't sure what she needed from him. Just a listening ear? Did she want him to call someone? Suggest a lawyer?

"Do you know what happened?"

"Apparently, he killed a pimp. Someone he knew while he was in the business. Not like they'll give me any details. I'm not even legally his guardian. But they had to call someone, and better me than child services, since *they* know nothing about him." Joss let out another sigh. "I don't know what I'm supposed to do about this."

"What did Luke say about it? Did he explain what happened?"

"He's not saying anything. Which is probably best because they'll just use anything he says to convict him."

"And he didn't tell you anything either?"

"I haven't talked to him. They haven't finished processing him yet, so he can't see anyone."

"He's allowed a phone call. He didn't want to talk to you? Did he call a lawyer? Public defender?"

"No. He didn't make a call. The cop who talked to me said that he hasn't had anything to say. Hasn't defended himself. Didn't want a lawyer. You know what's happened. Obviously, this pimp had contact with Luke in the past or was trying to pick him up."

"He'll probably get a lawyer in time. It's only the first day. Once he's had a chance to think about things, to talk to you and figure out what he's going to do…"

"Can you look into it?"

"What do you want me to do? Talk to the police? They won't tell me any more than they told you. They probably won't talk to me at all."

"No. I want you to find out what happened. Just ask around. Get the scoop from any witnesses."

Zachary tapped his finger against the table, thinking about it. "Sure… I'll do what I can to help. But the police won't want me talking to witnesses right now. They need to do their investigation first. And once Luke has been processed, he'll probably let you know what happened. He's just being careful right now. He knows how this works."

"They're going to railroad him!" Jocelyn snapped. "A kid like Luke isn't going to get any sympathy. They'll say he's in the business. He killed his pimp. He got into an argument over payment. Luke has got a record; they know exactly what kind of a life he was leading up until you brought him to live with me."

It wouldn't look good for Luke. Zachary knew that sex workers went to prison for much less. But he couldn't quite wrap his mind around what had happened.

"*Was* Luke back in the business? I know you were worried about him. What do you think happened?"

"I don't know. I'm not his mom or his babysitter. I don't always know where he is. I do my best to keep him out of trouble, but he's old enough to make his own decisions. I can't physically keep him from doing anything he sets his mind to. And he knows his way around. He doesn't need me to take him anywhere."

"I know that. I'm not saying that you should have kept him home or that you did anything wrong. You've been doing a great job with Luke. I can't think of anyone who could have done a better job with him. But you were worried that he might be tempted to get back into the life. The pull of the drugs and the money and positive strokes from the people he used to work for. Or a new boss."

"He's been out some nights. Not all the time, and not usually overnight. Just for a few hours. There's not much by way of entertainment around here. Popcorn and Netflix isn't exactly exciting for a kid who has been used to partying and the nightlife."

"So, he's drinking? Drugging?"

"I don't know. He says not, but…" Even though they were on the phone, Zachary could see her expressive shrug in his mind's eye. "Of course that's what he's going to say. Any addict who falls off the wagon is going to deny it to start with."

As Zachary had discovered with Tyrrell. Tyrrell had assured Zachary and Kenzie that he hadn't started drinking again. Until he'd disappeared on a drunken binge and Zachary had to track him down. He couldn't exactly deny it anymore at that point.

"But you must have seen the signs. If he was using again."

"He seemed fine to me. But if he stayed away for long enough to hide the signs… and those nights that he did stay out overnight…"

"Well… I'll find out what I can, but I don't know how much that will be. Do you think he'll talk to me? Once he's been processed?"

"No. Probably not. Kids are taught not to talk if they get scooped up. If you just keep your mouth shut, the cartel will get you out. Maybe you serve some time, but as long as you don't talk about anyone else… you can go back again when you are released."

Zachary made a noise of acknowledgment. His brain was busy, trying to figure out how he could do anything to help Luke. If the police wouldn't tell him anything, Luke wouldn't tell him anything, and Luke didn't even have a lawyer to defend him, how was Zachary supposed to get any information that might be helpful for Joss or Luke?

"I'll try to get in to talk to him later today or tomorrow," Joss said, lowering her voice a little, letting up on the anger that Zachary knew hadn't been aimed at him. "I'll find out what I can. I'll try to get him to get a lawyer and tell him to talk to you." She cleared her throat, but her voice still sounded tight as she went on. "You just had to bring him here, didn't you? You just had to go and let me get attached to someone. I care about what happens to him. You may think I'm a tough chick who won't let herself get hurt by anything…" That was certainly the image she tried to project. "But I do care about what happens to Luke."

"Of course you do," Zachary reassured her. "I'll do whatever I can to help."

3

After Zachary hung up the phone, he looked at Kenzie, shaking his head slowly.

"What exactly happened?" Kenzie asked. She pushed a few of her dark curls back over her ear, picked up her toast, and took a couple of bites, waiting for Zachary to fill her in.

"I don't know anything yet. Just that Luke was arrested for murder. Someone in human trafficking. Jocelyn doesn't know for sure whether he knew him from when he was in the business, or if this is someone that he's met since then. Maybe someone trying to pick him up. He's not telling anyone what happened."

"That's probably good for now."

"That's what Joss said."

"So… why did she call you? What does she want you to do?"

Zachary shrugged uncomfortably. "Look into it. I don't know what I'll be able to do or how helpful I'll be. But she's never asked me to help before, so I'll do whatever I can."

"Of course. I just wondered whether there was anything you *could* do."

"Probably not right now, but I can talk to him once he's been arraigned and everything. As long as he'll see me. Joss said she'll tell him to."

"If he lets *her* visit him."

Zachary rolled his eyes and nodded acknowledgment. "Man… Luke. I thought he was doing so well. I know Joss said that she was worried about him, that he might go back to the life, but… he seemed so strong when I talked to him. I didn't think he would."

"It's hard to wrap your mind around it. Like going back to an abusive spouse. I mean… he knows he's walking back into a violent, dangerous lifestyle, one that endangers him and where he'll be required to do things that he doesn't want to. And why? For drugs?"

"Among other things, yeah. There's an endless supply in the trafficking business."

"I thought he was doing well too. I'm sorry. You must be really disappointed."

Kenzie knew how hard Zachary had worked to get Madison and Luke away from the cartel and find them safe places to start over again, even going as far as planting false trails about both kids having been killed in the shootout during their escape attempt. He had hoped that they would be out of that life forever. But now Luke was right back in the middle of trouble again.

Kenzie reached across the table to put a comforting hand on Zachary's arm for a moment, then withdrew it. "So, what does this mean for the rest of today's plans?" she asked practically.

Zachary considered. "Nothing, really, other than being a distraction. I can't do anything right away, so we may as well just go ahead with our plans."

"Good. I think Tyrrell would be really disappointed if I showed up to pick him up without you."

Tyrrell had completed his program at the drug rehabilitation center, and it would be cruel for his brother not to be there to meet him and celebrate his accomplishment. Or to put it off for another day. Zachary needed to be there for Tyrrell, like he had promised.

He always needed to follow through on his promises to his brothers and sisters. They'd had to put up with enough crap from the parents who had abandoned them and the other challenges they had faced once put into the foster care system. They all needed him to be steady and reliable. A good big brother to Tyrrell, Vince, and Mindy, and little brother to Joss and Heather. Now that they were all back in his life again, at one level or another, he needed to show them that he wasn't the same Zachary as had burned the house down when he was ten, causing the dissolution of the family.

He would spend the rest of his life trying to make up for that.

"I have to be there for Tyrrell," he agreed. "I told him I would be."

"Are you going to eat?" Kenzie nodded to the granola bar and single-serving yogurt container on the table in front of Zachary. He needed to eat if he were going to get back up to a healthy weight and he couldn't take his newest meds on an empty stomach.

So he had to, despite the heavy, foreboding feeling that now twisted his guts into a solid, uncomfortable knot. Zachary breathed out slowly, trying to relax all of his muscles.

"Yeah. Of course."

He had started to open the granola bar wrapper before his phone had rung. He picked it up again and tore it open. He liked the chocolate chip granola bars, and now that he was on meds that didn't make him nauseated first thing in the morning, he could actually enjoy it.

Once they had finished eating breakfast, they got ready to pick Tyrrell up. They hadn't set up a specific time, but Zachary wanted to get to the rehab facility as early in the day as they could so that Tyrrell wouldn't be waiting around and they could spend as much time together as possible getting Tyrrell settled into his new life and celebrating his graduation with him.

Zachary drove. There was always a debate over which of them would drive, as they both enjoyed highway driving. Kenzie's sweet little red convertible was her baby, her pride and joy, and she loved any excuse to go out and show it off. Zachary's white compact, on the other hand, was meant to be as anonymous and unnoticeable as possible, looking like every other fleet car and rental out there. A solid, dependable ride that no one would even remember seeing later. Despite what Magnum, P.I. might have gotten away with in Hawaii, a private investigator couldn't conduct surveillance in a flashy red convertible. Vermont was not Hawaii.

Having enough space for Tyrrell and his bags necessitated taking Zachary's car. And taking his car meant that he got to drive, unless there was some reason to let Kenzie drive instead. When they had gone to the Lodge, he had been too wiped out to drive the whole distance, and she had taken over. But normally, taking Zachary's car meant he was doing the driving.

"I'm going to handle a few emails," Kenzie commented, taking out her laptop. "If that's okay with you. Did you want to visit?"

"I don't mind." Driving was like meditation to Zachary. It was one of the only times he could sit and do nothing and be happy about it. If Kenzie were paying attention to her email, he could probably go a little faster than he normally could drive with her in the car. Zachary's mouth twitched, and he had to make an effort not to grin at the idea.

"I saw that."

Zachary chuckled. "Saw what?"

"You'd better not get there in half an hour."

"Yes, ma'am."

The weather had been warmer the last couple of weeks. They didn't need to wait for the windows to defrost, so Zachary pulled out after ensuring that Kenzie had on her seat belt and was ready to go.

"Do you want music?"

"Whatever you want," Kenzie told him, her voice already far away, distracted by whatever she was reading on the screen.

Zachary turned on the radio and flipped through the saved channels until he found something good. By the time they reached the highway, he was already in the zone, blocking out all of his concerns about Luke and Joss and just how he could help Luke.

4

They didn't reach the rehab facility in half an hour. But it didn't take a full hour, either. Zachary caught Kenzie checking the time as they pulled up. She gave him a wry look.

"Time flies," she commented. "I expected to be able to get more done on the way here."

"It's supposed to be your day off anyway," Zachary pointed out. "You shouldn't be doing work email."

"Well, no. Not all of it was work."

Maybe she had checked her personal mail as well. Still, Zachary doubted that her bright red pursed lips and the small frown line between her eyebrows had been over something puzzling in her personal inbox.

"Maybe you'll be able to get a bit more done on the way home."

"Doubt it. The two of you will probably be jabbering like jays on the way home."

"Jabbering like jays?" Zachary raised his brows.

"At least I didn't say cackling like hens."

"We have a lot of catching up to do."

"And you'll have lots of time to do it. And you don't have to do it all today. I'm not saying it's a bad thing. You guys should talk and have a good time together. I'm just saying I know it will be distracting, that I can't focus on emails while you're having an interesting discussion."

Zachary smiled all the way from the car to the reception area. The lobby area that had been so bare and desolate when they had dropped Tyrrell off now seemed airy and was filled with bright sunlight, as if even the weather were celebrating Tyrrell's completion of the program.

"We're here for Tyrrell Goldman," Zachary told the receptionist.

She gave him a sunny smile. "Oh, believe me, I know! Tyrrell is over the moon about being finished and being able to go home with his family today." She tapped a button on her phone as she picked up the receiver. "And I would know who you are even without being told."

He and Tyrrell looked enough alike that people saw the resemblance between them and didn't need independent verification that they were siblings. Zachary briefly considered their shared genetic traits and the father they both resembled before pushing any thoughts of Berk to the side to stay focused on Tyrrell's achievements.

"He's here," the receptionist said into the receiver.

It was mere seconds before the security door to the right opened and a woman in burgundy nurse's scrubs motioned for them to join her. "Zachary Goldman?"

"That's me." Zachary gave Kenzie's arm a squeeze as they turned and headed toward the door. "And this is Dr. Kenzie Kirsch."

"Doctor." The woman gave Kenzie a respectful nod. "Glad to have you here."

"Don't worry," Kenzie said, to allay any anxiety the nurse might have about having an outside doctor in the facility. "All of my patients are dead."

The nurse looked at her, startled. "What?"

"I work at the medical examiner's office. The morgue."

"Oh!" The nurse laughed. "I see!"

"I don't have any kind of oversight here. I took a tour when we dropped Tyrrell off because I was interested in learning as much about your programs as possible, and I was very impressed. But there's no need to cater to me or even call me doctor. I'm just Kenzie here."

"Well, we're still glad to have you," the nurse said, but did look more relaxed about it.

She led them through a couple of short corridors to a common area where Tyrrell was sitting, waiting and talking to a few other residents. Like Zachary, he had dark hair and eyes, though his hair was not in a buzz cut like Zachary's, but a longer, shaggier style. He looked up at Zachary's arrival. His face split into a grin and he jumped to his feet.

"Zach! Bro! It's good to see you!"

He gave Zachary a vigorous hug and slapped him on the back. He turned to the other residents.

"My brother," he introduced, motioning to Zachary. "My big brother, Zachary. And this is Kenzie." He gave Kenzie a sideways shoulder hug. "Zachary and Kenzie..." he made a sweeping gesture toward the others to introduce them. "My buds. Worked our way through the program together."

Zachary nodded. "Good to meet all of you."

They made various comments and greetings. Zachary looked at Tyrrell, evaluating him, looking for any sign that he wasn't quite ready to leave the safety of the program yet. Of course, they had all talked it over before, but Zachary was worried. Tyrrell had seemed stable before too. Zachary hadn't had any idea that anything was wrong until it was too late. "How are you doing?" he asked. "You're ready to get out of here?"

"I'm ready," Tyrrell agreed firmly, giving a nod. "I'm doing really well. Don't know when the last time I felt this good was."

Zachary nodded, but he was still anxious, looking for cracks in Tyrrell's veneer. They didn't want to take Tyrrell away from the support of the program too soon. He needed to be ready.

"Are you ready to meet with Dr. Gable?" the nurse asked Zachary.

Zachary and Kenzie nodded. They both knew Dr. Gable and had met him on previous occasions. Zachary knew that today, Dr. Gable would be the one certifying that Tyrrell had completed the program and was ready to leave.

Zachary wished that meant that Tyrrell was cured and wouldn't have to worry about falling back again. But it didn't. He was a dry drunk. A recovering alcoholic, but never cured.

"This way."

5

They all went together to another room, one of the family visiting rooms like they had used before when they had taken Alisha and Mason, Tyrrell's children, to visit him. Comfortable surroundings, meant to look more like a living room than a doctor's office or exam room.

"Tyrrell Goldman," Dr. Gable greeted heartily and reached out his hand to shake Tyrrell's. "Can you believe it is time for us to say goodbye to each other already?" He was an older man, gray hair, wire-rimmed glasses, a lab coat that didn't quite cover his paunch.

"It seems like a long time, and like just yesterday," Tyrrell said. He looked around the room and at everyone assembled there. "I didn't think I would ever feel this good again."

"The time goes quickly." Dr. Gable sat down and motioned for them all to take seats. He laid a few papers out on the coffee table in front of him. "When Tyrrell came here, he was in pretty bad shape. Physically and emotionally." He looked at Tyrrell. "Over a month of very heavy drinking, and moderately heavy in the weeks before that. And, of course, his long history with alcoholism. It does a lot of damage to your system. Alters the way you think. Depresses your nervous system."

Tyrrell was nodding his agreement. He didn't seem to be embarrassed by the doctor talking about the specifics of the problems he'd had when he had arrived at the facility, as Zachary thought he might. But then, Zachary and Kenzie had seen. He had stayed with them for the few days between when Zachary had found him and when they had gotten him into the program. It had been a rough go.

"We have the results of some of the testing that you did and the medical examinations that were performed when you got here," Gable told Tyrrell, pointing to the stapled papers. "And pictures."

Tyrrell winced when Gable laid a few snapshots on the table. Zachary looked them over. They had been visiting Tyrrell regularly since he'd completed the first phase of the program. The physical changes had been gradual enough not to be startling. Still, when he looked at Tyrrell's admitting photos and remembered the way he had looked when Zachary had initially found him in that bar, it was a bit of a shock.

Tyrrell had grown gaunt during his drinking binge. Not as thin as Zachary when he went through his depressive cycle, but still noticeably thinner and less substantial than he was now. His eyes and skin had been dull, and Zachary remembered how he had done little else but lie around or sleep during the time he had been at the house. He had not been well. He had not acted like Zachary's brother.

Now, that mischievous smile was back. Zachary could see the twinkle in Tyrrell's eyes again, just like in the eyes of the six-year-old he had been separated from after the fire. Zachary leaned over and gave Tyrrell another hug.

"It's all thanks to Zachary and Kenzie," Tyrrell said. "Kenzie is the one who found this program and got me into it."

"The work has all been yours," Dr. Gable amended. "And it has been a lot of hard work."

Tyrrell nodded, not denying it. Zachary had seen their timetables, and knew that they kept the residents busy from before sunrise with programs, lessons, therapies, chores, and practical applications. If Tyrrell had made friends with the other residents who were there waiting with him, it was only because they had been able to talk while they worked and during meals and group therapy. There had been little time on the schedule for rest or recreation.

Dr. Gable flipped through one of the reports and read from one page, a narrative of the state Tyrrell had been in when he had arrived, the biggest concerns and challenges that the staff saw ahead of him. He put it to the side and picked up another, reading it aloud to Tyrrell. It was a graduation report listing Tyrrell's accomplishments and progress, the things that the other residents and staff admired about him, the areas he had shown strength in and the things that he needed to focus on going forward. Tyrrell's eyes shone proudly. He nodded as Gable reminded him of his responsibilities toward his children, the need to seek out gainful employment as soon as he could, and the need for ongoing therapy, mentoring, and group support. The facility provided employment counseling and other outreach services even after Tyrrell left. Dr. Gable gave him a brochure that listed various numbers to call and reminders of things to follow up on as he left the program.

"You said that you have a place to live," Dr. Gable said. "Fully independent?"

Tyrrell nodded. He looked toward Zachary. "It's Zachary's old apartment, where he lived before he moved in with Kenzie. He was still paying the rent and asked me if I'd move in there and look after the place for the first little while. It's rent-free until I get established, then working my way up to covering his payments to the landlord."

Zachary and Kenzie nodded. Zachary had been ready to terminate the lease on the apartment, and it seemed fortuitous that he'd still had it available to offer to Tyrrell. Kenzie had paid for Tyrrell's admittance into the rehab facility, and Zachary was making his financial contribution by covering Tyrrell's rent until he was making what he needed in order to support himself and pay his obligations for child maintenance to Lindsey. That way, Zachary didn't feel like Kenzie was carrying them. She was happy to put her trust fund to good use for Tyrrell's benefit, but Zachary wanted to do his part too.

Dr. Gable handed a medallion to Tyrrell. "That's a reminder of the time you have spent here and what you have learned in the program and marks the successful conclusion of your time with us. Keep it with you. Keep going to meetings. Don't get sloppy in your sobriety habits. Don't forget everything you've learned here."

"Thanks." Tyrrell rubbed the medallion with his thumb and then hugged the doctor. "Don't know what I would have done without you, Dr. Gable."

"You did the work. Keep it up. Keep working the program."

Tyrrell nodded seriously.

Zachary's mind wandered to Luke and how little support he'd had. What he'd been through in the years since his grandmother had died, and even before that when he'd been passed from one relative to another who didn't want to care for him, had been at least as traumatic as Tyrrell's early years. And his drug addiction was more serious than Tyrrell's alcoholism.

But he had only gone through a short, publicly funded recovery program and had only Joss supporting him and trying to keep him on the straight road.

Had they really thought that was all he would need? Zachary knew Luke sometimes went to AA or NA meetings, or had in the beginning, at least. Other than that, his support network was woefully inadequate.

Without the proper support, it had only been a matter of time before Luke would slip and fall back into his old ways.

6

Zachary?"

Zachary looked at Tyrrell, who was gazing at him questioningly. Tyrrell shook his head slightly.

"Everything okay?"

"Sorry. My mind was somewhere else."

"Not a good place," Tyrrell said worriedly.

"No, it's okay. I'm sorry. I shouldn't be zoning out in the middle of your whole graduation ceremony."

Zachary knew that Tyrrell would assume it was something to do with their childhood or with Tyrrell's hard fall off the wagon. That would get him thinking about the abuse, their father, and Tyrrell's own difficulties in being a good dad to his kids. A domino line of negative thinking that could eventually lead to another setback.

He tried to smile reassuringly. "Nothing to do with you. Just about a phone call I had this morning before we came to get you. Not something you need to be worried about. Just my ADHD brain. You looking forward to seeing the kids?"

Tyrrell's smile blossomed once more. "Am I ever! It was good to see them when they came to visit. But it will be even better when we can be in a normal setting. Where they can actually play and enjoy themselves."

Dr. Gable held out his hand to Tyrrell, and they shook, two-handed, both grinning. "You enjoy it," Gable told him. "And remember that it doesn't have to be perfect. Kids have up and down times. Storms blow over quickly. They make mistakes, and you will too, but you can both forgive each other and move on to something more positive. Just keep moving forward."

Tyrrell nodded. "I will."

"When you fall down and are disappointed in yourself, pick yourself up, dust yourself off, and give yourself a pep talk. You can learn from your mistakes. It doesn't have to be a disaster."

"I know. I'll remember."

"Good. You can call me. Make use of our outreach services. We're still here to help you to stay on track."

Zachary and Tyrrell jabbered like jays all the way to Riverbrook, where Lindsey and the kids lived. Where Tyrrell had also lived until his last setback. Kenzie sat back, eyes closed or looking out the window while listening to their chatter. Zachary had to admit that she had been right; it would have been impossible for her to try to work in that environment.

Even though they had visited Tyrrell regularly once he had finished the initial phase of his rehabilitation, it seemed like there was so much more to share with him. Tyrrell regularly contributed, telling them about this or that class or therapy session at the rehabilitation facility, about the other patients there, about the personalities of the various nurses, therapists, doctors, and other staff.

They were not talked out by the time they got to Riverbrook, but Tyrrell fell silent, watching out the window. Replaying his failures in the past, Zachary was sure.

"Think about the good times," he urged. "You had lots of good times here with the kids."

"I did." Tyrrell nodded immediately. "And with Lindsey, too. When we were first married..." They passed houses, a green area, and a strip of stores. "Things were so good. We had so much fun together, and everything was ahead of us. We had such plans."

And those plans had been shattered by Tyrrell's alcoholism. Lindsey hadn't known anything about his addiction or past when they had gotten married. All of that had come out later. Secrets and addiction were not a good foundation on which to build a marriage.

"You had good times together," Zachary repeated. "And you're going to have lots more time with the kids. Just think of all of the things Mason is going to try before he's an adult."

Tyrrell laughed. "That's assuming he makes it to adulthood. I tell you, sometimes I wonder how he's survived this long."

Just as impulsive as Zachary remembered being himself, Mason had a knack for getting himself in trouble. It was a dangerous world for kids, and wasn't easy for the parents of creative, out-of-the-box thinkers.

Zachary found the playground that Lindsey had described and pulled up to the curb, finding a space among all of the mom vans. Tyrrell's door was open before anyone else's. Zachary took his time unbuckling his seat belt and opening his door. He and Kenzie both delayed as Tyrrell walked over to the climbing equipment so that Tyrrell would be the first one that the children saw.

Mason was hanging upside down from his knees and started to scream. "Daddy! Daddy!"

There was confusion evident on the faces of the other children in the playground as they stopped their conversations and games and turned around to look at him. Mason dropped too fast from the monkey bars, landing in a heap in the sand but, before Zachary had a chance to worry that he might have broken an arm or hit his head, Mason was on his feet and running towards Tyrrell. Alisha, who had been playing a game of tag with some of the older kids, was fast on his heels. Despite her longer legs, she did not sprint past him to get to Tyrrell first.

Mason rocketed into Tyrrell with an impact that Zachary could hear from the sidewalk. But Tyrrell laughed and picked him up and swung him around rather than getting after him. Tyrrell walked to where Alisha had stopped and hugged her around Mason. "Hi, sweetheart."

"I didn't know you were coming here. I didn't know you were out!"

"I just got out this morning. I came straight here before going anywhere else." He kissed her on the forehead.

"You're out, you're out!" Mason crowed. "I missed you so much, Daddy! And now you're home!"

Tyrrell didn't point out that he wouldn't be moving back in with them. Mason already knew that. Zachary and Kenzie got closer and gave the kids hugs and pats on the back as they clung to Tyrrell. Mason was already bubbling over with all of the news about school, what he had been learning, the new projects he was working on, and any trouble he had gotten into. Tyrrell just held him close, nodding as he took it all in.

7

L indsey was standing a distance away. Tyrrell saw her and started walking with the children toward her. She didn't greet him with a hug or kiss, but nodded to him. "You're looking good," she commented, her voice flat.

"Thanks. I'm feeling really good. Physically and mentally. I'm going to beat this thing."

"Good. I hope you do."

They both understood that even if Tyrrell managed to beat his addiction and find a way to be happy and productive, they wouldn't be getting back together again. Too much water had already passed under that bridge. Zachary reached for Kenzie and pulled her into a gentle hug, reminding himself that he had someone now. After his divorce from Bridget, it had taken him a long time to accept the fact that they weren't ever going to get back together. Even when she beat the cancer and got healthy, there was no chance she was ever taking him back. He would never build a life with her. In their case, there had been no children to worry about. They would never have babies together like he had fantasized.

While he accepted that Bridget was now with Gordon Drake and Zachary was with Kenzie, he still couldn't help thinking sometimes about what it would have been like if they had stayed together. If things had worked out the way that he had hoped. And he still battled the obsessive thoughts or compulsions to drive by her house or see what she was doing.

Zachary shook off these thoughts and nodded a greeting to Lindsey. "Hi. Nice to see you again."

Their face-to-face interactions hadn't actually been very pleasant when he had been looking for Tyrrell. Still, Lindsey had apologized for that and thanked him for looking out for Tyrrell, something she didn't have the energy or desire to do. And she had appreciated Zachary and Kenzie taking the kids to visit Tyrrell a few times.

But Lindsey didn't behave the way that Bridget did toward Zachary, so that was a plus. He suspected she didn't even act that way toward Tyrrell, though she probably was more careful what she said and how she behaved toward him in front of other people than she was while they were alone. Living with Tyrrell's addiction, dealing with a man who had just walked off when their premature baby had been struggling for survival in the NICU, would not have been an easy job for even the most patient of spouses.

Tyrrell walked with the kids over to the climbing equipment so they could show him what games they were playing or introduce him to their friends. Zachary wondered how much their friends knew about the situation. Zachary and Kenzie sat down on one of the nearby benches to watch from a distance and Lindsey sat on the next one over. Not right next to them, but close enough that they didn't have to yell to be heard.

"The kids didn't know he was coming?" Zachary asked, though he already knew why.

"Would you have told them? I've seen them go through enough disappointment. They could have a nice time playing at the playground or have a great day with a surprise visit by their dad. Better than telling them that he was coming and then him not showing up. I already know what kind of a day they have when he doesn't show up like he promised."

Zachary nodded. "It was a nice surprise for them."

Lindsey mimed plugging her ears. "Mason's screaming, though…"

Zachary grinned. But he had noticed that she hadn't gotten after Mason for shattering everyone's eardrums. Better he was screaming in excitement than bawling his eyes out.

They all tried to relax. It was still chilly out, and sitting on the molded benches quickly made Zachary's tailbone sore. It had mostly healed, but was still tender if he sat down too hard. Or sat for long on cold, hard, unforgiving surfaces. He stood up and stretched, then leaned on the back of the bench while watching the playground.

"Too much sitting?" Lindsey asked. "Driving all the way out there and back?"

"Yeah." Zachary nodded. "How was your morning?"

"Nerve-racking. I'm always a wreck anticipating whether he will show up or not. Now that he's here..." she snuggled down into her coat. "I can relax. How was your morning?"

She probably meant how did it go at the rehab center, but Zachary's mind went to Joss instead.

"Didn't start out that great," he confessed. "I got a call from Jocelyn."

"That's enough to ruin anyone's day," Lindsey deadpanned.

Zachary chuckled. Joss wasn't exactly known for her sunny personality. She pushed people away from her and was frequently cutting and sarcastic.

"She wanted my help, actually. So, it wasn't too bad."

"Oh, that's good. What does Joss need help with? I got the feeling she is... fiercely independent."

"Yeah, she is." Zachary and Kenzie both nodded. It was a good description. Joss didn't want to have to rely on anyone else. It must have taken a lot for her to call Zachary and ask him for help. "It was... Luke is in some trouble, and she's hoping I can use my detective skills to help him out somehow."

"Luke. What's he done? Never mind, I probably don't want to know. Can you tell me exactly... who Luke is? Tyrrell tried to explain it to me once, but it was a bad time, or maybe he was drunk and not explaining it clearly. He's not her son, right? He's someone that she knew... way back when? They were both involved with the same organization or something?"

Zachary shook his head. "Not exactly. They didn't know each other back then. They didn't work the same area... though Jocelyn knows some of the players that are over the region... kind of like the godfather over Vermont or the northeastern states."

"Godfather?" Lindsey smiled and shook her head.

"I mean, nothing like that, but there is a hierarchy, and he was over the area that Jocelyn worked and the area that Luke worked. So she's familiar with some of those guys, up at the top."

Lindsey rummaged in her purse for a moment, but apparently did not find whatever it was she was looking for. She put it beside her on the bench. "And exactly what were they involved in? Tyrrell said something like trafficking, but I don't know if that means slaves of some kind or drugs, or what."

"They probably have their fingers in all of that kind of thing. But with

Joss and Luke…" Zachary readjusted his position, uncomfortable. He was glad he was on his feet rather than sitting down. He didn't feel quite so squirmy. How much would Joss want him to reveal about her life? She had been very open about it with him, but he wasn't sure how she would feel about a relative stranger knowing any details. "They were in the sex trade." He grimaced about the way it sounded. "They were trafficked. Both of them were in the business for years. And Luke was involved in recruiting as well. Bringing other young kids into the organization."

Lindsey's eyes were wide. "Here in Vermont? That kind of thing doesn't happen here."

"It happens here. It happens everywhere. You might think that people have to go to other countries to see the sex trade… but the United States is actually one of the worst."

"Here? Like, right in Vermont? There wouldn't be enough business here to support it."

"Here in Vermont. All over." Zachary didn't know nearly as much about the industry as Joss and Luke, but he'd had an education over the past year. Since learning that Madison was being trafficked.

"That's really sad. So how did Joss and Luke end up together? They're not… involved, are they?"

"No. Nothing like that," Zachary waved his hands as if he could stop her brain from going down that path. "No. Joss is helping Luke. Trying to help him… to stay clean and straight. To have a better life than he could have in the organization."

"How did they meet?"

Zachary shrugged. "That was me. Luke was involved in one of my cases and I went to Joss for advice a couple of times."

"She says you don't listen to her," Lindsey said, looking away from Zachary. She said it in a neutral way, not mocking or teasing, but she didn't really say it as a question, either. Something for Zachary to comment on. Or not.

"Well… yeah, she says that. I try to understand what she's telling me about how the industry works. And I respect her opinion and know that what she is telling me is the truth. But… her advice when it came to Madison and Luke was to stay out of it. To just leave them alone and not try to help." Zachary shrugged. "I couldn't do that. I couldn't just walk away from it, knowing the torture those kids were going through, the kind of life they had to lead. Even if I didn't understand it fully, I knew that much."

"I don't think I could have walked away either," Lindsey agreed. "But I probably would have gotten the police involved. Not tried to do it myself."

"I did get the police involved," Zachary told her emphatically. "As soon as I knew where Madison was, I got them involved. They asked her if she wanted to stay there or go back to her parents, and she wanted to stay there, so she stayed. And there was at least one cop there who was involved with the cartel or looking the other way. So once the shooting started—"

"The shooting?" Lindsey interrupted. Her voice had risen, and everyone nearby looked over at her to see what was going on. Mason and Alisha, attuned to her voice, turned and looked to her for reassurance. Lindsey waved at them to go back to playing with Tyrrell. "Shooting?" she repeated in a lower voice. "I thought you weren't *that kind* of private investigator. That's just on TV." She looked him over, eyes sharp. "You're not carrying a weapon, are you?" She looked toward Mason, as if afraid for him.

"I've never owned a gun," Zachary assured her, "and I never will. I wasn't the one shooting. And believe me, if someone is shooting, I am going the other way as fast as I can. Madison and Noah—Luke—decided they wanted out. I was helping them to get away from there. But this is the kind of boss that doesn't take too kindly to you leaving. They did their best to stop us."

Lindsey didn't say anything for a minute, just looking at Zachary and thinking about this. Her eyes moved over to Kenzie as if asking her to verify what Zachary had said. Maybe she thought he was just being a blowhard, pretending that he lived a more exciting life than he did. But being shot at had not been in Zachary's plans, and he didn't intend to put himself back into that position again.

"Zachary is very careful," Kenzie told Lindsey. "He wouldn't knowingly put anyone in danger. But sometimes… things happen. Situations develop quickly." She was probably thinking about the cases that she had been involved in too. Investigating that she had done while working at the medical examiner's office. Questions that she had asked that had triggered the wrong people to take action.

Lindsey looked back toward the children again, shaking her head. "It would have been nice to know that you were involved in this kind of thing before."

"I'm *not* involved," Zachary repeated. "I stay as far away from violent people as I can."

8

It was a bittersweet goodbye. A couple of hours wasn't a long time for the children to be able to play and visit with Tyrrell. But they were delighted that he was back out of rehab and that he seemed to be his old self again. The daddy who didn't drink was much nicer to them than the daddy who did.

Mason cried, despite trying to be a little man and hold the tears back. He snuffled and rubbed his eyes and said brave things, but it was obvious that his heart was breaking and he was worried about when he would see Tyrrell again and if he would still be sober the next time. Quiet Alisha just grew quieter. She said a polite goodbye and just stood by, waiting for Tyrrell to finish saying everything he needed to say to Mason. Eventually, Zachary, Kenzie, and Tyrrell walked back to the car together.

Zachary didn't say anything. He knew how badly Tyrrell must be feeling about having to say goodbye and wanted to comfort him. But he didn't want to fill the air with empty, meaningless words, reassurances that Tyrrell would see them again soon and that they would be fine and that he would be strong and be able to get a job and do all of the other things he was supposed to do so that he could see them regularly. What was the point in that? No one knew the future and, given Tyrrell's history, he probably *would* have another setback. Hopefully not for a few months, maybe even a year or two, but he had not had two consecutive years sober since college.

They all got into the car. Zachary turned on the radio to cover the silence. Tyrrell had been smiling and cheerful the whole time he had been with the children, even when saying goodbye but, glancing in the rear-view mirror, Zachary could see that his expression was now morose, deep frown lines between his knitted brows. Kenzie glanced back at him after several minutes of silence.

"It was a good visit," she told him encouragingly. "The kids were so excited to see you."

Tyrrell nodded.

"You'll be able to see them again soon. We can set something up at our house. Or maybe the wildlife park or something else they would like."

"I can set up visits with my own kids, Kenzie," Tyrrell pointed out. "I appreciate you bringing them when I was in the program, but I can work things out now that I have access to a phone again."

"Oh. Right." Kenzie bit her lip and looked out her side window. "Sorry, I didn't mean to imply that you couldn't handle it yourself. I guess I just got used to having them around."

"I'm just being cranky. It's just that..." Tyrrell didn't finish the sentence. Looking back at him, Zachary could see that he was struggling to sort out his thoughts and put them into words. As someone used to keeping secrets and running away from problems, it probably wasn't easy for him to try to express those feelings.

If his brain worked at all like Zachary's, a crash almost inevitably followed a good time, especially if it was something where he'd had to remain "on" for other people. Even though he enjoyed himself, as Tyrrell had with the children, he couldn't seem to hold on to that happiness. Instead, as soon as it was over, or sometimes before events had officially ended, his brain started to analyze everything that had happened, worrying over whether he had answered every question the right way, remembering where he had stumbled in an answer, not said something when he should, or embarrassed himself some other way. And it wasn't just the way that Bridget had criticized him after social events, even if he would have liked to put all the blame on her. His self-critical obsessive thoughts had started before ever meeting Bridget. He could remember it from a very early age. Maybe it had been exacerbated by Bridget's angry remonstrances and the many irritated foster mothers who had tried to bring Zachary up to be a polite and respectable young man, but the tendency to fall apart and disparage himself after a party or holiday had originated long before that.

"You're crashing," he suggested to Tyrrell.

Tyrrell looked in his direction, tilting his head slightly to consider it.

"Your brain is going through all of the things you did wrong or should have done better. Today and at other times. All of your failings."

Tyrrell's head bobbed up and down. "How do you know that?"

"I do it too."

Tyrrell cupped his palms over his eyes, leaning his head back against the headrest. "How do I make it stop? I know it was good that I got to see them today, but I almost wish I hadn't. I was calm while I was in the program. I had trouble after sessions sometimes, but we were so busy that it was just going from one thing to another and there wasn't really time to spend going over it all. At the end of the day, I would be so exhausted I would just fall into bed."

At that point, Zachary's hamster-wheel brain would happily have picked up with the hate-fest no matter how tired he was, going into overdrive trying to analyze everything. The more overtired he was, the harder it would be to shut off the voices and go to sleep. Tyrrell was lucky to be able to get straight to sleep after an overprogrammed day.

"Give yourself some time," Zachary said with a shrug. "Keep telling yourself that it was nice to see them so that you don't dread it next time. I don't really know more than that. You can talk about it with your therapist. Maybe they can give you some better advice."

"I know one thing that would calm it down."

They all sat in silence. Of course they all knew what Tyrrell was talking about. He was used to taking alcohol to numb the anxiety and self-recriminations. But he knew that he couldn't go back to it. Doing so would lead to more pain and heartache and would ruin everything he had accomplished in the rehab program.

Zachary pressed the buttons on the radio, looking for a faster song with a heavier beat to help fill the silence and distract them all from negative thoughts.

9

By the time they reached the apartment, the worst of the storm of emotions seemed to have passed. Tyrrell offered a few comments on his plans for the next few days and shared memories of some of the towns they passed through. Zachary pulled into the reserved space in the parking lot in front of the apartment building, feeling the satisfied "click" in his brain that he belonged there. He had been happy while he'd been in the apartment. Mostly. He was happier at Kenzie's, of course; that was his home now. But he'd felt good about living at the apartment. It had taken him a long time to get back on his feet after everything that had happened, but he had been able to move on and be independent again.

He let out a satisfied sigh. Kenzie heard it and looked at him, brows raised.

"Happy to be home?"

Zachary shrugged. "Good memories. I'd rather be with you."

"Of course you would," Tyrrell agreed. They all laughed. Zachary handed the apartment keys to Tyrrell and let him lead the way to figure out which key to use in the front doors of the building and in the door to his new apartment.

Tyrrell pushed the door open and there was a bit of a whoosh as the still air of the apartment stirred and mixed with the air from the hallway. There were a couple of flyers on the floor, and Tyrrell stooped to pick them up, then held them out toward Zachary. Zachary held up his hands.

"I don't want them. They're yours."

Tyrrell laughed and looked down at them. "Yeah. I guess they are," he said ruefully. He swiped back his hair with his free hand. "My first junk mail at the apartment." He still hesitated about what to do with it. He ended up putting it on the table to look at later. Zachary would probably just have tossed it out. But Tyrrell didn't know the neighborhood and might want to see what stores and restaurants the flyers were for.

Tyrrell took a deep breath and looked around, letting his breath out again slowly. "This is great, Zachary. You don't know how much I appreciate having somewhere to land. I'll make it up to you one day. Pay you back somehow."

"You already paid me back. By coming back into my life and introducing me to my siblings again. Before you came back, I didn't have anyone." He looked at Kenzie. "No biological family, I mean. I have Mr. Peterson—Lorne—and Pat. And I have Kenzie. But I didn't have any blood connections."

Tyrrell shrugged as if none of that meant anything. "So, how long were you here? Is this where you were when you and Kenzie met?"

"No. Two years ago, I was at the previous apartment. The one that..." Zachary trailed off.

Tyrrell looked at him expectantly. "The one that what?" he asked with a laugh. "The one that Kenzie didn't like? Did she make you get somewhere nicer?"

Kenzie squeezed Zachary's arm. "The one that burned," she told Tyrrell in a quiet voice.

Tyrrell's smile disappeared. "What?" He looked from Kenzie to Zachary, brows drawn down in confusion. "It was our old house that burned down. Back when we were little. When Zachary was ten."

"I know. And then there was another fire." She kept a close eye on Zachary, waiting to see how he reacted to the conversation. "Right after we met. Everything was destroyed. His wallet and ID too. It was a big mess."

"A pain in the neck," Zachary agreed. He wiped his perspiring forehead. He tried to focus on the details that Kenzie had mentioned instead of picturing the inferno, instead of letting himself go back there. "Do you know how hard it is to get your ID replaced when you don't have any ID? It took forever."

"How come you never told me that?" Tyrrell demanded. "Why wouldn't you tell me that you were in another fire?"

Zachary felt the heat of the first fire. Unimaginably hot, scorching his skin, the smoke filling his lungs. He had screamed for Tyrrell and the others to wake up, to escape the house while they still could, as he tried to squeeze himself into the narrow space under the couch for protection. Both times, he had been carried out by a firefighter. Carried out into the crisp, fresh winter air, so cold that it cut into his lungs already seared by the smoke.

"It's okay," Kenzie's voice told him. "Look around. Anchor yourself. What are five things you see?"

Zachary tried to see through the smoke and flames and confusion of the fires, both of them merging together in his memory and blotting everything else out.

"What do you hear?" Kenzie tried again. "Can you hear my voice?"

Zachary managed a nod. He could hear the sirens of that night, the crackle of the flames, his own strangled screams as he cried his throat raw.

"I can hear neighbors talking," Kenzie said. "Next door, I guess? It doesn't sound like they're arguing. They're just loud. And the ding of the elevator?"

Zachary heard the elevator and then the sound of footsteps in the hallway. He remembered the firefighters' heavy, clomping steps. Not like the light tread he heard down the hall.

"Yes," he whispered hoarsely. "Smell... fried food. Chicken? And... onions. Sweat." His own sweat, probably, rank with fear, clammy under his armpits and rolling down his back. Not smoke. The smell of the smoke was fading.

Kenzie rubbed his shoulders. "It's okay," she repeated. "Look around."

He blinked heavy-lidded eyes as if he were just coming out of a dream. The apartment looked just the same as it had moments earlier, but he felt like he had taken a journey back and forth through time. It was disorienting. Kenzie went over to the sink, ran cold water, and then filled a glass from the cupboard. She placed it on the table in front of him. "Okay?"

Zachary nodded. He was sitting at the table, though he couldn't remember how he had gotten there. Tyrrell hovered nearby, looking ready to jump into action but unsure what to do. Kenzie sat down in one of the other chairs, though she pulled it back and turned it at an angle so that she wasn't staring directly at him and he had a bit of space. Zachary picked up the glass and took a few gulps of the cold water, soothing the pain in his throat.

"*That* is probably why he didn't talk to you about it," Kenzie told Tyrrell.

"Uh… yeah, I guess so." Tyrrell flushed pink. He looked at Zachary uncertainly. "I thought that you didn't have flashbacks to the fire anymore."

He took another swallow of cold water. "I can be around a fire without being triggered now," he said hoarsely. "Not quite the same thing."

Tyrrell nodded slowly. "I didn't mean to do that," he said uncomfortably. "That looked like a bad one."

Zachary was thinking about it, wondering why it had been so intense, when he'd been able to head off most of his flashbacks recently, using techniques that Dr. B had given him to turn his mind to something else, or being able to anchor quickly before he became totally immersed in the experience. He sipped the water more slowly, not wanting to drain the glass.

"Double-whammy, I think. Because you were there the first time…" He turned his gaze from Tyrrell to Kenzie.

"And I was there when you fell asleep before the apartment fire," Kenzie finished. "Did you think that I was still there when you woke up to the fire?"

"I didn't know. I heard your voice—I dreamed that I heard you talking —before I woke up in the smoke. You *weren't* there…" He rubbed his forehead. "No. But I guess I got some wires crossed."

Kenzie nodded.

"It was like both were happening at the same time."

Tyrrell swore under his breath. "I'm sorry, bro. I shouldn't have asked you about it."

"It's okay. I *should* talk about it. Dr. B says that's the only way to get used to it, to get over being triggered. Just to look at it and talk about it normally, like this."

Still, his skin crawled and he was uncomfortable, worried that he might flash back a second time. Dr. Boyle said that he wouldn't once he was anchored, but he wasn't sure he believed it. His brain didn't always work the way it should.

"So you lost everything again," Tyrrell shook his head in wonder. "I don't know how you did it. You moved here afterward? How did you rent a place without any ID? How could you even get money out of the bank?"

"It wasn't easy. I couldn't get a place until my ID was reissued, and the bank was a whole other story. I had to see the bank manager and have someone swear an affidavit about my identity. They at least had a photocopy of my driver's license on the file so they could see my face matched.

And I waited until I got my settlement check because I wasn't really sure what I could afford, and had all of the costs of getting set up again…"

"Did you stay with Kenzie?"

They both shook their heads.

"No, I barely knew her yet. We'd been on a couple of dates, that's all. But one of the cops that I know, he put me up on his couch for a few days." Zachary shrugged. "Though… 'a few days' kind of became a few months."

"Well, yeah. With having to get all of that done first. You're lucky you didn't end up on the street or in a shelter. Or living out of your car." Tyrrell gave a short laugh. He had been living out of his car when Zachary had tracked him down. Though really, he lived in the bar and only slept in the car when he got kicked out of the bar.

"I was lucky," Zachary agreed. "Kenzie helped out. I don't know if I would have gone to Mario on my own."

10

———————

Joss called in the evening to tell Zachary that he should be able to visit Luke in the morning. Zachary felt pulled in two directions. He wanted to help Luke, of course. He wanted to see the boy and make sure that he was okay. But he also dreaded going to the jail and seeing him, knowing there was very little he could actually do. Joss and Luke were looking to him to solve this problem, to somehow get Luke out of the trouble he was in. But Zachary wasn't a lawyer, and it sounded like they had an open-and-shut case against the teen. He dreaded Luke's disappointment and the guilt of not being able to do the one thing Joss had asked him to.

It was a rough night, even taking sleep and anti-anxiety meds. Thinking about the visit with Luke, trying to anticipate what would happen and what to say to Luke to reassure him. Certain he wasn't going to be able to do anything to help, but desperate to do something. It didn't make for a restful night, even with chemical assistance.

Sunday was Kenzie's day to sleep in or at least to have a lazy morning, so she was just up, still in her dressing gown and blinking at her first cup of coffee, as Zachary was preparing to leave.

"Will the jail let you visit on a Sunday?" Kenzie asked. "And this early?"

"It won't be early anymore when I get there. And I checked their website. Looks like they still allow visits on Sunday."

"Seems like a wise thing to check before investing the time in driving down there."

"Yeah," Zachary agreed, checking his pockets for his keys.

"I mean... it doesn't sound like you talked to anyone and are only guessing that they'll let you in to see him. Don't you think you should call first?"

"What?" Zachary found his keys in a left-hand pocket, which was odd because he was right-handed. He shook his head, looking down at them. Maybe he had put them in his pocket while the coat was still hung up.

"You should call the jail. Make sure that you're going to be allowed in to see him before you drive down."

"Joss already made sure I'd be able to get in. I'm on a list somewhere as an approved visitor."

Kenzie rolled her eyes. "I still think you should do more than look at their website."

"It's easy to tell someone 'no' over the phone. It's a lot harder when they're right in front of you and had to drive a couple of hours to get there."

"But they could still tell you no."

"They could tell me yes over the phone and still tell me no when I got there too." Zachary shrugged. He was pretty good at talking his way into places, and he generally managed to get on with law enforcement officers, despite the reputation of his profession. He wouldn't tell them that he was there as a private investigator. He would just say that he was a friend.

"Okay..." Kenzie drew the word out and had that "Don't come crying to me when it doesn't work out" tone in her voice that he'd frequently gotten from foster moms. But things didn't work out the way he wanted when he tried to follow their instructions either. He might as well do things his own way.

"I'll try not to be too long," Zachary told her, giving her a quick peck on the cheek. "But even if I'm only an hour or two, then with the driving time..."

"Hopefully, you'll be home by supper."

Zachary nodded his agreement.

"Will you stop and see Joss as well?"

He thought about it. He had been so focused on getting through the visit with Luke that he hadn't thought about stopping in to talk to Joss.

"Maybe. I don't know yet. We'll see how the day goes. And she might not want to see me."

So far, she hadn't told him to get lost when he had just shown up on her doorstep without arranging something ahead of time, but she *had* told him to call the next time. She didn't seem to like meeting with him at her house.

"You never know," Kenzie said. "Though since you're doing her a favor, I would think she would show a little more appreciation and not just turn you away."

"Maybe. But we are talking about Joss here."

Kenzie laughed.

Zachary kissed her again and got on his way.

Zachary sat looking at the Kent police station when he got there. The trip had gone all too fast. He still didn't have any idea what to say to Luke or how to go about investigating what had happened in a way that would be beneficial to Luke's case. He would just have to find out everything he could and hope that would lead him to a solution.

Sitting in the car wasn't going to get him anywhere. If he lost the motivation to get out of the car and go into the police station, it was going to be that much harder. Zachary pushed himself to open the door and swing his feet out the door and hoped that the rest of his body would follow even though his brain was reluctant. The trick worked, and he locked and shut the door and headed into the police station without much more thought.

It was quiet. Apparently, not a lot happened there on a Sunday morning. There were no complainants gathered around the front desk, no shouting back and forth or ringing of phones. Just one cop sitting at a computer within view of the service window. Officer of the Day. Maybe someone who had screwed up and been punished by having to spend his weekend doing nothing but sitting and waiting. Zachary smiled as warmly as possible.

"Sorry, no services today," the cop told him. "Come back tomorrow."

"I'm here to see an inmate in the jail. He was just brought in recently. Luke—no," Zachary looked down at his notepad for the name Joss had given him. "Joseph Daniel Bryant."

The cop stood up and looked Zachary over. "You made arrangements?"

"My sister set it up."

The cop considered for another moment, like he might be able to come up with some excuse to send Zachary away. Then he reached for a rack of folders and thumbed through them. He pulled out one photocopied form and slid it across the counter to Zachary. "Fill that out."

Zachary had not anticipated having to fill out a bunch of paperwork to see Luke. He probably should have. The justice system ran on paper and red tape. Zachary was used to being able to skate by most of the paperwork requirements in Roxboro because most of the cops he dealt with knew him and didn't feel like doing extra work for a routine inquiry.

Zachary put the paper on the counter square in front of him and looked at the cop, who, after a moment, handed him a cheap stick pen to fill out the form. He stood there waiting as Zachary started to read through the headings on the form.

"I'm a slow writer," Zachary said. "You might as well read a book or something."

The young cop gave him a grin and sat back down in front of the computer. It was easier for Zachary to focus on each question and carefully scratch in his answers without someone hovering. He wasn't always so slow writing things down but, if he wanted someone else to be able to read it, he had to go slowly and form each letter with care. Sometimes even he couldn't read the chicken scratch that filled his notepads.

Eventually, he got down to the bottom of the page and went back to review each space to see if he had missed anything. When he looked up, the cop was looking in his direction.

"Done yet?"

"Yeah, I think so."

The young officer stood up again and took it from Zachary. Reading through the form, he asked a couple of questions and added notes to the spaces, sometimes striking out Zachary's answer completely. He glanced over it one more time, then took it back to the computer and started typing. He didn't seem to be transcribing all of Zachary's answers. Maybe just checking to see if the names matched up and what Luke's status was. He tapped a few more buttons and the printer beside him started to whir. He handed Zachary the printout. "There you go. You need to go around the outside of the building to the jail intake door. It's going to be locked. You'll have to press the buzzer. Takes a few times, sometimes. Don't come back and tell me they're not answering. There's nothing I can do about it.

Keep buzzing until they do. Give them that paper. If your inmate is available, they'll take you through the process."

Zachary looked down at the printout. "Okay. Thanks for your help."

"Have a nice day."

11

Zachary retreated, following the officer's instructions to go around to the other side of the building. There was a red panel with several warnings on it and a large button. Zachary pressed it firmly and held it in for a second. He released it and waited. Having been warned by the Officer of the Day, he knew it would probably be a while. If they were routinely slow to answer, they would probably be all that much slower on a Sunday, with reduced staff.

It was only a few seconds after his second ring that the door opened, startling him.

The uniformed woman who glared out at him was short, but broad-shouldered and stout. Zachary stepped back a little, feeling crowded.

"What is it?" she snapped.

"I'm here to visit...?"

She looked at his hand and snatched the printout from him. Her eyes ran back and forth, scanning the information on the page. "The kid."

Zachary nodded. "Yeah."

She made a sideways motion with her head and stepped back, at the same time pushing the door open wider for him. Zachary entered, and she led the way through a couple more locked doors to a bare-looking reception area. There was a chute; an empty doorway with counters running down both sides of it, like the metal detector and x-ray that he was used to going through at the Roxboro police department when he went to see Kenzie, or the security check-in for an airport.

"Remove everything from your pockets," the corrections officer told him, throwing a bin onto one of the counters. "Your shoes, belt, watch, and any jewelry."

"Should I take off my coat?"

She rolled her eyes. "Yes."

Zachary proceeded to follow her instructions. When he placed his wallet in the bin, she picked it up, flipped it open to look at his identification, and compared it with the printout. She put it back in the bin. Zachary felt vulnerable after taking off his shoes and belt, as if they were somehow protective. Like a suit of armor.

"That everything?" she asked when he was finished.

Zachary nodded. She pushed a button to start the conveyor belt and the bin disappeared into an x-ray. She stared at the screen for a few seconds longer than seemed necessary. Zachary shifted anxiously. He rubbed one foot over the other, wishing she would hurry up and give him his shoes back.

"Okay. Step forward. Walk slowly through the doorway."

Zachary obeyed. His heart sank at the warning beep and the light that came on at the top of the doorway. He looked at her. She picked up a wand and started to run it around his body.

"Usually just something like the rivets in your jeans or an underwire bra for women," she assured him. She paused at his elbow as the wand beeped. She ran it around his side again, and again it beeped in the same place. "You ever break your arm?"

Zachary looked at his arm as if it belonged to someone else. Eventually, he nodded. It had been a long time ago and he didn't remember any details. Still, he vaguely remembered that arm being in a cast that had banged into everything and had driven him crazy with itchiness. "Yeah."

"Got screws in it, didn't you?"

"I haven't got a clue." Zachary looked at the wand. "I've never had it trigger a security check before."

"Yeah, this is one of the most sensitive wands on the market." She stepped back from him half a pace. "Hardly anyone gets through here without it going off."

Zachary didn't know whether he found that reassuring or disturbing.

"All right, through here." She motioned to a steel door.

Zachary looked back toward the bin that held his personal items. "Uh, do I get back…"

"You'll get your stuff when you leave. If you want, we can go through the whole business of putting it into a locker, but you're the only one here. It's more efficient to just leave it in the bin and you can get it when you leave."

Zachary hesitated, thinking about his camera in particular. Since he had turned eleven, he'd taken a camera with him everywhere he went. First, the one that Mr. Peterson had given him for his birthday, and then, after the apartment fire, a small digital camera he had purchased to use for work. Mr. Peterson had given him another analog camera for his hobby pictures. He hadn't been allowed to keep a camera with him at Bonnie Brown or other institutions that he had been in, and maybe that was what was holding him back. He didn't want to feel like he was the one incarcerated there.

"Could I take it out to my car and leave it there?"

She rolled her eyes. "No, because then we have to go through this whole thing again. Do you want to leave it in the bin or put it in a secure locker?"

"Umm… a locker, I guess. There is some sensitive equipment in there…"

Not really. An off-the-shelf phone and digital camera. Not expensive or sensitive enough to warrant his paranoia. But hopefully, she couldn't tell the difference.

It took ten minutes to get everything transferred to a locker. Zachary was allowed to set the electronic security code so he would be the only one able to open it, yet he wouldn't have a key with him when he went in to visit Luke. As if they could have effected some kind of attack or escape with only a locker key. Then the CO finally took him through the steel door into a space that immediately felt like a prison. Stale air, dimmer lighting, concrete walls that looked like they had been painted over a dozen times, yet still didn't even come close to being clean. Zachary breathed slowly, concentrating on his breaths in and out. He wasn't exactly claustrophobic. But he didn't like to be locked up.

They zipped down one hall and into another. The woman indicated another door. "In here."

Zachary opened the door and found a visitor room with a table and two chairs, all bolted to the floor. The room was chilly, as if it were pulling in air directly from outside.

"Have a seat. I'll be about ten minutes."

Zachary wasn't looking forward to sitting in the stark, cold room by himself for ten minutes. But he had been through worse. He'd spent days at a time in the detention block at Bonnie Brown. He gave a brief nod and sat down in the chair that faced the door. He relaxed into it the best he could and closed his eyes. Maybe a nap. He'd had a restless night. Maybe if his brain was bored enough with the room, he could catch up on some sleep.

But his brain wasn't bored with the lack of stimulation. It decided instead to go into hyperdrive, anticipating danger.

"Just chill," Zachary breathed to himself. "Nothing is going to happen here." He took several deep breaths and tried to regulate his heart rate.

12

The minutes stretched out, and Zachary was pretty sure that the CO was gone significantly longer than the ten minutes promised. But that was the way things went sometimes. People didn't literally mean ten minutes when they said that. They just meant "soon." There wasn't anything wrong.

But Zachary's brain immediately began to run possible scenarios. It was jail. A lot of things could have happened to Luke. They might have found him hanging in his cell. He might have been beaten up by other inmates. He might have had an altercation with a CO. He could have died unexpectedly in custody. It happened. They had special terminology for such deaths. Excited delirium. Even if the person hadn't been excited or delirious. Zachary had been in detention at Bonnie Brown when a young autistic girl had died in the isolation cell next to his with her hands cuffed behind her back. Positional asphyxia. They hadn't had a word for it at the time. They said that she'd just died, some weird side effect of her neurodivergence. But the guards had hidden the fact that she had been handcuffed all night. By the time the medical team got there, the cuffs had been removed and she had been repositioned and covered with a blanket. The authorities who investigated it never knew what had really happened.

How would Zachary explain it to Joss if something had happened to Luke? How could he take that kind of news to her? And how could they insist on any kind of justice, knowing that Luke was basically a non-person in the eyes of the justice system? He couldn't get much lower in the eyes of society than a murderer, sex worker, and child predator. Everyone would be celebrating Luke's death.

The door thunked open, and the woman CO escorted Luke into the room. She didn't give him any instructions, but pushed him into the other chair and ran one of the chains connected to his shackles through the anchor in the table. Luke wore an orange jumpsuit that looked way too lightweight for the cool room temperature. Hopefully the cell block was kept warmer than the meeting rooms, which were not in constant use, but would heat up quickly with several bodies in them at once. Luke's feet were bare in what looked like flips flops intended for use in a locker room shower. Thin and soft, intended to protect him from fungus or other contaminants, but not warm or protective.

"You've got an hour," the CO told Zachary, then left them alone without a word to Luke.

Zachary looked Luke over. "Hey. How are you doing?"

Luke had a black eye, a nice shiner that looked about a day old. The bruising seemed to be spreading to the other eye, too. In another day, he would probably look like a raccoon. Luke was blond, his hair a little longer than Zachary thought was currently considered stylish. Even with his black eye, he was still handsome. *Really hot,* one of Madison's friends had said in describing him. He looked like someone who could have been in a boy band. A heartthrob. Clean cut, just rebellious enough to be seen as a bad boy. Just the type to lure teen girls—and boys—and coax them into a business that they never would have considered before they met him. It had clearly been at least a day since he had shaved. A fine stubble covered his jawline. More than peach fuzz, but Luke was still very young and his whiskers thin.

Luke looked away from Zachary, not answering. Zachary was silent for a few moments, waiting to see if that would draw Luke out.

"Joss called me. She is very worried about you."

Not even a shrug in response. Luke still didn't even look at him.

"She wants me to see if I can help you. Figure out what happened and how to get you out of here."

Luke stared up at the ceiling.

It would be a pretty quick interview if Zachary couldn't get any response from Luke.

"Luke. Please. Even if you don't think there is anything I can do to help, humor me. Joss wants me to do what I can. She cares about you. I do too. Other people care what happens to you. Don't just shut everyone out."

Luke lowered his eyes from the ceiling to look Zachary in the face briefly, then he looked away again. In that fleeting moment, Zachary saw pain and fear. Gone so quickly that he couldn't even be sure that he had really seen it. Maybe Zachary had just imagined it. He knew it should be there, so he had manufactured the illusion himself.

"Did you get any sleep last night? Have anything to eat?"

Luke shook his head. At least that was a response.

"Are you in a cell by yourself? Away from people who might hurt you?"

A shrug. Zachary wasn't sure whether that was confirmation or an acknowledgment that there were people there who would want to hurt him, but that he didn't care. He needed to act tough, as if he didn't care what happened to him. Zachary knew what that was like. Act vulnerable, and he opened himself up to more abuse. Act like he didn't care, and a predator wouldn't get as much of a kick out of harassing and abusing him.

"What do you need? Is there anything we could bring you?"

Zachary had no idea what the jail would or wouldn't allow, but it was just a tactic to get Luke to talk. See what he wanted, what he was thinking of, what he needed for comfort. Anything to get the ball rolling.

Luke remained silent.

"You're as quiet as Rhys," Zachary teased.

Rhys was mostly nonspeaking, and holding a conversation with him could be challenging. But at least he *tried* to communicate his thoughts, something that Luke had no intention of doing at the moment.

"What you need is a phone," Zachary suggested. The tool that Rhys used the most, outside of gestures. A few thumbed words and a gif or two usually helped Rhys get across the point he was trying to make. He didn't use sign language or an AAC, none of the systems that nonspeaking children were taught to use. It was as if Rhys couldn't use any standardized communication. As if doing so would make him too vulnerable. He had withdrawn and stopped talking when his grandfather was murdered, and it seemed that no therapy would ever help him regain what he had lost.

Luke just snorted and looked steadily away.

Zachary could feel the time slipping away from them. The CO had said that she would give them an hour. It didn't look like that was going to be enough time to get Luke's story out of him.

"Luke. Come on. Help me here. Let me do something for you. It's pretty hard to do anything if you won't say a word to me."

Luke shook his head.

"Who did you kill?" Zachary demanded, making his voice harder. Luke needed to listen. Zachary needed to be firmer with him. To insist that he respond. "Or were accused of killing? Tell me his name."

Luke's eyes flicked over to him briefly. Zachary watched him closely and saw a slight shift in his breathing pattern, a little flare to his nostrils. Readying himself. Luke cleared his throat.

"Eyler," he offered finally.

"Eyler? That was the victim's name? What's his first name?"

Luke shook his head. He clearly didn't know. Did that mean that it wasn't someone he knew well? Closely enough to know the man's last name, but not his first.

"And who is Eyler? Someone you knew from before?"

A hesitation from Luke. Tensing in readiness. Then looking away again and letting his shoulders fall slack again. Studied calm. Pretending to know nothing, to be unaffected by it all.

"So he was someone in Gordo's organization?" Zachary asked, hoping that the name of the big boss would shock Luke into reacting. Luke's eyes flew back to Zachary, then quickly away again. Good control. But then, he had been training to hide his feelings his whole life. From the time he was a little boy and no one wanted to be responsible for his care. For the years that he was in the trafficking ring and no one cared how he felt about anything, only about whether he did his job well or not. He'd had to hide his feelings if he was going to lure innocent young women and men into the organization and not give away his role until it was too late.

"Did Eyler recognize you? Come after you?"

No response.

"Were you attacked, Luke? I can see that you're hurt. Did he try to take you back?"

13

Luke's Adam's apple bobbed with a hard swallow. Zachary watched his face for any other indication of what he was thinking or feeling. He was good at reading facial expressions and body language, a skill he had honed growing up in an abusive home and foster care where it was essential to read the intentions of everyone around him, and a valuable skill for a PI, used to dealing with people who tried to hide things from him. Even clients tried to keep their secrets.

But Luke didn't make it easy. If anything, his expression flattened even more. He was like stone. His gaze was no longer on the ceiling or to the side. Instead, his eyes glazed and trying to meet his eyes was like looking into a mirror. There was nothing there to see.

"Luke." Zachary knew he was gone. Swallowed up in a flashback of what had happened with Eyler, or maybe in a memory further back than that, knowing Eyler in the trafficking ring or something that had happened to him when he was younger.

Or maybe there was no memory at all, but just dissociation. Luke had told him once before that it was best to just go somewhere else. Not to think about it. Not to form the memory in the first place, just to pull back and not be a part of the experience. He had learned to do it while being trafficked, just as Zachary and so many other traumatized kids had learned that there was only one way to escape when physically unable to protect themselves from the abuse.

"Luke." He touched Luke's hand, even though he knew it was probably against the rules to have any physical contact with him. There were lists of rules printed on plastic panels screwed into the wall, but Zachary hadn't bothered to read them. He'd stretched his brain enough filling out the long form at the police station.

Luke jerked back as though he'd been shocked. The chains clanked loudly, making both of them jump. Luke's jaw clenched and Zachary saw anger in his eyes for the first time. Fury at being touched or at being pulled back into the present.

"Tell me what happened," Zachary told him. "Let it out. It isn't going to help you to keep it bottled up."

"No."

"You've been accused of murder. This isn't some minor drug dealing charge. If you don't have a defense, you will go to prison for twenty years or more. Maybe for life. Is that what you want?"

Luke sat back in his chair, pulling on his chains in an effort to fold his arms into his body and get as far away from Zachary as possible. "Yes."

Zachary's brain hitched. He hadn't been expecting that answer. He thought he could talk Luke into seeing how serious the situation was. To show him that his only hope was to cooperate with Zachary, Joss, and a lawyer to figure out how to get clear of the charges, or at least to mitigate the length of the sentence.

"You want to go to prison?"

"Yes. So go home. Don't come back here. Don't bug me with your questions. Tell your sister too. I don't want anything to do with her. Not with either of you. Just leave me be."

"Why?"

Luke shook his head. He looked as confused by Zachary's question as Zachary felt about Luke saying he didn't want anything to do with Joss. Joss had been his lifesaver. The person who had been there for him for the past year, helping him to move forward and to stay out of trouble. He knew that there was a strong relationship between the two of them. An affection that ran deep. Not quite like a parent and child, but something similar. Maybe like the feelings that Zachary had for Mr. Peterson, though Luke's feelings were still seedlings, not having grown over decades like Zachary's. Still, he remembered how he had felt those first few weeks when he had been in Mr. Peterson's home, finding an unexpected ally, someone who cared about him even knowing his history. The first parental figure who really seemed to care anything about him, and the only one who had stayed a part of his life since.

"This is my life," Luke said. "Just stay out of it. Both of you."

"We don't want to stay out of it. Joss cares about you, Luke. She cares what happens to you. Let us help. Maybe you're right, maybe there isn't anything that we can do in the end, but we can at least try."

"Just back off."

Zachary shook his head slowly. "I'm not going to do that, Luke."

"It's not worth it. *I'm* not worth it."

"You are."

"I'm a rat. I'm sewer scum. Why would you want to help someone like me?"

"You're a person, and someone that I like and enjoy being around. And do you think that just anyone could live with Joss and put up with her attitude? That takes a special talent. That's someone worth defending."

Luke gave a bark of laughter. "I've never met anyone more real than your sister."

Zachary nodded. "She doesn't put a false face on for anyone," he agreed. "She calls it like she sees it. And if you don't like it... well, that's too bad. Take her as she is, opinions and all."

Luke's body language relaxed a little. His anger over Zachary touching him had faded. But the pain in his expression had not.

"Was it Eyler who hurt you? Is that how you got the black eye?"

Luke shook his head. "I don't know. I don't remember."

"Were you under the influence? Drinking? Drugs?"

"I'm clean. Not that it did me any good." His lips pressed together. "What was the point in going straight? This would have been easier if I had been high."

"Why don't you remember, then?"

"Just don't."

Zachary tried to see past Luke's mask. Could he remember and didn't want to talk about it? Could he not remember because he had dissociated during the experience or suppressed it afterward? Was he lying about being clean and had actually been blitzed out of his mind?

"How did the police come to arrest you? How did they know it was you?"

"I was there. They could see what happened."

Zachary winced inwardly. Being caught at the scene was not a good thing. Hard to get around that. "Were there witnesses?"

"No."

"Physical evidence? Your fingerprints? Your DNA?"

Luke shrugged. "Probably."

The police wouldn't have had a chance to process everything yet. But it didn't take long to compare fingerprints. If they had caught him in the act, they didn't need fingerprints and DNA to know that he did it. But they would be used in court to prove he was the killer.

"Why haven't you gotten a lawyer? You need someone."

"There's no point." Luke stared at Zachary. "Don't you get it? Why bother? Nothing is going to help." He closed his eyes as if exhausted. "Don't waste the effort."

"Don't give up. I know you wouldn't just kill this guy without a reason. That means there was some justification. That can get you a lighter sentence, if nothing else."

"You don't know that."

"What?"

"That I wouldn't kill him without a reason."

Zachary just looked at Luke.

"You don't know anything about me, dude," Luke pointed out. "You know nothing but what I've told you, and that could all be lies. I'm good at lying. I'm a professional. It's how I survived. Why would I stop lying just because I was talking to you?"

He was right, of course. Zachary didn't have any outside verification that any of Luke's story was true. An old woman who had said that Luke's grandmother had died and then he had fallen in with bad company. That was the only thing he knew about Luke from anyone's mouth but Luke's own. Or Madison's, which was the same thing, since she only parroted what he had wanted her to believe.

But Zachary believed that he knew the truth when he heard it. That he understood enough of the pain in Luke's eyes when he talked about his childhood and early days with the cartel to know it was the truth. And Joss had been in the business. She knew what it was like and everything she had said aligned with what Luke described.

He trusted Joss to be able to see through Luke's pretenses and know what the real deal was.

He met Luke's eyes. "I know you."

Luke snorted and looked away, eyes going up to the ceiling again, chin lifted in defiance. "You don't know me, man. You don't know me at all."

Zachary straightened. He rubbed the back of his neck, stiff from slouching in the hard molded chair. "Before long, our time is going to be up and the CO will be back to take you to your cell. Do you need anything?"

Luke's mouth started to form a word, then he shook his head and pressed his lips closed again.

"I'm sure they must allow me to bring some stuff in. Books. Candy. Writing paper."

Luke shook his head again.

The decision to close his mouth appeared to be final. He wasn't going to say anything else to Zachary. The sparse answers that he'd provided were going to have to do. Zachary wasn't going to be able to get any more details out of him. Luke wasn't assisting his own defense.

"Will you talk to a lawyer if we get you one?"

Luke again shook his head.

"You don't need to throw your life away like this," Zachary said.

Luke's chains jangled as he again tried to fold his arms over his chest but was defeated by the shortness of his tether. He sat like a statue, staring past Zachary and determined not to help him.

14

The CO again left Zachary sitting at the table in the meeting room while she dealt with Luke. Zachary wondered if she were the only one at the jail on a Sunday morning. There couldn't be a lot to do in a small-town jail on a Sunday morning, when the court and the police station were both shut down. Maybe the jail was empty some days, without even a few drunks to keep the bunks warm.

Zachary was eager to get out of the meeting room but knew that being impatient wouldn't move along any faster. Any anxiety or impatience with the process would just make it seem longer. He reviewed the few things that Luke had told him, trying to look at them from every angle and squeeze as much information from each word and gesture as he could. Once he got back to his car, he would write down everything he could before he started to forget. And he would write down questions that he needed answered and possible avenues to pursue.

While he was still analyzing each aspect of Luke's answers, the corrections officer returned. She stood in the doorway and nodded to Zachary.

"All right. Let's get you out of here."

Zachary stood, paused for a moment to make sure he had his balance, and followed her. She was inclined to walk at a quicker pace than he was, but Zachary didn't let her rush him. Walking quickly or jogging to keep up with her would just end up with Zachary tripping and ending up flat on his face. Since the car accident that had temporarily paralyzed him, he had worked hard to learn to walk smoothly again. However, it sometimes still felt a bit awkward. Running, climbing stairs, or things like walking backward were another story. His brain seemed to remember how to do these things, but his body didn't, and Zachary would inevitably get the movements out of sync.

The CO stood at the next door, waiting impatiently for Zachary to catch up with her. When he did, she swiped her card key and entered a code in the number pad. They were back out at the front in the check-in area again. She took him to the lockers and indicated the one they had put his personal items in. Zachary was relieved that the box clicked open the first time he punched in the security code. Part of him had been certain that it wouldn't work.

"What can you tell me about Luke's arrest and the charges against him?" he asked the CO as he slowly began to remove the items from the locker and to dress himself and put the loose items back into his pockets.

The woman didn't answer for a minute. She looked at Zachary, considering. "He didn't tell you?"

"No. I think… he's pretty overwhelmed at this point. Doesn't believe that it will do him any good to talk about it."

She shrugged her rounded shoulders. "Probably wouldn't," she agreed. "It's not going to get him out of trouble."

"It could help. If there are mitigating circumstances…"

She snorted. "As far as I can see, the only mitigating circumstance is that the guy he killed was a scumbag. Removing him from the streets was a public service."

"What do you know about the victim?"

"I can't really discuss the case with a civilian. But I imagine if you read the news, you'll find out plenty about his past convictions."

"Those are public record," Zachary agreed. "So it wouldn't be a breach of confidentiality to tell me that. I'll find out anyway from a couple of courthouse searches."

She considered this, watching Zachary buckle his belt back on. "I suppose so. Convictions for various assaults, sex trafficking, public intoxication. There are other charges that they weren't able to make stick…" She stopped, realizing that what they would like to have gotten him for probably wasn't something she should tell Zachary.

"That's about what I figured," Zachary agreed. "Any idea how far up the food chain he is? What his position in Gordo's organization is?"

Her eyes flickered at the mention of Gordo's name. Surprise that

Zachary knew who he was or that it was his organization that Luke had been a member of?

Zachary wasn't even sure how rank was determined in an organization like that. Were they similar to military ranks? To the *capo* and *consigliere* in movies like *The Godfather*?

"He wasn't at the top," the CO answered slowly, carefully considering her answer. "But he wasn't a street-level hood, either. He had people under him. He had power."

But he had let someone like Luke get close enough to take him down. Arrogance? Surprise? How had Luke managed it?

"What do you know about your friend's past?" The woman nodded in the direction of the jail cells.

"That he was a displaced child, grew up without a stable family environment. He had nowhere to go when his grandmother died and spiraled out of control, ended up in the organization. Recruited there by an older boy. Became a Romeo as well as a prostitute. Seducing younger girls or boys in order to bring them into the organization."

She nodded. "Not a nice kind of guy, even if he does look like a fallen angel. Don't get it into your head that he's the victim here. He killed a man. There's no question about that. He's got a sheaf of charges and convictions a foot thick. And probably a lot of them that aren't in our file because he's gone by different names and not all of his aliases have been linked together. He's been involved with the police since he was a young child stealing from the corner store. But he's not a child anymore."

Zachary was careful not to contradict her. As long as she was giving him information, he had to be careful not to argue with anything she said. "He's been living with my sister. She got him into rehab and has been keeping him out of trouble. Until now."

Surprise flashed across the CO's face. "Your sister?"

"Yes. Older sister. They're not romantically involved," he hurried to add. "She has some experience, though; knows how the business is run and the methods they use. So she was a good person to keep an eye on Luke, to try to keep him out of trouble."

"Your sister," the CO repeated, as if trying to convince herself that it was true. "I never knew that she had any family."

Zachary was surprised she knew anything about Joss.

"We didn't grow up together. I was in a different foster home. So were our other brothers and sisters. I only just met her a year ago."

"Well, *she* has a history too."

"I know. She's open about that. But she's not in the life anymore either. It is *possible* to get out."

She didn't deny this, but didn't confirm it either.

"Do you know what evidence they have against Luke for this... killing?"

She put her hands up. "I'm just the jailer. You'll have to talk to the investigating officers about that. Not me."

She knew more than she would let on, but she believed she was doing her job by keeping the details confidential. Zachary opted to stay on her good side. He didn't know how many more times he might be coming back to see Luke if he managed to get a toehold on the case.

"I appreciate all of your help. And you being here on a Sunday. That can't be fun."

She shrugged. "A quiet Sunday means that I can get caught up on stuff that I can't during the week. It's better than days when it's a circus here and everyone wants their business dealt with immediately."

Zachary had all of his personal possessions back, his shoes and belt done up, and winter gear back on. But he wasn't quite ready to leave. Worry gnawed at his gut. More than just concern for what kind of sentence Luke might be facing. There were many other things to be concerned about before Luke ever made it to trial.

"Listen," he said slowly, feeling his way carefully through the conversation. "I don't know anything about your jail or usual practices, so don't take this the wrong way..."

She pursed her lips, and frown lines creased her forehead. "What?"

"Is he safe here? I know that this is where he has to be, but he's young, and he's not a big guy. Is he... he's not in the general population, with adult criminals, is he?"

"Of course not. You don't need to tell me my job. Crap like that might happen in other facilities, but no one is getting assaulted in mine. Juveniles and adults are never mixed. Not in their cells, not in any common area, visitor room, nothing."

Zachary nodded, relieved. "Good. I don't want anything to happen to him."

She looked at him under partially closed lids, like there was something she was hiding and not sure that she would reveal to him. Zachary felt an itch at the back of his neck.

"What?"

"Even if he was in gen pop at the prison, he would be protected, you know."

Zachary frowned. "By the guards? The CO's, I mean? Is that what you're talking about?"

She shook her head. "He's marked."

"Marked how?"

"You haven't seen his tattoo?"

Zachary considered. He hadn't been particularly focused on Luke's body art. He had noticed Luke's ink in passing, but hadn't paid it much attention. "He has a few tattoos."

"Yeah. Well, the one on the back of his hand, that's the one I'm talking about."

Zachary tried to picture it. A couple of interconnected letters, he thought. Stylized like the big letter at the beginning of a chapter in an old manuscript, which always made it hard for Zachary to figure out what the first letter and word were supposed to be.

"Letters, I think."

The CO nodded. "A maker's mark from the organization he is in. Identifies who his boss or owner is, so everybody knows not to damage the merchandise. And to return him if he runs away. The other inmates would recognize it."

Zachary shook his head, unable to find the words to respond to this.

"He probably has it branded on his body somewhere, too," the woman told him. "Burned in deep so it can't be removed or inked over. That's what they do with the lower-level workers. He probably didn't get the ink until he had been with them for a few years, moved up in the organization to a respected position."

Zachary was nauseated by the thought of such a scar.

"The branding is intended to hurt for a long time. To remind them who owns them and keep them compliant."

His stomach gurgled. He swallowed and tried to get his thoughts back on track. "And what about... I'm worried about his state of mind. Knowing that he's looking down the barrel of a twenty-to-life sentence..."

"Most suicides take place in the first three to seven days. We watch them pretty carefully during that period. He's got nothing in his cell that could be used for a suicide attempt. You saw how he was dressed. Jumpsuit and flip-flops. A guy's gotta be pretty inventive to attempt suicide in our cells. But we watch 'em. Newbies like him are checked every fifteen to twenty minutes around the clock. And if he gets it into his head to try something stupid like diving headfirst off of his bunk into the concrete floor, someone is going to notice. He won't get far."

She saw Zachary's shock at the statement.

"They do that. Usually don't end up with anything more than bruises or a concussion, but other facilities have had fatalities. Someone crushes their skull, breaks their spine, or gets a bleed inside the brain. But not here. Ain't never had one of them in here."

Zachary swallowed. "Okay. Good. Thanks for looking out for him."

She nodded understandingly. "If I was him, I sure wouldn't want to wait around for my sentence. I'd be looking for the first opportunity to end it before that."

15

Disturbed by the CO's words, Zachary looked at his phone as he walked out of the jail and back around to the other side of the building where his car was parked, checking the time. He should make the best use of his time while he was in town, rather than having to drive back and forth or do all of his investigating remotely. He decided to go back into the police station to see what else he could discover about Luke and the crime while he was there. He had known that Luke would have a long rap sheet, but hadn't stopped to consider what else might be on it. He was, as the jail CO and Luke himself suggested, taking Luke at his own word. Of course he would show himself in the best light possible.

Luke had wanted to get out of the organization; Zachary knew that much was true. And he had admitted to committing plenty of crimes while he had been both a victim and a perpetrator in the cartel. He portrayed himself as being coerced and controlled, which was how it worked in the industry. But how much of their darkness had rubbed off onto him? He admitted to seducing other teens into the life, admitted that he had been doing it for years. What if after the first little while, he didn't have to be coerced anymore, but enjoyed the game? What if he had liked the power of moving up in the organization, the control he had over those boys and girls?

There were a lot of reasons to get out of the cartel other than the ones

Luke had given. He might have known there was a sting coming. Might have disagreed with someone higher up. Maybe he wanted to branch out into his own business. He could even have stolen money, drugs, or business from someone else in the organization and needed to hide out for a while. And Zachary had provided the perfect opportunity for Luke to do so; getting him out, making the other traffickers think that he was dead, and finding him a home and a new life with Joss. Zachary couldn't assume that Luke was quite as pure and well-intentioned as he had made himself out to be.

Zachary entered the police station and saw the same young cop as before. No shift change while he had been in the jail with Luke. The cop raised his brows.

"Something else I can help you with?"

"Thanks for helping me out with that. I really appreciate it."

The cop shrugged. "That's my job. Sort of why I'm here today. You're welcome, though. I take it you got in to see him?"

"Yes." Zachary leaned on the counter, trying to look comfortable and casual. "Do you know the kid I was in to see? Hear about what happened?"

"Yeah, heard something about it. He was processed through here, but I wasn't around at the time. Some of the other guys were. I only have it second or third hand." He nodded at his screen. "And what's on the computer."

"What are all of the charges, do you know?"

The man gave him an odd look. "Murder," he said with a shrug. "First degree."

"Is that it? Nothing else related?"

"You don't need to pile them up in a case like this. One charge is all you need."

"And the arresting officers, they thought it was pretty open-and-shut?"

The cop leaned back in his chair, making it squeak and squeal as he tested its limits. "Caught him red-handed. Knife in his hand, covered in blood. What's he going to say—that he was framed? He just happened along and thought that he would pick up the murder weapon, like in some stupid cop show on TV? That isn't the way it works. In ninety-nine percent of the cases, the perp is exactly who you think it is. It's just a matter of gathering enough information to hang them."

"Which isn't too hard in Luke's case."

"I think you can see that."

"Pretty clear," Zachary said encouragingly.

"I wouldn't want to be in his shoes right now." The cop apparently thought this was funny, letting out a snort of laughter. "Hell, I wouldn't want to be in those shoes anytime. Did you see them?"

Zachary forced a chuckle, nodding. "Not quite my chosen wardrobe either," he agreed. "And I'm not particularly discerning." He looked down at his jeans and shirt and scuffed shoes and shook his head, mocking himself. "Did Luke say anything when he was arrested? Anything to explain himself? To excuse what he had done? Or a confession?"

"Nah, Carruthers said he was dead quiet. Wouldn't answer any questions about why he had done it. Must have been a fight over business, is my guess. Two pimps working the same territory. Maybe one stole business from the other. A favorite john or something." The officer shook his head. "These guys are very *sensitive*. They get into a lot of fights with each other. Lash out. Usually, it's just some scrapes and bruises, but every now and then, you end up with a mess like this."

"They were both in the life?"

"I looked at their records, both of them. Long sheets, stretching way back. Maybe your guy was trying to horn in on Eyler's territory. First time he's been arrested in this part of the state. Thought he could set up his own business. Didn't know it was already covered." The cop shrugged. "Probably."

"I thought... that Luke had gone straight."

"What? He's not straight in any sense of the word." The cop laughed. "Been out of the picture for a while, but sometimes that happens. They travel or hide from someone who is gunning for them. But then they're back. They can't keep away from it."

"Luke has been staying with my sister. I would think that she would have noticed if he was setting up business again."

"Your sister." The cop's expression was immediately masked, as if he had pulled a hood down over his face. "Your sister is..."

"Jocelyn Goldman," Zachary said.

But the cop's lips hadn't been shaping a J sound. He had intended to say something else. He stared at Zachary, something uncertain about his manner.

Both he and the corrections officer had reacted the same way. The corrections officer had known about Jocelyn's past. She had wondered whether Zachary knew about Joss's history and had been surprised to hear that she had siblings.

"What do you know about her?" Zachary asked curiously, cocking his head slightly. He thought that Joss had been open with him about her history, but there was plenty that they had never discussed. Zachary wouldn't have wanted all of the gritty details about Joss's day-to-day life of being addicted and trafficked. Joss had the right to her privacy. Her dignity. She had the right to start her life over, free of that business and from having to explain it.

"The Old Lady? We all know her around here."

16

Zachary put both elbows and forearms on the counter and leaned toward the cop. "*The Old Lady?*"

"I know." The cop made a waving-away gesture. "She's not that old. In any other business, she'd still be in her prime. But in prostitution? She's an old lady." His mouth moved to add something else, then he thought better of it and closed his mouth tightly, eyeing Zachary.

It was true. Jocelyn had made it clear that the reason she was no longer in the business was because no one had any use for her anymore. She looked much older than her years, aged by hard living; smoking, drinking, drugging, and all of the abuse she had put up with since they were children. She'd been old beyond her years back then, too, the oldest girl in a family with six children, expected to keep them all quiet and out of the way of their parents. An adult by the time she was into her teens.

"So you knew her before she left the business, or not until after? Was she 'The Old Lady' when she was still working?"

The cop's eyes darted to the side. "Yeah. Don't know. She's been around a lot longer than I have. Never knew about her until the past few months. But other guys around here… they go back further than that."

"And that's who calls her The Old Lady?"

He didn't answer.

"How did you find out about her the last few months if she isn't in the business anymore?"

"She makes a pest of herself." The cop looked embarrassed to be reporting this. "She's always in here complaining about things. Pimps working in her area. Drug dealers. She's lobbying for this new law or that change in legislation. And if you arrest a hooker for something…" He rolled his eyes and shook his head. "The Old Lady is on a one-person mission to completely overhaul Vermont's prostitution laws."

Zachary tried to suppress a smile. So Joss had a secret mission, did she? After telling him to stay away from the human trafficking business, to look the other way and forget about trying to save Madison and Luke from it, she'd started waging war on them herself.

"She is a pain in the neck," the cop declared. "I knew there was going to be trouble as soon as I heard that kid was one of hers. No way this thing is going to just be quietly pleaded out and disappear."

"Luke isn't actually her son."

The young cop gave Zachary an odd look. "No, I know that. But she takes kids in. Cleans them up, sets them up in places of their own, helps them find jobs and all that. And makes life… uncomfortable for anyone trying to work her area. Any suspicious characters start hanging around near her place, checking into hotels, whatever, and we hear about it." The young man motioned to his computer as if Zachary could see the number of complaints Joss had filed over the preceding months.

"I didn't even know she was doing all that. I thought… there was just Luke."

"No way. The Old Lady is like a crazy cat lady, only collecting kids instead of cats. Luckily, they're not all crammed into her house…"

"How did all of this come about? How long has she been doing this?"

"I don't know. At least a year. Something like that."

That coincided with the approximate time that Zachary had brought Luke to Joss. Apparently, his action had triggered her social conscience and a desire to change the shape of things in the community around her. Or she'd felt the need to show Luke that there was a way to live outside of the trafficking rings. Or maybe she'd decided that the only way to keep them from seeing Luke and realizing he was still alive was to do everything she could to keep the cartels out of her neighborhood and out of Kent.

She had warned Zachary against doing anything that would raise the ire of the trafficking rings. It was a billion-dollar business and the bosses did not take kindly to anyone interfering with their profit. But apparently, that stricture didn't apply to Joss herself.

Maybe because she knew the players personally and had plenty of dirt on them, they thought it best not to do anything to hurt her. Who knew what kind of evidence she might have saved to the cloud or squirreled away in a safety deposit box that they couldn't get at, but that would come to light if she died. Maybe she had told them she had ways of reaching them and disrupting their business from beyond the grave.

"I didn't know," Zachary said, shaking his head and blowing out his breath in amazement.

The cop laughed. "You're the only one who didn't, then."

"I guess we need to have a little talk. She can bring me up to speed."

"She's a force to be reckoned with." The cop straightened some papers on the desk. "I wouldn't want to be in her crosshairs."

Zachary remembered how Joss had spoken about their father; how she had fantasized about killing him even as a child. And the way she spoke with such familiarity about guns.

The image of being in Joss's gun sights made him shudder.

Before long, he was on Joss's doorstep, seriously considering whether he ought to have called ahead for once instead of just showing up at her door. If she was waging war against the cartels, she might very well answer the door with a sawed-off shotgun. Or that PKM she had spoken so fondly of. He had already rung the doorbell, but he pulled out his phone, thinking maybe he'd better call her to let her know that it was him.

The door opened and Joss stood there looking down at him, her mouth a straight, thin line. But she was not cradling a machine gun in her arms, so that was a good sign. Zachary's mouth was dry. He nodded a greeting and cleared his throat.

"I've been at the jail. Thought I'd come and report to you, talk things over."

She considered for a moment, then nodded and stepped back to let him in. Zachary glanced around the small living room as he entered. There was no sign that anyone but Joss and Luke lived there. He couldn't see back into the bedrooms to see whether there were any other rescued teens sheltering there, hiding from visitors, until Joss could find another place for them to live. If there were, they hadn't left extra shoes on the mat by the door or anything else that gave away their presence to Zachary.

He followed Joss into the living room and sat down. She was watching him carefully, eyes sharp. "So?" she demanded, "What have you found out so far?"

Zachary sat on an easy chair. He didn't sit back in it, but perched on the edge, leaning forward. "Not very much yet. Luke doesn't have much to say. Wouldn't tell me what had happened. Wouldn't agree to get a lawyer. He's acting like he's resigned to going to prison for the rest of his life."

Joss nodded, her mouth twisted into a bitter shape like she had just chewed on a lemon peel.

"They, uh… they know you at the police station and jail."

She shrugged. "I'd hope so. I was just there making arrangements."

"It sounds like they've known you for longer than that, though. Like maybe… you've been waging a private war on the trafficking rings."

The hint of a smug smile replaced the bitter, puckered expression. "I told you; I know the business."

"So someone like me can't do anything to change things, to rescue people like Luke. But *you* can."

"You don't know anything. You managed to avoid ending up in the life. Lucky for you. But luckily for these kids, *I* did not. And I know where the bodies are buried."

Zachary swallowed and licked his lips. He wished she had offered him coffee. Or at least a glass of water. "Literally?" he joked, "Where the bodies are buried?"

"Sometimes."

The way she said it raised goosebumps on his arms, despite the temperature of the room.

"Why didn't you tell me any of this?"

"Why? What business is it of yours?"

"Well… maybe I could have helped you somehow. And I know it isn't any of my business, but you know I was trying to help Luke. To keep him away from the traffickers."

"You couldn't have done anything. Like I say, you don't know anything about the business or about any of the players. I do. I know what I can do, how far I can push. You won't listen to anything I tell you. You're too impulsive and you would just charge in there like a white knight, thinking you could change everything. I can't have my little brother showing up and making a mess of everything."

Zachary cleared his throat, uncomfortable. "Okay… maybe I would be too impulsive," he admitted. He knew it was one of his faults. It was the part of the ADHD package that had always gotten him in the most trouble. It had been highlighted on the very first psychological profile when he was ten and had been a problem ever since. Impulse control wasn't something that medication could give him, that he'd been able to develop through therapy, or that could be beaten out of him. Enough people had attempted it and failed. "But you could have at least told me what you were doing."

Joss just looked at him and made no further attempt to defend her position.

17

Zachary pulled his notebook out of his pocket and removed the pencil from where it was jammed in the coil.

"You know what happened, then. Tell me about it."

Joss raised her brows.

"With Luke," Zachary prompted. "Tell me what happened."

"I wasn't there."

"But you've been involved in this... disruption of the trafficking rings down here. So you know what it was all about. And you know the players, so fill me in on who was involved."

She gave him a wry look. "Is my little brother telling me what to do?"

"You asked me to help Luke. How can I do that if no one gives me the information?"

"Do you tell your clients what to do? They tell you what to do."

Zachary matched her smile. "Getting my clients to give me the information I need to do the job is something I do all the time. On every case. And I keep going back with more questions until I have all the information I need to do my job."

"That sounds like a threat."

"Yeah. How many times do you want me to show up here asking you more questions?"

Joss glanced over her shoulder at the blank wall. Zachary wondered what—or who—he would see if he could look through the walls. How many people was Joss trying to protect?

Joss returned her gaze to him. "Eyler. The guy Luke killed is named Eyler."

"I already got that much. Do you know his first name? Aliases? What he's been arrested for or what position he held in the organization?"

"You don't ask much, do you?"

"Just asking for the information I need to get the job done."

"Christopher. Christopher Eyler."

Zachary wrote it down, relieved to finally have some solid information. "Can you spell Eyler for me?"

"Spelling isn't my strong suit. I haven't ever seen it written out."

Zachary gave it his best guess. He was sure a few database searches would get him the right spelling. If Eyler had been involved in trafficking in Vermont for a few years, his name would be all over the place.

"And what is he in the organization? And… which organization? I don't know how they are set up. Are there rival organizations with different territories?"

"There are… smaller organizations under a bigger umbrella," Joss said, frowning as she tried to formulate an answer. "Independent operators, like franchises, controlled by someone higher up… but on a whole bunch of levels. Like a pyramid."

"With Gordo as the top boss in this part of the country."

She nodded, her eyes closing to slits. "Don't you go looking for him. You shouldn't even say his name."

"Why not?"

"Because people like that do not like to be known and named outside of their elite group. If word got out that you were sharing his name with the cops or spreading it around in your investigation, they could come after you. And you don't have any protection."

Zachary nodded and made a mental note of it. He wanted to help Luke if he could and help Joss with her cause. But he didn't want to end up being targeted because of it. He had to remember Kenzie and Rhys and other people around him who could also be targeted if he stirred things up and said the wrong thing.

"So Eyler was…"

Joss settled back, relaxing a bit. She rubbed her chin, thinking about it. "Luke started out at street-level. He moved up the ladder a little, acting as a Romeo, recruiting for his boss's stable as well."

"Right. He told me that. He was originally recruited by..." Zachary fished for the name in his memory. A year before, he'd had been a long, confusing discussion in the middle of the adrenaline-charged night of Madison's and Luke's escape. All of them, including Rhys, had been shot at. But Zachary had processed and re-read his notes and he had read them again after Joss had called to tell him about Luke's arrest, wanting everything to be fresh in his mind. "Connor. An older boy."

"Yeah. Ancient history. At that level, people don't survive for long. Luke is long-lived, for someone who wasn't able to advance much in the organization."

"And Connor's organization was taken over by Peggy Ann. Is that right?"

"She absorbed it, yes. And several others. With each 'takeover,' she advanced higher in the organization. So, Luke was no longer owned by a low-level boss, but a high-level one." Joss considered her words and revised her statement. "A mid-level boss."

Zachary had seen Peggy Ann. Not up close and personal, but close enough that he had no intention of running into her again or interviewing her as part of his investigation into what had happened with Luke. "Right." He made a quick note to make sure he remembered the discussion. "And where does Eyler fit in?"

"He and Peggy Ann were both about the same level."

"Does that make them peers or competitors? Do people get along if they are on the same level, or do they consider each other rivals?"

"You act like people are all the same. It's different for everyone. Bosses at the same level might exchange assets, refer business to each other, combine forces to form a bigger, more powerful organization. Or they might steal from each other, kill each other off, start rumors in the organization. You don't know. Even if two bosses appear to be cooperating, one might be planning to stab the other in the back. You could put your trust in someone just to have the rug pulled out from under you. You have to always be suspicious. Always assume that even if someone is helping you now or making a deal that benefits you both... that could change tomorrow. Or five minutes from now."

"Did Luke know Eyler? If Luke was under Peggy Ann, would he ever have had contact with Eyler?"

"I don't know."

Zachary needed a better answer than that. Joss and Luke had lived together for more than a year. Surely they'd had the opportunity to discuss different people they had both known. At least a guess. Joss could at least speculate on whether Luke and Eyler had known each other when Luke had been in the life.

But she could probably only give him the answer she already had. Luke wouldn't have killed Eyler if they didn't know each other. It wasn't a chance mugging. Somehow, Luke *had* known Eyler.

"And what did you know about Eyler?"

"What do you mean?" Joss's face was smooth and expressionless.

"If you've been spending your time fighting trafficking rings in this part of the state and Eyler was killed here, by someone you know, then I assume you know what he was doing here."

She scowled at his logic. "He was hoping to get established. The trouble with killing one cockroach is that there are a hundred more waiting to take his place."

"So even though you were successful in getting rid of whoever was here before Eyler, he wanted to fill the void. Snatch up new territory while it was available."

Joss nodded her agreement.

"And how did Luke get into the middle of this?"

Joss raised her hands palms-up and shrugged. "I don't know, and that's the truth, Zachary. He wasn't supposed to be involved with anything. Eyler wasn't supposed to know about him. Luke knew that if he was seen and identified…"

"Is it possible that's exactly what did happen? Eyler recognized him somewhere and went after him? Luke had to defend himself, and…?"

"Maybe. Your guess is as good as mine. Luke never said a word to me about having seen him. I asked Luke what happened, but he wouldn't say anything."

Zachary didn't have to imagine Luke's stubborn silence. He had just experienced it himself. "Can you speculate? You might say that my guess would be as good as yours, but you lived with him, I didn't. You knew more of what was going on with him. What he might or might not do. Who he was likely to run into. You know the business and players. I don't know any of those things."

"Yes. Maybe he ran into Eyler or one of his workers. Maybe he was identified when he was out at a club or a party. Traffickers often work those places. Drop a few recruiters and see who they can scoop up. If someone recognized his face…"

"Or saw his tattoo."

Joss looked at him, chewing on her lip. "Yeah," she agreed eventually and looked away.

"Do you have one too?"

Joss pushed up the sleeve of her sweater and turned her arm to show her the ink on the inside of her forearm. Unlike the fresh, clear lines and colors of Luke's tattoo, Joss's work was faded and fuzzy around the edges, the colors dull. It served to remind him just how long she had been trafficked. Decades had passed, and Zachary had never known what she was going through.

Her tattoo was not letters, but a red velvet crown with numbers below it. The numbers were so faded that Zachary could barely read them. He swallowed, looking at it. He didn't ask whether she had been branded as well or the meaning of the numbers.

"Would someone looking at that know..." Zachary's throat closed and he couldn't finish the question.

"Who I belonged to? Not a newbie. The low-level operators haven't been around long enough to recognize it. The established bosses? People all the way up the food chain? They'd know whose mark it was." She tugged her sleeve back down to cover it. "But the symbology is common enough for someone in the business to recognize it as a trafficker's claim."

Zachary nodded numbly. He wondered if any of the girls he had known over the years had borne a similar mark. He'd been in several institutional settings. Places a teen girl might be sent if she were considered a runner or promiscuous. How many girls had he met who had been trafficked without his knowing about it?

He had known girls who hooked, escaping foster or group homes to walk the streets, offering their bodies to escape the abuse or confinement. He'd always figured if they walked into it with their eyes open, that was their choice. But how many of them had been tricked, coerced, or physically forced into the life? Just because he never saw their bosses or organizations, that didn't mean they weren't there, watching, meting out punishments if the girls didn't do what they were told. Just because the girls said they could choose the lifestyle they wanted to, it didn't mean that they had.

Zachary touched Joss's arm where the tattoo was hidden beneath her sweater sleeve. His touch was light, just barely in contact with her. "Joss... you be careful. I don't want these guys hurting you."

"I can take care of myself."

"This is a nasty business."

"Says the initiate to the master."

Zachary shrugged. Of course it was silly for him to counsel her in something that she knew far better than he did. "I don't want to lose you. Not when I've just barely gotten to know you again."

18

Zachary closed his eyes and rubbed his forehead for a moment, trying to get back on track. "What did the police tell you about Eyler's murder? What do you know about what happened?"

Joss took a deep breath and released it. How much did his questions and his ignorance distress her? Did she fight flashbacks when showing him her tattoo? How much of her time did she spend reliving that past?

"It was in a hotel room," she said in a clear, flat voice. "Room was registered to Eyler. Don't know what Luke was doing there. There had been shouting, fighting, quite a disturbance. The police received several calls. When they got there, it was just Luke and Eyler, and Eyler was dead. Luke's prints all over the place. In Eyler's blood. On the murder weapon."

She stopped. Zachary waited, giving her time to pick up the narrative again, but she shook her head, keeping her mouth closed. That was the full story, as much as she was going to tell him.

Considering how little the cop at the police station had been willing to tell him, he was surprised at the details Joss knew. Had the police shared them with her or had she seen? Or had she talked to someone else who had firsthand knowledge? Maybe she knew people at the hotel. People who knew she was fighting against trafficking, or just a friend who was a maid or a girl who had happened to be at the hotel at the time.

"Any sign that there had been someone else in the room?"

"There are people in an out of a room like that all the time. Who knows who might have been there in the previous twenty-four hours. Just Luke and Eyler when the police got there."

"Do you know the name of the arresting officer? Or who is investigating the homicide? I should probably talk to them."

"I might have their names."

She didn't move to check her phone or business cards in her purse.

"What was Luke doing there?" Zachary mused. "What's been going on with him? Where has he been going?"

"I told him to be careful," Joss snapped. "We talked about it over and over. How dangerous it was for him to be identified by anyone in his previous life. I did everything I could to keep him safe."

"I know."

"It's a good thing I don't have any kids. How are you supposed to take care of someone who won't listen to you?"

He knew that she included him in this complaint. As bad as he felt about any pain and frustration he had put her through as a child, he knew he couldn't have changed his choices. He had learned not to trust anyone else. Not to accept their dictates just because they claimed to care or be in charge. He'd had to be independent and protect himself. He made a sympathetic noise but didn't excuse himself or Luke. Joss knew as well as anyone that a foster kid or throwaway had to make his own choices and live his own life, no matter how bad the consequences were. As she had told Zachary when they had spoken about it, she couldn't physically force Luke to do the things she thought he should do. She couldn't stop him from going out. She couldn't control who he talked to or if he chose to go back to the people who had trafficked him. All she could do was to try to be the voice of reason and tell Luke what the consequences of his actions might be.

Just like with Zachary.

19

Zachary looked at the time as he left Joss's house and returned to his car. While he needed to talk to the detective on the case, he doubted that he could get anywhere with the police on a Sunday evening. There hadn't been any activity at the police station. Everyone was home with their families and wouldn't appreciate being called by a private investigator getting involved in their open-and-shut case.

And if he spent another hour or two on interviews, he wouldn't have any time with Kenzie, and they tried to keep as much of Sunday as possible as couple's time.

He started the car engine and mounted his phone on the dashboard, plugging the charging cable into it. While he waited for the car to warm up, he called Kenzie.

"Hey, Zachary. How's it been going?" She sounded relaxed. Not worn out from being called in to work, not stressed about his taking so long to get home. She seemed to be in a good place.

Was evaluating the temperature of his partner something that everyone did? Or was it something Zachary did as a response to his experience with families in foster care? Was it normal or pathological? He pushed the question to the side and focused on Kenzie.

"Good. I'm not sure how much progress I've made, but I talked to Luke and Joss. I have a few details… a starting place, anyway."

"Are you… staying to do more today?"

"No. I'm on my way back. Just warming up the car and then I'll be on my way."

"Good. Then we'll still have some time together today. That will be nice. It's been quiet around here."

"Am I that noisy?"

She laughed. "No. You don't stomp or yell. But it's just different when you have someone else in the house with you. The friendly sounds of someone else floating around, doing their thing. Being able to have a conversation just because you're in the same room or having a coffee at the same time. I like having you around the house."

Zachary was glad she couldn't see him blush with pleasure in response to this observation. But she probably knew he would react that way anyway.

He thought about the case on his way back, talking aloud to himself about what he had learned and what he speculated or had questions on. He had recently learned how to dictate notes to his phone hands-free, which came in very handy on a highway drive. He dictated several notes to himself so that he wouldn't completely forget the things he had come up with while driving. It was like having a brilliant revelation in the shower and forgetting it as soon as he was dry. Frustrating.

The highway driving went quickly. Maybe a little more quickly than it ought to have. Zachary considered staying in his car for a few extra minutes longer so that Kenzie wouldn't think that he'd sped too much.

But she was probably watching for him anyway and would just laugh at him trying to obscure how quickly he had driven by hiding out in front of the house. It wasn't like she couldn't see his car the moment he pulled up in front of the house.

He saw her eyes flick toward her phone in her hand when he walked in to greet her. Noting the time, as he had feared. But she didn't comment on it.

"Hey. Glad you made it. Pizza just got here. You want some?"

Maybe she had not been checking up on his driving time, then. If pizza had just been delivered, she couldn't have been expecting him to take another half hour to get home. Zachary could smell the spicy tomato sauce, cheese, and warm, yeasty crust. His stomach growled. Had he eaten anything else since he had left the house? "That smells really good."

They walked together into the kitchen and sat down. Zachary got a message on his phone and took a quick peek at it before dinner. Something from Rhys. A conversation with Rhys would need all of his attention, so it would have to wait until after dinner. Zachary flipped through a couple of other messages before returning his attention to the table and realizing he had just sat down and let Kenzie take care of everything else. Plates, pizza, drinks. It wasn't like he'd left her with a big job, but he had to be more aware and not do that.

"Sorry. I spaced. Can I get anything else?"

"No, I think this is it." She shrugged. "You've had a long day. I don't mind. Not like I slaved over the stove all day."

"No, but you planned it all out, and I could at least have grabbed plates."

She nodded and didn't disagree.

They each took a slice and started to eat. After the first couple of bites, Zachary sighed, beginning to relax, his body and brain happy for the fuel after a long day of looking for answers.

"So, how did it go?" Kenzie asked. "You got to see Luke, I guess?"

Zachary nodded. "The usual red tape bureaucracy and procedures to get through before I could get in to see him. Pretty quiet at the police station and jail today." He took another bite of pizza and chewed. "I should have remembered to leave everything in the car. It's been a while since I did a jail visit."

"Oh, I wouldn't have thought of that either. But it's probably more secure to leave your stuff with the security at the jail than in your glove box, isn't it?"

"Yes. But some places don't even let you do that. You're just not allowed to bring anything but your ID and one car key into the building with you. But it's not like it would have been a long walk back to the car if they'd made me leave everything there. Just around the block. At some of the prisons, you park a couple of miles away and take a shuttle up to the facility."

Kenzie nodded. "How was Luke?"

"Not great. I didn't expect him to be, of course… it wasn't like he was frantic or crying for me to get him out of there. He would hardly talk to me at all. Very distant… They have him under suicide watch."

"Poor guy," Kenzie said with feeling.

Zachary nodded. It hadn't been that long since he had been in the psych ward in the hospital, under a watch himself. But he had admitted himself voluntarily, and it wasn't the same as being in jail. He had known where he was going and that it would be safer for him than trying to tough it out at home. He knew some of the staff there, knew the rules and procedures, and knew they would do their best to look after him.

"I've never had to face that," Zachary murmured. "The likelihood of being locked up for the rest of my life. I haven't been able to see past that moment, past the dark times, but... it's not the same."

"It would be pretty tough to face," Kenzie agreed. "A long time in a miserable place."

At least when Zachary had been locked up in Bonnie Brown or another institution, he had known that it would only be for a few weeks or months. Then he would have his freedom again. And that was what Luke had faced before. Small stints in the jail for whatever they had been able to catch him for, but not facing life imprisonment.

"I'm glad they're keeping an eye on him. I wouldn't want anything to happen to him. I mean... anything worse."

"What did he have to say?" Kenzie prompted, nudging him away from a deep dive into his suicidal periods or unhappy past. "What exactly happened?"

"He wouldn't tell me anything. More or less said that it was his own fault and to just leave him alone."

Kenzie shook her head. She wiped a splotch of tomato sauce from the corner of her mouth. "But you must have been able to find out some details."

Zachary gave her a half-grin. "I *am* a private investigator."

"Exactly. So what did Sherlock manage to uncover?"

20

———

Zachary toyed with his pizza. "Not many details yet. The victim's name is Eyler. He's in the trafficking business. Higher level than Luke, who was pretty much at the bottom, even after all of the years he had worked for them. He was staying at a hotel in town. Maybe looking at expanding his territory. Because Joss has been driving the traffickers out of town." He raised one brow at her.

Kenzie looked impressed. "I knew Joss was tough, but... how was she doing that?"

"Lots of complaints to the police. And from what I can guess, blackmail. Knowing that the worst offenders can't get to her because she has dirt on them."

"Sounds like a good reason to kill her. Remove the obstruction altogether."

"I didn't ask about details, but I would guess there is a fail-safe somewhere. Documentation in a safety deposit box or stored online and set to release if something happens to her."

"Smart."

"I don't think she survived this long by being stupid," Zachary agreed.

Joss might have been victimized and an addict, but she had never been stupid. She had somehow endured her traumatic childhood and decades of trafficking and was now strong and independent.

"No," Kenzie agreed. "I don't think she's stupid. She's always struck me as having a sharp wit, despite all of the abuse she must have put her brain through as an addict."

"Yeah. And apparently, she's been helping out other kids like Luke who were looking for a way out of the business."

"Really?" Kenzie laughed and shook her head. "I have a hard time seeing tough, independent Joss being a mother hen."

"Probably more like a mother bear." Zachary thought back to those early days while the family had still been together. Joss and Heather had both been surrogate mothers, taking care of him and trying to keep him out of trouble, which was a losing prospect. Joss had been fierce. She might have employed pinches or head slaps to keep Zachary in line, but she would also have stood in the path of an oncoming train to protect her younger siblings.

Only it had been their parents, not an onrushing train, that she'd had to protect them from.

"So after Joss runs the previous traffickers out of town, this other guy shows up, ready to set up his business," Kenzie suggested, returning to the narrative.

"Right. And something happens... Luke is there, for some reason, in Eyler's hotel room, and kills him. A knife, I guess, but I don't know the details yet."

"And how did they connect him to the murder?"

"Because they caught him there in the room. Covered with blood. His prints all over everything, knife still in his hand."

"Ouch." Kenzie shook her head. "Well, I'm not sure how you get him out of something like that. Find some mitigating circumstances and get the sentence reduced... work out some kind of plea."

"That's not going to be easy. Especially not when he is not cooperating."

"What does Joss know? Had this trafficker and Luke had previous encounters? Is it possible that Eyler had recognized him and was threatening him?"

Zachary shrugged, shaking his head. "Luke was in his hotel room. Eyler hadn't come after him. He'd obviously gone there looking for Eyler."

"Could it have been an arranged meeting? Maybe Eyler was threatening to expose him... for a payoff of some kind."

"A guy like Luke is more valuable as an asset than a blackmail target. He doesn't have much money, but he can lure and turn out new talent. Someone like him can bring in almost a million dollars a year. Eyler wouldn't get that kind of money by blackmailing him. Luke barely had any income living with Joss. He wouldn't be able to pay."

"Unless he got back in the business."

Zachary nodded. He fingered the notepad in his pocket. "If Eyler wanted something from Luke, then it was to have him working for him. Not blackmail." He was sure of himself.

Kenzie gave a nod, her eyes on Zachary's notebook, which he knew meant it was okay if he wanted to take out his notepad and write as they talked and ate. While they had decided on a rule of no phones or screens at the table during dinner in their couple's therapy, to reinforce their giving each other their undivided attention and communicating better, there were exceptions to the "no distractions" policy. One of them was that if they were talking shop, notebooks, paper files, and pictures or other files on their devices were permissible. Being able to discuss murder and forensics during dinner or a date was one of the things that had brought them together and which continued to keep them connected.

Zachary pulled his notepad out and jotted a few notes from his conversation before they could slip away from him.

"You think Eyler was probably going after Luke. To get him to work for him again," Kenzie said.

"He didn't work for him before. He worked for Peggy Ann. But Eyler must have wanted him. That had to be the reason they were together. Especially in Eyler's room. Eyler wanted to make him an offer... or to coerce him. But if there wasn't anyone else there, I don't know how he could have meant to persuade Luke."

Kenzie considered this, chewing slowly. She took another piece of pizza from the box and laid it on her plate. "You said before that Joss was worried about Luke getting back into the life. That he might be tempted because that was what he knew. It's hard work getting clean and then finding a way to support yourself."

"Yeah, that's true." He thought back to the previous conversation with Joss. "If he went to work for Eyler, he'd have money again. All the drugs he wanted. He knew his job and did it well, so he got praise and what Joss calls 'good strokes' from his bosses. He would have a social group; the other workers in Eyler's ring and the kids he brought up. I'm sure that living with Joss, he doesn't get much socialization with people who understand how he's lived, who normalize it. There are Joss and whoever she is trying to rescue from the traffickers, but he won't get approval from them like he would from people who are still in the business."

"So maybe he could be tempted. Maybe if Eyler promised him drugs, good pay, and a good position in his organization…"

"It might be enough to entice him over to Eyler's hotel room," Zachary admitted. "At least to talk it over." A feeling of heaviness accompanied the words. Luke had been working so hard. He'd done something few people would have been able to do, staying clean for a year after all of the years of addiction. But like with Tyrrell, staying clean for a year didn't mean he was cured. Both of them would fight addiction for as long as they lived.

Had Luke gone to Eyler, tempted by his offer? Was that why he didn't want to talk to Zachary about it? Because he had gone in a moment of weakness? Because he still craved the drugs and the approval? He needed more than Joss or anyone else straight could give him?

"I'll have to look into that further."

"How will you know if that's what happened?"

Zachary shrugged. "I'll ask questions. Start to build a picture of what happened before he killed Eyler."

"Poor Luke. After everything he has been through."

"Then it comes down to this." Zachary closed his eyes and saw Luke sitting across the table from him, gaze averted, small inside the orange jail uniform, facing the possibility of decades in prison. While it was true that Luke had victimized others, he was first and foremost a victim himself, a vulnerable child who had been twisted into something that had not been natural for him. "If that's what happened… I don't know how I'm going to be able to help. If he went there freely because he was interested in going back to work for Eyler and then killed him… How can anyone get a sentence reduced under those circumstances?"

"I don't know," Kenzie admitted. "I don't know of any defense or justification that would apply."

21

Zachary was feeling somewhat discouraged after dinner. Even though he had known from the time Joss called him that there wasn't much he could do to help Luke, he had still hoped to be able to find something. Something to show everyone that he had been right to help Luke get away from the traffickers in the first place, that he had a spark of human decency in him and deserved a second chance. Zachary didn't want to think that he had been conned by Luke, who had never planned to stay away from the life, or that it had been too late for Luke and he was irredeemable.

"Oh, got something from Rhys," Zachary said, sitting down on the couch and pulling out his phone while Kenzie picked up the remote to look for something they would enjoy watching together and that would hopefully distract Zachary from his funk.

He thumbed in his password and brought up Rhys's message.

It was a gif of a dog with popping eyes and the words "what's happening?"

Zachary considered his response carefully. Did Rhys know that something was going on with Luke and that Zachary had been looking into it? Or was it just a generic "What's up with you lately?"

He tapped in a non-responsive answer. *Hey, Rhys, just finished pizza with Kenzie*

Rhys sent back a big pink heart balloon. Zachary smiled.

"Rhys says hi."

Kenzie turned away from the TV screen to look at Zachary. He showed her the pink heart. Kenzie chuckled.

"Love to him too."

Kenzie says hi. How is school?

The dots that indicated Rhys was composing a reply started to blink at the bottom of the screen. Zachary settled into the couch, trying to get more comfortable and not aggravate his tailbone, which still hurt if he sat the wrong way. He looked at the screen to see what shows Kenzie was considering.

"*Unsolved Mysteries*? I haven't seen that in years."

"You interested? Do you like it?"

"Sure."

"It's not too much like work?"

"No. I don't have to solve these ones. Especially now that they're twenty years old."

"I like it when they have updates. That's always cool."

Zachary nodded his agreement. The phone vibrated in his hand, and Zachary looked down at it. A picture he had seen before. Luke. Cropped out of a picture Rhys had taken of Luke and Madison together. Zachary had first seen it when Madison had gone missing and Rhys had come to him for help.

His stomach tied itself in a knot. He tested the waters, not wanting to give away that something had happened to Luke if it was just a routine inquiry.

Did Luke call you?

Rhys quickly returned a large red X. *No.*

Zachary tried to figure out how to delicately ask what Rhys already knew. Had someone been in touch with him?

More dots appeared. Rhys composing a further response.

Another gif popped up. A toddler behind the prison bars of a playpen or baby security gate, holding on to the bars and shaking. Zachary swore to himself. Kenzie looked over.

"He knows about Luke."

"How did he find out?"

"I don't know. I thought that the two of them had broken off correspondence. The last few times I talked to Luke, he has said that Rhys isn't messaging him anymore."

Kenzie considered this. "Could he have been lying?"

"He's an accomplished liar. I can't say for sure I would know if he was. I keep wondering... about other things. The lady at the jail said that I don't really know him. Even he said so. I only know what he's told me about himself, and that could all be made up. I don't have independent verification of any of it. Except that he was in the trafficking ring and was Madison's Romeo."

"What reason would he have to make up all of the things he's said about his past?"

"To make himself look good. Make him look like more of a victim than he is."

"But as a teenager in the sex trade, he *was* a victim. There's no way around that. And they started him when he was how old? Twelve or thirteen? He doesn't have to make himself look like more of a victim than that."

"But that's what *he* told me. What if that is a lie? His age now, his age when he started out. What if he was never the victim but has always been a recruiter? Who is going to tell me anything different than he's said? There's no one to contradict him, so he can really tell whatever story he wants."

"Well..." Kenzie looked doubtful. "I suppose. But I don't know how he would keep such an elaborate lie going for a year. There haven't been any inconsistencies. Have there?"

Zachary didn't like to contradict her, but he'd been thinking about it and had to admit that there had been. "Yes... he contradicts his own story sometimes. I thought that was just... the drugs. The trauma. Dissociation. Getting confused about the timeline. It isn't hard to get mixed up when the abuse has been ongoing for so long. It all runs together and it's hard to remember what happened when and with who."

She nodded her agreement. "Yeah. Of course."

The phone vibrated again in Zachary's hand and he looked down at it. Rhys's last message was still on the screen, waiting for a response. Zachary gritted his teeth together and tapped out a brief answer.

Saw Luke today

A series of question marks popped up on the screen.

Zachary blew out his breath, not sure how much to tell Rhys. He didn't want to tell him too much in a text message. He should at least do that face to face. Though he dreaded the prospect. The last time he had gone to talk to Rhys about Luke, Rhys had not been happy about Zachary telling him to back off and watch out for Luke due to the danger of Luke pulling Rhys into the trafficking business as well.

And maybe that was why Luke had told Zachary that he and Rhys weren't communicating anymore. They had hatched a plan to keep him out of their business. Mollify him so that he wouldn't look too closely and see what was happening. Had there been indications that Rhys had still been in contact with Luke that Zachary should have seen? He really hadn't looked closely once Luke told him that Rhys wasn't talking to him anymore.

Had he been duped?

He's in jail and feeling pretty down, he texted Rhys honestly. There wasn't any point in telling Rhys that Luke was fine and would be getting out soon. Rhys would know or find out quickly that Zachary was not telling him the truth. *But he is safe. By himself, not a target. Guards watching*

It was a few minutes before he saw the blinking dots again. Kenzie pressed Play on *Unsolved Mysteries*, but Zachary didn't pay much attention to it. He kept looking at the phone, waiting for Rhys's response.

When it came through, it was succinct. *Wat happend?*

That was the big question. Zachary wished he had an answer for Rhys.

Trying to figure it out

Get him out

Zachary sighed. *Can't get him out. But trying to help. Find out what happened so we can work with his lawyer.*

Murder? Not Luke

In case Zachary didn't get it, Rhys sent Luke's picture again, followed by the red circle with the slash through it. Zachary knew that Rhys must be having a hard time with it. Just like Joss, even though she tried to keep on her tough mask and not show it.

He was arrested at scene with weapon, Zachary sent back. *He did it. But I'm trying to figure out why. What happened.*

The red circle came up on the screen again. Zachary tried to watch the TV, but kept looking down at the screen, waiting for something further from Rhys. When half an hour went by without Rhys sending anything else, Zachary switched over to message Vera Salter, Rhys's grandmother. Rhys's mother was in prison, and Vera was the one taking care of him. That gave Zachary pause, remembering what Gloria, Rhys's mother, had done and what she had tried to do. Rhys had been through enough trauma in his young life, stretching all the way back to the murder of his grandfather, which had effectively taken Rhys's voice away from him.

Vera, it's Zachary

It was a few minutes before there was any sign of Vera composing a response. She knew how to use the messaging apps, since that was one of the primary ways Rhys communicated. Still, there was no guarantee that she would have her phone within reach or notice that Zachary had sent her a message if she and Rhys were in the house together and she didn't need to keep her eye on the phone.

Zachary, is everything all right?

There's been trouble. Luke arrested for murder.

The dots started flashing immediately.

What? No! He's too young.

visited him in jail today. worried about Rhys. Keep eye on him?

Of course. Should I tell him?

He already knows. Was messaging me about it

How?

Don't know. Maybe still in touch with Luke?

Vera responded with a word Zachary knew she wouldn't use if they were having a spoken conversation, shocking him slightly.

I didn't think they were, Zachary typed, *but maybe they lied*

Yes, Vera agreed succinctly. And then there were no more messages from her either.

Zachary looked up at the TV and tried to get back into the flow of the mystery they were discussing. He was confused and thought they might have switched cases while he'd been focused on texting with Rhys and Vera. He kept looking back down at his phone, waiting for one of them to message him back. Rhys angry at him because Zachary had messaged Vera, or Vera letting him know that Rhys was okay. Or not okay.

But his phone did not vibrate again.

22

The next day, Zachary got up determined to get more information. He only had the bare bones of what had happened and he needed to know more. He started with a few internet searches, but word of the murder had apparently not made it to any of the news networks yet.

It was Monday, so Kenzie was back to work at the regular time and would be occupied all day, possibly even late. That gave Zachary plenty of time to get back to Kent to get some boots-on-the-ground investigating done.

There weren't a lot of hotels in Kent, so he knew it wouldn't take him too long to figure out which of them had been the scene of a recent murder and all of the drama that would have surrounded the arrest and investigation. The registration clerk at the Best Western directed him immediately to the non-chain hotel across the street, the International Rest Easy Suites. Zachary thanked the young man and crossed over to the other side. He didn't go to the registration desk there, but did a quick circle around the common areas on the main floor initially, then approached the front desk from the area of the elevators, which would give them the impression that he was a hotel guest.

"Excuse me... I was wondering where I would find the maids that cleaned the rooms over the weekend... Friday, actually. Friday night or Saturday morning...?"

There were three employees at the desk, and they looked at each other before the taller of the two men elected himself to answer the question.

"Is there some problem I could help with, sir?"

"No. No, not a problem. It's just that… my girlfriend, she put her rings down on the edge of the sink. I don't know why girls do that. And now she can't find them. I don't think anyone stole them," he hastened to add, holding up a hand. "But they might have gotten mixed in with the washcloth and towels…"

"If anyone had found them, they would have turned them in to the lost and found." The tall man turned and looked at the other two. "Any new rings in the lost and found?" he asked, as if it were not *his* job to know what was in there.

"Nothing like *that* found over the weekend," the young woman said, shaking her head. She smoothed her blazer in a nervous gesture. She gave the other two a significant look. Acknowledging that there had been *other* things of interest going on over the weekend. Zachary was sure it would have made a big impression on everyone. Even if the murder didn't make it to the news, it would undoubtedly be the talk of all of the hotel employees.

"I just wonder if I could talk to the maids and see where the towels and everything end up. My girlfriend is really upset, and even though it's her own fault for putting them on the side of the sink, I want to do what I can to help her."

"They probably went down the drain," the younger of the men suggested.

Zachary refrained from rolling his eyes. It wasn't nearly as easy to lose a ring down a hotel bathroom drain as it was to lose something like small stud earrings. Rings couldn't usually get under the edge of the stopper or through the strainer.

"I sure hope not. Or I'll be calling you to get a plumber to take apart the trap," he said with a laugh. "And the maids are…" He pointed randomly toward the elevators.

"We'll have to find out who did your room and speak with her," the tall clerk said unctuously. "You can't just go walking into the service areas and question the staff."

Which was exactly what Zachary wanted to do. "Oh, okay," he said. "Room 605. If you could find out for me."

He turned and walked back to the elevators as if to go back to his room. But when the elevator doors closed, he hit the basement level, not the sixth floor. Despite the man's response, all three of them had given away the location of the maid's service area, looking down or at the elevator, and then to the left. The left when he was facing the elevator was right when he got off, so he turned down the right corridor and headed toward the voices he could hear in the distance.

After passing several closed doors and branching service corridors, Zachary arrived at a break room where several uniformed maids were talking. They stopped when they saw him in the doorway.

"Hi. My name is Zachary Goldman, and I'm investigating the murder Friday night? Saturday morning? I'm sure you all heard about it…"

They looked at each other uncertainly, but there were several automatic nods of agreement.

"We've already told that other cop that we didn't see anything," a redhead complained. "None of us did. So just let us get back to our work."

Even though they had been standing around on a break talking. *Now* she had to get back to work.

"Yeah, sorry about that. We always end up going over the same ground half a dozen times. You wouldn't believe how often something is missed the first time. Or stories change, or people remember things later. We don't want to cause anyone any trouble, but I would appreciate your cooperation."

He didn't say he was a cop. That was their own assumption, based on the fact that he said he was investigating it and was dressed as they imagined a plainclothes police detective might be dressed. He wasn't going to disabuse them of the idea.

"Who was in charge of cleaning room…" Zachary pulled out his notebook and started flipping pages. "Hang on a sec… room…"

"Room 412," one of them provided impatiently.

"Right. Room 412. I see that." He flipped to a blank page in his notepad instead. "Who was supposed to be cleaning that room?"

"They had a sign on the doorknob," a Hispanic maid said. "No maid service. If people don't want their room cleaned while they are here, they put out a sign. Room 412 had a sign, kept it on the whole time they were here. So no one cleaned it."

"I see. What about now? I assume it has been cleaned now?"

"Not yet! Have to rip out the carpet and replace it. And sand and repaint walls. We don't clean until *after* all the work is done. Otherwise, we do it twice."

Blood soaked into the carpet and sprayed or cast off on the walls.

Zachary imagined it was pretty gruesome. But he wasn't going to leave it up to imagination.

"Could one of you let me into the room?" Zachary patted his pockets. "I think that one of the detectives was given a card key to get in and out, but I didn't bring it with me…"

The maids exchanged aggravated glances, but an older woman seemed eager to get a look at the notorious crime scene. She stepped toward Zachary, nodding. "I will do it," she said in a long-suffering tone for the benefit of her colleagues. But her eyes were bright, excited to be involved. "Follow me."

The woman's name was Mildred, and she had introduced herself and filled Zachary in on all of the details of her husband, children, and two young grandchildren by the time they finished taking the elevator to the fourth floor. She then fell silent, the gravity of the situation entering her consciousness.

23

Mildred led the way to the hotel room and paused there for a moment as if she might be having second thoughts. Zachary wasn't surprised. It was one thing to imagine the excitement of what might have happened in that room, a ghoulish interest in death and murder and all of the rumors that had been circulating through the hotel. But it was another thing for her to actually see it herself, to be walking in there with an investigator to see what had really happened.

"If you could just let me in," Zachary said. "You should probably not come in. We don't want to destroy any evidence."

She looked relieved and disappointed at the same time. "Well, yes, I suppose. I don't want to cause any problems with the investigation."

Zachary nodded. There was no sign or tape sealing off the hotel room, which meant that the police were finished with it. They had already collected any evidence that they were going to and had released the scene. The hotel could have it cleaned and sanitized and rented out already, if they had wanted to. If they'd been able to clean up all of the blood.

Mildred inserted her card key and pulled it out. The green light turned on, and she turned sideways to allow Zachary past her. He turned the handle before the lock could re-engage and pushed the door open.

"Thank you very much for your help."

Mildred murmured something about being happy to help and arched her neck in an effort to catch a glimpse of the mayhem inside the room. Zachary let the door shut behind him and then walked in.

Nothing had been visible from the door, so Mildred was out of luck in seeing something she could brag to her friends or gossip with her coworkers about. Although that probably wouldn't stop her. She could just make something up. A hall ran past the bathroom and then into an open sitting room space. It was littered with food wrappers and other detritus that Zachary didn't want to look at too closely to begin with. There was a doorway to the right and a kitchenette to the left. As far as Zachary could see, there were no obvious signs of the murder in the kitchenette. He opened the door to the bedroom and reached around the wall to turn on the light.

He could smell the blood even before he turned on the light. He squinted his eyes in preparation, knowing that the scene was going to be shocking.

There was, of course, no body. The victim's body had been removed Saturday morning. They had taken the blankets from the bed as well, so that only the bare mattress remained, soaked in blood, now a dull, rusty brown. There was cast-off blood from the knife on the headboard and wall, indicating that Eyler had been stabbed more than once. It was not a single stab wound or a slit throat. Zachary pictured Luke there with an older man. Bigger, maybe a bit pudgy around the middle, losing control and stabbing multiple times.

Why? Being stabbed in the bed made it doubtful that it had been a business meeting. An assignation? Had Eyler baited or insulted? If he was trying to get Luke back into the business, then there had probably been threats, an attempt at intimidation. He would have done better by bribing Luke, offering him drugs and the other things that the lowlifes used to lure young people into the fold.

Zachary entered the bedroom and walked around it slowly, looking at the window, the wall, the surfaces of the dresser, and around the bottom of the bed. The bedside units were not side tables with drawers, but open shelves, which guests would be less likely to leave things behind in. There had definitely been drugs in the room. There were wrappers and caps from syringes and a sort of burnt plastic smell still in the air despite the amount of time that had passed. There was a strap that might have come from a piece of luggage or might have been used as a tourniquet to raise the user's veins to make it easier to inject.

There were also long strings of condom packets on the bedside shelves and floor, some of them intact and others torn open and used. There were no used condoms on the floor or in the garbage cans, so Zachary assumed the police had taken them as evidence, along with the used needles. He studied the pattern of the cast-off blood and pulled out his camera to take pictures of it, then moved on to photograph the rest of the room. There wasn't a lot for him to go on, but it helped to get a feeling for the room and how things must have gone down.

There was another bathroom attached to the bedroom. Not a tiny one, but spacious with a jetted tub. Even though it was a fairly nice hotel, everything felt grimy and oppressive. The fingerprint powder smudging many of the surfaces in the bedroom and bathroom probably contributed to the feeling of everything being dirty. Red-brown handprints on the wall and sink in the bedroom gave Zachary pause.

Any personal possessions had already been removed by the police. Still, Zachary could see discarded makeup applicators and wipes and other personal products in the wastepaper bin, along with more long, skinny syringe wrappers. There were towels and washcloths missing, which he assumed had been removed by the police, since the maids had not yet done anything with the room.

There was no under-sink cabinet or medicine cabinet on the wall, all places where guests might accidentally leave something. The hotel's soaps and shampoos had been left in a basket on the counter, but the discarded bottles and wrappers were on the edge of the tub or in the garbage. The "no maid service" sign had been on the door for several days, so the amenities had not been restocked.

Zachary lifted the lid from the toilet tank for a quick check inside, but saw nothing out of the ordinary. He took the toilet paper roll off its holder, took apart the two sides of the springed cylinder, and found a cache of pills that the police had missed. He took pictures of everything and put them back.

He walked once more around the bedroom, looking for anything else that would give him some insight into what had happened there. He looked again at the messy living room and the apparently unused kitchenette. Lots of fast food and junk food wrappers and containers in the garbage cans and on the floor of the living room. Nothing that indicated the presence of salads or fresh produce, though he checked the fridge just in case anything had been left behind. It was empty. He checked through the drawers of the kitchen methodically, taking a picture of the contents of each one. There were only the bare essentials that someone might need if he took it into his head to cook. Maybe not even that.

Zachary looked through everything one more time, snapping a few more pictures, and then left the suite, headed once more for the front desk.

24

W hen he returned to the front desk, the tall man who had previously taken charge looked at him with a scowl of suspicion. This time, Zachary focused on his name tag, which gave only his first name. Arthur.

"Who are you really? You're not a guest here," Arthur accused.

Zachary nodded. "I'm investigating the death of your guest here the other day. Mr. Eyler."

"We already talked to the police about that."

"And I'm sure you answered all of their questions the best you could. But new things have come to light. Some things need follow-up."

"A couple of the maids said that you went down there. Interrogated them and talked Mildred into letting you into the room."

Zachary was lucky to have avoided security. But he'd figured it would take a while for them to figure out what was going on. By the time they got someone to the room to check up on him, he could be in and out. And he'd been right.

"I asked a few questions," he asked. "And yes, Mildred was kind enough to let me into the room when I asked."

"There's nothing there. The police have already investigated and taken all of the evidence. You didn't have any right to be in that room. It's burglary."

Zachary smiled cooperatively. "It isn't burglary when you let me in."

"I didn't let you in. A maid let you in. Because you lied to her." His mouth was an ugly red slash across his face. "You told them you were a cop, but you're not one of the police detectives investigating the murder."

"I didn't say I was a police detective."

"Whether you did or not, that's what you made them think. You intentionally misled them. Just like you lied and misled me with that rigmarole about your girlfriend losing her rings. Just who are you and what game are you playing here? Are you some reporter or thrill-seeking paparazzi?"

"I'm a private investigator," Zachary told him calmly. He reached into his pocket and brought out a stack of business cards. He separated one out and handed it to Arthur. "As I said, I am investigating the death of Mr. Eyler."

"Investigating it. But you're not police."

"No. I'm a *private* investigator."

"You can't be in here."

"I'll leave," Zachary agreed. He cocked his head slightly. "After you tell me why you're letting sex traffickers operate out of this hotel."

"What the—?" Arthur exploded. His face grew beet red. "What are you talking about? Just who do you think you are, throwing around accusations like that? We would never allow something like that!"

"You have been. Who knows how long this has been going on. Eyler was in town for a while. I don't know whether his predecessor used this hotel as well. I guess I'd have to talk to the staff to find that out."

"There's nothing like that going on here!"

"I just saw that hotel room. I can assure you, there definitely is."

"If there was, there was no way for any of us to know about it. How would we know something like that?"

"There are signs. He gets a room in the back overlooking the parking lot. He brings in a lot of young girls with fancy clothes or phones, but they never talk. Only he talks, and he pays in cash or with a preloaded credit card for a week or two at a time. There are noise complaints, music playing, people coming and going all the time, a lot of them men. Sound familiar?"

The other two hotel workers were crowding close, their eyes wide, listening intently to every word. Arthur's face, previously flushed, was quickly draining of color. Zachary tried to see over the high counter to see if there were a chair for Arthur to sit down on if he started to feel faint.

"The maids said that he keeps the 'no maid service' sign on the door all the time. So they don't get in there to clean." Zachary paused, watching him, examining his face for any tells. "You knew all this, didn't you? Maybe you weren't sure what was going on, but you had your suspicions."

"It's not my responsibility to know what guests are doing. What they do behind closed doors is their own business. It's the job of the police, not me."

"You cared enough to find out what I was doing."

"You're not a guest," Arthur said mulishly.

"You thought I was. And who do you think is supposed to report suspicious activities to the police?"

The other man leaned forward, inserting himself into the conversation. "I thought maybe they were models," he offered. "You know, real skinny with fancy clothes?"

Zachary studied him. "And you thought he was doing headshots out of a hotel room in small-town Vermont?"

"Well…" The younger man reddened almost as much as Arthur had. They had guessed. Of course they had. But they had kept out of it. Maybe because they were told to by management. Maybe because they didn't want anything to do with the police. Sometimes people learned from experience. One report to the police that came to bite them, and they would be far more likely to exercise caution the next time.

"It's disgusting," the young woman piped up. "I can't believe they would do that here. Gross."

"It happens all over," Zachary said. "Not just here. Not just this hotel. But we can't fight it if people keep looking the other way."

25

They all stood there uncomfortably, knowing that they hadn't said anything, but unable to justify it. This was good because then they would be more likely to help Zachary to make up for it.

"He was here for two weeks?" he guessed. Long enough for Joss and Luke to know he was there.

"Not quite, I don't think..." Arthur tapped the keyboard in front of him. "Oh. Longer, actually about two and a half."

"How many girls?"

Arthur looked trapped. He looked at the others. "I didn't really notice. Maybe three or four. Not at the same time; it was usually only one at a time. But three or four in rotation. I just thought... he was fooling around."

"None of the girls were ever together?"

"Well, just once or twice. It did happen. But not very often."

"So you knew that the girls knew each other. They weren't just girlfriends he was keeping from finding out about each other."

"Well..." Arthur scratched his ear. "I guess not."

"Could the three of you describe the girls that he brought in rotation?"

They looked at each other.

"There were two blondes," the woman said. "And that redhead. And a smaller woman who was Chinese or something."

"Is that it?" Zachary asked. "No brunettes? Other ethnic groups? Boys?"

"There was a Black girl." Arthur remembered. "She wasn't here very often. Tall. And skinny. All of them were skinny."

Zachary walked them through descriptions of each of the girls, getting as many details as he could. He didn't know whether it would be of any help to him in the end, but he didn't want those girls to be invisible. They had been ignored by the people who should have noticed them, should have reported suspected trafficking out of the hotel. They had been overlooked as if they were not real people.

Aside from the five regulars, the clerks thought that there had been a few others off and on, brought in for an hour or two and never seen again. And there had been other women who didn't have the same look as the "models." Older, hard-looking women who did not act submissive like the girls. Women who had worked their way up in the organization and now had stables of their own, probably. Peers of Eyler or maybe even over his head, there for business meetings rather than turning tricks. At least, that was what Zachary assumed. Some women stayed in the business for a long time, like Joss, but they were less likely to be working out of a hotel room, supervised by a handler. Zachary didn't know for sure what Joss had done as she got older. He hadn't asked her the details and didn't really want to know.

There had been a lot of men in and out and, while there had probably been some repeat customers, the employees couldn't describe any. They had seen the girls regularly, and the men mainly were let in a fire door from the parking lot; they didn't walk past the front desk.

Eventually, Zachary felt like he had probably gotten everything he could from them. Arthur and his coworkers had turned out to be a valuable source of information once he had gained their cooperation. Then he remembered one more thing. He pulled out his phone and went through his recent messages. He tapped on the picture Rhys had sent him of Luke to expand it to fill the screen and turned the phone to show to them.

"How about this guy? Have you seen him around?"

"Is he the one?" the woman asked in a hushed tone. "You know, the one that killed *him*?" Her eyes rolled up toward Eyler's room.

Zachary shrugged. There would undoubtedly be pictures in the paper and internet news by the time Luke got to trial. And his name and aliases. "Have you seen him?"

"I'm sure I've seen him around here," Arthur said with a nod.

"When? Can you remember?"

He shook his head slowly. "Anything other than the last day or two is just a jumble. I couldn't tell you which day."

"Friday? Were you on shift in the evening?"

"No, I was on during the day. And I don't think that's when it was. I'm sure it was longer ago than that."

"Days? Weeks?"

Arthur frowned, looking down at the picture, his forehead wrinkling. "I just can't be sure. I would say... last week, but it is so hard to be sure. I'll say something happened a month ago and then realize it's been a whole year."

"A week or longer?"

Arthur moved his head back and forth, thinking about it, then nodded. "Yeah. I would say so."

"And you?" Zachary looked at the other two employees. "Do you think you saw him?"

"He looks familiar," the younger man said and shrugged. "But I couldn't say that it was from here. Could have been here, or at a party, or on TV. I'm really not very good at faces."

"Do you think it might have been somewhere else?" Zachary prompted, pushing back on the suggestion. "What was he doing? Who was he with?"

The man closed his eyes, thinking about it. "I think... I don't think it was here. I can see him drinking or doing karaoke or something like that. Out with friends. Having a good time." He shook his head. "Not here."

"Do they ever do karaoke night here?" Zachary asked, with a nod toward the lounge.

"Yes, but I've never gone to it here. It's lame." He sent an apologetic glance at Arthur, who might be his boss or maybe just more experienced.

"There was another boy," the woman said. She looked at Arthur as if needing his permission to go on. "I kind of thought that he was the man's son. He came in with him a few times when he didn't have one of the girls with him." She swallowed. "I just thought he was his son. Right?"

Zachary shook his head. "Probably not. Can you describe him?"

"Oh..." She looked at the ceiling, thinking back. "I just thought... that's what made sense at the time. He was just a young kid, maybe thirteen. Um... dirty blond. About this tall..." She held her hand out beside her, at about her shoulder level. A reasonable height for a thirteen-year-old boy. Not too malnourished. "He would... have his arm around him, you know. I thought he got visitation some days or picked the kid up from karate because his mom couldn't that day. Something like that, you know?"

"And how did the boy seem?"

"I don't know." She shook her head. "What do you mean?"

"Was he… playing with a handheld game or his phone? Was he cheerful and bouncy with his 'dad' or sullen or pouty? Did he talk to him? Ask him for things or suggest things they could do while he was visiting?"

"No. No, none of that. He seemed… sleepy usually. Like he'd gotten out of bed too early or was tired after a long day. He never said anything. He'd just be there, under his dad's arm." She gulped and corrected herself. "Under that man's arm. Kind of… cuddling." She shook her head and nearly whispered. "I didn't know."

When he had all of the information he could get from them, Zachary pulled out a couple more business cards and handed them out.

"Please let me know if you think of anything else. Or if you see any of these people again."

26

Zachary checked his messages when he got out of the hotel. He had kept his phone on "do not disturb" while he'd been conducting his investigation at the hotel so that he wouldn't be distracted by any calls or messages. There were no personal calls, but there was one number with no ID and a voicemail message. Zachary played that and found a testy message from a cop who identified himself as Detective Richards. He wanted to talk to Zachary as soon as possible and didn't sound too pleased about it.

Zachary decided to try the police station and see whether he could see Richards face-to-face rather than talking over the phone. It was harder to just blast someone and refuse to listen to anything they said. Much harder to "hang up" on someone standing there in front of you.

He was at the police station in a few minutes, greeted by a different Officer of the Day from the one who had been there Sunday morning. Rhodes, by his name badge.

"I was wondering whether Detective Richards is in," Zachary inquired politely.

"Do you have an appointment?"

"I don't, but he was trying to reach me earlier. He left a message on my phone."

Rhodes pursed his lips, considering. Apparently, he hadn't had to make the judgment as to whether to screen someone Richards was trying to reach before. He was used to the appointment/no appointment dichotomy, which was easy to manage. "Uh… if you'll give me a minute, I'll see if he is available."

He took a few steps away from the service counter toward one of the desks, then turned around, looking embarrassed. "Uh… I didn't get your name. I guess I'm going to need that."

"Zachary Goldman. It's on the Eyler homicide."

The officer's eyes widened slightly at that. Zachary saw him give a tiny nod of affirmation to himself. Yes, he was doing the right thing. Rhodes was going to want to talk with a witness on the Eyler case. Zachary imagined they probably did not get a lot of homicides. And the ones that they did get were probably mainly domestic disputes or drunks. Not sex trafficking.

He walked over to his desk and picked up the desk phone. With his back to Zachary and his voice low, he dialed an extension and had a short conversation. He hung up the phone and returned to the service counter.

"Detective Richards will be right out. You could have a seat while you're waiting…" Rhodes motioned in the direction of the single row of chairs lined up under the window in case Zachary had missed them.

Zachary walked over to the window and looked out at the street, watching the traffic and pedestrians passing by outside. He would probably be spending more time than he would like in a hard plastic or metal chair; he would avoid sitting until he had to.

Detective Richards didn't take long to come through the locked security door. He was an older man with a military bearing and a slight gut. A formidable, no-nonsense kind of guy.

"Goldman?"

Zachary nodded. "That's me."

"This way."

Zachary followed him through the security door and down the hall to an interview room. Zachary was glad not to be chained to the table as Luke had been. Not so happy to see that he had been correct about the hard metal chair that would not conform to his body shape and ease his healing tailbone.

Zachary sighed and sat down anyway. Might as well not start off the interview appearing uncooperative. He tried to sit with his weight on one side rather than balanced in the middle. He should have brought one of his special pillows with him, but that would have been embarrassing. He'd rather be physically uncomfortable than mocked by the big policeman.

"You have some identification?" Richards demanded.

Zachary had to get back up to work his wallet out of his back pocket. He opened the flap to show his driver's license and handed it to the detective.

Richards barely gave it a glance before handing it back. Just ensuring that he wasn't dealing with a kook, Zachary supposed. Or that if he was dealing with a kook, he would at least be sure that he knew who he was talking to, rather than trusting that Zachary hadn't given him an alias.

Zachary sat back down and again tried to make himself as comfortable as the metal chair would allow. Richards didn't sit immediately.

"Why don't you explain to me your interest in the Eyler homicide," he suggested.

No hint as to what he already knew. Keeping his questions open-ended.

"I know Luke," he explained. At Richards's blank look, he elaborated. "Your... suspect. Uh..." He felt for his notebook to double-check the name Joss had given him. "Joseph Daniel—"

Richards waved Zachary's fumbling answer aside. "Bryant. I doubt that is the name he was born with any more than Luke. So, okay, Luke. How do you know Luke?"

"I know him from a previous case that I was involved with. I can't give you the details, but that's when I met Luke for the first time. Joss called me to let me know that he'd been arrested and to see if I could find out anything that might help him."

"Who is Joss?"

"Jocelyn Goldman."

Unlike the others, Richards didn't make any sign that the name meant anything to him. Either he wasn't plugged in to the grapevine, or he had a much better poker face than the jail CO or the cop that Zachary had talked to on Sunday.

"Luke has been staying with her. She has a history... and was helping Luke to stay clean. Helping him to start a new life."

"You know about his history."

"Yes... I know what he told me about it, anyway."

Richards studied him, frowning, then nodded. "Exactly right. You have no idea whether the stories he tells are true. Chances are, they aren't. They're just stories he made up or heard somewhere else. Thought he'd recycle them for his own use. He's a con man, been in trouble ever since he could walk."

Zachary was silent on this point. He shifted his position slightly and tried to change the direction of the conversation.

"I was hoping you could give me some of the details of the case against Luke. Well, not details, of course. Just the general gist of the case. Anything more than what has appeared in the news?"

"If it hasn't been in the news, then we didn't release it to the public. You're not here so that I can share my investigation with you."

"No, of course not," Zachary agreed. It wasn't like he'd ever had police cooperate with him or feed him information. Or at least, very rarely. He wasn't expecting it to be that easy.

"I have some information that you should probably know," Zachary told him, extending an olive branch. "Things that may be important to the case."

"You haven't figured anything out that we haven't already covered," Richards dismissed. As if Joe Public never managed to figure things out before the police. Zachary had been involved in too many other cases that the police had given up on or been wrong about to believe that for a second.

He just sat there, waiting for Richards's curiosity to get the better of him.

Show up at a police station and start bragging about how he knew things that the police didn't or how he figured something out, and they would write him off as a kook, like he was one of those psychics who called in with tips, insisting that they knew the whereabouts of a murdered or missing child. But hold back, act as if he didn't care to tell the police anything, and sooner or later...

"What information?" Richards asked grumpily. "And just so you know, I've already heard about your antics at the hotel. Impersonating a police officer is against the law, you know."

"I didn't tell anyone that I was a police officer. I said I was investigating the case. If anyone asked whether I am a cop, I let them know that I was a private investigator."

"You intended them to believe you were a cop, no matter what you said."

Zachary shrugged.

27

Richards stared at him, trying to intimidate him. But Zachary just waited it out. The silence again worked in his favor.

"What do you know?" Richards asked again. "Or think you know?"

"I know that Eyler was trafficking girls out of that hotel room. I'm sure you already figured that much out, but I did get descriptions of some of the girls he has been taking there. Maybe that would be helpful in finding out what happened around the time that Eyler was killed. There may be witnesses that haven't come forward."

"I see. Is that it, then? Descriptions of some hookers?"

"Trafficking victims," Zachary corrected. "Vulnerable minors. Not criminals."

"I didn't say they were criminals."

"I wonder how many DNA profiles you are going to get from the condoms and needles that you recovered at the scene."

Richards rolled his eyes. "At least a dozen, I'm sure. But all of that is beside the point. We already know who killed Eyler. Your friend Luke. All of the rest of this is just distraction. I don't need more witnesses. I don't need more DNA profiles to identify all of the johns and every other piece of filth that has been in that hotel room while Eyler has been pimping out of there. We'll process it all because this is a homicide case and they'll want everything they can get to shore up the case, but we don't need it. Your boy was caught red-handed, Mr. Goldman. Smoking gun in his hand."

Zachary must have frowned at that, because Richards backed up and clarified.

"I mean that figuratively. I meant the knife. Which was *literally* still in his hand when he was caught. And his bloody prints all over that hotel room."

"Mmm." Zachary nodded. "That's something I was wondering about."

"What?"

"If you had just killed someone and had their blood all over you, why would you go around the room touching everything? And why would you still be holding the knife in your hand while you did it? I mean… was this a fetish? Was he confused or hallucinating? If he was actually doing something… like trying to cover up what he had done or searching for something, then wouldn't he put down the knife? He wouldn't be walking around the suite holding on to it."

"That's what happened. Don't ask me why your psycho friend did what he did. Because there's something wrong with his head, obviously."

"Ah. Right."

"He has a history. Trauma. Head injuries. Overdoses. All of that stuff does a number on your brain. I wouldn't expect him to behave logically, like you or me. Criminals like him do all kinds of crazy stuff. Laying down and going to sleep in the middle of a robbery. Trying on the woman's panties. Ordering pizza. You would think that people would just run after doing something like that. That they would wash their hands and leave the knife there and sneak off before the authorities could get there. But the guy is not right in the head. That's just the way it is."

Zachary had to admit that he'd heard stories like that. It was true that criminals often did crazy, illogical things. Especially if they were on drugs. But he knew Luke, and Luke had not struck him as being that kind of person. He had been an addict, so it was entirely possible that he'd been on something and had a complete break from reality, hallucinating or paranoid.

"Was he high when you arrested him?"

Richards shrugged. "He tested clean. But who knows? He could be on some new designer drug that we don't test for yet. Or, like I said, brain damage from previous episodes. The kid's drug history goes back years."

"He seemed fine when I talked to him. And when I've seen him before. He doesn't act like he has brain damage."

"You can't always tell. Someone could be able to carry on a perfectly normal conversation like we're doing now, but not have any judgment, or flip out and go schizo on you thirty seconds later. You go to some of these mental hospitals, and you think the person you're talking to is a nurse or orderly, and then find out they're one of the patients. Who knows what delusions this kid could have?"

Zachary shifted uncomfortably. He did not like the way that Richards was talking about mentally ill patients. Zachary understood that Richards was just speaking of his own experience. But Zachary had been in the psych ward himself and wished Richards wouldn't be quite so cavalier and dismissive.

"Are you having Luke examined by a psychiatrist, then?"

"That's not my job. That will be up to the lawyers."

"He's in your jail. Isn't it your responsibility to make sure that's the appropriate place for him? If he should be in a psych ward…"

"No. Again, that's a job for the lawyers. The kid is safe in the jail. Nothing is going to happen to him there. If he needs a psychiatrist or medication or therapy, his lawyer can worry about that."

"He doesn't have a lawyer yet."

Richards shrugged. "Still not my concern. I arrested him, which means he goes to jail. That's the way the system works."

Zachary could argue it. A cop could certainly invoke Title 18 and have Luke evaluated. But Richards had no interest in doing so. He wasn't concerned about Luke's mental state, only about making sure he was off the street.

"So… are you interested in any of the information I learned at the hotel today?"

Richards scowled. "I really oughta arrest you for impersonating a police officer."

Zachary waited a few seconds. "So you're not interested?"

Richards sat down in the other chair. Zachary didn't know whether this was because psychologically, the cop was now putting him on the level of a peer rather than someone he was trying to show authority over, or if his feet were just tired from standing.

"Fine. What did you discover at the hotel? Besides the obvious, I mean. We already removed all of the forensic evidence, so it isn't like there was much left there for you to find."

"If I was you, I would do a more thorough search of the suite."

Richards's face got a shade redder and he looked ready to explode.

Zachary set his phone on the table, unlocked it, and tapped the screen. He found the pictures of the pills he had found in the bathroom and showed them to Richards.

"In the toilet paper holder."

Richards swore, a single, angry syllable. Zachary couldn't help shifting back slightly, instinct telling him that Richards was going to take a swing at him. But Richards kept himself under control. He picked up Zachary's phone and swiped through pictures in both directions, checking out all of the photos of the hotel, before handing it back.

"Is that all?"

"I didn't do a thorough search. Just looked around. I was only there for a few minutes. I wouldn't be surprised if there is more to find. I'm not confident that the site review was as... rigorous as it should have been."

"Uh-huh. It isn't like we didn't have all the evidence we needed against your friend. I'm not sure what the probative value of some pills in the bathroom is. We already knew the place was full of drugs. You're not saying that these pills belonged to your friend, are you?"

"Well, no. But I like to have a full picture of the situation, not just how things looked at first glance."

"Even when that first glance was of a kid holding a bloody knife over a bloody corpse?"

Zachary shrugged. He hadn't found anything that would exonerate Luke or would give him an argument for a lighter sentence. But it was early days. It would be months before Luke's case went to trial. As urgent as it felt to get him out of that jail and back home, that wasn't the way things were going to work out. He was going to be in jail for a long time and, after conviction, in prison for even longer. He wasn't going to be going home to Joss.

"What about the descriptions of the sex trafficking victims that were working out of that suite?"

Richards sighed. "I don't see what the point is, but yes, give me the descriptions, if you have them."

"I imagine there is security camera video too. You can probably find each of them on the video if you look."

"You think so? This guy was a pro, not just some hick hiring out his girlfriend. They use doors that don't have security cameras. If there is a camera in an elevator or hallway that they don't want to be caught on, it's easy to spray or smash it. They wear hats or hoods and keep their faces turned away from cameras. They know how to avoid video cameras."

"Maybe some of the nearby businesses, then. They wouldn't have been worrying about those. There was a car lot nearby. Some convenience stores. I'm sure they all have video."

Richards made a motion for Zachary to get on with it. He flipped through his notepad to give Richards the descriptions of the prostitutes that the hotel workers had taken note of.

"They could be witnesses. You don't know if Eyler was alone when Luke… was there. One of these people may have seen something important. Something that throws an entirely different light on what happened."

"It's not a matter of throwing a different light on it. We know what happened. A hooker's perspective is not going to change the facts of the case."

Zachary bit the inside of his cheek, trying to keep himself from reacting to Richards's disdainful words. "It could."

"And do you really think that we'll be able to find these girls?" Richards motioned to the notes he had just written down, transcribing from Zachary's notebook. "They are going to be long gone. They will have left town. Maybe even the state. Whoever is taking over from Eyler, they'll have those girls out of reach by now."

Of course they would. Why would they keep them around to talk to the cops? They had plenty of experience moving people around the country. Zachary sighed. Those girls would never be heard from again.

28

S o, you think that Luke killed Eyler *why?*" Zachary asked.

"Because he was caught red-handed."

"No, I mean… why would he do that? Why would he kill Eyler? What was his motive?"

"We don't need a motive when we catch him red-handed. This isn't some detective show on TV where you have to figure out everyone's motivations. The fact is that ninety-nine percent of the time, the person who killed the victim is exactly who you think it would be. The challenge is in gathering enough evidence for them to be arrested and convicted. Trying to figure out who is the murderer is just for dramas. Cheap novels and TV detectives."

"But don't you want to know? Don't you want to understand what happened? For the jury, at least?"

"I'm not the one who has to present it to a jury. I'm just the one who needs to charge him and coordinate getting the evidence. It goes to the prosecutor and he takes over. We have a lot of forensic evidence to be processed, which will take months, but I already know exactly what it's going to show. It's going to show that Luke killed Eyler. The rest is just extraneous and unimportant."

Zachary shook his head. The circumstances of the case mattered. Richards might be satisfied with "we know he did it because he did it," but Zachary was not. He needed to understand what had happened. Once he could put it all together in his head in a way that made sense, he would be done with it. Until then, he would keep asking questions.

"Look," Richards said, "there's not that much to understand. Criminals kill each other all the time. It saves us a lot of paperwork and the taxpayers all of the money it would have taken to keep Eyler in prison for thirty years. That's a good thing. We're grateful to him for that. But there's no great mystery here. You can ask 'why' a hundred times, but in the end, it doesn't matter."

"You think it was a business deal gone wrong."

"Of course I do. They were both in the business. Prostitute kills pimp. Usually, it's the other way around, but we'd rather the pimp was the victim. It doesn't matter whether it was because the kid wanted to set up shop on his own and Eyler wasn't going to let it happen. It doesn't matter if it was over Eyler withholding pay or drugs or trying to get the kid to do something he didn't want to. It doesn't even matter if it was jealousy because Eyler favored another hooker over him. Luke confronts Eyler, they yell and scream and Eyler ends up getting stuck. By the time we get there, it's all over and all that's left to do is take Luke into custody and Eyler to the morgue."

"Luke wasn't working for Eyler."

"I don't think you can know that. He could have been."

"He wasn't," Zachary said, with more certainty than he felt.

"Then he was trying to branch off on his own. Not a good idea when there is another boss in the area, but the kid thinks he's got a chance. Eyler sends for him, and either the kid is stupid enough to go confront him face to face on his own, or Eyler sends out the goon squad to bring him in."

Zachary raised one finger, objecting. "If Eyler's men brought Luke, then where were they when Luke killed Eyler? Standing by watching?"

"I'm sure they didn't think that he was a danger. Unarmed kid, been in the business for years, he knows how to behave."

"And that doesn't bother you?"

"Eyler was a big guy. Capable of looking after himself. Overconfident, maybe. I'm sure he didn't think Luke was any danger to him."

"It just doesn't make any sense," Zachary insisted.

Richards shrugged. "It doesn't have to."

It was clear that Zachary wasn't going to get anywhere with Richards. Each was sure of his own position. Richards knew that Luke had done it and that no one had been able to see it coming. Zachary was equally sure that Luke would not have put himself in that hotel room without a very good reason.

After ending their interview, Zachary wanted to see Luke again. Maybe now, knowing more of the details of the case, Zachary would be able to get something out of him. If Zachary could only identify mitigating circumstances around the murder, at least it would be a start. He would have something to go to Joss with.

Since Zachary had already filled out the required forms on Sunday, the officer at the front desk told him he could go around to the jail and they would let him visit Luke. Zachary found the door locked as he had the previous day. He had thought that it might be open on a weekday. But then, it was a jail. He should have expected it to be locked up tight.

They were, at least, faster to answer the door buzzer than they had been on a Sunday. Zachary had left as many of his personal items as possible in the car this time so that he didn't have to give much more than his shoes and key to the male CO who checked him in.

"You're here to see the kid?" the hulking man questioned, looking down at the clipboard in his hand after ensuring that Zachary was not bringing any contraband into the jail.

"Yes. That's right."

"Come with me."

Zachary followed him to a visiting room that was pretty much the same as the one he had been in on Sunday. Zachary decided to stay on his feet until Luke got there, to save him having to sit for so long on the uncomfortable chairs. The one at the police station had been bad enough.

The CO had been turning to leave, but he paused, looking back at Zachary. Zachary didn't move, waiting to see if he wanted something. The CO turned back around.

"Siddown."

"I just thought I would stand while I'm waiting. Been sitting all day…"

The man shook his head. "Sit."

"Okay." Zachary gingerly lowered himself into the chair .

"If there's going to be trouble with you not following the rules, you will not be allowed to visit."

"I didn't know it was a rule. Sorry."

The CO pointed to one of the plastic panels bolted into the wall with its long list of rules that must be followed during visits. Zachary hadn't read it and didn't plan to, but he pointed his nose toward it anyway. The CO waited another moment, then nodded and withdrew, shutting the door behind him. Zachary sighed and waited. He was going to be pretty sore by the time he got home.

It seemed like a long time before the CO brought Luke in. Half an hour or even forty-five minutes. Zachary didn't wear a watch—and wouldn't have been able to wear it into the visiting room—and he didn't have his phone with him, so he didn't have any way to verify his feeling about how much time had passed. He knew from past experience that his ADHD or meds could cause a sense of time distortion.

The door opened and the CO walked Luke in, one big hand holding on to Luke's arm in what looked like a painful grip. "Sit," he ordered, while at the same time shoving the slight teenager into the other chair, not waiting for compliance. A puff of sound escaped from Luke when he hit the chair, but he didn't voice any complaint. He waited patiently for the CO to anchor his shackles to the table. The CO walked back out and stationed himself outside the door, occasionally looking in the narrow window with wire mesh crisscrossing through it.

Zachary forced a smile. "Hey, Luke. How's it going?"

The bruises seemed to have set in darker in the twenty-four hours since Zachary had seen him. The oversize orange uniform made him seem small and insubstantial. Zachary worried again how Luke would be treated while he was in jail, and later, after he was convicted, in prison. The CO said they would keep him safe, but things happened sometimes. Security holes. Things that the COs were aware of and let slide. A series of mistakes that left a vulnerable teen at the mercy of bigger, more violent men.

Luke picked at a scab on his arm, not looking at Zachary.

"Rhys was asking after you."

That got Luke's attention. He looked up. Clearly, this was not what he had been expecting Zachary to say.

"Yeah?" he asked. "How is Rhys?"

"He seems fine. Very concerned about what's happening to you."

"Well, you can tell him I'm fine. Gonna be a long time before we can see each other again."

That was one positive aspect of Luke's arrest, at least. Zachary didn't have to worry about Luke luring Rhys into the trafficking business.

"I thought you told me that Rhys wasn't answering your messages. That you weren't in contact with each other anymore."

"Yeah, I did."

"Was that just a lie?"

Luke shrugged and didn't answer, leaving Zachary to wonder. Someone had told Rhys about Luke being arrested. Was it possible that person had been Luke himself? Joss had said he hadn't called anyone, but she might not have known. Or had someone else filled Rhys in?

"I went and had a look at the hotel," he told Luke.

"Nice place, hey?"

"It *was* nice," Zachary admitted. "But what was being done out of there was not."

"That's just the business. Gonna happen whether it's a nice place or a dive."

"Every hotel? You think every hotel is being used for trafficking?"

"Most of them."

Zachary didn't think that could be the case. But that had been Luke's life experience. Probably circulated from one hotel to another for a couple of years until he was trusted enough to be out on the street unsupervised to do the dirty work of bringing new talent into Peggy Ann's stable. Or Connor's, if he had still been around then.

"Well, anyway... I saw the room. Why don't you tell me what you remember about it?"

"About the room? Nothing special. Big. Fancy tub. Nice surroundings; johns like that. Makes them feel like they're not down in the sewers like they are."

"I meant what do you remember about the murder? About Eyler."

"Fat slob hadn't changed. Lives in a pigsty. Hardly ever washes. Treats his assets like crap."

"You knew him when you were working with Peggy Ann? Or before that, with Connor?"

Luke gave him a sharp look. "Why?" he snapped.

"I'm trying to get a picture of what happened. How you knew each other. Your history. What led up to him being killed."

"You don't need to know anything that happened. All you need to know is that I stuck the pig. Did the world a favor by taking him out. Should have done it years ago."

"Why didn't you? What pushed you into it now?"

"He was just the same. Nothing changes, just the names of his victims. Made me sick."

"Seeing that he was still trafficking?"

"I knew he would still be trafficking. No one gets out of that voluntarily. Not someone in his position, making money hand over fist. Why would he quit a good thing?"

"Why did you go to Eyler's hotel room?"

"To kill him."

Luke's answer was just a bit too quick.

"How did you know where he was staying?"

Luke hesitated. He shrugged, but Zachary could see him trying to come up with an explanation. "I still... hear things. If you know the business, you see and hear things that other people wouldn't. I knew he was in town. It wasn't hard to find out where."

"How did you know he was in town? Did you run into him?"

"What difference does it make?" Luke objected again. "I killed him. I don't need a deal or a softer sentence. I don't care about that. I always knew I'd end up in prison sooner or later. It's pretty amazing that I made it this long without any long stints."

"So, knowing he was in town, what made you find out where he was staying and to go kill him? Why wouldn't you keep your head down so that no one would recognize you? You blew all of that work you did on starting fresh. Let everybody know who you are. You seemed like you were doing really well with Joss. That you had... a new direction. Were excited about it."

"Excited? No. It was kind of... novel to have this new life, not to have to do any of the things I used to to survive. And your sister is great. But it wasn't the way I wanted to live the rest of my life."

"I didn't know that Joss has been rescuing other kids."

"So what? You don't own her. She doesn't have to tell you everything she's doing."

"I didn't say she did."

Luke jerked on his chains, making them clang loudly against the anchor. "Why are you even here?" he demanded, raising his voice. "I didn't ask for anyone's help. I don't want your help or help from any do-gooder! Just stay out of my life." Luke swore, standing up abruptly.

Zachary jumped back, even though he knew Luke's chains would keep him on the other side of the table. It was a reflex reaction, that instinct to protect himself.

The door opened and the CO strode in. He grabbed Luke by the shoulder and shoved him down, dumping him back into his chair. "Stay there!" he barked, reaching for the chains to untether him. "You keep your hands still, or you'll meet the business end of my taser."

Luke continued to swear and cuss. Zachary wasn't sure whether he or the CO was the target of Luke's words. The CO unlocked the chains from the anchor and pulled Luke back to his feet. He looked at Zachary as he started to push Luke toward the door. "Don't bother to come back, got it? Don't need people who are going to rile the prisoners up."

"I didn't—"

"Stay there. Until someone comes back for you."

Then he pushed Luke through the door and let it close behind him.

29

When he eventually got back to his car, Zachary tried to ignore the off-balance feeling that the encounter with Luke had left him with. If he thought about it too much, he would end up getting anxious and emotional. He hoped that by ignoring his body's visceral reaction to Luke's explosion, he could keep forging ahead and the uncomfortable, off-balance feeling would right itself. Just like riding a bike. If he tried to stay still or go too slowly, he would wobble all over. But if he just bore down and sped ahead, staying upright was easy.

But emotional confrontations were not like riding a bike.

Zachary pulled out his phone and checked for new messages. There was a voicemail from a number that he didn't recognize. He played it back and was quickly distracted from the meeting at the jail.

A soft woman's voice. "Mr. Goldman, I hope you don't mind me calling. You said that if I found out anything else about the… the unfortunate death we suffered recently, I should let you know, so I thought I should. It's Mildred, from the hotel. The maid service. I was the one who took you up to the room…? I guess you know that. Your memory is probably better than mine. One of the other maids here, she was on the floor when they were fighting. You know, *them*; before the police came. Okay, so call me back or stop by. Thanks. Bye."

Zachary gathered that she was trying not to use inflammatory words like "murder." They probably had strict instructions from management that they should not mention Mr. Eyler's untimely death anywhere they might be overheard by guests.

He drove back to the hotel rather than calling Mildred back. He was going to need to see the other maid's face and body language and didn't want to be trying to coax her to talk over the phone. Especially if, like Mildred, she had to be circumspect with hotel guests nearby.

He texted Mildred's number when he got there.

It's Zachary. I'm here at the hotel. Where you want to meet?

It was a while before Mildred was able to text Zachary back, which was not a surprise.

There is a coffee shop down the street. By the car lot. Meet us there.

Zachary sent a thumbs-up back and got out of this car. He could walk the block to the coffee shop. He had been spending way too much time on chairs that aggravated his tailbone. It was time to stand up for a while and, hopefully, it would stop throbbing.

He waited outside, watching the foot traffic on the street, paying attention to what stores and facilities were close to the hotel. When he eventually saw the two women in maid's uniforms walking down the street toward him, he went into the coffee shop.

It was mid-afternoon, and the coffee shop was not too busy. There were plenty of tables open, and the chairs looked much more inviting than the ones at the police station and jail. Zachary joined the short line at the cash register and, as he got to the front, the two maids entered. Mildred led her friend up to Zachary, looking anxious and awkward.

"Hi!" Zachary gave them both a warm smile. "What can I get you?"

"Oh, nothing..." the smaller maid said, shaking her head. "I don't need anything."

"Well, if we're going to sit down and talk in a coffee shop, we should at least pay for our time. I'm going to have a coffee, but if you want a muffin or some juice..." Zachary motioned to the display case and notice board. "Whatever you feel like. But you should have something."

"Well... okay."

Mildred gave Zachary a smile and nod of approval. He ordered both women what they wanted, and they took a corner table where Zachary could see anyone coming in or going out of the cafe.

"I am Rosetta," the smaller woman offered, nodding to Zachary a little shyly.

"Nice to meet you, Rosetta. You can call me Zachary. Mildred said that you were around before the mur—before Eyler died. and maybe you might have heard some of what was going on."

Rosetta nodded. She dropped her eyes to her tea and thought about it.

"I understand there was an argument. Quite a disturbance. Several people called the police about it."

"Yes. They were very loud, lots of yelling and screaming, not trying to stay quiet so that other people would not hear them. You could hear them several doors down." Rosetta shook her head. "I was cleaning a room just across the hallway. I was very frightened. Worried that they might come out and find me listening to them. They were... very violent people. I could tell. I did not want to be in the middle of things."

"No," Zachary agreed. After being shaken just by Luke's sudden change in mood, he could well imagine how a loud altercation would feel threatening to the small, vulnerable maid cleaning the room across the hallway. "That must have been really disturbing."

"Yes."

"Can you tell me about what you heard?"

She played with her teabag, not looking at him. "I hear... the big man shouting. There is always music playing," she told Zachary. "All the time. We get complaints about it sometimes. But he pays for a week or two, in cash, and I think..." She trailed off and looked at her companion uncertainly. "I think maybe he pays extra for the complaints to go away."

Zachary sighed, thinking about Arthur and the other staff members at the front desk. And there would be other people there on the other shifts. A little bit of extra cash spread around to ensure things went smoothly for Eyler and his business. He made fistfuls of money as long as he was operating. There was plenty for expenses like paying the hotel staff to look the other way and pretend not to know that something illegal was going on in that room.

"You're probably right," he told Rosetta. "He probably did."

She looked reassured by this. Mildred didn't say anything to contradict her or tell her that she should not be talking out of school.

"Because of the music, you cannot usually tell what is going on in there. It is covered up. But the big man..."

"Eyler."

"Mr. Eyler... he is very loud when he is angry. He is easy to hear over the music."

"Could you tell who he was angry at? Who was in the room with him?"

She shook her head. "They were too quiet to hear over the music and Mr. Eyler's shouting. I know there is someone else there... but I cannot hear."

Zachary nodded. "Could you tell what Eyler was yelling about? What had upset him?"

"He was yelling about... 'I take care of you,' and 'You owe me. You do what I say.'" She shrugged, looking down at her tea and fishing the teabag out. She took a small sip but didn't look as if she even tasted it. "So, I thought maybe... a girlfriend or a child." Her eyes swam with tears. "He was very loud, very angry."

30

How long did the fight last?"

"I don't know. A long time. I was trying to get the room done and to move to the next one... but I didn't want to be in the hallway if one of them came out. I didn't want them to see my work cart, so I pulled it into the room. And I waited." She dabbed at her eyes, her hand shaking. Reliving the trauma, adrenaline pumping again, fearing for her own safety and whoever was on the receiving end of the abuse.

"It's okay," he assured her. "You're safe here. Whatever happened, no one is going to come after you. No one knows what you heard or that you are talking to me. Eyler is dead and his people have pulled out. They'll want to fly under the radar for a while now, not attract police attention."

She nodded gratefully and used her napkin to soak up the tears that were leaking from her eyes.

"You are very brave to step forward like this. I appreciate you telling the truth, even when you are scared. Someone needs to hear what happened."

It was a few minutes before she seemed to get herself back under control. She swallowed and nodded and patted Zachary's hand. "You are a very nice boy."

Zachary's ears got hot. He rolled his eyes up to the ceiling, trying to control his reaction, but it clearly didn't work; Rosetta and Mildred both laughed at his red ears and face.

"Uh, thank you. Did you see anyone come into or leave the hotel room? Or were you in the other room the whole time?"

"I did not see then. Other times, I saw people come and go. They were very busy."

"Did you ever see a young man go in there?"

"With the big man, yes."

Zachary hesitated. "Which one? There was a younger one, maybe thirteen, and an older one who looked… nineteen or early twenties."

"Oh…" She looked surprised at this. "I only remember the young one. I thought… his son. It must have been his son, I think."

Zachary didn't correct her misperception. Like the clerk at the front desk, she had jumped to the easiest, most comfortable solution. People didn't think of boys being prostitutes, of young boys being trafficked just like girls. So they saw a different relationship. An affectionate arm around the shoulder, a whisper directed in the boy's ear, and they saw Eyler as a father figure rather than a predator. Just as the hotel clerks had preferred to think of the girls as models rather than trafficking victims.

Zachary nodded. He found Luke's picture on his phone again and showed it to her. "Did you ever see this one?"

"In the lobby maybe, or on the elevator… before the shouting. He didn't go into Mr. Eyler's room when I started my cleaning. But I thought he would."

"Why?"

"That is the room people were coming and going to. Other suites on the floor were rented to families. Older couples. They tried not to put too many people on the floor because of the noise and complaints. I see him again… when the police were there. When they found Mr. Eyler dead. The boy was there, and they arrested him. I was peeking around the door…"

"Yeah. That's who was arrested. But I'm trying to figure out what happened. If there is a way to get him off with a lighter sentence. Was Eyler making threats? You were afraid of him. Do you think there was reason for Luke to be afraid of him too, in the room with him?"

Her eyes got wide. "Yes, yes, of course. They were fighting. Mr. Eyler was shouting. I'm sure he was afraid."

"Was there anyone else there? Any of the men that you had seen go into Eyler's room before?"

"I don't know. I don't think so, or they would have been there when the police came. I did not see anyone else come out with the police."

Zachary nodded. "I really appreciate you taking the time to talk to me about this. It's helpful to get some inside information on what actually happened that day. There's nothing of note in the papers and, of course, the police won't tell me anything."

"You're working for the young man?"

"Sort of. But he won't tell me anything either. It makes it pretty difficult to find anything out."

"Well… I'm sorry for him. I hope you can do something to help him. He looks like a nice boy, but that Eyler—he was not."

Zachary wrote additional notes in his notebook as he thought through Rosetta's story. He had decided to go for a walk while he worked things through. As well as his tailbone being sore, he was also restless and anxious, his ADHD making him feel like he might explode if he had to sit any longer. He considered taking one of his ADHD pills, but they were extended release and it was too late in the day to take one without it interfering with his sleep. A brisk walk would help. And if he couldn't think of anything else to do while in town, highway driving always soothed his need for constant motion and helped him focus his thoughts.

He stopped every block and so and jot down another note, then walked off briskly again. He was out of shape. His shoes pinched and rubbed uncomfortably and his legs tired long before he expected them to. He needed to get more regular exercise. He could at least think about walking places around town instead of automatically hopping in the car whenever he needed something.

His mind roved back and forth over the case. What Joss had told him. Rosetta's story, the bits he had learned from Richards, and Luke's reactions to his questions. It wasn't a lot to cobble the whole story from. He had an overview of the crime and what had happened that day, but none of the details. None of the events that had led up to Luke's meeting with Eyler in his hotel room that day.

Rosetta had been able to provide some details, and Zachary couldn't shake the feeling that the other staff at the hotel could fill in more. They had seen the comings and goings of Eyler and his guests. Had Luke been there before? Had he gone to the hotel with the specific plan to kill Eyler? Or had it been for something else and things had gone sideways?

Zachary was sure that Luke hadn't intended to work for Eyler. And he hadn't planned on going into business and competing with Eyler. Those were two things he was absolutely certain of.

As much as he could be.

Zachary flipped through his notebook to find the information he needed. He called the hotel and asked for Kurt, the younger man who had been on shift with Arthur and the young woman when Zachary had questioned them. He was put on hold for a moment, then heard the man's cheerful greeting.

"This is Kurt. How can I help you?"

"Kurt, it's Zachary Goldman. The private investigator."

"Oh," Kurt's enthusiasm dulled. "Hi."

"I was wondering if you had remembered anything else about Luke. Where you might have seen him before."

"Yeah. I was planning to call you. But now is not a good time."

"When are you off?"

"Another hour."

"Can I take you out for dinner? Coffee? A drink?"

"Huh. You might not want to do that, if you don't want to tarnish your reputation."

"Oh?" Zachary was taken aback. "I'm not sure what you mean. Is there somewhere we could meet that you could talk freely?"

"I don't know."

"Your place?" Zachary offered, hoping that would make Kurt more comfortable. "Wherever you want."

"No. Maybe… there's a bar where we might happen to run into each other. Do you know the town? It's O'Callaghan's, near the highway."

"I'm sure I can find it. You'll be there in a little over an hour?"

"Yeah. That should work."

"I'll see you there."

31

Zachary waited a while, hoping that Kurt would already be at the bar so that Zachary wouldn't attract attention to himself, a stranger in town hanging around waiting for someone. Kurt had sounded pretty jumpy about the two of them getting together. Still, he had picked a public place to meet. Somewhere they might be seen. Whatever he was worried about, it didn't seem to be that one of Eyler's men would show up and teach both of them a lesson.

He walked into the bar and waited for a moment, blinking, for his eyes to adjust to the dimness of the interior. He spotted Kurt at the bar, looking as if he were just there to drink alone. No glance toward the door to see if Zachary had arrived yet. Not obviously waiting for someone else to join him before placing his drink order. Just a young man out for some refreshment after a long day at work. And Zachary imagined their shifts were probably quite long and tedious, dealing with complaints and travel-weary guests all day.

Zachary walked up to the bar and took a stool two down from Kurt. "A Coke," he told the bartender. "And... I don't know... nachos?"

"Loaded?"

"Yeah, sounds good."

Zachary didn't look at Kurt, waiting for him to take the initiative. Kurt sipped his beer, not looking at him. Zachary was willing to wait and let him pick his timing.

The bartender placed a tall glass of Coke in front of Zachary and, a minute later, handed him a large plate piled high with nacho chips, cheese, and toppings. Zachary eyed it dubiously.

"That looks good," Kurt commented.

Zachary slid it toward him. "Help yourself. There's no way I'm going to eat all of this. I was thinking of an appetizer, not a full meal!"

Kurt snagged a few chips and munched on them.

"Zachary Goldman," Zachary introduced himself. "Just passing through town."

"I didn't think I'd seen you here before. Kurt."

Zachary nodded. "Nice to meet you."

After a moment, Kurt slid over to the bar stool next to Zachary and helped himself to some more chips. He made small talk with Zachary for a couple of minutes, his eyes jumping from the bartender to the other patrons, to the door, and back to Zachary's face. He started to relax eventually, his beer glass refilled and half of the chips eaten.

"We have to be careful," he explained to Zachary. "I didn't want people to think that we were dating."

Zachary raised his brows. "Oh?"

Kurt shrugged and nodded. "They know at work that I'm gay. But that doesn't make it okay to talk about it at the hotel. I'd get in real trouble if I started talking about bar hopping and parties and *that kind* of behavior."

Zachary nodded. He'd been in gay bars before, working cases that necessitated it, and he knew that, despite the relaxation of anti-gay legislation, there was still a lot of anti-gay sentiment alive and well in Vermont. And probably all over the country. It was not comfortable being targeted by bigots. More than that, it could be dangerous. Zachary had landed in the hospital the last time, working the Jose Flores missing person case.

"I think we're safe here. For now."

Kurt nodded. He took a couple more nacho chips. "I didn't run into Luke at karaoke."

"Okay. You want to tell me about it?"

"He was out... socializing. Not drinking. He said he didn't want to have to go through detox again. But he wanted to be out and to meet people his age who shared his interests."

"He was lonely."

Kurt agreed. "Isolated. He couldn't just stay home with that old lady all day. He would go stir crazy."

"What did she think about that?"

"She didn't like him going out. Figured he was going to get himself into trouble again. But she couldn't control his life. He has to *have* a life, not just be locked up inside all day."

Kurt broke off, and they were both silent for a few moments, realizing that Luke was now locked up inside all day and likely would be for years to come.

"He was going out to bars and other entertainment spots looking for company."

Kurt nodded. "Nothing wrong with that. It's practically a national pastime. When you're gay or bi, it's a little more complicated. Feeling people out. Trying to make contact with the right people. People who will be interested, not disgusted or violent."

Zachary nodded.

"Last thing you need is some guy waiting for your outside of the bar," Kurt said, "just waiting for you to show your face."

"Yeah. I get it."

Kurt studied him, forehead creasing. "Are you—? I didn't get that vibe from you."

"No. I'm more than happy with my girlfriend. But I was on a case. Trying to get a lead on a guy in a gay bar. And a group of neo-Nazis followed me when they saw me leave. Decided to teach me a lesson."

Kurt's face went white. "Are you kidding me? And you were there by yourself?"

"I was. I didn't think anything would happen to me outside. Once I left the bar, I thought I was home free. Walk to my car, go on to the next place."

Kurt shook his head back and forth slowly. He swore. "You gotta look out, man. Go with friends. Get a cab or ride share right outside the door. Don't walk away from a place like that alone."

Zachary shrugged. A little late for that advice now. Though he had been warned at the time. "I guess I learned my lesson. Not the one they wanted to teach me, maybe, but I'll be a lot more careful the next time."

"How bad was it?"

"They were interrupted by a good Samaritan. I went to the hospital, but didn't stay over. No broken bones or ruptured kidneys." Zachary said it lightly, though he hadn't been laughing about it at the time.

"Don't joke about it, man. You're lucky. Not everyone survives a stomping like that."

"I know. I was lucky for the passerby who decided to do something about it."

"Really lucky."

They were both quiet for a time, nibbling on the nacho chips and sipping their drinks.

"Luke was good people. Charming. I enjoyed being with him. Hanging out, dancing, whatever. We weren't serious. Just friends. He wasn't looking for a commitment. I got that."

Zachary nodded. "He's always seemed like a good guy to me."

He realized after saying it that it wasn't entirely true. In fact, the first time he had met Luke, he had seen him as a monster. Someone who was taking advantage of a young girl. Holding her hostage and pimping her out. There hadn't been anything he could do at the time but call the police, and Madison refused to leave Luke, so there was nothing the police could do either. But then Luke had reached out. Had sent a message to Zachary under Madison's name, saying he wanted out. And from there…

"Heart of gold," Kurt agreed.

"Did he tell you about his past? His history?"

"No. He didn't talk about it. I knew there had been some bad stuff in his past. Stuff that he didn't open up about, but I was okay with living in the present. Everyone has stuff in the past that they would rather not talk about. Nobody lives a blameless life with nothing to be ashamed of."

"True."

Kurt rotated his glass on the bar, turning it around and around as he contemplated the time he had shared with Luke. "I did know… that there was a lot of stuff he didn't want to talk about. I knew he'd drank and used a lot; that was why he wouldn't touch anything with alcohol in it. And if we were out somewhere and the drugs came out, he would suggest leaving. He didn't want to stay around it, be tempted. I figured that was probably where most of his shame came from. But I also knew… addicts, out on the street, no family to look after them… a lot of them end up turning tricks to get drug money. Especially if they're queer. One vice feeds the other."

"But he didn't tell you about that?"

"No. He kept that door closed, and I was happy to comply. We were having a fun time together. Didn't need to spoil that with a lot of sordid details."

"But then… something happened," Zachary suggested.

"Yeah."

32

———

S omebody recognized him?" Zachary guessed.

Kurt looked surprised. He nodded and took a sip of his beer.
He wiped his mouth with the back of his hand. While his voice
was cool, it looked as though he were trying to hold back tears. Anger or
grief or pain? Zachary couldn't tell.

"Yeah, we were out passing the time, getting some moves on. Actually,
there *was* karaoke." Kurt laughed. "I'd actually forgotten that. But we
weren't singing. Just cheering on the people who were. Or making fun of
them."

"I'm not the type to get up in front of an audience," Zachary confided.

"I need a few drinks under my belt before I will. So we were just
listening, enjoying the show, and then this guy is in front of Luke, stepping between him and the stage, getting in his face. Luke was ticked. But
this guy keeps banging the drum. Saying he knows him. Calling him
Noah. Grabbed Luke by the arm and held him, looking at his hand,
saying that he had to come back."

"How did Luke respond?"

"Said the guy was crazy; he didn't know what he was talking about.
But the dude kept hanging on to him, tapping the tat on the back of his
hand, saying things like he's owned. He's bought and paid for. That he has
to go back again."

Zachary nodded, waiting for the rest of the story.

"Luke said it was just a tat he'd picked out of a book. That it didn't mean whatever the dude thought it did."

"Was he convinced?"

"No. No way. Luke pulls away from him, threatening to make a big scene and have the guy arrested if he doesn't keep his hands to himself. The guy lets him go but immediately starts making phone calls. Luke was really freaked out. He said he had to go. Had to disappear before the goon squad showed up. Didn't want to be taken back there. Wherever *there* was." Kurt sighed and shook his head. "Was it with Eyler? Is that who had owned him?"

"No. But he knew Eyler from before. His boss and Eyler knew each other. Did he say anything about Eyler? His name? Did this guy who came up to him know who he had worked for? Was he one of Eyler's men?"

"Whoa, whoa," Kurt held up his hands. "Stop there, man. I don't know. I don't know anything. He didn't tell me who he had worked for or who the other dude worked for or anything like that. I told you; he didn't want to talk about that part of his life, and I didn't want to know. You think I wanted to go over all of that negative stuff and sit around being miserable with him? No, we were there to have a good time. To put everything else behind us and just enjoy being together."

Zachary nodded and tried to slow his brain down. He needed to know those things, but Kurt wasn't going to be able to provide them. He had been happy to be kept in the dark about all of the murkier stuff in Luke's past. Zachary needed to look beyond those logistics and just get the best picture he could of what had happened.

"Okay. What happened? Did he get out before the goon squad showed up?"

"Yeah. He ran. We both ditched the place. Went in different directions, then met up again somewhere else. He said that he'd lost the guy and everything was fine."

"Was he worried about running into him again? That he wasn't safe here anymore?"

"No. He said he'd need to stay away from that bar for a few days, until he was sure that no one would be there looking for him. That's all. He didn't act like he was worried about anything. He never mentioned *Eyler*."

"What did the guy who confronted him look like?"

"Tall, black hair, medium brown skin. Maybe Hispanic, I don't know; I didn't hear an accent. But some of those guys speak better than we do."

He didn't match any of the descriptions that Zachary had been given so far. "Did Luke call him by name?"

"No. I don't think so."

"And did this guy ever show up at the hotel? One of Eyler's guests?"

"Nnno."

Zachary heard his hesitation. "What? You think you know where I could find him?"

"No. It's not that. I did think that I saw him at the hotel once. But I'm not sure it was the same guy. I was drunk that night. I'm not a good witness. I couldn't swear that it was the same guy."

"People don't look the same when they're out in the open under good lights as they do dressed for the nightlife, with dance lights flashing, in the dimness of a bar."

Kurt tipped his glass toward Zachary. "You got it. Exactly. I just couldn't be sure whether it was the same guy, or just a nightmare, or a trick of the light. We didn't talk about him afterward. Pretended like it had never happened."

"And this guy that you saw at the hotel, was *he* associated with Eyler?"

"I'm not sure. He came in from the back. Went up the elevator. He could have been going to see Eyler. Or he could have been going anywhere else in the building."

"Well… your story confirms one thing, and that is that someone recognized Luke. Someone knew that he was here and knew that he belonged to one of the trafficking rings, even though it wasn't Eyler. Eyler might have seen it as an opportunity to acquire a good asset."

Kurt looked like he had something else to say. Zachary looked at him, waiting.

"That wasn't the end of it," Kurt said.

"Oh?"

"I heard that Luke was in a fight in another bar a few nights later. I wasn't there, so I don't know who it was or what happened. But something was going on. Maybe the guy found him again, tried to take him away, and wouldn't be put off this time. Maybe he decided he didn't care if the police got called, that he could force Luke to go with him before the cops would get there."

"You don't know who it was, though."

"No."

"How did you hear about it?"

"Just through the grapevine. People talking about it. Whenever there is something interesting going on, it gets spread far and wide through the clubs. Even faster in the LGBT community. It's a way to protect ourselves, make sure everyone knows what is going on."

"But it doesn't sound like you got a lot of details."

"No. Wish I could tell you more."

"Which club was this at?"

"Oh. Maybe you could find something out there. Maybe someone over there saw."

Zachary nodded impatiently.

"It was the Duck and Dog." Kurt shrugged and rolled his eyes at the name. "It's usually pretty safe there. They got good security. If it had been somewhere else... who knows what would have happened."

Kurt pushed his empty glass toward the bartender, who exchanged it for a full one. He tapped his fingers on the edge of the bar before picking it up to drink it.

"I didn't know," he said. He flicked a glance at Zachary and then away again. "I really didn't. I knew Eyler was up to something shady but, like I said, I thought they were models or something. That he was just operating an unregistered business out of the hotel. Ducking taxes. Something like that. I didn't know he was trafficking those girls. I would have said something."

Zachary nodded and didn't contradict Kurt, but wondered whether it were really the truth. It seemed like it should have been pretty obvious what was going on in that hotel room.

"And with this guy and Luke... I didn't think it was that serious. We kind of laughed about it. Mocked the guy. Said that he was crazy if he thought that one person could belong to another, like a slave. Wasn't there a war fought for that? You know. Just being kind of silly about it. I never thought that... I never thought there was something serious behind it. That someone wanted Luke that badly, that they thought they owned him and had the right to dictate what he could do. I thought it was all just drama. Some loony. And when I saw him at the hotel. I didn't know for sure it was him. It could have just been someone with a resemblance."

That was a lot of excuses for not seeing the evidence of human trafficking right in front of him. But there were a lot of people who didn't think that human trafficking existed in the United States. Or that if it did, it was only illegal aliens, or that it only happened in the big cities. They didn't want to believe it was happening right in front of them.

"I'll follow up with the Duck and Dog. Maybe they can tell me what happened with Luke. What this altercation was that he was involved in."

Kurt nodded. He rubbed at his eyes with the heels of his hands as if he had just woken up. "Thanks. I feel horrible that I missed all of this. I just thought... Luke had done drugs in the past. Maybe this guy had too, and it scrambled his brain. I didn't take any of it seriously."

33

Zachary could see that he was going to be quite late getting back to Kenzie in Roxboro. He had tried to pack too much into one day. But he didn't want to go back home without seeing what he could find out at the Duck and Dog and to have to return to Kent just to do that. The bar wouldn't be open in the morning, so he would have to return in the evening another day. He would have to be late getting home to Kenzie two nights instead of just one. Better to get it over with, even if he was tired after the long day.

The bar was open when he got there. Initially, he just sat down with another Coke and watched the early patrons arriving. He knew he should probably have something more to eat, but the nachos with Kurt had killed his appetite and nothing else sounded good.

He nodded to the bartender, who was puttering around behind the bar trying to look busy until the bar filled up.

"I hear you had some excitement here the other day," he commented.

"Excitement?" the bartender raised his brows. "What excitement?"

"Some kind of altercation. Between a young guy I know who lives in town and some... outsider."

The bartender studied Zachary and shook his head. "You don't live around here either. I haven't seen you here before."

"No, I'm from Roxboro. Just here for a visit. But... my pal is in trouble, and I'm just nosing around, trying to get a bit more information about what happened. Because what else am I going to do? Just let him rot away in jail?"

"In jail? If I'm thinking of the same night as you are, no one was arrested. It was over quick, mostly verbal, and the two of them just got bounced." The man shrugged. "Hardly something to write home about."

"Yeah, unless he got into another fight with the same guy later on. Then… things might have escalated."

The bartender looked interested. "I hadn't heard about that. Really? Again that night?"

"No, a few nights later. So now he's sitting in a jail cell." Zachary shook his head. "He's a nice guy. It really wasn't his fault."

The bartender leaned on the counter. "Luke, right? That's the guy?"

"Yeah." Zachary smiled. "You know him?"

"Sure. He's been around here a bit the last few months. You get to know the regulars. He'd never made any trouble before. It surprised me."

"How much did you see?"

"Well, I don't have the best vantage point here. I was busy with my job, so I didn't see how it started. Just a brief scuffle, and then it was all over and they were both tossed out." The bartender's eyes scanned the bar patrons. "Now, if Cathy is around…"

Zachary looked around as well, though, of course, he had no chance of identifying Cathy, whoever she was. There were not a lot of women in the bar. But the evening had just begun. There would be more later as they finished their dinners and trickled in.

"There," the bartender said, pointing across the room at a young woman in what seemed to be a combination of punk and goth. She looked in his direction, maybe sensing that someone was watching her or talking about her. The bartender made a jerk with his chin, inviting her over to join them.

Cathy made her way over to them and looked Zachary over. She looked at the bartender. "What's up? He's not exactly my type."

Zachary felt his face getting red and hoped it wasn't too obvious in the dim lighting of the bar. The bartender snorted.

"The other night. A week ago, or whatever it was. When Luke and that other guy mixed it up…"

She nodded. "Yeah."

"You were here, right? Did you get it?"

Cathy nodded again and studied a chip in the black nail polish on her thumb. "Sure. Of course."

The bartender spoke to Zachary. "Cathy, here is our aspiring videographer. Always got her phone or camera out, capturing anything interesting that happens while she's here. Has made some good promo cuts for us. She hypes the bar. We endorse her videos. It's a good arrangement."

Zachary looked at Cathy, impressed. "And you got footage of the fight between Luke and the other guy?"

"Yeah. Sure. Most interesting thing that has happened here in a few weeks. Fights always get people's attention." She adjusted a large shoulder bag, pulling it from her side to her front. She dug around in it, muttering. She pulled out a tablet and set it up in a display position on the bar. Zachary watched her tap through a few screens and scroll through a long list of videos. She tapped one, and Zachary bent closer, his eyes focused on the shot of Luke and another man he didn't recognize, facing off against each other. Squaring up to each other, fists clenched, ready.

Luke's face was white and hard. Unbruised. The other man was not Eyler, whose face Zachary knew from the sparse news articles reporting his demise. The man didn't have his build, either. Eyler was frequently referred to as a big man or as fat. The man on the screen was older than Luke, but he had a fighter's build. Narrow hips, broad shoulders, biceps that were well-defined but not bulging. He had a dark goatee, hair buzzed as short as Zachary's, and an expression so hard it looked like his face had been chiseled out of rock.

At first, it was impossible to tell what the two men were saying, with the music and conversations going on throughout the bar. But as people noticed what was going on, they stopped talking, watching to see what would happen.

The older man reached for Luke, grabbing him by the arm and twisting it to look at the tattoo on his hand.

"...think you can set up business here?" he demanded, shouting to be heard. "You're out of your depth, kid! This isn't your territory and you ain't got the cred to run anything."

"This *is* my territory," Luke argued, jerking his arm away and giving the other man a retaliatory push. "Mine, not his. He's been in town what, two weeks? I was here way ahead of him, and he's not setting up on *my* territory."

"You've got no assets. A few washed-out girls you picked up and think you can turn? You got no experience running a business like this. Being able to bring them into the business isn't the same as being able to run it yourself," he sneered.

Luke didn't argue the point. "You tell your boss that this is my territory, and if he doesn't get out, I'll take him out myself!"

Zachary went cold at the words.

On the screen, the drama continued. The older man laughed in Luke's face at the threat, taking a step closer to him. He shoved Luke. Luke swung back with a hard fist, and the two of them engaged for a few blows, falling back away from each other before the bouncers pushed their way through the crowd to put a stop to it. A bouncer grabbed each of them and hustled them toward the door. The men did not fight against the bouncers, who were two or three times Luke's size.

Zachary could hear Luke still shouting at the other man. "You tell him if he doesn't get out of Kent, I am going to kill him!"

Then they were removed from the scene and pushed out the door. Zachary hoped that the bouncers followed them out the door to ensure they didn't kill each other on the sidewalk outside.

But they hadn't killed each other outside. Luke had killed Eyler in his hotel room.

"Well." Zachary stared at the image frozen on the screen when the video was over. "That was certainly better than trying to get bystander accounts."

Cathy grinned at him. "Good video, right? It's made a lot of views."

Zachary looked at the screen and started to take in a few other details that he hadn't noticed before, too focused on the video itself.

"This is online?"

"Sure."

"It's public?"

She nodded. "That's the best way to get people to see it," she pointed out dryly.

If the police conducted their investigation thoroughly, they would find it. And that would be the final nail in Luke's coffin. A public threat against Eyler. A demonstration that he was prepared for physical violence, if that was what it took.

Zachary had no idea how he was going to spin that.

34

Zachary needed to talk to Luke. To really talk to him, with Luke actually involving himself in the conversation and answering Zachary's questions. Zachary's list of questions was growing.

But the jail would not be open to visitors so late in the day. And Zachary might have problems getting back in to see Luke. Luke's angry outburst at the end of their last conversation had resulted in the CO telling Zachary not to return. At that time, he hadn't thought much about it. He hadn't planned to go back so soon and figured that they would forget any trouble by the time he returned.

He sat in the car, thinking. After a few minutes, he tapped Kenzie's name on the phone and waited for her to pick up.

"Late night tonight," Kenzie observed as soon as she picked up. Zachary felt bad for not getting in touch with her sooner, but he had been right in the middle of the investigation. Everything seemed urgent and he didn't feel like he could take the time.

"It is. And I'm trying to decide what to do now. I've made progress today, but I need to talk to Luke again tomorrow. See if I can get some answers now that I know a little bit more about what happened before the murder."

"And you don't want to come all the way back here, just to turn around and go back in the morning."

"I can if you want me to. We could still spend some time together tonight and have breakfast together in the morning."

"But it's a waste of time and gas. And I assume you're not getting paid for this job."

"I wouldn't ask Joss to pay for this. I'm the one who brought Luke to her in the first place. In a way, I started this whole thing."

"Well, not intentionally." Kenzie gave a short laugh. "You certainly didn't do anything wrong by helping Luke to get away from the trafficking ring and finding him a new home with Joss. None of us could know how things would turn out."

"I wish I could... go back and change things."

"What would you change?"

"I don't know." Zachary thought about it. He had done the best that he could. Would taking Luke somewhere else have been any better? Another family or friend who could take him in? A rehabilitation program? He knew that there were organizations that helped sex workers get off the street and start a new life, but he didn't know if they dealt with young men as well as women, or if Luke would have been open to going through a program like that.

Even knowing what would happen down the road, Zachary couldn't see any path other than the one he had taken. He didn't know how things could have worked out any differently. Luke had been trying...

But when he thought about the Luke he had seen on the video Cathy had recorded, he had a chill. Luke saying that it was his territory. Luke threatening to kill Eyler if he didn't get out of town. All along, Zachary had been telling himself that Luke would never get back into the business, and he certainly wouldn't decide to start turning girls out on his own. He knew what Luke had gone through, how much he had wanted to escape that life when he had grown so attached to Madison.

Or at least, he knew what Luke had told him. Maybe none of it was true. Zachary didn't know those things for himself. He only knew what Luke had told him and what he had believed from his interactions with Luke. He had never actually seen any of it.

Had Luke just been stringing him along the whole time? Was he just as warped and twisted as the man he had killed and, rather than protecting himself, had just been trying to take over the territory himself?

"Zachary?"

"Sorry." Zachary tried to focus on Kenzie. "I don't know. The more I find out, the less I think I know Luke and what I'm talking about. I thought I knew what I was doing. I thought I knew what kind of a kid he was. But all of this has made me wonder."

"I was really concerned when he came to the hospital with Joss while you were there. And he was there at the same time as Rhys. I couldn't understand why he would come back here when he knew how dangerous it would be if one of the people he knew in the past was to see him and recognize him there. Why would he take that chance? And I was worried for Rhys, of course. I always worry that Luke could lead him into a relationship that wasn't good for him. That boy has been through enough trauma in his life."

"Yeah." Zachary's heart thumped hard in his chest when he thought about Luke exposing himself and maybe putting Rhys at risk as well. But Luke was in jail now, and he wouldn't be getting out any time soon. Rhys was safe from him. From that one danger, at least. "Did you know… that they were still in contact?"

"I thought Rhys stopped responding to Luke's messages."

"So did I."

"They were still talking?"

"Looks that way. Or there was an intermediary that was passing messages back and forth between them."

Kenzie made a noise of disgust. "I can't believe them! I suppose you just can't believe anything teenagers say. They go through this period where they are so rebellious and secretive, wanting to try everything out for themselves…"

Zachary remembered Joss's complaint that he wouldn't listen to anything she said, but would make up his own mind and disregard her warnings, even when he knew that she was more knowledgeable than he was. Had he ever grown past that "seeking independence" stage? Or was he stuck emotionally and had never matured?

"I remember… lying and hiding a lot of things from my foster families or group home leaders. Not listening if I wanted something and someone told me no." He grimaced. "Incorrigible, just like my mother said."

"Don't go down that path. You know that what your mother did and said was unfair. You never talk like that to a child. And you don't abandon them and say that you don't feel like taking care of them anymore, either. *Don't* judge yourself by what your mother said."

"She's not the only one. There were plenty of others who couldn't manage me. Who wouldn't keep me because I wouldn't behave and do the things they said to. Even with the Petersons, when I would go back to visit

Mr. Peterson to get his help in developing my film, they would say—his wife especially—would tell me to call and set something up instead of just showing up on their doorstep." Zachary paused, swallowing. "But I never did. Right up to the time that they separated and Mr. Peterson wasn't there anymore. I just showed up and expected him to be there and able to work with me." Kenzie made a noise, starting to respond to him, but Zachary went on. "And then when I found out he wasn't there and got his new address, then I went over to his new place and showed up on *his* doorstep."

Kenzie laughed. Zachary wasn't sure what was funny about it. It was painful, looking back and seeing how disrespectful he had been. That despite how kind and accommodating Mr. Peterson had always been, Zachary just hadn't seen the need to do what they asked. If he had called ahead, they could tell him no. If he just showed up, they would have to let him in. Mr. Peterson had never turned him away.

"I can just see you doing that," Kenzie said, still chuckling. "But you have changed since then. *Now* you call them ahead to set up visits."

"Usually." There had been a couple of times when Zachary had not called ahead, too emotionally overwrought. And Mr. Peterson and Pat were always accommodating and said he was welcome to drop in any time. "I mean… I'm an adult now, so I have to behave like one. Or I should, anyway. But I still feel like that. Like that little boy or teenager… that… I just want what I want, and I don't think of anyone else's feelings."

"I don't think you do that very often. Sometimes you get overexcited or you know what needs to be done and just do it. But I'm not sure I can think of anyone around here who thinks of other people *more* than you do."

Zachary scratched his head, trying to reconcile the way he saw himself and the way Kenzie saw him. He sighed. "Do you want me to come back tonight? Or should I stay here?"

"You sound done-in. I think you should stay there. Get yourself a hotel room and relax. Have a good sleep tonight. I don't think you need to drive all the way back here and then back out in the morning. I'm going to head to bed before too long anyway. Call me in the morning, and we can video chat for breakfast."

Zachary felt the smile spread across his face. He liked that idea. They could still have their morning routine. He could still talk to Kenzie before work and see her smiling face. "But I thought phones were not allowed at the table," he teased.

"This is an exception. Do it. We'll have virtual breakfast together."

"Okay. I will."

"Good. And call me tonight after you get situated. Just so I know you're settled for the night. If you want, you can tell me about what you found out today. But if you're not up to it, we'll just say goodnight."

"Okay." Zachary nodded. "I will."

35

Zachary had to admit to being anxious about going to the jail again in the morning. He kept remembering the rough CO, how he had shoved Luke around and threatened him. He had told Zachary not to come back again. What if he were on duty again? What if he were the one in charge of inmate visits and told Zachary that he was banned from the jail and wasn't allowed to talk to Luke anymore?

But there was no guarantee that the same staff would be on every day or even every weekday. They might take other shifts. They might be rotated regularly. It could be the woman CO who had helped him on Sunday or someone he hadn't met yet. And it wasn't like they had a wall of shame where they displayed the pictures of everyone who wasn't allowed to visit the jail. He doubted if they even had a list on the computer with the names of everyone they wanted banned from visiting.

Or maybe they did.

And if they did, had his name been added to the list? Or was it just an empty threat?

He eventually decided that the CO was probably just blowing hot air. He had a quick temper and a job that allowed him to push people around physically. He probably couldn't be bothered to deal with administrative lists. Chances were he had forgotten all about his sharp remark toward Zachary. Inmates got into arguments with visitors all the time. That was why they had CO's watching the visitor room in the first place and so many rules written on the wall. Luke's meltdown had been minor, probably forgotten by the CO as soon as Luke was back in his cell.

Zachary was getting used to the security check at the jail. Having to be wanded every time, and the CO performing the check asking him whether he had ever broken his arm. Try as he might, he couldn't remember how he had broken it or whether he had known that they had put screws in it. He only vaguely remembered how annoying the cast had been. But then, all casts were annoying, and he'd had enough of them to know that.

His heart fell when he saw that the same CO brought Luke to the visitor room as had brought him the previous day. He pushed Luke down hard into the seat, making him wince. "There'd better be no more nonsense like yesterday," he warned. "You want to end the conversation; you just give a wave. Don't need to act like a spoiled two-year-old." He looked at Zachary and favored him with a glare. "Didn't I tell you yesterday not to come back here?"

Zachary shrugged. "I don't know, did you? There was a lot of yelling going on. I might not have heard you."

The CO gave a short bark of a laugh and, despite his objection, let Zachary stay there and stepped back out of the room after anchoring Luke to the table.

Luke was glassy-eyed. Tired? Or had they drugged him after his outburst of the day before? Some facilities were very free with chemical aids, with a doctor on staff who happily wrote out scripts for whatever the security staff said they needed to keep the population quiet and compliant.

"Hey," Zachary greeted. "How are you doing today?"

Luke shrugged. His head wobbled slightly, but Zachary didn't know whether it was intended as a head shake or was just an involuntary movement.

"I made some good progress yesterday. Trying to find out exactly what happened with you and Eyler on Friday and in the days before."

"You're not a lawyer. Don't need you."

"You want to just rot in prison? I would think you would welcome the help."

Luke shook his head. "I didn't ask for you to be here. Just tell Joss... no. Leave me alone here and just focus on the others. This experiment didn't work." He raised his eyes and looked into Zachary's for a moment. "Did you ever think that it would?"

Zachary tried to read Luke. Was he basically a good kid, like Zachary had thought, who had been victimized and coerced into doing something that was against his nature? Or was he predatory and just making up lies to make Zachary feel sorry for him?

He knew that Luke was charming and a good liar, and still, looking into his face, could not see the guile. He knew what Luke had done, how he had victimized other teens, but he couldn't see the darkness in him.

Was Luke *that* good of a liar?

"How long have you known Eyler?"

"I didn't know him."

"You did. You knew who he was and what he was doing. Why would you kill him otherwise? You went there specifically to confront him."

"Why would I do that?"

"I don't know. I can't figure it out. At the Duck and Dog, you said you wanted Eyler out of your territory."

Luke was definitely surprised by Zachary's knowledge of what had happened at the bar. His eyes widened slightly and his jaw clenched. He shifted his gaze so that it was over Zachary's shoulder at some invisible point beyond him, keeping his face blank. "The Duck and Dog?"

"You got into a fight with one of Eyler's men, and you told him to tell Eyler to get out of your territory or you were going to kill him."

"Then why are you still asking questions?"

"I want to hear your story."

Luke shook his head. "No."

"You talked to me before about your past. When we were trying to get Madison way from Peggy Ann and the rest of them."

"Did I?" Luke's voice was far away and unconcerned.

"Do you remember telling me about Connor?"

Luke's eyes went back to Zachary's face. He licked his lips. "Who?"

"You told me about how Connor was the one who seduced you and brought you into the cartel. How he lured you and turned you out like you did with other kids later."

Luke didn't answer. Zachary looked for any tells. A small nostril flare. Constricting of his pupils. Anything else that would give him more information about how Luke was feeling. He worked his way into the conversation slowly, trying not to cause a blow-up like the day before.

"You remember Connor, don't you?" he asked gently.

Luke's mouth formed the beginning of a denial. Then he closed it, pressing his lips tightly together to keep any words from escaping. Zachary waited.

"You fell in love with him," he prompted.

"Yeah," Luke admitted finally, unable to deny his feelings toward Connor. "He looked after me. Said all the right things. Did all the right things to pull me in. Gave me drugs. Protected me. Of course I fell for it. Just like any of the kids I turned out."

"Because when you take a kid that no one cares about and lavish attention on him, that's the natural reaction."

Luke nodded his agreement. "Works every time, even on someone like Madison, who had two loving parents. But they lived separate lives. She was by herself a lot or hanging with her friends. Lonely people make good targets."

Zachary took a deep breath. "What happened to Connor?"

36

The muscles in Luke's jaw jumped. He looked away again, trying to maintain his impassive expression. "Told you. He died years ago."

"How?"

"What does it matter? Everybody dies."

"Was it drugs? Something to do with the trafficking? Cops?"

Luke's gaze shifted to his hands, and he studied them as if evaluating a manicure job.

"Was there a connection?"

Luke looked at him, forehead creased. "Connection between what?"

"Between Eyler and Connor."

He hadn't liked Luke's previous reaction to this question. It stuck in his head, and he wanted to figure out why. What had his brain caught on to that he hadn't recognized consciously?

Luke's eyes looked like they would burn right through Zachary. Zachary had been right; this was a sensitive line of questioning. One that he had to handle very carefully.

"What was the connection?" he asked gently.

"I don't know." Luke's shoulders rose in an annoyed shrug, then stayed high, making him look hunched and protective.

"You're not fooling me. I can see there's something there."

Luke was silent, staring back down at his hands again. Zachary tried not to look at the CO standing on the other side of the door and wonder how much time they had left to visit. He could try to wait Luke out, but he wasn't sure that was the right way to get Luke to talk.

"Why won't you tell me? If you cared about him, don't you want to talk about him? About how much he meant to you and what happened to him?"

"Connor has nothing to do with this case. I told you he died years ago."

"I know. But I think there is still a connection between him and Eyler. What is it?"

Luke shifted and leaned back in his chair, slouching dramatically, trying to make it look as if he were not tense or upset by Zachary's words. "Connor once... belonged to Eyler."

Zachary felt a small thrill at the confirmation. His instinct had been correct. Even though no one had identified a connection between Connor and Eyler, Zachary had just felt like whatever was between Eyler and Luke had not started when Eyler had moved into town and started up the business but had been festering for many years. Way back to Connor. Zachary nodded slowly and thought about Luke's answer, trying to sort it out.

"He once belonged to Eyler? But then what happened?" Zachary didn't exactly know how transactions were managed or hierarchies shifted in the trafficking business. Was it like a pro sports team? Was it a rigid structure and discrete transactions? Or was it a flow, constantly shifting and changing in a liquid state?

"When I met Connor, he was with Peggy Ann."

Zachary nodded. He had seen Peggy Ann, so he had a picture in his mind of the severe, angry-looking woman. Women who rose up in the ranks in the trafficking business were hard. Harder than the men.

"But he told me about how he had originally been with Eyler."

"Did Eyler bring him in? Or did someone else under Eyler bring him in?"

"Don't know. But it wasn't like it was with me. Eyler had Romeos turning new kids. But he also did grabs."

Zachary shuddered. "Is that what it sounds like?"

Luke nodded. "At least with what I did... I could say that it was their own choice. Maybe I lured and seduced them, but deciding to turn tricks was always their own choice. I never forced anyone into it." He closed his eyes, those long, almost feminine eyelashes contrasting with his pale skin. He swallowed and looked back up at Zachary. "But I never grabbed anyone off the street. Eyler, he would go out in a van with a couple of goons, and they would look for someone out walking by herself, on a lonely street. Pull over, grab her—or him—and drive off."

Zachary imagined the terror, dramatized on TV many times over, of being grabbed by strangers, thrown to the floor of a van, bound and gagged, and spirited away. The victim's family would never know what had happened to him.

He licked his lips, shaking his head. "That's awful. Is that what happened to Connor?"

"Yeah." Luke's eyes flitted around the room. "He was on the street, homeless, had been kicked out by his folks. You know." He shrugged with one shoulder as if he didn't care. "Like lots of kids. It happens. But when there are guys like Eyler around…"

"It's not safe. But when you met him, Connor wasn't being held captive anymore. He wasn't being forced to stay."

"There are different ways of forcing people to stay. You don't need chains and shackles." Luke rattled his chains against the anchor. "There are plenty of better ways. Eyler got him hooked. Crack, probably. And Eyler was a real sadist about controlling the supply. Liked to see his assets suffer. They'd be going nuts in withdrawal. Would do anything to get more product. They would do whatever he wanted for the next hit."

Zachary shook his head in sympathy. "Those kids' lives are ruined just because they walked down a street alone."

Luke nodded. "Wasn't the only thing he did, either. Like I said, he was a sadist. The slightest infraction, just looking at him the wrong way or taking too long to answer. Being sick. A bad report from a john. And he'd take it out on them. Beat 'em bad. If they refused a job, he'd torture them. Do whatever it took to make sure they did. Between jonesing for the next hit and bein' messed up… they'd do the job."

That was more how Zachary had pictured the human trafficking industry before he had learned about the psychological conditioning that was used by Romeos like Luke.

"You might think that they would run the first chance they got," Luke said. "As soon as they were free and out of sight of an overseer… but that's not the way it works. If you're living in fear and craving your next hit, you don't run. You stick to what's safe and will get you more product. Doing exactly what you're told. Doing everything you can to show your boss that you're loyal. Do what you're told. Report on others. Ingratiate yourself."

"And that's the kind of life Connor had been living. So when he targeted new kids by giving them love and attention, he saw it as doing them a favor. Saving them from having to go through that kind of torture."

Luke considered this, gazing up at the ceiling. He nodded slowly. "Yeah. I guess. That's probably how he felt."

"How did Connor go from belonging to Eyler to belonging to Peggy Ann? How does that happen? Is it just… like a sale of a product?"

"Sometimes. Different bosses might do swaps or sales. Keep moving kids around to make it harder for the cops to track them. Get rid of someone who isn't a good fit for their business. Or a troublemaker. With Connor… it was a little different."

Zachary waited for the story. Luke was clearly finding it easier to talk now, with the conversation focused on Connor instead of him. Maybe he'd never been able to tell this to anyone before. Never been allowed to talk about the person who had brought him into the life, to grieve him when he died. It was important for people to be able to talk about loss. Or so Zachary had been told by Dr. B.

"What happened?" he prompted when Luke didn't continue immediately.

Luke tried to scratch his neck, but the chains wouldn't let him move his hands that much. Instead, he stretched and rolled his shoulders, thinking about it before jumping into the story.

"Connor wasn't doing real well with Eyler. Maybe if he'd taken the softer approach, it would have worked. But Connor was always in trouble with him. Resisting, rolling his eyes and dissing Eyler, passed out when he was supposed to be working a job. I don't know what the last straw was. Connor never really said. Maybe he didn't even know. Something happened and Eyler and his thugs beat the life out of Connor. Dumped him somewhere in the alley or a sewer. Left him for dead."

Zachary's eyes widened at this description. Eyler must really have been at the end of his rope with Connor to dispose of him like that. With the cash that each asset brought in, getting rid of a kid was blowing hundreds of thousands of dollars per year.

37

"But things obviously didn't work out like Eyler had expected," Zachary said. "Connor survived."

"Yeah. Imagine that was a pretty big shock to him." Luke snorted. "Someone found him still alive and Peggy Ann decided to see if she could save him. Big risk. I don't know why she did it. She would have known that he was a pain in the neck. That Eyler had intentionally dumped Connor. To put any time and effort into saving him and seeing if she could still use him once he recovered... she must have seen something in him that Eyler hadn't."

"Different perspective. Maybe she thought he'd respond better to other methods. That he'd be grateful to her for saving him. She must have figured that he could bring in some money, or she wouldn't have done it."

"Yeah. The bosses, they don't do anything out of compassion or any human feelings. Not that I ever saw. This was all before my time, so I only heard about it. She nursed him back to health. But then she had to deal with her bosses about whether that made him hers or not."

Zachary frowned. "If Eyler left him for dead, and she was the one who put all of the effort into helping him, then why wouldn't she be his new 'owner'?"

Luke shrugged. "If you saw a car pulled over to the side of the road with its flashers on and no one around, and you decided to tow it to your place and fix it up, does that make it yours?"

offoffP.D. WORKMAN

Zachary tilted his head, acknowledging the point. "Okay, yeah. I guess it wouldn't. But I figured that legal title and... moral title in a criminal organization would probably be a little different."

"Yeah. That's why they had a big discussion about it. Whether Connor was still Eyler's property even though he'd thrown him away, or Peggy Ann's because he would have died if she hadn't picked him up. It's not the kind of thing that happens very often in an organization like this."

Zachary didn't imagine it did.

"So... that's how he went from being Eyler's asset to being Peggy Ann's," Luke said with a shrug.

"He must have been grateful to Peggy Ann for saving his life."

Luke fixed Zachary with a stare. "You think so?"

Zachary had to reconsider, thinking about what kind of a life Peggy Ann had saved him for. Turning tricks for her instead of Eyler. Recruiting other young people. While Peggy Ann might not be as violent as Eyler, she wasn't exactly a mother hen. She had to be just as tough as any of the men in the business. Tougher. It wouldn't have been a picnic. Maybe Connor would have preferred that he had just died.

"He would tell me not to complain," Luke said. "If I got talkative and said how much I hated Peggy Ann or what kind of a boss she was... he'd remind me that it could be a lot worse. She would punish me if I screwed up, but her punishments didn't compare to Eyler's. And she was a lot more careful with the drugs. She didn't give as much as Eyler did or withhold it as long, so we didn't have the big spikes and crashes we would have if we'd been working for him. Still enough to hurt if you didn't get your next fix, enough to convince you to just shut up and do what she told you to. But not curled up on the floor screaming."

It wasn't the first time that Zachary had counted his blessings that he hadn't gotten hooked on drugs coming up through foster care. There had been plenty of opportunities. Plenty of his foster siblings or group home inmates knew where to buy and had stashes hidden in the house. There had been enough offers of something to take the edge off by apparently well-meaning friends. But he had managed to avoid them.

"What happened to Connor? Did he overdose? Or was it something related to his injuries?"

If Connor had died "years ago" as Luke had claimed, then he probably hadn't been with Peggy Ann long. Perhaps Connor had never fully recovered from the beatdown.

Luke shook his head. "Come on, man..."

670

"You don't want to talk about it. I know. But you'll feel better if you can share it with someone." Zachary hoped that was true, and it didn't just traumatize Luke more to have to relive it. "I think it's important. All of this feeds into what happened when you went to confront Eyler in his hotel room."

Luke raised his eyes to meet Zachary's for a moment. He had said from the start that he had killed Eyler and didn't want any help from Joss or Zachary. He had accepted spending the next few decades in prison. Maybe the rest of his life. There was just the tiniest glimmer of hope in his eyes when he looked at Zachary, and Zachary hoped that what he had said was true and it would be helpful to show mitigation. Maybe Connor's death had nothing to do with Eyler or the confrontation in his hotel room. But surely how Eyler had treated Connor, whom Luke had loved, had something to do with how he had reacted. Maybe there was some mitigation. Something that would make a prosecutor or jury consider a lighter sentence.

"Eyler always resented Connor and anyone associated with him. Guess he was jealous, seeing how profitable Connor was for Peggy Ann after Eyler had discarded him. He resented the bosses deciding that Peggy Ann was his new owner and didn't have to give him back or pay anything for taking him."

Zachary nodded, making a noise of agreement. It made sense. Eyler felt like Peggy Ann had stolen something from him and shown him up. Zachary could understand why he would resent her.

"Because Connor brought me in, Eyler always treated me like trash too. Whenever he or his men saw one of us—Connor or one of his stable—they always harassed us. Goading, threatening, sometimes getting physical. Nothing serious, because then Eyler would get sanctioned. Just little stuff that they could get away with. Trying to make our lives miserable."

"He and Peggy Ann worked closely together?"

Luke shrugged. "Yeah... both worked the same territory. Competed for business. Didn't usually deal with one another, but sometimes. We saw each other, had to deal with both of them operating in the same area."

"That must have been difficult."

"Our lives were difficult, with or without Eyler. Bosses, cops, johns, addiction, being assaulted. Eyler was just one more thing. Just one more... predator to look out for."

His voice had gone flat. If he were anything like Zachary, that note in his voice meant that he had shut down his emotions. They were becoming too much, and he couldn't deal with them. He had talked before about dissociating, separating himself from his experiences. Zachary suspected he was now looking at everything from the outside. His time with the cartel, dealing with Eyler, talking to Zachary; he was no longer part of it, but watching it all from a distance where he didn't have to feel the pain and emotions.

"So… what happened to Connor? What did Eyler do?"

It had to have been Eyler. Luke wouldn't have talked about how Eyler was bullying and harassing them otherwise. It wouldn't have been part of the story. Had the supposedly mild physical abuse become more? Eyler had let his resentment of Connor take over?

Luke stared off into the distance. A thousand-yard stare, like Zachary wasn't even there. Like they weren't confined to the visiting room but were out on the highway, looking far down the road.

"Eyler hired him for a side job. A special assignment."

"Could he do that? Wouldn't he have to get Peggy Ann's permission?"

"Yeah, of course. But he didn't. It was a secret; Connor couldn't tell anyone about it. Eyler offered him a fortune. Thousands; I don't know. We didn't make that kind of money. Just enough to survive, with the rest of it going to our bosses. But he offered Connor some outrageous amount for this special one-time deal. All he had to do was keep it a secret and, of course, Connor would if he wanted the money."

"But you knew about it?"

"He didn't tell Peggy Ann or anyone who might report back to her. But him and me were… I told him not to take it. We both knew what kind of guy Eyler was, and if he was offering money like that, there was risk involved. Big-time risk."

"You mean risk of being found out? By the cops or Peggy Ann?"

"No. Physical risk. Some high rollers, they'll pay a lot to have their special fantasy fulfilled, but that's routine. The boss will make all of the arrangements and take all the money. The asset only gets the usual rates. If the boss is offering more… it's because no one else wants to take the risk with this guy. That it's worth the beating they'll get for refusing the job."

"Why would anyone consider it, then?"

"Because… for Connor, the money meant… the possibility of getting out of the business. Having enough to go somewhere far away and start a new life. Free and clear, with a new identity, somewhere the organization would never be able to find him."

"He wanted to get away from Peggy Ann?"

"From her, and all of it. He'd nearly been killed. And when he recovered, it was to the same life. Just a different personality. It was better, but it was the same."

Zachary nodded slowly. Maybe it was something like going from one foster family to another. Things could get better, but other things could get worse. And some things stayed the same no matter what family he went to. He never felt like he belonged in the families he went to. He would always be the outsider. The new kid. New at the home, new in school, never staying in one place long enough to form a real relationship with anyone. He knew he would never become part of a forever family. That everywhere he laid his head, it was temporary. That wherever he went, there would be predators, but he wouldn't know who they were until they revealed their true colors, and then escape was impossible.

"He took this job, even though it was risky, thinking that he would be able to escape the life."

Luke nodded.

Zachary's stomach was in knots. He knew he needed to continue the questioning, but he knew he would be horrified when he found out what had happened to Connor. He knew it would be heartbreaking and awful and that he wouldn't ever be able to forget it once Luke told him. He couldn't bring himself to prompt Luke to go on with the story. There were a few minutes of silence, and then Luke went on anyway. Maybe, as Zachary had said, he needed to tell the story.

"He didn't know who the john was. I don't think Eyler ever told him. Not before he left that day. Maybe right before they met... but I doubt that Eyler would have risked Connor backing out once he got there."

Luke drew a circle on the table with his finger, going around and around, trying to stay in that far-off place he had gone to and tell his story.

38

This john... he was bad news. He had messed up hookers before. Did some real damage. As a boss, it's not worth servicing a dude like that, no matter how much money the payoff is. If you lose an asset, or they're in the hospital for months, it's tens of thousands of dollars."

"But if it's not your asset..."

"Yeah." Luke's face was flat, unflinching. "If it's not your asset, then it's worth the risk."

"He'd put... assets... into the hospital for that long before?" Zachary tried to imagine the kind of damage Luke must be talking about that would sideline someone for that long. Or to be written off as a complete loss.

"People said he'd done more than that. I don't know where all of the stories came from, how many of them were true. But if they were... some of the kids he'd hooked up with... they never came back."

Zachary shuddered, flashing back to Archuro. Zachary had been bound and shot up with drugs, unable to move, while the sadist told him all of the things that he planned to do to Zachary both before and after his death. All of the little rituals that he enjoyed and how long it would take. That the torture would last for days before Zachary's body finally gave out. And even then, Archuro would not stop.

Luke's eyes had focused on Zachary. Zachary's reaction to the revelation must have surprised him. He had expected an exclamation from Zachary, shock and dismay, not this silence. Zachary gulped. He wished that the jail would have let him bring a water bottle in with him. He felt so parched he could hardly speak. And it was not just a side effect of his meds.

"He was embargoed," Luke advised, continuing with the narrative when he knew that Zachary was still following him. "That means that none of the bosses would supply him. They had all agreed to freeze him out. Force him to go somewhere else for satisfaction."

Zachary nodded silently.

"Connor never came back," Luke said without inflection.

"Did they… ever find his body? Do you know for sure that he's dead? That Connor didn't just take the money and go?"

Luke took a deep breath and let it out. "Yes. They found him. The cops. Eyler must have dumped his body once it was all over. Left him in some farmer's field so he wouldn't be associated with Eyler. Cleaned him up to try to hide his involvement. Cops said it didn't matter. They could still tell that he'd been bound and drugged. Some special cocktail the john cooked up to incapacitate him."

Zachary felt cold. Nauseated. He looked at the door and at the CO standing on the other side, wondering if he should signal him. If he were going to be sick.

"He was cut up," Luke went on. "Like, this guy was a psycho. Something seriously wrong with him." He shook his head. "And there's something seriously wrong with the psycho who feeds him another victim. Eyler knew what he was. Everyone did." Luke swallowed hard. "Eyler intended for Connor to die. I know it."

And Luke had finally avenged Connor's death of years before. Eyler was lucky that the vengeance hadn't been well-planned-out and executed. That he hadn't been made to suffer the way the Connor had. For him, death had come quickly. Much more quickly than he had deserved.

It was a long time before Zachary could force himself to speak. Luke didn't seem to notice the silence. He just sat there, lost in his memories or trying not to be drowned in them.

"What did Peggy Ann do when she found out?" Zachary finally asked. "There must be… you said that the bosses got together to decide whether she was Connor's owner or not. There must be some kind of consequence for someone who… poaches another's boss's asset and ends up getting him killed."

"Yeah, sure," Luke agreed. "They put restrictions on his business. Sort of... put him on probation. Wouldn't let him advance or grow his base. Kept him back for a few years. That let Peggy Ann get ahead of him. But now... Well, you found out, right? He's expanding. He's taking on new territory, adding to his stable, setting up shop in *my town*. After all he did, he's operating like nothing ever happened. He got his revenge on Connor and on Peggy Ann. And on anyone who was close to Connor. He deserved to be punished. Really. Not just a temporary setback, but really punished."

"Killed?" Zachary questioned.

"Yes. I'd kill him twenty times over if I could. The only thing I regret is that I couldn't torture him like that john tortured Connor."

The CO returned to take Luke back to his cell. He looked back and forth at Zachary and Luke, both silent, and raised his eyebrows, but he didn't ask any questions. Probably he was just pleased that Luke hadn't exploded again. Luke waited, his body slack, while the CO unlocked the chain that anchored him to the table and stood and walked like a sleepwalker when the CO ordered him back to his cell. The CO took one last glance at Zachary and walked away without saying anything.

Another CO took him back to the reception area of the jail and gave him his belt, shoes, and key back. Zachary walked back out to his car and sat in it for a few minutes, his whole body shaking, fighting all of the images of Archuro and trying to discount the similarities between the two attacks. Was that how Archuro had started out before moving to kidnapping immigrant men to fulfill his horrible fantasies? Or had he been doing both at the same time? Zachary couldn't imagine that two men had been operating in Vermont simultaneously, doing what Archuro had done. When the cartels had refused to supply him with any more victims, he had gone out hunting on his own.

Eventually, Zachary put his key in the ignition and started the car. Warmth flooded through his body that was more than just the car heater kicking in. The sound of the engine meant freedom. The ability to get away, to go wherever he pleased, away from anyone who wanted to harm him. And it meant that in just a few minutes, he would be speeding down the highway, his brain calming and body relaxing. And then he would be home with Kenzie.

39

H e hadn't taken into account the fact that he had gone to the jail to see Luke as soon as visiting hours began. While the interview felt like it had lasted forever, it had not, and the day was still young when he hit the Roxboro town limits. Kenzie was still at work and would be for hours. There would be no one waiting for him at home.

That left him feeling rudderless.

He went home to an empty house. He remembered to disarm and reset the burglar alarm, despite his anxiety. He went into the living room and opened his computer to check his email. He looked at the date and the calendar to determine whether he had anything scheduled. If it were Wednesday, he had therapy with Dr. B. And it would be a good day for a therapy session; she could help him break out of the dark abyss he found himself in. But it was not. Zachary cast around for someone else to call.

He thought of Rhys, but he would still be at school. Mr. Peterson was his go-to for someone to talk to and ground himself and was almost always available. Still, Zachary couldn't talk to him about anything to do with Archuro. Archuro was too closely connected with Mr. Peterson and Pat, and Zachary wouldn't take the chance of sending Pat back into that same dark hole as Zachary was struggling to get out of.

There was plenty on his task list and his email inbox was undoubtedly overflowing, since he had been so focused on Luke's case for the last few days. He wasn't even sure when he had checked it last. But Heather had taken it upon herself to monitor his email while he had been in the hospital, and that had worked out so well that he had asked her to keep an eye on it going forward, to make sure that he didn't lose track of things. She was very organized and had become his right hand in Goldman Investigations.

Heather.

Few people in his life could actually understand what he had been through with Archuro. She had been assaulted when she was a teenager and, having no emotional support at that time, had been forced to go on as if nothing had happened and hadn't been able to actually deal with the pain and find the strength to deal with it until just a year ago when she had learned of Archuro's attack on Zachary. It was hearing about his experience that had drawn her to him.

Of course, Joss had probably had to deal with assaults just as bad or worse, but he had a pretty good idea that if he went whining to her, she would just tell him to lock it in the vault and quit being such a baby.

Zachary found his phone in his hand and Heather's name up on the screen before he was even aware that he had decided to call her. He tapped her picture and listened to the ringtone. He hoped that she wouldn't be out shopping or doing some work for her husband. Zachary didn't pay her full-time wages or give her enough work to occupy all of her time; she wasn't waiting at his beck and call.

"Zachy," Heather greeted cheerfully. "Hi. How are you?"

"Feathers." Zachary smiled, comforted already just by hearing her voice and their childhood nicknames.

"What's up? I haven't heard from you for a while, and you sound… like you're somewhere else."

"I just needed…" Zachary's voice cracked. He wasn't sure what he wanted to say to her. He didn't really want to tell her the dreadful tale of what had happened to Connor. He didn't want to burden her with Luke's case and the meager chance that he would ever get out of prison after what he had done. Instead of finding mitigation in what Luke had done, Zachary had instead managed to establish that there were preexisting bad feelings between Luke and Eyler and a clear motive to kill him. Not exactly what Joss had been hoping for. "I just wanted to hear your voice."

"Aw. Rough day?"

Zachary found himself nodding. "Yeah. It kind of has been."

"What can I do? Anything I can help out with?"

"No. Tell me what's going on that I need to do. I haven't even looked at my email."

"I noticed! It's okay, there hasn't been anything really urgent, or I would have called you. There's employment screening stuff for you to look at. I did the basics, but you need to do the deeper background. And there are a few insurance surveillance jobs, if you want to take one of those on today."

"Surveillance. Yeah, that sounds good." Watching to see whether accident victims were walking, running, or lifting grandkids or groceries when they were supposed to be disabled by a car or workplace accident; that was something he could easily spend a few hours on, but it wouldn't take a lot of thought. He could sit in his car, listen to some music on the radio, and just watch someone else's life instead of thinking about his own.

"Okay. I think we've got three. I'll send them to you, and you can see if they are at home."

"Or out playing tennis."

"Right," Heather agreed with a laugh. "Will that help? Are you sure you don't need anything else? I've got time to talk, if you want."

"Um… yeah." Zachary let out his breath slowly and tried to relax his shoulders. "I don't want… you don't need to hear the details, but… just something that's brought it all back up. The assault. Archuro."

She swore, which made Zachary chuckle to himself. Too often, he saw Heather as a timid little housewife, an empty nester who would never say a bad word to anyone. He sometimes forgot the little firecracker she had been when they had both been small or how fierce she had been when finally confronting her own attacker. She was no little church mouse, his Feathers.

"Point me at whoever triggered you and I'll let them have it," Heather threatened.

"It wasn't intentional," Zachary said, "and I was kind of forcing him to talk about something that he didn't want to, so it's my own fault. I didn't expect it to…" He swallowed and cleared his throat. "I didn't think it would be… so similar to what happened to me."

"Are you okay? Do you want me to come there? We could go out on surveillance together; you can show me how it's done."

Zachary was taken aback. "Really?"

"Sure, why not? I don't have anything that *has* to be done for the rest of the day. It won't take me that long to get there. You can have some lunch and relax for a bit. Take a look at those backgrounds if you need something to occupy yourself with, and then we can go out together."

The idea of spending the afternoon with his big sister was very attractive. Instead of just stewing by himself, waiting for Kenzie to get home and rehashing the conversation with Luke over and over again in his head, he could talk with Heather. Show her how to conduct surveillance, find out how she was doing, talk about the mischief they had gotten into together when they were kids and Heather was supposed to be keeping him out of trouble but sometimes instigated it herself. He found her easy to talk to and she would know to avoid the subject of Archuro unless he brought it up himself.

"Zachary?"

"Yeah. That would be really good, actually."

"Okay. I'll hit the road here. See you after lunch."

Zachary said goodbye and she disconnected. He looked at the phone for a moment and thought about checking his email and social networks, but decided against it. Heather had reminded him that he had to eat. He'd had only the bare minimum for breakfast, the food he had to eat to ensure he was not taking his meds on an empty stomach. If he got distracted by his email, he would forget to eat lunch, and Heather would definitely give him a lecture when she arrived. He opened the freezer door to see what microwavable meals he and Kenzie had stocked.

40

Heather gave him the first address, and Zachary didn't need the GPS to find it. He was familiar with the Montpelier community and quickly found the quiet street the subject lived on. He pointed out various places that they could park to watch the house, and detailed the positives and negatives of each.

"We might have to use a few of them. Move around a few times so that people don't see the same car sitting there for a couple of hours. This car blends in really well, but if someone goes out shopping and sees us sitting here, and then they get back from shopping and we're still here, they might get suspicious."

Heather nodded. "Yeah. I notice that kind of thing, and it makes me nervous. Not like it used to; I used to be really paranoid about it, because of…" She trailed off.

Because she hadn't known who her attacker had been and had always been afraid that he would return one day to hurt her or one of her children. Now that she knew he was behind bars, her life had changed.

"We'll take a quick look behind the house too. See if there's a car in the garage, anything suspicious in the garbage, what the back exit looks like. There are no stairs in the front, so it's easy to access if he really is injured, but it can be a big tip-off if he has to use stairs to get to his car and there's no lift. According to the medical report lodged with the insurer, he can't get around without a walker or wheelchair."

He drove down the block and navigated to the alley, driving slowly until he identified the same house from the back. There were no stairs, but he hadn't expected there to be. It didn't appear to be built on a hill, so if the front was flat, the back probably was too. But sometimes there were surprises behind.

There was not a garage, but a gravel parking pad. The car parked there matched the description of the one registered to the subject's wife. The subject's car had been damaged badly enough in the accident to be written off and, since the insurance company had not yet paid the claim, he probably had not had enough money in savings to buy something new. Or he wasn't able to leave the house, so they no longer needed a second vehicle. Zachary pointed each observation out to Heather so she would know what sorts of things to look for.

"Do we really need to check the garbage?" Heather asked, looking at the bins.

"We're not going to do a detailed comb-through. Just have a quick look to see if he's bought a home gym lately or something else that would indicate he is able to do more than what he says."

"But how would we know who it was for? His wife could buy a home gym."

"If there is one, we'll have to see whether we can see it through the windows and see who is using it."

"You can do that without being seen?"

"Easiest way is one of these…" Zachary opened the glove box and pulled out a tiny camera. "It's very unobtrusive. Stick it to the window when they are out of the room, and it broadcasts a signal to my phone. I can see what's going on without having to be peering in the window with my camera. I can leave it there for a few days until I'm sure one way or the other, then remove it again when I'm done."

"Have you ever gotten caught?"

"With one of these? No. Caught surveilling a subject…?" He shrugged. "Yeah. It happens."

"What do you do?"

"Bluff. Get to my car and take off. If worse comes to worst and they call the cops, then I have a PI license, can show them that I was there on legitimate business and not just a stalker or a burglar casing the place out."

Of course, that line did not work if he were actually watching someone for personal reasons and was caught out. If the subject was his ex-wife, for instance.

Before getting out of the car, Zachary picked up another small electronic device from the glove box. Heather opened her door and also got out.

"What's that?"

"Tracker." Zachary glanced up and down the back alley, then crouched down and placed it on the inside edge of the car's back bumper. He felt it click on the metal and tried to wiggle the tracker. It wouldn't move. The powerful magnet held it firmly in place. "You want to put it where you can retrieve it again quickly, but it isn't visible to anyone just casually looking at or under the car. Hopefully, the subject doesn't have an oil change scheduled or some other car maintenance, because if they put it up on a lift, it's a lot easier to see."

"If this is his wife's car, why do you need to track it?"

"It appears to be their only car. That means that if he goes out, whether his wife takes him to a doctor's appointment or he goes out to play golf, he'll be in this vehicle. If he's in that much pain, he isn't going to take the bus or walk far. He could take an Uber, but if someone has a car available, they'll use it. We don't know if we might need to come back here to do a detailed garbage search or something else when they are both out. If we can track their usual daily schedule and tell when they are farther away from the house, it's much safer. Today we came in blind, not knowing whether he would be here or not." Zachary looked at the house. It was impossible to tell whether both husband and wife were home or not. "Once we've watched them and seen who is using the car when, it will be much easier."

Heather nodded. She was looking around nervously, not wanting to get caught.

"Don't look like you're not supposed to be here. Act calm and casual, like you live here or are visiting your friend. If you look anxious, people will want to know what you're up to. If you act like you're supposed to be here, you'll be invisible, unless they have other reasons to be suspicious."

Heather took a deep breath and forced herself to stop moving and looking all around. "Okay. Sorry. I'm not used to fieldwork."

"You'll catch on. After you've sat on your butt for six or eight hours, you stop worrying so much about getting caught. You get to the point where you would prefer to get caught…"

Heather laughed. Zachary walked over to the garbage and recycling bins. He opened the garbage bin lid. "I'll check this one, you see if there is anything interesting in the recycling."

The contents of the garbage bin were all in black bags. While Zachary appreciated not having to sift through loose garbage, he much preferred it when they used the clear bags. He pulled each bag out and put them down on the ground, then quickly opened them, shifted the contents around for anything large or suspicious, then popped them back into the bin. Heather rummaged around in the cardboard and plastic containers in the recycling bin.

"I don't see much here. Mostly just grocery packaging."

"Anything medical?"

"No, not that I've seen. But they'd need to put that into the garbage or medical waste, wouldn't they?"

"Not the outside packaging. Anything sports related?"

"No hockey sticks."

Zachary laughed. "Okay." He put the last garbage bag back into the bin. "Nothing obvious at this point. We'll go back out front. There were some good parking spaces there. If they come out, it will probably be through the back door to the car. From where we are parked in front of the house, we can see the back door if it opens because it is on the side of the house. Then we watch the tracker to see where they go and fall in behind them once they're a few blocks away."

"Aye-aye, sir."

41

Zachary looked at the time on his phone as he shifted restlessly, trying to find a more comfortable position. They had changed parking locations a few times and had each taken a walk around to stretch their legs and take a look around the neighborhood. But Heather wasn't used to surveillance and, even though he was enjoying their time together, Zachary's tailbone was also signaling that he had been sitting in one place for long enough. He tapped his screen to log his time, then called Kenzie at the medical examiner's office.

"Hey, how are you doing?" Kenzie greeted. "Are you going to be home tonight?"

"Can I have a friend over for supper?"

Kenzie laughed. "Well, I suppose so, if you promise you'll get your homework done."

Zachary chuckled, happy that she didn't seem to be stressed by the suggestion that he bring someone home with him. "I'm with Heather."

"Oh, great! Yes, I'd love to have Heather over for supper. We can talk about you."

"Hey, that wasn't what I was planning!"

"Too bad. Once you put us together, it's out of your control. Are you at her place, then?"

"No, she and I went to Montpelier for some surveillance. Spent the afternoon together."

"You were done with Luke pretty quickly, then?"

Zachary felt his smile disappear as she reminded him of the interview with Luke and what had happened to Connor. "Yeah. And I wanted to get home. I'll... I guess I'll tell you about it later."

"Sure. You okay?"

"I'm fine. We've been keeping ourselves occupied. Do you want me to pick something up on the way home? Then you don't have to make anything or wait for delivery."

"Sure. Get whatever you guys like. You know what I like."

"Okay. See you in a couple hours."

"Take care. See you soon."

He hung up and realized that he hadn't asked her how her day was or whether she would be off in good time. Since she had agreed to dinner but hadn't told him to hold it until later, he had to assume that she would be home in good time to share a meal with them.

"All set?" Heather stretched and rolled her shoulders. "I'm glad you decided it was time. My muscles are getting really cramped."

"You have to build your way up to longer stakeouts. This wasn't too bad, but I can't sit for much longer."

Zachary started the car and pulled away from the curb, giving the house one last look before they left. He was always sure that something would happen right after he left. While surveillance jobs could be hard, he had a difficult time breaking away sometimes, wanting to stay for just five more minutes in case something happened.

They got out to the highway in a few minutes. Heather didn't make any comment about Zachary's driving speed.

"What about Tyrrell?" she asked. "Do you want to invite him over for dinner too? That would be fun."

"Uh... well..."

She looked at him, evaluating his reluctance. "We don't have to if you don't want. It was just a suggestion."

"It's just... I know that when he's around me, it makes him think about when we were kids, and all of the crap that went on... and the problems he has with his kids... and if I end up talking about this case with Luke, and I have flashbacks, then he feels like he has to be the strong one... I just don't want to put all of that on him. I want him to have the chance to recover and get back to a normal life."

Heather nodded. "You don't have to explain, you know. It's okay to just say no. I'll accept that."

Zachary thought about that. He'd lived in too many places where a flat "no" would earn him a punishment. Sometimes just a loss of privileges, but often a physical "reminder" to watch his mouth and his attitude, or even being slapped into isolation at Bonnie Brown or locked in a room or a closet at a group home. He had learned to be pretty careful how he answered, never saying no if he could help it.

"That still… doesn't feel safe," he confessed. "It's not you. I know you would never do anything to hurt me. But…"

"As long as you know I'm fine with it. If it doesn't feel okay, then do what does. But you don't have to be afraid that I'll be upset or won't let you make your own choices. You're allowed."

Zachary nodded. "Thanks."

He stared at the road and the cars ahead of him, letting himself slide into the meditative driving state that soothed his anxiety.

***

Kenzie liked Thai and Heather said that she did too, so Zachary bought several of their favorite dishes at the local Thai restaurant. Zachary wasn't sure what time Kenzie would be home and hoped that the Styrofoam dishes would keep everything warm and fresh until she did. But he supposed they could be microwaved if they got cold.

Heather sat on the couch beside him when he opened his email inbox. He had her emails to him filtered into a special folder because he had found that she was really good at keeping him organized and on top of the email requests that came in from clients. He read through the summaries and notes that she had made for him before starting the rest of the email.

"You need a better way to track your tasks," she told him as she watched him sift through the emails and add a couple of items to his task list. "If you use an app where you can send stuff to it directly from email to your task list, labeled with the client name and the type of task it is, you don't have to keep all of the details in your head or search for them in your inbox."

Zachary rubbed the back of his head. "Yeah… I suppose that would be good."

"You'd be able to see immediately what stuff you had to do on the computer, what calls you had to make, what errands you had to run and surveillance you had to do. And it would all be tied back to the original email so you could just click once to re-read the details."

"Do you have an app that does that?"

"Look." She pulled out her phone and started to show him through her task management app. "And you can set dates and alarms so that you only have to see what to do today, and if you get sidetracked, there are reminders. My son always had to have alarms."

"Yeah. I've been doing that with the calendar. Trying to remember to put all of my appointments into it with alarms so that I have enough time to get places even if I forgot about it. It's good… if I remember to put everything in it."

"It works for tasks too. Why don't I set up an account for you? I can set up the projects and contexts, and I can add tasks and notes to it directly instead of emailing you about them. Because we're duplicating the work if I email you what needs to be done, and then you add it into the app. I'll show you how to send emails to it and label everything, and then you can add tasks directly to it as well."

Zachary shrugged. He was glad that she was offering to set it up and organize it. If the structure were already set up and she just told him what to do, it wouldn't be so overwhelming. He tended to put off big projects that were tedious and required a lot of organizational effort. Then he ended up forgetting things or hurrying to do them at the last minute. "Sure. That sounds good, if you really want to set it all up."

She smiled. "I like organizing things. It's like solving a puzzle."

"You know what else is like solving a puzzle? Being a PI," Zachary deadpanned.

Heather laughed.

Zachary heard the garage door opening. "And there's Kenz. Good. Everything should still be warm."

42

Zachary stood up and walked into the kitchen to greet Kenzie and start opening the food containers. Kenzie stopped him when he gave her a kiss, holding his face still for a moment to look into his eyes.

"You're okay?"

He nodded. "For now."

"The talk with Luke didn't go well?"

"I'll tell you about it."

Heather joined them in the kitchen, and they worked together to set the table and spread out the delicious-smelling food so everyone could help themselves. Zachary's stomach growled. He had gone for so many years on medications that suppressed his appetite or made him nauseated that it always surprised him when he felt hungry. He put his hand over his stomach, immediately wondering whether he had remembered to take all of his meds that morning. But it was too late to worry about it now. He might as well just enjoy the meal.

They all sat down.

"So... how was your day today?" Zachary figured he'd better make up for not asking her when they had talked on the phone. "I suppose that when we have company, we're not allowed to talk about dead bodies at the table."

"Only in the most very general terms," Kenzie agreed, giving Heather a wink. "I did have dead bodies today, yes."

"Did you do an autopsy? Or just… test samples and administrative stuff?"

"Did an autopsy this afternoon. But it went quickly, as you can tell, since I'm home in good time. It was pretty routine. A doctor who wanted to know how an experimental protocol had worked."

Zachary took a bite of noodles and chewed them slowly. "I assume since the patient was dead, the experimental protocol was a failure."

"Well, not necessarily. It wasn't the protocol that killed him. And the doctor will have to check our x-rays and measurements against what he did at the last check-up to see any growth or shrinkage. But the patient died of pneumonia, not directly from the disease or treatment."

"And you don't think that the pneumonia was a side effect of the treatment?"

"Not directly. But either the disease or the protocol could have weakened his system and made him more susceptible. Or made it so that he couldn't fight it off."

Zachary nodded. If they had been alone, he would have asked her for more details. They both enjoyed talking about the clues that she found while performing her job, and anything that Zachary might be able to ask her about the forensics in a case he was working on. Kenzie was always careful not to give him any names or identifying facts.

Heather and Kenzie discussed non-medical things for a few minutes, catching up on each other's lives and running through the usual gamut of weather and other routine small talk. Zachary was focused on the food on his plate, not really following their conversation, but he felt Kenzie's gaze when she turned to him. He swallowed the food in his mouth without chewing and it went down in a lump. He chased it with a couple of gulps of water.

"And things didn't go well with Luke today? Or is it something else?"

"It's both, I guess." Zachary took a smaller sip of water, irrigating his suddenly dry mouth. "Things didn't go the way that I had hoped with his case. Instead of finding anything that would help him, the details that I've found out just make it worse. More nails in the coffin. And also… a personal connection." He took a deep breath and tried to decide how to explain it and how much he wanted to say in front of Heather. It wasn't that he minded her hearing anything about his assault so much as his not wanting to say anything that would bring back what she had suffered when she had been attacked as a teenager.

"You think that Luke planned to kill that guy?" Kenzie asked. "Is that what you mean?"

"He went to Eyler's hotel room, knowing that Eyler had caused Connor's death. Connor and Luke were really close. I can't see any reason Luke would go to Eyler's room other than to take revenge. He'd uttered threats in public. Said that if Eyler didn't get out of town, Luke was going to kill him."

"Ouch." Kenzie nodded. "That looks pretty bad for Luke."

"Maybe he just went there to see if Eyler had left," Heather suggested. "Or to… encourage him to go."

Zachary shook his head. "Luke didn't have any way to convince Eyler to go. He could threaten, but he didn't hold anything over him. He didn't have any leverage, and Eyler was bigger and more powerful than he was."

"Then how could he have thought that he could kill him?"

Zachary frowned, thinking about it. He took another bite of the food. It was good, but he could barely taste it, too focused on Luke's case and all the loose threads that the story still presented. "Well, he did, so obviously he could. But I don't know where all of Eyler's men were. He should have had some security around him. I don't know how Luke could have caught Eyler off guard."

"Well, I suppose if Luke is a good enough shot, then he didn't have to get too close," Kenzie offered.

Zachary shook his head, holding up a finger to refute this. "He wasn't shot. He was stabbed."

"Stabbed." Kenzie's lips pressed together. "Well, that is up close and personal, unless he's a knife thrower."

"No. Don't think so. He's a street rat, not a circus performer. The detective didn't give me any details of the injuries. And it's an active investigation, so a request for information wouldn't go anywhere. But it was obvious from the blood spatter that he was stabbed more than once."

"Maybe he's really skilled with a knife and Eyler didn't know it," Heather suggested. "Maybe he didn't know that Luke carried one and didn't think Luke would attack because he was smaller…?" Heather didn't know any of the background of the case, but she had obviously picked up what she needed from the little Zachary had said. Maybe knowing less helped her see clearly, instead of being impeded by all the relevant and irrelevant facts that Zachary knew.

He was thinking, running through pictures in his head. Trying to remember everything he had learned in his brief visit to the crime scene. A crime scene from which all of the evidence had already been removed. No body, no murder weapon, none of the things they thought were relevant or might have trace evidence on them.

"What are you thinking?" Heather asked after a moment.

"That... he wasn't carrying a knife."

"How would you know that?" Kenzie asked. "Is that what he told you? You know that he could be lying about any of the details."

"Oh, I know he's not telling me all of the facts," Zachary assured her. "He won't tell me anything about what happened. Just that he killed Eyler."

"He *didn't* tell you that he wasn't carrying the knife?" Kenzie persisted, not having gotten a clear answer from him.

"No, he didn't."

"Then how could you know?" Heather asked. "The police? Was it in the news?"

"No. It was in the drawer."

He looked up from his plate. Both of the women looked baffled by his statement. Zachary tried to backtrack to give them the information they were missing.

"It was a suite with a kitchen. Just a small one. I took pictures of all of the drawers." He pulled out his phone and navigated to the cloud storage where he had saved the pictures from the kitchen. He flicked through them, looking at the photos of the drawers in particular. "There is a cutting board. But no knife."

They all exchanged looks.

"Well..." Heather considered. "You know how hotel kitchens are. They're never fully stocked. They're always missing something that you need. In my experience. When we vacationed with the kids, we used to like to book hotel rooms with a kitchen so that we could make food there instead of paying for fast food all the time. And they were always missing a pot or pan, or a pancake turner, or oven mitts. The knife might have disappeared weeks or months before and never been replaced."

"Maybe," Zachary admitted. "But if Luke went there unarmed..." His brow furrowed and he shook his head, trying to figure it out.

"What?" Kenzie asked.

"Why would he go see Eyler unarmed? If he intended to kill him, then, of course, he would take a weapon."

"Then he probably did. Heather's right. The kitchen knife has probably been missing for a while."

"Maybe. But it would have made more sense for him to get a gun. A way to kill Eyler from across the room. Not having to get within arm's reach of him."

Zachary had another bite of the Thai food, then pushed his plate away from him an inch. He wasn't going to be able to get any more of it down.

"What *did* Luke tell you?" Kenzie asked. "Or don't you want to talk about it?"

"He told me about Connor."

"Oh, right. You did say that. And Eyler killed Connor?"

"Yeah, indirectly. Supplied him to a john that he knew was dangerous. Who had assaulted and possibly killed other prostitutes."

Heather shuddered. "How horrible."

Zachary was glad that he had decided to stop eating. Talking about Connor brought back the rest of the emotions he had been trying not to deal with and made his stomach tie into a tight knot.

"The thing is... what Luke told me about it..." He looked at Kenzie, trying to anchor to her and keep his voice steady. "It sounded like Archuro."

Kenzie gazed at him for a moment, unblinking, as she tried to make sense of this. "You think... that the john who killed Connor might have been Archuro?"

Zachary nodded. Kenzie did not ask for all of the details of the similarities between the two cases. She knew better than to ask for the details of what Archuro had done and said. Zachary had never been able to voice them to her or to anyone else. But she had seen his scars and she knew some of what Archuro had done to the other men he had killed. Zachary had been trying to think of how to convince her without explaining the parallels to her, but Kenzie seemed to accept it at face value. He was the one who would know.

"It could be, couldn't it?" he asked Kenzie. "Archuro didn't live that far away. He could easily have... hunted there. There's nothing that says because he picked up his own victims some of the time, he couldn't have hired from a trafficker at others."

Kenzie nodded. "It's not unusual for a serial killer to have hired and possibly killed prostitutes in the past. Sometimes it's people in that community who recognize it and clue the police in."

Like with Jose and the other men who had disappeared from Archuro's hunting area.

Heather touched Zachary's arm. "But he's in prison now. He's not going to hurt anyone else."

Zachary swallowed and nodded. That was, of course, aside from the damage that he'd already done. Zachary would probably suffer from his encounter with Archuro for the rest of his life.

43

Zachary already had his phone in his hand from looking at the pictures he had taken at the hotel so, when it vibrated, he looked down at it, even though their usual rule was no phones at the table. A notification that he'd received a message from Rhys flashed across the top of the screen. Zachary looked at his plate and the rest of the food on the table.

"Do you mind if I take this? It's Rhys. I'm kind of... finished with eating, and..."

"And with talking?" Kenzie suggested.

Zachary nodded. He needed some time to himself. Heather had helped him to hold things together until Kenzie got home, and he'd been able to tell them the bare bones of what he had learned from Luke, and now he needed space. Kenzie knew him well.

"Go ahead," Kenzie agreed, waving him away. "Heather and I will catch up on all of the gossip."

He thought they had already done that, but she was giving him an "out," and he would take it. He picked up his plate to scrape it into the garbage and put it in the dishwasher. "You can leave the cleaning up for me. Just... remind me in an hour if I forget."

"Heather and I can manage it. It isn't like there are any pots and pans to scrub."

"Okay… well…" he shrugged, looking at the food and dishes left on the table, "just let me know if you need a hand."

Kenzie nodded and again motioned him away. Zachary retreated to the bedroom, where he could chat with Rhys without being distracted by the conversation between Kenzie and Heather.

He stretched out on the bed and brought up the messaging app to see what Rhys had sent.

A picture of Adele with the word "hello" superimposed on it.

Hi. How are you doing? Zachary tapped back.

He hoped that it would just be a conversation about Rhys and what he was doing at home or school. Not about Luke and what was going on with his case.

Of course, that hope was immediately dashed when a picture of Luke appeared on his screen.

First, how are you? Zachary insisted.

He waited for the dots to appear on the screen, indicating that Rhys was composing an answer. Was he doing something else while holding the conversation? His homework or talking with Vera? Or was it taking that long for Rhys to identify his feelings and start to formulate a response?

Eventually, a picture of a basset hound appeared on the screen, its droopy mouth and wrinkles making it look sad. Very similar to how Rhys's mouth naturally fell into an unhappy frown. Zachary waited for a minute to see if there were any words to go along with the picture, but apparently, Rhys wasn't able to formulate anything verbal.

Sorry you're feeling bad. It must be very hard for you.

Luke's picture appeared on the screen again. Zachary sighed heavily.

I'm still working on finding a way to help him. He's in a bad situation.

Then finally, Rhys's first words. *u help him*

I'm doing my best. Trying to come up with answers. But he is not talking to me.

There was no immediate response. Zachary closed his eyes and rubbed his forehead and the space between his eyebrows. He hadn't noticed the headache until then. He was tired and frustrated, irritated at not being able to help Luke and angry at him for refusing to help in his own defense. Also stretched thin by his flashbacks to Archuro and the assault.

The phone vibrated. Zachary opened his eyes and looked down at it.

There was a picture of a flower. A daisy, he thought, except it was purple and he didn't know if daisies came in colors other than white. What did that mean? Rhys was sending him a peace offering? He was mourning?

Zachary hit the question mark and sent it, asking for more details.

But the answer back from Rhys was just as cryptic.

Aster

Zachary blinked and tried to think of what Rhys was trying to tell him. The word didn't connect up to anything he could think of. He got up and went back to the kitchen to talk to Kenzie. The two women paused in their conversation and looked at him.

Did that mean they had been talking about him?

Probably.

They were his partner and his sister. While they each had their own interests and were friendly with each other, the primary connection between them was Zachary. And he provided them with lots of material to discuss.

He handed the phone to Kenzie. "Can you make sense of that?"

Kenzie looked at it. "Aster?" She looked back at Zachary questioningly.

He shrugged, at a loss.

Heather looked interested. "An aster is a flower," she said. "I learned that living with the Astors all those years. Even though that's not where their name came from."

"Do they look like purple daisies?" Zachary asked.

"Yeah. Or it can be a girl's name. I can't think of anything else off the top of my head." She looked curiously toward the phone. "How is it used?"

"Just by itself. But it *could* be a girl's name." Zachary took the phone back from Kenzie, nodding. "I'll try that."

He returned to the bedroom.

Sitting down on the bed, he tried to figure out what to say to Rhys.

Is Aster a girl?

Rhys responded with a picture of a girl floating several inches off the floor. Was that significant, or Rhys's form of *well, duh*?

I don't know Aster

It was a few minutes before Rhys responded with a picture. This time, a selfie taken by Luke, with him and a young woman in the frame, their faces close together so that he could capture both of them.

Aster.

Zachary felt a thrill go through him at this new bit of information. Exactly who was Aster and what did she have to do with anything? She was clearly a friend of Luke's. In the background was a blur of lights and moving bodies. A bar or nightclub. While Luke looked old enough to drink legally, even though he was a teenager, the girl looked younger. Maybe sixteen. Her face was a little round. Cherubic. Just enough baby fat to make her look like a mischievous little angel. She smiled into the camera, enjoying her time with Luke.

If they were close, why hadn't Luke mentioned her? Because he wanted to keep his relationships private? He must have known that Zachary didn't want him and Rhys to be friends, or he wouldn't have lied to Zachary, saying that they weren't communicating with each other anymore when they were. Maybe he figured Zachary would try to take Aster away from him too. And he was right. Zachary wouldn't want that angel-faced young woman to be pulled into the trafficking world either.

He tapped another message to Rhys. *Luke didn't mention her. Are they BF/GF?*

Considering Rhys's attraction to Luke, it was probably insensitive to ask him if Luke and Aster were boyfriend and girlfriend. But where else was Zachary going to get that information? Joss hadn't mentioned Luke having a special girl, so Zachary had to assume she didn't know about Aster.

friends, Rhys texted back succinctly.

But would he know? They only communicated by electronic messages, so Luke could get away with not telling Rhys they were intimate partners.

Where is she? Where does she live?

He received back an animated gif of a dog that looked like Scooby-Doo shrugging. *I don't know.*

Do you know how to contact her?

No answer

Aster was not answering Rhys's messages. Did that mean that something had happened to her? Or was she in danger? Hiding? If she was close to Luke, she might be too scared to come forward, to share what information she knew about what had happened.

Do you know anyone else who might know?

Rhys sent the picture of Luke and Aster again. Luke knew. That wasn't terribly helpful when Luke was not talking to Zachary. But maybe if Luke thought Aster was in danger, he would. Zachary drummed his fingers, thinking.

Can we talk? Can I come over? he eventually typed in.

A bobble-headed dog nodding gave him the affirmative.

44

Rhys was apparently watching for Zachary. When he pulled up to the curb, Rhys opened the door of the house and stood waiting for him. Zachary walked up the sidewalk and fist-bumped with him as he entered. Vera was reading in the living room. She looked up long enough to welcome Zachary, but apparently figured it was best for her to just stay out of the way for now and give the two of them room.

Rhys led Zachary into the kitchen. He stuck his head in the fridge and rummaged around while Zachary sat at the table. Rhys pulled leftovers out of the refrigerator and stacked them on the counter. He pointed to Zachary and raised his brows. *You?*

Zachary shook his head. "Kenzie and I had Thai tonight. I'm stuffed."

Rhys nodded and prepared his evening snack. In a few minutes, he sat down at the table with a heaping bowl of food. He shoveled a couple of forkfuls into his mouth before his eyes finally met Zachary's. He moved his hands wide, eyebrows raised. *So…?*

"I want to know about Aster. How you met her. How Luke met her. Anything I should know about her."

Rhys frowned. He pointed to Zachary and then made a zero shape with his hand, looking questioning. *You don't know anything?*

"Nothing."

Rhys thought about it some more, munching away. He started thumbing through pictures or videos on his phone. Eventually, he showed

Zachary another picture. Luke was front and center, but someone was standing in the background behind him.

"Was this the first time you saw Aster?" Zachary guessed.

Rhys pointed at him with a pistol-shaped hand. *You got it.*

"But Luke already knew her."

Rhys nodded his agreement.

"Had they met at a club? Or somewhere else?"

Rhys shrugged. He indicated the picture again off-handedly. *First time I knew anything.*

"And Luke didn't tell you where they had met?"

Rhys shook his head.

"Do you have any idea? A guess?"

Rhys flipped past the photo of Luke and Aster and the next couple of pictures and then showed it to Zachary. Clearly a dance floor. Kurt had said that Luke had been going out to meet people and not be so isolated. He needed to be with people, not just at home alone with Joss.

"Dancing? Or drinking?"

Rhys nodded at the first, then shook his head emphatically at the second guess.

"Not drinking? You're sure?"

Rhys shook it again. Kurt had also said that Luke wasn't drinking. Just out to have a good time. To socialize and make new friends. Zachary remembered how difficult it was moving from one place to another as a child. Landing in a place where he didn't know anyone and had to start all over again. It got to be too hard after a while. So that he didn't even want to try. He just kept his head down and tried not to do anything to irritate his guardians, and otherwise to be invisible everywhere he went.

"And Aster? She was just looking for some company too?"

Rhys nodded.

"What do you know about her?"

Rhys scratched his chin, considering. Eventually, he took a deeper dive into the photos on his phone, searching for something he remembered. Zachary had hoped to see snippets of conversations between Rhys and Luke or Aster, but apparently Rhys wasn't going to share that. Maybe he had deleted his conversations with Luke to ensure that his grandmother wouldn't find them and realize Rhys and Luke hadn't ended their friendship after all.

Eventually, Rhys handed the phone over to Zachary.

Zachary studied it, frowning. It was a picture he knew, of Luke—at the time, going by Noah—and Madison. Madison had gone missing and Rhys had been concerned about her. He'd had some inkling of the fact that she was involved in trafficking and that Luke wasn't really just the attentive boyfriend everyone thought him to be. It was before Rhys had been attracted to Luke. Or at least, before he'd let anyone know it.

Zachary tried to bridge the communication gap. He'd asked Rhys to tell him about Aster, and Rhys had shown him a picture of Madison. Aster, then, was like Madison. Zachary's gut tightened at the thought.

"Do you mean that Aster was being trafficked too?"

Rhys nodded and took another bite of his meal.

"By Luke?"

Rhys shook his head adamantly. He crossed his hands in an X and pushed them away from him.

Zachary was relieved at that answer. At least, temporarily. Rhys could be wrong. Luke and Aster might have kept those details from him. Luke was a good liar. And when Zachary had first found Madison, she had not understood what she had gotten herself into. She was doing her boyfriend a favor, and Luke was carefully leading her down the path, with each step getting her more and more comfortable with doing things she had never dreamed she would be doing before she had met him.

"Do you know who she is under? Who her boss is?"

Rhys mimed stabbing himself in the heart and slumping over dead. Zachary found his meaning pretty clear.

"Eyler?"

Rhys nodded and pointed at Zachary.

Zachary swore. "Eyler was Aster's boss? She worked for him?"

Rhys made a motion behind his back. Zachary tried to fathom his meaning.

Rhys held one fist upright, then grabbed his wrist with his other hand and pulled it up as if lifting himself up.

"Helping hand?" Zachary asked. "Rescue! Aster was rescued from Eyler?" Rhys was nodding his agreement. "Aster was working for Eyler, but she was rescued?"

Rhys pointed at him, nodding.

Zachary took out his own phone and looked at the picture that Rhys had sent to him of Luke and Aster together. He studied her face and tried to remember the descriptions of the hotel clerks of the young people who had been in and out of Eyler's suite. Blond girls. One of them with a rounder face, like a fresh-faced farm girl. Had they been describing Aster?

He looked at her, looked at Luke, looked at the background. They had been laughing and enjoying themselves, dancing. What had happened between that moment and Luke entering Eyler's hotel room to kill him? Why hadn't he just stayed with Aster?

After gazing at the picture for a moment, he went to his browser and searched for the Duck and Dog. Rhys leaned in, trying to see what he was doing. Zachary found the website for the bar. A series of video thumbnails ran down the side of the screen, and Zachary looked for the fight between Luke and the other man. It wasn't there, but he could see reasons for the bar not to put that particular one on the website. He clicked on another and, as he had hoped, it took him to the videographer's social media channel. Looking down the list of videos, he was able to find the one of the fight. He turned his phone slightly as he watched it so that Rhys could see it as well.

Rhys watched the action and made several gestures of surprise. Zachary played the video again. He watched it two more times. The flash of movement was difficult to see, but Zachary managed to pause the video and step through a few frames at a time to get a reasonably clear still from the first few seconds of the video. He showed it to Rhys and pointed.

Rhys nodded his agreement. At the very beginning of the recording, Luke was pushing a young lady back and stretching his arms to block the other man, protecting her.

Aster.

She was the reason for that fight.

"Where is Aster now?" Zachary demanded.

Rhys spread his hands out, palms up. *I don't know.*

"She could be in danger. You need to tell me. If we're going to get this all straightened out, I need to talk to her."

Rhys shook his head, eyes wide and innocent, shrugging dramatically.

"You've been messaging with her."

Rhys pushed his phone toward Zachary, pointing to it and motioning for him to look at his phone and find any messages. So he had deleted them, or they were in an app that was hidden or protected. Zachary didn't bother to pick it up.

"She's the one who told you that Luke had been arrested."

Rhys hesitated, then gave a slight nod.

"And then what? Have you talked to her since then?"

Rhys shook his head and made the familiar hand gesture. *No.*

"It's pretty hard for me to do anything if everyone keeps lying to me and withholding information from me. I thought you really cared about Luke."

Rhys opened his mouth. "I do!" he blurted.

"But you're not doing anything to help him. Aster may know a lot of the details that we're looking for. She was around, hanging out with Luke, and knew Eyler. *She's* the connection, not Connor."

Rhys mouthed the name "Connor" and shook his head.

"Connor was... someone in the organization that Luke was close to, who was killed by Eyler."

Rhys's brows went up in surprise. So, there was still plenty that Luke had not told Rhys. It made sense for him to withhold anything too personal or too ugly to tell the younger boy about. Luke had, so far, kept Rhys well out of the way of the trafficking business.

Rhys picked his phone back up and thumbed a brief message.

DON'T KNOW WHERE

Zachary took a deep breath and let it out slowly. If Rhys didn't know where Aster was, it didn't matter how firm and persuasive Zachary was. Rhys still wouldn't know.

45

Heather had gone back home after supper, so it was just Kenzie when Zachary returned from his visit with Rhys.

"Did you find anything out?" Kenzie asked. She had put on her pajamas and was rubbing cream into her heels.

"Not a lot, but a little more progress. There was a girl."

"Aster?" Kenzie asked.

Zachary nodded. "Aster. A girl that Luke was trying to protect who had been trafficked by Eyler."

"Do you think *that's* why he went after Eyler?"

"I guess so, yes. I thought that it was because of Connor, but I couldn't figure out what would have triggered him to kill Eyler now, when Connor was killed years ago and Luke did nothing about it then."

"Maybe he feels more empowered now. Or is afraid to see the same thing happen again. So... he jumps into action and confronts Eyler."

"And that does not end well."

"Or it *does* end well," Kenzie said, tilting her head to the side slightly. "Eyler is eliminated."

"Well... yes," Zachary admitted. "He can't prey on any more girls—or boys. But Aster is still out there somewhere, and there are plenty more people prepared to step in and take over where Eyler left off. And Luke is headed for prison, maybe for the rest of his life. Is anything really any better?"

"No. I know. I just thought… Luke got what he wanted. And it sounds like this Eyler was worse than most. Why would he provide Connor to a john that he knew was dangerous?"

"Because he wanted to get back at Connor."

"What did the poor guy do?"

"He used to be owned by Eyler. But he caused such problems that Eyler beat him and left him for dead. Only Connor had the gall not to die, and one of the other bosses took him in. And then—"

"There's an 'and then'? How many lives did this guy have?"

Zachary nodded. "And then he turned out to be a really valuable asset for Peggy Ann. When she didn't have to pay anything to Eyler for him."

"Then…" Kenzie paused as she tried to sort the narrative out. "How did Eyler arrange for Connor to see this dangerous john?"

"Promised him enough money that he'd be able to break free and start a new life somewhere else, with a new identity. It was a side gig. A secret from Peggy Ann."

Kenzie shook her head. "Then Eyler really did want to get back at her and Connor."

"Yeah."

And that was the kind of man who'd had Aster in his stable. Zachary remembered Luke's description of how harshly Eyler treated his assets and shuddered to think about what Aster would have gone through at his hands. Possibly snatched off the street, drugged, beaten, and turned out.

It wasn't a particularly nice thought to dwell on before going to bed.

Despite Zachary's concerns, He didn't sleep too badly. At least, not compared to his worst nights. After waking up, he worked on the deep background checks that Heather had mentioned he needed to do. And was finished two of them by the time Kenzie woke up and rolled out of bed.

She got her first cup of coffee from the kitchen and stood there looking adorable with her sleep-mussed hair and pajamas, rubbing her eyes.

"Are you going back south again? Looking for this Aster?"

Zachary nodded. "Yeah. I don't know if I'll be able to find her, but… I need to try. Knowing what Madison and Luke and Connor went through… I can't just leave it alone, thinking someone else will help her. I have no idea if she's back in their hands or hiding. She could still be in town, or she could be long gone. If she's skipped town… that's probably the best thing for her. As long as she didn't leave a trail for anyone to follow."

"But where would she get the money to leave town?"

Zachary nodded at the question. "Yeah. They're pretty careful about how much spending money they give to these kids. Keep them close to home. And if they think they're going to run, or if they do run and get caught…"

"I hope you can do something to help her. But don't be too hard on yourself if you can't. You can't take care of everyone."

Zachary flashed a look at her and nodded. He knew she was probably thinking about his fixation with Bridget and her babies. It was a battle every day not to think about them and to go by the house to check on them. His need was so deep and primal, he knew it bordered on being pathological.

Forget bordering; he knew it was well into obsessive territory.

It was true that Zachary couldn't help everyone. But if he had let that stop him in the past, there were a lot of cases that would have gone unsolved. It was being obsessive about a case that led to him being able to find the things other investigators had missed and to chase them down to a successful conclusion, even when at times it had put his life in peril.

"Don't do anything dangerous," Kenzie said, her mind apparently running in the same track as his. "Slow down and think before you put yourself into a bad situation."

"I won't do anything dangerous," Zachary agreed.

And he would try not to.

When Luke saw Zachary waiting in the visitor room, he stopped and pulled back, turning his head away to indicate to the CO that he didn't want to stay there.

"I got nothing more to say to you, Zachary."

The CO looked from one to the other, brows raised.

"You need to talk to me if I'm going to help Aster," Zachary told him.

Luke stiffened. He looked at Zachary in disbelief. "How did you…? You gotta stop, man! Stop digging and just stay out of it."

"Staying or going?" the CO asked Luke sharply.

Luke hesitated. He wanted, of course, to say no and show Zachary that he was still in charge, even if he was in jail. He wanted to assert that Zachary couldn't know anything or do anything unless Luke decided to speak to him. But if everything he had done had been for Aster, then he couldn't very well abandon her to her fate now.

He let out his breath in an angry huff. "Stay," he announced.

"Get in there, then." The CO shoved him forward. Luke lurched forward and managed to avoid falling despite his leg shackles. He sat down. The CO anchored him into place and left them alone together.

"How are you going to help Aster?" Luke demanded. "What's wrong?"

"I know that you rescued her and were trying to help her. That's why you killed Eyler, wasn't it? To protect her from him? So that what happened to Connor wouldn't happen to her too?"

Luke stared at him, face impassive, and didn't answer one way or the other.

"Aster is missing. If she's been taken by the cartel again, I need to know that. And where they're likely to stash her."

"Missing? She's not at the—" Luke cut himself off. Zachary actually saw him wince in pain from biting his lip. He scowled at Zachary. "How am I supposed to know whether you're telling me the truth or not? She's supposed to be safe. What do you mean, she's missing? Who told you she's missing?"

Zachary could see that not having all of the details made it impossible for Luke to refuse him. Luke had to assume that Zachary knew more than he did about the current situation. Zachary was on the outside, where he had freedom of movement and could talk to who he liked. If Luke could get any information on the inside, the pipeline was probably pretty slow and unreliable.

"How am I supposed to tell whether *you* are telling the truth?" Zachary countered. "I know one thing, and that is that you haven't told me everything I need to know. Especially everything about Aster."

"I haven't told you *anything* about Aster," Luke said grumpily, slouching down in his chair.

"Yeah. Exactly. Why not? If I'm going to help you—" Zachary could see the expression on Luke's face that he was going to protest that he didn't want or need any help, "—or help Aster, then you need to tell me everything. You can't just sit there and say nothing."

"No one asked you to get involved in this case."

"Yes. Joss did."

Luke sat there fuming. "She should have left you out of it. I told her to just let it be. I told her and told her to keep it in the family."

"I *am* family."

"Not that kind of family. The kind of family that chooses each other. Joss never chose you."

Zachary was stung by the comment. On the one hand, he knew that Luke meant they were only thrown together by an accident of genetics. But on the other hand, he felt as though he had been rejected by everyone in his family after the fire. Even though the social worker had never said the other children didn't want to be with him anymore, Zachary couldn't help but wonder if that was were case. She had told him in the beginning that he'd be able to see them after everyone was settled, but then that never happened. Of course the children hadn't had any say in what families they went to. But the fact that they had never been reunited as children gutted him.

No one had wanted him. His entire family had disappeared from his life.

Refusing to be distracted from his goal, Zachary sat there as if Luke's words hadn't hurt him and repeated. "Where would Aster go? Or if the cartel got her again, where would they take her?"

"She didn't have anywhere else safe to go. That's why she was with—" Luke again stopped himself. This time Zachary actually saw a fleck of blood on his lip.

And Zachary knew where she was supposed to be. They had just been talking about it. *Joss.* Zachary's biological family, but Luke's and Aster's chosen family. Luke had told Joss not to get Zachary involved, because Zachary would find out about Aster.

And that could change everything.

46

Luke's face was as white as a sheet. He could see that he had given Zachary too much information. He, who had told Joss not to give anything away, was the one who had put his foot in it. He scowled furiously when Zachary waved for the guard to take Luke back to the cellblock, but there was nothing he could do to stop Zachary.

Back in the car, Zachary forced himself to sit and consider the possible outcomes. The pros and cons of going to Joss's house now that he had the rest of the information he needed. Kenzie would have been proud of him for stopping to think before he dove right in.

But in the end, he dove in anyway.

Joss answered the door and scowled at Zachary. "What are you doing here?"

"We need to talk."

She stood there for a moment, more to let him know that she had the upper hand than because she actually didn't want him to enter, Zachary suspected. She sighed deeply, took a quick look behind her, then opened the door wider to let him in. Maybe it hadn't been a power move; maybe it was to ensure that anyone who had been in the living room had time to clear out and hide in one of the bedrooms until he was gone.

Zachary followed her in. He stooped to put the box he held onto the coffee table. "I brought donuts for the girls," he said in a voice raised loudly enough that others in the house would be able to hear it.

Joss's eyes blazed. "I don't know what you're—"

"Did someone say donuts?" A tiny slip of a girl, a blond teen, stood in the doorway to the hall, peering around the wall to scope out the treats.

Joss opened her mouth to rebuke the girl but, before she said anything, the girl flitted into the living room and opened the box. "He brought the good stuff," she called out to the rest of the house. "And look at that, I'm the only one home. I guess I get all of them."

There was movement from the other rooms. The other girls came into the living room, some of them slowly and cautiously, and others boldly, a tall one pushing the others out of her way so that she could reach the donuts first and have her pick. Zachary looked carefully at each of them, looking for Aster's round farm girl face and seeing if any of them might match the description of one of the girls at the hotel.

But Aster was not there.

"Is this everyone?" Zachary asked.

Joss was glowering at him. "Anyone ever tell you you're a pain?"

Zachary chuckled. "I might have heard that a few times."

"You guys shouldn't have come out," Joss told the girls severely. "You're supposed to be keeping a low profile. We don't want people to know that you're here."

"There's keeping a low profile," the small blond said, licking chocolate glaze off her fingers, "and there's missing out on donuts."

The others giggled and nodded in agreement. Most of them were painfully thin—the result of drugs, neglect, and a society that idolized thin as beautiful. The traffickers wanted girls that the johns thought attractive, and fat wasn't on the list of desirable qualities. It gave Zachary hope that Aster had not been with the traffickers for very long, or she would have lost the comfortable roundness of her cheeks. If she hadn't already become conditioned to the rules of the trafficking ring and bonded to her boss, maybe it would be easier to get her out and give her a chance at a normal life.

Zachary turned his attention back to Joss, who was looking down at the box of donuts and eventually bent over to pick one out before sitting down to talk to Zachary.

"So... Aster..." Zachary ventured.

The other girls quieted, the jokes and giggles dying on their lips.

Joss shook her head, frowning. "Who told you about Aster?"

"I keep my sources confidential. I was hoping that I would find her here. She's not with you?"

"She should be. She was supposed to be."

"And Luke thought she was safe here?"

"Did you tell him she wasn't?" Joss's voice rose sharply.

"I asked him where she was. Then I figured out that she was here. Or that Luke thought she was here."

"I can't believe he told you."

"He didn't. At least, he tried not to, but he gave it away."

"My brother, the private investigator."

"I do have some experience in worming information out of people. I'm pretty... persistent."

"That's one word for it," Joss said sourly.

"You're the one who asked me to help."

"To help find a way to get Luke off or get his sentence reduced. Not to interfere in other things."

"I'm doing my best, but how can I do that when I don't have the full story?"

"You do. I told you everything you need to know."

"No, you didn't."

She avoided his eyes, looking at the girls seated and standing around the room.

"Did she go somewhere else?" Zachary asked. "Or did something happen?"

"She wasn't careful enough." Joss looked significantly at the young girls. "They need to follow the rules to stay safe."

"Do you know where she is?"

"I know who she's with," Joss corrected. "Location—no."

Zachary's stomach twisted.

At least Eyler was out of the picture.

But there were still plenty of predators out there who would be happy to add another girl to their offerings. Eyler's territory was open. Who would try next? Who would take it over?

711

47

Zachary wasn't familiar enough with all of the players in the trafficking business. He only knew one of Eyler's close competitors. One who had outstripped him while he had been on probation with the cartel, climbing the ladder and growing her business while Eyler was held back.

"Tell me it's not Peggy Ann."

Joss rolled her eyes and let out a sigh. Another expression of her disgust at Zachary figuring out things he wasn't supposed to know about.

"We have to get her back," Zachary said, his heart giving an extra thump or two as it sped up. He remembered the burn marks on Luke's shoulder, the looks that both he and Madison had shared when they talked about her. Peggy Ann might be more civilized than Eyler, but that wasn't saying much. She would still use drugs and pain to force Aster to do what Peggy Ann expected her to. Maybe Aster would be lucky, and there was a more experienced prostitute like Luke helping her out, showing her the ropes and ensuring that she didn't get into too much trouble. Someone who could make sure she knew what to do to avoid getting hurt.

"We?" Joss repeated. "How are *you* going to get her back? You don't know where she is. If you try to go in there guns blazing, you're going to get killed."

"Maybe there's a way we can negotiate for Aster."

"Do you think that I'm not already doing that?"

Zachary was a bit taken aback by her vehemence. But if she had been fighting to get Aster back the whole time Zachary had been investigating Luke's case, she was undoubtedly tired and frustrated. Of course she would be irritated by Zachary's ignorant suggestion.

"How can I help?"

"There isn't anything you can do to help. You don't know anything about this business or about Peggy Ann."

"I know a little," Zachary protested. "It might not be much, but I've been figuring it out. I know about Eyler and Peggy Ann. And Connor, Luke, and Aster. I know about Luke running into one of Eyler's men at the club and defending Aster."

Jocelyn stared at him. She frowned. "Who is Connor?"

"Connor was one of Eyler's assets, but then he ended up with Peggy Ann, and Eyler wasn't happy with that. Got his revenge by setting Connor up with a john known to be dangerous." Zachary raised his brows at Joss. "You haven't heard the story before? About how Eyler got sanctioned by the cartel? He wasn't allowed to advance...?"

Joss frowned and shook her head. "I heard that, of course. But... Peggy Ann didn't have anything to do with that."

"No," Zachary agreed. "She didn't know about it. Connor took a job on the quiet. She didn't know what was happening until it was too late."

"You're sure? Connor was Peggy Ann's asset?"

Zachary nodded. "According to Luke. I don't have independent confirmation, but that's what he says happened, and he was around at that time and very close to Connor."

"I heard about it... I was still in the business, then. But I was pretty messed up, and I don't remember much other than that a boy was killed and Eyler was punished for it because the john was supposed to be embargoed."

"Well, that's the story that Luke tells. Eyler tried to kill Connor once before. Left him for dead. But Peggy Ann nursed him back to health and he was working for her. That pissed Eyler off because Peggy Ann was using his asset without having had to pay him anything, and I guess Connor turned out to be pretty good at recruiting other kids, like Luke."

"He was Luke's Romeo?"

Zachary nodded.

"Then he would know." Joss sat there, frowning, a deep crease between her eyebrows.

"I think I smell something burning," one of the girls teased. "Smoke's coming out her ears, those gears are turning so fast."

Another girl slapped her arm. "Leave her alone!"

"I'm just teasing!"

Joss turned her head to glare at the two girls, and they were immediately silenced. She looked back at Zachary again. "Was Connor's murder ever solved?"

"No. But the organization knew who it was. They knew the john and they knew it was Eyler who had set it up."

Joss nodded. "But the police? They didn't know? Eyler didn't go to prison for it."

"No, he tidied things up so the police didn't know where Connor had come from."

"If someone were to tell the cops that Connor belonged to Peggy Ann…"

"Oh." Zachary understood in a flash. "Then they would go after her for the identity of the john—"

"And after her as an accessory. Because if she owned him, then she must have set up the meet."

"But she didn't know anything about it. It was Eyler."

She shrugged. "So? He's not around to confirm Peggy Ann's story. Not that he would anyway. Nobody has any proof. It was years ago. As far as the cops are concerned, whoever set up that date is partially to blame for the outcome. Prosecuting the pimp who set it up would be a warning to anyone else in a similar situation. 'You put together a match and something happens, and we'll come after you.'"

Zachary nodded slowly. "You think you can get to Aster if you get the police to arrest Peggy Ann? It's kind of a long shot."

"Yeah, it would be," Joss agreed dryly. "Especially since it would probably be months before they were ready to make an arrest. They're not going to do anything on my say-so. They have to get evidence to back it up first. By that time, getting Aster away would be a lot harder. No. I'm just thinking… maybe Peggy Ann doesn't want to hang on to the girl if there's that much risk." Recognizing that Zachary hadn't yet caught up, she filled in. "If there's a risk that *someone* could tell the cops that she was involved in Connor's death."

"You're going to blackmail her?"

The girls were whispering back and forth, not loud enough for

Zachary to make out what they were saying. But they were obviously surprised or concerned that she would consider it.

"I think I could make it part of the negotiation process. Up until now, I haven't had much leverage. But with something as explosive as this, I might be able to push a little harder."

"You need to be careful," Zachary warned, worried at this suggestion.

"Look who's talking!"

Zachary laughed weakly. "Well, I didn't say you should do what I would. I would try to be careful. It's just that sometimes…"

"You go off like a bull in a China shop?"

"I try," he protested. "I stopped to think about it before I came to see you today."

"And you figured I wouldn't answer the door with a Glock in my hand? Shoot first and ask questions later?"

"Well, I was right, wasn't I?"

Joss pushed her long shirt aside to show the butt of a gun protruding from a holster on her hip. "Were you? You're lucky I'm not as impulsive as you are, or you could be in a world of pain."

Zachary cleared his throat. Sweat broke out on his forehead. "Do you really think you should be carrying that around?"

"With these girls to protect," Joss indicated the teens, "do you really think I shouldn't?"

It was difficult to argue the point. Zachary wiped his forehead and smiled weakly at the girls. "You haven't had to use that, have you?"

"Do you think I would tell you if I had?"

Another good point.

Joss waited for him to voice any further stupid questions or objections, but Zachary was finished and stayed quiet.

48

J oss excused herself to make a call or reach out using some other method to contact Peggy Ann. Zachary was left sitting with the girls, who giggled and stared at him and whispered to each other. Zachary could feel his face getting red. He hadn't been in such an awkward situation with a bunch of girls since he had been a teenager himself.

"Are you really Madam's brother?" one of them asked him. She laughed and looked away again, blushing herself.

"Madam?" Zachary repeated. Remembering how Luke had been arguing with Eyler's man about territory, his gut twisted. The cop he had talked to at the police station the first day had said that Joss was rescuing girls and kicking the traffickers out of her neighborhood, but what if she were setting up shop herself? What if her "rescuing" was just taking girls away from their bosses and using them for herself?

"It's a joke," the girl said, shaking her head. "It's funny because she's *not*. She's just helping us out. She doesn't want us to be in the game. She's not in it herself."

"Not anymore," another agreed.

"But you know that she used to be like you," Zachary said.

"A loooong time ago," the first girl giggled.

Zachary opened his mouth to point out that Joss had still been in the game until quite recently, then closed it again. Joss didn't need him telling stories on her. And maybe they just meant she hadn't been young and beautiful for a long time.

"Well... I am Joss's brother, yes. But until recently, we hadn't seen each other for a long time. We didn't actually grow up together. Not after I was ten, anyway."

"She acts like she doesn't like you," one of them told him. "But when you're not here, that's not how she talks about you."

Zachary raised his brows. *Was that so?*

He knew Joss wasn't quite as tough and cold as she pretended to be. But it was hard to catch the flashes of affection, and they were gone so fast that he was left wondering whether he had imagined them.

It was a while before Joss returned to the living room. The girls had gone their different directions, but a couple were still in the living room, chatting and reading books.

Joss's cheeks were flushed and her eyes bright. She looked surprised to find Zachary still there.

"You're going to have to go. I can't leave you here with the girls."

"Where are you going?"

"To see if I can get Aster back."

"I'll come with you."

Joss shook her head. "No, you won't. Why don't you go home? I'll let you know if I need anything."

"You need me. I'll help you with Aster, and then we'll get this thing with Luke straightened out."

"What makes you think Aster has anything to do with Luke?" Joss shook her head. "It's nice of you to care, but stick to one thing at a time."

Zachary laughed. "You don't tell someone with ADHD to stick to one thing at a time. It's impossible."

"Well, maybe, but I don't need you to do anything else. Just trying to help Luke. And if that's not possible..." She trailed off and shrugged. Not the shrug of someone who didn't care, but of someone who was carrying a heavy burden.

"If I'm going to help Luke, then I need to talk to Aster."

Joss stopped in her preparations to leave and looked at him. "Why?"

"Because I think she knows about it. She was there when Luke got into a fight with one of Eyler's men. I want to hear what she has to say about it."

Joss gave her head a quick shake. "Then you can talk to her when she gets back. If I can get her."

"I'll help," Zachary repeated.

"I don't need you."

"No, but it looks better if it's both of us together."

Joss appeared to consider that for a moment. "I don't think so," she decided.

"You're going to go see Peggy Ann all by yourself? And you get after me for doing stupid things? It's not smart to go there by yourself. *She* won't be by herself. When I saw her when we were rescuing Luke, she wasn't by herself. She had a guy with her. Some... troubleshooter, Luke said."

"You're going to come along to be my troubleshooter?" She gave a short laugh. "Can you even shoot?"

"I won't be shooting. You're the one with the gun. But I think... it just looks better if you have *people*. One person by yourself, she might decide to do something on impulse. If there are at least two of us, she has to think it through. She doesn't know me. She won't know if I'm carrying or what my skills are. Who I know or whose protection I might be under. There's a lot to think about if you don't know a person."

"You're hoping she doesn't just blow both of us away and ask questions later."

Zachary took a deep breath and blew it out. "Yes. And I'm trusting that you've already laid the groundwork to make her think twice about that."

Joss nodded, conceding the point. Zachary figured that if Eyler and the previous trafficker hadn't eliminated Joss, she had enough dirt to worry them.

"Fine," Joss said finally. "But you do what I say and no arguing. This is not exactly... the safest mission."

Joss gave the girls various instructions on what they needed to do and on avoiding detection and other security issues. Zachary guessed from the rolling eyes that it was all ground Joss had covered more than once before. But he had to hand it to her—the girls were safe and comfortable. Joss had told Zachary before that there was nothing he could do to get kids away from the trafficking rings permanently. But there she was, with five of them. And up until recently, Aster and Luke too.

He followed Joss out to her car, a black SUV with dark windows that would make it easier to transport people without their being seen. Zachary climbed into the passenger's seat without comment and let Joss get on her way. Too much talking right away, and she'd pull over and make him walk back to his car. He was sure of it. He waited until they were well on their way on the highway before speaking.

"So, where are we meeting her?"

"You'll see."

"You think she'll deal? Let you have Aster?"

"Maybe. She wasn't happy talking to me on the phone, but she's agreed to meet. That's more than I expected."

"You think it's a trap?"

"If she could guarantee that nothing I know will get out after I'm dead, yes. But she doesn't know what arrangements I've made to disseminate information about her and the rest of the organization if something happens to me."

"And you *have* made arrangements, right?"

She looked at him for an instant, then turned her attention back to the road. "Of course."

Zachary couldn't tell from the flat tone of her voice whether she really did have all of those safety measures in place or whether it was just a bluff.

If Zachary couldn't tell, then how could Peggy Ann? She had to assume that there was a chance Jocelyn was telling the truth. She had to protect herself and her organization.

Zachary watched the road. It helped him to relax, despite the fact that they were going to face a dangerous woman who was part of an organized crime syndicate that would just as soon see him and Jocelyn both dead. He had faced criminals before. But not usually this way. Not intentionally confronting them with the truth and trying to coerce something out of them. He really did *try* to stay out of trouble, even if it did seem to always find him.

"Can *you* shoot?" he asked Joss.

"Would I carry a gun if I couldn't?"

"A lot of people carry guns who can't."

"Well, I'm not one of them. If you're going to carry, you should know how to use it. And not just a couple of test fires at a tree stump or on a gun range. You should practice regularly and not be afraid to use it."

He wasn't sure whether he was reassured or not. It was good, of course, that she knew what she was doing and was comfortable using a weapon. But he really didn't like the part about not being afraid to use it. He was hoping that she wouldn't use it today.

49

The area that they drove to was not a neighborhood that Zachary had hung out in or done any jobs in before. The houses were huge, some of them with full-sized tennis courts or swimming pools, which were not at all common for Vermont. Zachary stared at the towering mansions.

"You're meeting her at her house?"

"One of them."

"I can't believe… she lives somewhere like this."

Zachary had only caught one glimpse of Peggy Ann before. She hadn't exactly been a society lady. She'd been dressed fashionably in a red leather jacket, but not made up to look glamorous. A sour-faced, hardened woman who had a job to do.

"Where did you think she would live?" Jocelyn demanded. "You think she's going to be in some run-down rat hole? She may put her girls up in places like that, dirty little places that could be condemned at any minute. But the kind of money that she makes on the backs of these kids is not just a few extra dollars. This is… an empire."

Zachary swallowed and nodded. He'd read the stats about human trafficking, so he shouldn't have been surprised. He knew that it was a billion-dollar business. Of course mid-to-high-level bosses would make enough for a fancy house. Or several fancy houses. They wouldn't choose to live in the drug and rat-infested dens they kept their employees in.

Joss checked the numbers on the gates with the one on her phone and eventually pulled to a stop in front of one of them. She checked the number one more time, then inched close to the speaker with a red call button. She pushed the button firmly and kept it held in for a few seconds longer than Zachary would have dared. She was not trying to be polite and inconspicuous. She was there for a reason and believed that she held the upper hand.

"Who is it?" a male voice inquired.

"Joss."

They had undoubtedly been told to expect her, so the pause while the security guard pretended to check a long list of authorized guests was just for show.

"One moment, please."

He clicked off. Several minutes passed without any further response.

Joss rolled her eyes and put the car into "park." She picked up her phone and started to thumb through content and read.

"Yes, you may enter," the speaker finally announced.

Joss didn't move or acknowledge the guard.

"Hello? Are you still there?" There was a murmur as the guard talked to someone else in the room. "Hello? Miss… Goldman?"

Joss continued to play with her phone.

There were a few more squawks from the speaker. Looking around, Zachary spotted several surveillance cameras. They could see Joss and the fact that she was ignoring them. Eventually, Joss put her phone away and pressed the button on the speaker again. Probably making the guards jump if they were close to the speaker on their end and expecting her to speak rather than to ring the bell.

"Yeah, it's Joss. Is she ready yet?"

"Come in," the voice responded. The gate clanged and started to move.

Zachary smiled to himself. Power play met with power play. Joss knew how to give as good as she got. They drove along the winding drive. The leaves were just coming out on the trees. It was still cold at night, but the trees knew it was spring. They reached the house, and Joss drove part way around the parking area so that the van was not neatly pulled into one of the stalls, but in the middle of the lane, pointing outward. Good for a quick exit. Though Zachary suspected that if there was trouble, they wouldn't make it all the way to the van.

Joss got out of the van. Zachary stepped down and walked along beside her.

"You keep your mouth shut," Jocelyn warned. "Let me handle this. You're just here for appearances."

"Yes, ma'am."

She glared at him.

The door was opened for them before they had to knock or ring, by a man who was not dressed like a butler on TV, but more like a hood, in jeans and a jacket. He looked the two of them over.

"Miss Goldman," he said curtly, with a nod. "And who is this? He shouldn't be here. You shouldn't have brought anyone."

Joss shrugged, looking bored. "Look. I have an appointment. Is Peggy Ann ready or not? I'm not going to deal with a bunch of delays and nonsense. Ready or not?"

He nodded, his head at a bit of an angle as if he were considering something else or didn't really want to say that Peggy was ready. "We'll need to search you."

"You will not," Joss snapped. "Where is she? Upstairs?" She motioned to the grand staircase on their right.

"We can't let you walk in there with a concealed weapon. We need to protect the boss—"

"I'm sure she has a gun of her own. She certainly doesn't need you stepping in to protect her from a washed-up hooker. She's not helpless."

"Well, no!" the guard agreed, his neck turning red. "Of course not."

Joss pulled back her shirt, tucking it behind the gun on her hip. "There's mine. She'll have hers. But she knows that if she kills me, she loses. All of the information I've collected over the last few decades gets spread all over the state. Even farther than that. And if I shoot her, how am I supposed to get what *I* want?"

"It's our standard protocol. It's routine. We *have* to do it."

"That's bull. Peggy Ann knows I'm not going to meet her unarmed. So quit the nonsense. No more stalling."

The man looked at her for a moment, then shrugged. He apparently knew that Joss might not cooperate and had a standard protocol for *that* too.

"In her office. At the top of the stairs and to the right."

Joss headed for the large staircase without any expression of thanks. Zachary moved briskly to keep up with her. It wouldn't do to have him trailing behind her like a lost puppy. He needed to look like he was supposed to be there and was strong and prepared to deal with whatever nonsense they might like to throw at him. The staircase was curved so that the stairs were wedge-shaped rather than rectangular. The stairs were deeper than standard household stairs. While they were probably easier to walk up and down in a ballgown, they were the wrong distance apart for Zachary's stride, and he had difficulty figuring out how to take them comfortably. He was fine with walking and going up and down regular stairs, but the physiotherapy he had done after injuring his spine had not covered stairs that were the wrong distance apart. He lagged behind Joss by a stair or two all the way up, and she was waiting for him and glaring when they got to the top. Zachary didn't bother trying to explain the reason for his awkwardness.

They entered the hall together. Jocelyn put her hand on the doorknob of the first door to her right and looked back at Zachary to make sure he was ready.

His heart was pounding hard, but he was ready. They were just there to talk, after all. And whether they succeeded in getting what they wanted or not, they would walk away in a few minutes, safe and sound.

50

Joss pushed the door open without any apparent hesitation. Zachary admired her. She was tough as nails, that was for sure. She was not cowed by anything. She stepped into the room ahead of him, but he was close behind, and then moved up beside her so as not to be relegated to a subordinate position.

Peggy Ann's desk was large and ornate. Very dark, maybe black walnut, with fancy carved edges. The kind of thing Zachary might expect to see in the White House or a museum. It looked heavy and very old, but was polished to a high sheen.

Peggy Ann sat behind it. She was a petite woman with dark hair and a hard, angry face. She pretended to be engrossed in her work and unaware of their arrival. Or at least, unconcerned by it. There was a man standing a few feet away from her. A goon with a thick neck, his arms folded across his chest, looking like the bouncer at a biker bar. There were only the two of them. So their numbers were matched, even though it was clear that there was no way Zachary would ever be able to fight someone that big and well-muscled. At least Joss wasn't outnumbered. It looked better.

Joss marched up to the desk, not waiting to be acknowledged. Zachary stayed with her. He could have stood back like the goon and tried to fade into the background, but he wanted to be right there with Joss, presenting a united front. So that to Peggy Ann, it would *feel* like two-to-one, even if it wasn't.

"I'm here to talk," Joss declared. "Don't try to put me off with the fake work you're trying to finish."

Peggy Ann looked up, her pen still hovering over the paperwork. "Who is this?" she demanded. "You were supposed to come alone."

"We didn't discuss that. I brought my acquaintance with me. I'm sure you don't mind. You're surrounded by your men." Joss looked around, sneering at their surroundings. "Like you're afraid of getting assassinated or something."

"I'm not afraid," Peggy Ann corrected coldly. "I merely take precautions. Like you, wearing that gun like a talisman."

"Your guy downstairs wanted to see it. It's not like you thought I was going to come here unarmed."

"This is tiresome," Peggy Ann said, pushing her papers to the side. "Are we done with the posturing?"

"I'm not here to show off. I'm here to get Aster."

"Aster," Peggy sneered. "What kind of a name is that?"

"It's a flower," Zachary offered.

Joss turned and gave him a poisonous look. She had told him to keep his mouth shut, and here he was already jumping into the middle of her negotiations without being asked.

Peggy Ann gave a harsh laugh. "Can't keep this one under control, Joss? I thought I remembered you being better at getting men to do what you wanted."

Joss stared at Peggy Ann, not taking the bait. Zachary didn't know whether Peggy Ann actually knew anything about Joss's past. He was pretty sure that Joss hadn't been in Peggy Ann's stable or in any way associated with her. But it was a small world. She imagined that the different players heard about what workers were good and which were troublemakers, about who belonged to whom and what their special talents might be. And Joss had been in the business for a long time. Long after the blush of youth had faded.

"Aster," Joss repeated icily.

"I don't know what makes you think that I have her or would give her back to you. If you can't keep track of your own girls…"

"You know she is mine."

"I know she was Eyler's," Peggy Ann countered. "I'm not sure how that would make her yours."

"Eyler is dead. She left him before he died and came to me. I told Eyler and everyone else to stay out of Kent."

"It's not yours, dear. Living somewhere doesn't make it your territory. You have to *earn* territory."

"I have. I took it from Maxwell and I won't let anyone else operate there. It's the desert; you're not going to get anything out of it. Ever."

"Because the almighty Joss says it is so?"

"Yeah. I know you. And I know the organization. If people infringe on my territory, I will use what I know to get rid of them."

"Snitch to the cops, you mean."

"Whatever it takes. A few well-placed words here and there can ruin a business. You get a reputation for mismanagement and unhappy clients, raids on your cathouses, girls who won't stay or who refuse clients... it's not long before your name is mud in a small, close-knit community."

"I'm not worried about you," the small woman said, straightening her papers and putting down her pen. "You and your rescued girls and little house in the suburbs. You think you could take down someone like me?"

"Aster."

"You ridiculous woman! Aster is mine now, and I will use her to control you. If you cause problems, she is going to suffer for it."

Zachary's stomach twisted at the thought. That pretty young girl, being used as a pawn by Peggy Ann. Being tortured if Joss didn't do what she was told. And of course, Joss wouldn't do what she was told any more than Zachary would.

Joss didn't blanch or turn a hair at Peggy Ann's threat. She looked utterly unaffected. "I know about Connor."

Peggy Ann raised an eyebrow and looked at Joss as if she didn't know what she was talking about. "Connor?" She feigned ignorance. "Who is Connor?"

"You know who Connor is. A boy in your stable who died at the hands of a john."

"Oh..." she tilted her head to the side, brows drawn down, "that sounds vaguely familiar. But that was years ago."

"The case is still open. The police would love to have some new leads on it."

Peggy Ann shrugged. "Nothing to do with me. I can't help it if someone makes a date outside of my purview. I do my best to protect my assets, you know, but sometimes things are out of my hands." She looked down at her shapely hands with their red, manicured nails as if distracted by them.

"There is no way that Connor could have been introduced to that john without you. And you knew, like everyone else, that he was embargoed. But you let it go ahead. You contributed to his death."

"Even if that were true—and of course, it is not—the police would never come after me for it. I didn't make the arrangements."

"You had to know about it."

"I did not. But if I had, I would still not be guilty of anything."

"You have withheld information about the commission of a crime. If you had given the police what you knew, that scumbag would be rotting in a prison cell. But instead, you let him go free. All of you who knew about his previous crimes and about him torturing Connor to death just turned a blind eye and pretended it didn't happen."

"The appropriate action was taken at the time," Peggy Ann said smoothly. "I was not in the position that I am in now. I did not have the power to change anything. Eyler was responsible, and he was the one who was disciplined. Regardless of any of that..." Peggy Ann made an airy motion with one hand. "The police cannot arrest people for what they know. Knowing who committed a crime is not a crime."

"You contributed," Joss insisted. "He was your boy. If I tell the cops you set it up, they will come after you."

"I had nothing to do with it," Peggy Ann said sharply, her voice rising. "I had no knowledge until it was too late. You think I would have let one of my top assets be slaughtered like that?"

"You think you can convince the police of that? Once they know that you owned him, they'll know that *you* arranged for the date between him and the john, and they'll come after you."

Peggy Ann shook her head. "That is not going to happen. I am not afraid of the police."

Zachary could feel Joss's frustration that she was not making any headway with Peggy Ann. And Peggy Ann was probably right. Even if Joss told the police that Peggy Ann had been the one to set up the encounter between the john and Connor, the chances that Peggy Ann would go to prison over it were very slim. They would have to prove Peggy Ann knew the john was dangerous.

51

There are rules in this organization, right?" Zachary asked.

Peggy Ann and Joss both looked at him in irritation. Joss's mouth was a thin, straight line. She would take the stuffing out of him once they were out of the house. It was the second time he had spoken up, and this time was a bigger infraction.

"We have rules," Peggy Ann agreed. "And we have our own system for dealing with infractions. Eyler was disciplined, whether or not anyone thinks he deserved a harsher punishment. And that's the end of it. We don't deal with the justice system."

"There must be rules against stealing other people's assets. Like when you took Connor from Eyler."

Peggy Ann looked at Joss. "Who is this guy? I didn't take Connor from Eyler! Eyler disposed of him and I took care of him on my own. This was all adjudicated years ago. It's ancient history."

"But *Aster* isn't ancient history. And her case hasn't been adjudicated."

There was silence in the room, like everyone had taken a breath in and held it. Zachary looked deliberately from Joss to Peggy Ann.

"Didn't you take Aster when you knew she belonged to someone else?"

"You're an idiot!" Peggy Ann snapped. "You don't know what you're talking about. Aster was Eyler's, and he's dead."

"And who gave you his assets?"

Peggy stared at him through narrowed eyes, not answering. Zachary's heart was thumping hard. Joss and Luke had both indicated that Peggy and Eyler were competitors. Luke had told him before that when one trafficker died, his boss absorbed his business. So Eyler's girls would not go to Peggy, but to Eyler's boss. More than likely, Peggy Ann had snatched Aster and she was only bluffing about it being a legitimate acquisition.

"Besides," Zachary went on, going all-in on his own bluff, "Aster wasn't Eyler's anymore. She was Joss's. Eyler gave her to Joss before he was killed."

"He did not," Peggy Ann said tightly.

"She kept running away. Joss was... trying to convince Eyler to leave town, and he didn't want anything else to do with her. So he said that Joss could have Aster. He didn't want to have to deal with her anymore."

Peggy Ann's eyes cut to Joss, considering this. Joss's chin went up a little, challenging her. Neither one said anything as they measured each other up and Peggy Ann weighed this new story.

"There had already been trouble between you and Eyler," Zachary pointed out. "Are you really going to try to convince Gordo that Eyler gave *you* Aster?"

There was a gasp from Joss when he said Gordo's name. Zachary belatedly remembered her warning not to even mention it out loud.

His use of Gordo's name seemed to have the same effect on Peggy Ann, whose face drained of color. Zachary decided to push it further.

"First, you take Connor from Eyler. He's furious, but the organization rules in your favor and says that you can keep him. Without having paid or traded Eyler anything. Then you supply Connor to an embargoed john, and he's killed, getting lots of attention from the cops. And now, someone knifes Eyler in his own hotel room and you somehow acquire one of his girls. You think that Gordo is going to give Aster to you? Why? Because he gave you Connor? You screwed that up royally, didn't you?"

Peggy Ann's face was a white stone mask. Zachary didn't even see her signal her bodyguard but, out of the corner or his eye, he saw the big man peel himself away from the wall and take a run at Zachary.

Zachary was much too slow to react. Never athletic even as a teenager and having had to relearn how to walk and move after his spinal cord injury, his reaction to seeing the guard come at him was delayed by what seemed like hours. Before he could turn and attempt an escape, the guard had a tight hold on Zachary with his beefy arm wrapped around Zachary's throat. Zachary first gagged and then tried to inhale and found his air supply had been cut off.

"You want *another* body to explain?" Joss asked coolly.

Peggy Ann didn't say anything, but must have made a sign to the bodyguard. He released the pressure on Zachary's throat, allowing Zachary to take a deep breath.

"I don't know what game you're playing at," Peggy Ann growled, "but those accusations will not stick. I'm well-respected. I follow the rules and everyone, including my bosses, knows it."

"You think you're safe," Zachary's voice was higher than usual and raspy. "And then someone stabs you in the back." He tried to remember exactly what it was Luke had said. "You put your trust in someone, and they pull the rug out from under you. How many people in the organization do you really trust not to turn on you the first minute they smell blood in the water?"

"Get them out of here," Peggy Ann said. "I need to think. Lock them up while I figure this out."

The guard released Zachary's throat, but held on to his arm. He jerked his head at Joss, indicating that she should go with him. Zachary didn't know whether to hope that she cooperated and came with him and kept him company or made a break for it, realizing that the guard would be occupied with Zachary already and would not be able to go after her. She probably couldn't make it out of the house, but she could try.

Joss took a quick look around the room and did not try to run. She went along with the guard, with Zachary, out of the room, down the hall, down the stairs, and down another set of stairs in the back of the building that led to a cool, windowless basement.

52

"What the hell was that?" Joss demanded when the guard left them, shutting the door behind him. "Didn't I tell you not to say anything? You were supposed to be here just for numbers. Just for moral support. Not to insert yourself into the middle of the discussion and stir things up! You haven't got a clue how things work in an organization like this!"

"You weren't getting anywhere with your threat to take it to the police," Zachary pointed out, trying to stay calm in the face of her anger. As the oldest child, tasked with the responsibility for all of the others, Joss had been a disciplinarian. If he stepped out of line, she was fully within her appointed family role to smack him around or impose whatever consequence she thought appropriate. And while she had only been a child, some of those punishments had served as very painful lessons he would remember for a long time. It wasn't easy to face her fury without flinching.

"Maybe not," Joss snapped. "But at least with my approach, we would be leaving here alive."

"Without Aster."

"There was only ever a slight chance that we were going to be able to get her. I wasn't counting on it."

"Well…" Zachary tried to think of a bright side to the situation or an excuse for doing what he had done. But he couldn't think of either. He sat down on the floor, his back against the wall. The cold floor was really going to be a pain. "We're not dead yet."

"Always little Miss Sunshine, aren't you?"

Zachary closed his eyes, thinking that it would only be a few minutes before Peggy Ann figured out the best way to dispose of them. But after sitting there like that for what he estimated was half an hour, he was getting too restless to stay still. He opened his eyes and looked around, cataloging everything he could about the room. There wasn't much to see. It was probably intended to be used as a storage room. Hard tile floor over concrete. No windows. No furniture. A suspended ceiling, above which they could probably see the pipes leading to the upper floors if they were to pop one of the tiles. There was a plugin on each wall, but no cords plugged into them. The walls appeared to be poured concrete rather than wallboard. Not something anyone could break through.

A good room to hold someone prisoner in.

Maybe when Peggy Ann had built extra storage rooms into her basement, she had planned to use them as temporary detainment areas. As a human trafficker, she would frequently have people on her hands who needed temporary housing while she and the other traffickers dealt with business arrangements. Zachary didn't think she would use her house for them regularly, but she might occasionally need to house a person or two.

The bodyguard hadn't needed any prompting as to where to put them when Peggy Ann had said to lock them up.

"What are we going to do?" he asked Joss.

"*Now* you want my direction? What we are going to do is wait here like sitting ducks until she decides what she wants done with us. Then we're not going to have much choice but to go along with whatever she decides."

They sat in silence.

"Do you really have a system set up that will leak information about them if something happens to you?" Zachary asked.

Joss looked at him and didn't answer.

Zachary felt his pockets. "They didn't take our phones. We can call for help."

Joss paid him no attention as he turned his phone on and tapped the phone app.

No service

"There's no signal down here," he told her.

"Brilliant."

Of course there wasn't any signal. Joss hadn't even needed to check. But then, she had been in the business for a long time. As she had been trafficked, she had probably sat in a number of rooms like that one. Completely cut off from the world. So much that she might start to wonder if the rest of the world even existed anymore. Whether everyone other than her bosses and johns she dealt with had ceased to exist.

We are going to sit and wait.

Something changed even before Zachary could hear footsteps in the hallway outside. A drop in the air pressure when a door was opened, maybe. Something stirred and alerted his animal brain that someone was coming.

Joss looked up too, and they both strained their ears, then eventually heard the footsteps. Just one set, Zachary thought. Not the two people that would be required to handle them both securely. But then, maybe all he needed was a gun or a couple of pairs of handcuffs. Zachary wasn't exactly a ninja.

It didn't occur to him until then that they hadn't even bothered to take Joss's gun from her. Joss had gone with the bodyguard as directed and had not tried to shoot her way out. She had been put in that room with him without protest, and she hadn't discussed any escape plan with Zachary while they had been in there. But what was she going to do? Shoot whoever opened the door to get them? And then what? They wouldn't be able to get out of the building without running into other members of Peggy Ann's crew. Zachary didn't know how many bullets a gun like Joss's had, but it wasn't a TV show. They weren't going to be able to shoot their way out.

The door opened. Zachary followed Joss's lead and stayed sitting on the floor, waiting. It was a different man, not the bodyguard. He looked at the two of them and scowled.

"Get up. Time to go."

"Where are we going?" Zachary questioned as he got up. He couldn't help himself. Even though he might not want to know the answer, he couldn't just follow without asking.

"Shut up."

Zachary glanced at Joss, hoping for some sign from her as to what he should do. She got to her feet, saying nothing. She didn't reach for her gun. She didn't complain about their treatment or ask what was happening. She looked as if this were all routine. Boring, even. He didn't know how she could not show any anxiety over what was going to happen to them. His guts were writhing so bad he didn't think he could stand up straight to go with the man.

Joss touched him lightly on the back to usher him ahead of her. He was soothed by her touch, even though it was fleeting and she barely touched him. Just feeling her there, knowing she was behind him, was comforting. She didn't have to say anything. He knew that she was telling him to stay cool and not say or do anything stupid. In his head, he promised her that he wouldn't.

They went with the man, back upstairs to the main floor, then up the grand staircase to the second floor, and into Peggy Ann's office. She wasn't there. The room was empty.

"Sit down." The man pointed to the upholstered chairs in front of Peggy Ann's desk. Zachary looked around. There was another door in the corner of the room. It did not look like a closet.

"Is that a bathroom? I could really use one... you know... while we're waiting..."

The man rolled his eyes and gave a nod. Zachary got up, made a beeline to the door, and let himself into a small, sparkling clean bathroom. He let out a sigh and was as quick as he could be, not wanting to be caught with his pants down—literally—when Peggy Ann returned to deal with them.

He returned to his seat in the office, feeling much more relaxed and human. He was still anxious and had no idea how everything would play out, but felt more in control of himself and his body. Joss gave him a look of exasperation when he sat down beside her. Zachary shrugged. Despite his varied childhood and private investigator experiences, this was not the way he was accustomed to being treated.

The door opened and Peggy Ann walked in and sat down at her desk. Zachary assumed the big, black desk made her feel stronger and more secure. It was physically imposing when she was not. She looked directly at Joss.

"Take my advice and don't ever bring him here again."

Joss raised an eyebrow but didn't say anything. Zachary's heart started to thump, finally hopeful. If he and Joss were going to come back, they would have to be alive. There wouldn't have been any point in saying it if Joss and Zachary, or even just Zachary, was going to be dead.

"You are going to stay away from anyone in the organization." Peggy Ann leaned forward on her desk, her jaw set, speaking through gritted teeth. "You are not going to keep stirring things up and getting in my way. You are not going to communicate anything to… anyone over my head."

As Joss had suggested, Peggy Ann would not even say Gordo's name.

"Is all of that understood?" Peggy Ann barked.

Zachary was nodding, but Joss sat there impassively. "You seem to think that you're the one with the negotiating power here."

Peggy Ann's face flushed a deep red.

"I have no desire to have anything to do with anyone in your organization," Joss said. "When I left, I planned on never having contact with any of them again. I don't want any of you operating in Kent. If you do… then expect me to get irritated by it. And that means I will have the cops in your business any time I can. And that any girls who come to me for help are going to find asylum and are not going to be forced back into service."

The tendons in Peggy Ann's throat stood out. She tried to stare Joss down, but Joss looked unconcerned.

"I know all kinds of things about you and the organization. All I'm asking for is peace and quiet. For your kind to stay out of my town and leave me alone."

Peggy Ann seemed to be speechless. Eventually, she signaled the guard. Zachary braced himself for attack. Fists, gunshot, or another arm around his throat. He didn't know what to expect. But the guard stepped out of the room. There were voices in the hall, and then the man returned. Leading a blond, round-faced girl by the arm.

Aster.

Zachary didn't know whether to believe it.

Maybe all three of them were going to be executed. That would show everyone not to threaten a cartel boss in her own house. Maybe Peggy Ann had decided she didn't care what would leak out once Joss was killed.

"Go." Peggy Ann made a flicking motion with her fingers. "Take her and go."

Zachary was the first one to his feet. Joss was slower to get up. She nodded vaguely in Peggy Ann's direction.

"Thank you. I trust we won't have to see each other again."

She looked at the guard as they approached him. "Let her go."

The man looked surprised. He looked at Aster, then released her arm. Joss touched her gently on the shoulder.

"Come on. Let's go."

Aster walked beside Joss. Zachary brought up the rear. They walked out to the car without a word. The sky was beginning to get dark. Zachary opened one of the back doors and slid in, letting Aster ride shotgun. Aster's arms were crossed and her hands pulled into her long sleeves. She walked like a zombie, uncertain as to what was going on, without a will of her own. Zachary didn't say anything as Joss shifted the car into drive and hit the gas. When they got past the big, barred gates, he sighed in relief but still didn't speak until they got to the highway.

"That was... something."

Joss glanced over her shoulder at him. "You did okay," she said grudgingly.

"I did good?"

"You did good."

53

Zachary sat back. Joss didn't give out praise lightly. He couldn't remember the last time she had praised him for anything. He wasn't sure she ever had. It was a new experience.

He watched the scenery pass by the window, feeling drowsy. The after-effects of the adrenaline. Now that he was safe, it was time to replenish his stores. He watched the soft glow of the sunset changing from oranges to deep blue, with the stars creeping out.

"Wake up, baby brother. I'm not carrying you into the house."

Zachary rubbed his eyes and looked around. He hadn't intended to let himself fall asleep.

"Though I probably could," Joss went on. "What do you weigh? A buck? Buck twenty-five?"

"I don't know," Zachary groaned. He stretched and stumbled out of the car. Though, of course, he did know. The doctor tracked his weight closely, making sure he didn't stall in his weight gain.

Joss opened Aster's door and encouraged her to get out and go into the house. She must have fallen asleep too. Zachary could certainly understand why. He was exhausted after just a few hours languishing in Peggy Ann's basement room. Aster had been there for days, or maybe somewhere worse. Jocelyn had said that Peggy Ann would not have her girls living in the house, but somewhere else. Some dirty little apartment like Madison had been living in when Zachary tracked her down. Probably several of them in one apartment.

Zachary let Joss and Aster go ahead of him again, Joss nudging Aster along until they reached the house. The outside light was on, and the door, when Joss tried it, was unlocked.

The other girls were watching for them and crowded around Aster when she walked in the door, hugging her and greeting her with high-pitched, excited voices. Aster stood there, seeming not to even be taking it in. Eventually, the excitement died down, and Joss led Aster to the couch and let her sit down. The other girls were quiet, whispering to each other.

"Why don't you girls go clean up the kitchen and let me talk to Aster?" Joss directed.

Eventually, the other girls left them alone. Just Joss, Aster, and Zachary. Zachary studied Aster with concern. He wasn't sure whether she was drugged, hurt, or traumatized. Maybe all three. She seemed very distant and unsure, curled up into herself.

"Can you tell me what happened?" Joss asked gently. Zachary appreciated this soft, gentle version of Joss. He didn't jump in, but let Joss take charge. She was the one who knew Aster. Zachary only knew her from her pictures.

Aster shook her head.

"Come on," Joss coaxed. "I need you to tell me what happened. You left the house? You were supposed to stay here and keep safe." Joss shook her head. "I blame Luke for always going out, making you feel like you were missing out on something."

Aster sniffled. "Not Luke's fault."

"Not this time, no. You made that decision for yourself. What was it? You wanted to go out to meet with friends? Dance? Where did you go?"

"No. I just... I wasn't feeling good. I needed to get some fresh air. That's all." She blinked; eyelashes wet with tears.

Zachary's heart went out to her. Who knew what she had been through at Peggy Ann's hands and, before that, with Eyler. Was she one of Eyler's "grabs"? Someone he had just snatched off the street and forced into working for him? Where had she been before that? With her own family? Homeless on the street?

Joss frowned at Aster, the crease between her eyebrows deepening. "You weren't feeling good and needed some fresh air," she repeated flatly.

Aster nodded. She rubbed both eyes with the heels of her hands.

"Sounds to me like you were jonesing."

"I never said that!" Aster's voice rose in pitch.

"Tell me you weren't."

Several seconds passed in silence. Aster shrugged, her lips forming a pout. "Maybe. I needed some air. I couldn't just stay cooped up here."

"So you went for a walk."

"Yeah."

"To get some fresh air."

"Yeah. That's what I said."

Joss shook her head. "You can't BS an old addict. An addict doesn't go out for fresh air. She goes out for drugs."

Aster's mouth twisted into a snarl. "No."

"Yeah? If I tested you right now, what would I find?"

"Peggy Ann gave me something. That's not *my* fault."

Luke had said that the traffickers would get new recruits addicted to get them to do what they wanted. Someone hurting for a fix would do almost anything for the next dose. But Joss's expression was hard. She wasn't buying Aster's excuse.

"You didn't go out for a walk. You went out to buy."

"No." Aster shook her head again, tears falling down her cheeks. "I didn't!"

"Why do you think there are rules about staying in the house? When you go out there, especially to buy, people can see you. They're watching for you, and they'll act the moment they see you."

"I don't have any money."

Joss was being too hard on Aster, assuming she knew what had happened based on her own experiences. But Aster wasn't Jocelyn. Zachary opened his mouth to interrupt and point this out. Joss was victim-blaming, acting like it was Aster's own fault she'd been kidnapped by Peggy Ann's goons. It wasn't Aster's fault that she'd been targeted. All she had done was go out for a walk to clear her head.

54

Joss shot Zachary a look before he could voice his opinion. "You don't need money to get drugs if you know the right places to go," she told Aster, but Zachary knew she was talking to him. "The people to go to."

"You think I wanted to go back there?" Aster's voice was teary. "You think I deserved what I got?"

"I think you needed a fix and would do anything to get it, including turning yourself back in to the organization, because you knew they would give you what you needed if you went back to work for them."

"You think I wanted to hook?"

"I think you needed drugs."

"It might be easy for you," Aster snapped, "but it isn't for everyone. Just because you managed to get out, you think it means anyone else can. As long as they're strong enough." She wiped her nose on her arm. "But not everyone is as strong as you!"

"I don't expect you to just go cold turkey all by yourself. There are other people here to help you. I told you about the detox I could get you into. You didn't have to just tough it out without any help."

"You're all high and mighty. Think that you're better than any of us."

Joss shook her head. "Where do you want to go? Whatever program you want, I'll get you into it. Or back to your family. You just say what you're willing to do, and I'll help you."

"I don't know." Aster pulled at a lock of hair and wrapped it around her finger. "I'm not like you."

Joss sighed. "Until you're ready to commit... I can't help you."

"You're kicking me out? Well, why not? You already kicked Luke to the curb."

Zachary looked at Joss, shocked by Aster's accusation. Joss shook her head. "I didn't kick Luke to the curb. I didn't kick anyone out. I haven't kicked you out. Luke isn't here because he got himself into trouble. That had nothing to do with me."

"Is he okay?" Aster continued to sniffle. "If anything happened to Luke..."

"Okay? I guess he's okay. He's alive. They'll make sure he stays that way so they can take him to trial and put him in prison for twenty to life. Sure, he's fine."

A fresh burst of tears from Aster. "He's the only one here who understood me. He cared. He would go out with me, and we would just have a good time, and he would listen. He—he was a really good listener."

"I wish he hadn't taken you out. Taking you where you could be seen, where Eyler's men could find you and take you back or report to him on your movements... he didn't do you any favors. He put you in danger."

"It wasn't Luke's idea. It was mine. He just came along to keep me company."

"He should have told you to stay home."

"It's all my fault. If it wasn't for me, he wouldn't have..."

Aster was the reason Luke had gone to see Eyler. To tell him to back off and leave her alone. He knew about Eyler through Connor, and knew what had happened to Connor. He didn't want to see it happen to another kid, especially fresh-faced Aster, who was happy to hang out with him and dance. She had met Rhys virtually and exchanged messages with him. They had sent photos back and forth. Involved Rhys in the happy times, even though he couldn't join them, and it all had to remain a secret from Zachary, Vera, and Joss. Luke took on the role of her protector.

"Luke made his own choices," Joss said. "And some of them were not good choices."

Zachary rubbed the bridge of his nose, thinking over his notes and the various interviews he had done since first finding out that Luke was in trouble.

"Where were you the night Eyler was killed?" he asked Aster.

"I was here!" Aster looked at Joss for her to confirm the fact to Zachary.

Joss nodded. "She was here."

"All night?"

Joss's eyes slid over to Aster. "Why?"

"Are you sure she didn't go out for a few hours to get drugs or do something with Luke?"

Joss leaned her head back and sucked in her cheeks, studying Aster. "I can't sit up all night making sure that no one leaves her bed. I check at night. I know who is here in the morning. But if they sneak out and put themselves in danger, there isn't anything I can do about that."

"I didn't," Aster insisted. Fingers poking out of her sleeve, she pulled on a lock of hair, twisting it around and around.

But Zachary was starting to put it together. For years, Luke had stayed away from Eyler. He didn't go after the man when Connor was killed. He'd probably only been fourteen at the time, small and vulnerable. Not able to face off against a big man like Eyler. When he had gone out with Aster and been approached by someone wanting to take her back to Eyler, Luke had been quick to defend her, but he didn't kill the messenger or go to Eyler's hotel room to confront him at that point, at the peak of his anger. He had made threats, but he hadn't been violent.

But a few days later, he had gone to Eyler's room. Possibly unarmed. And had killed him.

Why?

"You went back to Eyler," Zachary suggested to Aster. "You were looking for drugs, and you knew he had the good stuff. Eyler was more generous with drugs than most of the bosses. Gave you more, higher-quality stuff. You didn't have any money, but you knew he would give it to you if you went back to work for him."

"He was a pig," Aster spat. "First client of the night was always him."

Joss nodded her understanding. "And once you'd satisfied him, you would get your drugs. The next dose, anyway."

"He was…" Aster covered her mouth to hide her expression. Her eyes squeezed shut and more tears ran down her face. Joss looked unmoved by her emotion. Joss had been in the business for a long time and had probably seen it all. She was of the opinion that the best thing to do was to compartmentalize. Lock it away in a box and, if possible, don't revisit it. Aster covered her face with both hands. "He likes to hurt," she said, voice muffled by her hands. "He said not to tell anyone, but the things he does..."

She sobbed, unable to tell them any more. Zachary looked at Joss, wondering if maybe he should leave. Maybe Aster would be able to tell Joss more, woman-to-woman. Zachary being there was probably hampering her. Joss gave a slight shake of her head, surprising him. He raised his brows in question, but stayed where he was.

He was the one who Aster has started talking to, so maybe something about him made her trust him. Like she had trusted Luke. She hadn't stayed at home with the other girls, relying on their help and association, but had gone out with Luke to have a good time.

"He hurt you," Zachary repeated. "Luke said he was like that. He enjoyed hurting his girls. Or making them suffer by withholding drugs."

Aster nodded.

"What did he do to you?"

Joss widened her eyes at Zachary, asking him if he really wanted to know.

Of course he didn't. Zachary felt sick asking the question. He didn't want to know what sorts of torture Eyler enjoyed. Zachary didn't want to think about the things that had been done to him by Archuro. He didn't want to know any of it. But Aster had been waiting for him to ask.

"He had..." Aster was gasping with sobs, her sentence broken up into bunches of words, "... a knife. Kept threatening... me and he'd start to cut me... and I screamed. He'd cover my... mouth or kiss me to muffle it... laughing. No one... would hear... me over the music..." She took a deep, shuddering breath, trying to collect herself. "I wouldn't do it... tried to get... away. Said I didn't want to... but he put his hands... around my throat..."

She broke off, sobbing more. Zachary had been trying to keep himself aloof, to be alert to the fact that she could be lying and dramatizing to make herself look good. Some people were great at turning on the water-works and garnering sympathy. But he didn't believe that Aster's distress was faked. He touched her hand tentatively and, when she didn't pull back, he covered her hand with his own as if he were trying to warm it up.

Joss moved as well, first putting her hand on Aster's shoulder, and then moving it to unbutton the top couple of buttons on Aster's blouse. There were dusky bruises around Aster's throat. She was not lying about the fact that he'd choked her.

Aster turned her hand to hold Zachary's, her grip painfully tight. "He

743

was gonna kill me." She breathed shallowly, no longer sobbing, but forming her words carefully. "I knew he decided I wasn't worth his time and was gonna kill me."

Zachary could have tried to argue, to say that she couldn't know what Eyler had intended, that Eyler surely wouldn't dispose of a valuable asset so soon. But Luke had told him Connor's story. Maybe he'd told it to Aster too.

55

T he knife was right there," Aster squeezed harder, making Zachary wince. He was worried that she was going to end up breaking bones. But he was too engrossed in her story to make her let go. He didn't want to do anything to interrupt her. She had started to unburden herself and, as she got it out, she was calming down. She was no longer sobbing, maybe past the point where she could feel the fear and anxiety anymore. "I guess he thought it was out of my reach, or that I would pass out right away. Maybe he just thought... I wouldn't dare."

Zachary nodded, encouraging her to go on.

"I could reach. And I... I just drove it in as hard as I could. He kind of... collapsed on top of me, and I rolled him over. And I stabbed him again. I don't know how many times, until he stopped moving or making noises."

Zachary pulled his gaze away from Aster to look at Joss. He wondered, at first, if Joss had known this all the time and been part of the cover-up. But Joss's pale, pinched expression told him she had not. She had believed that it was Luke, had not guessed that Luke was covering up for someone else.

Aster had been there at bed check, and she had been there in the morning when Joss got up. Joss hadn't guessed that Aster had been gone for several hours in the middle.

"When did Luke get there?"

"Not until it was over. I was trying to clean up. Get all the blood off so I could…" she sniffled, "go home." She let go of Zachary's hand and looked down at her own palm. It was crossed with several deep cuts. Zachary realized that both he and the police had failed to recognize the significance of Luke's unmarked palms. He had not been the one to drive the knife into Eyler again and again, his hand slipping from the handle to the blade.

"What did he do?"

"He said Eyler had been shouting." Aster shook her head at this thought. "I don't even remember that. I just… I was so scared. I just wanted him to stop, to let me go. I went because I needed drugs, but he was going to kill me."

"Luke told you that Eyler had been shouting. When? Was he shouting at you before you killed him? While he was choking you? Or when you stabbed him?"

"I don't know!" Aster's voice cracked. She waved his question away in irritation. "Who cares? He said people would be calling the police. He told me I had to get out of there before the cops got there. They couldn't find me with Eyler's body. All covered with blood. *Luke* was shouting at me, telling me how I should have kept Eyler quiet so no one would call the cops." She was outraged at this. "How was I supposed to keep him quiet?"

"He was worried about you. Trying to keep you safe."

Aster nodded. "I know. I just… I was so messed up. I couldn't think straight. Being attacked like that, and him dying… I just wanted to go home and hide."

"And he got you out of there before the police showed up."

Aster nodded. "Told me to be quiet. To take the stairs down. Pretend…" Aster tried to suppress a smile. "Pretend like I was sneaking out on Joss." She wiped both cheeks.

"Maybe if there'd been less sneaking out, this wouldn't have happened," Joss pointed out.

"I know. But… Eyler shouldn't have done that. He shouldn't have tried to kill me!"

"No," Zachary reassured her. "He shouldn't have done that."

Joss rolled her eyes at Zachary. He sighed. "What are we going to do?"

Joss rubbed Aster's back. "I'll call a lawyer. He'll tell us how to get this sorted out."

"I'm not going to jail," Aster said, sniffling and wiping her eyes, which were getting very red and puffy. Looking at the bruises on her throat,

Zachary wondered how many other marks were on her body from the encounter with Eyler, who liked to hurt people.

"Honey, it was self-defense," Joss told her. "You're not going to go to prison."

"But *Luke* is," Aster protested.

"Luke isn't going to prison either, because he wasn't the one who did it. We've been trying to figure out how to get his sentence reduced all week. You should have told me what happened."

"Luke said not to say anything. Just to go home and pretend that I'd been home all night. So that's what I did. I did what he said. He said he would get me off."

Zachary shook his head. "He shouldn't have interfered. This mess could have been avoided if the police had known what happened from the start."

56

Zachary made a large carafe of coffee in the kitchen and helped himself to a mug. He looked at his phone and frowned when he realized how late it was. It had been dark when they had reached Joss's. He should have been home long before. He was already too late to have supper with Kenzie. He was surprised that she hadn't called him. He tapped on his phone and text apps, which were not showing any alerts or recent calls. That never happened. Especially if he was so late getting home. He tapped Kenzie's name to call her, and the phone just gave three beeps and told him that the call had failed. He looked at the service icon in the top corner to make sure that he had coverage.

No service.

Zachary swore. Joss, pouring herself a cup of coffee, turned and looked at him. "What?"

"There's something wrong with the phone. No service."

"Try shutting it off and restarting it. Sometimes if you've been out of service for long enough, it stops looking to preserve battery life."

Zachary swore again, but this time just in his head. He shut the phone down, watching for everything to disappear from the screen, waited for a slow count to ten, and then held down the power button. By the time it finished going through its warm-up cycle, he could see that he had service bars. The counts of his missed calls and new texts rocketed up. Which meant he was in big trouble.

"You're looking a little green there, little brother."

"Yeah, I missed all kinds of calls and messages. Kenzie is going to think I drove off a cliff or something."

"You'd better call her."

"Good idea."

She smirked at his sarcastic tone. Zachary stared up at the ceiling rather than looking at Joss or any of the girls going in and out of the kitchen, helping themselves to coffee or trying to talk to Aster or Joss. No one wanted to talk to him, which was good. He had enough problems to deal with.

"Zachary?" Kenzie's voice was high-pitched with worry.

"I'm here. I'm sorry, everything is okay."

He braced himself for a stream of invectives. And Kenzie would be right with all of them. He'd been stupid. He should have noticed the time hours ago and checked his phone to see what was wrong with it. He should have called her before supper to tell her where he was and what was going on. He should have acted like an adult and let people know what was going on, instead of just dropping off the face of the earth.

"You're okay?" Kenzie repeated, sounding thick and choked up. "What happened?"

"There was no service. For a while. And I didn't realize that my phone hadn't reconnected when I got out of there. So I thought… I don't know what time I thought it was. I should have noticed how late it was getting. I'm so sorry."

"Did you check your messages?"

"No. I saw there were a bunch, but I just called you first. I can listen to them later."

"Yeah, and laugh at how freaked out your partner was getting. You missed therapy. Dr. Boyle called."

He hadn't even thought to call her and cancel. He'd lost track of what day it was or where he was supposed to be. He had been so caught up in the developments of the case that he'd been oblivious to the rest of the world.

"Oh, no. I lost track."

"Your calendar reminders should still go off, even if you're out of service."

"Yeah, they probably did. I've just been so focused on everything else, I never heard or felt them."

"Well, call Dr. B and let her know you're still alive. We were really worried."

"You know I'm okay right now," he pointed out. "I'm not depressed."

"You could have had an accident. Or something to do with that trafficking ring… Or something might have upset you. You were really having a hard time after hearing about what had happened to Connor. I didn't know if things had gotten worse. I don't know. I was imagining all kinds of things."

"I'm so sorry."

How was he going to tell Kenzie what had actually happened? That he'd been sitting in a basement wondering whether they were going to execute him or if there was any chance of escape. He had never really thought that they would just let him and Joss walk out of there with Aster. It had been every bit as bad as she had worried. Because he thought that they could just walk into Peggy Ann's house and negotiate for Aster's release because of some secret information that Joss held. Which he was beginning to think was just a bluff. Sure, she had worked with the cartel for a long time, but did she really know enough to have them all convicted? And if she did, did she really have the information secreted away somewhere with a release protocol if she disappeared? He was beginning to doubt all of it. She was just really good at head games.

"Where are you, then? Are you coming home?"

"Yes." Zachary pulled the phone away from his face for a moment to look at the time. It was already late and, in the morning, he was going to come straight back to talk to Luke again. "I'm at Joss's now. I'll get on my way."

"Maybe you should stay over there. Are you alert enough to drive?"

"I just had a big cup of coffee." He hadn't yet finished what was in his cup, but he would before he hit the road. "I won't fall asleep."

He expected her to tell him again to just sleep over on Joss's couch. But she didn't. She must have really been worried about him and wanted to see him, even knowing that neither of them would get very much sleep before going back to work in the morning.

"I'll be back as soon as I can," he promised.

"Don't speed. I'll see you when you get here. I'll be okay now that I know you're fine."

"Good." The guilt was a tight knot in his stomach. He knew, despite her calming words, that she'd been really upset. He didn't know whether she had gone as far as to call the police, maybe a personal call to Campbell to find out whether he knew anything. She wouldn't have been able to file a missing person report yet, but she could have called around to hospitals and morgues.

"You're going?" Joss questioned after Zachary ended the call.

"Yeah. I didn't realize that there was a problem with my phone and it had gotten so late. She was really worried. I want to get back there and reassure her that everything is fine."

Joss nodded.

"What about you?" Zachary looked toward the living room where Aster and the other girls were talking. "Are you going to get any sleep tonight?"

"No. I don't expect so. Need to get things straightened out with Aster. She's coming down hard. It isn't going to be a soft landing, and I'm going to have to talk her into talking to a lawyer."

"Do you know what's going to happen?"

"She'll probably have to turn herself in, but should be able to get out on bond because it was self-defense and nobody's going to be crying for justice for that scumbag."

"I'll be back in the morning to talk to Luke."

"Maybe we'll see you over at the jail, then."

"Good luck."

Joss nodded. "You too. I don't know that I'd want to be facing Kenzie after that stunt."

"It wasn't a stunt!" But with the way she had stood up to Peggy Ann, unflinching, he knew that Joss would never have had any problem facing Kenzie's anger, no matter how bad. He had to keep reminding himself that Kenzie wasn't Bridget and wasn't going to react like she would. Bridget would have torn a strip off of him when he called. She would not have been polite and requested that he come home. He probably would have had to sleep on the couch for a month.

57

Zachary parked the car and, by the time he had opened the door and climbed out, Kenzie was standing in the open front door waiting for him. He walked as quickly as he could without getting overly awkward and tripping. When he reached her, he put his arms around her and pulled her in close.

"I'm sorry, I'm so sorry."

"Shut up. Quit apologizing and just hold me."

"I am."

She gripped him tightly, pressing herself against him. Zachary remembered how worried he had been when Tyrrell had disappeared. Not that he had known the first day, or anywhere near the beginning. By the time he knew Tyrrell had disappeared, it had been weeks, and Zachary was frantic to find him or to find out what had happened to him. He tried to imagine what it would be like to suddenly not be able to get ahold of Kenzie. If phone calls and texts and every other imaginable method failed and he had no idea what had happened to her. It was inconceivable. He had no idea how he would have handled it. A nervous breakdown, probably.

Eventually, Kenzie's grip on him relaxed and she pulled back a little. "Better come in. The neighbors are going to be wondering what's going on."

Zachary stepped into the house. Kenzie touched his face, looking into his eyes. She took a deep breath and let it out. "Do you need anything? A bite to eat before bed? I don't suppose you remembered to eat, if you didn't even think to look at the time."

"No. But it can wait. I'm not hungry."

"You're late on your night meds."

"Uh, yes." Zachary nodded his agreement. And she was right to point it out, because he needed to take some of them with food. "I guess I'd better have something small, then."

She kept a hand on his arm all the way into the kitchen as if to reassure herself that he was okay, that he was there, not just a figment of her imagination.

"What can I do?"

"Sit." She pointed to his chair. "I don't want you in the way today. I don't have the emotional resources."

If he were helping her get things ready, it should be less for her to deal with, not more. But Zachary kept his mouth shut and didn't argue the point. He had asked her what she wanted, and she had answered clearly. Arguing opinions was not going to do anyone good, particularly when they were both so drained.

Zachary sat down as he was told. He looked through the doorway to the living room to check his car through the window and make sure that it was safe. He didn't even remember shutting and locking the doors, but he could see that they were all shut. He pulled out his key fob and hit the lock button a couple of times to lock and arm it. Then he noticed the dark form lying on the couch in the dim living room.

Tyrrell.

It made sense, of course, that he had come over when Kenzie had called around looking for anyone who might have heard from Zachary. He had been there to support her and do what he could to try to track down Zachary, just as Zachary had once helped to track down him.

"How long has Tyrrell been here?"

"Early evening. Dr. B called to say that you had missed your appointment, and I wasn't really worried for a couple of hours. I know that sometimes you just get distracted and might have forgotten about it. But when you didn't come home and didn't answer any calls or texts, we started to get concerned. I couldn't find you on that app. Location unknown. I guess that's just because you didn't have service, but I was thinking all kinds of things."

Kenzie warmed up some leftovers, put them on the table in front of Zachary, and filled a glass of water before sitting down to join him. She didn't have anything to eat, but she sat and stared at him. He ate a few bites of the food and tried to think of what to say other than to apologize again, which she was tired of. He downed his night meds and looked down at his plate, considering whether he was going to eat anything more. Maybe a couple more bites, just to make sure that the pills didn't give him heartburn or nausea.

"So… find anything out today?" Kenzie asked casually.

"Um… yeah. Big day." Zachary took a deep breath in and let it out. "It wasn't Luke who killed Eyler."

"What? Are you kidding me? But he admitted it."

"He was covering to protect someone else. I'll get his story tomorrow. I just… believed everyone who said that he had done it."

"Well… there was plenty of evidence pointing in that direction. Found holding the murder weapon, dripping with blood."

Zachary nodded. "But that didn't mean that he'd just killed Eyler, like they said. There was a few minutes between the disturbance and when the police got there… enough time that he should have been out of there. He could have ditched the weapon in a sewer grate and gone somewhere to arrange an alibi. But he didn't do that. He intentionally stayed there to get caught so that the police wouldn't be looking for anyone else."

58

L uke." Kenzie shook her head. "Somebody needs to give that boy a talking to."

"You and Joss can flip for it. Or maybe you should both give him a talking to and hope that it will actually stick."

Kenzie nodded her agreement. "So, how did you figure that out, Mr. PI? You were still convinced this morning that he was the culprit and were looking for ways to get his sentence reduced."

"Well… I went looking for Aster, the girl in the background of the video. And I guess… that triggered the rest. Started all of the dominoes falling."

"Well, good job for noticing her in the video. I guess no one else did."

"Oh, I'll have to message Rhys tomorrow. He was the one who gave me Aster's picture so I *could* recognize her. He'll be glad to hear that Luke will be getting out."

"I'm sure he will," Kenzie agreed. "What happened when you went to talk to Luke about her?"

"He gave away that Aster was supposed to be at home with Joss. So, I went to Joss's to find out."

"And was she there?"

"No. Turns out that she had gone out… looking for drugs."

"She's an addict?"

"Most of these kids are. It's one of the ways the bosses keep them on the hook. Keep them supplied with drugs. If they ever try to leave, they have to leave that supply pipeline behind. If they ever refuse to do a job, their boss withholds the drugs. An easy way to keep them under their control."

Kenzie nodded. "These poor kids. When I think about the stuff that they have to go through."

"They're not all kids. Joss was in the business for a long time."

"I know, but they generally start as kids. That's the best time to get them. When they are the most vulnerable. And what happens after that... well, it's not exactly their fault. Once they're trapped in this cycle of addiction and abuse, and with how powerful these cartels are. It's scary."

"Yeah. So, she went back looking for drugs. Back to Eyler. One thing led to another..." Kenzie didn't need to know all of the sordid details of what had happened to Aster. "And she ended up killing him in self-defense. Luke shows up, gets her out of there, and covers up for her. Taking all of the heat himself."

"But if it was self-defense, then it was justified. She can get off free, or with a minimal sentence."

"Yeah. I have to talk to Luke about it tomorrow. I don't know what he was thinking. He should never have been there in the first place, but when he saw what had happened, he shouldn't have stepped in like that. It would have been better if Aster had stayed and faced the cops, told them that she had been attacked."

"Wow. That's quite a revelation. You managed to track down Aster...?"

"Uh, yes. She had been picked up by another trafficker. Peggy Ann." Zachary frowned, thinking about it. "I don't know whether she just wanted to run Aster, to pick up another asset for free, or whether she did it to try to control Joss..."

Kenzie's eyebrows went up. "To try to control Joss? How? In what way?"

"Well, Joss has been rescuing girls from the organization. She had rescued Aster already and she was living at the house with Joss. She's got a whole house full of them. Joss has been a thorn in the side of these traffickers, calling the police to report them, trying to drive them out of town. I guess maybe Peggy Ann figured that if she got her hands on one of these girls, she could hold her hostage. Force Joss to back off."

"Jocelyn doesn't strike me as the type to be intimidated too easily," Kenzie said dryly.

"Uh… no. You should have seen her today. I couldn't believe the way she stood up to Peggy Ann and her goons."

"Oh…?"

Zachary licked his lips. He should have kept his mouth shut. He should not have told Kenzie that he had seen Joss stand up to the traffickers. If he explained the details to her, she would not be happy about it. She would realize that all of her worries about him when he had been unreachable had been justified. And then the next time she couldn't reach him, it would be that much harder for her to believe that everything was okay and he just happened to be out of service or not have noticed her phone call.

He took a sip of the water, looking around the kitchen, trying to think of something else to tell her about. If he could just distract her so that she wouldn't realize he had not answered her inquiry…

"But how was your day at the morgue? I've been telling you all about my day, but you haven't told me anything about yours. I shouldn't be monopolizing our time together." He looked at his phone to see what time it was. "We should be in bed."

"Tell me about Joss facing Peggy Ann." Kenzie's voice was even and firm. Zachary swallowed.

"That's kind of a long story. We should probably leave it to tomorrow, so we can get a few hours in tonight. If you want to be in good shape for work…"

"Whose idea was it to confront Peggy Ann? And why were *you* there?"

"It wasn't my idea," Zachary protested immediately, and was glad that he could tell the truth about this point. "Joss decided that the only way she was going to be able to negotiate successfully for Aster's release was to go in person."

"Really."

Zachary nodded eagerly. "Yes. It was her idea, not mine. I didn't just dive into it."

"And… she asked you to go with her?"

"Well…" Zachary looked down, studying his fingernails. He needed to take better care of them. A couple were ragged and needed to be smoothed down with an emery board. He thought that he had probably messed them up on the concrete in the basement room. While he had done his best to copy Jocelyn's lead and remain calm, it had been hard to keep his body still and under his control, and he had scratched and scraped at the concrete floor while trying to think his way out.

"You volunteered?"

757

"I couldn't let her go by herself. That would have been too dangerous. Just Joss, and all of Peggy Ann's crew? I had to go with her, at least make it look like she had other people behind her."

"Because it isn't as easy to shoot two people as it is to shoot one?"

"Well…" Zachary struggled to explain his thought processes to her. "You see… Joss has been threatening these guys. Peggy Ann and the other traffickers. Telling them that if they don't get out of her territory, she is going to leak information about them to the police." Kenzie opened her mouth to respond, but Zachary held up his hand to stop her, not yet finished with his explanation. "And she has said that if they kill her, the information will leak out after she dies. That she's made contingency plans so that killing her won't solve their problems, it will make them worse."

Kenzie looked bemused. "Okay…?"

"So… I needed them to see that she wasn't alone. That she had friends and other people behind her. That she wasn't just bluffing, but might have set up this plan to have other people spread the information if she died."

"But you couldn't very well spread it if you were dead."

"Well, we never said it explicitly that way. It was just… to give an impression. And I knew that Peggy Ann wouldn't see Joss alone, that she would have at least one other person in the room to keep her safe. It would look unbalanced if Joss met her by herself."

Kenzie stared at him, processing this. "And you managed to convince Joss of this?"

"Yes."

She shook her head slowly. "You and Joss thought that the best way to get Aster back, rather than going to the police about this girl being held hostage by human traffickers, was to go and confront this boss face-to-face."

59

Zachary chewed on the inside of his cheek. The way that Kenzie said it made it sound so ridiculous. "The police are already trying to get enough evidence to prosecute these people. They've already got all different agencies trying to shut them down. Going to them about this one hooker that we think is being held by this one pimp against her will won't get anything done. When Madison was with Luke, and I got the police to go to bust him, there was nothing they could do. She told them that she wanted to stay with him, denied that anything was going on, and they didn't have any evidence, any way to take her back away from him. It would have been the same with Aster. If they could find her—and Joss and I didn't know where she was being held—then she would just say that she was there by choice."

"Why? If she was being held against her will, why wouldn't she say so? If she knew that the police could get her out, and she could go back to Joss, that's what she would do."

"No. She wouldn't. They are conditioned to only do what their bosses tell them to. If they don't, the drugs will dry up, they will be hunted and beaten, their loved ones will be killed. They don't have control over their own lives. They have to do what they are told."

"If Aster turned on Peggy Ann and told the police that she had been held against her own will, then they would arrest Peggy Ann. She wouldn't be able to do anything to hurt Aster."

"She'd bail out in a day. Or her goons would go ahead and track down all of Aster's friends and family and hurt them. She wouldn't be able to get drugs anymore and would have to find a new source. Even if she tried to stay away from the organization, they could still have hurt her. And if they did track her down in person…"

Kenzie could fill in that part herself. She looked like she still wanted to argue that Joss and Zachary should have gone to the local police, but didn't have enough ammunition to do so. "So, you and Joss formulated this brilliant plan to go negotiate for her release."

"It worked," Zachary pointed out, a little stung by her remark. "We did it. We managed to get Aster out of there. She's back with Joss. And Peggy Ann knows that Joss has dirt on her that would make her look bad in front of her bosses, not just give the police a reason to arrest her."

"What dirt?"

Zachary waved his hand, tired and not wanting to get into it all. If he could just gloss over what had happened at Peggy Ann's house, they could get to bed. He really wanted to just lie down with her and cuddle and let the stress and anxieties of the day roll away.

"Another time. I'm beat."

Kenzie grunted, dissatisfied. "When exactly did you lose your phone service? You forgot to mention that part."

"Uh—when we were at Peggy Ann's. And I didn't realize that my phone hadn't reconnected when we got away from there."

"Does she have a signal jammer or something? How can she make calls if she has no service? I don't see how you could run a cartel like that without any phone service."

"Well, even with a jammer, there could still be places where she *could* get a signal. Or she could shut it off when she wanted to make a call…"

Kenzie stared at him, clearly seeing that he was just throwing out whatever he could to distract her from the fact that he wasn't answering. "I think there's more to it than that," she said quietly. "Don't lie to me. You know the ground rules we laid down in couple's therapy. If you don't want to answer, tell me you don't want to answer. Don't lie to me."

"I didn't lie…"

"Are you going to tell me the truth? Or tell me that you don't want to answer?"

Zachary considered, weighing one against the other. He could just tell her that he didn't want to answer, and they would be done with that part of the conversation. Kenzie would be forced to talk to him about other things rather than continuing in the same vein after he had told her no. But then she would know that he was keeping something from her, and she would probably guess that it was because he had been in danger and didn't want to tell her about it.

He sighed. "It wasn't because of a signal jammer. As far as I know. There could have been one, but… there was a lot of concrete in the building. It was probably blocking the signal."

"Were you in some kind of bunker? Or is this some kind of industrial building?"

"Uh… bunker would be a closer guess. We were in the basement. For a while."

"I see."

She probably did see far more than he wanted her to know.

"We were fine. No one hurt either of us. We were just… detained for a while so that Peggy Ann could figure out what to do and get Aster back from wherever she was being held. It was good, really, because it meant that she was considering what Joss had and deciding how to respond."

"Or whether to take the chance of just getting it over with and killing both of you. Take the risk that Joss was bluffing or that the information wouldn't be enough to get her in trouble."

"I don't think that was ever a serious consideration," Zachary told her uncomfortably.

"No? You felt safe and secure the whole time you were there?"

Of course he hadn't, and Kenzie knew it. She saw right through him, even when he tried to shade the truth. It was a wonder she had gone into medicine instead of into private investigation like he had. She would have been brilliant at it. Or maybe a psychologist or one of those behavioral analysts. She was better at reading him than anyone else was.

Zachary shook his head. "I'm sorry. I know we put ourselves in danger, but we were trying to rescue Aster. But it was… a calculated risk."

"I don't like it. I got a taste today of what it would be like to have you drop off the face of the earth and never come home and, in case you're wondering, I didn't like it. That really freaked me out. Please…" Kenzie's voice was breaking, "don't put yourself into dangerous situations. And check your phone more often."

Zachary got a lump in his throat at Kenzie's emotion. He nodded, feeling like an even worse heel than he already had. He knew he needed to be more careful to check in with her. Too often, he lost track of time when he was working on a project and didn't think to call Kenzie and let her know where he was or what he was doing. But then, she didn't often call him during her workday either. Sometimes at lunchtime, and then again toward the end of the day to let him know how late she was running so he knew when to expect her home. The rest of the time, she did her work and he just assumed everything was fine.

But Kenzie wasn't a private investigator, poking into people's lives, putting in hours on surveillance, or trying to negotiate with human traffickers. There was a bit of a difference. Unless she told him otherwise, he assumed that she was at the morgue, working on the computer or assisting with an autopsy. Not out somewhere she might be putting herself in danger.

"I'm really sorry about the phone," he said miserably. "I wish I had realized earlier that you weren't able to reach me."

She nodded. Looking at the clock on the wall, she let out a sigh. "Well, you're right. We'd better be getting to bed. I already know I'm going to be tired in the morning. Might as well at least get a little bit of sleep under our belts." She stood up, scraped the remains of Zachary's dinner into the garbage, and put his plate in the dishwasher.

"I'm not planning on wearing my belt to bed," Zachary attempted humor, hoping she wasn't too tired to appreciate it. "Are you?"

Kenzie gave him a light slap on the arm as she walked by him. "You're going to be sharing the couch with Tyrrell if you're not careful!"

60

Zachary was up before Kenzie in the morning, as usual. He had managed to get a couple of hours of sleep, but his brain was too active, running through everything that had happened, trying to sort out all of the little unanswered questions about the case, and then wondering what was in his email inbox and whether he was falling behind on his other work. He still had surveillance to do. And deep background checks. There might have been other stuff that had come in since he had looked at his inbox last.

He had forgotten, while in bed, that Tyrrell was on the couch, which was where Zachary usually sat to do his work. He looked at the lump under the blanket for a moment, considering. He did not want to wake Tyrrell up. Even if he suggested that Tyrrell retire to the guest room, which would be more comfortable than the couch, Tyrrell might not get back to sleep. Zachary didn't want to do anything else that might affect Tyrrell's fragile mental health. Too little sleep could lead to depression, and depression could lead Tyrrell back to the bottle.

He picked up his laptop from his work table. He could sit at the kitchen table, but the light might wake Tyrrell up, and the table was not at a good height for him to use his computer. Instead, Zachary retreated down the hall to Kenzie's home office and set up there. They hadn't ever discussed this being Kenzie's territory, somewhere she wanted for herself. She had never told him not to use it, but he still felt a little guilty for assuming that he could use it for his own purposes without getting her permission first. He would have to seek her forgiveness later.

Pushing the discomfort and distraction of a new environment out of his mind as much as he could, Zachary opened up his laptop and started to work.

When he saw that his inbox was nearly empty, he just about had a heart attack, thinking he had been hacked. But he saw an email from Heather about their new workflow and opened it up. She had set up the project management account that she'd said she would, and listed the URL, login, and password, as well as the fact that he could download it onto his phone. Each actionable email that had come into his inbox had been sent to the new program, where it was sorted by client and type of task, linked back to the original email. Junk had been routed to the spam folder, and anything that was personal or she thought he might want to read had been filed into a new "personal" folder.

Following Heather's instructions, he processed the new emails that had arrived in his inbox since she had last looked at it, sending them to the project manager app or the appropriate folder. Then he stared for a minute at his empty inbox, analyzing the anxiety he was feeling. This time, it wasn't worry that he was forgetting something important or was buried under an avalanche of email. Instead, it was because he'd never had an empty inbox before and felt like he'd become unimportant or invisible. The many emails in his inbox had always been a testament that people wanted him, needed him, or considered him important. It felt like he had been erased. He clicked on his personal folder and looked at the emails there. He still had people who felt like he was an important part of their lives. They were just in a different folder now.

He tried to shake off the unsettled feelings and clicked over to the project manager to see what he needed to do.

"Ah, here you are."

Zachary was startled at Kenzie's voice. He swiveled the chair to turn and look at her in the doorway. "I hope you don't mind; T was still on the couch and I didn't want to wake him. I can move somewhere else if you want. The guest room or kitchen table."

"No, this is fine. Why shouldn't you use the office? I always thought you preferred the couch, but you can use the office whenever you want. As long as I'm not using it, I mean, and honestly, that's not very often. You need it more than I do."

"It's your space, though. I don't want to just take it over."

"No, it's fine," she waved a hand at him. "Please do. Use it whenever you like."

Zachary stretched and arched his back. "It is a better setup than hunched over my computer on the couch."

"Yes. I hate to think of what kind of problems your bad posture will cause in the future. You should be using an ergonomically correct setup. I have a chair and desk fitted to me at work so that I don't end up with carpal tunnel or back problems. Even the autopsy table raises and lowers so that I'm not operating at the wrong height." She looked Zachary and her desk over with a critical eye. "If something doesn't fit right, or you're getting a sore back after using it for a few hours, let me know. We can get a better chair. You could even use a standing desk, if you wanted to. There are lots of options."

"I don't think I would like a standing desk. I like being able to sit down and relax."

She nodded. "Whatever works for you. Some people find that a standing desk helps them to focus better, or to move around more. With your ADHD, you might even find it helpful. It doesn't mean you can never sit. Just that you have options."

Zachary nodded. "I'll just finish this search, and then I'll join you for breakfast." He looked at the system time on his computer. It was later than they usually ate breakfast. "Do you still have time?"

"Yes. I'm not giving up my coffee or my breakfast."

"I'll leave this." Zachary looked at the screen one more time, then closed the lid to force himself to break away from the screen and focus on Kenzie and real life going on around him.

He followed her out to the kitchen, and they worked together as usual to set the table and get out what was needed for their preferred breakfasts. Toast and marmalade for Kenzie, and a granola bar and whatever else Zachary could get down after taking his morning meds.

There were a few noises from Tyrrell, and then he sat up, rubbing his eyes, to look around.

"Oh! You're back!" Tyrrell bounced up from the couch and made a beeline for Zachary. He clasped him tightly. "Where were you yesterday? You had us worried."

"Sorry," Zachary gave his brother a squeeze. "I had phone trouble." He glanced at Kenzie and didn't fill in any other details. Tyrrell didn't need any extra stress.

"Is that all? Man, you should have called!"

Zachary and Kenzie both gave him a look.

"On someone else's phone," Tyrrell clarified, laughing.

Zachary nodded. "Yeah. I should have. I lost track of time and didn't realize how late it had gotten. As soon as I did, I called Kenzie."

Tyrrell shook his head. He punched Zachary lightly on the arm as a reprimand or to reassure himself that Zachary was really there, then considered his own state. "Sheesh. You'd think I slept in my clothes. I'll at least go wash up."

He went down the hall to the bathroom.

"You're going back to talk to Luke this morning?" Kenzie asked.

"Yeah. Need to get his full story. If he'll tell the rest to me now that we know half of it. I can't believe he fooled everyone with his phony confession."

"I don't think anyone can be blamed for assuming that the guy holding the knife dripping with blood was the killer."

61

Zachary was so eager to confront Luke with the truth that he forgot all of the protocols for getting into the jail and kept having to repeat everything. He hadn't left his personal items in the car. He went through the security gate too fast and didn't hold still properly when the CO tried to wand him to confirm that the extra metal in his arm was what was setting the metal detector off, rather than that he was trying to bring a weapon or some other contraband into the jail.

"You're so jittery," the CO complained. "Are you high on something today?"

"No. Sorry. Just… I know that Luke didn't do it. I'm going to talk to him about it to get all the details of what happened. Before long, he'll be out of here."

"But then we won't be seeing you every day anymore," she teased, her face still serious. "Aren't you going to miss us?"

"Definitely," Zachary agreed.

He tried once more to hold still while she checked him with the wand, and eventually she nodded.

"Okay, you're clear."

"You already know I have metal in my arm. I don't see why it's such a big deal to wand me each time."

She rolled her eyes. "Because it could be something else. You get our guard down with the first few visits, then bring something in. You certainly look like you could be up to mischief today."

Zachary laughed. "I'm not, I promise. I'm just excited that we're going to get him off. You'll see."

She escorted him to the visitor room, and one of the male CO's came in with Luke. Luke looked at Zachary for a moment, considering whether to stay and talk to him or not.

"Come on, Luke," Zachary invited. "This is probably the last chance you're going to get to talk to me here."

Luke frowned. The CO hooked him into the anchor and left the room. "What's that supposed to mean?" Luke demanded.

"I mean that you're not going to be here anymore."

Luke's eyes went back and forth across Zachary's face as if trying to read him. He didn't like this new development, didn't know what to think of Zachary's announcement.

"We found Aster. She's back home with Joss."

"Uh… good. Glad to hear it. I wouldn't want anything to happen to her."

"You like her, don't you? Quite a bit."

Luke shrugged. "Yeah, sure. She's a nice girl. Lots of fun."

"Is she the only one who would go out with you? Dancing or to the bars or clubs? The rest of them listened to Joss and followed her rules?"

"No one followed them all the time," Luke said with a hint of a laugh. "She makes *lots* of rules."

Zachary allowed himself one short foray into the past, smiling as he remembered Joss bossing them around, telling them all of the rules, either of what they were supposed to do when they got home, or the newest game that she and Heather had cooked up. Yes, Joss had liked making rules back then. Trying to fence them in so they couldn't get into any trouble. But Zachary always managed to get into trouble. As much as she wanted the order and control that rules would provide, it didn't happen.

"Yes, I'm not surprised. But Aster was just a little bit more special to you?"

Luke considered the question, looking at it from various angles, frowning at Zachary and trying to see what he was getting at, what he was trying to pull over on Luke. "I like her," he said finally. "Like I said. She was fun. Funny, intelligent, rebellious."

"And you were protective of her. When one of Eyler's men saw her and tried to take her back to him, you defended her. Wouldn't let him take her away."

"I would do that for anyone," Luke said firmly. "No one should be owned or made into a slave."

If anyone knew what he was talking about, it was Luke. He knew what Aster had faced if she went back to Eyler. He had known all of the dangers and tried to keep her from making that mistake. He remembered Connor and, Zachary was sure, wanted to prevent the same thing from happening to anyone else. But especially not to his new friend, Aster.

"Tell me about the night Eyler was killed."

Luke shook his head.

"Did you hear Aster leaving? Or did you wake up and realize she was gone? Maybe she messaged you to let you know where she was going, so you wouldn't be worried."

Luke shook his head slowly. "I don't know what you're talking about."

"You knew you had to keep her from going back to him. He couldn't be trusted to keep her safe. He was sadistic, hurting the kids in his stable if he felt like it. And you probably knew that Aster had already had some trouble with him. Worried that she might be going down the same path as Connor had. What if Eyler decided that he didn't want her around anymore? What would he do?"

Luke's face was white. "Why would I think that?"

"Because he was. He decided to kill her. To strangle her to death while she was at the hotel. Then, no more trouble from Aster."

Luke rolled his eyes. "He wasn't trying to kill her."

"She has bruises around her throat."

"It was a fetish. He would have let go."

"Aster said he was trying to kill her."

Luke took a deep breath in and released it. "She's not very experienced. She would have learned. Like we all did."

"That's why she stabbed him. Because he was strangling her. It was self-defense."

"You don't have any proof of that. There's no evidence to back that up."

"There's Aster's own story."

"The cops need evidence. Not just a confession. Confessions are a dime a dozen."

"She and Joss are going to the police today. They may be here in the building already. Aster is going to confess what really happened. And once they re-examine the evidence and confirm her story, they'll release you. You can go back home."

"While she goes to prison? No."

"She won't go to prison. It's self-defense. It's the law."

"And you think the cops are going to believe some teenager? A hooker? They won't. They think we're all liars. Making up stories. They only believe what they see with their eyes. And you know what they saw with their eyes?"

"You, holding a bloody knife."

Luke nodded and sat back in his chair, looking smug.

And of course he was right. The police had immediately believed what they had seen. They didn't look any further than that. But they would have to know that there was a competing story. They would have to look at everything again to see which story held up under scrutiny. And Zachary believed that they would accept Aster's story. It made more sense than Luke going over there after years of avoiding Eyler, unarmed, killing him with a kitchen knife found at the scene.

Besides, Aster had cuts on her hands and Luke did not.

62

"Tell me what happened when you followed her," Zachary coaxed. "I know everything else. Just fill in the details."

Luke stared at him for a long time. "This is confidential," he said eventually. "Like lawyer-client privilege. You can't talk to anyone about it. If you repeat anything, I'll deny it. Say that you made it up because you wanted a relationship and I turned you down."

Zachary gulped. He hadn't been expecting that. He would never repeat Luke's words to anyone in authority without his permission, so he really didn't have to worry about it, but just the thought of some of the people in his life or of his clients thinking that he'd been pursuing an illicit relationship with a teenage prostitute was enough to make his heart pound like it had been announced all over the media. It would destroy his business. His friendship with Rhys. Who knew how many other people in his life would believe it? Hopefully, most of those he was close to would recognize it for what it was, lies to discredit him, but who knew how many friends he would lose because of it?

"I'm not going to tell the police. That's up to you," Zachary told Luke, trying to keep his voice as calm and soothing as he could despite the tightness of his throat.

Luke nodded slowly, still watching Zachary as if he might suddenly change his mind or give some indication that he was lying.

"You followed her to Eyler's hotel?" Zachary asked. "Or did you know that's where she was going?"

"I had a pretty good idea she needed to score, and that was the easiest source. She didn't know a lot of other people in town. She could have found something on the street, but then you never know what kind of quality you're getting. Eyler, she knew he had the good stuff."

"Didn't it bother you that she was going to him?"

"Of course it did. You think I wanted her having anything to do with that piece of—" he broke off, shaking his head adamantly. "She had gotten away from him. She was safe with Joss. We could have helped her. We could have kept her safe from him if she would just stay away. I get that there were too many rules, that you have to get out sometimes before you go buggy... but going back to Eyler? But she was desperate. I understood it even if I didn't like it."

"And you didn't confront her or follow her to the room?"

"I knew where she was going. I didn't need to be right behind her. I figured I'd hang around there while she did whatever she had to do to score some dope from him, and when he was done with her... I'd try to get her back home to Joss's."

Zachary didn't ask for further details, letting the silence do its work and get under Luke's skin.

"She went up and I hung around downstairs for a while. Didn't figure she'd be down right away. Eyler would want his turn with her. Watched the doors to see if he lined up some clients for her. Didn't spot any. I went upstairs just to take a look around, see what the setup was. Whether they had the whole floor. If there were any of his goons around."

Zachary hadn't thought to check whether Eyler had booked more than one room. He probably had, if he wanted to have several of his stable working at the same time under his close supervision. He would need more than just the room he was sleeping in.

"Did you see any others?"

"Didn't see anyone patrolling the hallways. Couldn't tell whether the other rooms were all occupied or not. Everyone was out of sight." Luke's eyes went up to the ceiling as he told his story. "Eyler was yelling. The guy was supposed to be a professional, but he was bellowing over the music that was supposed to cover up the noise of what was going on in those rooms. Berating her for leaving him, for thinking she could go back to him for drugs without any punishment. Calling her every filthy name he could think of." Luke licked his lips. "Gem of a man."

Zachary gave a short laugh. "Oh, yeah."

"With him being so loud, I figured people would be calling the police or the front desk complaining about him. I mean... there was no doubt he was out to hurt her. You could tell, listening to him, that he was going to do something to her."

"But you didn't go in."

"We've all dealt with guys like that. Best to let it blow over. The ones that blow up like a bomb are usually over it quick. He'd figure Aster had learned her lesson. And with the noise he was making, I figured the cops or at least hotel security would be along before long to put an end to it. It was best I wasn't in there when they got there. No point in trying to tangle with Eyler or get myself arrested."

Zachary nodded his understanding.

"And then..." Luke pursed his lips and seemed to be searching for the words. "I never heard anyone make that kind of noise before. I've had some pretty vocal clients, but not anyone who sounded like that."

"When she stabbed him?"

Luke nodded. "He... screamed and screamed. I wasn't sure what to do. Kept waiting for someone else to come and take care of it. Thought security would be there any minute, but they weren't. Just the music playing then... couldn't tell what was going on in any of the other rooms, or whether the hotel staff were going to take care of it. He could have paid them to look the other way no matter what noises came out of his rooms. Probably did. Money will get you a lot of privacy in a place like this. People are happy to look the other way if they're getting something out of it. They'll chance losing their jobs because it's worth it..."

"And then..."

"No one was coming. I broke in. Those doors are easy to bypass. Went into the suite, through the living room area into the bedroom..."

"And found Eyler dead and Aster shell-shocked," Zachary suggested. Aster had said that she hadn't even been aware of Eyler yelling at her, had no idea how much noise he had made when she had stabbed him. That showed that she was traumatized. Had perhaps dissociated to escape the abuse.

Luke rubbed his chin. "Eyler was dead all right. And Aster... naked, covered with blood, shooting up."

Zachary shuddered at the mental picture. So desperate for her next fix that she hadn't bothered to tend to any other necessities first.

"I got her into the bathroom. Yelling at her to get cleaned up and dressed so that she could get out of there before the cops showed up. She was moving so slowly. Like she didn't have any idea what she had done or that there was going to be trouble. Got the worst of the blood washed away and helped her dress. She was so high she would have walked right out of there starkers. And trying to get her into her clothes… it was like dressing a toddler. Arms and legs going every direction. Distracted, flirty and playing around…"

Zachary could hear the anxiety in Luke's voice over how long it had taken to get Aster presentable. He could feel the time pressure, knowing that the police could be there any minute.

"I told her to go home. To go straight back to Joss's and wait for me there. Not to tell anybody what had happened. I didn't know whether she'd be able to follow my instructions or whether she would just wander around the hotel or out into the street. But I couldn't take her myself. I needed to… clean things up a little."

Zachary remembered the handprints in the bathroom. Smudges of blood all over the place. The police hadn't lifted Aster's prints there. "You intentionally put your prints over hers."

"Yeah. Anywhere I could see. It was a mess. But I knew if they caught her, she was going away for a long time. Eyler might be scum, but they would still want to make an example of her. Hookers can't just go around killing their bosses or anyone else they think is being abusive. Society says that if you put yourself into that position, choose that lifestyle, then you better be able to take what they dish out. There are consequences to your choices."

"That's victim blaming."

Luke raised a brow. "And…?"

"Well… I thought we were supposed to be past that. That we're more civilized now and understand about abuse and PTSD and the way that these predators control the people they traffic."

"Welcome to my world," Luke snorted.

"And then the police got there before you could finish obscuring all of the evidence and leave."

"I'd done enough to make it work." Luke's chin lifted slightly. He *had* done a good job. He had done what he had set out to do, ensuring that the police saw only the evidence that he had planted.

"Yes, you did. But now… it's time to admit what really happened. Aster is going to confess. When they investigate her story and realize that it is true, you're going to get out of here. You need to confirm her story instead of saying that you killed Eyler. She'll get off. She still has bruises on her neck. There will be proof that he was trying to kill her, and she can get off with self-defense."

Luke stared at Zachary, chewing on his lip. "You really think that they'll believe her? The guy deserved to be killed. I'm happy to take the heat for it, if it keeps Aster out of prison."

"You killing him because of your past and what happened to Connor will send you to prison for decades. Even saying that you were defending Aster or trying to keep Eyler away from your neighborhood is going to get you time. But she was being assaulted. She's allowed to defend herself under the law. No prison time for her."

"If they believe her."

"She has the injuries. You need to give them the same story as she does. They'll believe her."

"You think so?"

Zachary nodded. He could understand why Luke was so distrustful. For a lot of years, the police had pulled out all the stops to prosecute the victims of human trafficking rather than the traffickers or the johns. Prostitutes were seen as the lowest sort of criminals, despite how they were victimized by the traffickers. The tide had turned, with a number of states adopting the policy of prosecuting pimps and johns and providing counseling and services for the victims. Hopefully, there was enough awareness of the issue that no court would consider putting Aster in prison for what she had done.

But there were always wild cards.

"I'm *sure*," he told Luke. "She's going to be okay."

63

After he finished his visit with Luke, Zachary texted Joss as he walked around the building to the police station to see if she had taken Aster to the police station.

Dealing with it now, Joss replied.

He walked in through the front doors of the police station and looked around. He couldn't see either one of them; they must have already been taken to another room and were giving a statement, or waiting to give a statement to a policeman.

A cop walked out of the secured area to bend down and talk to the officer of the day, and Zachary realized it was Detective Richards, the homicide cop on Luke's case.

"Detective Richards."

Richards looked at him and didn't recognize him immediately. Then he clued in. "Goldman, right? What are you doing here?"

"I was just checking in with Joss. I knew that she was planning to be here with Aster this morning."

He nodded. "Yeah, the girl is making her statement." He rolled his eyes. "That's quite some story."

"It's not just a story."

"Yeah, well, if we find out that she's lying and that you're the one that fed the story to her in order to get the kid exonerated...."

"It isn't anything like that. I just followed the evidence to her. I didn't know she existed before I started. And once she told what really happened, we made arrangements for her to talk to you."

"You really think she did it, not the boy."

"Yes. And she's got the bruises to prove it."

"She can't prove where she got the bruises. They could be from anywhere."

"Well, maybe her DNA was found on Eyler's body. Or maybe his is under her fingernails."

Richards shrugged. "We'll see where the evidence leads. It can take months to get DNA back."

"How long do you think they're going to be in there?" Zachary nodded toward the offices and meeting rooms.

"Couple of hours, at least. To do it right."

Zachary looked at his watch. "I'll pop back in later, then."

"Why? They don't need you here. You don't have any direct testimony to add to her case."

"No. I just want to see that what I started... ends well."

"It won't be over for some time. But you do what you like. No skin off my nose."

Zachary could have sat in his car for a couple of hours doing what work he could on his phone and laptop. But he decided to reward himself for bringing the case to a successful conclusion by taking some time off for his own photography, which he hadn't been spending much time on lately.

He worked his way through several parks and open spaces, exploring the spring growth, stalking and snapping pictures of birds and squirrels, and watching people who were out enjoying the pleasant weather. Not people who were just hurrying from one place to another, with work or family trouble on their minds. No cheating spouses. People who actually looked happy and relaxed.

He returned to the police station when Joss said they would be getting out soon and met them when they returned to the public welcoming area.

"How did it go?" Zachary asked immediately, checking both of their faces. Aster was pale, probably not feeling very good after whatever drugs she'd been on the previous evening had worn off. She looked tired, but not upset, not what he would have expected if they had told her that she was going to have to serve time for Eyler's death or hadn't believed the story she had told them.

Joss nodded, giving a grim smile. "Aster did what needed to be done. I'm sure it will all work out. One less scumbag for us to deal with here. Maybe now they'll leave my girls and me alone."

"You need to be careful," Zachary warned her. "Don't antagonize them. You're lucky that so far, everyone has backed off when you said that you have information that could be detrimental to their business. One day…"

"Someone might decide to shoot first and ask questions later?" Joss finished. "Take me out and take their chances with the rest?"

Zachary nodded.

"I know." Joss sighed, folding her arms across her chest. "Believe it or not… I sometimes have trouble backing down once I've drawn a line in the sand."

Zachary chuckled. "Oh, I think I can believe it."

She pretended to punch him in the shoulder. "Don't get so cocky. Why are you looking so cheerful and pink-cheeked, anyway?"

"Just been out doing some photography. I forget sometimes how much I enjoy just getting outside with a camera."

"What do you take pictures of? It wasn't a job?"

"No. Just some wildlife. The local flora and fauna. And a few of people. It's nice out."

Joss nodded as she exited the building with Zachary and Aster. "It is nice." She put her hands on her hips for a minute, taking in a lungful of air. "The trouble is… it doesn't stay like this. Sooner or later, a cold front rolls in, the sky gets dark, and everything changes."

"So, I should enjoy it while it lasts?"

"So you should always be prepared for what's coming next."

Did you enjoy this book? Reviews and recommendations are vital to making a book successful.

Please leave a review at your favorite book store or review site and share it with your friends.

Don't miss the following bonus material:
Sign up for mailing list to get a free ebook
Read a sneak preview chapter
Other books by P.D. Workman
Learn more about the author

DON'T MISS A THING! GET THE LATEST NEWS AND A FREE EBOOK

Your First Taste

PDWORKMAN.COM/SIGNUP

PREVIEW OF
UNLAWFUL HARVEST

More books will be coming in the Zachary Goldman Mysteries series, but they are not ready for preview yet!

The next book in the timeline after They Came for Him is Posed for Death, book #6 in the Kenzie Kirsch Medical Thriller series.

If you have not started the Kenzie Kirsch Medical Thriller series yet, read Kenzie's origin story in Unlawful Harvest. Here is a free preview!

CHAPTER 1

MacKenzie reached for the ringing phone, trying to drag herself from sleep, but her hand encountered only the empty base of the phone, the wireless handset missing.

She pried her eyes open while feeling for it on the bedside table, knocking off keys and a glass and an empty bottle and other detritus. She swore and blinked and tried to focus. Where had she left the handset and who was calling her so early in the morning? The phone rang five times and went to her voicemail. Too late to answer it. She sank back down onto her pillow and closed her eyes. Whoever it was would have to wait.

But no sooner had it gone to voicemail than it started ringing again. MacKenzie groaned. "Are you serious? Come on!"

She turned her head and squinted at the clock next to her. It was hard to see the red LED display in the bright sunlight. It was almost eleven o'clock. Certainly not too early for a caller, even one who knew that she would sleep in after a party the night before. She rubbed her temples and scanned the room for the wireless handset.

There was a man in the bed next to her, but she ignored him for the time being. He wasn't moving at the sound of the phone, so he'd probably had more to drink than she had. She slid her legs out of the bed and grabbed a silk kimono housecoat to wrap around herself. The caller was sent to voicemail a second time. MacKenzie took another look around the bedroom without spotting the phone, then went out to her living room, also bright with sunlight streaming in the big windows. Outside, the pretty Vermont scenery was covered with a fresh layer of snow, which reflected back the sunlight even more brilliantly. MacKenzie groaned and looked around. The newspaper was on the floor in a messy, well-read heap. The remains of some late-night snack were spread over the coffee table. Some of their clothing had been left there, scattered across the floor, but no phone.

It started ringing again. Now that she was out of the bedroom and away from the base, she could hear the ringing of the handset, and she kicked at the newspaper to uncover it. She bent down and scooped up the handset. She glanced at the caller ID before pressing the answer button and pressing it to her ear, but she knew very well who it was going to be.

No one else would be so annoying and call over and over again first thing in the morning. She couldn't just leave a message and wait for MacKenzie to get back to her, she had to keep calling, forcing MacKenzie to get up and answer it. Her mother didn't care how late MacKenzie might have been up the night before or how she might be feeling upon rising. It was a natural consequence of MacKenzie's own choices. MacKenzie dropped into the white couch.

"Mother."

"MacKenzie. Thank goodness I got you. Where have you been?"

Her mother had been calling for all of two minutes. Where had MacKenzie been? She could have been in the bathroom, having a shower, talking to someone else on the phone, or at some event. Granted, she didn't go to a lot of events at eleven o'clock in the morning, but it *could* happen. Mrs. Lisa Cole Kirsch had a pretty good idea where MacKenzie had been. In bed, like most any other morning.

"What is it, Mother?"

"It's Amanda. She's sick."

MacKenzie nodded to herself and scratched the back of her head. One of the things that would definitely set Lisa into a tizzy was Amanda being sick. She worried over every little cough or twinge that Amanda suffered. She had good reason, but it still made MacKenzie roll her eyes.

"What's wrong with Amanda?"

"I don't know. Maybe it's just the flu, but I'm really worried, MacKenzie. The doctors said to just wait and see, but they don't understand how frail Amanda is. They think that I'm just overreacting and being a hypochondriac. You know that I'm not just a hypochondriac."

"I know. So, how is she?"

MacKenzie had to admit that even though her mother worried about Amanda, her worry was well-justified. Amanda's health could get worse very quickly, and with the anti-rejection drugs suppressing her immune system, she was prone to picking up anything that went around.

"She's not good. She was up all night, throwing up, high fever, she's just not herself. I called an ambulance at eight o'clock. She just can't keep anything down and I don't like the way she's acting. So... weak and listless."

MacKenzie felt the first twinge of worry herself. Amanda had spent much of her life sick, but she was a fighter. She usually did her best to look like nothing was wrong, not letting on unless she was feeling really badly. She would laugh and brush it off as just a bug and smile and encourage MacKenzie to tell her about what was going on in her far-more-interesting life. MacKenzie closed her eyes, focusing on Lisa's words.

"But the doctors don't think that there's anything to worry about?"

"No, but you know... they never do. She has to be at death's door before they'll admit that there might be a problem."

"Have they given her anything or did they just send her back home again?"

"They've got her on an IV and have said that they'll keep an eye on her. But you know they don't really think there's anything wrong. They're just humoring me."

"Yeah. Do you want me to come?"

"Would you? I'm really worried."

"Okay. I'll need a few minutes to get myself together. I'll be there as soon as I can."

"Thank you, MacKenzie. I don't know what I would do without you."

The sad thing was, Lisa would do just fine without MacKenzie. Even though she said that she needed MacKenzie, MacKenzie wouldn't really be able to do anything that Lisa couldn't do herself. She'd been dealing with doctors for a lot of years, and though she didn't pick up on the medical jargon as quickly as MacKenzie did, she could hold her own very well and was stubborn as a mule when it came to Amanda's care. She would protect her baby at all costs, and Amanda would get the best of care whether MacKenzie were there or not.

But if Lisa wanted the extra comfort of having MacKenzie around, who was she to argue? She didn't have anything else going on that prevented her attendance, and even if she did, it was easy enough to beg off of any event with an excuse, especially if the excuse were that Amanda was sick. MacKenzie had used it as an excuse even when it wasn't true. Although technically, even when Amanda was feeling well, she was still sick, so it wasn't really a lie.

MacKenzie hung up the phone and put it down on the brass and glass side table. She scrubbed her eyes with her fists, and when she opened them again, Liam was standing in the front of her.

"What's up?" he asked. "Everything okay?"

He hadn't yet recovered anything more than his boxers and, for a minute, MacKenzie just let her eyes rove over the piece of eye candy, remembering the night before through a slight haze of alcohol. They had gone to the Cancer Society fundraiser, had made the rounds there and let themselves be seen, and then had returned to MacKenzie's apartment for more drinks, some real food, and private entertainment.

"MacKenzie? What's up?"

"Amanda. She's in the hospital and Mother wants me to go over there and reassure her." MacKenzie yawned.

Liam bent over to pick up the various items of clothing he had dropped the night before. "Is she okay?"

"I'm sure both Amanda and Mother will be just fine. But she sounded pretty worried, and she said that Amanda was listless, which isn't like her. A really bad flu, maybe. I hope that's all it is."

"I was going to have a shower before heading out. Do you want it?"

MacKenzie weighed the options. Amanda was in the hospital, so she would be getting the best of care. Did it really matter whether MacKenzie had to wait an extra ten minutes for Liam to shower before she got herself ready?

"Or," Liam suggested, a dimple appearing in his cheek, "we could shower together and be done twice as fast."

"I have a feeling I wouldn't be out of here very quickly if we did that," MacKenzie laughed. They could easily be another hour, and Lisa would be on the phone again, ringing insistently, demanding to know where MacKenzie was and why she wasn't at her sister's side yet.

"Okay," Liam agreed. "So, do you want it?"

"Yes. I guess so. I need to pull myself together even if I am just going to the hospital." Lisa would not want her to show up looking bedraggled. She'd expect MacKenzie to be well turned-out even if it were the middle of the night, which it wasn't.

Liam nodded agreeably. He pulled on his white shirt from the night before, but didn't put on the pants or the rest of his outfit. "Shall I make you some breakfast while you're in there so that you can get out more quickly?"

"Would you? Just a couple of pieces of toast and some juice," MacKenzie requested, heading toward the bathroom. She looked back over her shoulder at him. "And coffee."

He smiled. "I think I know by now that you don't start any morning without coffee."

"Well, I need to fortify myself with *something* this morning before facing my mother."

She had a quick breakfast while Liam got into the shower, but he wasn't out by the time she was finished. She poked her head into the bathroom.

"Will you be much longer?"

She could see his shadow through the shower curtain as he turned his head toward her. "Oh... I can just lock up when I leave. You can go ahead."

MacKenzie shook her head. "I don't like to leave people here when I'm not around. Sorry. Can you be quick?"

"Yeah, sure." His tone was agreeable, but clipped. He obviously didn't appreciate that she didn't trust him enough to leave him alone in her apartment. But MacKenzie had been burned in the past by people who didn't respect her privacy, and she wasn't about to leave him there without supervision. She didn't know him well enough. Just because she could go with him to an event, and maybe bring him home afterward, that didn't mean she knew enough about his essential character to leave him there alone. She valued her privacy and there were a few things around the apartment that were quite valuable. Not that she thought Liam Jackson was going to steal them. She knew where to find him if he did. But it just wasn't good policy. If she didn't notice that something was missing right away, she might never be able to track it down again.

"I'll just be two more minutes," Liam promised.

"Thanks."

She went back to the bedroom and, since she had the time and couldn't leave until he was finished, she actually went ahead and pulled her bed into some semblance of order. It didn't look as good as when the maid did it, but it was better than leaving it all rumpled. She would appreciate it when she got home later.

If Lisa could only see her now. Twenty-seven years old and actually making her own bed. On a roll, she went into the living room and picked up the newspaper, which she threw in the garbage, and her clothes, which she threw in the laundry. Liam was out of the shower but not yet out of the bathroom. She threw a random assortment of dishes into the dishwasher and had the place looking pretty tidy when Liam made an appearance, dressed, hair wet but neatly combed, and his face still stubbly, not having taken the time to shave. She stood on her tip-toes to give him a kiss. "Thanks. Sorry about having to rush you out of here. It's my sister. Mother wants me there, so I have to make sure she's okay."

Liam nodded, looking down at her and letting his fingers linger on her jaw for a moment. "That, or you got one of your girlfriends to call to break up the party so that you could get rid of me."

"Ugh. I wouldn't do that when I was still in bed."

He smiled. "Give me a call later, then. Let me know how it goes. And we'll see each other again... soon."

They didn't have anything lined up, no dates, no fundraisers, nothing on the horizon. Liam was a nice guy, good looking, and MacKenzie might add him to her regular coterie of admirers, but she hadn't made up her mind yet. She wasn't one hundred percent sure that he was her type. Whatever that was.

After seeing him out the door, she put on her coat and winter gear and headed for the hospital.

When she managed to find her way to Amanda's hospital room, not in the renal unit where she usually was, Amanda was asleep. Lisa sat next to the bed, watching her sleep. Not reading a book. Not looking at her schedule for the week. Just watching her sleep. MacKenzie would have gone crazy. She couldn't stand to have people staring at her.

"Hi, Mom," she said softly.

Lisa looked over at her, automatically making a motion for her to be quiet before she evaluated MacKenzie's voice and the deepness of Amanda's sleep and decided that she probably wasn't being too loud after all.

"How is she doing?" MacKenzie looked over her kid sister. Amanda was twenty years old, but when she was asleep, she looked about ten. She was shorter than MacKenzie, and MacKenzie wasn't exactly an Amazon herself. Amanda was small and elfin, and people often mistook her for a kid if they weren't paying attention. She had a beautiful face, when she was feeling well. She wasn't looking too bad. Her weight was good, her cheeks round rather than sunken like they had been when she'd been through her worst times. She had long, dark hair that got tangled if she didn't take care of it, which was hard to do when she was in a hospital bed all day, but she didn't like to cut it short so that it would be easier to take care of. She said she needed her strength, like Samson.

Amanda was pale, and that bothered MacKenzie. But if she had the flu and had been throwing up for hours, then of course she was going to be pale. It was just a virus. She would be feeling better soon.

"She's sleeping," Lisa stated the obvious. "She's been so sick all night… I'm glad she was finally able to drift off. Maybe she's on her way to feeling better."

"Probably just a bug."

"Yes. Hopefully."

There was an IV hanging, but Lisa had said that Amanda needed it to stay hydrated. It didn't necessarily mean that she was back on some treatment again.

MacKenzie pulled the other chair in the room closer to her mother's and sat down. Amanda had been given a private room, of course. There was no way she was going to be left in some hallway or emergency room curtain. Lisa would see to that.

"Do you want to go get something to eat?" MacKenzie suggested.

"Well…" Lisa's eyes flicked over to Amanda. "I don't know. I don't want to leave her alone."

"I'm here. And you haven't had anything to eat, have you? You've been with her since last night?"

"Yes, you're right."

"Well, you're not going to be any good to her if you're fainting from hunger or all angry and irritable from low blood sugar. So go. I'll be with her if she wakes up. She's not going to be alone."

"Are you sure?"

"Why don't you take advantage of the fact that I'm here, because I'm not going to be here all day. Go have something to eat."

"Okay," Lisa agreed, but she still made no movement to get up, watching Amanda with worried eyes.

"She'll be fine for now. I'll have them page you if something happens."

"Would you?" Lisa brightened at that suggestion. She could go have something to eat and still be sure that Amanda hadn't taken a turn for the worse. She clutched her purse on her lap, then nodded and got up. "Thank you so much, MacKenzie, I appreciate you coming and being here for your sister."

"And for you," MacKenzie reminded her. "Don't you try saying that I never do anything for you."

"I would never say that."

MacKenzie raised her eyebrows as her mother left. She might say it and she might not. But she would certainly imply it the next time she wanted MacKenzie to do something for her and MacKenzie had something else going on or didn't want to be there.

Lisa's heels clicked sharply as she walked away. MacKenzie watched her go. She leaned back in her chair and looked over Amanda once more. The hospital chair was far from comfortable. She was going to have to get used to it if she were going to be there for a few hours.

"I should have brought a book," she murmured to Amanda. She hadn't thought to bring anything with her. She'd just gotten herself together and headed over. And she couldn't go down to the gift shop to pick something up. Not after dismissing her mother and saying she'd stay with Amanda while Lisa was eating. MacKenzie sighed and resigned herself to just sitting there and napping while she waited either for Amanda to wake up, or for Lisa to return from lunch.

CHAPTER 2

She had nodded off, and when she opened her eyes and rubbed the stickiness away, she realized that Amanda was awake, her head turned to look at MacKenzie.

"Oh, hey sleepyhead," MacKenzie greeted.

"Hi," Amanda said in a soft little voice. MacKenzie waited for the rejoinder about how MacKenzie had been falling asleep in her chair. But Amanda didn't tease her. MacKenzie bit her lip. That was what Lisa was so worried about. Amanda might look like she was just a little tired, but that shouldn't change her personality. Her lassitude suggested that there was something more wrong, not just a twenty-four-hour flu bug. She shouldn't have been experiencing that level of fatigue with just a virus.

"How are you feeling?"

"I think I'm better now," Amanda said faintly.

MacKenzie waited for her to go on, but she didn't. "I guess you had a pretty rough night of it,"

Amanda nodded. She turned away from MacKenzie again and her eyes closed. MacKenzie frowned watching her. It was just the flu. Just a fever and throwing up. It could be any number of viruses. They had her on IV. She was going to be just fine.

Lisa returned, and looked worriedly over to Amanda lying in the bed, as if she had expected her to be sitting up talking by the time she got back.

"She was awake for a minute," MacKenzie said. "She didn't throw up, so that's good news."

"I think they put something in the IV to stop her."

"Oh. Well, that's good. At least they're taking it seriously."

"She really does need to sleep," Lisa said, but MacKenzie knew she was trying to reassure herself. They were all used to Amanda's high energy level. Even when she was sick, she still joked and teased and tried to keep everyone around her in a good mood. She didn't like long faces around her hospital bed.

"If she was up all night throwing up? She sure does. I was up half the night and I could still use a few more hours of sleep. And I wasn't throwing up."

"You were up late?"

"I was at the fundraiser."

"Oh, the one at the Phelps's house?"

"Yeah. That one."

"Who did you take?"

"Liam Jackson."

"He's a nice boy."

"He seems that way," MacKenzie agreed. She focused on looking out the window on the opposite side of the room. She didn't want to blush and have Lisa detect it. MacKenzie smiled and raised her eyebrows as if she weren't thinking immoral thoughts about Liam Jackson.

"How is Daddy?"

"You know your father. Always occupied with very important meetings with very important people."

MacKenzie nodded, smiling. Lisa hadn't said it in a way that was sarcastic or critical, but with a little bit of humor, as other women might talk about their husbands' interest in cars or collectibles. *Boys and their toys.* Was that how her mother saw Walter's lobbying? As a hobby that occupied her husband and kept him out from underfoot?

"Does he have anything interesting going on right now?"

"I'm not sure what he's working on. I don't really pay much attention, unless it is something that could have an impact on one of my causes."

Lisa always had plenty of causes on her agenda. There were an infinite number of foundations, societies, and fundraisers that needed her attention and support. Lobbying kept her father busy and fundraising kept her mother happy. MacKenzie just didn't know what it was that kept *her* happy. When was she going to find her way in life? She didn't want to be a lawyer, lobbyist, or politician. But she didn't want to be a socialite or drum-beater either. She had done well enough in school and had taken enough classes in college to get herself a degree, but that hadn't helped her to find her place in the world. She wasn't passionate about anything.

Lisa's eyes were quick and perhaps took in more than MacKenzie had expected. She reached over and patted MacKenzie's hand. "You'll find something," she said. "You're just a late bloomer. You need to be patient and give yourself some time."

"When you were a kid, what did you think you would be when you grew up? Did you have any dreams?"

Lisa shrugged and looked away from MacKenzie. "I don't know. I wanted to be a wife and mother. I was never really interested in a job. I felt like children were my avocation." She shrugged. "I know that's not a very popular answer these days. We're supposed to think big and take the bull by the horns, to make our mark on the world. But I can't help but think… that the marks being made on the world wouldn't amount to very much if it weren't for the mothers."

MacKenzie gave her a smile. "The hand that rocks the cradle, and all that?"

"Yes. Exactly. Mothers shape the thinkers and the soldiers. The scientists and the astronauts and the Nobel laureates. They all had mothers. They all had people to help them along the way and give them support at various parts of their lives, like a mother would, even if they didn't have a mother. I happen to think that's a very important position."

"Of course," MacKenzie agreed. "I never thought that you should be required to give up your family and have a high-power job."

"I could have, you know," Lisa said. She obviously didn't want MacKenzie thinking that she had only stayed home to be a mother because she couldn't do anything else. She had chosen to be there and not to hire a nanny to raise them. That had been her choice, not a fallback position.

"I know, Mother. You have a brain. You're very organized and I'm always amazed at what you can accomplish. I know you could have chosen to do other things."

Lisa nodded, satisfied.

MacKenzie looked back at Amanda. They had been lucky to have a mother who stayed home to look after them. Amanda probably wouldn't have survived without a strong, proactive mother watching over her. How many times had Lisa been the one to take her to the hospital and insist to the doctors that something was wrong, and she wasn't taking Amanda home until they had figured out what it was? She had insisted that Amanda wasn't just a whiner or a hypochondriac, but that she was really ill. She could have died if they hadn't been forced to dig deeper for the answers.

MacKenzie and Amanda hadn't really been playmates. MacKenzie had been too much older than Amanda to consider her a real friend and peer. Instead, Amanda had been MacKenzie's baby as much as she had been Lisa's. MacKenzie had been fascinated with her care and had happily fed and changed her. It was like having a living doll. MacKenzie had never even liked dolls. But she liked having stewardship over the tiny new person in their home. Lisa had encouraged her interest rather than shooing her off to go play or insisting that she diaper her dolls instead of her sister.

At first, no one had known that anything was wrong. Amanda got sick a lot, but children picked up viruses everywhere, it wasn't really that unusual. As she got older, she didn't outgrow it, and MacKenzie realized that she was sick a lot more often than MacKenzie or her friends, or little Amanda's other friends. She remembered the day when she had been out at the playground with Amanda, about nine years old by then, and MacKenzie a teen. Amanda had been playing tag or grounders or some other schoolyard game on the climbing equipment with her friends, but she had to sit down at the edge of one of the platforms, her face white, trying to catch her breath and get up the energy to go back to the game. The other girls teased her for calling timeout too often and told her that she couldn't be safe, but there wasn't any point in tagging her while she sat out, because she wouldn't run after the rest of them and the game would grind to a halt.

MacKenzie walked over to Amanda.

"Mandy-Candy," she singsonged, "what's wrong? Don't you want to play anymore?"

Amanda was breathing shallowly, too fast. "I want to play," she protested, her arms folded across her stomach, "I'm just too tired. I need a break."

"Do you want to go home?"

Amanda looked at the other girls still playing and having a fun time on the playground equipment around her. She looked sad. Not just sad, but desolate, as if they had all run away and left her behind where she could not follow.

"I guess so," she said finally. "I can read, I guess."

"Do you really want to?" MacKenzie pressed. "I'm not saying you have to. If you want to stay and play…"

Amanda shook her head. "I can't," she said hopelessly. "I don't know how they can run around all day."

MacKenzie sat looking at her as the seconds ticked by, a knot growing in her stomach. She walked home slowly with Amanda, back to the big house on the hill. It was a long way for a child who didn't have any energy left. Partway there, MacKenzie boosted Amanda up onto her back and carried her piggy-back to the house. Amanda lay against her, body limp, arms around MacKenzie's neck.

When they got home and MacKenzie settled Amanda in bed with a book, she went looking for Lisa. Lisa was, luckily, home for the evening and not on her way out to some fundraiser.

"Mother… I think something's wrong with Amanda. I mean… really wrong."

Lisa looked at her for a long time, then finally nodded. "I do too. And I think it's time we found out what."

So many doctors had said that Amanda was just a girly girl, that she didn't want to participate in activities and was overly sensitive to every little ache and pain that came along with growing up and roughhousing with friends. There wasn't really anything wrong.

But when they had insisted that it was time to figure out what was really wrong with Amanda and that they weren't going away until they got some answers, everything changed.

And it would never be the same again.

***

Unlawful Harvest, Book #1 in the *Kenzie Kirsch Medical Thriller* series by P.D. Workman can be purchased at pdworkman.com

ABOUT THE AUTHOR

P.D. Workman is a USA Today Bestselling author, winner of several awards from Library Services for Youth in Custody and the InD'tale Magazine's Crowned Heart award, and has published over 80 mystery/suspense/thriller and young adult books, including stand alones and these series: Auntie Clem's Bakery cozy mysteries, Reg Rawlins Psychic Investigator paranormal mysteries, Zachary Goldman Mysteries (PI), Kenzie Kirsch Medical Thrillers, Parks Pat Mysteries (police procedural), and YA series: Tamara's Teardrops, Between the Cracks, and Breaking the Pattern.

Workman loves writing about the underdog, who the reader may love or hate. She has been praised for her realistic details, deep characterization, and sensitive handling of the serious social issues that appear in all of her stories, from light cozy mysteries through to darker, grittier young adult and mystery/suspense books.

> P. D. Workman, does not shy from probing the deep psychological scars of childhood trauma, mental illness, and addiction. Also characteristic of this author, these extremely sensitive issues are explored with extensive empathy, described with incredible clarity, and portrayed with profound insight.
>
> — KIM, GOODREADS REVIEWER

Some of Workman's titles have been translated into Spanish, French, Portuguese, German, and Italian.

Workman began writing at an early age and is a prolific reader as well as writer. She is also passionate about teaching and learning, expresses her creativity through art and cooking, and loves exploring the Calgary parks and green spaces where the Parks Pat Mysteries are set. She was a legal assistant for many years and has done extensive charitable work.

Workman was born and raised in Alberta, Canada, and is married with one adult son.

Please visit P.D. Workman at pdworkman.com to see what else she is working on, to join her mailing list, and to link to her social networks.

If you enjoyed this book, please take the time to recommend it to other purchasers with a review or star rating and share it with your friends!

facebook.com/pdworkmanauthor

twitter.com/pdworkmanauthor

instagram.com/pdworkmanauthor

amazon.com/author/pdworkman

bookbub.com/authors/p-d-workman

goodreads.com/pdworkman

linkedin.com/in/pdworkman

pinterest.com/pdworkmanauthor

youtube.com/pdworkman

Find P.D. Workman's books at

PDWORKMAN.COM

Scan the QR code below